BACKSHADOW

A Novel

Julie Mann

Library and Archives Canada Cataloguing in Publication

Mann, Julie, author
Backshadow : a novel / Julie Mann.

Previously published in electronic format.
ISBN 978-0-9949277-0-5 (paperback)

I. Title.
PS8626.A59B33 2015   C813'.6   C2015-907592-0

Printed and bound in the United States of America

*At least 1 in every 3 women globally will be beaten, raped
or otherwise abused during her lifetime.*
*—United Nations Development Fund for Women
2003*

*For all the women living with shadows,
and for Paul.*

Character, like a photograph, develops in darkness.
—Yousuf Karsh

A being must carry the shadow to embrace the light,
and blend these vital breaths to make harmony.
—Dao De Jing

Aneeta
Delhi, India
1996

Ever since the first time, the nights have haunted her. Perhaps because night is a reminder of what she lost with darkness around her. But neither dark nor light are of any matter in things now. The sun and moon, the shadow planets, they cannot change what has taken place. What has been taken.

There is a first, a second, and a third time. And on. With each approach he becomes even more bold, more sure of himself. For a while she recalls, recounts, relives them by ticking her fingers. It is a juvenile form of accounting for a problem well beyond her. In years. In maturity. In experience. But she does not quite know what else to do with it. Beyond giving it some order.

She tells herself that she will seek help if it does not stop. By the time she runs out of fingers. That she will find the strength. The courage. To speak. She will. *She will.* But then she muddies things when she starts to wonder what sorts of things should account for a whole finger, and what might account, say, only for a knuckle's width or two at most. Is a rough succession of kisses the same as a hand inside her pants? Is a hand in the pants worth less than a finger that is pushed into her? If two fingers, is it then different? If he himself enters her, the trespass is worst. Or is it? Does she measure by pain? Or by the use he makes of her body? If her hand is covered and squeezed around him, around his hard and throbbing self, is it counted the same as a violation of her body?

Because she cannot form a clear system of appropriate values, of currency for compare, she eventually loses what she considers an accurate weighting of trespass entirely. Knuckles and folded fingers are not good markers, not adequate or accurate. And they cannot account for the emotions that stay with her. Long after.

When she has run the course of fingers she merely convinces herself that she is not sure. And because she is not sure, how can she possibly bring it forward? What should she say? If she herself is confused. About what counts. What is offence, and what is not. Until she can be sure what exactly to do, she begins to keep up a simple tally in her diary margin. Simple, because now she counts everything the same. She keeps track only of each time he comes. Not what exactly happens in each of those times. Small, neatly ordered strokes along a perfectly straight horizontal in blue ink. Not sure any longer what is right, what is wrong, what she should do, she simply watches the crosses of the growing rail line in between two stations. And so, in this fashion she keeps building it, the collection of perpendicular slashes that square the line of time that marks her life. Sometimes she thinks of it in terms of the government's plans for rail expansion. For added service into the more remote communities. To the outlying rural villages. How far will it go? How far afield can it possibly traverse? She tells herself, convinces herself, that like a rail line it must be finite. Logically has to be. That at some point must lie an end. After which it will be no longer. Each time she adds a stroke to her paper she sends her focus into the future, to look for that day. To scour the horizon. For the end of it. To hope that soon she may catch a glimpse. Of the potential for a terminus.

Did she want for Dev Uncle to do this to her? No. Ask for it? No, of course not. Sometimes it is what he tells her. That she is asking. With her eyes, with her lips, with her budding womanly body. That it is her fault. That she has brought it on herself.

One morning not long after the first time, he had caught her coming from her morning bath. Openly, he had stared at her nakedness. With a wolfish smile and heavy-lidded longing in his features. For what seemed an eternity she had stood rooted to the spot, dripping water from her hair upon the cool polish of marble, so that it pooled slickly around her unmoving feet. He had taken full advantage of her reaction. Admiring her childish yet narrow hips and the small tuft of finely curled hair sprouting from between them, the blossoming flesh of her breasts with their nipples erect in the cool of the air. In regaining her senses she had fled for the safety of the bathroom and the lock upon the door.

He had come to stand on the other side of the door, so close that she could hear the heaviness of his breath. In a carefully controlled voice he had told her that she would not always have walls and doors to hide behind. With her heart thrashing wildly in her chest she had leaned her whole weight against the door. Even though she knew she had not the strength to stop him if he wanted to pursue her there. 'I will call to the others. I will shout if you do not go this minute.'

'And what will you do if they come? What will you tell them?' he had inquired in a measured tone that clearly showed his mocking.

Does she? Tempt it? Bring it upon herself? Inside of her a silent ongoing conversation runs. A gnawing within her withering conscience. And points a weakly accusing finger. Have you asked him to stop? Yes. I have begged. Pleaded. Do you ask in the right way? What is the right way? Does he continue? Yes. Then it is not the right way. But what is? The. Right. Way. Certainly not the ways she has tried. What avenues are left? Indeed. Indeed, what avenues at all? Do they not all come to the same confounding end?

Her reactions swing in wild pendulum extremes of grief and rage and pity. He has betrayed her. Her trust, her love. It is no mistake, no accident. He knows what he is doing. To her. Time and again. It has become familiar territory; he passes boldly through the boundaries. Re-mapping permissions. Going where his hands have no business. Taking what does not belong to them. Possessing what is not his to possess. He has blackened her. Soiled her. Ruined her. And he has done so without remorse, without care. Thieving.

One day she comes to a stark and jagged realization: The only count, the only trespass that was ever truly worth noting was the first. The first time. So now, why protect? Why guard? Why fight? What has been taken is not coming back. Not ever.

And yet, like a prisoner, she keeps up the tally. Pointless as it may be, there is comfort in knowing that one stroke will eventually be the last. And when he comes for her again and again and again, she does the only thing she can do to give herself a place to pin hope, she coaxes herself into diversion. Disappears into her imagination. So that she has the sense of leaving her body. On little bird wings she floats away. How will it look? Sound? Feel? The sweet freedom she pictures. Sunrise atop a peaceful hill station. The mountains alive with birdsong. Fresh. Clean. She does her best to devote her senses entirely to this simple means of escape. She wraps herself in it. It is the only control she can take in the matter. To have her mind leave. And find a place elsewhere. Away. From him. From the ugliness. She carves a mental world apart. Where she cannot be touched. To leave the nightmare behind. Because she knows now that time cannot be turned back. It marches only forward.

Kameko
Tokyo, Japan
1996

It is a single lipstick stained handkerchief, still with its sharply ironed creases, that destroys her childish illusions of family like a magician's house of cards. Her volatile teenage heart jumps at the discovery, for the meaning of it is plain. Hastily, she bends and snatches it from where it lies to silence its revelation, to deny it. A truth exposed to her by an accident of chance. Somehow it has fallen into the open. She wonders how long it has been there. She wonders why fate has chosen her to find it, to know the meaning it shares. Holding the flimsy square of finely woven cloth that is stitched with a design she recognizes, she considers the story it portrays. She draws it to her face. The elements are unmistakable. She knows the reek, the look of transgression. The alcohol and perfume intermingle with the scent of Father, and with the laundry soap Mother uses.

It ignites anger in her. Eating at her like a poison, crawling acidly through her veins, eroding the openness of her heart. Crumbling a girl's love for her father. Transforming him, this man who had carried her upon his shoulders on many a Sunday afternoon family outing in the park, a man who indulged her with tiny decorative dolls at *Hinamatsuri* or brightly coloured kimono and delicate silken obi for *Shichi-Go-San*. On such occasions she had seen the pride that shone in Mother's eyes. She remembers as a little girl how she would grasp both their hands. And walk between them. But was it she alone who had bound their affections? Who held them together? Even then?

She pushes the cloth into her book bag. On her way to school she disposes of it in the trash bin behind the noodle house. In the warming air of spring she thinks now that the sky does not look quite as blue, the budding trees do not seem somehow as appealing, the scent of their new growth is not as fresh.

Even with the stained cotton square out of her sight, out of her possession, she finds she cannot ignore its silent confession. Her desire to know becomes insatiable. To see not just a piece of the puzzle. That is the only way she can figure out what to think of things, of him. And so she resolves to take the train into town after school; hide herself in the great spires of Tokyo concrete. To wait and follow him from his office until his footsteps reveal all there is to know. She feels compelled to see truth with her own eyes. She naively hopes, somewhere deep within herself, that it might dispel her original conclusions. Perhaps she will find that things are not at all as she has believed. Perhaps her upset and her confusion will have been in vain. And her loyalty will be restored. Or perhaps what she sees will agree with the way her senses have jumped. Instinct tells her this is the more likely finding. Her head knows it even if her heart hopes differently.

Four nights she stands waiting. Shivering like a fool in the closing darkness and cool night air. Four nights of homework and study she sacrifices before she has her answer.

He leaves the office building alone. Walking swiftly and with purpose among streets crowded with others like him, suited, hurrying still, to destinations unknown. She follows closely. Focusing on his head and shoulders so that she does not lose him in the crowded flow of the sidewalks. With gritted teeth she surges along with the waves of city people until his form takes a turn. It is a nondescript bar he enters, just off the mouth of an alleyway in the Shinjuku. She stops herself at the corner, not knowing what to do next. Not having planned anything other than to follow. Several people mill about in the doorway of the establishment. Smoking, talking, bantering in a loud, half-drunken way. From the suits they wear she assumes them to be salarymen like Father. Perhaps he is just visiting a bar for outings with work colleagues and some hostess has used the handkerchief. Or perhaps even a work friend has made use of it. Innocently. This is understandable, acceptable. And maybe why he would not have been troubled about it being found at home. If there was something, surely he would have taken care to hide it better. There is one window. She thinks it over. But what if? She doesn't want the attentions of the other men in the doorway to follow her, nor does she want to alert Father to her presence. Should she? Just to see? After all, that is what she has come for. What if this is her only chance? To settle things in her mind. She can't turn back now.

The door opens to reveal a couple in silhouette; talk, laughter, and music spill out and around their shadowed form. The one half cuts a familiar outline, the top portion of his torso anyway, before it joins in the shadow. Kameko is left bare, exposed, knowing that they are likely to pass within paces of her face. Her instinct is to look down, stare at the ground, to let them walk by. To avoid recognition. She had never considered that he would be leaving the bar so quickly.

Father's voice finds its way to her. And her ear hears something different in it, a melodious quality. He is talking animatedly, with a life Kameko cannot remember ever having seen before between Mother and he. The woman at his side is laughing and gazing up at him. And then, his laughter—how different, how full, how free it sounds. He had offered his arm when they had emerged from the club, and she holds it now, elegant and easy. As they approach the opposite side of the alleyway, Kameko draws herself tight to the concrete and the dimness of the building shadow. Lights of neon bathe their faces in an alternately red and blue-white glow. Both are smiling. They are comfortable and familiar. And affectionate. She cannot tell whether the woman is younger than Mother in the unsuitable light, but she can see her grace, the shapeliness of her figure, the fineness of her features. The glamorous life of a mistress; a stark contrast to the life of a housewife. It could not have been more plain, this distinction.

But more unsettling, more unexpected, is the feeling that is clear even without being able to clearly discern their faces. In their bodies alone. A display that has never been evident between her parents. Not that she could ever recall.

Happiness is etched into his entire manner. He is different behind his father mask and his husband mask. This she is not prepared for. She watches until the figures are swallowed by distance and the throng. She looks up into the buildings steepled around her and clutches her coat around herself. A chill begins to creep into her now. The fire of her fury is slowly ebbing away, leaving her drained and more confounded still. She does not know what to think. Has she satisfied her curiosity? Yes. But is she satisfied by what she has seen? Has it confirmed him as the villain in the way she thought she needed it to? Wanted it to? She fights the urge to cry. Bleary-eyed and disconsolate, she makes her way along the street to a telephone. She dials the number without hesitation. The pickup at the other end is almost instantaneous, reassuringly so. 'Hai. I fell asleep on the train. Missed my stop.' Her voice is wooden, her words stilted. Like a liar. But there are no questions. She turns from the phone box and numbly begins to make her way to the train station.

Mishima had written of seeing as a meeting between the eye and being, with the ability to transport a person to a realm visible to no one. And so it has. Seeing has left her stranded there, in the shadow realm, with no remedy but silence. For what is not spoken of cannot offend, cannot dishonour, cannot disappoint. She resolves then that she will make this disappointment hers alone in order to keep the harmony between them. For the sake of *tatemae*. In exchange for a time before, when she had been the one to disappoint.

Gregory
Durham, California
1997

In the muddy early hours of morning the television is still on. Home shopping. Again. Commotion's all but robbed it of sound, making the movements of the images seem unreal and dreamlike. He roars, like some kind of animal, from the kitchen area behind. She strains, but she cannot hear Mama at all. Not even the sound of her crying. Just him. What the hell is he banging on? There is a thudding sound. Like a cupboard door opening and closing again and again. The crack of dishes on metal.

She has to be there. Fury's no good without an audience, without a target. Fear pricks her spine. Her pulse throbs heavy and fast at her throat. Her footfall is quiet on the musty gold shag carpeting.

The inside of the trailer is small. Tonight, though, the distance from front room to kitchen seems a long way. Things are giving over to the fight; the crisp split of wood, the snap of hard plastic, the shatter of glass. And, getting closer, she hears water. Splashing. But there's no reaction from her. No pleading, no begging, no preaching, no attempts to pacify him. Nothing. Gregory's gut has opened into a pit. She picks her way swift and careful. As she makes for the noise, the Louisville Slugger beckons from its resting place beside the easy chair. His most prized possession. Something inside tells her to pick it up. There's the shush-shushing of blood in her ears keeping time with her heart, and needles spiking at the back of her neck. Sparks of silver pop and bleed in front of her eyes. She doesn't think what she might do with the bat, just has a sense that she ought to have it.

The wooden shaft is at her side, downward pointing in the grip of her right hand, as she steps forward. The scene is framed in the narrow opening between the rooms. A dirty trail of ketchup-stained dishes clutter the countertop, along with a fry pan and an array of cooking utensils. There's remnants of what must have been dinner. The Heinz bottle stands at the end of the line. Cupboard doors are flung wide, contents litter the floor in jagged pieces.

They are together at the sink. Mama and he. His back is to Gregory where she is coming in on them. He doesn't see her. He is pressed up against Mama. He has her bent back awkwardly against the sink. As if he were dipping her, like in a dance. He's curved over her; together they make almost an arch. She can't tell about his arms and hands, what he's doing with them. Except that she can see them reaching. Straight out. Ridged cords of muscle. What Gregory can see of Mama is her legs. Straddled by his. Twitching. Pushing. Slip-sliding on linoleum. And her arms, Mama's arms flail, in wild flapping motion up towards the top of him. His shoulders. They try to slap at him. Her hands are opened wide. There is a gurgling sound and the slosh of moving water coming from the sink. Making its way weakly to where she stands, at the back of the scene. The observer. The sound from Mama is dying down. Water noise comes in short fits. Shallow bursts of bubbles signal breath leaving, departing. Deserting. Her legs are slowing in their spasmodic strain. Her arms begin a defeated downward drift. A slow round of liquid runs in a puddle between Mama's feet.

And then she hears a gentle humming in her head. The voice of a child. Singing. Like she used to do. *Jesus loves me.* How she used to protect herself. From the sounds. *This I know.* The sounds that have haunted her for so long. *Little ones to him belong.* She was afraid. So very afraid. *They are weak, but he is strong.* His sound is overpowering it now. Washing away the overlay of the simple melody. Darkness falls heavy on her. The dark of all the nights gone before. She doesn't have much time if she's going to save Mama. She's not moving anymore. And there's no sound from her. Gregory raises the wood high above her head.

Mama crumples into a lifeless heap to the floor. And Curtis wheels around. To find her. A flood rips through Gregory. The intensity of which she has never known. Like a dam burst, this molten heat burns in her veins, rushing, pushing and drowning out everything else. Everything. His face is mottled purple and red. He's screaming, yelling, reaching for her, grabbing. She's backing away. Backing up. He's still coming. She feels herself raising her arms high, again and again, thrashing it down, his Slugger, wherever it happens to land. He is moving. Scrambling. *Yes, Jesus loves me.* She needs him to stop. Needs to make him stop. She needs to get to Mama. Needs to find out. If she's still alive. Needs to know he won't finish them both. His hairline is bloodied. By her, she knows. It is too late. She has to. Or he will. She is panting. Backed up into a corner. His hands, fists, are blindly swiping at her. There is the sound of the bat, hitting. Hitting not what is was made for. It is thick, the sound, a dull thudding. Wood meeting flesh. Over and over and over again. His movement toward her is slowing now. Blood covers his face. He drops to his knees. The sound of the melody is rising up. She can hear it again, the small voice in song. *Yes, Jesus loves me.* He falls forward onto the floor. Blood, like tomato ketchup, oozes from under him. Seeping along the speckled linoleum. Across one, two, three tiles it flows. Creeping toward where she is. Her face is hot, her heart thumping out of her chest. Finally, he is still. She is gasping for air, and the sound is mixed with whimpers. *Yes, Jesus loves me.* The words of the child begin to fade. She regards, in disbelief, the bat she still holds. Its surface stained and slick with the briny pulp of him. Spatters have been thrown all around the room. On the walls, the ceiling, the far reaches of the kitchen floor. The breath she draws is tangy with the scent of iron. She lets it drop, the shaft of wood. His beloved baseball bat. She remembers his words from so long ago. *Means more to me than you'n your mama put together. Was the life I should've had.* It falls across his legs.

Gregory tiptoes around his body and moves toward Mama. To see if she can find signs of life. It isn't until she coaxes a sputtering breath from waxy blue lips that she reaches for the phone and with trembling fingers dials 9-1-1.

English 50
Bay City Community College
San Francisco
September 2002

Aneeta

There is an energy about the man who will lead the class. Good energy. A warm positive flow. He spills into the room, like water into an open space, filling it with a presence that is genial. Pleasant. These are the words that come to her. He is handsome in a very American way; light eyes and hair, broad-shouldered and tall. There is a little whisper somewhere within. To remind her. That especially with men it is not a matter of how the outside may look. Wariness returns. She wonders what might hide beneath the visible. Instead of simply being afraid, she is mixed in her emotion. Curiosity piques as well, questions. She recognizes the little bird inside; a spirit long dormant. And feels a flutter of wings.

He is holding a sizable stack of papers and books. Corners at the base of the pile stick out in some disorder. Because his hands are full he gives the door a backward shove with his shoulder, letting momentum take it to a satisfying meeting of wood against wood. There is a rush of air through open windows when the door closes, blinds and flapping cord lengths tap against window frames as the exiting gust flows into the grassy tree-dotted expanse beyond the building.

He strides to the front of the room where he deposits his load of materials upon the tabletop. He shrugs out of his navy coloured blazer and drapes it across a chair back. His movements are relaxed and unhurried. He talks as he makes himself ready. 'Good evening.' He casts his smile to each and every being in the room, taking them in with his welcome. His voice is deep and rich, with an edge of a western nasality. 'Welcome to English 50. I don't like to refer to it as English 50, because to me it says nothing about the course. I'm sure I'm not the only one who finds it just a bit strange that language can be objectified by some arbitrary number. However, I use it this once in an effort to make sure that you've found your way to the right class, like you weren't expecting nuclear physics, or calculus or something.'

There is a ripple of laughter. He turns his back to them, facing the dusty expanse of chalkboard. 'You can laugh, but it happens more than you might think.' He is writing English 50, and then, underneath, in a larger line of squarish block capitals he writes: Introduction to Creative Writing. He says, as he begins a third line, 'My name is Neil Turner.' T-U-R-N-E-R he completes in a swift, practised spill. He turns to face the group; places the bone of chalk on the desk.

'In this class we'll play with the arrangement of words to give something meaning. We're going to spend our time doing that in a variety of ways. To expose you to a breadth of style and form. We're going to read and discuss some of the works of the more notable writers of our day, and we're also going to share our own works, if you will, in order to gain insight and to, hopefully, foster creativity within the group. That, in a nutshell, is it. In this class we'll talk, we'll read, and we'll write. Sound like what you expected?' Several heads nod. With hands on hips at the front of the room, he is now more closely surveying the group assembled before him. 'Good,' he says to the spare response. He brings hands from hips into a sharp, quick clap to dispel the remaining chalk grime and signal his intention to move on.

'I'll get administrative housekeeping out of the way first of all, and then we can get on with things. The college likes me to take the roll at least on this first meeting in an effort to keep their records neat and tidy. Tell me if there's something else you want to be called and I'll make a note. I should also warn you that it takes a while for my mind to put faces and names together, so give me a couple of weeks. I don't mean to be rude, but at the outset I may have to point and just say, *You*. Remember that matching game you used to play as kids? Where you turn the card over and then have to remember where you last saw its mate to make a pair? I never won that game. I got blasted every single time. It pleased my older sister to no end.' Again, there is a light trill of laughter.

There is a certain appeal in his manner. In the way that he treats them almost as equals, includes them in his discourse. He seeks and seems to care for their opinions. He is not overtly stuffy, nor does he have the sense of stern condescension she is used to in a teacher. Not like the sisters at St. Mary's. Maybe it is that he gives the impression he is one of them, like them, that he seems not to be held to the relationship of instructor to student, that his will be an interactive instruction where they are all intended to be linked in common pursuit, one to another. She decides she likes this idea, this unique approach to learning. She is suddenly glad she had seen the posting for the class on the library noticeboard. She is excited at the prospect of rediscovering the imagination in herself.

Gregory

A quick scan, unless there are stragglers, has the count at 12 women, 9 men. Turner looks like an okay kind of guy. Not too uptight, and not too full of himself. She is feeling just the slightest bit surprised, pleasantly. Of the women, one or two look suburban housewife, carefully made-up, hair-did, manicured, a little bit too ready to giggle—on a get-out-of-suburbia pass. There's a handful of younger ones, girls, collegiate-like, or what she expects of that type. A few of the guys are like that too. Then one sort of bohemian hippie chick, lost in the sixties kind of vibe. How she imagines a writer might actually look—peasant skirt to her ankles, strappy brown leather sandals and a tank top. Judging from the show of nipples through ribbed cotton, no bra. The guy front and center—greasy hair down the back side of his neck, ruddy complexion and lined face—seems, in looks, like the oldest of them, even more than the prof. How must that be for someone? And why would you put yourself here, in this kind of environment. Why now? What for? There's a meathead looking guy to her right, close kind of crew-cut, long-ish tattoo of twisted flames stretching out of his t-shirt sleeve and down his arm. A real mix of people. So that she feels she doesn't stand out as much as she worried she might. She is buried in the middle of the arrangement of desks, in a position that lets her blend into the group. More easily than if she were on the periphery.

She wonders what the good doctor has told this guy, Turner, about her. To get her in on a freebie run. What he'd said to him. 'Got a patient who's got a bit of a writing thing. Killed her dad, you see, with a baseball bat.' Isn't there some confidentiality thing that says Gedge couldn't do that? But they're friends, Gedge'd said, so who knows? Who knows how far the red tape and secrets-are-safe bullshit goes? Would he've kept it quiet? Or told him a little, without the gory details, sort of to ease her in without raising too many eyebrows? Hers is the kind of story she imagines a typical kind of man wouldn't keep locked inside of himself. Once it's put on him. Though shrinks are different. Not so easily offended by ugly shit. It's their stock-in-trade. She's going to have to ask him what he said, how much he told him, this Turner guy, though she should know from the way he handles her when she comes up in the roll call. When he calls her name, she ought to be able to read it, from the way he says it.

'Abbott, Gregory.'

'Yeah,' she answers and slides down a little in her seat. His eyes meet hers and take her in swiftly, only his eyebrows register surprise, and it is fleeting. Better than she thought. Not such a big deal. He mustn't know much. Either that or he's pretty damn cool with things, things that most people aren't.

Around her she hears other voices as he moves systematically down the list. 'Bratten, Manfred.' The red-faced older guy answers. 'Elva, Madelena.'

'Maddy. Hi.'

'Maddy,' he notes aloud and marks on the sheet, holding it to his leg to make the correction.

'Franklin, Randall.'

'Make it Randy.'

'Randy, okay. Randy.' He adjusts again.

Names and names and names. She looks down at her notebook where it sits on her desk. *What's in a name?* Shakespeare. From GED class. Inside. She contemplates the oddness of sitting here. That it strikes her almost as surreal.

'Freeman, Mike.'

'Yup.' Tattoo guy. His answer is snappy. Almost a bark. Maybe ex-military.

'Hillborn, Andrew.'

Head of crazy curly hair, sharp nose and heavy dark-framed glasses shoots a skinny white arm in the air to grab attention. 'Andy, that's me.'

'Okay, Andy.'

'Malik, Aneeta.' He looks up. 'Is it Ma-lick or Ma-leek?'

'Ma-lick,' she responds, running the sounds together. This girl is utterly beautiful. Long and willowy. Even her voice is low and melodic. Tinged with accent. Sounds foreign. Exotic. Like her looks. Waves of rich brown hair. Creamy mocha-coloured skin. Like an overshot of milk to coffee. In fact, more like milk with a shot of coffee, and not the other way. Her eyes make her look almost otherworldly. In the sense that they don't match. With her skin. They aren't brown, which, given her look, one would expect. Far from it. Instead they are this pale grey-green. And shaped almost like the eyes of a cat. Wide, with a fine lengthening pull at the ends. Must be relatively new here, otherwise would the accent still be so evident? The girl tucks her hair behind her ear on one side and looks shyly down at her desk.

'Rathner, Ruben.'

'Got me.'

'Tanaka, is it Ka-mee-ko?'

The voice is soft. The girl, a doll-like Asian with ebony hair framing delicate features, looks like a frightened rabbit ready to dart down a hole. 'Hai. Yes.' Her head bobs a few times and then nods a small bow. She looks fragile, like porcelain, like one of those statuettes ladies collect. A china doll. The kind that shatter into a million tiny pieces if they're let go of. That's what this girl reminds her of. And looks so young, like a child almost. She sits very straight in her seat. Proper, and upright. With a rigid and seemingly unnatural posture. She just holds herself. Like an orphan waiting for someone to claim her.

Kameko

She had been worried that she might find it difficult, the people and the language intimidating. In Japan she would no longer be young enough or competitive enough after such a length of leave. In some small way she hopes that a return to learning might give her a sense of some purpose, some direction, some sense of belonging. That it might lead her to rediscover a part of her that has been lost.

The man heading the class is not what one would expect. Not what *she* would expect. He is more like a character from some engaging American novel. Her professors at Waseda had all been what she considered elderly. Elderly is a graceful and distinguished word. Old is perhaps truer. Though not as gentle. Grey-haired eggs, they were. With worn, sagging faces. Sprouting unruly hair from ears, eyebrows, noses, between knuckles. They were brittle in their tones, gruffly soldiering through their teaching deliveries. To know, to understand, must come from experience. So, of course, those who had lived most were given the task of instructing. There was a set form of thought, forum was not encouraged, questions were not typically welcomed. Like a mother bird to its fledglings, they spat up the same already digested food over and over, in the hope that one day the young before them would repeat the cycle. Everything the same. That is the flow of harmony. That concepts, ideas, be accepted as they were put forth.

With some, threads of senility were beginning to weave themselves through the one-sided lectures they delivered. One she remembered, Ogawa-san, used to routinely lose his train of thought in recitations. So that he would have to pause and ask the students to reiterate the idea of his last statements. At which point he would, stroking his chin, say more to himself than to those in the lecture hall, 'Ah, yes.' And, looking blankly on his audience, he would presently return to his dictation almost as if he had not missed even a moment, so much committed to memory was his discourse. Clouds of stifled giggles were disguised by shuffling papers, groaning seats, and a chorus of clearing throats.

She isn't sure that this class is what Shiro would have had in mind when he told her she should get out more. It is recent, this leaning, to do things that might also appeal to her. Perhaps, if she is honest, it is a small act of defiance. Though it is also true that since coming to San Francisco they have become distanced from the hold of the stricter conventions, the traditional roles of husband and wife. He has allowed her to work, and has encouraged her, even pushed her, to forge new relationships. It justifies her presence here, in this class. If she chooses to believe that it satisfies his wishes. She is careful in this way, to think and consider things in the proper order, to think of her husband first. Even if she has intentionally neglected to seek his permission.

'I write because I love it. But it doesn't pay all the bills.' There is some laughter from the other students. 'I teach to pay the bills.' This time his own laughter is layered among them. 'That I teach writing helps me to like what I do. It's a balance thing. Kind of like a marriage.' A trill echoes around the room. Kameko expects it is from those married in the group, those who perhaps have attained the balance he speaks of. The same kind of equilibrium that for she and Shiro is proving elusive, hidden like some treasure in a children's game.

Gregory

He's on the edge of the wooden table intended to function as a desk. Arms crossed over his chest, he's got one foot planted on the floor while the other swings slightly in mid-air. 'I'm not a fan of saying *don't* in writing. As in life, I think rules are meant to be broken, conventions challenged. That's what makes things creative, dynamic and vibrant. I would very much encourage you to experiment with words as a medium of expression. Let's see where that takes us.'

The light in the sky has dimmed to dark. This is so unlike what she had pictured. She is surprised to find she's actually looking forward to doing what he's suggested. Except for the part about having to share and discuss what she puts on paper. Writing's her therapy for a lot of shit that she doesn't really want to offer up for public consumption. Hell, she has enough of a time dissecting it with the good doctor. *Hey guys, here's a little ditty I wrote about what I can do with a baseball bat.* She can just about imagine suburban housewife reaction.

Turner is still talking, and from the looks and sound of things everyone is just sopping the whole spiel up. He has a kind of presence, a charisma, she'll give him that. 'I'm going to expect you to write in different forms and along different parallels, but those are basically the only parameters I'll ascribe to what you're doing. The most important thing I'm going to require of you weekly is to engage in an open discourse. I realize how intimidating that might seem to some—' *No shit, Sherlock*, she thinks, wondering if the comment applies to her alone, '—but the hope is that we can learn from one another. Believe it or not, after 12 years of teaching I'm still learning from my students. And yeah, I started when I was fresh out of high school.' Laughter. 'Joking,' he says mildly, putting up his hand. More laughter. He definitely knows how to work it.

'Nothing is ever wrong, so don't be afraid to push boundaries. Sometimes we'll chat about writers who done good—bad English, I know—writers who got it right, whose work is admired and respected, and widely read: across genders, generations and cultures,' she sees Beauty, the exotic with the grey eyes, nod just the slightest, 'and we'll talk about why you think that might be the case.' He smiles expansively in Beauty's direction. What hot-blooded hetero man alive wouldn't?

'Along with doing it regularly—' he gets a laugh out of pretty much everybody that time, 'yeah, ha-ha—the best thing you can do for your writing is to read; anything and everything. Read with a critical eye. I mean, really turn every single bit over in your mind. What's good about it, what you like, or conversely, what's maybe not so great. I don't care what it is, just read! It could be city billboards, restaurant menus, letters, newspaper articles, poetry, fiction, non-fiction, I don't care. It all adds to who you'll become as a writer. The library or, depending on how deep your pockets happen to be, the bookstore ought to be your new favourite hangout.' A few more titters, and just the smallest hint of a smile from China Doll.

'Okay, for next week: I'd like each of you to bring a passage from a published work that you admire or might have particularly enjoyed—perhaps even that you feel describes you in some sense—to read and discuss. A gentle beginning that, I think, will give us all some insight into one another. As people first. And writers second. What do writers write most about? People. And in a broader context, the human condition. That's what makes us relate to things we read, that's also what motivates us to write what we write.' There is some shuffling of belongings at his natural finish.

'So, in closing the first of our sessions, I want to leave you with something as profound as it is banal. Something that bears keeping in mind when you put words together creatively. It's exceedingly obvious, but crucial to every single written offering. It's that every piece of writing, without exception, has three common elements—a beginning, a middle, and an end. The beginning, it's got the hook that pulls us in, piques our human interest, our curiosity; the middle gives us something to sink our teeth into; the end is meant to give us the sense that we've made a journey, and that along our journey significant development has taken place. Sounds simple enough, right?'

He stands. 'That's it for our intellectual ground-base tonight. But before you go, I'm handing out a course outline,' he removes a slim sheaf of paper from the pile on the table and takes it to Manfred, the red-faced guy, who happens to be the closest of the group to the front of the room, 'with a formalized schedule and format for the course. In the upper right hand corner you'll find a phone number: my office. And office hours. Once you've got yourself a sheet you're free to flee.'

Gregory
5 days later
Office of Arthur C. Gedge
Doctor of Psychology
San Francisco

It's still very warm in the city. The sky is that colour of unmarred true blue that comes with serious heat even though summer is almost gone. It's hard to believe she's been outside the brick and barbed wire more than three months. She sits in Gedge's office, waiting on the doc. The windows with their glass-lights are opened to their fullest to try and capture whatever air might be moving. She likes looking at the pattern the colours throw on the walls. Every now and then there is a whisper of a breeze. Gregory can feel it, just barely, as it dances along the tops of the hairs that line her forearm. She gets up and walks to the water dispenser in the corner of the room. Pulls down on a cone-shaped cup. Chooses the darker blue handle. For the cold water. Crazy. Water dispenser with a temperature choice. So simple. This one or this one. What do you feel like? Cold or not so? How shrink-ish. A mind-fuck for the patients. Like lab rats. Which one to choose?

The door opens after a short tap of warning. 'Gregory.' She turns away from the blue tinted cylinder, holding the cone of water in her hand. A bit of pressure could send it up and over the rim. She watches it as she makes her way to the chair before his desk, the way it shivers with movement.

'So?'

'So.'

'How've you been?'

'Good. Pretty good.'

They sit, square to one another. Her on one side of the desk, he on the other. She drinks the cup. He reaches across for it. 'Here, let me take that.'

'Sure.' She crumples it. Hands it over. He deposits it in a garbage underneath his desk. She wipes the back of her hand across her damp brow. She is sweaty from the bike ride over. Does not really relish the trip back. Up those hills. In the heat.

He regards her, like he is looking for some clue. Some indicator to start things off, to give their conversation a direction for the day. She is used to the way this works now. It irritated her at first. He calls it finding a starting point for things. In the absence of one being offered first by her. He used to always have to initiate. Lately not as much. But she lets him have his look, his wander over her features, the instinctive actions of her physical behaviour, see what there is to see, from the outside.

'Started class last week.' He doesn't seem surprised. Is it catalogued? In her file? In his memory? Has he seen Professor Turner since?

'How was it?'

'Good.'

'How'd you feel before?'

'Before, when before?' She is playing a bit with him now. She knows what he's asking. But, thing is, the answer's not so easy to figure. 'Uh, guess the truth is, a couple of days before I almost talked myself out of going.'

'But you went.'

'Yeah. Had to give myself a bit of a rough pep talk first.'

'Don't be so hard on yourself, Gregory.'

He uses her name comfortably. Usually people don't. Most can't.

'If I wasn't hard on myself I'd have crawled into a little hole by now.'

'Why do you say that?'

'Just…it's easier, you know? To insulate myself. From things. Anyway, point is, I went.'

'So that was good. You managed to get past your fear.'

'Yeah, I guess.'

'It will get easier, you know.'

'Sure as hell hope so.'

'How was the class?'

'I liked it. For the first time and all.'

'And how did you feel, being among the other students?'

'Nervous. Transparent.'

'But did it go away, that feeling? As time progressed?'

'Yeah, some. Good people watching.'

'What do you mean by that?'

'Just that it's a different group. Not all college crew cookie-cutter cutouts is all.'

'Did that make you feel more at ease?'

'Yeah. It made me feel like it would be, well, like I wouldn't stand out so much.'

'Do you think you stand out?'

'Yeah. That all the wrong things show.'

'You think that among a more uniform day-school kind of college grouping you might feel more obvious.'

'Yeah. It was a bit of a relief. And Turner,' she clears her throat and shrugs, 'he seems like a decent guy.'

Gedge smiles a bit at the compliment. 'He is.'

Under her arms is slippery with perspiration. 'Um, I have to ask, 'cause I kind of, well, the thought crossed my mind sitting there, when he took the roll, you know…'

'Yes?'

'Well, how much he knows. I mean, about me. You must have told him enough to get me into the class, but…well…it made me really uncomfortable, the not knowing.'

'You have to realize, Gregory, he understands that I'm bound by confidentiality.'

'Yeah, and so that means you told him what?'

'We met for coffee, I said I had a patient that I felt had talent and who, I thought, could benefit from his class, but without the means to pursue it independently.'

'Okay.'

'I asked him if he would do me a favour.'

'Okay.'

'He agreed.'

'And?'

'That's it.'

'He didn't ask any questions?'

'No.'

'So what kind of info, details, did you give? To get me on the list?'

'I gave him just your name. The telephone and address, et cetera, are care of this office.'

'Oh.'

'Are you okay with that?'

'Yeah, I suppose. So basically he knows that I'm your patient, that's all. And that he's doing you a favour having me there.'

'That's about it. Whatever else comes during the course of his class is entirely up to you.'

She nods thoughtfully at the knowledge. That her secrets are safe. Well, except for the fact that she's in therapy. But that's not so unusual.

Gedge is looking at her to see what effect all this is having. What her mental processes are doing with the information. 'Now that you know, how do you feel about it? What I've told the professor?'

'I guess it makes me more comfortable. Like I'm okay to go back. Like everyone won't be looking at me funny. For some sign. That I'm a crazy killer or something.'

'But you're not, Gregory. I thought we had established that. I thought you had accepted that.'

'I know, I know, but it's not so easy. It's habit—wondering what others see, what kind of conclusions they might draw. If they know the ugly side of the story.'

'It's up to you what they know, or what they will know of you.'

'Thanks.'

'There's no need.'

'Still.'

'Then—you're welcome.'

The Beginning:
A Three Cornered World

The knowledge that we are responsible for our actions and attitudes does not need to be discouraging, because it also means that we are free to change this destiny. One is not in bondage to the past. All this can be altered if we have the courage to examine how it formed us. We can alter the chemistry, provided we have the courage to dissect the elements.

Anaïs Nin

Gregory
Durham County Lock-Up, California
1997

Her visitor. She has known who it would be. Only one person it could be. It shoots through her. Mama. She's not prepared. For the moment she'll set eyes on her. The first since she'd splintered their lives into a million tiny shards. The only thing she knows for sure: there is no fix for what she's done.

What must Mama think? Feel? What could she say? What can be said after, to a woman widowed by her own daughter, her own flesh? What?

She could still feel the weight of wood in her hands, soft and smooth. How she'd turned it, the shaft of the bat, gripping it hard. She could still feel the thrashing, the swinging movement. The hit of gristle, of bone. And she could smell it: the fight, the dinner, the blood. Like it's a downdraft coming through the prison vents.

Her hands. She flips them over in her lap. Splays her fingers wide. Hands of a killer. They hold no sign. Of what they're capable of. The shackles on them are clunky and brutishly oversized. They bite where skin is thin over bone. Seems unlikely, she thinks, turning them at an angle, lifting them as far as the chain lets her, to even imagine.

She functions in a daze, the hours she's awake. There is a sense that she's swallowing down sand, sand that pours and sifts over her insides, settling porridgey and dense. Her brain whirs like a wheel in mud, spinning itself uselessly round and round without taking to anything. Like a motor missing the gears. She is exhausted, and yet agitated. Shaky.

She feels like she ought to offer apology, but knows she won't mean it. It'd be hollow, empty. She simply needs, in this visit, this meeting, to make certain that Mama is okay, that she's going to be okay. That she'll be looked after. She has to summon enough energy to talk Mama through things. It's the only thing she can do now for her.

The person she sees through the wall of plexiglass looks hardly anything like the woman she thought she knew. The woman whose secrets she shared. The woman whose suffering she's lived next to all her life. Mama is birdlike, frail in appearance. She has the look of a child; disoriented and unsure in the strange surroundings. She is young-old in a way that pierces Gregory. Fear runs sharp and plain through her features, her expression, her body moves.

As she sits, her hands butterfly. They travel from face to neck to the invisible of her lap and then back again. Mama's face is drawn, pinched and tight.

23

Angular lines pull at red rimmed eyes, eyes that hover over blackened half-moons. Skin crepes at her jawline and gives her a worn look that adds years to the thirty-six already lived.

Her neckline is covered. It will take weeks for the last of him to die down. Even with him gone, Mama's still programmed the same. The paisley pattern of the too familiar scarf, a rainbow of reds and purples and orange, wraps the entire length of neckline and on into the collar of her cotton long-sleeved blouse. The scarf finishes with a jaunty bow. The happy look is a lie. She knows what the flesh looks like under the disguise. Handprints mapping out the hold he had on her. At the top edge of fabric Gregory can see the beginnings of a purple-blue cloud peeking out of the scarf's charade, their shades a testimony to the freshness of the event. A rush of nausea twists in her. The gypsy scarves Mama called them. She made it a bit of fun between them. Dressing up in all sorts of scarves. Until Gregory'd come to realize the real purpose of their *play* was to hide the marks, the injuries. Bruises, cuts, welts, stitches, broken bones. To stop the potential for whispering, for questions.

With a quivering half-smile Mama lifts the earpiece uneasily to her. *Oh Mama, I am so sorry, and yet I am not, not at all.*

'Gregory, I...' Mama turns to look behind her. At guards, at the other visitors. She leans in to the glass. 'I don't like this. This place. I feel...' she turns again and whispers, 'like everyone is staring. Like everyone knows. It doesn't feel safe. It doesn't feel right.' She is fingering the knot of her bow.

'Mama, you need to be calm.'

'Gregory, how can this be happening? How?'

'Mama, I need you to listen. Mama?' Mama's breathing is fast, panicky, in her ear. 'Mama! How're you doing? Did you let them take you to hospital?'

Carefully, Mama circles the truth of it. 'Well, I...I told them I was feeling fine, you know. They told me that I might have had some injury related to drowning! To drowning! But I...I told them I was fine. Fine! But they...they insisted. I didn't know what to do. What was I supposed to do? I knew he'd be so angry with me. Oh God, he would've been so angry. And then...they said... they told me...he was gone.' She whispers the words. 'Gone.' Mama looks up very slowly and into Gregory. 'And...well, I didn't know what else to do. They took me on down to General with sirens and all. On a stretcher in the back. All sorts of machines and things they attached to me. It was all a bit much, you know? I told them I was okay. God, he would've been so angry.' Her eyes drop and she raises a hand to smother her emotion.

'Mama, I just need you to tell me, okay? So you let them check you over?'

'Oh, they made such a fuss. And I told them I wasn't really sure what it was they wanted since I was feeling fine.'

'Mama, you were not fine. You needed to be seen to. To find out whether there was damage. That couldn't be seen. To the brain, lungs.'

'I mean, drowning, Gregory? I told them that it was ridiculous. He never would've let me drown.'

'Then what was he doing, Mama? What the hell was he doing? What then—if you think he wasn't drowning you? What?'

Her speaking is jittery. Nervous. 'I didn't have any broken bones. Didn't even really get bloodied anywhere. Just some bruises. Only bruises. He didn't hurt me real bad. Not too bad. It wasn't bad at all. I just didn't…understand all the fussing…all the fuss they were making.' The thin veneer of composure begins to crumble. 'Oh. Oh. Now where? I can't…I just need a Kleenex. Just…' She is rifling frantically through her handbag, jerkily reaching with her free hand, 'I can't seem to…I…I don't think I can do this. I don't want to do this. Why? Why?' Her mouth yaws wide, the ends pull down. The hand flies up to cover it. Trembles there. Fingers fluttering like butterfly wings. Mama is coming undone. 'Why, Gregory? Why? Why did you have to?' She whispers the questions without looking up. Gregory can feel heat burning her eyes. She cannot cry. Not here. Not now. She turns to look quickly at the guards, hoping the sight of them will hammer down the urge.

Drawing a crumpled wad of tissue from the inside compartment of her bag, Mama wipes streaming tears from her cheeks. 'I can't believe he's gone. I can't believe it.' She is shaking her head—no, no, no. She says it again, this time barely above a whisper, 'I can't believe it.' Her head drops and her hand rises to shield her eyes. Suddenly it is impossible for her. The second. The moment. Reality. She heaves with her anguish. Sound rises up and stalls in her throat; her knuckles are mottled white around the handset. 'He never would have killed me. I know that. He loved me. He didn't mean to hurt…' Attempts at keeping her grief private are slipping. 'He didn't mean it. He needed me to help…him.' Words are buried between hiccupping sobs.

Gregory holds the receiver still, but feels strangely distant. Removed. Mama's grief does not belong to her. 'If it was my time, I was ready. Gregory, don't you see? I was ready. Maybe…maybe if the good Lord had taken me home, maybe it would've been all he needed. All Curtis needed. To change. Then I would've achieved what God wanted for me in this life. You see? Maybe it was meant to be that way.'

'And what would you've had me do, Mama? What're you saying? That I should have let well enough alone and watched it be you? That I shouldn't have been interfering in the plans you thought you might have had with God? That I should've been okay with it? Because there was some greater good involved? He was trying to kill you. Killing you. And yes, he would have. I swear it. The way he was going, he would have.'

'He would've stopped. You didn't know him like I did. Yes, he loved me. Times it may not have seemed…' her talk is broken, confused. 'But he loved me. We…we understood each other. He didn't need to die. He shouldn't have died. It wasn't right for him to die….' She is rocking in the hard plastic of the chair. Back and forward. Little movements. She holds tightly to the limp Kleenex, hand gnarled around it.

Guilt gnaws at Gregory. Around raw edges. But only for the way she has rearranged Mama's life. Not for him. If she was in that place again she would've done the same. What if? Her mind swells at a horrifying thought. It's like she's been kicked in the gut. Icy spider legs trail up the back of her neck, into her hair. God forbid she should consider the alternative. That he'd lived. Where he's concerned, she is flat. Spent. Tinny empty.

'So many questions.' Mama is whispering again into the handset, but Gregory can hardly make it out.

'Mama?' she queries.

'There are so many questions. And, I don't know. I just don't know...' Now she is weeping quietly, a soft mewling.

Gregory needs to bring her around. 'Mama.' She says it sharp, prying into her grief. 'Did you do like I told you and call Lil?' Her voice is pleading. She needs to know Mama's taken care of.

Mama nods, 'I got her at the bakery this morning.' Lips tremble and her chin puckers. 'She's...she's coming. Said she would get someone to mind the shop and drive right on down.'

Gregory had never, not for one moment, doubted Lil's rally. She lets herself wonder, selfishly, what Lil would have thought at Mama's call. She imagines her sinking heavily onto the stool by the counter. By the sunny yellow of the wall with the telephone. Hands clotted with flour and sticky dough. She doubts the news would have rocked Lil. She'd known it would come to tragedy eventually. Though this? Maybe not this very way.

Gregory
Yreka, California
1993

She'd needed to get out. She just couldn't stomach it. The clumsy chaos of it. The wild of limbs striking out. The smacking sound when there's a hammered connection between flesh and bone. And Mama's weak defence, her pleas, her prayers, her cajoling. Saving herself has always seemed selfish. But what good can she do? What the hell good, anyway? Damn, she wishes Mama would up and walk away. Get out. For good.

Gregory huddles tightly against the damp of the morning cool, leaning into a railing post. She holds her sweatshirt neck over mouth and nose to try and capture the fleeting warmth of escaping breath. Shivering against the bite in the early spring air, she tries to think of something other than being cold. Or tired. She wonders how long she's been waiting. Plays a mental game of countdown. The darkness is changing around her, lightening ever so slightly. Or is it imagination?

Why Lil's, why the bakery where Mama works, she doesn't rightly know. Usually she'd rather be alone. But she trusts Lil. It's an instinct she's got, deep in her gut. That, and she's limited in her options. As in, this is it. She's tired of running. This door with its fading red frame will be open before dawn. And it'll be open to her. For warmth, shelter, comfort.

The run of shallow stairs backs onto a gravel laneway behind the row of smallish, tidy buildings whose pretty facades face onto quaint Main Street. Here, she's kept hidden from prying eyes. From questions. From the regular, slow cruise of black and whites. She pulls her knees more tightly in to try and keep the chill from creeping through the gaps in her cramped shape. She has tried to close her eyes, to rest, but the sounds and shifting shadows keep her on guard.

Night is receding, it isn't a trick of her eyes. Slowly, slowly it is giving way. She hears footsteps. The crunch of loose gravel. She raises a silent prayer. *Please, please let it be Lil.* The figure rounds the corner and suddenly stops. Baron, Lil's constant canine companion, gives a low rumble in the back of his throat. His ears point high and his sharply curled tail stands to attention with warning. For just a fraction he waits before the scent of her makes her from foe into friend. His tail wags in greeting and his head drops. With a slow whine he approaches and his warm tongue licks at her frigid hand. 'Hey, Baron. Hey,' she says quietly as he leans into her. Lil had rescued him from a shelter after her husband Al's death on tour in the Arabian Gulf.

A woman now on her own, Baron provided protection and companionship.

'Saves my sanity, he does.' She'd named him—she'd laughed telling them—for the shepherd in his breed mix and for his upright and dignified bearing, even though he was nothing but a cuddly teddy bear.

'Dear sweet Jesus, Gregory! You just about had my heart at a standstill! What in heaven's name are you doing here?'

Lil had given Mama a place to work that was also a place of refuge. For them both. The small bakery had given Lil's sisterhood as much as it had given a paycheck. Mama didn't have to hide with Lil. Between them there was a bond founded on compassion and knowing that came without judgment. There was a shoulder in times of need, a ready ear, an unquestioning friendship. With Lil there was no need for secrets.

'You come inside this instant and get yourself out of the damp. God, it creeps right through your bones. And you in just a sweatshirt? It's a wonder you're not a solid block of ice. Get to your feet, girl, and get in here.' Lil moves briskly through the door and into the narrow hallway, flicking lights as she goes. Gregory follows, Baron proudly strutting at her side. His head is cocked, his eyes are bright with the light of excitement at having unearthed a friend so early in his day.

'Sit down, Gregory. Just right here, while I make you something warm.' Lil moves with familiarity around the perimeter of the worktop island to fill a kettle and set it to boil.

'Now then, let's take that hood down and have a real look at you. He didn't come at you, did he? He'd better not dare, that man. I'd have the police on him so fast, he wouldn't have a clue what hit. Your mama, Gregory, she's coerced me into an understanding. Of leaving things be. For her sake. But a child's a different matter altogether.'

'Lil, he didn't get me. Wasn't out for me. It's just the regular thing. I left and…and I just didn't feel like going on back. I feel ashamed, actually, thinking about it. I should've gone back to look in on her after.'

Lil sighs, 'You know, Gregory, I want to help her, I really do. That man truly makes my blood boil. But she's going to have to want to help herself first. That day's gotta come soon, God love her. Hon, much as I want things to be different, I cannot save her, just like you can't. It's going to have to be down to her. So help me, though, if he beats up on you—'

'I'm okay, Lil. Really. I just…I just needed to…just get away from it. That's all.'

'Your lips are blue, Gregory. Give me your hands,' and Gregory, who has not strength for anything other than to simply do as she is told, passes them stiffly into Lil's custody.

'You are freezing, young lady. Absolutely freezing. Just how long have you been leaned up against my back rail like that? You foolish young thing.' Lil rubs furiously at Gregory's numb skin.

'Who's counting, Lil?'

'Why, I'm counting, that's who! Here I am trying to bring life back to your limbs and you're full of sass. You're going to be impertinent with me, young lady, at a time like this? What were you thinking? Why did you not come on up to the house?'

With Lil's scolding and the back and forth banter Gregory can feel herself thawing, regaining her senses. Once the kettle is boiled, Lil fixes a steaming mug of tea and sets it before her. Gregory wraps her hands tightly around it to let its warmth travel through her. She lowers her face to the steam coming off it. Her hands are shifting in colour from blue to reddish-pink. A slow sigh escapes.

'Get some of that liquid to your insides,' Lil urges.

'Last thing I wanted was for some eager beaver rookie on night patrol to pick me up. Cops are totally predictable. Whatever they stumble into the tin badges think they've got a right to fix. If that's the case, then we're gone. Pulling out. Headed for the road. Before ink's even dry on the report. I kind of like it around here. Wouldn't mind staying a while is all.'

'Kind of nice not having to be all alone this morning. Isn't it, Baron?' Baron barks. It makes Gregory smile. 'Well, seeing as you're here, kiddo, might as well make a helper of you. I'll put you to work. Just as soon as I've fixed you one of my special Mexican omelets. We'll be a team today, you and me. I'll give Mrs. Bosworth at the school a call to let her know you'll be out for the day. Don't believe you'd be much for thinking today, not after the night you've just had. Right?'

In the corner, Baron wags mildly and whines as though he's understood the mention of breakfast. They both laugh a bit at his expectancy. His tail marks a happy sideways arc against the floorboards. Lil readies eggs, cheese, tomatoes, onions. 'The man is a monster, plain and simple. No two ways about it. Deserves to be behind bars. Man who beats a woman's nothing short of the most evil creature on the face of this planet. But you know that it is absolutely not my intention at all to have Curtis running off. I'd rather keep you two close. Oh, if Al were alive, he'd teach him a thing or two about being a man. By God, he would.' Lil is chopping and cracking and whisking like there is no tomorrow. Baron has stood up and walked to where Gregory sits. He puts his head gently, knowingly, into her lap. He looks up at her with sympathy in his liquid eyes. She takes a hand from the mug and strokes him thoughtfully.

There's a sizzle of butter running in a hot skillet. The smell of it makes Gregory's stomach rumble. Baron's ears prick at the sound. 'It's just me, silly,' she tells him affectionately, rubbing him under his muzzle.

'Hon, I'm sorry, I am. For sticking my big old beak up into it, but it just makes me so damn mad, it does. He does. You know it is more than a person ought to ever have to deal with. You shouldn't have to be in the middle of this kind of mess. I've said it to your mama. She's always making excuses for him. Telling me how he's trying to change. How he just needs another chance.' Lil sighs and shrugs her exasperation, 'I don't know, Gregory. As God is my witness, I do not understand her.'

She finishes dropping the last of vegetables and seasoning and cheese onto the cooking eggs and brushes the back of her hand along her forehead. 'You starting to shake that chill off? Getting a bit of warmth to your bones?'

'Yeah, I'm better.'

'Your lips still look blue, but there's colour rising in your cheeks. You're not as ghost pale.' Lil flips the omelet expertly. 'Sure as hell hope she's all right.' She squints at the wall clock, 'I'll give her till 9. And if she's a no-show I'll try and get her on the phone.' She moves into the racks of utensils, pans and forms. Picking and choosing with a familiarity and an instinct for the baking needing to be done. She exhales loudly as she goes about arranging her tools in the way that she likes them. Rolling pins here, pie pans there. And the muffin tins. 'No good can come of her being with him. After he does this time and again. No good whatsoever.

'You know,' Lil begins, her expression brightening, 'I've just had a thought. A damn good one, I think. Any time you want—I mean it—there's my office. You know the room at the top of the stairs, in the attic? I've got a little couch there, and, you know, the basics. It's nothing fancy. I used to spend a lot of time there myself right after…well, right after I lost Al. Couldn't bear being home on my own, all alone, or lying down there in our bed. But now? It doesn't get used much. Hardly at all, in fact. I don't want you spending another night,' she gestures, her thumb raised in hitchhiking motion at the back door, 'out there.' Lil turns and busies herself at the sink, her back to Gregory, 'I'll leave a spare key out back. There's a little hook under the porch for my dust pan. That's where it'll be. You make sure and use it. Whenever there's trouble. Even when there's not. No need to ask, okay? And I will be sure and tell your mama I've said for you to do it. To have your space.

'Now, let's you and me and patient-as-Job Baron eat up, and then get on with what needs doing, so I'm ready to deal with your mama when time rolls to.'

Baking with Lil is a much-needed diversion, one that wraps her in simple, undemanding comfort. Lil teaches Gregory how to work her hands. Shows her that they are capable of creation. Worthwhile creation. In every successive pinch of salt, cup of flour, every roll and push of dough, every carefully carved round and resulting fresh loaf or pie, cake or cookie, there is a sense of purpose, satisfaction, and a growing confidence.

Lil doesn't ask questions when she shows up. Even if it's during school hours. She just gives her a job, puts her to work. If Mama's working and tries to say something Lil simply shushes her quiet.

For Gregory, the tiny attic room is a slice of heaven. She'd conjure just about any reason or excuse to be there. Lil seems pleased that she comes around more often. She leaves notes posted on the walls, a tiny pillow embroidered with 'Home Sweet Home' on the worn but welcoming couch. Sample soaps, a hairbrush, toothbrush and toothpaste crop up seemingly out of nowhere; followed, over time, by a Spring Lilac mist, dried flowers in a vase, a tube of sheer pink lip gloss, a portable CD player.

It is in the haven of her tiny attic tower that she stumbles across it. A scrap of coloured tissue, torn from a larger whole, wrinkled with use. Its hue is a tender and inviting blue. She holds it to the light of the tiny window that is carved into the gable of the roof, and is taken by the way it gives itself over to the light. How together they cast the same colour into the room itself. So enchanted is she by the effect that she tamps the edge of tissue into the tight closure of the window frame. She's seen coloured glass like this before. Little pieces made into big picture windows in some of the churches of towns they've lived in or passed through. Sometimes, too, in fancy shops. Once in an antique confectionery filled with rainbows of candy. Never, though, has she seen from the inside what light can do with colour.

She keeps an eye out for similar paper. In the art studio at school she pulls discarded clippings from the waste bin, quickly stuffing them into pockets or flaps of binders or books. She begins to assemble a collage of scraps. A tumbled jigsaw pattern that grows across a good half of the window, the misshapen edges adding character in their lack of uniformity. The light behind it throws something pretty and delicate onto the walls. It gives her something. Though she can't say what. Out of this collection of mismatched, jagged-edged bits and pieces rescued from the trash she's made something worthwhile, something beautiful.

When Curtis comes whooping in one night saying he's got work further south, it's no big surprise. Time they were moving, he says. He talks about things being better, making all the same old promises that never come to pass. For the first time she can recall, Mama mounts a half-hearted protest. To stay. Saying she's gotten to like the place. But he can see through her. 'Don't like that old bakery bitch. Don't want her getting up in our private business. In our family stuff.' He says it with a hard tone. 'You been getting too friendly like I always warn you against, and I don't want her talking. 'Sides I've gone ahead and accepted the position already, look bad if I were to back out. Thought you could at least find it in your good heart to be happy for me. They're mentioning the possibility of management someday. Be a step up. An *opportunity*. See, I got management talk in me. I got the right words for it. There's not a thing that's keeping me here. Not a single thing.'

Lil edges around it with her customary matter-of-factness, though her voice is tight. 'If you ever need anything, you hear, anything at all, you know where to find me. I mean it. Call, write, send smoke signals, I don't give a damn. Call collect. Just, please…You don't want to be on the hook for making an old lady lonely. I need to be needed.' Lil puts her hand to Gregory's cheek, brushes her tears away and gives a half-smile. 'Be good, kiddo. Bear up. And for God's sake, stay out of that man's way.'

Gregory can only nod. Baron whines, sensing that something isn't right. She presses her face into him, soaking his ruff with her tears.

'I hope that I don't hear from you because he's managed to lay her in a pine box. God in heaven, you hear me?' she raises up her plea to the sky. 'I pray he doesn't kill her. I'll never forgive myself for standing by like she wanted.

'I'm going to say one thing to you, Gregory, you listen and hear me good. Baby, I know you feel it's your job to pick up the pieces, but your mama's life doesn't have to be yours. Your mama's dear to me, you know that, but you can't be held up by her choices. Just you remember that. You need to make your own life. It won't do you any good to go and get yourself lost in hers. Her battles? Her war? It's not yours. You do your best to steer clear of it, won't you? And remember, I'm here. Any time at all.' Lil looks hard into her eyes, 'You need me, I'm here. For the both of you. Don't forget it, okay?'

Curtis is whistling to himself as they pull out of town the last time, the reflection behind them blurred and shrinking in the Chevy's rearview mirror.

Gregory
Durham County Lock-Up, California
1997

How they move she'd never noticed. Black pointed arms shaking hands. One by one by one. Like a politician along a campaign route. Tick. Tick. Tick. It burns into her brain. Time. Just the passing of it, of seconds, is boggling when it's all a person has.

She tears her eyes away from the black and white wall clock and considers the room. To try and divert her attention from fixing on the waiting. Everything is coated in the same bleakness. Old and worn; dirty with human discontent. The table's pebbled oatmeal surface tells a weary tale—of palms pushing papers back and forward; hands pressing against it for a sense of stability; fingertips thrumming, keeping rhythm with the clock; the pounding fists of outrage. Fear, anguish, fury, sorrow. She imagines that the inside of this room has seen variations of the same scene over and over and over again. Hundreds of times. Thousands of times. Futility is the common thread in them all.

She looks down, the grotesque tangerine hue pulling her eye. It is so at odds with her mind's processing of the rest of the surrounding dreariness of this place. She closes her eyes against it, the brightness of the prison kit, but behind her eyelids the same things replay over and over. In fragments, shards, little pieces of the whole. Without order. Digging at her.

They have tried to give her meds. For pain, for sleep, for shock, for anxiety, for depression. Their reasons for her need are endless. So many different pills. Names she cannot get her tongue around. *Are you depressed? Are you feeling depressed*, they ask her. She does not know. She is numb. Somewhere drowning in darkness. Voices fade in and out. *It will make things better. Make the process easier. They'll help. You'll see.* 'No.' She says it, but it is stronger than she feels. She shakes her head. She is terrified, but she cannot lose herself. She needs to hang on to reality. As hard as it is.

She has accepted her fate. But she will not give in to it. Her back is starting to hurt where she has been pushing it into the hardness of the rigid frame of the chair. As she looks around again she knows they are watching. From every corner. Through every piece of mirrored glass. They will search her following her visitor. Making her squat, cough, fingering her, pushing at her. Gloved fingers poking and prodding. She tries not to dwell there. It's part of the process. The rules. She is a part of their machinery. A cog in the wheel. She hears the louder tick and pull of the hour hand as it rearranges itself on the black and white face. Another hour gone.

She waits. For one Kendall Busch. Public defender. He fits in with the slow swamp around her. *If you cannot afford one, one will be appointed for you.* They first met, herself and Kendall Busch, at her booking and arraignment. A furtive meeting. Little by way of exchange between them. She remembers not much. Just the sight of him. His mouth moved at her, for her, like a recording set to the wrong speed. She'd tried to follow the process. To fill in the blanks. Strange, the way the system worked. We'll condemn you for what you've done. Then we'll pretend to want to help you.

There's a shuffle of shadow beneath the base of the door. Interrupting the motley fluorescence. An earsplitting buzz slices through stuffy silence, the lock giving way to her visitor. She finds the sounds on this side unnerving. Hard. Harsh. They burn into her brain. Perhaps it's the way sound travels from stone to steel and back again. There is nothing to soften it.

Kendall Busch is unkempt and shabby. His threadbare sport jacket hangs from sloped shoulders. He is without a tie, and his shirt collar pulls open to one side. She can see stains from the skin at his neck on the frayed edges of fabric. His trousers are creased and too wide for his frame. The brown leather of his belt is adjusted under the extending bulge of his middle-aged waistline. The whole of him is like a sigh. Defeated.

He settles in the chair opposite her, the tabletop dividing them, and takes to shuffling paper in a manila folder heavy with history. He does not raise his eyes to look at her. Instead, he clears his throat. She can see he is uncomfortable. Can read it. Written all over him. He continues to fumble until he finds a thin stack of paper, stapled in one corner. She sees her name and his name. He takes it from the folder and taps the edges against the tabletop. He flips quickly through the pages. A vein of ice runs through her.

'Uh, Gregory,' he starts awkwardly, with uncertainty in his voice. His eyes flick once more over the top sheet, she sees his lips move slightly, forming words in silence. With more firmness he begins again. 'Gregory,' he raises his eyes up for the first time to meet her own and plunges into what has brought him, 'I've had a meeting with the prosecutor and with the judge. This morning.' He pauses. 'We had quite a lengthy discussion,' he offers, no doubt to show the effort made on her behalf. And she knows, suddenly, what will be next. 'Uh, the prosecution, Gregory, has offered a plea bargain in your case. One that is worth consideration.'

He clears his throat again and raises a hand to the bridge of his eyeglasses, adjusting where they sit on his nose. 'We talked in some depth about the circumstances of this case, your case. We talked about your history, and about you both, meaning yourself and your mother, and your, uh, situation…what you've endured over the years. Unfortunately, the prosecution can make that work in its favour. Because it speaks to motive. And they both feel, the judge and the prosecutor, that given your psych assessment, there is nothing to suggest that you weren't in control of your faculties at the time. At the time, uh…' Pause. She senses his hesitation as he struggles for words. Words to state the obvious. The obvious that he seems to feel he must tiptoe around. As if she is somehow unaware. 'At the time you took your father's life.'

His hands again begin to shuffle file papers, telegraphing his unease. 'Then there's the question as to whether or not the use of force was reasonable. There is some disagreement. In that regard.' Halting. Reading. Studying. 'Gregory, the prosecution isn't disputing what took place, and that you were required to step in and take action to stop it, but they are saying that the amount of force used to stop the strangulation was greater than necessary. What they put to the judge when we talked, Gregory, is that this killing was less about you saving your mother's life and more about your own need for retribution. And that, of course, and the outcome, the homicide, goes to their point of excess. It is, however, very hard to nail down, in these cases, what the outcome would have been if the force used were within reasonable limits. So that mitigates their stance some.' He sighs; puts the papers down. He regards her through grease-marked lenses. 'Suffice it to say, Gregory, the prosecutors feel that Curtis ought to be alive today.' Her body spasms involuntarily with the statement.

'Then there's the matter of the Emergency Room release forms. Gregory, the fact that your mother signed those forms over the years released Curtis from all culpability. The fact that she didn't wish to press charges against him, ostensibly for injuries she allegedly sustained at his hand, well, it damn near exonerates him.'

'Might as well have had a gun to her head.' A ribbon of frustration threads slowly through her.

He clears his throat again, 'Look, I know. For what it's worth, I get what you're saying. I'm not saying that what he did, what he did to you both, was okay. But you have to understand that to the law this is like one great big puzzle. And all its parts have to be accounted for and accommodated. And weighed up the same. That's what the judge has to do here.

'The plea, Gregory, all things considered, is one I think is pretty fair. Given the charge and the sensitivities of circumstance.' He plunders on now, not waiting. He wants to be rid of his burden. 'Since you're a first time offender with no prior history, they're willing to accept a plea of guilty to manslaughter. Five years is what you'd get, credit for time served, credit for behaviour, a year's parole after. They're recommending Garden State Correctional Facility for Women. It's one of the better ones. Good reputation for inmate rehabilitation. Not so large a population. Conditions are better than most. Clean. Programs and therapy. GED. Your chances are better. I'm recommending that you think on this deal carefully. I truly don't think there's anything to be gained from a trial. I think you'd do worse out of it, in my estimation.'

He sounds like he's describing a vacation. Like she is planning on going on a trip. Some trip. She'll take it, the plea. It's the price to be paid. Comparatively, it is small. She is nodding. Cannot bring herself to speak it. Her agreement. But he knows. He sees it. She adds up the time. When she's done she'll be free to start again.

Gregory
San Francisco
September 2002

Why should she give a shit what they think? Any of them. Even him, Professor Turner, for that matter. It should be a simple assignment, not the noose around her neck she's made it out to be. If this is the way it's going to go with her week after week, she's sure to have a nervous breakdown before term's end. Doc Gedge said she might find it liberating. The good doctor. Always quick with the prescription. But not having lived with the illness, does he really know the best remedy? Can he?

Fuck it, she thinks. *I can do this.* Then, just as quickly, the direction of thought changes. *I can't, I'm not strong enough, I'm not ready.* Then: *What are you hiding from? What are you still hiding from? When are you ever going to be ready if not now? Are you going to spend the rest of your life hiding? Hiding from everyone and everything? Stop being such a coward, a chicken shit.*

She needs to just pick something. Not labour it. So she chooses. Because she can relate. The dreams, the loneliness, the conflict and confusion. She feels Steinbeck's words, his ideas, his characters, so keenly.

> *A guy sets alone out here at night, maybe readin' books or thinkin' or stuff like that. Sometimes he gets thinkin', an' he got nothing to tell him what's so an' what ain't so. Maybe if he sees somethin', he don't know whether it's right or not. He can't turn to some other guy and ask him if he sees it too. He can't tell. He got nothing to measure by. I seen things out here. I wasn't drunk. I don't know if I was asleep. If some guy was with me, he could tell me I was asleep, an' then it would be all right. But I jus' don't know.*

She realizes somewhere in all of this, that she is hoping to impress him, Turner. Why, she's not exactly sure. Maybe so he's not sorry he let her be there. Not sorry he granted Gedge the favour to begin with. Or could be so he doesn't think she's stupid. So he sees she's got a brain, is a thinking individual. That she can keep up, can hold her own. She snaps the light off. Her decision's made. Her insides are setting about unwinding. Was it so hard, really? Worth all the anxiety? Breathe it out. Her shoulders give a little. She circles them once, twice, and shrugs up to release the tightness. With her hands she reaches and squeezes the juncture where the flesh of them meets the base of her neck, kneading them like she would pie or bread dough. She pushes back in the chair, scraping it gently across the creak of floorboards, and stands, stretching into the dimness and the shadows that come with the evening.

Gregory
Durham County Lock-Up, California
1997

What's in a name? A lifetime of pain and of condemnation. A history. A push, and a reason why. A name. Is the starting point for her. For the story. For who she is. The choices she's made along the way. And it is a reminder. Always a reminder. Of him.

He'd chosen the first two of her names. He'd allowed Mama the third. But once a person got done wading through the first two—the strangeness of them—the third didn't much matter. Like an afterthought. In life there's not many an occasion to even get to it. Her third name is Rose after Mama's own mama. She'd never known her. As for her mama, she had more sense than to try and interfere in what Curtis wanted once his mind was made up about something. And it was definitely fixed.

He would tell it with a thorny, twisted satisfaction, his end of the story. Every time he got the opportunity. To make sure she knew just what she was to him. That she'd been named for the two things he wouldn't have on account of her coming: the first, a son, and the second, a bike. Gregory was the name he wanted for a boy. And he only wanted a boy. A girl didn't figure into things. Not at all. The Harley was after a Harley Davidson Motorcycle. Hence the name, her name. Gregory. Harley. Rose. Abbott. She was his reminder. A constant reminder. That festered deep in his gut.

A yellowed and stained photograph went everywhere with him in his tired billfold, the Harley he'd been saving for. A terrible beautiful beast all chrome and fire and ego. He'd talk about the extra work he'd been taking on, all so he could have that bike. Made a deal with the owner, so as he could pay for it a bit at a time. How he'd had a plan. Picking up extra shifts at the gas barge, doing yardwork for people around town.

'If it weren't for Ruby and her wide open legs nailing me,' he'd say, 'things would be a whole 'nother ball game. Best believe she knew just what she was doing. Me, I was considered quite a catch. Letterman in baseball. Led the team to the pennant. I was the heaviest hitter they'd ever seen. No shortage of girls would've liked to have worn my jacket. Could have had my pick. But she was a whore. Even though she pretended different. Preacher's daughter, virginal, innocent. All bullshit. She was just as loose as any other.'

What might have been, the prospect of it, had fermented into something bitter, something that went down a little like fire. Maybe that was why he'd taken to drink like he had. To drown in it, to try and forget.

'Actions got consequences, I know. I wasn't ignorant about things. But I begged her, I did. Would have done anything, anything, to change things from the way they were. Woulda' done anything to change things.' His tone would become ragged mean, 'But I seen the glint in her eyes. When she told me no. That God would damn her to hell. If she were to kill it. Kill the baby she was carrying. Though she didn't give much thought to how God would feel about what got her into the mess in the first place. With her legs spread. Tried talking sense to her. No sense there, I come to realize. No, she had to have it her way. Had to hold me back.

'She had the best of me like I know she planned. She'd have it, and I'd have her. Stuck. With the whole shooting match. Because her daddy, preacher man, he didn't want her neither. Knowing what she'd done. How'd that have made him look? Nope, her own family didn't want nothing of her. I got stuck, you understand, dumped with the whole mess.

'Could've given her a good old hit to the belly. Considered it more'n once. League scouts were looking, sniffing around. I'd have been a great asset. To any team. Good enough to go pro. Now look what I got to show for things. On account of the stupid bitch, your stupid, selfish mama, who wouldn't think on anyone but herself.'

Times she'd find him swinging his old bat in the yard. Times like that she'd just set back and watch. Keep herself hidden away from his eyes. Usually he'd have had a few before he'd take it out. That old Louisville Slugger. Faded blond woodgrain covered with a layer of life's grime. Parts of it were clean worn away, the edges of the slender end curred from what once had been circular, chipped over the trail of their journeys. Splinters husked along the shaft where it'd caught against something sharper and harder than itself.

Was the booze in him, she guessed, made him do it in the open. Made him more sure of himself. So he didn't see the silliness of what he was doing, swinging at nothing. On his imaginary diamond, the field void of players, he'd take up the stance. All serious-like, eyes slitted and fixed on the distance, mouth vexed in a grim line, looking, searching out the pitch to come at him from an unseen pitcher atop a mound of distant, invisible earth. Sometimes she'd hear him talking. Fixing the play or setting the field like an announcer at a big league game.

He'd reach the bat back and up some. Swaying with the drink in him. He'd hold it, elbows square, circling the tip around. And then, with sheer might, he'd slice through the air: reaching, driving, pushing to the full extension of his arms, aiming for some formless point.

Sometimes he'd swing it just the once, sometimes more. When he wasn't out reminiscing, he'd set it by his easy chair. Always kept that Slugger close to hand, to stir the bitters in his heart.

It was always the same song. One Mama'd taught her when she was really little. When she was scared it would come out of nowhere to play through her—

> *Little ones to him belong*
> *They are weak, but he is strong*
> *Yes, Jesus loves me…*

Funny how it'd help to calm her. Just a simple song.

She remembers. Time upon time. The fights between Mama and Curtis. A collage of images kaleidoscopes before her. One blends into another blends into another and another. Times she had listened. Times she had, in horror, watched. When she was still too young to run from it. To leave. She'd hide in the darkness of a cupboard or a closet, under a chair, or table, or the nearest bed. In one place—she can't recollect anymore where it was they were living—she used to climb into the small cabinet under the bathroom sink. Hunch beneath the piping. Comforted by the tightness of the space, and the metallic curves she shared it with. She remembers the aches in her coming out of it. The way her back would pain her with the straightening of it. The needles she would feel in her feet and the spider pinches that would crawl prickingly up her legs.

Or through a crack of some opening, where light bled the scene in on her, she'd see their jerky two-step. Hear the sickening sound of force on flesh. The fluttering cries. The sound of pain. Sometimes she couldn't help it, there'd be a warm release of pee, her own pee, running down the insides of her legs from the shock of a blow connecting with target. From the weight of the fear pressing in on her. Hands up. To cover her mouth's whimper. Then on up to her ears. To cover the sound. Pressing tightly. Ever so tightly. As if the pressure might banish it. Holding still. Ever so still. So that her muscles ached from the tightness of being held not moving. That's when she'd first started humming the song. To keep from hearing. To try and settle herself.

One time she can recall so sharply. She's screaming. Calling out to her. 'Mama. Mama!' Sobbing. Begging. Reaching out for her hemline. The flowers on her dress. Faded flowers. Crying for him to stop. 'Daddy! Daddy, please no!' There's the hardness of the blow to the back of her head. And falling, falling. Into the wooden corner of the table. There's baby teeth dotting worn linoleum. She can see the flecks of pattern with teeth lying in between. And blood. She's scrabbling about, burning the skin of bare knees; still screaming, scraping the little bits of ivory into the reddened palm of her hand. Crawling between dancing feet, she takes cover in the underside of the kitchen table, her lost, loose teeth folded tightly within her pudgy, sweaty and bloodstained grip. In her head there is a thick and heavy ringing. Criss-cross, she sits. Legs folded underneath. Back straight. Smoothing the flowered fabric of her nightgown over trembling knees with only one hand. Again and again, this way and that. Smooth and smoother. Damp under her palms. Until not a crease remains. Whimpering at the shock of rawness that throbs in her mouth. Where her tongue passes over bare gum.

Stringy flesh floating where ivory had once held fast. Salty tears mingle with the iron tang of her blood. The song lilts through her, in a little-girl voice. *Little ones to him belong, they are weak, but he is strong. Yes, Jesus loves me.* A silly, clumsy girl is the story Mama offers after, when she has a need for explaining things. At the school. At the grocer's.

Being out of it made her able to go back in. She'd reasoned this in her heart. To give her guilt over to the back seat. Guilt for leaving. Running. Hiding. When things would go bad. It was so she could help fix Mama after. Gregory was the only one Mama's shame would let in close. The only one Mama really had.

Sometimes, to lift Mama's spirits, they'd take the scarves out. Mama's gypsy scarves. She had a whole case full. They'd tie them on arms, wrists, ankles, knot them over hair like a turban or around the forehead like a bandanna, make kerchiefs or looping bows at the neck. Mama'd say gypsies wore bright colours and patterns to show their love for life, their zest for excitement and adventure. Eventually Gregory had come to realize that the scarves were not so much about loving life as they were a way for Mama to hide the dark side of her life. That they were not so much about dressing up as they were about covering up.

'Forgive him, for he knows not what he has done.' That's what Mama would pray. Afterward. Once upon a time Gregory used to believe Mama was right. She couldn't say exactly when, for her, things had changed.

Aneeta
San Francisco
September 2002

In the bottom of the case, beneath layers of brightly colored silk, lies a thin assembly of effects. She turns these over in her hands gently, as if to be less careful might turn them to dust.

There is a small pouch of jewelry. Everyday pieces. Not the high quality dress kind; not the kind that need to be kept in a safe or safe deposit box. These, the only ones she now has, include a few thin bangles of gold, several necklaces and a number of pairs of modest earrings clawed to semi-precious or imitation stones.

A small box of dark wood with a pattern of gold inlay on the top holds a meager collection of photographs. Herself and Asha, holding hands in the courtyard. Her parents' wedding. The family when she was yet a baby. Her grandparents. Also in the box her fingers touch the tiny little elephant. She takes it out and sets it upon the floor and then returns her hand to probe still farther into the case that has come so far with her. It does not take long for the fingers to find what it is that they seek. She has kept a number of books, her favourites, but none feel to the touch as this one. The slender leatherbound volume of *Gitanjali*.

Aneeta opens the cover gently. On the thick vellum of the inside cover the faded, spidery hand reads:

> *Dearest Aneeta,*
> *May these words take life as you live your own.*
> *Your loving father*
> *1990*

The year of his death. She was just a child. This is all she has left. Aside from the memories, the photographs, and her dreams. The songs of Rabindranath Tagore. Images and ideas that seem to look into her soul. As if they have felt her pain, walked her journey, suffered her trials. Is it possible that the wheels of life turn in the same circles again and again? For that is how it appears. And the only way she could reason that the words can offer so much meaning to her after such a length of time from being put to paper.

But, she thinks, there is more reason that they resonate so deeply. For they are a possession that binds her to Papa. She can feel his wisdom flowing through them. Water poured into an empty vessel, filling her up. Relieving her parched insides, insides made brittle by doubt and hardened by fear.

She need look no further, there are no words that have moved her more, or meant more in all that she has read.

The time that my journey takes is long and the way of it long.
I came out on the chariot in the first gleam of light,
And pursued my voyage through the wildernesses of
Worlds leaving my track on many a star and planet.
It is the most distant course that comes nearest to
thyself.

Aneeta
Fresno, California
2001

They are alone. In the room they will share. His eyes study her intently where she sits, on the edge of the bed. She is cold. From the air, and from the fear that holds her. The first night a bride spends with her husband is a sign of the life that is to follow. How many times has she heard this? And now. Here she is. Instinctively, she shivers.

He turns to press the lock on the door. Then he swivels back to her and begins to pull his shirt from his waistband. His fingers release the buttons, one by one. Slowly, lazily. A sly smile spreads across his face. His tone is hard when he speaks. 'So.' So. She can see muscled, coffee brown skin where fabric now gapes. Her heart beats so swiftly that she thinks it might be visible through the silk of her blouse. Her chest is tight. So tight. As if the garment, which was tailored perfectly to her form, had somehow in minutes shrunk itself two sizes. 'Let me just set a few things straight. So that you know where I'm coming from. And where we stand. Firstly, I don't intend to play games. There's no being coy with me. I know how these things are supposed to work. For the new bride.' The words that follow shake her. 'But I'm not buying any excuses. You're no innocent. No virgin. I know that much. So don't go giving me all that shy crap. Save the act and spare me the tears. You're bought and paid for now. You're mine. And I don't care what went down with you back home because you belong to me. Don't look so surprised. As long as I leave you able to cook and clean, nobody'll have a thing to say about it. Got it? Nobody in this household'll even care. So don't bother trying to look for any sympathy or a shoulder to cry on.' He laughs. It is a sound that cuts her. 'Own family couldn't wait to get rid of you. Have you taken off their hands. Little too convenient, I'd say. So, the way I see it, if we cut through all the beginner bullshit I think we might get on okay.' He stands and pulls his belt free from his trousers. He pulls the zip and lets them drop. He wears nothing underneath. She is shocked at his openness. Frozen in place. His eyes fire with something wild.

He moves swiftly toward her and pushes her backwards on the bed, hard. She hears herself gasp. Deftly he flips her onto her front and jerks her back so that her legs trail over the bedside. She is suddenly facedown in piles of rumpled bedding. Her hands furtively find a tenuous hold on the top coverlet. Her brain pulses with the heavy rush of panic. In what seems a fluid singular motion he strips her bottom half. Silk and undergarments are cast aside. 'I'm not big on foreplay, but you'll get used to it.' She squeezes her eyes tightly shut and winces as he urges her trembling legs further apart. A wet hand runs the length of the division between her buttocks, slowing to coldly circle the opening. Fear grips her. An old, familiar sensation. Hands grab roughly at the flesh of her hips and pull her hard to him. Pain augers through her. She feels split open like ripe pomegranate flesh. Burning sears her insides. Claims her. Over and over again. The rhythm calls to mind the pounding of a heavy mallet. Like the ones streetside shoemakers use for softening leather hides. Every so often he punctuates the force with a groan. Her teeth are gritted against the jolting intensity. All she can do is wait. It is her duty. A wife's duty.

Her mind casts backward. Across oceans and continents. A distance that she had thought, believed, could bring change. Despair is entirely pointless. Tears have no fitting place. There is only one place for the laying of blame. This time it belongs squarely with her.

At his rough falsetto cry, relief fills her. Movement stops. Breath pools around them, an ebb and flow current marked by the deep pull of exertion and a shallow layer of panic. Her jaw aches with tension and she realizes that her teeth are clamped hard-edged together. He steps from his place at her back and throws himself onto the bed. Dark eyes stare skyward. Dully he speaks: 'Go and clean yourself up.'

She slides back, and draws herself weakly up. Legs tremor and threaten to give way. Like a newborn calf just free of its mother's womb, she picks her way toward the sprawling bathroom. She is grateful that it is their own, within the bedroom they share. That she will not have to face any of the others in the household.

'Bet you never had it like that before, huh?' he manages thickly, as she reaches the threshold. She does not turn, does not speak. Grateful for at least a temporary sanctuary, she steps from carpet onto tile and closes the door. She looks at the small metal latch protruding from the brass doorknob. There is no sense in using the lock. Her mind replays his voice with dark clarity. The smooth, unaccented curve of his American English. The words crash violently through her, *You're bought and paid for. You're mine. As long as I leave you able to cook and clean, nobody'll have a thing to say about it, nobody'll care.*

She leans over the basin. A hot pulse throbs in her backside. It mimics the one she can see in the expanse of mirror. The one that beats under the thin skin by her collarbone. If she didn't physically hurt so much at this moment, she may actually have laughed. What might her new husband make of that? She wonders if she might be going mad. For thinking of laughter. At a time like this. Obscene as it seems. Perhaps, though, it is appropriate. If only to mark the brutal irony of it all. For the sameness in difference. And for acknowledging the truth of what she has just now discovered. That she has simply allowed herself to be traded from one nightmare into another.

Aneeta is 13
Delhi
1996

He lies down, his body hard against her. She is almost lost to sleep. Almost. And then, startled by him. His presence. She has not seen him approach. She cannot see his face. But she knows it is him by the name he whispers. A pet name he has given her. *Rani.* Though there is something different in the cadence. That is foreign. It is low in his throat. She can feel the air from his nose at the base of her neck in puffs of heat. Lips brush her lightly there. And linger. Not in the way of uncle to niece. It is not that way at all. There is an intensity of heat that comes from him. That radiates into her.

Everything within her screams: *What is he doing? This should not be happening. Should not. Be happening. Should. Not. No, please. No! Just stop. Stop!* A sweet smell chokes her nostrils. She knows it is the scent of whisky. A drink that he likes. A drink that Papa had taken sometimes. A hot hand reaches out and settles. All of her tightens. Silently, she is praying: *Please. Please, don't do this.* Let it be merely a dream. A bad dream. Panic keeps her paralyzed and mute; eyes squeezed tightly closed against the darkness. A wounded ache spreads through her. The buzzing of inner chaos rushes like ocean water in her ears. Her heart hammers like a frantic drumbeat.

Cloth is a weak barrier. Easily overcome, it is pushed aside. Layer after layer. Bedclothes, nightgown, undergarments. The searching hand is insistent in its exploration. In the way it crosses from territory to territory. It knows the way it wishes to go, travels without hesitation. It travels down and down, boldly across her abdomen, beneath her navel, to the place between her legs. She clenches them as tightly as she can together, but it is not enough. Her will, her strength, is no match. He simply pushes his way through, beyond. Tears escape her pinched eyes, hotly rolling down her cheeks. His hand is so much stronger. She cannot stop him. He creeps into the untouched parts of her. To invade her. His breath comes in quick short bursts as his body rocks against her. A tongue licks at the back of her neck. In lazy flicks, it reaches up toward the base of her earlobe. She wants to scream, but does not dare. She pulls her shoulder up, wincing. Lips against skin curl upwards. Climb into an invisible smile. A sick smile. She cannot think. *What to do. What to do?* There is a sudden white-hot pain within her flesh. She can feel his body jerking, twitching. A shudder engulfs him.

Childhood floats away from her then, lost like a broken gossamer web on an invisible breeze. Innocence stolen by a thief she has both loved and trusted.

Aneeta
Delhi
1990

Her first written work at school was entitled: *My Life as a Bird*. In it she fancied herself something of a chica-roo, a fine-feathered little creature flitting from tree to tree at will, stopping only to amuse with a lofty how-do-you-do to the world laid out beneath her. Unsettled, Mummy called her. A child, Papa had corrected.

From the time I shake myself awake
My days are always fair
I live a life of fancy
A life without a care

In a leafy tree-top
I flit from branch to branch
I sing a happy little song
And dance a happy dance

They say of me
Beneath the tree
Such a fine and cheerful fellow
So ready is this little chiri
To chirp a tune in hello

But nothing in the world below
Will ever tempt me down
For I'm up above the worries
Of a life upon the ground

The ideas had brought mirth to both of her parents and her teacher, Sister Harbans, too. 'That girl,' claimed Papa, 'has a fertile imagination.'

In the minds of the sisters her creativity more than made up for her entirely absent punctuation in the piece. Punctuation, they said, can be taught. Creativity is inspired. Inspiration is divine. They felt she had been given a gift. And said as much. That it would be a terrible thing to waste. That her abilities in composition had far exceeded their expectations for a child of such a tender age. That in spite of the sheer whimsy of it, it was clearly recognition of the guidance that a belief in the Almighty could give to a child.

Mummy, once she had recovered from her laughter, cautioned, 'Let us hope when the time is right she shall put her wit to some use and not simply flit away from us like a silly sparrow. I prefer a child to have her feet firmly anchored to the ground. Not floating in such lofty ideals.'

'When the time is right, my pet,' Papa had soothed, 'she surely will come down from the clouds.'

'Papa is not coming home. Ever again.' Asha had told her this harshly. Then given her shoulders a shake, a strong one, a jerk that made her neck snap. Mummy was taking it in turns to be so, so sad and then so, so angry. Papa, she overhears from mourners, had died of heart attack while sitting behind his desk, with a raft of commodity papers spread before him.

'Isn't it like Bakshish,' they say, 'to die immersed in his work.'

'I hope that he has left them well set at least.'

'Do not be so foolish. Bakshish was a man of wealth. He would have been well-prepared for every eventuality. He was a planner. A fine mind.'

'So, so smart a man.'

'I hear the man had much money. Funds here and there. Rupees, dollars, pounds sterling.'

'Really? I heard Hindujas were going to buy him out.'

'I hear he was planning to retire. Soon-soon.'

'Goodness!'

'Hindujas?'

'A very smart man. Brilliant. Too sad.'

'It must be very big. His company and dealings.'

'That is what I have heard.'

'Where have you heard?'

'He must be very successful if he has gained interest from the Hindujas.'

'Yes, but for how long will the riches last? He is not earning anymore.'

'I hear the brother will take over.'

'That is true.'

'A strange one, the younger brother, no family of his own.'

And so the whispers went in their secretive way, round and round, one giving way to another and another, trading stories and speculation.

Heads wag somberly forth and back. 'Such a sad thing. For his girls.' Sympathy-laced compliments are offered like candy, 'Such a good girl. Such a sweet child.' Aneeta is pinched hard on the flesh of childish cheeks and crushed to pillowy bosoms of wailing women she does not recognize. Turbaned men young and old, with palms together, bow their heads before her in silence, taking it in turns to pat her hands and the top of her head before moving to line the walls of her home. She picks at the decoration on her chunni and practises holding it mysteriously to her face in the way she has seen the women do with their saris to cover false tears. She cries the very same kind of cry. The aunties coo at her like doves along the garden wall, 'Poor, poor beti. Poor, poor child.' And the wailing starts anew, rising into a chorus pitch that reminds her of the yowling of cats who gather in the night.

Again, the whispers come to her, follow her—from tight clusters, from leaned in heads behind raised finger fans, from ladies serving trays of tea, from the kitchen where bubbling pots are tended and food is readied.

'Sushma is a young woman yet.'

'Hanji.'

'Look at the hair. Not a speck of grey.'

'She has lived an easy life. That is why she does not show her age.'

'Not like the rest of us. Hunh? Never a problem, never a difficulty.'

'Perhaps that is why the fates have seen fit to take her husband from her.'

'This is the way sometimes, the way of balance.'

'Hai, what a thing to say!'

'No, I am only meaning that sometimes this is how fate works.'

'We shall see what comes. How she fares. It will not be so easy. Not anymore.'

'With girl children, one never can be too careful.'

'And now without a father.'

'Sushma has no choice but to see to things herself.'

'Hai, now that Bakshish is gone she must make these girls into the most wanted of brides. For her own future to be settled.'

'The noises of gossip, hai, how they can ruin a life. Give not one tongue something to wag about.'

'It is true, every two eyes have a mouth. But if they are filled only with sweetmeats, then the words that follow can be nothing but kind.'

Aneeta
Delhi
1996

The sky is spun with woodsmoke and the last golden threads of sunlight. Drumbeat pushes the procession through the congestion of the streets. The excitement is infectious. A chorus of horns make a disjointed melody. Clapping and shouting join the rhythm of the wedding party marchers. There is joking and laughter. A fraternity forms around a heavily brocaded and scarlet-turbaned groom who looks anxious in spite of the knot of happy revelers. Hands rise up in a sea around him. Cheers ring out and boomerang back among the growing throng.

The mare was not Raj's idea. He was not one for show, but his family had insisted. It would not be right, they protested, to have our son come to his wedding in any other way. In the home of a magistrate Aneeta is unsure whether much of one's desires in life were open to negotiation. At least they had not forced an elephant. They had used Asha to coax him to agree to a short ride through the Delhi streets to the Colonnade Room. Of course when she had said how lovely it would look he put aside his protests. In the interests of pleasing his bride-to-be.

Tonight is a show. A grand spectacle. A wedding the size and importance of Asha's would be talked about for weeks. It is, Aneeta imagines, for she has never actually attended one, no less glamorous than a Bollywood premiere. Friends and relations have flocked from near and far, as they do on such occasions, but due to Asha's father-in-law's position much of Delhi society has also turned out to witness the particularly auspicious marital alliance of Rajnish and Asha. The green eyes of envy are certain to be in ready supply; eyes that would eat, dance, drink and whisper.

Mummy has always warned that lives could be undone almost as simply as a bow on a gift. Ruin, she would say, preyed on weakness, and like the best hunter, had the uncanny ability to know just where to set a trap. When it came round to marriage time every family hoped and prayed that fate was smiling, that some unknown Pandora's box did not open itself to taint things. For, as she and Asha were regularly reminded, a family's reputation was impossible to repair.

Mummy had done well by Asha. Aneeta has heard it again and again. From aunties, from uncles, from everyone—the opinion is consistent. Mummy has married her up beyond even Asha's imagining. Anyone's imagining, really. Raj is dreamy and good looking in the movie star sense, a law firm partner with plans to follow the path of his father. A very nice boy. Very, very nice boy. In fact, the word she has heard used any number of times is *perfect*.

She waits and watches from behind a pillar. Not entirely proper, but not forbidden either. Mummy is preoccupied with other things. Aneeta fingers the folds of finely woven peacock-coloured silk wrapped around her and does her best to look less a girl and more a young lady. She breathes deeply of the jasmine-infused smoky air. Raj has come to a sideways stop at the edge of the walkway. The horse dances this way and that, eyes wide and black at the noise and rush of people that close in around the arriving groom.

Very gingerly Raj shakes a golden boot free of the stirrup, and with a wide leg arc over a rump piled high with adornments and decoration, he dismounts. A great cheer rises up. Gamely he poses beside the horse for those who yell of their desire for snapshots, but excitement is clear in his face and prompts him, after a quick awkward slap of the horse's neck through layers of flower garland, to make his way toward the great white marbled building where his bride shyly waits.

A choppy singsong reaches out from the light and into the thick dark of the settling Delhi night. A melody beckons from beyond the stories-high pillars, at the top of the broad red-carpeted stairway. In its thrall, the young turbaned groom puts a hand to the heavy gilded kirpan hilt at his waist and floats with the human throng of well-wishers who propel him up the steps.

Flashbulbs are intent in capturing every moment as he is craning to see beyond the human chain of women at the doorway to the massive ballroom. 'Hey mister, you want your wife? You have to pay!' Lady relatives demand silly sums of money and threaten to remove his boots, or not to let him pass. He offers a wad of rupees to pacify them. It is clear to any watcher that he will stop at nothing for the girl of his dreams. Nothing else matters. He is as bewitched by her as she is besotted by him. The Prince and his beautiful Princess. It reminds her of childhood storybooks. Across the crowded hall Raj finally spies Asha, steps beyond the chittery ladies, and strides toward her. To take his place by her side. The beautiful and happy couple. Their eyes speak a silent language one to another. It is there for all to see. Love. It is the hope of every girl on the continent; near and far, far and wide. A twinge of jealousy flares just for a fraction of a moment and then dies within her. She is pleased for Asha-didi. Truly. For the dream-come-true marriage. The handsome groom, a wedding like this, the important family, the cinema kind of happy ending.

Tonight, though, in Asha's radiant wake, Aneeta is content with her small step toward womanhood. A shimmer of *oohs* and *aahs* had greeted her growing-up appearance in a sari this evening. My-my's and all sorts of compliments. She had tried hard to remain serene, not to let a ridiculous childish grin come over her face. Even now, the memory makes her smile. She stands straighter, wondering if her Prince Charming is somewhere in the watching crowd, maybe he cranes to catch a glimpse of her without her knowing. The heavy gold of the necklace that dips into the hollow at her throat pulses with the eager beating of her heart. Aneeta makes a wish and looks quickly into the heavens to pin it upon a star. She hopes that fate might one day smile just as favourably in her direction.

Fate, however, has something else in mind. It is in the night. After Asha's wedding celebration. The first time he touches her. In that way. In the way that transforms her. From innocent to soiled. Like a spilled inkwell, the trespass clouds and bleeds through every part of her. It covers over all of the magic. All of the beauty. All of the wishing.

Dearest Papa-ji,

Is it possible for you to see words on paper where you are? I do not know. Perhaps this is an impossible request, but I need your help, your advice. And I cannot think what else to do, where else to turn. And so, I shall write of my dilemma in a letter, which afterward I shall burn. For I must keep the confession that follows a secret, at least in this world.

If you were here things would surely be different. I miss the way things used to be. Before the harshness of fate snatched you away. Before peace was shattered. I used to try to wish you back. I used to think my love could do it. When it didn't work I wondered if I loved you enough, or if maybe you didn't want to come back. I've realized, I think, that I'll have to settle for remembering. If I squeeze my eyes tightly shut I can imagine your face, smiling, warm, looking into mine. I can hear the way your voice used to softly wrap around me, to hold me close. I can feel your beard; my hand in yours. I wish that time could be unwound. But wishing, I know now, is nothing but a wanting child's foolishness.

Perhaps because you are no longer among us, I can feel safe in telling you what I can share with no other. Would you believe if I told you things of Dev Uncle? Horrible things. Unthinkable things.

He has hurt me in a way that I cannot heal from. It is a wound that cannot be seen by the eye, but it has taken me over and it is worse than any other harm I can possibly imagine enduring. And what could I do? What can I do? All is lost. I am lost.

I am so ashamed. I am worthless, soiled, no better than a piece of used rubbish. A girl like me brings nothing but bad luck. I am a plague upon my family. And I fear nothing more than the day when my secret might dirty us all.

I beg of you, Papa, please give me some guidance, some sign, for I know that I cannot go on like this. I beg of you, I beg of God, or of whatever powers might be where you are, to hear my plea. Tell me what I should do. Tell me how to go on.

Gregory
English 50
San Francisco
September 2002

So the gang's back for the second installment. There's a bit of a buzz traveling the room as people, now sort of familiar, smile at others, offer 'Hi' to seatmates, pull books from backpacks, bags, oversized purses, slender zippered cases. There's a vibe of eager mixed with nerves.

He breezes into the room. He is in a loose fitting short-sleeved shirt and a pair of khaki shorts. Wearing a pair of leather sandals. Surprisingly, they don't look too bad. What kind of guy can actually get away with sandals? Turner makes straight for the blackboard, front and center. In oversized letters he writes:

How do I know what I think until I see what I say?
E.M. Forster

He turns to them and with a wide smile apologizes, 'Sorry for the duds. Supposedly, however, clothes don't make the man. It was the faculty welcome back shindig. Undercooked hamburgers, warm beer and all. Love it. Love the campus life.'

He walks back behind the table and starts to spread books and papers across the expanse. 'So. We ready to begin?' He moves forward, hands on hips, surveys the group assembled in tidy vertical rows.

'Why don't we...' he muses, and motions with one arm, 'move our chairs out and into more of a circle. It's geometry far more conducive to discussion.' Again, the ready smile. Does this guy ever stop? Wake up one day and think, I've got nothing to fucking smile about today? This golden boy? Doubtful. Looks as though his whole goddamn existence is charmed.

The thought has hardly made its way from his lips and people are already on the move. Standing, shuffling. Physical shape shifting. Humans morphing into something that looks more egg than circle. Here and there funny indentations out of synch with arcs before and after it. Adjustments are made.

Gregory pulls in on a corner and ends up with the crew-cutted army type on her left and the hippie looking Boho Chick on her right. Beauty and China Doll are across, on the other side of things. Maybe gravitating toward one another. She notes that both are flanked on the outer sides by the suburban Barbies, overteased blonde hair by Beauty and beside China Doll a plumpish, mousier version, cardigan carefully knotted at her neck. What's the bet that inside the Barbie 2 designer handbag there's also a designer wallet where, front and center, there's a flip out of at least three, if not more, gap-toothed critters grinning out from some creepy faked-out photo studio background. She's too good for Wal-Mart. And for Sears. JC Penney too. Probably some private photographer. More than likely. She can see that in her.

Turner pulls a chair to rest in front of the table and his things. He crosses one leg easily up and over the other in a closed V and balances a notepad on the bend in his knee with a pen poised mid-air overtop. 'Much better. This is much better. Now we can all see each other, talk to each other, get the most out of this exercise.'

He switches gears imperceptibly, though the language of his body does not change, languid and unpressed. 'The quote on the board. Forster. A brilliant English novelist. Way ahead of his time, made commentary on class, social structure, sexuality, even race. He held up a rather damning mirror upon our tendency toward hypocrisy. Room With a View; A Passage to India.' Pens are scratching. 'The quote, I think, most appropriately sums the workshop style we're going to engage in today. The more you talk, the more you'll think. The more you think, the better you'll come to terms with your own ideas and opinions. So don't be afraid to talk!' A hum of agreement makes its way around. Yes. *Yeah*, she thinks. *I get it. Talk.*

'Okay, so enough of me talking at you. It's you guys I want to hear from. Anyone willing to start?' There are creaks and groans of protest from the chairs, the shifting in seats a sure signal of nerves. Faces purposely void of expression and commitment are looking around to see who might take up the pole position. 'I feel like that teacher in the Ferris Bueller movie…Anyone? Anyone?' he chuckles, 'Come on people, let's get over these first date jitters and get on with things.'

Mercifully, the crew cut beside her breaks the answering silence. 'Yeah,' Turner says pointing to him with an open blank in between.

The guy volunteers, 'Mike.'

'Yes, Mike. It was on the tip of my tongue. I told you you're going to have to give me a few weeks. For names to settle in. Thank you, Mike, for being so fearless and accommodating. What've you got for us?'

Mike reads something called *Beer Can* by John Updike: '*This seems to be an era of gratuitous inventions and negative improvements. Consider the beer can…*' A smart critique on beer top popping. There is a good round of laughter. Especially from the guys. Out loud and from the gut. Even from the uptight nerdly looking ones, who want to be included in the manliness of it all. Eagerness bubbles to the surface then, and talk, commentary, questioning begins. A wading into the unknown. A little humour breaks the ice. A point for the crew-cut guy, Beer Can Mike. You're smarter than you look, she thinks.

The group brings Turner a real mix. She can see the desire for approval shining in their eyes. She wonders if hers will look the same. She just doesn't want to make a fool of herself is all. Blonde Barbie, teased and sprayed, channels Jackie Collins—*Lucky*. God. But Turner finds something positive to say, even though Gregory thinks he must have been scraping. Commercial success. The often disconnect between literary recognition and the business of writing.

They hear Ken Follett. Dean Koontz. Shakespeare from one of the more intellectual guys, who, it turns out, is a budding thespian slash writer slash waiter. He reads it projecting his best put-on English accent. Turner is smiling. Dig in.

Boho Chick brings Margaret Atwood. Apparently, both are Canadian. Boho Chick herself and Atwood too. *A Life Before Man.* She reads about a woman whose lover has committed a gory suicide. Turner enthuses on Atwood's long and golden literary history; her incredible character portraits.

Manfred of the Red Neck brings James Joyce, which Gregory likes. Dark, sinister, a bit of an edge. There's Virginia Woolf. And Lewis Carroll's *Alice Through the Looking Glass.* Turner is like an excited child in it all, delighting in the divine literariness of it. 'Yes. That's it. Exactly. You are amazing me.' She wants to laugh at him. He sounds so effusive, so rah-rah. Give the man some pom-poms.

'Gregory.' All of a sudden she goes cold. How did he remember her name? 'What's your offering?'

'Well…' she looks down and takes the sheet of paper into her hand. She sees it tremble in her grasp. Swallows hard. *It'll get easier—* she hears Doc Gedge at the back somewhere behind her. Indistinct but distinct. Not really there. Her psyche's pep talk. Hopefully enough to ward off a complete breakdown. Which, at this very moment, she is on the verge of. This is Round 1. If she can just…If. She's on the pullback of the catapult. Turner is watching her expectantly, but the pleasantness, the invitation, has not left his facial expression. '*Of Mice and Men*, I chose,' she stumbles, 'by, uh, John Steinbeck?' *Great grammar.* Her voice sounds halting, barely audible. But she suspects it is because of the loud ringing in her ears. Faces are turned toward her. Intent. *What the hell are you looking at?* Instinct rears up. Fear. *Don't make a fool of yourself. Don't.* She steels herself against the stampede of uncertainty. *Just do it.*

'A few miles south of Soledad, the Salinas River drops in close to the hillside bank and runs deep and green. The water is warm too, for it has slipped twinkling over the yellow sands in the sunlight before reaching the narrow pool. On one side of the river the golden foothill slopes curve up to the strong and rocky Galiban mountains, but on the valley side the water is lined with trees—willows fresh and green with every spring, carrying in their lower leaf junctures the debris of the winter's flooding; and sycamores with mottled, white, recumbent limbs and branches that arch over the pool. On the sandy bank under the trees the leaves lie deep and so crisp that a lizard makes a great skittering if he runs among them. Rabbits come out of the brush to sit on the sand in the evening, and the damp flats are covered with the night tracks of 'coons, and the spread pads of dogs from the ranches, and with the split wedge tracks of deer that come to drink in the dark.

There is a path through the willows and among the sycamores, a path beaten hard by boys coming down from the ranches to swim in the deep pool, and beaten hard by tramps who come wearily down from the highway

When she lifts from the page the room has gone quiet. Turner has his eyes closed and is leaning back in his chair. He has his fingers laced and across his chest, he is smiling broadly. She feels a tightening in her chest, seeing his reaction. Looking down, she starts out again. It feels like a journey. Like she is there. Isn't that precisely what she loves about Steinbeck and his voice? From the very first words of his she'd read. Every shading and fleck and nuance, she gets it. She feels, reading the passage now, transported in time and place, the way Turner looks.

> *'A guy sets alone out here at night, maybe readin' books or thinkin' or stuff like that. Sometimes he gets thinkin', an' he got nothing to tell him what's so an' what ain't so. Maybe if he sees somethin', he don't know whether it's right or not. He can't turn to some other guy and ask him if he sees it too. He can't tell. He got nothing to measure by.'*

Stop. There is a sliver of nothing and then the present resumes. 'Mm-mm-mm. What a landscape Steinbeck paints. You feel like you can sink right into its rhythm. Can't you feel it? You can tell the man was intimately tied to that dirt. That his feet were well and truly invested in that stretch of ground. Just as an aside, a trivia point—did you know that Steinbeck used to sign his letters with a flying pig logo? His Latin motto—I love this—*Ad Astra Per Alia Porci*. In English: To the stars on the wings of a pig.

'Gregory, a fine offering.' She felt the flush but would not yield, keeping her face to her paper, struggling to banish it before it's written for all to see. She's not like that. Not the kind to let a little praise affect her. Praise is for the weak. The needy. Somebody other than her.

Kameko

Professor Turner does not still for long, he moves like a honey bee among spring flowers, gathering from them all. His enjoyment is clear. 'Who haven't we heard from?'

It is a wise way, this idea of sharing, to open the course. It offers insight into each individual. And in such a manner that people are willing, even eager to give. Shyly, she raises her hand. Wanting to open some part of herself. 'Yes,' he smiles his agreement at her.

'Yes.' Her voice is quiet. She struggles against her hesitancy, her instinctive inclination to draw inward. She looks down at the paper she has prepared. Clipped to it is the 1000 yen note. She takes the money and holds it up. 'He is Natsume Soseki,' she says. 'The family name is Natsume. In Japan we say the family name first, so really his name is reversed in America. Actually, Soseki was a pen name. Kinnosuke was the true given name.' She nods.

'In Japan he is a very famous and well-respected author. Of the Meiji Era.

This is the time when his writings were published. Mm,' she scrambles to order the digits in her mind and to say them in the correct arrangement, 'in the nineteen hundreds, at the beginning. He is said to be Charles Dickens of Japan. He studies for some time in England, but there he is unhappy. So he returns to Tokyo. He is a master of Haiku and also Han poetry and fairytales.' There are some solemn nods. And bodies leaning in to hear her. She can feel the smile that has traced itself across her face. Gentle and agreeable.

'You can see how important he is, and handsome,' she giggles slightly at the handsome reference, though she is not sure why. 'He was very influential in shaping Japanese literature. He is writing about nature and people mostly, but also about duty and about culture. About life and difficulty. He uses words very beautifully, in Japanese and also in English. This is why I have chosen him for sharing today. And he is known also as a teacher; a professor and scholar and writer.

'I am reading from his *Kusamakura* novel. In English, *Grass Pillow*. One of his most well-known novels. Mostly I find it good because, even though it was written so long ago, it has meaning for everybody. Even today.' She looks up into their silence. Sees the waiting faces. The way they are listening. To her. To what will come from her. A sudden sense of strength prompts her.

'However you look at it, the human world is not an easy place to live.

And when its difficulties intensify, you find yourself longing to leave that world and dwell in some easier one—and then, when you understand at last that difficulties will dog you wherever you may live, this is when poetry and art are born.

The creators of our human world are neither gods nor demons, but simply people, those ordinary folk who happen to live right next door. You may feel the human realm is a difficult place, but there is surely no better world to live in. You will find another only by going to the nonhuman; and the nonhuman realm would surely be a far more difficult place to inhabit than the human.

So if this best of worlds proves a hard one for you, you must simply do your best to settle in and relax if you can and make this short life of ours, if only briefly, an easier place in which to make your home. Herein lies the poet's true calling, the artist's vocation. We owe our humble gratitude to all the practitioners of the arts, for they mellow the harshness of our human world and enrich the human heart.

When I had lived in this world for twenty years, I understood that it was a world worth living in. At twenty-five, I realized that light and dark are sides of the same coin; that wherever the sun shines, shadows too must fall. Now, at thirty, here is what I think; where joy grows deep, sorrow must deepen;

the greater one's pleasures, the greater the pain. If you try to sever the two, life falls apart. Try to control them, and you will meet with failure.'

She bows to indicate that the passage is finished. There is quiet around her. Suddenly she is very conscious to be fixed at the center of the attention. It is not a natural position for her, but she is surprised to find she does not dislike it. She is pleased to see some faces long with thought, some heads nodding. Some faces are down, hands flying across paper. 'Even after nearly one hundred years from the time he has written *Kusamakura*, his words still have much meaning for me about life, even living here in America where it is very different from Japan. I hope that you have enjoyed the offering. Maybe in the passage there is meaning for some of you too?'

The professor is looking pleased, 'See, that's the beauty, the absolute beauty of great writers. They have the ability to touch so many of us regardless of time, of place, of circumstance. Simply, perfectly, with such relevance and largesse. Yeah, it gets to every single soul, doesn't it? Incredible. Terrific. Thank you for opening our eyes to that.'

And within her it suddenly seems as if candlelight has been re-ignited in a darkened room. Making her world perhaps an easier place in which to dwell.

Kameko
San Francisco
2002

She stands waiting for the elevator. As seconds pass, she catches herself shifting from one foot to the other. Such is the agitation she feels. When the doors slide sleekly back she finds herself face to face with an American woman, unmistakably pregnant, who must have come from one of the parking levels below ground. She has long blond hair that curls luxuriously down her back, and pale blue eyes. She wears office clothing, a neatly tailored jacket and skirt; it does not hide her advancing condition. If anything, it shows to greater effect her rounded form. There is a twist of longing in Kameko's belly, low and sharp. The woman looks startled to see someone standing before her. Their eyes lock for an instant and then drop. Kameko steps in and turns her back to avoid staring, concerned that her expression might give her away. The doors slide closed. The 23 on the number panel is alight. Both are going to the same floor, the same place. Kameko's stomach tightens. Could she be? From the same office? From Okura. The office her husband leads. Her mouth opens on silence. Then closes itself. She feels like a fish yanked from the water, left to gape awkwardly on the sand. She should turn. Inquire. Pleasantly. *Will this be your first child? Why, your husband must be so pleased by your good fortune.* She will watch carefully for signs. Signs that might betray her situation. But before she can urge herself to turn and speak they arrive at floor 23. The doors slide back. The woman excuses herself and steps swiftly past, vanishing behind a door near the far end of the corridor. Kameko moves slowly out and looks after her. Long moments after she has disappeared.

She is sent by the woman at the main Okura reception desk beyond the heavy glass doors to explain herself. Mr. Tanaka is not to be disturbed. 'But I am his wife,' she has protested. The voice, the words, do not sound like her. She stands before a desk central to the room and senses the stares and whispers of the people that buzz in busy orbits around it.

    'I am terribly sorry. Mr. Tanaka is not available just now. ' The smile of the matronly lady is kindly, with notes of pity and apology. The small rectangle of plastic fastened at her breast, on the same side as her heart, proclaims her Ueda-san. Kameko wonders how long ago it was that she came to this country, how long she has worked for Okura. Probably all her working life. Maybe there was no success in marrying her. That is often the path of the Office Ladies and Welcome Ladies. Lonely women make loyal and dedicated employees. There is a large stack of papers and a box of clips open on her desk. Another neat pile is rising beside, the papers having been collated and clipped. She reminds Kameko of a dog tethered to a gatepost. For the purpose of warding off the unwelcome. Again, she repeats that she is Shiro's wife.

'And, may I ask, had you made arrangements to see him?' Her tone is one of admonishment. Her head is inclined a little bit to one side. As if she thinks one would not simply be so presumptuous as to arrive during the workday unannounced. Without having made inquiries as to a husband's schedule for that day. It is a gross oversight. One cannot expect to be accommodated on this basis. Such is the message in the tilt of Ueda-san's head. The gesture is very clear to Kameko.

'No.' Kameko's voice is low. Embarrassed. There is heat in her cheeks. Her head is bowed. She is like a chastened child. She should have known. She holds on to the picnic box with two hands. The handle is smooth but she can feel the clamminess transferring from her hands.

'Oh dear!' the lady clucks. 'This is a most unfortunate situation. I am sorry for your trouble. Tanaka-san is a very busy man. As I am sure you know.' She is shaking her head, wagging it back and forth. 'But, may I say, it is very good to see a wife doing such a considerate thing for her husband.'

'Yes,' Kameko replies absently.

The woman continues, as if she had been encouraged, 'To be committed to his care, as you obviously are. Mindful of our traditions. Sometimes Western ways can be confusing, overpowering. I can see that you are not like that. It is refreshing to see such a thing.'

But she is not there simply to provide Shiro's lunch. There is a wave of guilt that mingles with her embarrassment. Not in the way this woman thinks. She has come with the lunch as a pretext for seeing with her own eyes the man he is at his place of work. Though for what purpose she cannot be sure. Just that she has wanted to see. With her two eyes. History replays in her. The jaunty steps of her father. As a younger man. And the woman who looks on him adoringly. The shared laughter. Laughter that never rang out in her home.

'To see that duty maintained,' the woman babbles on, 'I would say that Tanaka-san is fortunate. I am sure he will be very appreciative of such consideration.' Would he? It hardly seemed likely. He would probably think her intrusion an annoyance. That is what she has become. To him. 'And of your efforts.' Kameko nods a small bow at the compliment, even if it is far from truth. 'I'll bet his favourite items are prepared in here.' She can almost imagine the woman's lips smacking with anticipation. 'Why it almost makes me long for my own lunch break. But I am sure not to have something as fine as what you have organized. As what a wife does out of love.' Kameko has to avert her eyes.

What response would she give? If she weren't such a coward. If she was able to throw off the constraints of convention and the requirement for niceties.

Oh, Ueda-san! The idea is almost laughable. The basket is purely for pretense, you understand. Hardly a full bowl of rice inside and some two-day old fish left from a dinner my husband never arrived for. I ate my own portion alone. She wondered what the woman would say then. Certainly it would stop her nosiness and preaching. Kameko has half a mind to let it out. To put an end to the trail of sticky-sweet comments. But she knows to do so would be horribly rude. The poor woman is hardly worthy of such disrespect.

'Mrs. Tanaka, you may leave the box with me. I will personally assure you that he will get it. Just as soon as possible. So that nothing becomes spoiled.' She reaches a hand out to where Kameko stands, not moving, still clutching it to her.

'Oh. Oh, yes. That would be…fine. Thank you.' Again she bows.

'Would you care to write a message to go with it? I, myself, am a lover of poetry. Perhaps just a few lines? Since I know your feeling for your husband.'

How could you? How could you know? Her insides cry out in indignation. 'No, no. It is okay.'

'Not even so much as to express your good wishes? I find it is always more thoughtful when a note, however small, is included. Even though I doubt it is the case that he would be unsure as to the box's origin. With such a thoughtful woman for a wife. Think of his delight at discovering the lunch with a special note.'

'No. I do not think…no, he will know.' She has no desire to coddle delight in him. Just the opposite effect, in fact, is what she hopes. He will see from the haphazard manner of it, when he opens the box, that the lunch was merely an excuse. That is the message she wishes him to receive. It is far more poignant than any words.

'Oh, all right then. May I ask, have you traveled long?'

'Excuse me?'

'To get here. Have you traveled long? Because I would recommend that for future visits you might wish to make your husband aware of your plans. I am sure he would be happy to receive you. Especially if it were to mean more lunches would be brought to him. A man is easily satisfied by way of his stomach,' Ms. Ueda rubs her own belly in a childish circular motion and beams brightly. 'But I can see that you already know this is true.'

Kameko's smile trembles. The woman's words echo discordantly within her. Her reply, of course, is empty. No more than illusion. 'Yes, of course. Of course, I know it.'

Kameko
Tokyo
1996

Her given name, Kameko, means tortoise child. The tortoise being a symbol of long life makes hers a desirable name for its auspicious meaning. Except in the schoolyard. There were other names, too, that inspired silly humour, but for some reason the children never let her forget her reptilian origins. *'Turtle, turtle on your way, why are you so slow? No one else in all the world, takes so long to go!'*

Mother looked confused when she told her of the children's fun-making. Father had chuckled in his thin, gravelly way and said, 'But Kameko-chan, the little tortoise will outlive them all and surely have the last laugh.'

In her, the taunts inspired a certain sense of determination. Made her feel as though she had to prove something. And so she had become a dedicated student. Always working hard. To make a point to all of them. In the way that children feel they must in their innocence. She is at the top of the standing in every school—elementary, middle school and now high school.

The same need had once driven her study of the violin. 'Father, one day I will be the best violinist in Tokyo. I will practise and practise until it is so.' Again, Father had laughed in his throaty way, not from his belly, with real feeling, as she had heard other men do, but with a control that sounded almost disbelieving. As if he was merely placating her. 'Of course, Kameko-chan,' he had agreed, knowing how very unlikely her claim.

Many a parent prayed for the gift of prodigy. Mother was no exception. And Kameko was good, very good. She wanted so badly to be a performing violinist. To stand at the front of overfilled concert halls and to play music. To have people exclaim over her talent. How proud she would have been. How proud Mother would have been. And Father. She would not have to have been ashamed of her name in a situation like that. Not at all. And because of her fame even the children would realize that they had been mistaken in taunting her.

Mother, convinced that of the millions of pleading prayers raised up by Japanese parents the rare and raw talent of prodigy had been bestowed upon her only daughter, sought an endless array of private instruction. In the early years, Kameko fared well in festivals and competitions, gaining a level of local notoriety. Until, at age eleven, when gawkiness had overtaken cuteness, when crooked and oversized teeth were peppered with the gaps of those recently lost, the rising star had slipped. Fallen back to earth.

Her instructor, Akiko-sensei, of some repute himself as a professional player, felt compelled to share the truth as he saw it. He had not meant to be intentionally unpleasant about it Kameko did not think, but it seemed to take Mother that way. After one particularly bad lesson, one in which her fingers stumbled all over themselves hunting and pecking for the right notes like a chicken in the yard, he very solemnly explained, 'You see, Kimura-san, with prodigy Japan likes its truly gifted in the form of a little child, one who can, through their fingers, convey the experiences of a lifetime. That ability, Kimura-san, it is indeed a gift. It cannot be learned. It must be present without and in spite of learned technique.' As if anticipating her protest, he raised his hand to beg her silence and attention. Kameko had stood numbly in the corner, half-hidden by her music stand, wishing that she truly could draw herself into a shell, as her namesake would have, and disappear. Matter-of-factly Sensei had continued, 'For if it could be learned, there would be nothing exceptional in the quality of it. The listener wants to gasp with the impossibility of it. That these performers are hardly more than babies, and can be adorably packaged in pristine tiers of silk ruffles or in the earnestness of tuxedo tails, is what makes them extraordinary.' His message was clear. She had gulped at tears and shifted weight from one foot to the other in horrified embarrassment.

She was not one of them. And her dreams were not to be. For a time Mother was truly devastated, and then devastation had been replaced by disbelief, by question and doubt. She went seeking other opinions, asking that Kameko be able to play for other instructors, other schools, other tutors. Sheepishly, Kameko went along. Still she did not find the agreement she sought. Mother had hoped from at least one, maybe more, a bubbling of enthusiasm, a damnation for the idea of Akiko-sensei. She received thoughtful opinions that Kameko was good, that she had potential if she wanted to dedicate most of her waking moments to perfecting the craft, but that she was not a natural prodigy.

Kameko recalled how she had felt so sorry for Mother's disappointment, her upset. Responsible. Guilty. For failing her. That, for Kamkeo, was worse even than her own sense of loss. And it made her determined to somehow, someday, make up for the sad way that things had turned out.

'Earth to Kameko! Come in, Kameko!' Akira laughs, 'Wow, has that math result got you all worked up?' They are in the school cafeteria. Lunch break is almost over.

'You haven't eaten anything,' Misako comments.

'How do you expect to grow up big and strong?' Akira, her dear and crazy friend, jokes.

'I am not much for eating. Not today.'

'Are you on a diet? Little Miss Skinny is on a diet!' Akira calls out through hands shaped like a megaphone.

'Stop that, Akira! You're no better than those election callers,' Misako scolds her.

'Those really annoying ones that end up waking me up on the weekends? Here's a thought: Maybe, subliminally, they've brainwashed me to sound that way.'

Yuki laughs. 'Ha! It wouldn't come as a surprise.'

'If all else fails, maybe I'll have a future shouting messages for the bully boxes.'

'I'm just not feeling up to eating,' Kameko says.

'What about your poor brain?' Yuki asks her. 'How are you going to have the energy or wits to cram for the history test at the end of the week?'

When she confesses it, her reason for distraction, her friends laugh at her naivete. 'O-ho!' Akira chortles. 'Sweet, innocent Kameko has just found out that her father is a dirty old man!'

A heated flush rises to her cheeks. She wills it away. But her anger at it showing itself serves only to make it worse. 'No, that's not it.' She had hoped to feel better by talking about it, but she is beginning to wonder if it has been a mistake to have brought it up.

'Don't tell me you think he's unique. He's just like a million other men who can't stand the nags they married. So he went out and got himself a doll to play with as well! Look at it this way, Kameko, he is relatively okay looking. With a good job. If you look at things *relatively*...maybe it would be more strange not to have a mistress. Mistresses come with the territory. You know it. For the big *sararimen*,' she bats her eyelashes in an attempt to appear coquettish. Giggles at Akira's acting lighten the tension. 'Come on, it's the duty of the housewife to be blind in the interests of keeping the family happy. It's in the good-wife, wise-mother job description!' Akira suddenly pulls a sour face, 'But believe me, it's not a job I ever want to have, no sir! I'm not going to let some man jerk me around like a puppet on a string. I'm going to live life for me! I'm going to write my own ticket. Just watch me. Go where no Japanese woman has gone before!' She waves her arm broadly across an imaginary horizon.

'Of course you are, Akira, of course. From you, I can believe it!' Yuki giggles. Akira's comic faces once again make them all crumple with laughter.

When silliness subsides Kameko assures her oldest friend, 'With a crazy face like that everyone will run to make way for you!' The ringing of the bell brings the chatter to a finish. Hurriedly they gather books, lunch leftovers and belongings, and head to class.

Akira leans in to Kameko, they are head to head as they walk the hall, 'Take my advice dearest little Kameko-chan: Concentrate on school. Use your brain. Make your own future. Don't be one of *them*!' Akira fixes her face into a crooked sneer and chants loudly with a clenched fist pumping the air, 'You know what they say, the good-wife and wise-mother must live her life for every other. But I say to hell with being stuck in the *nurumayu jotai*! Why settle for a lukewarm water situation and let the grime be forever on your skin? If the water's not hot enough in the marriage tub, a woman should get on out. Or better still, don't bother getting in! There you have it. Fight the good-wife stereotype!'

It is Misako who gives her arm a gentle squeeze with a small smile. 'It is the way of things,' she says in a thoughtful murmur, 'but it hurts us sometimes.'

She puts one hand to her chest, over her heart, and shrugs, 'Even though it is not for us to be hurt.'

The teacher nods sternly at them, the look very clearly disapproving, as they noisily enter the classroom. When he turns to write on the board Akira sticks her tongue out at his back. This, as always, results in the desired trill of laughter. The teacher turns swiftly to find out what is the cause of the giggles behind him. It is the way of Akira. Akira's Law they call it; it is her nature to thumb her nose at tradition, at the ways that are accepted. If there is to be a leader of the little group, it is definitely Akira. The four take to their assigned seats and open their books in preparation for the day's lesson.

With Akira's words ringing through her mind, 'Don't be one of them—the stereotype!' she realizes that she wants a life for herself as far from her mother's as humanly possible. Study. Study hard. It is the one way, the only way. To have a choice in life. She imagines Mother's placating voice:

> *'Have you had enough rice, then? Would you care for more fish?'*
> *'Shall I make you some tea?'*
> *'Come, let me get you something to eat.'*
> *'Is this how you like it?'*

She is a good woman, the kind of woman that is praised, the kind that lives an empty, selfless existence; *tsukushizuma,* the go-all-out-wife. Kameko suddenly feels scornful of the anxious-to-please passivity of the housewife maiden. *Sorry Mother*, she apologizes silently, *for thinking of you in this way. But I don't want to end up as simply a foolish puppet. Akira is right, I don't want to be that stereotype.*

***Aneeta**
English 50
San Francisco
September 2002

She is one of the last to read. When he calls on her, her heart pounds. She remembers the elocution exercises that the Sisters had insisted on in school. The drills. The memorizations. The winning recitations. She never won. She was always too fast in her speech. Her words would string themselves together like a rope and her mouth would fly, with hardly a breath, until she reached the end, until her knees were ready to buckle under her. Sister Cecilia was gentle in her criticisms. 'If only you were to slow that overeager tongue of yours, child, you would surely do very well. You have a melodious intonation. Give the ear and the mind a chance to appreciate it more fully.'

She is not worried so very much that they should hear *her* voice in this classroom, but that they should hear the beauty of the voice of Tagore. As she begins her throat is tight, 'I am going to share with you some of the poetry of a man of my country. He is, in origin, Bengali. From the southernmost portion of India. His name is Rabindranath Tagore. I will read two of the pieces from this volume.' She shows the cover of *Gitanjali*. Memories flood her mind as she sets the book on her desk. She swallows hard and tries to heed Sister Cecilia's caution.

> *'Thou art the sky and thou art the nest as well.*
> *O thou beautiful, there in the nest it is thy love that encloses*
> *the soul with colours and sounds and odours.*
> *There comes the morning with the golden basket in her*
> *right hand bearing the wreath of beauty, silently to crown the earth.*
> *And there comes the evening over the lonely meadows*
> *Deserted by herds, through trackless paths, carrying cool*
> *Draughts of peace in her golden pitcher from the western ocean of rest.*
> *But there, where spreads the infinite sky for the soul to take her flight in,*
> *reigns the stainless white radiance.'*

Her tone wavers and thins,

'There is no day nor night, nor form, nor colour and never, never a word.'

That the last line is whispered is unintentional. Any louder and surely she would have crumbled. She hurries to begin the second of the songs, hoping to tamp down the rising swell of tears.

> *'That I should make much of myself and turn it on all*
> *Sides, thus casting coloured shadows on thy radiance—such is thy maya.'*

She blinks rapidly in an attempt to banish hot liquid she can already feel starting to leak at the corners of her eyes. She never considered this. That to hear and speak these words would have such a great effect as this. Such a bittersweet and potent reminder of home. Of Papa. And times that were simple, happy. Times that were without fear. When the little bird in her was yet uncaged.

> *'Thou settest a barrier in thine own being,'* her voice catches, *'and then*
> *Callest the severed self in myriad notes. This thy self-separation has taken*
> *body in me.'*

She should have chosen differently, chosen some passage less personal, less a part of her. How daft and terribly childish she must appear. A simple reading and she ends up in tears.

> *'The poignant song is echoed through all the sky in*
> *Many-coloured tears and smiles, alarms and hopes; waves*
> *Rise up and sink again, dreams break and form. In me is*
> *Thy own defeat of self.'*

It is possible to be moved by written works, she is only an example of that. Let it be explained in that way. That it is the beauty of words and images only, and not the way they touch the rawness of truth in her.

> *'This screen that thou has raised is painted with*
> *innumerable figures with the brush of the night and the*
> *day. Behind it thy seat is woven in wondrous mysteries*
> *of curves, casting away all barren lines of straightness.*
> *The great pageant of thee and me has overspread*
> *The sky. With the tune of thee and me all the air is*
> *Vibrant, and all ages pass with the hiding and seeking of thee and me.'*

Sheer force of will brings to her lips the briefest of smiles and a short laugh that sounds nervous and embarrassed. It is declaration that she is finished. She raises what she hopes to be a brave face and looks into the yet blurred sea that circles around her. She is not prepared for the sympathy in the professor's eyes, nor for the way it silently cuts through her melancholy.

As her message shifts to tell of the poet himself, she begins to regain composure. 'Tagore was considered quite a genius. His artistry with words is considered deeply profound and moving. As you just saw.' A polite and indirect apology for her public display. 'He was very much revered all through India. His verse transcended caste and religious divides. Among Western circles, too, Tagore was well-respected. He was extremely well-traveled in Europe and America. He was held up in prestigious literary circles, and also in the scientific community. He corresponded with the likes of Einstein. It was rare, especially at that time, in the early 1900's, to find one who could do well in two such opposing spheres. He was the one,' she forces a smile, 'to give Gandhi the name Mahatma, meaning great one, out of his deep admiration.' There is an audible sigh from somewhere in the group. 'He won the Nobel Prize for Literature in 1913. The first of our nation. It was a great point of pride in India's history.'

Professor Turner is still watching, she can feel his eyes travel her profile. She turns, ever so slightly, and lets her hair fall, like a curtain, to shield the side of her face.

The Canadian woman with a wild mass of copper hair volunteers, 'That was so beautiful. So beautiful. And you read it…so *beautifully*. I could really, like, feel it.'

'Aneeta, thank you. Truly.' The professor puts his hand lightly to his heart and gives her a small bow. His smile has returned. The seriousness is gone. 'I think we've got a couple more, am I right?'

The class moves on. She gladly goes with it. Buffeted along. The next reading is from *To Kill a Mockingbird* by Harper Lee. She is glad to be listening, to let her mind be pulled away from its sorrow.

It isn't until they are packing up to leave that he approaches her. The professor. She is startled by him. His closeness. His voice is low, 'I'm sorry.'

'I beg your pardon?'

'I'm truly sorry. Obviously the reading,' again his hand is to his chest, 'held a great deal of emotion for you.'

She does not trust that she can keep feeling at bay. In light of his gentle concern. She swallows. Looks down. The group is trailing out of the classroom. Only a few are left, still gathering belongings as she is. She concentrates on putting things into her sack. 'Yes,' she replies, shy of his attention.

'It's a beautiful volume you read from. Is it in English? Or were you translating for us?'

'This one is English. The original was in Bengali, which, unfortunately, I cannot read or speak.' She closes the bag and forces herself to smile. Her mouth is tight.

'So where did you get this one? Here? I have a thing for rare books. If I can find something as surprising as that around here I'd love to know where.'

'No. This one…it was a gift from my father. A very long time ago.' She blinks rapidly against fresh tears.

'Ah. I see. I felt really bad…seeing you cry. It made my heart go out to you.'

She slides the thin sleeve of leather into place with care. 'No, I should be the one to apologize…after such a display. It…was silly.'

'I feel like I should do something to make you feel better. After all, it was my stupid assignment that made you cry. There's nothing I hate more than seeing a woman cry. Can I make it up to you? Maybe buy you a cup of coffee? Or do something to restore you to a sunnier disposition?'

'No.' It comes out abrupt and harsh. Sharp. An embarrassed flush rises to her cheeks. Not wanting him to think her rude, she attempts to temper the response, 'But thank you. It's very kind, but unnecessary.' Swiftly she closes her bag, nods her good- bye, and, feeling much like a deer trapped in a thicket, carries herself in what she hopes looks a relatively normal gait from the room. She can feel the gaze that follows.

She sits at the bus stop. Beside her an older dark-skinned woman shares the wooden bench, with a flowered kerchief tied under her chin. Tightly curled hair shot with fine threads of silver peeks from the edges of the fabric. The woman is muttering something to herself as she leans forward to look out; first left, then right, she peers down the street. In anticipation of the bus, Aneeta thinks. Every so often there is a stern harrumph of disapproval as she settles back again to wait.

After some minutes pass, she turns to regard Aneeta through thick eyeglass lenses that so magnify the appearance of her eyes behind them Aneeta is reminded of the eyes of the large carp Ranna would bring from the fish-wallah at the bazaar. With indignation the woman sputters, 'Wasn't that bus coming at ten minutes to the hour? It's five minutes to. Not s'posed to be late as this. Goodness. It sure does throw a schedule out of whack. Prob'ly got caught up in some kinda traffic. But this time of day? I wonder. Some trouble must be makin' him late. Huh. Some kinda trouble.' The woman shakes her head in dismay. It is clear she expects no reply from Aneeta, merely a sympathizer in her complaint. What would the woman have had to say of riding Delhi buses if here a five minute delay is cause for concern?

A car draws alongside the bench and stops. The window lowers smoothly. A familiar voice reaches out, 'I can't leave you here like this. I mean, I feel so bad, so responsible. For what happened.' He looks so assured in his posture behind the steering wheel of this sleek and stylish car.

The woman turns to Aneeta, 'This your husband?' she intones. Aneeta vigorously shakes her head. 'Your boyfriend?'

'No.' Aneeta shakes her head once again.

'You know him at all?'

'Yes.'

'You do?' She sounds incredulous at the fact she has unearthed.

'Yes. He teaches…a class I am taking.'

'He does?' The woman stretches the does out into 'duhzzz'. Her oversized eyes are squinting at the driver of the car by the curb. 'You her teacher?'

'Yes, ma'am. I am.'

To neither one in particular she says, 'Sounds well-mannered, you ask me. Not anybody ever cares 'bout what I got to say, but there you go.' She shrugs broad shoulders.

'Would you humour me,' he continues, 'so I don't feel so lousy. Let me at least try and cheer you up.' Aneeta looks the other way down the road wishing for the bus to round the bend, but she can't help the slight smile.

'Mm-hmm. This here's a stubborn one. I can tell it. Mister, you got some work ahead a you. Can tell that's the truth.'

'Aneeta,' he beseeches, 'let me buy you a cup of coffee. Or tea. Whatever you like.' He is leaning himself away from the steering wheel where his arm is draped, his face is framed in the window opening.

'Handsome too,' the woman says less loudly, leaning in Aneeta's direction. Self-consciously, Aneeta tucks a length of hair behind her ear. Then in a louder voice the woman says, 'Honey, let the man do somethin' nice for ya. '

'Thank you.' He acknowledges the vote in his favour. 'There's a café just around the corner. Please. Just twenty minutes of your time. Promise. No shop talk. Just some corny jokes to lift your spirits. So I can rest a little easier. Scout's honour.'

'Looks nice enough to me.' The woman shrugs again. 'But I can let the authorities know if I see you on missing persons. Seems harmless though. Given him a good lookin' over. Never seen him on America's Most Wanted. Better than wastin' all evenin' on this bus we been waitin' on.'

Aneeta slowly rises. Again she looks left. No bus. She has a year of classes ahead with this man. What harm could come of it? Only a cup of tea. The dilemma silenced, the decision made, she moves toward the door he pushes open for her. Just once, she looks back at the woman still perched on the bench, who is now smiling her way. With the backward flick of a hand she says to Aneeta, 'Now you let him do somethin' nice.'

They sit, in the small coffee shop, he with a cup of coffee, she with tea. 'So. I just wanted to say sorry.'

'So you've said. But, really, there is no need.' Aneeta looks down into the mug of steaming tea, inhaling its jasmine vapour. Across from her he watches, his smile warm. She is uneasy with this attention, his attention.

'I'm glad you brought that collection, Tagore's, to share. I feel badly, obviously, that it made you cry. That was never my intention when I asked you to choose a piece that meant something to you.'

'No, it was silly that my emotions took me over like that, embarrassed me.' She lifts the mug to her lips, lowers her eyes and drinks.

'It's a strong person who can feel so openly.'

'I didn't feel strong.' She smiles weakly.

'Sorry. No shop talk. I believe I promised corny jokes.'

'You did, yes.'

'Would you like to hear some?'

The question surprises her a little. She didn't know exactly what she had expected. But not truly the delivery of jokes. 'Well, since we're here. Wasn't that the premise?'

'Okay. Ready yourself. Because I,' he volunteers proudly, 'just happen to be the corniest joke-teller around.'

'Really?'

'Here I go.' He clears his throat in mock seriousness. 'How does an elephant ask for a bun?'

'How,' she says softly, faintly smiling, 'does an elephant ask for a bun?'

He hefts a golden forearm to his nose to mimic an elephant trunk and nasally asks, 'May I have a bun, please?'

She can't help but laugh. It is so very childish—no, not childish, but rather childlike, this way of his. He is gazing at her again, grinning. She looks down at her tea, suddenly shy. Surely they are close to twenty minutes into the arrangement she'd agreed to. And yet, she finds herself not wanting to leave.

'You have a beautiful smile.'

'Thank you.' She blushes at the compliment. Her mind passes the sentiment gingerly back and forth like a fragile package that does not belong.

'I'll have to tell you another. For another smile. A repeat performance. At least one more. Then I know we're on the right track. Then I can feel that I'm delivering the levity I promised. So,' he muses, 'here's another: How do you catch a unique bird?'

She ponders a moment, 'I really couldn't say.'

'You 'neak up on it. Get it? You-neak up on it. Unique?'

She puts her hand to her mouth and laughs behind it. 'Oh dear.'

'See, I wasn't lying. These are the corniest of the corny, are they not? But I got you. I know you're laughing. Back behind your hand. I can see it in your eyes. They give you away.' He turns away then from the tiny two person table where they are sitting and says loudly to no one in particular, 'See, I got her laughing. She likes my jokes.' A few people look his way, amused, perhaps.

Aneeta lowers her hand, 'Do you often appeal to complete strangers?'

'Whenever I can. Strength in numbers, you know. I like playing to an audience. From a very young age my folks had me figured for either an actor or a comedian. Joker, thespian, teacher—it's all the same thing.'

'Really?' She smiles up at him.

'Essentially. So, I have to ask, now that I have you in a better frame of mind, what part of India are you from? Obviously you're not Bengali since you admitted you don't read it.'

'I…am from Delhi, New Delhi.'

'How long've you been here, in the States?'

'Not very long.' She isn't prepared for his questions. She should have been, but isn't. Her words sound rushed and hasty. Like a child trying to cover misdeed.

She looks down. She does not wish to be thought badly of. By him. And she does not wish to feel badly about herself. Or guilty. About what is left behind. She loses herself for a moment in the past, until he interrupts by clearing his throat, and brings her back to the present.

'Sorry for getting too personal. Just cut me off at the pass if I'm poking my nose where it doesn't belong. Changing the subject entirely, what made you want to take creative writing?'

'I guess a number of reasons. I very much enjoy literature, the study of it. And I liked to write creatively, in my school days. But actually, the main reason, to tell the truth, is that I also need to better my English. My written skills could use some,' she searched for a word, 'polish, perhaps. It's been quite a time since I left school and I fear I've lost a great deal.'

'I'd certainly be happy to help you out with English. In your writing. I mean, if you need. At all. Any time. Any time at all.'

She laughs at his silliness. 'I may just need it, the help.'

'Consider me at your service,' he says with dramatic flourish.

'I think I have finished my tea,' she says gently.

'Right. Of course. Could I get some more hot water? Another cup? Anything?'

'You are very kind. You really did not need to go to this trouble just because I shed tears in your class. But I think I should be going. I'm afraid I've overstayed the twenty minutes of your invitation.'

'Well, I hadn't meant the timing literally. I wasn't sure how much it would take to get you feeling better. And for me to overcome my guilt.'

'I think that we can say we've had some success on both counts, yes?'

'And I am terribly relieved at that.' Again, she finds herself laughing in his company. He stands and moves around to help her with her chair. Her coat. A current runs through her at his closeness. How long has it been since she has laughed? Allowed herself to laugh? Too long. Too terribly long.

Aneeta
Delhi
1996-2001

She is in a market. It seems familiar. She tries to place it. But cannot. She sees a run of shanty stalls. They remind her of some that stretch through alleys along GB Road. Where girls are paid. For sex. She weaves a slow circle. Where am I?

Now she is among fruit and vegetable vendors. Somehow along the same alleyway. She knows it is not right, but the image persists. Their wares are polished and piled high around her. The pyramids of foodstuffs seem taller even than she is. They seem not to stand straight, but to lean inward as they rise. Hawkers are shouting at her as she passes through, clamouring for her attention. The passage is very narrow. She is not sure what she is to be shopping for, though she is certain that if she brings nothing back with her Mummy will be angry. A flutter of panic stirs.

In the high-gloss sheen of an eye-level aubergine she catches sight of herself. Her hair is crudely shorn. She is wound in black fabric. Black, an ill omen. Black is reserved for the impure, the disavowed, the disgraced. Her breath catches. Instinctively she reaches to her head. Her hair is gone. Gone. What remains is in odd patches. It is coarse. Like small needles. She wonders how this happened without her knowing.

Louder and louder, the wallahs call for her attention. 'Miss. Miss!' 'This way, Miss!' 'This way, Rani!' When she hears it, her nickname, she turns quickly in fright. In the process she feels herself knock something. The towers begin to tumble. A finger points at her with a shout. Hands reach out grabbing, pulling. Then she is running, through the narrow lines of the marketplace. It is a labyrinth that closes and opens and shifts in an endless maze. There is no way out. Fingers curl and claw at her. She can feel their spidering along her skin. Cutting into her. She is frantic, but she does not know which way to turn. To free herself. Chappals slap madly against the stone underfoot. Her breath is coming in gasps. She cannot slow. They are coming for her. They are chanting, shouting at her back. 'Whore! Filthy whore! Disgrace to your name! To your family! To your caste!' And then rising to the top of the chorus she hears clearly, so very clearly, Mummy and Asha's voices too. They stand out among the other cries. She looks over her shoulder at the angry faceless mob that pursues her. Fists are shaking in the air.

'Please,' she pleads, 'please!' A wall of cobbled stone materializes before her to block her way. To stop her. She gives a push at it wildly, but it is solid. She presses her back up against it. With greater urgency she begs, trying to make herself heard over the din, 'Please! What do you want from me?'

'Kanjari! We want you to do what is right! What you must!' In one ear it is

Mummy she hears, in the other one, Asha. In the background there are jagged edges of cruel laughter. And then she is choking on the unmistakable smoke of kerosene fire as it snakes hotly around her.

From her sleep she is jerked awake in a panting cough. She feels like she is suffocating. She gasps desperately for breath. She can feel a presence beyond the mosquito netting. Real? Or imagined? This is how so many nights are for her. Fear lies in heavy layers upon her; rest eludes her.

Her mind conjures noises. A scraping that comes from somewhere above. The sound of water trickling. A far off creaking. And from beyond, a trill in the darkness. The chowkidar security watch patrol. Outside the gates, one signals to another. Nightsounds close in around her. Her chest is still tight with the dream.

The phantom of him steps softly around. So that there is no relief to be had. Actual or imagined, he is always with her. Like a permanently on-duty chowkidar. With no interest in protection. Just interest in un-detection.

Once, she had broken a tiny elephant figurine Papa had given her at her birthday. She had been inconsolable. Papa had told her it was a big girl gift because it was fragile. She had been so proud to receive the exquisitely fashioned miniature with its tiny jeweled headdress. To be considered a big girl. Until she had knocked it from the table and it had shattered on the marble floor. He had assured her that it could be fixed. But after it was glued she had still been able to see fine hairline cracks. She had known, in her little girl-big girl way, the weakness that such damage inflicted. That it was there to stay. That it could never be fixed entirely. That it had become a part of the figure itself. It would never be the same. Not as it first was, ever again.

Like the figurine, she feels broken into little pieces. She is living a schizophrenic existence. Voices have taken up dialogue in her head. They conduct a silent ongoing interrogation. But there are no ready answers to their questions. Around in endless looping circles they travel.

The idea of death blinks slowly in her conscience. There is some opaque promise in the idea of a release from shame, the thought of a way out. She turns the idea over and over inside her mind, like a gift, a neatly wrapped and bowed possibility. It comes to consume her. In Sister Helene's science lectures, as worktables lined with plaited pairs of upturned faces consider the elements of the periodic table, her heart skips and quickens. CN, the elemental sign for cyanide. Lethally potent. Sister taps at its position with her pointer stick, in a slow 1-2 rhythm. Tap. Tap. Not easy to get, however. And then there is phosphorous, symbol P, and thallium, Tl. Implicated in more than a few murders. Bromine, Br. Arsenic, As. Tap. Tap. Lethal elements march their way into her brain. Settle down into thoughts. So many poisons in appropriate quantities would surely do the job. Hadn't she very recently heard of a child killed by ingesting roach poison? In the villages pesticide tablets are often used. Surely not too difficult to come by, these items of everyday convenience.

Or then there is the matter of hanging. A reliable means for sure. From a ceiling fan, or backyard tree. Even from a well. Two out of three are immediately available to her. Except that she would rather spare them finding her in this way, having to cut her down.

She wonders if she would have courage enough to simply step into the turbulent Delhi traffic. To sacrifice herself to a passing bus or taxi or rickshaw. But in such a scenario she could not be certain, she realizes, of the result. The train would be more likely to bring a decisive end. It is a common thing to do. But would enough be left to identify that it was she who had perished? It is inconceivable that there be a question as to her fate, not knowing worming its way through minds, images, imaginings of those she loves. She would need to be certain of things being finished cleanly.

But ideas turn on themselves and birth clouds of greater uncertainty, suffocating courage and purpose. One, in particular, confounds her. In death, whispers of gossip and speculation would no doubt run rampant. After all, what prompts a young woman, a child of such a family, more blessed by far than many, to take her life? In the wake of the certain questioning and curiosities, shame would still shadow her memory. Shifted only by degrees. For in such a course, truth would remain invisible. And spare the guilty. Spare. The guilty. That he should be spared is an outcome she finds impossible to reconcile.

She was always his favourite. Everyone knew it. Everyone. He made it no secret. Perhaps it had been part of some plan. Perhaps he had always intended for it to be that way. And he was not discouraged in his attentions. Rather maybe encouraged, now she thinks, by her blind childish excitement.

He had come often to visit. More after Papa's passing. In a way, his increased presence and his added attentions helped to ease the burden of loss. His spoiling of her brought happiness at a time when it was in short supply. Which is why it went down all too easily. Like a tin of favourite sweets.

He would hardly have stepped through the front gates and into the courtyard before she would throw up cries of his arrival to whomever was in the house. 'Mummy, it's Chacha-ji come to visit! Dev Uncle is here! Mummy, Asha, come! Dev Uncle is here!' She would besiege him rather like a puppy. 'What have you brought for me? What have you brought for me?' He would hide treats in a pocket or in his hand or his case, and she would have to search him for them. She loved to rummage through every possible hiding spot she could find. He would tickle her under her chin, under her arms. But was it more than that? She can't recall. Did his fingers touch her other places? That she did not notice at the time? That she did not see would eventually become sinister? She didn't know now what to do with those memories. Where to put them. Between belief and disbelief. Between innocent affection or underhanded manipulation.

He would lavish her with little trinkets, sometimes toys, even things more grown-up and ladylike than she deserved, sparkling bangles or a vial of sandalwood essence. 'For my little Neeta Rani,' he would say. His nickname for her. She was his princess. She used to feel so proud to hear it. So important. 'Thank you, Dev Uncle. Thank you, Chacha-ji.'

Maybe it was his way of winning her favour. All those years ago. He had made her love him. Trust him. Unable to deny him. Because he had her heart. Maybe *now* is a return for his affections of *then*. That because of a history of giving he feels justified in taking.

'So sorry for interrupting, Aneeta Miss, but your mother has requested that you serve tea. She and your uncle wait in the front room.' Aneeta looks up from her school books with a start. Ice floods her veins. 'Miss?' the housemaid questions gently, interrupting the wheeling of thought.

Does she see it? 'Yes, Mina?'

'Achcha. It is nothing. No matter. I will wait in the kitchen.' Aneeta nods and watches Mina depart, the wind catching her saffron chunni, her silver anklet jingling lightly with her steps. As she reaches the door she turns back to look once again, her eyes searching, but clearly knowing not what they are looking for. At last, with a face that shows her puzzlement, she turns her attention away and to the steep slip of stairs that lead into the rest of the house.

Aneeta lets out a deeply drawn breath. A breath she has held. Her heart jumps like a panicked mouse. The rooftop had been one of Papa's favourite places. Into the air she whispers, 'I wish you were here, Papa. I do so wish it. Then things would be different.' She moves toward the door, school things clutched tightly to her, chilled by what she has been summoned to do, the role she must play.

She leaves the books on a tiny hallway table inside the door and goes to the tiny water closet to splash some cool water on her face. She fears that Mina has seen into her. Her mask had faltered, slipped. But a slip on the face is not nearly so plain as a slip of the tongue. Mina knows no more than what she has seen.

She tries to make her expression as natural as possible in the mirror's mocking reflection. A complexion without upset. She smoothes the front of her tunic and turns to make her way to the kitchen. When she gets there Ranna is readying the tray for her and Mina is arranging laddu and burfi on a small plate.

Ranna raises her head with a half-smile that reveals an uneven tang of stained and pock-marked enamel, 'So, Mina has found our lost child.'

'Yes, she has found me.'

'I was worried you had run away and left us.'

'Leave you? Why, I would never do that,' she jokes stiffly in return.

'Take it now, before the tea goes cold, or Mummy will not be happy.' The tray passes from worn domestic hands to the young, which tremble slightly as they receive it. The contents give her upset away with a jingle from both porcelain and silver. A thick salt-and-pepper eyebrow rises up. 'Uncle is here for tea,' Ranna adds, 'if Mina has not told you.' Mina looks directly at Aneeta as Ranna adds the last bit of information. They can see there is something, the way the looks pass between their eyes. She turns quickly and urges herself away from their unspoken questions and toward the front of the house.

'Ah, Aneeta, here you are. What has been keeping you? Dev Uncle has come to visit and you are not even polite enough to come and greet him. It used to be that you were the first to greet your Chacha. And now it's almost impossible for you to be found.'

'I was at the rooftop. Studying.'

'Studying. You see?' Dev reassures, smiling, 'A good student. A beautiful girl. She wants only to please her Mummy. Motives are pure. Nothing to worry for.'

'And you didn't come before now? When you must have seen Uncle arrive? I wish I could share your certainty, ji. How strange you act these days, Aneeta.' Mummy tuts at her.

'Mummy. Uncle-ji.' This is all she can muster by way of greeting. She struggles to keep the battle that rages within her invisible to the eye. She hopes the tremor in her voice is noticeable only to her own ear.

'You see? Hardly a word. This is what I am saying. Like a ghost, she is.'

She tries to keep things from rattling on the tray. Uncle and Mummy seem in fine spirits, talking around her as if nothing has happened, nothing has changed. And she can do nothing. Nothing to save herself from it. She lays out the food and prepares to pour. Her jaw is firmly set, her teeth the hard soldiers of her tension.

'Aneeta. *Rani.* I know how much you wish only to please,' Dev cajoles in a too sweet voice. He turns to Mummy, 'I wonder if it makes her unhappy that I still use her pet name. Maybe she finds it too childish. But I am so fond of it.'

Mummy laughs. 'I don't think a girl ever tires of being thought of as a princess, Dev.'

'Ah, well,' he pauses, 'so long as Aneeta doesn't ask me to stop.' She looks up for a moment to find him smiling easily. Inwardly, she seethes. Disgust sours in her throat. Standing before him she pours tawny liquid into the fine white china cup. Though she longs, instead, to hurl the steaming tea upon him. For it to disfigure him, marr his false smiling face and scar him forever, the way he has scarred her.

Before he takes the tea, he eases a square box from his breast pocket and places it lightly on the tray she holds. Cup and box stand side by side. Trembling. A token? A payment for his guilt? Or is it that he thinks that such a thing might make her agreeable, pliable, like a lump of clay? 'For you,' he says simply, at last taking the tea. It occurs to her the sheer obscenity of it. In Mummy's presence. No shame gnaws his conscience. Her face burns with the upward scarlet creep of humiliation and fury.

Without acknowledging the gift, Aneeta moves to fill Mummy's cup. 'Why, Aneeta! You've not even thanked Uncle for his kindness. Hai, what kind of rudeness? Perhaps he has spoiled you too much. You forget your manners! I do apologize for her rudeness, ji.'

He waves a hand dismissively, 'Don't scold her too much. I have the feeling her mind is right now somewhere else.'

Mummy chimes firmly in, 'Open it and offer proper thanks for the kindness of your uncle and his unnecessary generosity. Show him that you are not totally undeserving of his affections.' Her tone is warm in front of Dev Uncle, but Aneeta can feel the scathing in her rebuke, can feel the steeliness in the eyes that follow her jerky movements to finish the service in an adequate manner.

She wants to scream that no amount of trinkets could ever undo what had been done. But she knows that she will not. And he knows this too.

'Honestly, ji, I don't understand it. She must have taken leave of her senses.' Mummy sighs.

Numbly, Aneeta sets the tray on the sideboard and snaps the box lid back on its hinges to reveal a gold bangle, delicately etched with a simple, feminine patterning.

'Eh, Rani? What do you think, for a most beautiful young lady? I hope that an uncle at least can get the fashions of the moment for a favourite niece.'

'It is very nice, thank you.' She offers the words woodenly, knowing it is the least that Mummy will expect from her tongue. The inside of her sighs in crumbling defeat. He is right. As much as she hates it. Hates him. And moreover hates him for assuming it to begin. He has been right in his assumption. She'll say nothing, scream nothing. Not spit or throw hot tea. Or throw his precious box back at him. If only for Mummy's sake. She cannot. He knows it. And he is reminding her. 'Mina interrupted me in the midst of my afternoon studies. I must really get back to my revision.' Without awaiting a reply, she takes the tray up and swiftly sweeps out the room into the cool of the hallway, leaving the bangle behind. To at least show him. That she cannot be bought. She is so preoccupied with anger and revulsion that she runs blindly into Mina. With a thick clang the tray somersaults from her grasp and onto the marble floor. Issuing a half-gasp, half-cry in a fit of frustration, Aneeta bolts for the stairs. Voices below become quieter, tinny-sounding, as she climbs. At the top she reaches out almost savagely for the door, desperate for the limited expanse of rooftop freedom.

At her back she hears Mina: 'My fault, Sahib. Sorry, sorry. I knocked her. So sorry. I will clean it.'

Sushma's exasperation follows, 'Hai! You see? What has taken hold of that one? What to do? I tell you it is not easy with this girl!'

Aneeta can already hear the clearing of shards of broken china as she steps into the warmth.

Later, he comes to find her. She is immersed in the schoolwork spread before her, but for his presence she has a sixth sense awareness. She shivers involuntarily, gooseflesh radiating outward along her arms, hair rising at her neck.

'Hmmm. So here you are,' he says lazily. He closes the door and walks across the space, looks down to where his car sits in the courtyard. He leans his shoulder confidently against the wall opposite where she sits. She can feel him watching her, studying. She keeps her head down, looking at the notes spread before her. She will not give him her attention until she herself chooses it. A small flicker of power. A seed that is germinating within her. It makes her feel a boldness that is new, different.

'Here I am,' she answers with a thin thread of sarcasm. Mummy would have been dismayed by such impertinence. Finally she looks up, finds his eyes. Narrows her own.

'So.' He shifts his gaze from hers to nonchalantly consider the landscape of neighbouring rooftops before circling back to find her again. 'That was quite a display earlier. Not the wisest of choices. Given the circumstances. I thought you understood. How things would work. How you would be the one to suffer most.'

'You think I'm not suffering? With what you've done, what you do?'

'What *I'm* doing? Not alone, Aneeta. These things cannot be experienced alone. The way I see it and the way *they* would see it is that you are just as guilty as I. Maybe more.'

'I didn't want for this to happen.' Her voice rises. 'Ever! It was not me! Not me who began this.'

'But you did nothing to stop it? Think how you would look.'

'And what should I do? Besides beg and plead and cry. Every time. Every single time.'

'One could argue that you went along with it. Especially if it were to come to light...' he squints into the distance, smiles, 'after all this time.'

'What choice did I have? What choice was there? Even now you remind me. Even now.'

'Ah, we always *have* a choice, Rani. It's what we do with that choice in what fate deals.'

'You know, Uncle, from the way you spoke during tea, in front of Mummy, you must be very sure. That I will never open my mouth. That I will always be the frightened little girl. Who will never speak out. To spare them, to spare myself. I wanted to throw the tea in your face.'

He chuckles easily at her. 'I'm glad you didn't. My dhobi would have had an awful time removing the stains.'

Words spring out of her fury. Words that speak of a wisdom and cunning that she wasn't aware she even possessed. 'You work hard to make me think nobody will believe me. Or that I will bring such unbearable shame on my family. If they were to find out. So on and so on. You tell me this, remind me, every time there is a chance.' She says sharply, '*I am the one who would be on the losing end. If truth were to come out. This is one point you never fail to make. To keep me down. To keep things the way you would like to have them. No matter the way in which things go today, tomorrow, next week, next month, next year—I will always be the loser. Tell, don't tell. I will, I won't. For so long you've seen my words as empty. But you see, maybe I am growing wiser, Chacha-ji. What I have realized, that I didn't really think about before, is that losing does not come in degrees. The outcome for me, well, we know what it is, what it will be. That it can't be changed. What I'm trying to say, to tell you, is that I've had enough time being the frightened little girl. You've taken everything from me! Everything I was, everything I had, everything that I could have been. The woman I wanted to be. Longed to be. You've denied me all of that, and I hate you for it. As much as I once loved you. As much as I trusted and believed in you. And now look—I am nothing! Just a handful of dust. Because you've taken it all away. You've left me with nothing more to *lose,* Chacha. Did you ever think of that?'

He shifts his weight from one hip to the other. It is not much, but it is something, and she has seen it. She repeats the words more slowly, watching him as they make their way to where he stands, watching them register in his understanding. 'Nothing. Is left. For me. To lose.' And her eyes hold his in silent warning. She has stepped directly into the heart of the battle.

'We'll see, Rani. We'll just see. How much courage your heart actually holds. You forget just how well I know you.' He smiles again, but she sees it is forced, that there is uncertainty in it.

It is not improper that she would want to visit her sister without a ready reason or some occasion. Mummy had seemed, in fact, quite pleased at the idea. As if her elder sister, somehow, might fashion her into a more agreeable child.

She smoothes her uniform tunic with clammy, nervous palms. The sitting room in which she waits has the look of hardly being used. There is an atmosphere in this house of unmistakable affluence, with touches of refinement that are not found even in her own home. She settles onto the edge of an overstuffed divan, careful that her skirt keeps its place over her knees. 'I'll let your sister know that you have arrived, Miss.' The housemaid retreats.

Several heavy silken tapestries hang imperiously from the wall, depicting well-known clashes from history, the noble Raj emerging victorious in the final scene. She knows them to be antique. The ceilings are very high and give the illusion of disappearing into an infinite space. The air is cool, the work of the stone along with the enormous air conditioning generators that lurk behind.

In spite of the chill in the room her face feels hot. Her insides are like a shaken Fanta soda. Unlike what Mummy and Asha think, hers is not truly a social call. It is perhaps even manipulative, and for that she does feel sorry.

'Neeta! How wonderful it is to have you visit!' Her elder sister steps into the room looking elegant and radiant. She is loose and fluid in her movement, almost like a dancer. Silk and scent swirl about her. She exudes an aura of sophistication and confidence. 'But you've grown taller again! You must be taller even than Mummy now. What does she have to say about that when she is having one of her stern chats? With you looking down on her! Oh my!' She laughs lightly.

The sound of it ripples around the room. Aneeta envies the way it must feel to enjoy that kind of happiness.

'Come, let's sit. I have fresh laddu for our tea. How are you? How is school coming along? Why, you must be very nearly done!' Aneeta speaks in thin ribbons about school, the Sisters, revision, not really sure what she is saying, attempting polite coversation when really, her mind is fixed on what she has come for. The maid enters the room, interrupting the conversation with an elaborate tray of tea and snacks. 'Promise you won't tell Ranna or she'll have a go at me for spoiling your appetite.'

'She will take vacation soon, to see her nephew in Madras.'

'I can't remember that last time she actually went on vacation. It seems like she is always stationed in that kitchen. How very strange it will be in there with her gone,' she muses, 'but a good chance for you to practise some cooking skills!' Asha nods, 'It is a good thing to at least know the basics. For your future life as a wife.' Asha smiles and bites into a soft laddu.

Aneeta flushes, her own laddu, a sweet she adores, sitting untouched. She feels the quickened tempo pulsing at her neck. Heat fires anew in her cheeks and burns at her neckline. 'Why must it always be about what a woman can do for a man, Asha? Why must life always be about pleasing them? Or being good enough? Why is there no need for a man ever to measure up?' Frustration, long held back, is flaring in her, 'Why is it never the other way?' Asha's expression registers surprise at the sudden outburst. 'Why is it always that the woman has to be the one sacrificing?' Her tone sounds petulant and immature to her ear.

'Is this about growing up? Is it about the pressures of your future? Just look at me. Look at how happy I am.' She gestures around the room at the world that she has become a part of. 'I know a similar arrangement will be made for you.' Asha's voice dips into a low whispered reassurance while a hand reaches out to lightly take Aneeta's own, 'You mustn't worry about such things needlessly.'

'It is more than that, Asha. More than just worries about marriage. If ever there is to be one.'

'Of course there is! Silly girl, why on earth would there not be one?'

'There is something…Asha? I need to tell you something.' Like an unraveling thread of cotton, words begin to flow. 'It is of Dev Uncle.' Aneeta gathers what tender courage she can muster, knowing that her decision to share the dark secret that has kept her for so very long could well cost her everything she holds dear. 'He comes to me when he knows no one is watching. He touches me, Asha. Places where he should not.' Aneeta watches horror and disbelief overpower the beauty and radiance of only moments before. Each revelation, she can see, pushes her sister further and further from her. In heart, in mind, and in spirit. 'Asha, he does things he should not. Forces me—'

'What are you saying! You…stop this instant! Stop! I don't want to hear this!' Asha's voice shrills in denial, in shock, in the fury of outrage.

Aneeta looks into the crisscross weave of the fabric covering her lap, where her hands are lying numb, where her sister has let them drop. 'He forces himself on me,' she whispers thinly. 'And I hate myself. And I die. Over and over again, I have died. I wonder how many more times it is possible to die, Asha.' She looks up.

Asha no longer looks at her, but gazes into the distance, somewhere beyond the doorway of the room. Her expression is grim. 'You are wrong,' Asha says without emotion. 'It cannot have happened as you say it.'

'But it has,' she pleads. 'The first time was on the night of your wedding!' Asha's head whips back. The association is like an icy slap.

'He is our uncle, Aneeta,' Asha says with sternness, 'how could you do this? He has known us since we were babies!' Her voice rises sharply, her tone is accusing, 'And you were always his favourite! You!' She looks up at Aneeta, her eyes are narrowed, as if trying to see beyond what is at the surface of Aneeta's expression, trying to read something deeper. 'And this is how you repay him? I just can't believe it. This…story. I cannot believe what you are telling me. No! Not Papa's brother!'

'I cannot say why, Asha. I have tried for so long to think of why.' She raises her hands in a weak gesture of helplessness.

'But you should have done something. Something to stop it. You should have stopped it!' Asha's voice is belligerent, demanding. Her face has turned chalky, making her lips seem overly red. They are harsh with the colour drained from her skin, like her tone.

'Believe me, I have tried everything I could think of!'

'He wouldn't!' Talk plays out in a disjointed choppy wheel of back and forth false-starts. 'He wouldn't do this…unless. Unless you had…Why are you telling me this? Why?'

'I couldn't keep going, Asha. I needed help. For so long I've been alone with this. Afraid. I can't…I don't want to be afraid anymore. Please. I never meant to hurt you, I just needed…I just hoped…I don't know. That if you knew, at least…I am sorry, didi. I think perhaps…I should go.' Aneeta is hoping that her sister might stop her. But Asha is silent. 'It's best, I think…that I go.' She stands and smoothes her skirt carefully, as if it is a task that requires great attention. Asha does not rise. Does not look at her. Aneeta wills back tears. 'I am truly sorry. I only hope…you can forgive me. I can find my own way out. Goodbye, sister.'

The change is irreversible. What had begun a meeting between sisters will finish an encounter between two never more separate in existence. It is just as he had warned her it would be.

She drops wordlessly to the floor at her mother's feet. In a gesture of humility and respect she reaches out to touch the softness of skin between sandal straps. Her mother looks startled at the mark of deference. Her featherlight greeting is a symbol out of the ordinary. A silent signal.

She has started it. Now she must finish. It is painful, the anticipation of what will come. Maybe, she thinks, she will be wrong about the reaction that will greet her news. Though Asha has already tempered that hope. A hope that instinct had told her was foolish and impractical. There are ways such things are dealt with, unpleasant matters. Just as every morning the dirt is swept from the floor, so she knows, too, that her confession will need to be cleared up somehow and kept from tainting others.

Upon her head she feels the light touch of her mother blessing her. Would she have blessed me if she knew? The answer is certain. As certain as the change of day into night.

With a deep breath, Aneeta raises her head and meets her mother's eyes. Aching, grieving, she tells it, what needs to be told, from the beginning.

Unlike Asha, Mummy says nothing. Simply purses her lips into a thin, hard line. Aneeta reaches out again, instinctively, for the feet, but this time her hands are kicked away. Abruptly, Mummy rises, and with her Aneeta does too. In a need to somehow plead, placate, appease.

A hand slices the air and sharply, decisively, meets the flesh of Aneeta's cheek. Shock registers on Mummy's face, her mouth opens, but no sound, no words, come out. Aneeta's hand instinctively goes to the searing outline that is left behind. Is it possible to see a whole being wither like a flower before one's eyes?

She wishes she could do or say something to ease the pain. But there is nothing. Somewhere beyond she hears a door close. Nothing is left. It is all done. Opened and closed. It is too late to wonder if hers has been the right choice.

Kameko
Tokyo
2000-2001

Life is brief
Fall in love, maidens
Before the raven tresses begin to fade
Before the flame in your hearts flickers and dies
For those to whom today
Will never return

She had been reviewing a term paper when her phone had rung. She rarely received calls from Father. None, at least, that had not been solicited or forced upon him by Mother. Though Mother has tried her best to be the glue in between them, their bond has weakened to such a degree that they have little of any importance to share with one another.

The briefest of pleasantries are exchanged. She listens for Mother's voice or steady noise in the background. She can hear nothing of her. Nothing to suggest her presence at all. It is entirely unlike him to call to indulge in chit-chat.

When he finally confesses his true reason for calling, she is stunned. The news takes her breath and crushes her chest as if an elephant has sat upon it. His call has not been engineered by Mother, but by circumstance. 'She is ill. With little time. The doctors have told me. I have not told her as much. I am telling you.'

She is dying. Cancer. A scan because of some unusual underarm and shoulder pain has shown it dotted throughout her chest and shoulders. And there is a tumour in her brain. It has already claimed too much of her; is too far along to be treated. She has a year, eighteen months at most. Make the best of her quality of life until the end is what he has been told.

'We have to do what we can to make her happy. I need you to help me. We must attend to her. To her wishes. To make her time…not too trying. Not to hasten…' his voice breaks and she is startled to think that he might have been momentarily overcome, 'the sickness.'

One evening not long after, they sit, the three of them, at the table. The remains of a picked-at meal before them. The atmosphere of death, like a dinner guest, sits heavily in their midst. With every turn of the conversation the visitor is silently acknowledged. The invisible ghostly presence decides the direction of so much more than simply the dialogue of the moment. It captivates and consumes them, closing the eyes to any reality other than the single certain strain it plays.

Father brings it up. But Mother's eyes, so bright, like glittering onyx buttons, watch her intently. 'There is a boy. The son of one of my customers. His father is in a senior position with one of the *Sogo-Shosha*. Big company. Okura. Many international dealings. His son, too, is a *Shosha-man*. A graduate of Tokyo University. Todai. Like his father before him. It would be nice for you two to meet. His father has seen your coming-of-age photo. The one I keep on my desk. He has suggested—'

'Yes,' Mother breathes eagerly, unable to hide the excitement in her voice. 'You should meet. It would be very nice, to meet a boy like that.'

Kameko indulges this wish, as she feels she must. Even though it is not something she would have sought for herself. Strangely enough, she finds herself pleasantly surprised by Tanaka Toshiro. He is polite and intelligent. Charming. Rakish and handsome. With waves of thick hair that frame an elegant face; square jaw, definite cheekbones, a sleek, angular nose. They go for walks. Dine together. See films. Talk of books they have enjoyed and professors they have not. They laugh conspiratorially about traditional parents and the influence of modern ways. Shiro shares with her his hopes and dreams. For himself. For his future. The career path he has mapped out. The opportunities available to him as part of a multinational firm. She finds him refreshingly candid, ambitious, and without the overbearing ego she has expected.

When talk turns to marriage it is almost a relief, for it becomes clear that this has been Mother's desire all along. With time uncertain it feels as if one is fighting a frantic battle against an invisible tide. Almost as if she is racing against death itself. And it has made her single-minded in her determination that she should not disappoint her mother. That in some way, fulfilling this last wish might at least partly make up for the times that life already had.

Akira asks her if she has been abducted by aliens, if they have sucked her brain out through her ears. Loudly demands to know, for all around them to hear, if this is truly her friend Kameko, or some crafty impersonator, she the victim of some intergalactic cosplay gag. But joking quickly gives way to a more serious appeal. 'Kameko, you have to listen to yourself! The drivel that's coming from you! That this guy is different. Japanese men are never different, Kameko. The role is always the same. They're just looking for another Mommy. This guy, he's a textbook case. Modern Tokyo man? No different than his father or grandfather's generation. Going to be the big,' flexing her muscles, Akira twists up her face like a cartoon hero, 'Super-salaryman someday. Doesn't give a shit about anything but his rise to the top. Having a wife is just one of the steps along the way. Then the baby. Good-wife, wise-mother. Come on, Kameko, you know it! You've lived it. Think about it. How happy was that fairytale?'

'How can you say that? You don't know him. He's different.'

Akira's laugh is bitter, 'No, he's not different, you're different. You've gone all crazy in the head. That's what infatuation does to us. Makes us blind. A little bit kookoo. It's a temporary form of insanity. Listen, I'm here as your friend, as possibly your best friend, because I don't give a shit what you might think of me for saying this. As a true friend it's my job to try and steer you straight. You know, the others told me to leave you be. Not to say anything. Misako said you had enough going on with your mother's illness. That we shouldn't begrudge your happiness, that you need something to be happy about. But, Kameko, look at me! This isn't it! You're not being true to yourself. What did you work so hard for? Just so it could be flushed down the toilet by getting married? This is not right! Your head isn't clear! Focus on your mother, sure. You have to. I get that. But don't give everything else up!'

'What choice do I have?'

'You have a choice. These are her last days. I'm sorry to have to say it, but soon she'll be gone. You, though, will have to live with your choice. Then what? Don't do this! Please. Think about yourself. Your life. It's only just beginning. Talk to her. Tell her. At least try. Maybe she'll understand. She might surprise you.'

But Kameko knows in her heart that her decision to fulfill Mother's wish, to do what she can to make her happy in these last days of her life, is not a matter of choice, it was never a choice. It is her duty. She can't expect Akira to understand. Akira, who would not be governed or guided by old ways, by tradition. Who, as a matter of principle, refused to swim with the current, always against it. That was her way—Akira's Law. Defiance.

Akira was found hanging from the overhead lamp in her dormitory room at the university. There was no note, no indication, no explanation of why. Akira's roommate had said that to see the room it was as if she had just taken a break from studying, and on some whim had decided that death was a good out. 'We had exams coming, and there were some course papers due. But I just don't get it. She was always so prepared. It wouldn't have been that big a deal. In reflection, she had been really grumpy for the last few weeks or so. You know, before she…well, before she decided to end it. But other than that, nothing was different. I mean, she always had the potential to be touchy about things, but that's just the way she was, wasn't she?' Kameko was sorry for the poor girl who turned like a spinning top, riddled with questions, needing to talk the confusion out of herself.

Akira had been top of her class at Todai. It was no surprise to any who knew her. Choosing death over what she had spent her young life working for, the life she had wanted for herself, that was the biggest surprise.

Haunted by the last time she had seen her friend alive, Kameko is wracked by guilt at the argument they'd had. She goes over it again and again in her mind. Sifting through stale, now meaningless words and memory fragments, she searches for some clue, something she might have missed. Even though there is no difference it can make now.

She is sick, too, at having to face Akira's mother. To pay her respects. With her only daughter gone, the woman is now left to face her remaining years alone. Akira's father had left when Akira was little more than a baby. It explained a great deal about Akira's personality, the hardness of it. The black and white ledger she seemed to live by. It was tidy, unsentimental. So why had she done something so obviously steeped in emotion?

Maeda-san is predictably overwrought at her daughter's tragic death. 'I am so sorry. So very sorry.' What could Kameko possibly say to ease the woman's pain? 'She…Akira was a wonderful girl. Terribly smart. Determined and hard-working. And…I…we…all loved and admired her greatly.' The chrysanthemum trembles in her hand. She bows low. As Maeda-san reaches out to Kameko her knees suddenly buckle. Sobbing, she is helped up and led away to another room by some dour-faced woman Kameko does not know. Sorrow butterflies in her breast as she watches an inconsolable Maeda-san retreat. Her moist hand grips the reedy flower stem as she makes her way across the room to the small shrine. Her eyes linger on Akira's stern-looking image, and she finds she cannot help but think what her friend might have said at that moment— 'God, just stop with the circus already! It's all such a farce.' *But you have no say here anymore, Akira. You've made that choice. We used to think you were so strong, Akira. So why couldn't we see it? Why couldn't we see how frail and fragile you really were?* She knew what her friend would have said with her couldn't-care-less sort of manner. That Kameko had been too distracted to notice.

It is Misako who comes to her after, whose confession shakes her to the core.

'She came to see me. Told me she intended to confront you. About the whole Shiro thing. About your decision to marry.'

'She came. She was very sharp. The last time we spoke. Hot-headed. It was just like her. Akira's Law, remember?'

'She wanted to try and talk sense to you. That was what she said. And to tell you…' Misako halts and, softening her voice, begins anew, 'to tell you…that she loved you.'

'We loved each other, the four of us,' Kameko argues blindly.

'Not like a friend. In the other way. Like,' Misako sighs, 'to have fallen in love with you.'

'Loved me? I don't understand.' Kameko shakes her head, feeling wooden.

'You hear, but you don't listen. She loved you. Was in love with you.'

'But, I…never knew.' Her senses are struck dumb. 'I…had no idea!'

'She was going to tell you. To try and get you to stop from going ahead with marriage. She knew you would try and please your mother. She wanted to talk you out of it. Or at least talk you out of rushing into it. Without considering what it meant for your future. Without considering yourself.'

'She tried. But...I didn't know. She never said anything. It was all about Mother. And Shiro. Our talk.'

'I don't think she knew how you'd react. She wasn't sure what you'd think of her having feelings for you. Mainly, though, she just wanted to slow what was already in motion. That was her first intention. She hoped if she could be honest and tell you, maybe you would see things differently. As you know, it didn't go so well. Between you. She was quite upset at how it had turned into an argument. She wanted to try and be softer, gentler, not so much like herself. So after, in her mind, she thought she had blown it. This is what she told me. That she pushed too hard. And pushed you further away. I told her to try again, to see you. This time to be more understanding of your position. To open her own heart to you in the process. I know you, Kameko, if you had known you would have been sympathetic. Then she might have felt she had done what she needed to. Then maybe it wouldn't have hurt as much as it obviously did.'

'But she, I mean...I never did. See her again. We never met again...after we had argued.'

'Would it have changed things for you? Could you see yourself in a relationship with her, loving her?'

'I'm just...very shocked. I think I would have been too shocked to react properly. I may have hurt her more.'

'But that's just it. She would not have wanted a *proper* reaction. Just, I think, for you to know. And to let it sit with you for a while. Before going ahead and making your decision. One way or the other. That may have been enough. I don't know. We'll never know. But her feeling obviously ran deep. Deeper than she felt she could show. Deeper, perhaps, than she could live with.'

They are married, she and Shiro, two months later. Under the spring blossoms. His parents seemed to have no objection at the speed of things. She presumed that they had been told. Perhaps when there was no overlooking the undeniable physical changes in Mother. Father would likely not have wanted to bring it up before. Would not have wanted it to be seen as a reason for initiating the match.

Misako gives her a little hug, a sweet-sad smile. Leaning in gently, careful not to spoil her elaborate white wedding attire, equally careful with her words so that tears would not come to line Kameko's whitened face. 'It helps to remember there is sunshine, that it is warm, that it is comforting, that it can save all the world around from being dark.' The sentiment, though meant to encourage, only causes the rise of guilt. When tears begin anyway Shiro smiles at her, presuming that her emotion is for him, for them. Not knowing, never knowing, that she cries her tears instead for Akira. For young life lost, for the waste, for her part in letting it happen.

She battles to regain composure, to overpower her sorrow. Emotion, she feels, makes a being transparent like glass. Under its influence she worries she might lose her sense of place. The daughter and new wife mask might be taken over instead by the ugly self mask. She refocuses herself on the present. Akira is gone. Only shadows of her remain. There is no force left that might alter her course. Or shake her resolve. This is her duty, a debt she owes, feels compelled to pay. Before it is too late.

Mother has practically disappeared before their eyes with the passing of the seasons. Now, as everything around is beginning to bloom with new life, Mother is nearing death. She is little more than a shell, shrunken to the size of a fine-boned sickly child. Yet she smiles through her pain. 'Today you have given me life again. To see you marry was my greatest longing, my only wish.' Kameko turns Mother's words over and over again inside herself as reassurance of what she has chosen, what she has done. It is the right thing. The selfless thing. Damn Akira for trying to take that away, for casting a pall over it all, in death even as she would have in life. She recalls Akira's sharp condemnation: *The argument about not having a choice? About circumstance and duty? That crap is only an excuse. An excuse that covers up how foolishly blind you're being.* But circumstance couldn't simply be weeded out in things. Life was inextricably linked to it, affected by it. Misako had agreed: 'We do the best we can. Even though we sometimes lose our way, circumstance comes along to awaken us. To give us direction, to show the path that is intended for us.'

Gregory
Garden State Correctional Facility
1997

Incarceration. Such an ugly word. There is no mistaking the new. Faltering steps. Pillow and blanket, markers of the intake process. Plain as if there were a drawn target. Never let it be said that the State never gave. Then the march to the wolves, hungry creatures that can sense the tang of fear in the knot of fresh meat, the weakness. Guard towers vault the skyline. A lattice of barb and metal canopies the walk. As far as the eye can see there are walls, an eternity of walls. Walls to divide, to segregate, to keep in, to keep out. She struggles to take it all in. Understanding is a cold creeping floe. Foot after timid, weary foot. One in front of the other, a wending snake of orange. This is only the beginning.

'Abbott!' Strip. Squat and cough. Pat-down. Casual feel-up. She grits her teeth, thinks *don't react*. De-louse. Shower down. Med work-up. TB test. Kitted into a different set of prison orange. Always they look like they've been cut for a three hundred pound gorilla. 'What? It's no fashion show in here!' is the comment when she asks for a smaller size. Yeah, but I'd prefer not to have my ass hanging to my knees for the next five years, is what she feels like returning. She lets it come through her eyes instead of out of her mouth.

Her orientation: *You're young, you're down for a long time, stay out of the shit that goes on and you'll be fine. I always say to the newbies your tour is going to be what you make it. If it starts shitty it'll stay shitty.* The phrase sounded like something Curtis would say. Her face must have transmitted something. *Why're you looking at me like that? It's the best advice I can give someone starting out. Do the time right and it'll do you right. Play things the wrong way and it won't come to any good. Don't fall for any of the funky in-house shit that can land you up to your ass in gators, there's plenty of it.* For just a minute the lecturing officer stopped and stared hard at her. *You'll do okay. May be young, but I think you got it covered. You'll be fine. Just hang tough.* The last thing Gregory'd expected was a pep talk.

Pay close and careful attention. This is a game that has to be played smart. Has to be played to win. Just like the outside, the inside has its own set of rules. Its own code of conduct. Feathers ruffle easy. When squawking rises, trouble comes down swift and sharp. She's been warned. It's the code inside that lives, breathes, and keeps each and every one of them. Ignorance is not excused. Even for the new. Don't ask, don't tell. Don't trust any that do. Best to get it right from the start. There are two levels to life inside. It is clear that the inmates are the pulse of this being, but administration, with its own agenda, figures in some. And, funny enough, one relies on the other. Kind of like a playground see-saw. Except that this is no playground and serving a prison sentence is no kiddie game.

She thinks strategy to herself: Watch without looking, without seeing. Carry features without fear. Hold straight and tall. *I am not afraid. I am not afraid.* Eye contact is the *fuck you factor*. It needs to be used with caution. Keep the face bland, the eyes empty. Don't be caught up owing anything to anyone. Needy is weak. And weak is preyed upon.

'Darling!' the guard walking with Gregory singsongs. 'We've got fresh meat here for ya.'

'Mmm, just what I've been needing, Robutsky. Must've read my mind. I always knew it'd be damn near impossible to keep my cannibal tendencies from a bright one like you.'

'Yeah, yeah. All your book learning and it'd make sense you'd be a little bit squirrelly upstairs.'

'Careful or we'll pull a *Lord of the Flies* on you guys one day. I've got friends, you know.'

'Yeah, but your friends don't know shit.'

'Whatever blows your skirt up, Robutsky, or twists your g-string in a knot.'

'Abbott. Darlen. And Darlen. Abbott. You ladies play nice.' All five of his fingers press themselves into her back. As if she were made of playdough. His shove gives her a slightly winded sensation.

'Donkey Kong asshole,' the woman mutters. 'Why I oughta,' she raises up her fist and shakes it at the bars. Robutsky is already gone. Gregory can hear him calling out to some of the women down the corridor. 'Always trying to get my goat, that one. You look dazed. Shell-shocked. You okay? He's just a bit of a wiseass. Bottom of the heap. He can't do nothing but try to piss you off. It's kind of a game more than anything.' She extends her hand. 'Darlen, Claire, or the outside version, Claire Darlen. The idiots can't resist the proximity to *dar-ling*. Welcome to the State's institutional welfare system, your home away from home for the next —how long you down for?'

'Five, I guess, pretty near five years.'

'Shit, that's a tour,' she replies with something that Gregory thinks might be concern in her eyes. 'Well, until we part, I hope we can co-habit peaceably. He said Abbott, right?'

'Yeah.'

'And your first name would be?'

She is tempted to lie, but thinks better of it. Her name might actually buy her some credibility in here. Just for once she finds herself semi-relieved to have it. *A fine legacy, Curtis.* 'Gregory.'

'Gregory.' She does not sound surprised at all in the way she says it, the way it rolls with her sound. 'I like it,' Claire says approvingly. 'Welcome to frikkin' paradise, Abbott, Gregory—as defined by our overbearing, paranoid, dumb-ass leader of the moment. It does my petty and hardened heart some much-needed good to have a laugh at Republican expense.'

Gregory estimates her age to be mid-twenties or so. From the look of her. Claire is mousy and bookish thanks to thick, dark-framed eyeglasses. She's got a determined personality and an edge to her humour. Several inches shorter than Gregory's five eight, she makes up for her smaller size and frame with a hard sort of look that says, *Don't underestimate what you're dealing with.*

The day Gregory arrives Claire's already been inside eleven months. 'I don't count the days. It's just too depressing for me. But some do—days and hours and minutes and seconds. Anything that shaves a little from the total, that gets them seeing they're closer to the end.'

It's a tight living space that contains a feeble-looking set of metal bunk beds butting up against the concrete wall that separates them from similar spaces on either side. B Block 211. There is an eye-slice of plexiglass carved into the reinforced metal of the door that during lock-up will show no more than a scrap of what's beyond it. Claire speaks and motions like one of those QVC presenters Mama liked to watch, 'This here's your walk-in closet.' Life has to be contained in a battered metal footlocker or else it becomes a ticketable offence. 'Down the hall a ways, your recently refurbished—if you count an already peeling coat of paint refurbishment—spa bathroom with all the amenities. Don't mind the mould and mildew, they add to the charm and authenticity of the place. Hope you're not allergic. And from the Ladies of Garden State Welcome Wagon, my gift to you, these lovely high-fashion shower sandals. All the rage on the inside because you never, under no circumstances ever, want your skin coming in contact with that tile. Lucky for you they're one size fits all. And my last mate, girl gone home, left them behind. Here.' Claire reaches the plastic slip-ons forward with a smile. Gregory must have a funny look. 'Seriously, they're a gift, no strings attached. Once girls know you're new you'll get them giving you things, the decent ones at least. To help you ease in. It's the way we roll, most want to help. A sort of jailhouse sorority. We've all been in your shoes. You'll get to know pretty quick which gifts you want to take and which you should turn away, if you know what I mean.

'In case you're wondering, and from the look on your face, I expect you are, I'm not a nutcase. I take the piss only because it's one thing that keeps me from getting depressed. If you don't have a sense of humour about these things, then you've got nothing.'

Claire's is the upper bunk. To look out the window. 'I like the natural light,' she tells Gregory, 'and to be able to see out of this motley hellhole. And I like to imagine, when I look out, all the wire and shit, the towers, that it's an illusion, that it isn't actually there. I kind of use my mind to erase it. It took me a while to psych it up, but it works. So I can get the green of the grass and the blue of the sky, without all the interruption of the prison add-ons. It's a bit of a trip, but it helps.' She shrugs. 'Got to do what works. Hold on sanity can be a bit slippery at times.'

Claire coaches her: 'Some of the guards can be real assholes about things they write up. Dust on the light fixture. Corners not tucked right on the bunk. And, of course, every damn one of them has a different version of what's right and what's not, what's clean and what's not. I say, think about the guard that's the biggest prick—you'll get to know fast—and clean to their standards. That's the safest bet. Get written up enough and there's a tour of seg in it.'

For now, keeping her possessions contained is simple. Gregory has space to spare in her locker. 'It'll change. When your paperwork's through and you get some outside money you'll get a commissary account. Collect shit. You'll be surprised how fast it all fills up. One crazy-ass down in A has nothing but squeeze cheese in hers. Go figure.' Claire has obviously noticed her looking longingly at the rows of books she has neatly lining the bottom portion of her locker. 'You can borrow them. I don't mind. Most of them I've come across in here. Some I get from work; I do admin and tutoring. I get some sent in. You get, you give. And there's a shelf in the common room, but it's typically stacked with romance novels and shit. I don't know if that's your thing or not. Still, got to keep an eye out. And there's the book program that comes. Some of the guards bring in too. You wouldn't believe how important a little variety becomes in here.'

It's her first official inside shrink date; Ellis, the name of the doc. 'I notice that you don't have anyone on your visitors list. Sometimes it helps, you know, in working through things, to have the face-to-face time with people who know, who know *you*, who care.'

'I prefer it this way. I got myself into this mess and it's me that's got to deal with it.'

'I understand your desire, Gregory, to fix what you seem to see as your problem, but honestly, it's not yours alone. It's more complex than that. I think you're shortchanging yourself, but I will respect your wishes. If you should happen to change your mind or your feeling, we can re-visit things. You say the word. For now though, maybe we should look at your desire for solitude and use it to clean house. Metaphorically speaking. Maybe instead of visiting with someone else, since you seem reluctant about it, maybe the person you need to be getting in touch with most is you. Perhaps after you get more comfortable with yourself you'll want to extend that reach a little. To include others.'

'And just how do you propose I do that, get in touch with myself?'

'Think of it as a personal kind of stock-taking exercise. You know the supply warehouse? Well, every six months they have to inventory what's there. It's for planning; so they know when to reorder, catch problems or buying patterns, so they don't get caught short. What they do is they count and make a physical note of everything in that warehouse. Every single item. So that's my analogy of what I'd like you to do. Or start doing. Do a stock taking of the inventory you're keeping in your mental and emotional warehouse. All the stuff you've got stacked up inside. I'd like you to note it down. Words, images, memories, sensory experiences. All of it—anything and everything. The goal of the exercise is to bring you closer to letting it go, freeing yourself, leaving it behind you. But the by-product is that it will also help you ready for what's ahead.'

'Who else is going to see it? Are you going to have to show it to someone?

Could it affect my time, or sentence? Could I get written up for anything?'

'I can assure you, it will not be used against you.'

'Yeah? And how do I know I can actually trust that's the truth?'

'I can tell you that I have a professional oath to uphold. There will be no repercussions based on anything at all that you may choose to bring forward during the course of therapy. Okay?'

'Yeah. Sure. Whatever you say.' *Trust*, she thinks, *is what gets a person fucked.*

'Now, I think the first thing I'd like you to consider, dealing with the most recent events first, is to write all your feelings, memories, everything holed up in your brain, your heart, your being, put it in a letter. I know, I know. Just,' he raises a hand, 'hear me out. And I want this letter to be written to your mother, who, as I understand it, shared in the same cycle as you. But here's the thing—it's up to you to decide whether or not you want to actually send the letter you write. You don't have to, and there will be no pressure to either, because that isn't the main reason for this piece of writing. What I really want you to use the letter for is to explore your emotions and thoughts related to your family circumstances. Let it all come out of you and flow through onto the paper. I'm not worried about grammar, spelling, anything like that. I'm more concerned that the process brings about some form of release for you. That's step one, the first step. All right?'

'I guess.'

'You don't sound convinced.'

'Well…it's just words. My words, stuff I already know. How's that a help?'

'Because you think it's static, one-sided, right? Because the person you're really interacting with is only you, and you're sure that you know you? You'd be surprised, Gregory. Often the fiercest of our emotional battles happen inside of us, and we're not even aware they're going on.'

'Yeah, that's shrink-talk for *Gee, Gregory, let's find out just what kind of nutcase you really are.*'

'Not at all. Writing is a legitimate therapeutic tool. Do it as honestly as you can, no holding back, and you will feel better for it, because of it. I can promise you that. Don't question why you're writing what you're writing, don't overthink, don't analyze, don't criticize, just get it all out.'

'An exorcism.'

'A little different, but yes, I guess a bit like it, in some respects. Though instead of having outed a foreign body, I think you'll come to find that you will actually gain a fuller, more complete self. Make any sense at all?'

'Some.'

'I'll even supply the notebook to get you started.' He slides a ruled school exercise book across to her. 'Try and make some time for it every day from now until our next session.'

'It isn't like I've got a whole hell of a lot of other shit going on in here, have I?'

'So use it, the time. Use it. To do this. For yourself. In the outside world who gets the chance for genuine uninterrupted introspection? To turn the magnifying glass inward, instead of focusing on what's going on in the outer orbits around us.'

'You're sounding very *Twilight Zone*. It's a wonder you're not the one in therapy.'

He smiles. 'Here's my final point to consider, yes? A big one. It's not that we are *subjected* to circumstance that is merely ours to endure, it is what we *do* with what we are given that truly counts.'

'Yeah, okay, whatever.'

'I'm not saying it will be easy. It won't. You have to commit to not giving up. Even if it gets hard. Because it will. And it will be painful. But it will eventually get easier too. In time. Do something with your circumstance, Gregory. Take from it, don't let it take any more from you. '

Dear Mama,

I am writing this particular message on my doctor's recommendation. For therapy. He's looking for me to let go of some of my feelings, my baggage. Stuff he thinks might be in my head and my heart that might keep me from healing. I guess it's more about just getting things out. Into the open. Where I can look at them, so I can see myself more clearly. So I can get started with moving on.

I'm going to write things as they come. And I'm going to be as honest as I can. If you should ever come to read this, Mama, know that I didn't write these things with any intention of hurting you.

I am glad Curtis is gone. Dead. That's the truth. And I'm not sorry, either. I can't find sorrow or sadness in me for him. He may have been my daddy, but I can't find anything good inside myself for him. I am relieved. Relief is the biggest thing I feel that's tied to him right now. Like a huge weight's been lifted off me. I hated him. For taking life away from us. The good parts of living. For making us hurt. For making us live scared.

For as long as I can remember, I felt like it was my job to protect you from him. To step in and fix things after. My biggest fear was what he might do to you, what might happen if I wasn't there for you. When I needed to be. The idea that I had to keep you safe, it was what kept me going. You were my purpose, Mama. Because I couldn't get you to give up on yours.

I grew to hate that you would try and make me pray for him. Especially after he'd hurt you. Maybe I didn't hate it so much at first, when I was younger, because I believed you when you said it was our duty to help him. Because we ought to love him. Ought to forgive him. As I got older, though, I hated the way you tried to cover

94

for him and what he had done.

I can recall the first day I stood up to him. Showed him I wasn't afraid. Day he smacked me in the face and I didn't cry. Not a single tear. He couldn't make me cry. He saw it. He knew it. My belly opened up and I had this crazy urge to laugh in his face, at the shocked look he had. That's when things changed inside of me.

I kept hoping that one day we'd just pick up and go. Run away, live with Lil, move someplace he'd never find us. Like some adventure from one of my books. I had all these 'escape' options planned out for us. Not more than fiction, I suppose. I guess my imagination got the better of me. In my heart I knew you'd never leave. I never understood it, but I knew it.

Now you don't have to run. You're safe. To me, that's all that matters. I only hope you can forgive me for what I did, for taking away your purpose in life.

Gregory

She gets on with Claire. They're similar in their approach toward survival inside. They haven't talked, really, about the details of outside. They live for here and now. Day-to-day. That's enough. Therapy's the only thing that forces her to go back. In the name of fixing her head.

On the wall beside the upper bunk Claire keeps a few small snapshots. Patches of colour on an otherwise blank stone wall. They're posted right beside where Claire's pillow is. Perhaps it's a relief of boredom for her, wondering about Claire's photos. Over time, though, it gets so her mind burns with wanting to know the actual stories.

In one picture, Claire, in jeans and a t-shirt, shyly smiles out from under the arm of a much taller man. The gesture captures his arm slung casually, warmly, about her shoulder. They both look pleased in the camera's view. Her hair is longer in the picture, and she wears no glasses. She is, Gregory thinks, really very pretty. Especially without the heavy dark frames she wears inside.

Beside it is a photo of a young boy. In this freeze-frame she can see enchantment, merriment, in the child's squinted eyes. His hair licks up in the center, almost as if it is suspended on air, in the midst of a jump. He is elfin in appearance. His pleasure is so ripe and full that it makes Gregory herself want to smile at it. With it. Almost wishing she could share in some of his gladness. She can't help but feel just the slightest twinge of envy.

It is months before she gets up nerve enough for asking.

'Claire?'

'Hmm?' Claire is lying on her bunk, concentrated on reading *War and Peace*. She is about one quarter through. After carting it around for the last couple of weeks she's taken to calling it a sledgehammer. 'I swear, it's building my biceps,' she'd said, 'I'll probably end up looking like a professional wrestler before I'm through.'

Claire's sat up, looking at her, her finger keeping the place, ready to go back to the story. Gregory isn't sure how come she's stepped out on this ledge now, she is actually surprised that the question has inched its way out of her. But since she's started it, toe in, she might as well leap.

They've shared so much of themselves just by virtue of being and living so close. Bodies in undress, menstrual cycles, bodily functions, the ravages of sick. But nothing so intimate from the other side. It's kind of like an unwritten part of the inmate code—Don't ask. She's always been good at reading people, but inside everything's the same, and the details that give a person colour, give a perspective, an identity, that's all missing. Blank space.

'The pictures on the wall. Your snapshots.' She gestures. Would Claire open herself or firmly close the door on that other world? 'I mean, I see them staring out from the wall and they seem so, so real, so lifelike almost, and it...it's got me wondering.'

Claire folds her page corner and lets the book slide solidly to the mattress. She looks at the pictures. Smiles at them smiling out at her. 'Me with my dad.' She has turned herself around on the bed, to slowly trace the edges of worn paper. Then her voice goes thready and light, like a wind whistling through a field of husk, 'The boy is my son.'

Gregory starts at this information. She doesn't know why, but the thought hadn't occurred to her. 'Your son?' Her voice inches up.

Claire speaks his name softly as she gazes at the image, 'Jace. His name is Jace.' Of course the resemblance between mother and son is clear in hindsight. Gregory's surprised she hadn't seen it winking at her before. His features are all of his mother, but in miniature form, covered up some by the babyishness of him, in the fullness of his face and in the cheeks, the mischief in his eyes. With time, she suspects Claire will more fully emerge in his looks.

'He's five here, in this picture,' Claire says.

'I can see you in him.'

'Mmm.' Claire is wrapped now in remembering, tracing the shape of him with her finger. She pulls her face back to meet Gregory. In her eyes there is pain, fluid and dark.

'I'm sorry for bringing it up, Claire. I didn't mean...I just...He looks so happy, and just looking, you know, you can almost feel it too, his happiness.'

'It's not your fault. They're out here in plain sight. It helps me, seeing them.' She gives a rueful smile, 'I'm missing so much. So much of him. I get so down sometimes, so angry with myself for letting this happen. My choices got me here. I have to take responsibility. But every single day I try and look forward and think about what we'll still have. When I get out. It keeps me going. I can't make up for the time I've lost, but I'm damn sure going to make every minute of our future count. That's what I live for. In here.'

'Yeah,' Gregory whispers. 'And his...daddy?' Gregory cringes as she says the word.

Claire's laugh is brittle. 'He's long gone. Met him at college. My senior year. He was doing this-and-that. An entrepreneur. The big man on campus, except that he was only on campus to chase skirts. He wasn't actually going to school. He was an opportunist. With a goofy sort of charm. I was an easy lay who happened to be stupid enough to get pregnant. That was definitely not in the cards. At the time I was very tempted to terminate, but something in me, this crazy sixth sense, told me that I just couldn't. Sure as hell wish that sense would've been in working order for the rest of the shit I did for him.

'I was a mule for him. Drug mule. God, it was a rush when we were first starting out. And such easy money, so easy you would not believe.' Claire sighs. 'And I got greedy. I kept doing it while I was pregnant, figuring it was the perfect cover. I mean who in their right mind would suspect a woman *with child* of carting a kilo here or there? And then after he was born, I'd leave Jace with a sitter some days to do a run for him. Shit, I'd even pump and leave breast-milk for the baby, I mean I was so *on.* I thought I had everything covered. Not just the bases, the whole damn field. I was doing this the smart way. For the money, for my kid, for our future. I *chose* to be blind. The funny thing,' she says with a smile, 'is that even though I knew I was breaking the law, I thought it was okay because I was doing it for all the right reasons—the American Dream and all that bullshit. Never ever in my wildest nightmares had I ever considered getting caught. I had all these crazy sky-high plans. I figured I would choose to walk when I had gotten enough from it. But how much is enough? Is it ever enough? I don't know. And when I got nabbed? Bastard was gone like a shot. Must've sniffed the bust on the wind or something like that. And even then, even though he was happy to leave me with the whole goddamn enchilada, I couldn't bring myself to turn over on him. Far as I know, stupid Feds still haven't caught up with the asshole. Anyway,' she sighs, 'coming up on the end of my cautionary tale—I was lucky and got a safety valve qualifier that kicked me out of the mandatory minimum circus. Every day I say a prayer of gratitude for that.

'I've learned—with lots and lots of time to think—that being angry or bitter about the situation doesn't help me any. I think knowing I've got someone to live for, someone who needs me on the outside, it's what keeps me sane.'

'But Jace?'

'With my dad. In the valley. Got a farm. Dad was willing to take Jace. I don't know what I'd have done otherwise. To lose my kid to the State would have been unimaginable. I could never have lived with it. I'll be forever grateful to my dad. For what he's done. For Jace, and me for that matter. The fucked-up great white hope.'

'But you don't get visitors.' It's more statement than question.

'I don't want him here,' she whispers. 'I mean, I got no odds with the ladies. I'm no different, no better, than any woman in here, but I don't want him seeing Mommy this way. In here. I want to shield him from it as best I can. Even though my dad doesn't necessarily agree, he respects my wishes.' She gives a bit of a chuckle. 'My hard head comes from him. Right on down his family line. He knows better than to argue the point, one bull head against another.' She does her best to smile, though the tremble in her lips is a giveaway. 'That's why I'm looking forward to making up for lost time.' She turns palms up as if to say, that's what I've got, that's me.

'You, Gregory?' Claire inquires. 'Who you got waiting in your wings for this to be past?'

Something in Claire's face or voice makes her want to let it out. Because Claire seems not to be afraid of the truth. She is matter-of-fact with it. And set on leaving it behind her. Because, for some reason deep in her gut, she trusts Claire. And it is such a relief to be able to have that.

Aneeta
Delhi
2001

The sun rises and sets. The moon traces a familiar path across the Delhi sky. She hears of things only second-hand. In the kitchen. From a breathless Mina. She can see the anger in Ranna's being, in little things; the way she punches at the roti dough and mutters to herself, in the noisy way she bangs things about. There is to be a marriage. They are looking for a boy, a family. Outside of India is preferred. This is how it has been decided the problem shall be resolved.

She can only imagine how a matrimonial advertisement might read. Scraps of phrases occur to her. She crafts a harsh version in her mind.

> *One fair, homely, convent-educated girl—slightly used— requires*
> *Brahmin boy outside of India or sub-continent to save industrialist*
> *Delhi family from reputational ruin. Certain imperfections overlooked*
> *in favour of speedy alliance.*

In actuality, the words will play on illusion. To hide the necessity for marriage. To hide that the bride offering is less than ideal. A screen of ink on paper. To improve her chances. All of their chances.

Aneeta looks from the coriander she has chopped to near oblivion and into the gaze of Ranna, who says nothing of what she has done to the poor herb, but whose eyes glisten with unshed tears. It is a startling message of sympathy. Aneeta has the urge to reach out and touch the woman's hand across the expanse of rectangle in appreciation for the affiliation she feels, but place keeps her from the impulse as the moment slips past.

She is pragmatic enough to know not to expect a version of Asha's fairytale for herself. Only a sweet bargain will make her desirable. Defect would have to be traded against defect. So long as family name and image emerge intact.

The sundown comes on her inertia the day Mummy arrives at the door of the kitchen to announce it: 'We have found a boy. In America. California.' That daughter by blood and staff are lumped together for the delivery is highly uncharacteristic. Ranna's mouth gapes, wide and crooked. The wedge of knife in her hand falls to the block with a clatter. Mina raises a food-stained chunni to cover the lower half of her face where it ripples in the sharp pull of breath behind it. Aneeta can only wonder how the news has registered across her own features.

Marriage is a plausible exile; the miles are a form of insurance. At the very least, it is allowing her to begin again.

The wizened old bichola creaks in on bent hips, rocking left and right, the fabric that wraps her bulky frame moving side to side in jerky rhythm with her. Thick and raspy comes the command: 'Bring the girl!' The matchmaker is the shrewdest of inspectors. Like a hawk, it is her duty not to miss anything.

She has never seen the woman before, she is sure. Usually there is some connection—to some outer reach of a distant blood web. Or then again, given the circumstance, maybe not. Maybe they would prefer that there is no link, nothing to spark the potential for gossip.

Out of hallway shadows, having spied Aneeta, the bichola wheezily harrumphs toward her. She stops several paces away. Her eyes are squinted, hot with the glare of scrutiny. Slowly, they travel down and back up again. In methodical study, the woman separates her attentions into smaller parts, breaking the landscape bit by bit. Aside from the slight whistling of her breath and an occasional grunt, she says nothing. She is fully absorbed in her work. Taking in and sizing up the details before her.

A gnarled hand extends outward, waving her closer. 'Come,' the voice cracks. 'Let me see you.' As if what she has been doing until now is not considered seeing at all. 'Turn around,' she orders, and Aneeta shyly obeys. There is less there, at one's back, that can be hidden, but it, too, requires a measure of time.

'Auntie,' Mummy interjects and pushes forward, 'let us go into the front room, where there is more light and you can sit. Come, hunh? It is more comfortable.' The old lady's chappals slap softly as she changes her beady-eyed bearing to follow Mummy's retreating figure.

In the glow of afternoon light, the old woman closes in once again. As she draws near, Aneeta notices milky rings around dark irises, hairs sprouting from a wart just by the left ear, an odd tooth that protrudes into a carved indentation in the flesh of her lower lip. The woman reaches out and rubs, not unkindly but with some force, at Aneeta's cheek. Then she regards on herself, with one squinted eye, the fingers she has rubbed with. No doubt to see if some of the lightness of Aneeta's complexion is due to make-up. The flaws in her, however, are not of the surface level variety. They are not readily available to the naked eye. But the eye that saw through? Now that was entirely a different matter. She wonders how much of her, the inner her, is outwardly on show. Does she project a fear, an uncertainty? A woundedness? Maybe a vulnerability, that perhaps shows in her eyes? Like a dog can smell fear, will the bichola sense that something lies hidden in her?

'Hair down. Take your hair down.'

Mummy breezes into the room with a tea tray as Aneeta frees her hair from its thick coil at the nape of her neck. 'Auntie,' she interrupts, as the woman's fingers lace themselves through the length of hair, 'why don't you come and sit. Rest for a moment. I've brought tea and some fresh vegetable pakora.'

The old woman lets the hair go and waddles her uneven bulk toward a chair, lowering herself into it with a heavy 'unngh.'

'You don't feed her enough!' The bichola's pronouncement grates accusingly. 'She is skinny. Like a boy. She has no figure, no curves.' It is as though she is little more than a piece of livestock for barter, no different from any cow or goat, except, perhaps, in value. Eyes follow closely as Aneeta moves around the slender width of table to serve the tea and snacks to them both. Contentedly, the woman stuffs pakora into her mouth and loudly slurps the scalding amber liquid. Aneeta is both relieved and grateful at the shift in attention.

When plate and cup are empty, the old woman caws, 'Horoscope is okay. Good. Boy's family is satisfied. And she is well-mannered? Wanting to please a husband?' She does not wait for Mummy to answer, her questions are meant to be taken as statement of expectation. 'The family wants no trouble. They want also a girl to be homely. This one, she is pretty. Sometimes means trouble, hunh? They like pretty, but want homely too. What about schooling? Lessons? Can she cook? They want someone to cook. There is a brother. Older. He is married. But the girl is modern. American-born. The family, they miss things from India. If they are getting their bride from here they want her to be the way they remember a girl should be. To have certain skills, certain personality traits, to be traditional. Respectful. Modest.'

'Of course,' Mummy replies. 'We are a traditional family. That is how she has been raised. With solid roots. We are very much in agreement. Very much of the same mind.'

'The filth that affects young girls these days, pah! Such disgrace! What has become of virtue?' Aneeta feels a thick ribbon of ice winding its way through her, curling from her feet upward. The woman raises her head and narrows one eye in Aneeta's direction. A penetrating concentration shows in the knitted effort lining her face. Aneeta tries to keep her expression mild and her eyes unwavering under the renewed study, but she fears she must look wooden, especially under such a practised eye. Intently, the bichola watches her. She knows not to look away; hands seek comfort in the fabric pleats of her sari, hiding her worry in the folds.

Abruptly, the old lady turns and barks in staccato cadence, 'The mother will come here.' She jabs at the air with a crooked finger, 'To see her.' She nods after the stern proclamation, in little swooping bobs, as if agreeing with some silent invisible partner, and reaches for another pakora. And so, the first hurdle is past.

She comes within the month. From America to Delhi. They behave like long-lost sisters, Mummy and the woman who may one day be her mother-in-law. Anju is her given name. Arora, the family name. It plays like a scene out of a Bollywood cinema production. A chorus of hai-hai's and tinny laughter; leaned-in embraces cushioned by thick pillows of air.

With wide, frozen grins the two women carp at one another about this and that, that and this, all the common orbits, while mental measuring sticks try to figure just whose standing really is best. Of course concessions are graciously extended to the boy's mother. As they must be. Small points willingly forgone in favour of loftier goals and objectives.

There is a wave of melancholy that takes her as the prospect of marriage becomes more real. If this match is settled, she will be jetted to the other side of the world entirely. With oceans and continents in between. She thinks of all the things she will be leaving behind, all the things that mean home to her, the things that she will miss, the things that she loves. She thinks of Papa with sudden yearning, and tears spring to her eyes. She blinks quickly in an attempt to banish them and tries to focus her mind on what she has heard about America, on what it must be like in California. In pretense she reaches a finger to one eye, gently tugging at the outer corner of the lid as if something is irritating it, in order to brush telltale moisture away. But Anju's eye is keen, and the furtive motion does not go unnoticed. It draws conversation to the colour of her eyes. 'She wears contact lenses?' Mummy is asked. Could it be that she suspects some trickery? It sends a shiver up her spine. Hers is a more serious deception by far. Though perhaps less easily discovered than some cosmetically altered characteristic. Perhaps.

'No, no. The grey? It is natural. Unusual, but natural. She has come by it on my side. My mother,' Mummy replies, misunderstanding the reason for the question.

'Indeed unusual. I just wondered, perhaps.'

'Colour is hers.'

'Eyelash,' Aneeta volunteers, holding up a fingertip to excuse being caught on the verge of tears.

'Oh. Achcha. I see. Eyelash.' Neither woman balks at her explanation. They are immediately back to their sport.

'With such good looks from both sides I will have beautiful grandchildren. Maybe the grey will then come into our family too.'

After little more than a month Anju returns with husband and son. Her youngest son. One of two he is. Just as she is. Youngest daughter to youngest son, this marriage. For the first time, Aneeta sets eyes upon Jovin. The man who is to be her husband. Her initial impression, one forged only by the eye: he is handsome, arrogant, and very much accustomed to having his own way. Female guests have swooned over him, but unlike Asha's Raj, who would have graciously conversed, flirting lightly and humouring them, Jovin chooses to ignore their attentions entirely. The only person with whom he is indulgent is his mother.

'So why a handsome and successful man from America is coming to Delhi for choosing his wife?' She hears the whispered questions.

'Bhai, what are you saying? Our Aneeta is something special. A real beauty. It is not every day one comes across a girl as fair. Or with such light eyes.

Or from such a respectable family, with convent education and traditional values.'

'The girl from India, she will not disappoint a man as his bride. Especially not in America.'

She sits quietly captive, submitting to the time-consuming mehndi ritual. Talk turns around her, almost as if she were not present to hear it at all.

'These American girls they are too-too much for the female liberation. They have looser morals, no values, cannot even make a roti, hunh?' Heads nod, laughter erupts, thighs are slapped in hearty agreement.

'To say nothing of a curry, or a decent pickle!' More laughter rolls.

'Why would he not choose the best we have? These girls are good girls. I tell you, this is the kind of girl that mothers want for their sons.' A low rumble of agreement sounds at this pronouncement. For just a moment she longs to burst out that she is not the good girl they think. Her face burns at the thought of her secret, at the thought of how fast opinions would change.

The fault for what has happened under this roof would never fall upon Dev Uncle. In history, black is black. And white is white. In cases like this one, grey is simply a colour for unusual eyes. As much as she is afraid of it, of what being a wife will be like, about the man chosen for her husband, a man she does not know, it is her only hope.

She looks down to study the elaborate designs that decorate the backs of her hands and slender wrists, vainly trying to halt yet another flood of hot tears. In misplaced sympathy the mehndi artist pats her arm. Well away from the pasty patterning that slowly dries itself into her skin. 'Beti, it will be okay, you will see. This husband he will give you good care in America, such a good place for beginning a new life. I have a cousin. Pretty girl, like you. She has married a taxi driver in California.' The woman says it proudly. 'She says to me it is a very good place. But you, you will have rich and handsome husband.' She nudges Aneeta's silk draped thigh. 'You will be able to have lots of babies. Beautiful babies, na? Look at you. You must smile! He must not think you are sour like a karela melon. Smile, girl. You are so lucky, hunh?'

There is clapping, singing, mirth and laughter, as at all such occasions. This time, though, the festivities are for her. And yet, she cannot share in the excitement, the joy, the gaiety. Instead, she wears her pretense at happiness like her heavy wedding jewels. For now. Later they will be put carefully away. Jewels and a shy bride's smile.

I miss you, Papa. The words echo inside of her, like little threads, weaving in and out, in and out. There is a sensation of emptiness in her middle that seems to run the length of her; from the thrumming pulse at the dip of her gold-laden neck to the bottom of her belly. As if the decorated outer layer of her is but a shiny lacquered shell. With nothing of substance beneath it. Hollow.

By her husband's side in the temple she keeps her eyes and face down. She concentrates on the resplendent red silk that drapes gracefully over her crossed legs. Now and then there is a squeeze of her shoulder or slight pat on the back, an encouragement from one of the guests. But the gestures are faceless and blank. Behind her. Now, and forever. Rupee notes circle above her and Jovin's heads and flutter, like falling leaves on the wind, into the crimson catch before her and the ivory of his own.

She stumbles during the traditional walk around the altar. Before God and all that is holy. Before all of the eyes upon her. In a moment of panic she grabs at the fabric that drapes down from his shoulder into her hands, fabric that links them. She has clutched at it to keep from falling. It pulls at him, and he slows and stops. For just the slightest of pauses. But he does not look back at her. To see if she has recovered her footing. Or to check that she is okay. When he feels the time is adequate, he simply begins to move again. He gives her no greater consideration. Such a little thing it is. Just a single lost look.

Gregory
Garden State Correctional Facility, California
1998-2001

A 4 a.m. wake-up call. She walks with a small group huddled against the pre-dawn sepia. And trades one brick outline for another. The bite of the air at this time of day keeps her alive. Shoots adrenalin through her senses. The shock of it. Gives an edge to her thinking. She sees embers of cigarettes flicked out into the darkness of the yard. They walk quiet; most are still too tired for the work of conversation. She prefers it, silence.

During intake an entire life is reduced to one 11X14 document. They flatten a human being down to a string of numbers plus related effects; a standard and simplified format. Name, birthdate, place of birth, health, work experience, additional skills. Most times it's how placements are set. It seemed natural, her being assigned to the kitchen. Between her time with Lil and her almost 12 months at Suzie Homemaker's Homestyle Baking commercial crap-erie, her latest and last outside post after dropping out of school, she has experience.

She gets on with the kitchen chief, Dorinda, and doesn't mind working for her. Inmates have come and gone. One day there, next day not. Some released. Some reassigned or transferred. *Make better use of their tal-ents*, is how Dorinda says it. Gregory has fast become one of the senior staffers. She's good at what she does. Which, she assumes, is why she's kept there. It's considered more work than some of the other stations. She shrugs it off.

Prison food is uninspired and staple in consistency. There are days she doesn't blame a person for not wanting what's on offer. They don't have a whole lot to work with. Menus are pasty with starch, so that they can be extended to their limit. There's a lot of commissary cooking that goes on between meals in the block units. With the food inmates can buy up using their own money. Some of the women can concoct their own dishes using commissary snacks and the little bits of contraband they manage to smuggle out of the dining hall. Creamer, pats of butter, odds pocketed from a meal are stashed and saved for use in creative prison recipes. Guards seem only to care about catching the bread and fruit that walk out of the hall. On account of the hooch they can be made into.

Dining hall is the place plans are made, kites and other items passed, favours exchanged, seeds of gossip planted, turf enforced. A touch here, smack there; there's kissing, fondling, holding of hands. Things can go from not to hot in the blink of an eye. And hunger sometimes has a way of making people act a little more crazy than usual. The women are loud and overly animated in this environment. Like a bunch of barnyard chickens, which is why dining hall is dubbed The Hen House. For all the fussing and noise. All the preening and posing and strutting around.

Guards station themselves in pairs around the perimeter. They joke and chat. Rovers move through the inmate group, the lines, the food stations. Sniffing for signs of trouble. The Hen House has the biggest bang potential if there's plans for shit to be disturbed.

'According to the CalCor Bible,' jokes Claire, 'thou shall be fattened and turned to sloth by way of refined dietary starch. Carbs to keep the peace! That's how they maintain a more agreeable populous inside the walls. Starch 'em up so they're dozy and docile.' Claire's earned the nickname Nutrition Nazi for her outspoken views on what she calls 'the decided lack of honest-to-God real food'.

'Dollar-for-dollar, raw food is probably cheaper than all this processed shit they send in. Call me a dissenter for voicing an opinion or for asking that we get something *real* every once in a while, or a Bark Bitch for mouthing off on the wilted salad and limp carrot sticks, I don't care. Doesn't bother me. It's actually sort of a compliment. It means they're getting my message. When it comes right down to it, chow is all about the money and the power. Nothing against you, Abbott, I know you girls are doing the best you can. But the only way things are ever going to shift around here is if some mouthy-assed capital B—and right now that's me—is willing to make some noise. Sing the song long enough, one day they won't be able to ignore it. Come on, you've got to at least like my style!' Fruit and vegetables are a luxury. And they are beggars. On the inside. Food, while necessary, isn't a priority for the powers that be. Gregory has to turn away those that beg for seconds, bigger helpings, or ask for extras. To give in once, even once, would forever establish her as negotiable.

At the end of the shift she removes the heavy utility canvas apron ties from her waist and where they circle her neck. When she peels away the thick web of netting around her head she rubs at where it has left a red trench running across through skin of her forehead. She waves in the direction of Dorinda and with a hitchhiker's thumb gives her a look of *Okay?* to signal her departure. Dorinda nods and gives a shooing motion with a latex-gloved hand. Okay. No point in saying anything or yelling across all the fussing of the kitchen. Bodies moving here and there. From counter to counter. Across the row of sinks, with faucets in full flush. There's the clang of pots and pans, and all manner of chopping, grating and whirring that would have swallowed any words before they got to an ear that needed to hear them anyway. Today there's one girl, new, assigned to chopping duty who is fighting to pull at her knife, the chain tangled up in a snarl. The way they're tethered the knives barely reach the cut counter as it is. The rise of her cussing tops all of the other kitchen noise. The girl is jerking angrily on the chain, as if that's going to make a difference. *Honey, if it could get broken that easily...* Dorinda, having been alerted by the loud and loose language, stands hands on hips with a disapproving look, watching the scene play out. It would be funny if it weren't so damned pathetic. Gregory has yet to make up her mind if this one is just suffering from *The Syndrome,* as it's jokingly called, that makes a person come unglued some this side of the walls and wire, or whether she has a few marbles jangling in her upstairs.

No way would she want to be in charge of this misfit team, Gregory thinks, as she moves toward the open cubbies gridded along the back wall. But Dorinda's got the right mix of tough in her. To keep things smooth. She calls the girls she likes 'Baby', the ones that cause trouble or don't do the job right she calls 'Miss Thang'. Most of the women coming through the kitchen like her. All of them have a healthy respect for her. Nobody with any sense messes with her. Some, the toughs, call her 'Señor', but she's not like that. She doesn't take any shit, but she doesn't screw anyone over either. And she doesn't appreciate the 'admin honkeys' messing with her world. Rumour has it Dorinda's ten in to twenty years for shooting point-blank a member of the Bloods gang at his initiation killing—for trying to earn his colours by finishing Dorinda's son in a drive-by. Problem was, the kid got out of the car to get his shot off and was obviously slow on the trigger. Dorinda, with a mother bear's protective instinct, had taken matters into her own hands. 'Didn't want for the kid to die in it. That wasn't it at all. Just wanted to keep my son alive. What's so wrong about that?' The law didn't see things the same way. 'My boy, he's never been up in the gangs, never been trouble to nobody. And they choose a gang boy's life over that? That boy's rap sheet was longer than he was tall.'

But Dorinda's no cold-blooded killer. 'Tell it to the State,' she'd mutter, 'write it to my useless jackass congressman. Least I've still got some life left when I get out of here. Least I got that much. Maybe some grandkids, even great-grandkids by then. Something to live for. Make it worthwhile.' She'd sent her son to Idaho to live with a cousin. 'Compton just ain't no place for a young man growing up no more. Better to pave the whole place over and put a freeway right through it. That's what I'm saying. The way the gangs have changed things. Might as well cover the whole place up with concrete.'

Gregory wraps lifeless ties around the folded apron middle and tucks it, hairnet secured at the top, into the cube that is hers. She counts herself among the lucky for the sentence she is serving. Turning to leave, she pushes hard against the heavy door and steps out. The slow closing arc takes the kitchen chaos bit by bit, but she can hear Dorinda's voice rising up in the last sliver before the door seals itself. She pauses just for a moment to clear her lungs and her mind. To shake her head at the crazy girl fighting with the knife. Flipping out at it. Now it seems okay to smile a little. Because no one can see. Looking up into the blank hazed blue, she blinks at the sharp brightness of it. She circles her shoulders a couple of times, shrugs them up tight and shakes them out. After a deep drag of outside air she begins the return walk to B block.

She keeps eyes keen as she crosses the length of the yard from corner to corner, careful to pick her way around the groups. On the court women play 3-on-3. The Beef Brigade, as they're called, pull themselves up on the chin-up bar, pump iron, and otherwise mill about. Some jog around the field of unevenly shorn grass. Still others play an impromptu soccer match. There are a handful of wooden tables and benches where women have settled into card games or talk while others stand idly by. Watching. Or not. Idleness. A sure bringer of trouble. Creator of problems.

There's an edge to the action in the yard. The invisible tension keeps her on her toes, and keeps her moving. One foot in front of the other. Looking like she's got something that needs doing, somewhere to be.

It's no small victory to move from the wait list into the GED class. How it happens so fast she thinks is down to Claire, who works in the education office. Claire brushes off thanks with a shrug. 'Don't mention it—and I mean that literally too. But you need to put all the goddamn book reading you're doing to work on something. Otherwise it's no more than passing time. Best to log it on something useful.'

Cecilia Alvarez, the GED teacher, may be a small woman, but she sure packs a power punch. And it's clear she's got no fear of the group of convicts sitting at her back. Most outsiders wouldn't be so sure of the group or what they're dealing with.

On the first day, when she has finished writing her name, the course name and the major sections they will cover on the whiteboard, she turns and smiles. Hers is not a closed smile. There is nothing tight or false about it. She claps her hands, but it isn't until she starts to talk that she really grabs their attention. Maybe it is because she comes across sure, strong, bold. There's something Gregory can't put her finger on, but this woman has an aura of credibility, like she knows them, gets them.

'Listen up, everybody. I'm going to make this speech once and only once. This is how it's going to be—This is my classroom. My classroom. Not yours. I run the program here. And you don't run me. I don't care one iota what goes on in the population among you ladies. This is my turf. You come in here to learn. There are others more than happy to take your place if you decide you don't want it. Take a minute and think good and hard. I want that decision made now, so we've got a group with serious intentions. Be sure in your mind, in your heart, in your gut, whatever you use for deciding things. Now, once you've made that choice, if you elect to stay, this is what I've got to say to you, I'm going to lay it down as plain as I can—you come into this class and you leave your ego, your petty squabbles, you leave the rest of your world at the door. There's no kite passing, no chirping, and no fighting.' There are looks exchanged and a low running murmur. 'That's right, you *know* what I'm saying,' Alvarez is nodding her head. 'In this classroom— regardless of whatever shit goes on beyond these doors—' there are a few *oohs*, 'in this classroom, my classroom, we have a mutual respect for one another, and for the process of learning, understand? Make trouble and you…are…out. No questions, no exceptions.' The whole room falls silent, save for some shifting in seats.

'This is a big step, going for your GED. The even bigger step was realizing you need to have it. I applaud you for that, I do. But don't think that this is a free ride, just because you're inside. If anything, it's going to be tougher. Because some stripe-tied ninny *out there* is going to be more critical of you ladies, not less. And he, ladies, or the uptight she-counterpart in the cubicle next door to his, is going to see things differently than one who has had the chance to become acquainted with your charming and dynamic personalities. Everything in your life, once you've been a convict, is going to be an uphill battle, that's just the way it is, so better get used to it. This is no different. You will be singled out and judged. They won't go easy on your bad self, they're going to go harder. So, having said that, it's best you understand right off and up front that I am not going to spoon-feed you. In this class you have got to pull your own weight. As I said before, there is a waiting list for this program. It is a privilege to be a part of it. Treat it as such. That means, do the work. *Want* to do it. Always do your best work. You don't want to make the effort, then don't keep your ass warming up one of these valuable chairs. That's what it's all about in my books, ladies: effort. If I think for even one minute that you're dead weight, if I even sniff that this is a coaster for you, or that you don't want to be here, or if you come in bringing trouble, you're out the door. And you are never,' she pauses and takes the time to look at each and every one of them, from one side of the room to the other, 'and I do mean never, welcome back. Understand? Capisce? Comprendez? Yeah, you got me, I'm speaking your language, right?' She is looking at Carmelita Lovilla who is giggling, 'You think I can't, princess? You just go ahead and try me.'

'I'm sorry,' Carmelita says laughing, 'but you're so damn cute when you're acting tough.' The rest of the class laughs. Even Cecilia Alvarez laughs, and then, with a sharp eye, she fires out something Spanish that for a moment surprises Carmelita who finally replies in Spanish herself.

Alvarez says, 'All right, enough of the heavy. Let me give you a bit about me. Since you think I'm so *cute*.' She smiles directly at the still sheepish looking Carmelita. 'I've been where you're sitting. I may be cute, but I'm not perfect. I did my own GED inside. Don't be asking what fool thing I did to get me doing time, I did it. It's done. That's how I see each one of you too. This is a clean slate. I see you shaking heads, wondering what the hell I'm doing back up inside the fence. Point is: you get, you've got to give, sister. This is my giving right here.'

Aleda Johnson, a D-blocker, pipes up, 'Chapel's across the yard, I think you took a wrong turn somewhere.' There are a few snickers.

'Think what you want. My being here shows you that if I could do it, any of you can. All of you can. But it's about choice. You've got to make that choice and then do something about it. For yourself. Not for anybody else. Not your boyfriend, husband, lover, pusher, pimp. Not for any of them; they won't care, won't want you to have this little piece of paper. Why? Because it gives you power. Changes up the cards in your hand, yes it does. It gives you choice. But first you've got to choose to work hard and then do it.'

'Just do it!' someone behind Gregory choruses.

'Exactly right. Just do it! Nike got something right, except that attitude's probably partly to blame for you being in the can in the first place. However, in GED class it's probably a damn fine motto.' She stops and looks appraisingly at the group. 'I think we'll get along just fine. And I think it helps that we all understand each other, yes? Without further ado: Welcome, ladies, to picking up where you left off in your learning. Welcome to the first day of the rest of your life. Because this single piece of paper, it *will* change your life. GED makes you a somebody. Got it? Ladies? Gents?' There are a few laughs. 'Show me your hands, put them up in the air, way up, if you get it. If you've got a gripe, there's the door. Feel free to go.'

Cecilia Alvarez is true to her word. In the first weeks there are a couple of women out the door, including Aleda Johnson. After that, they really dig in to learning. She's an enthusiastic teacher and a cheerleader for them all. It makes them almost hungry to please her, and it tightens their bond as a unit. They call her Miss Cecilia. The name suits her. As Carmelita Lovilla would say, it's 'cute'.

She waits while the room empties and then approaches. 'Uh, Miss Cecilia?'

'Gregory.'

'I...I've been really struggling with the *Midsummer Night's Dream* essay.'

'How have you been struggling, Gregory? We've covered it pretty extensively in class.'

'Yeah, I know. It's not that. It's just...well...I've kind of got a thing with it.'

'That's not at all unusual, Gregory. It's very much a different language from the English of today. But I thought we had managed to modernize the tale in our discussions, to bring it into the present. So we could understand and relate to it.'

'It's not in the way that you think, my trouble with it.'

'Oh?'

'It's...personal.'

'I see.'

'I mean I get it, the language, but I'm having trouble trying to get past this...problem. We were studying *Midsummer Night's Dream* at high school and I had...well, I had this bad experience. I got to thinking about this...individual who hurt me back then, well, I thought of him kind of like Bottom...because making a bit of a joke made me feel better about things, you know? But now it's like I've got this black hole in my head because of the connection my brain makes between the way I kind of channeled my hurt and anger at the time into Bottom. And every time I think about the play I find myself back there and it sucks up all the energy in me and leaves my brain dark. I've tried, I have, but it's just this huge mental block that's keeping me from being able to write about it.'

'Well, Gregory, you're not tied to the Shakespeare. If you want you can choose something different. If it's really giving you that much trouble. I mean, this exercise isn't meant to be debilitating. Though, Gregory, the block is something writers all butt up against at one time or another, often times it's just symptomatic of the act of writing. When there's emotion tied to that block, sometimes writing is the best tool to help us to break through it. Yes?'

'Yeah, I know. That's what the therapy doc tells me too. And I am doing it. Writing more. To deal with things. But with this, I can't think clearly about the assignment without the other stuff interfering and it's like someone pulls a switch in me, and all the essay ideas, they just go blank.'

The air is thick with pot smoke and the sweet of alcohol. She didn't know the boy having the party. What with the whoop and the overhead high-five, it was plain he did. There's a girl looking like a rag doll, passed out in a corner. Mouth wide. Skirt shoved up to reveal an edge of lace. Bruises along thigh flesh. The girl is ignored by the crush around her. EMF is singing—You're unbelievable. Oh!

She remembers climbing a shallow set of stairs; holding on to the hand behind his back. He leads along a dark hallway. Past silhouetted couples in the shadows. Near the end of it he pushes through a door, pulling her with him. A sudden pang wrenches her gut; mushrooms into a blast of panic. There is a sofa. He pushes her onto it. She is protesting. Trying not to let fear take over. Trying not to piss him off. Trying not to sever her fragile ties of belonging.

He grinds at her. She can feel the hard outline of him. The heat. Nirvana winds up on the stereo. Smells Like Teen Spirit. He grunts with the effort of holding her. She is squirming, straining against him. One arm pins her wrists together over her head. The other works at the button and zipper on her jeans. He pushes them roughly down, down, down. It happens so fast. So smooth. So easy.

No! With a surge of strength she gets an arm free. She swings hard, heart pounding, and cuffs him on the side of the head. She connects with a thud. The hit is forceful enough to catch him off-guard. She smacks at his face, yanks a fistful of hair. She is kicking and slapping and writhing. There are the sounds, the ugly sounds, flesh against flesh. Guitars rage and roil. She pulls her leg up and jerks her knee hard into his groin with an upward jag. Sudden and smart. His howl. His oomph as he loses air. Hands free her.

Music is tremoring through the walls, the floor; a deep base beat makes her body vibrate. Legs scramble for traction. A braided rug burns skin away. Clumsily she finds her feet. Grabs at cotton and denim pooled around her ankles and stumbles out of the room, out of the illusion.

Monday: Boys in lettered jackets laugh and exaggerate pelvic thrusts. Falsetto voices and bursts of raucous male laughter taunt. Cheerleader girls, with perfectly painted faces and tossed tresses, sneer. She tries for cool, unaffected. Moves numbly from class to class. Keeps the couldn't-give-a-shit challenge in her features.

English class. With Mr. Eager. 'Eager for English' his first day joke. Nobody had laughed. She liked the class. And Shakespeare. Normally. Soliloquy is the order of the day. 'Though there is no true protagonist in A Midsummer Night's Dream, critics generally point to Puck as the most important character in the play. Why do we think that is?' Her mind fumbles. Hands go up. 'Yes?' A hand is selected and viewpoint delivered. In rises and falls. Something slivers into her pain then and takes hold. The idea of the asshole as the ass, Bottom. It's almost poetic.

Every time she remembers, she thinks of Bottom and gets Mr. Eager's kind of hoppy voice reciting in her head:

But a dream. If only.

'Gregory, I'm not going to push. Go with something different. Just don't cop out and be bringing me some fool piece on *Green Eggs and Ham* or something.'

'No, I wouldn't.'

'Got something in mind as an alternate?'

'Well I was thinking maybe…Steinbeck? *Of Mice and Men?*'

Miss Cecilia looks at her appraisingly, 'You've read it?'

'I have.'

'Got a copy?'

'Yeah, I mean, my…my cellmate, Claire, does.'

'Oh right, I forgot. Claire had mentioned to me that you two were mates. Well, you picked one of my favourites. It'll be tougher for you without all the background discussion, but I'll okay it. Maybe if Claire's willing, chew through it with her. Really dig through the themes for symbolism and significance. Think hard on the reasons for the sub-stories and the ways the characters fit together. And the time period, the way it influences things. I absolutely think if you work hard you can do it justice. I'll look forward to your draft.'

After three rewrites and heavy back and forth with Claire, she eventually earns an 'A' for the essay. At the top of the paper Miss Cecilia writes: 'Exceptional work, Gregory!' Beside the comment there is a happy face. Exceptional. Her. Her guts flip at the crazy idea of it.

Seven months and eighteen days later, she has done it. The classroom is paper streamered. She doesn't know how Miss Cecilia has managed it, bringing decorations in from outside. Somehow, too, there is a *Congratulations GED Grads! You Did It!* cake that has Dorinda's name written all over it. Gregory knows it's Dorinda because just the other day she'd caught her squirreling away a little pack of shaved coconut. 'Hey, Dorinda! That coconut was for tonight's pudding.'

Dorinda had snorted at her, 'Ain't nobody going to miss a thing like coconut sprinkles when they got pudding already. And don't you be going on about nothing, you hear? There's a far better thing I got to be using this for. Far better.' She had turned her back with her head high and an air of secrecy. This frothy and divine looking cake has been edged in coconut. And on top, beside the spidery icing writing, coconut has been dyed with food colouring and made to look like little fountains of celebratory fireworks.

There are tears, hugs, and congratulations within the group. Even Miss Cecilia has been spied dabbing at her eyes as she passes out results envelopes and recognizes each one of them with a few words about their personal achievements. Pictures are taken by one of the guards.

Some weeks later the prints are up on the noticeboard. What surprises her about the snapshots of that day is that she looks happy. Genuinely happy. In fact, the whole group does. There is a serious group photo and then a goofy one of all of them acting camp. Gregory's idea of silly was a set of rabbit ears over Miss Cecilia's head. The euphoria is clear. In all of them.

Now she finds that the first taste of learning has made her hungry, has made her want for more. She goes back twice a week to Cecilia Alvarez for the study of literature. She dives back into reading, indulging in most everything that comes her way. More Steinbeck and Orwell, some Faulkner and Hemingway. She goes back to novels she'd missed out on at school. Harper Lee's *To Kill a Mockingbird*, Francis Scott Fitzgerald's *The Great Gatsby*. She disappears into tales of worlds and times apart with the likes of Brontë and Austen. She works her way through all of Claire's locker books and even her magazine subscriptions, reading about the world unfolding outside the prison gates. A very quiet older inmate they call Mouse swaps old issues of National Geographic in trade for the news magazines. The photos give her a view of places she's never seen, so far beyond what she's known.

Writing comes to her more regularly. She is journaling fact and dreams and memories. Putting ideas down, whether there's sense in them or not. Doc's been right, doing it opens her up. Like there's some vault in her she's unlocked. Hard as it is at times, it lets her climb inside, under her skin, to have a good look on parts she never even knew she had.

She finds it isn't all tied to the past anymore, what she writes. Sometimes she tries to make sense of what's to come. Or what she'd like to come. She lets herself hope.

The Middle:
The Process of Becoming

Last night I wept. I wept because the process by which I have become woman was painful. I wept because my eyes were opened to reality.

Anaïs Nin

Aneeta
Fresno, California
2001

Her first impression of America is formed in the tubular glass and steel corridor. Moving along, the group of them, in a pack of belonging, she thinks of the way cows travel across dusty earth in passels bound by indistinguishable but undeniable commonality.

On paper she now belongs to this family. She lets motorized walkways push her along. Her father-in-law has papers ready in his right hand. On the top, a narrow strip of mint green is longer than the others. She has been told that she should simply remain quiet. She looks down at the simple gold band dotted with a delicate filigree of tiny diamonds. The symbol that binds her to Jovin. Her husband.

They approach a wicketed cage, not unlike many in Delhi. Except to say that this one, with its very high, thick partitions, looks far more authoritative and stern than any she has encountered before. The transparent walls are so dense that they distort one's vision, lending an out-of-focus cast to outlines beyond. Or perhaps it is only a trick of her eyes; fatigue from the journey.

A heavy, uniformed man sits behind glass. Her father-in-law places his papers before the unsmiling officer and lays, very carefully, passports out over top, in a precise fan. She notes that her passport is the one most hidden by the way he has placed them. Though the peek of foreign lettering makes it stand out from the others.

Hers is the first he attends, slipping it out from under the stack. *Aneeta Kaur Malik* he reads, loudly, haltingly. He mispronounces the middle name *Cower*. Her unmarried last name he splits, into two twanging parts. She remains silent, as she has been asked. Tentatively, her father-in-law clears his throat. For his part, Jovin stares blankly into space. Into the distance. He stands furthest from her, on the other side of her mother-in-law, who has twisted her face into a sort of grimace-smile that conveys an exasperated lack of tolerance with the man before them. Jovin does not even seem a part of them. A part of her. A husband.

'So what purpose brings you to the US of A?' he asks blandly, studying the details at the front of her passport. His lips purse and eyes squint as they gather in her image and compare it to the likeness before him. Paper to flesh. Flesh to paper.

Her father-in-law speaks quickly in a furtive tone that belies his discomfort. 'She,' he indicates Aneeta with an incline of his head, 'has married my son.'

'S'atso?' the man leans back in his chair, prompting squeaking with the rearrangement of his bulk. He raises his eyes to take them in, in their disjointed array. A touch of something plays across his lips but does not let itself show enough so that she can tell what it is. Mirth? A sneer? Concern? Doubt? One minute it is hinting at his features, the next moment it is gone. He turns his attention to her. Looks at her carefully, like the old bichola all over again. She expects that the fabric of her suit is a rumpled mess. She has not had the opportunity to change or even straighten it in the overly cramped confines of the tiny airplane lavatory. Suddenly self-conscious, she tries unobtrusively to smooth at her torso without letting her eyes drop.

'We have required documentation for her.'

'I'll be the judge of that, sir, if you don't mind. Why'nt you show me what you've got.' Her father-in-law fusses with the papers. A shaky thumb and forefinger separate marriage papers and immigration documents from the rest.

'I'll take those. We'll have a look through 'em. Make sure everything's in order. I'm gonna ask that y'all follow me.' With that, he rises. The springs of the chair groan at their sudden release. He flicks a switch on the side of the slender post at his side. It turns a lighted 7 that marks his place in the row of agents to dark.

She hears a heavy latch click. He opens the side panel of his cubicle, turns sideways to ease through it, and steps down from a raised platform. With her documents in hand, he begins to walk through the high-ceilinged hall. They trail obediently after. Aneeta catches an exchange of looks between her in-laws. Jovin, she notices, does not engage in their silent conversation of the eyes, staring instead directly at the back of the uniformed man. Fellow travelers from other kiosks regard them with a mix of curiosity and sympathy. Some she recognizes from the flight.

He ushers them into a small room with a wall of glass on one side. The front side. Outward looking. He motions them to a bench and closes the door with a firm and solid sound that seals them off from what lies beyond the perimeter. They are like a zoo exhibit, on display for those in the open space. Across the moving tide of people Aneeta spies a sign in thick black lettering, *Welcome to the United States of America*. It is decorated by a ring of tiny stars. She feels anything but welcome.

Officer 7 moves toward a nearby clutch of other similarly dressed men and women. Some sit at desks. Some stand behind counters with lines zigzagged in front of them. She watches the man who has deposited them here. Watches as he jocularly converses with colleagues. Watches as he takes a place behind one of the counters. At a computer screen. Back and forth he flicks through papers and passports. He spreads them along the space in front of him. She can see him shifting them in order. Reconstructing details to confirm the story they tell.

It is then that she whispers, 'Is everything all right then, ji? Is this the way it is supposed to happen?'

Her mother-in-law's eyes narrow. Her father-in-law replies in barely more than a hiss, with viper-like intensity, 'How would I know this, do you suppose?'

Officer 7 is now striding back towards the fishbowl room. By his side is someone else this time; an also-uniformed, dark haired and olive skinned woman.

To Aneeta's eye they are an odd couple. He tall and she small. She terribly slim, he bulky and wide. The door opens. Hall noise bursts in with them. It breaks the stilted discomfort. The woman wears a small tag with 'Mercado' upon it. Aneeta notices, as she looks to Officer 7, that he wears a similar badge. It reads 'Bonner'.

'Aneeta Malik?' the slight woman queries, though she already knows. She says Malik in the same way as he, Bonner, has. In two parts. Broken in the middle. Ma-lick.

Aneeta nods and whispers, 'Yes.'

'Follow me.' From the way her in-laws look it is obvious that this is unexpected. Control floats up and suddenly out of reach on butterfly wings. Chiffon flutters at her back as air blows past her. She moves after the retreating figure of officer Mercado, past Bonner who holds the door.

They had been assured the paperwork was complete. Rupees were discreetly handed-off at appropriate levels to ensure that the processing of the documentation had occurred with almost unheard of speed. She wonders if there is something that might make her unwelcome. Ineligible. Inadmissible. What if the door to the US of A, as Bonner has called it, is not open to her? A tremor shivers through her. Maybe it is a small oversight. Perhaps easily corrected. Perhaps. They enter another room. With a narrow table. A chair on each side. Bonner stands at the threshold. Mercado nods to him and he shuts the door, taking his leave. She motions Aneeta to a chair and takes the seat opposite.

Meekly, Aneeta settles into the hard frame. Mercado regards the papers before her. The papers Aneeta recognizes as her own. Her passport rests to one side. There is a quiet tick-ticking of a clock in the corner. 11:18. Almost a full day since her departure. She is coated in the grimy, oily film of travel. Her eyes are dry and hot, she longs to close them. Cold coils in her.

'Miss Malik.' The syllables are not broken this time. Though they are jerky, they are not separate.

'Yes.' Her voice is soft, so soft.

'I'm going to ask you some questions.' Officer Mercado's voice is loud and slow and deliberate, as if she suspects her of having some hearing impediment. 'Do you understand?'

'Yes.' A little bit stronger now.

'Can you understand what I'm saying?'

It seems a silly question given that they've come this far. 'Yes.'

'Will you need a translator?'

'No, I shouldn't think so.' With some assurance.

'You seem to speak good English. Where did you learn?'

'At school.' It is foolish, but she has the urge to laugh.

'So you are educated?'

'Yes.' She knows enough not to offer more than is asked.

'To what standard?'

'I have my Class 12 certificate.'

'For a young woman…' Mercado, studying the documents, trails off. 'Will you be pursuing more education? Here in the United States?'

'I am not certain.'

'You do not wish to?'

'I don't know.'

'How come?'

'Because I don't know about my husband's family. About what they would expect.'

'So this marriage was arranged?'

'Yes.'

'By whom?'

'By my mother.'

'Really?'

Aneeta hears grains of skepticism. 'Yes.'

'So if your mother, as you say, undertook to arrange things, how did you come to hear about your husband?'

'We had a bichola.'

'Excuse me?'

'A…' Aneeta fumbles for the right English term, 'a wisewoman, elder, what you might call a matchmaker. To help find a suitable match for me.'

'You weren't interested in finding a potential husband yourself?'

'It is not always the way.' She smiles a little to cover her voice sounding false.

'I see. So this man? Your husband. He's an American citizen?'

'Yes.'

'Born in the States?'

'I think.'

'You don't know?'

'I'm not…certain.'

'On what basis did your families see you as a suitable fit? You know, given that you were looking for a *match*.' Mercado exaggerates the emphasis on match.

'In standing, I suppose. Position, caste. We were considered equals in worthiness.'

'How long have you known one another?'

'Just since we were introduced.'

'And when was that?'

'A couple of weeks from our wedding.'

'So it was all already organized?'

'It happened very quickly, our families agreeing. We hadn't much of a chance.'

'I find it hard to believe that an educated young woman like yourself has married a man without at least getting to know him a bit first.'

'This is sometimes the way we do things.' She thinks, *the way circumstance sometimes forces us to do things. To fix things.*

'Hmmm.' Mercado's response is non-committal. 'So just how did you know that this was the man for you? If you knew nothing about him, or hadn't had the chance to get to know him?'

'I…relied on my family's judgment.'

'You have that much faith in them? I don't know that I could trust my family to pick the guy I'm supposed to spend the rest of my life with. You seem like a smart girl. How could you be sure?'

She shrugs to dispel the inference, but cannot quell the uneasiness rising within her. 'I know that they want what is best.'

'So they send you halfway around the world to a man you don't know.'

'On the outside it would seem so, but it is not so unusual.' She nods to show that she is not at odds with the bargain they have struck on her behalf. It is a better bargain than if she had stayed. Better by far.

'So you've said. You understand the implications of the visa you've got papers for?'

'I'm sorry?'

'Your spousal visa.'

'Oh, yes…I think.'

'Let me refresh your memory for you. Just so we're sure you understand. So you're well aware.'

'Okay.'

'That you are involved in a genuine marriage relationship.'

'Yes.'

'With one,' Mercado pauses and looks to the papers, 'Jovin Singh Arora.'

'Yes.'

'And that he is responsible for you. What does your husband do here in the States for a living?'

'He works in the financial industry.' There is pride at being able to ally herself with such an important field.

'Doing what exactly?'

'I…well…I cannot really say.'

'Meaning you don't know? Because the financial industry is pretty big. Employs huge numbers. Workers in all sorts of capacities. I mean, he could be a bank teller. Or an accountant. See what I'm saying here?'

'I see.' She nods for Mercado as a knot expands in her stomach.

'Love him?' The sudden sharpness of the question catches Aneeta by surprise.

Her words form themselves slowly around her hopes, her fears, around what she does not yet know. 'He is my husband. Of course.' After a pause she continues, in the way a more carefree bride perhaps would, 'I consider myself very fortunate.' She nods her conviction to Mercado, for the outside world, and for the not at all certain part within herself. *I am fortunate. I am. To have such a chance.*

'I see. And that's all?'

'Is it not enough?'

'For your sake, Miss Malik, I hope it is.'

Gregory
Garden State Correctional Facility, California
2001

A voice barks into the morning on the public address, 'Darlen!' *Claire!* Gregory looks up at the PA box on the kitchen wall with a start. 'Report to the CO station.' *What?*

Dorinda is looking at her across the kitchen. 'Go on. Go on and find out. Git! Find out.'

'Are you sure?'

'Sure, I'm sure. You go on. I'll take care in here. Now go!'

She makes her way in a hurry out the door, down the steps and across the yard. She doesn't dare run, but she walks as fast as she can. Fast as her legs'll take her, to get back to the Block. When she gets to the cell Claire is frantically stuffing things into a sack. 'What the…?'

'Holy shit!' Claire gasps at her, 'Ho-ly total mother-shit! I'm so glad you came. So glad you got here. I don't believe this. I…I mean, I knew…but I didn't…'

'Claire! You're making no sense at all. You're talking gibberish. What the hell's going on? What do they want with you? I heard your name on the PA. You haven't done anything crazy, right? So what the…?'

'What's going on? What's going on? They're sending me home! Shipping me out. Right now! And I had no goddamn idea! I mean…no idea. With my ten percent and good time…I knew I was close…but I mean, this is crazy…I had no idea…it's like I won the lottery all of a sudden. Oh my God, I'm buzzing! This is fucking insane! Can you believe it? I'm going home! To see my boy, to hold my boy! My baby! I'm going to be free! And, holy shit, have a decent meal! And a goddamn marathon hot bath. And sleep in my own bed! I can't believe it's here, the end. I'm here, I'm here…I'm done!' With a squeal Claire flings her arms around Gregory and starts hopping, bouncing, like some lunatic kid all sugared up.

'Whoa…whoa, Claire! For a sec…stop bouncing! Shit, I was freaked! I thought something was *wrong!*' Gregory is wound up inside like a spring coil.

'No! No, nothing's wrong! It's good, all good. And I…I'm so glad you got here before they got on my case. I'm leaving the books, okay? All of them. What you don't want, you just pass them on. And my shower shoes, and toiletries and… God, I just wish I had the chance to be better prepared. So that I could've made a list. About who…you decide, you know, who needs what. Holy shit, I just can't believe it! I'm going *home!*' She puts her hand to her forehead in disbelief, 'It's not sinking in. It's not. I guess not till I'm out the gates, past the goddamn wire. Until I can't see it anymore. Oh my God!'

Gregory sinks heavily onto her bunk. Claire's bed won't stay empty for long. They'll reassign it within days. Claire gone. The idea winds her like a hard blow to the gut. She swallows down a growing knot, prays she doesn't lose it. Claire looks wildly around the small space, 'Aww, screw it! I don't need any of this stuff! What'm I doing trying to pack old laundry soap and commissary?' She laughs. 'God, I'm going to miss you!'

'You won't.'

'Here, I'm...' Claire grabs a piece of paper and scribbles on it madly, 'I'm going to write the details of my dad's place. So you've got them. If I don't hear from you...if I don't hear from you...I am going to hunt you down, Gregory Abbott, I mean it. I'll track you clear across the country if I have to!' She thrusts the paper at Gregory. She keeps her eyes down, pretending to read what Claire's written, but her vision has gone blurry. 'Oh wait a minute,' Claire laughs, 'you can't go that far, can you now? Your ass belongs to the State of California, just like mine. You write, call, or something, or both...hell, I don't know. Just do it, or like I said, I'm coming for you!' Claire is half-laughing and half-crying and shaking her head the whole while.

'You sound out of your head, better calm it, Claire, or they'll keep you in, just for spite. Shove you in seg for going looney on them.'

'They would not dare. I am telling you, they would not dare! C'mon bunkie, what say you walk me to the desk?'

'Yeah. Sure.' She cannot break down. Cannot lose it.

'Oh...my...God...you've got to promise to give Dorinda a great big hug from me, for letting you come in the middle of your shift.'

'Yeah, sure.'

'That about all you can say, Abbott? Yeah...sure?'

'Nope.'

'Well, there's a huge improvement on the scale of dynamic response.'

Gregory wishes she had the guts, the strength to say what she is actually feeling, to tell Claire how much she is going to miss her. How she didn't think she would be able to go it alone. But she doesn't want to break down. Not in front of the guards, not in front of other prisoners who might see. And she knows it's not fair to Claire, to put that kind of trip on her, so she tries to keep herself even, to hold everything back. Keep the emotional rocket barreling through her in check. Locked down tight. 'Glad you approve.'

'Wiseass.'

'Better than being a dumb-ass.'

'I'm going to miss you, wiseass, dumb-ass, or whatever.' Claire's voice is starting to shake.

'Nah, you're not. 'Cause having me around would mean you're still caught up in this flea trap. Get a grip, Claire.'

'I know, I know. But still... I will miss you.'

'Only because you've been living on top of me for years.'

'Yeah, but it got so...so...comfortable. I'm totally freaked. No counts, no bars, no more living with every minute of the goddamn day accounted for. No freakin' orange! Holy smokes, I am going home. Home! Outside. Free! I don't know if I can handle it. I don't know. This is flipping ridiculous. I'm scared! I won't know what to say, the right things to say. Or what to do. I mean, I've forgotten what it's like to be civilized. And I…hell, I don't even *know* my kid anymore. What's he going to say? What if he doesn't want me around? What if he hates me?'

'He won't hate you, Claire.'

'How can you be so sure?'

'I just am.'

'God, I hope you're right. I really hope so.'

'End of the line, Darlen.' It is CO Joe on desk duty, a guy everybody likes.

'Joe! They're sending me out!'

'So I hear, Darlen, so I hear. I told them they made a mistake.'

'What?'

'Kidding, just joking. Darlen, loosen up, will ya? Ladies, you got a minute to say your good-byes. They want me getting this show on the road. Just so as you know though, I won't say nothing if I don't see nothing.' Joe purposely turns his back and hums as he takes to shuffling some of the papers stacked up for recycling.

Claire grabs her tight. 'You can do it, Abbott,' she whispers into her. Gregory feels a warm damp patch on the skin of her neck. Tears? Is Claire crying? 'You just do what it takes to get to the other side.'

'I will.'

'And promise me I'm going to hear from you. Don't you dare say yeah… sure…or I'll throttle you right here and now. Got me? And then I won't be going anywhere. And it'll be your damn fault. How's that for guilt? Tell me you promise.'

'I promise,' she whispers.

Claire backs away some to look at her. Their arms are ladder locked. When she steps close again she leans in, so their foreheads are touching. Gregory can smell her, can feel the heat of her body. She tries frantically to commit details to memory. So she can keep something of her. Claire's eyes look into Gregory, past what they can see, and hold her. There is worry, there is fear, there is tenderness. Gregory can feel herself beginning to tremble, to crumble, at the idea of loss. The loss of Claire. She takes a shuddering breath, keeping everything else tightly reined, so tight that she wants to explode behind the drag of air she pulls into her lungs. Everything is slowed down. Walls and bars dissolve around them, where they stand. Claire gives her a half-smile, but her eyes are sad, wet. Claire's lips reach out for hers, soft and warm. Gregory's breath catches. Time stalls. Inside she is heaving, keening, breaking. She can feel the rhythm of Claire's pulse in the kiss. Everything unsaid floods through. She can understand Claire, suddenly, in a way that words would never have allowed. Not in the chaos of this, of what's going on. When Claire finally pulls away, Gregory's lips stay soft and warm. She can feel heat rising; the choking lump in her throat, the tears stinging her unblinking eyes. *I will not cry. I can't. Can't.*

Claire offers a shy smile. 'Take care of you.'

'Yeah.' Gregory tries her best to keep it together, to stay looking cool, to try for a look of some sort of happy. For Claire's sake.

'Sure,' Claire mimics, her eyes still concentrated on Gregory.

'Okay, Darlen?'

'Okay, Joe.'

'Let's head on down this damn brick road one last time then, shall we?'

Claire lifts a hand in silent farewell. Gregory does the same. She can't trust her voice. *Suck it up. Suck. It. Up. Don't break. Don't.* The hurt behind her ribs is blazing and knife sharp.

Claire turns to Joe. 'Yeah,' she says to the guard, grinning, 'sure.' Gregory stands until they are buzzed through. Claire turns and waves one last time as they round the corner, and then she's gone. Every part of Gregory aches. Suddenly her mind imagines Claire in the sunny setting of the picture with the boy. The boy, whose hair is licked with motion. And she pictures him running, knees and arms and legs in motion, fluid with joy and excitement, once again wrapped into his mama's eager, waiting arms. She knows she is selfish to be unhappy, to be feeling this way. If she cares for Claire as much as it feels like she does. Realizing it shifts things, just a little bit. Because she wants that joy for Claire.

Kameko
San Francisco, California
2001

Relief had come with death, but grief was not content to let her go. A dullness takes her over, seeping through her, out of her. As if her heart is pumping it through her veins, pushing it through her pores. The pervading hollowness makes her feel as though her body is brittle and fragile. Exhaustion drags at her.

Marriage provides an amiable companionship. It helps her pass the worst of times. It offers an escape. With a halting fluidity, life transfers its previous attentions, those of a daughter, to those of a wife. If it wasn't for Shiro, the distraction of a new relationship, the eagerness to please, the need for company, she didn't know what turn her own life might have taken. She had decided, in the end, to leave school, to forgo finishing in favour of caring for Mother. When death had finally come for her, it was reassuring to have the rest already settled. To know, without having to think or decide anything, just what came next. Life with a husband, living for a husband, is a simple rhythm. It does not force her beyond her shell. The monotony of the everyday is somehow a comfort; a salve for insides twice torn by grief.

When news of Shiro's transfer to San Francisco comes, just as the blossoms are blooming again, Kameko is grateful. Grateful for a shift in focus, for a fresh canvas upon which she can begin to define the texture and the detail of married life. It would give them a freedom, she and Shiro, if not forever, then at least for a time. Distance would give them the chance to find a way forward, in a heading entirely of their own making.

'We should,' he says with a hesitation that shows his obvious discomfort at broaching the matter, 'try to have a child.'

'Oh yes, we should.' She'd breathed out, all of a sudden wanting with an intensity quite foreign to her.

'My mother. Has been asking.' It is halting, the intonation of his words, giving away his embarrassment. 'It is pressing on her. She would like to be a grandmother, to tell her friends something of it, some news. It is not that I worry what she or others think, but for us I think it would be nice.'

'Nice. Yes.'

'It would be okay for you?'

'Yes. It would.'

'There is nothing else you'd rather...' he trails off leaving the half-question hanging above them.

'No, I think I would like it for us, a child. A baby.'

'I am relieved. Because we never spoke. Before. About it, about babies, children, you know. I wondered about school. My mother, in her not exactly nice voice, said to me: *How much time has it been? For you two lovebirds to be in that empty nest? Have you not had enough pleasant times together? So you are only two. How long can it continue to be so interesting? Shiro, please tell me you are not the modern types who do not want to make a family.* That is the way she put her words. Of course, I reassured her. But it startled me for a time. Because I did not know. Of your preference. For family or not.' He smiles lightly, his eyes raised in a look of questioning.

It touched her, the care he took in approaching the matter, his evident awkwardness. 'I prefer it, family,' she says, smiling.

'She asked what you are doing. After the move and after the adjustment to the city. If you are healthy, eat well, sleep enough. She knows the challenges of work for me, from my father. But she was concerned for you, your health. She just wants...Well, she is a woman, so obviously I cannot understand her direction. Yes, is what I answered her, you were well. Doing better. *Kameko does not consider returning to school?* she asked. No, no, I told her. She felt relieved. She didn't think it worthwhile in America. Even to pass the time. I told her that you're...we...are good, content. Happy.' He nods at Kameko. '*Then you should try,* she said to me. Imagine me talking with my mother about such a thing. Yes. Yes, I told her. What am I to say? I just want to be rid of her on the telephone. To stop these questions.' He laughs. 'She has never pried so much before. You can see that this is a matter of some importance to her. *Talk to Kameko,* she says. I'll talk to her, I said. I promised.'

He sounds comedic in the way he presents it. She stifles a giggle. He throws up his hands. 'What?' Then his face became quickly serious. 'I would like a child,' he says with his eyes searching her own. 'We are far from Japan. It is a good thing, too—to be far from my mother's eyes and ears.' He smiles and holds up a long and elegant finger to indicate his sturdy point. His voice softens, 'It would be a good thing for you, for us. A baby. To give you something. To fill your days. To gobble up the nights and rob us of sleep.' There is amusement ribboned in his tone.

'I think we must try very hard to make this happen.' His eyes twinkle. 'We should make appointments to...work on this project of yours...ours.' She laughs out loud and gives him a playful slap on the shoulder for his silliness. 'No, but I am serious,' his eyes widen in mock surprise. 'And you hit me for that? I am, as they say in the West, at your service. Shall we get down to this very important business? I think now, and...' he rubs his chin thoughtfully, his joking obvious even though he is attempting a more solemn display, 'certainly at every opportunity. I think you should follow me, to practise.' He takes her by the hand to lead her, laughing, to the bedroom.

Aneeta
Fresno, California
2001

Edges are bleeding into one another the way water might cloud ink on paper. The wall calendar in the kitchen flips, page to page, from one American landscape to the next.

There are times she has walked past the telephones in the house wishing that on the other end someone might want news of her. But there is no familiar voice reaching out to her across the miles, no ear to hear her stories, to greet any news of hers with joy or surprise or pleasure, no one to ease her longing, her homesickness.

It is best a clean break. That is at the heart of it. Keeping things clean. Distance was a best-case compromise for a worst-case difficulty.

She is no longer her mother's daughter. She has become somebody else's problem. A problem passed along. By marriage. Though she begins to see how it might appear strange that she has no contact with her own blood. Which is why she eventually asks for sheets of aerogram paper and postage stamps.

No one disputes her desire to write. In fact, they are likely thankful for her thrift. Overseas postage is far cheaper than overseas calling. She has noticed her mother-in-law passing behind her, eyes covertly trying to read over a shoulder. The letters she pens are meant for Mummy and Asha mostly. Sometimes she will write to others to show variety, if someone were to be curious. The messages are always pleasant in tone and theme. She tries to carefully balance informing qualities with inquiring qualities. She talks of weather, the house, the neighbourhood and neighbours. She responds to fictitious queries and asks after relatives or other news.

That the letters would never reach their destination, that they never would be deposited in a post-box, only she would know. Only she would know to expect no replies. Though it is falsehood, there is no malice intended by it. And when her correspondence is written, sealed and addressed, she secretly tucks the paper into the depths of her suitcase. Let them believe whatever it is that they will.

While head and heart know that her written words are purely a charade to keep wondering at bay, she begins to enjoy the crafting of a parallel existence. A pleasing incarnation of life. In words upon paper.

Each weekday has much the same tempo. Stockbrokers begin early. This is Jovin's position in the financial industry. *Investment Specialist* is what it says on his business card. Now she knows. Now she could have answered the question the Immigration Officer, Mercado, had asked. He and his elder brother, Narinder, both work for the same company. They have to be to their office before the markets of the east get underway, and there is a time difference of three hours east to west. They drive for forty minutes on the freeway. Unless the traffic is bad. Or the weather. Then it is longer. Sometimes they take only one car. Other days they each drive. Schedules after the markets close some days separate their paths and bring them home at different times. When Jovin returns home later than his brother he often has the sweet scent of liquor on his breath. It is a scent that stirs dark memories.

Dadi-ji, as she calls her father-in-law, is usually in the midst of morning prayers by the time she bids Jovin goodbye for the day. Her sister-in-law, Samar, does not awaken with Narinder. Narinder shrugs his shoulders into a dark suit jacket and accepts a cup of steaming tea from her hands. Jovin's jacket hangs on the chair back beside him. Whomever reaches the room first generally switches on the television set perched on the kitchen countertop.

The news in the still dark pre-dawn hours of the morning is rarely good. She was horrified the day she saw tall towers in New York City erupt into flames and smoke; people, soot-covered and bleeding, running through the streets in panic. Pictures of the lost and the heroic had flashed in turns across the screen. That morning they had rushed through everything. The world seemed to be coming slowly undone. The same ugly images looped again and again. A heaving pit had opened in her stomach. But she had felt a profound sense of awe at the determined solidarity among the people.

Since that day, however, she has taken to turning the small set off as soon as the brothers leave. She tiptoes past her whispering father-in-law and goes back into the room that she and Jovin share to ready herself for the day ahead. She leaves his breakfast waiting for him in the kitchen for when he has finished his morning ritual. Like Samar, her mother-in-law elects not to awaken so early.

She is the imported wife. 'Fresh out of the village,' her sister-in-law jokes in a voice that seems unnaturally loud. There is always laughter to accompany the comment. It is a pointed reminder of her position in the household. As the foreign bride of the youngest son.

The only one to show any softness to her is her brother-in-law, Narinder. Or perhaps it is imagined. Because he simply isn't as harsh as the others. He does not boss her around, or speak too loudly, or call her names. He simply lets her be. No orders, no requests. She sometimes wonders about the personalities of the brothers. How, for siblings, they seem not very much alike. But just as quickly as the thoughts come, she shakes them away. It is pointless to dwell on the differences between them.

She has caught Samar's eyes hot upon her after some exchanges with Narinder. She shrugs her shoulders to show her sister-in-law that there is nothing behind it, any kindness he might show her.

She understands now the bichola's words about the family wanting a traditional girl. Tradition inferred that a girl would be acquainted with place and hierarchy within a family and would be accepting of her status and what was dictated by it. Now that she is caught up in the web she understands it perfectly.

As the wife of the youngest brother she is expected to be responsible for much of the housekeeping. She is expected also to cook and to launder. The words of the old matchmaker echo over and over in her. Mummi-ji, as her mother-in-law Anju wishes to be called, misses no opportunity to remind her of the duties she is expected to undertake. Her words needle Aneeta, even though they are cloaked in false cheer. 'Chee, girl, you think that these dishes are going to wash themselves? If only it were so.'

They seem surprised that she cannot drive. Displeased, in fact. Here, there are no drivers. In America, California, people must drive themselves. They want her to fetch groceries and see to other errand-running. 'How will she get around if she cannot drive? She cannot expect someone to always be able to take her.' Dadi says this to no one in particular and tuts to lament the fact. 'She was supposed to be a help coming here,' he says. Dadi-ji has said she needs to learn, and take a test for driving. To make her useful to the household. This is a land of many cars. In this family they have four. Two Mercedes, a Toyota, and Samar's red, convertible BMW with a license plate that boldly says *Samar*. Cars snake in orderly rows in and out of grid-lined California streets and highways in so carefully organized a manner. Not like the craziness in the streets of Delhi. Not at all.

In this country it turns out that having a household staff is a rarity. A middle-aged Mexican couple, Raoul and Maria, are the only outside help the family employs. They come three days each week. Raoul works outside the house in the modest gardens and tends to the exterior needs of the house. He is narrow and wiry in stature. His motions are fluid and birdlike with an element of grace and softness, but with a certainty in them. He attends to his outside domain with unhurried ease, but he is not slow either; there is conviction in his attentions that shows his dedication. She is able to see the yard from the laundry area and from the kitchen—that is how she is able to study him. At midday, he approaches the back door where his wife meets him with a container that holds his lunch. The smells that emanate from the tiffin-like vessel are heady with spice and the fresh scent of coriander, so much so that they make her mouth water. Maria is slight and small with luminous brown eyes and warm golden-brown skin. She wears her hair pulled into a tightly netted bun in a way that accentuates the high draw of her cheekbones. Her hands are chapped from work. She will touch her husband lightly on the shoulder as she hands him his lunch, and he will reach up and cover it with his own, just for a moment, before he is gone again.

On the days they are at the house Maria attends to inside duties. It is a pattern clearly well-established. She works her way through all of the rooms methodically. Picking-up, folding, cleaning windows, dusting; she seems never to be still. Last of all in the cleaning routine is the vacuuming. After each room, Maria carefully backs out of the perfectly gridded area and closes the door after her. Almost as the untouchable Dalits used to have to do. In an altogether different time and place. A world apart. Aneeta supposes that the closed doors signal to Anju that Maria is finished with a certain part of the house. Sometimes Anju will fling a door wide and tread upon fresh vacuum streaks, destroying without hesitation the tidy rows of Maria's handiwork. With a loud 'Maria!' she beckons, intending the woman present for an impromptu inspection of the selected site. Aneeta can see the tension in Maria, the way her hands clasp and unclasp while Anju speaks, can hear it in her fervent 'Si, si. Si, Señora. As you wish.'

It fast becomes apparent to Aneeta that Raoul and Maria both are entirely in Anju's employ. They answer only to her. The others are not involved with such household concerns. Anju issues direction; it is she alone they consult as to the nature of their duties. She has overheard Samar demand that some task be done for her, but Maria, with head bowed, had deferred to Anju, 'Si, Miss. I will ask Mrs. Okay? Then I will do it.' Only Narinder has kind words for the couple if his path should happen to cross theirs.

Over a succession of days spent together there is an easiness that begins to grow between them. A sense of comfort. When he comes to the back door to collect his lunch, Raoul gives her a smile if she is present, and a nod of his head. He retreats to a sliver of shade in the yard to eat before resuming his duties.

Aneeta notices that Maria does not stop during the workday to eat, unlike her husband; that they only ever bring one container. It leads to their first exchange beyond the duties of the day. Maria has spent an entire morning polishing Anju's brass pieces, scrubbing goblets, statues and intricate renderings of Indian deities. Aneeta can see perspiration dotting her hairline, can feel the ache in her own wrists just from watching the woman's industry. 'Please,' Aneeta volunteers, thinking she must be hungry, 'let me make you something to eat.'

Maria is so startled by the interruption of Aneeta's voice that she drops the toothbrush she has been working with. It lands with a clatter upon the newspaper covered tabletop. In an attempt at reassurance Aneeta offers, 'I'm feeling hungry myself. I'm going to warm some vegetables from last evening's dinner. Could I warm some for you as well?'

She regards Aneeta with some uncertainty before answering, 'No, Señorita. Gracias. I have eaten already.' And presently returns her attentions to the darkened v-channels on the leg of an elephant statue.

'At least let me make you a cup of tea. Please, I insist.'

Maria looks up. And nods at Aneeta. 'Tea. Si. Okay, I will have some.' It is when she puts the porcelain cup down on the table that Maria looks up at her and offers the slightest of smiles.

Aneeta stands to sip her tea, watching as Maria changes hands with the toothbrush to intermittently drink from her cup. They are two women alone in the kitchen, separate, yet also together. There is peace in the knowledge that someone shares this moment. It makes her want to hold on to it for as long as she can. Without a word, she slides into a chair on the opposite side of the table. Maria's face is surprised as she picks up a worn scrap of cloth, daubs it with sickly green polish, and begins to rub.

Her mother-in-law discovers them there some time later, when they are almost at the end of the task; only a few pieces remain. Anju's face is like a storm cloud, so rapid in transformation that it is impossible to read. Both Aneeta and Maria have stopped scrubbing to wait on her reaction, rags suspended, hands gripping cloth and metal. Without a word to either, Anju simply turns on her heel and leaves. Slowly, they let go of the breath they have held in her presence, and share a knowing look. It is the beginning of friendship.

Somehow Maria and Raoul temper the rest of her life. Anju has said she expects Aneeta to assist in the work she has for them each week. As much as she is exhausted by the household labours that they undertake, she find she enjoys the time she spends with them. She has learned to change a lightbulb. Mop the floors to an acceptable shine. To choose ripe lemons from a tree in the yard. To stitch a button. She learns simple words of Spanish: *Hola, gracias, por favor*. They laugh at the clumsiness of her tongue with the different sounds. But she can tell they are quietly pleased. They—Raoul, Maria and she— are left to their business, so long as at the end of the day the work Anju wants done is completed satisfactorily.

She has discovered that the neighbours on one side of the house are a white couple and on the other, an Asian family. The fair-skinned woman has long, golden-blonde hair. She raises a hand in greeting to Aneeta when she sees her and Aneeta returns the same. Over time, she notices that the woman is going to have a baby. She observes her changing shape, the way she has slowed in her movements. Across the fence that divides the two families she can see contentment in the woman, the way her hand naturally comes to rest on her swollen abdomen, the way she smiles down at it.

Jovin is slowly becoming more open with her and more talkative. There is a familiarity growing between them. Even Anju is becoming more agreeable. Only Samar is different. She makes no attempt to veil her displeasure. It is clear in the way her eyes flash. The way she pokes with her comments. Over everything and nothing at all. Not unlike what she had seen between Anju and her own mother, she senses it is a competition of sorts. And it is her place to concede. As the newcomer, the new wife. She knows the order will not change, but she hopes, with time and adjustment, her sister-in-law might. And so she does her best to please her. Even going so far as to cook dishes she knows Samar favours. Aneeta tries, if not to make her happy, at least for a tenable air of peace between them.

Narinder is understanding, apologetic even. One afternoon he sits Aneeta down at the kitchen table and makes an attempt to explain. Samar is at a salon having her nails manicured. Jovin is away at the gym. Her mother-in-law and father-in-law are at an anniversary party. 'She's going through a tough time right now.' He sighs and runs a hand through the wave of dark hair. She feels a sentimentality towards Narinder. She has taken to calling him Bhaji, to give him the respect owed an older brother. And out of a sense of gratitude. For his kindness, his mild manner; for his efforts to smooth rough edges between she and Samar. She sees, too, the way he attempts to balance the wishes of his parents against those of his modern wife. 'She's feeling a lot of pressure.' Aneeta is drawn to the hurt in his eyes. 'We've been married for two years now. You know the Indian way. We should have a child by now, or at least be expecting. Mom's really pushing.' His laugh is sad, slow. 'You, of all people, know what my mother can be like.' He looks up, with an apologetic half-smile. 'They think she should be pregnant. We should be pregnant. But Samar wants to go back to school. Not to have to start a family right now. If you guys…' he lets the thought trail off without finishing it, though his inference is clear. She looks away, embarrassed at the intimation. 'Anyway,' he pauses, 'with you in the picture we thought it might give Samar, us, some breathing room. I shouldn't be burdening you with all this stuff. I just thought it might help if you knew where she might be coming from in all this. That's all…that's all.'

She opens her mouth to speak, to reassure, to say that it is all right. That she understands. But before her lips can form the words he scrapes his chair back and stands. As he leaves the room she hears his weary sigh.

Kameko
San Francisco
2002

Often, she dreams of stroking a child's face in the moonlight. In the mind's vision she gazes adoringly at the blank canvas that is this child, holding a petal-soft hand whose fingers find and curl around her own. Lifting the infant to her, she nestles the warm bundle tenderly against her yielding flesh, skin to skin. The child eats from her, hungrily, with tiny fluttering swallows. She hears the sigh of her own exhausted satisfaction. It is like nothing else, the greatness of the love she feels for this miraculous new life.

Shiro's suggestion of a child had appealed to her. It is something she had not previously given a lot of thought to. Though she hadn't really thought that traditional marriage would suit her either. What would she have done with a Humanities and Literature degree anyway? Probably gone to work for a big corporation in some obscure position more about fetching and carrying cups of tea for senior staff members than contributing intellectually to some greater idea, some bigger purpose. The idea of it seems rather pointless now.

But having a child is meant to be simple. An extension of marrying. The next in successive progressions. It is the logical expectation. The couple becomes a family. Almost, it occurs to Kameko, a little bit of a mathematical equation. Wife plus husband equals baby. It is most simplistic in form, in ideology, and plain figures. Not so, however, in achievement.

Every month when she sees the blood she curses it. Her emptiness transforms them both. Shiro has become frustrated with her, losing patience with her moods and fears. The practice they had once laughed about has trailed off.

He is beginning to turn himself away. She tells herself it is because of the new job, greater responsibilities. She is miserable without him and miserable when he is home with her. He is annoyed around her, sharp with his words. He leaves the apartment earlier, as the light is coming over the bay, and stays away longer, until she can see, often through bleary eyes, the lights twinkling in the distance. There are nights when he does not come at all. She excuses it, even welcomes it. Considers it her punishment. After all, she is deficient as a wife if she cannot also be a mother. On the surface she tries to keep *tatemae*, her pleasing outside face, while invisible waves of shame, hopelessness, frustration, exasperation wash through her like the tides. The cycle repeats itself over and over again, weakening and transforming her.

In another dream, one that comes now with increasing regularity, she sees a park in winter. One she used to walk through near the university. Her mind paints the sky a melancholy grey; all is bitterly cold. Naked trees claw at the gates of an invisible heaven, barren, desperate for life within their limbs. It troubles her, this scene, for it shows no sign of vitality in its landscape. Even the water below the misty and faded vermilion arc of a narrow bridge does not move; ice is crusted in crystalline patches on its surface. She stands still at the center of the span, rooted in place. All other colour starts to fade into grey. As if life is leaving it, draining away. She hears the hollow wailing sound of fleeing sea birds who have lost their path from the water's edge. She senses that she, too, is lost; she does not know in which direction she should move. All the while the ice is creeping up in her, prying with bony fingers into her soul, claiming her bit by bit.

'You should go out.' He says the words sharply, with what sounds like condemnation.

'I do go out.' She argues defensively, even though she knows it is hardly true.

'I mean go out and do something.'

'What something?'

'I don't know. Something different than what you do now. Maybe shopping.'

'Shopping?' She is incredulous at his suggestion. How it trivializes the very nature of things.

'Or make some friends. I don't know. You've got to get out. Get the idea of a baby out of your head. Set it aside.'

She bites down hard on her tongue and bows her head. 'Yes, I suppose it is right. Right of me to move on.'

'That is not what I am saying. Just, that…feel the air, maybe see the colours. Of the season. The city is quite beautiful. You do not see it because you refuse to look. You should open yourself to other things, let the course be more natural. Maybe then…' He trades off the mundane with his admonitions, mixing the two to soften them, but the meaning of his words comes through. Like an arrow it lodges in her heart.

'Yes. Natural. Yes.'

He shakes his head, his exasperation clear. He stands, suddenly, shoves his chair back. In minutes she hears the apartment door slam.

She cannot blame him for his frustration, for leaving. What kind of good wife is she? She has hardly served him a palatable meal lately. The cupboards are poorly stocked. She is content to let supplies dwindle to nothing before her eyes, resistant to going marketing to replace them. She is distracted. Preoccupied. While ironing she had burned a good necktie right through, lost to some vision in the mist on the bay that had drawn her eye. When her attentions had turned it was too late. Dior. She had placed it gingerly in the bin and wept. Foolishly wept. For so much more than the lost band of silk. She had taken the trash out to the chute and pressed it down. Hard. Listened to it slide away. Until the sound had eventually faded to nothing. She should go to get him another one. But she does not care to. He has many others. There is really no need.

Familiarity is increasingly strangled between them. Once open windows are closed, bolted, covered over. Both are tiptoeing around as if they are picking a way over sharp edges of broken glass. Afraid of each other, afraid of themselves, afraid of truth.

Shiro arranges the appointment. But he does not accompany her. These are women's matters. The idea of fertility offends his masculine sensibilities. But how does he know, she wonders, that the fault for the matter, the lack of conception, lies only with her?

She has been received and processed in the office very efficiently. The waiting area reminds her of a Tokyo department store. Very bright and white with chrome and glass. Fine for shopping, but otherwise not so peaceful or reassuring. She is overwhelmed by all of the questions and the information they require. Details that are embarrassing and personal. She sits with the clipboard on her lap, flipping the paper from one side to the other. Searching for things she knows, understands, things she can fill in the empty blank spaces. She wants to cry. For some time she simply sits clutching it to her, not moving. Finally, she musters the courage to ask.

She approaches the transparent reception desk. 'Excuse me, but I am sorry. I do not know all of these things. So I don't know what to do for filling in this information.'

'We just need something for our files,' a pleasant and pretty blonde woman with a deep suntan reassures, 'so that we can start a record for you.' A wide smile.

Kameko offers a small nodded bow. 'So then it is okay that it is not all finished?'

'Oh, don't worry, most people can't complete it all. You just put in what you know. Insurance information. Any medical history, treatments, menstrual info. Check off any diagnostics you've already had done. The doctor will be able to fill in some of the blanks. If you're done I can take it for you.'

Around her in the expansive waiting area some women are whispering with ill-at-ease looking husbands, partners. She is lonely for Shiro, for some company at least, but also glad he is not here, it would be too uncomfortable. She has chosen a seat beside a tall chrome and glass case that holds magazines and medical literature: *Fertility and You, Family Matters, Pregnancy: What Every Woman Should Know, It Takes Two to Make Three*. It hides her. From the other eyes that are in the room. Eyes cannot help looking. It is a matter of natural curiosity. But it is never pleasant to be like a specimen under a microscope.

'Mrs. Tanaka?' She starts a little at her name. A woman has stepped into the room from behind a central inner door. She is dressed in sloppy blue. A smock top and wide-legged bottoms held to the waist by a drawstring at the front. The woman looks down at the paper file in her hand and holds the door, waiting for Kameko to gather her things. As Kameko approaches she looks up and offers a smile. 'Mrs. Tanaka, please follow me.' She stops at another door down the hall a ways, knocks once, and opens it. She lets Kameko pass through and motions, 'Please undress and slip into the gown. The doctor will be with you shortly.' Then she is gone.

Behind the door Kameko sits. Waiting. Her stomach rumbles its discomfort at the situation. Why does breakfast seem so distant a memory? Her hands and feet are cold. The green gown she wears is open at the back and she feels the cold of a draft coming from somewhere. She re-adjusts herself on the table so that the air cannot reach her bare skin so easily and hugs herself against it. Her clothing is neatly piled on a white leather chair in the corner of the examination room. Her underwear and camisole are hidden carefully in the middle of the garments.

A clip-clop of shoes in the hallway stops outside. The door opens on a beautiful dark-haired woman in a white lab coat. 'Good morning,' she opens a folder to reveal the form Kameko had laboured over, 'Mrs. Tanaka.' She smiles. She has a warm smile in spite of the coldness of the surroundings. There is a heavy chain that lies in the hollow of her breastbone. She wears a rich red dress beneath the crisp white. Her feet are clad in fashionable heels. She scans the paper quickly. There is not much to digest. 'You're here Mrs. Tanaka because,' her voice drifts and she looks up, still with a smile, 'you have some concerns regarding pregnancy? In particular, from what it looks like here, conception?'

'Yes,' Kameko responds shyly.

'And you are how old? Let me see 19,' she trails off into as she calculates, 'so you are 25 now. Yes, you would be 25. Right?' She nods at Kameko. 'And you've been married for a little less than two years?'

'Yes.'

'Trying to get pregnant for how long?'

'More than one year.'

'Okay, and before that used birth control?'

'Yes.'

'What form?'

'Condom. And,' she thinks, rubs her fingers together to give motion to her thought while she tries for the word, 'sometimes jelly.'

'Okay. Used them regularly when you were active?'

'Yes.' She nods but thinks there were probably times, too, when she had not used birth control. And never considered the outcome. Or lack of outcome.

'Ever had an abortion?'

'No.'

'Miscarry? That you were aware of?'

'No.'

'Ever experience an ectopic pregnancy? A pregnancy where the egg develops outside the uterus? That you're aware of?'

'No.'

'When did you get your first period? Can you remember?'

She casts her mind back. What year had she been in at school? 'I think 13, maybe.'

'Okay. And the symptoms, the flow, would you say that they were normal? From the beginning?'

'Yes, I think so.'

'No heavy clotting, discharge, odd spotting, unusual cramping?'

'No.'

'And in duration, how long?'

'Just, maybe…5 or 6 days?'

'I'm going to try and get a feel for your family background. Factors that might affect things. Where are you from?'

'Tokyo.'

'Ah, nice. I visited Tokyo during a summer break from college one year. I loved it. You were born there? '

'Yes, in Tokyo.'

'Any siblings? Brothers or sisters?'

'No.'

'Do you know how old your mother was when she conceived?'

'No.'

'Do you know whether your mother had a similar experience?'

'No.'

'Miscarriage? Or a history of miscarriage?'

'I don't know.'

'Do you think you could ask her?'

'She is…' she pauses to choose her words, feels the squeeze in her chest, 'Mm. She has died. Recently.'

'I'm sorry. Very sorry to hear that.' The doctor asks more gently, 'Is there maybe someone else you might ask about her history? Your father? An aunt, perhaps? It might give me a clearer picture.'

To ask Father would be laughable. He would not have concerned himself with such things. 'No. There is no one.'

'Okay. I didn't mean to pry, I just want to get an feel for what might be the situation with your reproductive experience, the more I know, the better I can assist.'

'My parents had a baby, me, when they had been married for three years, I think. Maybe four.'

'Okay, so a little bit further along than you and your husband now. Mrs. Tanaka, I'm going to do some tests. On your blood. Check your hormone levels. Plot your cycle. A routine pap and cervical test. We'll look for sexually transmitted diseases, not to alarm you, since if you've been using condoms as birth control it's unlikely, but we want to be able to rule them out. We'll book an ultrasound, initially probably only an abdominal one. If I have concerns about any results I'll maybe look to do a transvaginal as well.'

'Oh.'

'I know I've been doing a lot of talking, asking a lot of questions, but Mrs. Tanaka, I want to assure you that none of this, even the delay in conception, is unusual. I do want you to know that. It is possible after I run all these tests, that we'll find nothing that points to you not being able to conceive naturally. Quite probably, when the time is right, it will happen. You *will* conceive. Given the recent trauma associated with your mother's passing, it may be that the stress on your body is simply hampering your ability to become pregnant. For the moment. It may be tied to that, it may not. It could be that this is simply your body's answer to handling emotional stress, the upset of it. You understand?'

'Yes. So, I may still become pregnant?'

'Right now, Mrs. Tanaka, I would say that it is possible. But we're going to have a closer look at things before I can speculate with any certainty.'

'Now, aside from the office appointments, we'll also arrange for the various tests I've recommended. My nurse will draw some blood for the initial work-up before you leave today. I would say my advice to you in the meantime: be patient. Relax. Enjoy life as a newly married couple. Enjoy sex. Don't dwell on the prospect of getting pregnant. The pressure you put on yourself can be defining in cases like this. Shift your focus. Take your mind off it. Take up a hobby, keep yourself busy. Sometimes, Mrs. Tanaka, the difficulties stem from little other than trying too hard. Sometimes it's just a matter of the pressure that keeps it from happening. Okay?'

'Yes.' Her voice comes out, a whisper, threaded with possibility. It could be. It could still be. For her. For them. It could be real. One day.

'Let's get you to lie down with legs in the stirrups and I'll take a culture.' Kamkeo lies back, warming with the news. 'That's it. Now move up, up. And a little more up, slide your bottom right almost to the end of the table. I know it feels strange. There. That's it, there.' Kameko hears a drawer opening, the snap of gloves and tearing of paper. 'I'll just check your ovaries first. I'll palpate vaginally with pressure on the abdomen. The jelly will be cool. It may feel just a little bit crampy. Deep breath in. Here we go. Good. And fine.' She feels it leave her, the sensation of fullness. 'There.' Then the running of water into the rounded steel basin. The faucet is suspended high over it so it gives almost a musical sound when it reaches the curve, cradled there for an instant. 'I'm just warming the speculum. And again: speculum in, deep breath, relax. You'll feel a scrape as I take the culture. There we go, we're done.' A snap as the cylinder is closed with the sample inside. 'All right?'

'Hm. Yes.' Kameko turns her head on the pillow and the doctor pulls the sheet back over her. Her cheeks are hot.

'Okay,' the doctor pats her thigh. 'That's it for today. You may find you have a little spotting after the scraping. It's not cause for alarm. You can go ahead and get dressed. I'm going to have the nurse come in a couple of minutes to take blood samples. Then when you're ready she'll take you back to the front office and we'll book the appointments we need.'

'Yes. Thank you. Thank you.' She has raised herself to her elbows.

'No problem. We'll see you again soon, Mrs. Tanaka. And please, as

I've said, don't worry. If something irregular should show up, we'll notify you immediately and we'll work from there, but don't assume that there is something wrong. Okay, Mrs. Tanaka?'

For some reason the sound of her married name digs at her, and so she volunteers, 'Kameko.'

'I'll see you soon then, Kameko.' The doctor smiles.

Kameko tries to smile. 'Yes. Soon.'

There are nights, most often at the end of the week, that he leaves her. At home. He doesn't talk to her about where he goes on these nights. Nor does he inform her in advance that he will be out for the evening. It is a husband's entitlement. Not to have to explain. Sometimes Narinder accompanies him. Samar often leaves too, though she drives her own car. Engines thrum to life and pulse their way urgently, excitedly, out of the garage, down the drive and quickly out into the street. Like ants they seem to scurry away, with haste and intention. She is left.

On such nights, when Jovin finally clatters into the room they share, he is bathed in stale smoke and the sour-sweet tang of alcohol. He wakes her with the noise he makes, the banging about, the smell, the way he sinks heavily onto the bed to remove his shoes, his shirt. She sees the way his frame sways, the jerky way he moves. It does not take many nights like it for her to realize that he intends to disturb her into waking. He crashes about with disrobing and in the toilet before he throws himself roughly down on the bed beside her. Where he expects to find her, his wife, awake and obliging.

There are times when he no longer has control enough of his body to get what he wants from her. 'Bitch, look what you do to me!' His eyes narrow accusingly. His words slide thickly together. She tries to make her expression sympathetic but without pity, which, she fears, might further anger him. She is afraid of him then, even though there are others nearby. Because of his air of unpredictability, his anger, his blame. On those occasions she tensely holds herself still, barely daring to breathe, wishing the moment past, praying that he is taken quickly by slumber.

Bit by bit, she gathers pieces of these evenings. Samar takes great pleasure, like holding a carrot to a hungry mule, in dangling scraps of information. 'Out.' 'Party.' 'Friends.' It is a clear point of satisfaction for her sister-in-law, this superior play. While Aneeta plies the brothers with tea and tablets for headache, toast and eggs, she listens. On these mornings Dadi-ji is like a child vying for a bedtime story. He hangs on their words, the tale they tell. This is how she eventually comes to understand.

'Where was it?' Dadi-ji will ask. Details begin to emerge.
'You know Jagtar's Uncle Satish?'
'His sister's son. Opened Tandoori Palace. About six months ago.'
'Quite sizable. With rooms in the back. For private parties, banquets.'

'We were about thirty last evening. But the room could quite easily hold a hundred.'

'Achcha? Really?'

'Think the guy thought he could get off watering his booze. And charging full price.'

'Thought nobody'd be able to tell the difference.'

'Randy was so pissed he went and picked up a case of Red Label and brought it back in, box and all. The big man.'

'Just got himself a 500 SL too. A black one. Real beauty.'

'Hunh? He a doctor?'

'No, Dad. Works for a tech company. Big money around town.'

'Got himself a load of options at start-up. Now he's exercising.'

'That's not the only thing he's exercising. See the cat he left with? He kept tucking the green into her all night. Blondie Double D. She gave him quite the ride.'

'Gori?' Dadi is incredulous.

There is a Cheshire Cat grin from Jovin. 'His mummy would have such a cow if she knew the way he messes around.'

'Not like he's going to marry her. Just having some fun. He'll go back to being the good son.'

'They are looking,' Dadi-ji interjects, head wobbling, 'Auntie is consulting a matchmaker. She wants a girl from India.'

'Yeah. He'll stop pissing around at some point and take the plunge. If he wants his inheritance.'

'Why should he stop? Just don't get caught,' Jovin gives a sly grin, 'with the proverbial pants down. How many girls'd Ravi hire? I saw four. But they all looked alike. I know one of them was Candy. She gave me her card. But I kept calling others Candy and they were really getting pissed for some reason.'

'Think there were about six. Though who were those other ones? There was a bunch who came in late? Real mouthy and loud.'

'Can't really be sure. Too focused on my game.'

'You are so full of it!'

'Yeah, whatever you say, big brother.'

'Quite the party.'

'Vik got so drunk he passed out in the middle of a hand.'

'Oh my God!' Dadi-ji sounds horrified, but wears a half-amused looking smile.

'Yeah after he got himself slapped for coming on too strong with one of the girls. She kept yelling something about cash up front. She was a bit of a freak. Might've been on something. She stopped mid-song once and just tried to stare him down. Tassels dangling and all.'

'Hard to be serious when you're looking at a thong and tassels.'

'Basi lost his shirt at the table. Man, he shouldn't be allowed to play poker.'

'Hey, you did okay, little brother.'

'Yeah. I wait till everyone's pissed and then I cheat!'

'Yeah, well feel sorry for Basi. Leela's pregnant again. His parents paid extra for the early ultrasound 'cause they're so desperate for a boy. And it's another girl! Third one! Trying to convince her against it, but Leela won't agree to do anything about it. That guy is destined to die poor.'

'Unlucky bastard. You know his parents won't let up until they get a boy. Somebody needs to give him a box of condoms! Man, my head is killing me this morning.' Jovin calls to her, 'Aneeta, get us a few more headache tablets, will you?'

'Of course,' she answers softly.

From them, it sounds a bit of fun. Even to Dadi-ji. She cannot think why it turns her stomach so. It is hardly new, the idea. That boys should be allowed to be boys. Let them play as they wish. Because eyes and ears will always choose to excuse. Because this is simply the way boys are.

An uneasy sensation comes over her. Familiar but unwelcome. Old feelings shaking hands and how-do-you-do-ing where they have no ties. Old nightmares left over from troubles elsewhere. In another place. Another world.

Women circle the front room chattering noisily. Men spill out of the back of the house, beyond the kitchen, joking and laughing.

Aneeta watches, not without a sense of satisfaction at the way the people seem to be enjoying the fresh samosas she has made. She has re-filled the platter twice already and still they are eating. Anju had supervised the preparation earlier in the day, issuing commands throughout the process: 'More potato!' and, 'Not so much spice, girl! They are California Indians, not masala mongers like you are used to!' and, 'Roll, girl! Dough should not be so thick! With your arms! Push harder! Hai, what shape is this? No one likes too much pastry in their mouth, the edges they will leave behind if it is too much.' Remonstration as opposed to demonstration. Aneeta had only to follow instruction and endeavour to give as little as possible for her mother-in-law to poke at with her sharp tongue.

She moves carefully with her tray of steaming cups to see to the guests. She cannot imagine Samar playing such a role. At least in this way Aneeta is useful to her mother-in-law. Which, she thinks, must count for something in Anju's internal balance of credits.

Most of the women in the room are Anju's age and older, but several have also brought along with them younger women, either daughters or daughters-in-law, although Aneeta is not yet certain which is which. Nor who is connected to whom. Some join her to ferry food and other items back and forth from the kitchen. Tea is drunk, fresh is boiled, refilled, and again drunk. Previously piled high stores of food are rapidly disappearing. Somehow it feels a measure of worthiness, an endorsement of sorts.

Anju instructs her to touch an elderly auntie's feet and she complies. Over her lowered head Anju says, 'You know how these days we are losing the respect.' She receives an awkward pat on her shoulder. In Punjabi she hears that she is a good girl. Very pretty, if a bit skinny.

'Like Aishwarya she reminds me,' someone says, 'the eyes, maybe, because they are light coloured.' She keeps herself concentrated on serving. Tries to keep a pleasant smile in place. The women talk around her in shifting, swirling tides of words and pointed laughter.

Inquiries about her are directed to her mother-in-law. *Where did you find her? Where is she from? Family name? Brothers-Sisters?* A new daughter-in-law is a curiosity, but a mother's point of pride rests with sons. Anju talks glowingly about the boys. About their work. Their money. She does not miss a chance, any chance, to mention a new computer for Dadi or the big screen TV, the new satellite dish. Interestingly, she says nothing about Samar. There are no questions from the aunties about her either. Samar seems a subject best skirted around.

'You know, I never eat samosas at home. I have to watch my waistline these days. And the creep of my sugars. This is what my son says to me. Lucky thing to have a son who is a doctor.'

Loud satisfied slurps smack at the pleasure of another's undoing. '...up to some kind of dirty business. I heard it.'

'And lost his job, too!'

'Always lands on his feet.'

'Maybe not so this time.'

'...two girls and now another.'

'Chee, but he will be ruined by having to marry them all off!'

'...an embarrassment to the parents.'

'I have said it myself. It was a terrible mistake. But what can you do?' Anju looks like a cat with a bird amid the speculation.

The chorus of tuts and hai-hai that greet unfortunate hearsay sound far too pleased at the mention of unpleasantness. It is a staging for deconstructing lives, this. Into building block circumstances. For dissection and closer inspection. Tongues cluck. And feast on fresh samosas, sweets, and gossip. Confidentially. Conspiratorially. It serves as a reminder. Of what can happen when secrets come to light. A shiver runs up her spine. An old-ghost shiver that has crossed the thousands of miles with her.

As the day begins to turn, leaving lean-to hugs are exchanged and air kisses are planted on a warm breeze. Teetering and still tittering women make their way out of the front door. Men pair up to form husband-wife duos that venture in slow parade to various vehicles. Top of the scale is Mercedes. Always Mercedes. Then BMW. Aneeta recognizes symbols upon the bonnets of some of the cars that fill the drive. No Ambassadors here. Nor Maruti. According to Dadi-ji, Europe makes the finest cars. One by one, automobiles come to life and manoeuvre down the street.

Aneeta watches the procession from the windows and begins to gather the remnants of the afternoon. With the last of the guests gone, Anju shuts the front door with a weary moan for effect. 'I tell you, these parties, they are so, so much.' She raises a fleshy arm and gingerly probes her yet crisp hairline. 'Too much, I think. You don't mind, do you?' It is not meant as a question. And so there is no need for an answer. Only for doing. With a final sigh for emphasis her mother-in-law turns and walks away, leaving Aneeta to the trifle of tea things—a graveyard of empty cups and soiled plates; scattered golden crumbs and swipes of chutney; paper napkins and crumpled bits of sugary foil.

'I want to go back to school.' It is a missile. Fired without warning from Samar's glassy red lips. Lips that are used to making demands. Lips that are used to getting what they want. Her words shatter the peace of those already seated for dinner.

Aneeta nearly drops the pot she is carrying. In surprise. At the lack of warning. And the sharpness of Samar's statement. She can see she is not the only one caught off guard. She places the heavy pot, with hot mat underneath, onto the table, easing it to the middle. A mild curry, very hot. But only temperature-wise. Hot yet mild, the way Samar likes it. Everything the way Samar likes. She tries not to look. Does not raise her eyes.

Anju's shrill erupts like a siren wail. 'What? What do you mean you want to go back to school?'

Aneeta lays the spoon on a towel beside the pot and silently backs away.

'I *mean* I want to go back to school.'

'What school? Where? Why?' Anju screeches in the way of a threatened parakeet.

Narinder holds his glass at his lips to shadow, for just a moment, the grim expression on his face. Then he takes a long draw of rum and Coke.

'Whatever for?' roars Dadi-ji. Samar squares up on her chair. She is clearly, by the set of her hard facial expression and defiant reddened pout, ready for whatever attack the idea may be due to bring.

Looking around at them like this makes Aneeta want to laugh. The groping, futile sputtering of the parents looking for some raft of logic to cling to, the spoiled child tantrumming her way toward what she wants. She feels sorry for Narinder, who obviously does not want to be caught in the middle of the upset.

And then Jovin is throwing himself suddenly into the ring. 'Mom, take it easy. Let's try to be calm about this. Take it easy.'

'How can I take it easy? Hunh? Crazy, this girl is. Crazy!'

Aneeta watches and listens while her husband tries to ingratiate himself with both sides, 'I know, I know. It's a surprise...to you.' Just the slightest pause. One that would hardly be noticed if one weren't listening carefully. One hardly obvious at all in the noise of the upset. Then a smile. 'But you can't tell me that it's beyond the realm of possibility. I can see why she wants to do it. Samar's a smart girl. Don't be so quick to judge. Hear her out.'

'How? How can she do this to us, I ask you?' With a practised look of anguish Anju widens her eyes woefully.

'It's not about you,' Samar rails back. The vehemence of her tone makes Aneeta cringe. 'It's about me. Me! And I want this for me.' It is clear that Samar does not care a whit about the hornet's nest she has stirred.

145

'Selfish girl! Bone selfish,' Anju caws. 'Only ever thinking of herself. Narinder, what have you to say about this crazy girl? She is your wife. Can't you have some control? Tell her how she should behave.' Beside her Dadi-ji is waggling his head in disbelief. His face is raked with redness and Aneeta can see a stand-out vein pulsing doubletime where his neck meets the collar of his shirt.

She marvels at Jovin—in one breath appeasing his parents, in another acting as ally to Samar. Samar looks quite at ease in the midst of the chaos. Every now and again as they rally, Jovin reaches to give Samar's hand a touch with the tips of his fingers, very lightly, quickly. Narinder has not reached for his wife once. Nor spoken in defence of her. There is no touch between them. Not even a look. He seems an island unto himself in the midst of the mutiny.

'My husband supports me in this.' It is Samar's first mention of him. A triumphant, scorning claim. Now he has no choice. But to make his opinion known.

'Please, Narinder,' Anju begs. 'Please tell me that you don't agree with,' pointing an accusatory finger in Samar's direction, 'her foolishness. Son, please! Arre, please!'

'What do you want me to say? She's my wife. I want her to be happy.' He sighs. 'I want you to be happy too. But if this is what she wants right now, then so be it. What kind of life would we have, Samar and I, if I don't also take her into account? You knew, Mom, that she wasn't the kind of girl who was going to settle down and have babies overnight. So kids, grandkids, will have to wait a little longer. I'd rather she was ready before we start a family. That she doesn't do it just to satisfy you and then decide the timing was wrong and be miserable about it.'

Anju's attempts at pleading are becoming strained, anger again seeps through her thinning beggar's cloak. 'But that's why you get married. To have babies. Getting married means the selfishness has to be left behind. She doesn't need more letters beside a name to have babies. There is no sense in it.' Anju sulks like a spoiled child. 'How much longer, I ask you, are you going to make fools of us? A shameful mockery. We can barely show our faces. People talk about us, you know. What is the matter with Anju's daughter-in-law? Saying horrible things! Hai, can you live with that?'

'I have the right to decide when I'm going to have babies. It's not some communal decision that you have any say in. It's my body, it's my choice, so you had better get used to it.'

'Hai! This girl!'

'Son, talk sense to your wife.' Dadi will not look at Samar. His tone shakes with anger. 'She has a Bachelor degree, okay. With us that was okay. Now she needs to be a wife. To be respectable. It is your duty, to your mother and I. We have been patient. But this? You can't expect us to be agreeable about this, Narinder.'

Though it is clear she will not win the battle today, Anju dives back in, 'Already Gurjit flaunts her little grandson in my face and Pinkie, her daughter-in-law is having twins. Twins, imagine that. Why am I being cursed, I ask you?'

Samar rallies, 'Oh stop with the melodrama, will you? Make Miss

Fresh-Out-Of-The-Village have your grandbabies! Isn't that what she's been raised for? Isn't that why you brought her here? Because you wanted *traditional*?' Roughly, Samar stands. She has had her say. And her husband has agreed. What better way to keep hold of the upper hand in things than to walk away leaving a stunned Anju with her jaw on the ground and Dadi-ji ranting to no one in particular about sacrifice and the dictates of history. Like kindling wood upon a kerosene fire it has flared predictably. What is left will smolder weakly; eventually the flame will die out, and with it, their opposition.

Narinder's head is in his hands. The glass in front of him is empty. She watches Jovin rise and follow Samar's path to the hallway. Dinner sits in its place on the table, long since forgotten.

It is the first thing she presses him on. In the aftermath of Samar's scene. And she harnesses Dadi-ji's displeasure in her attempts to persuade him. Harnesses it and uses it. 'I need to drive. Even your father says so. To get the shopping and to do other errands, to help. To drive is the only way. Teach me.'

He begins taking her out in the little silver car that doesn't see much use. A Corolla, it is called. Not all of the time is spent on instruction. In truth, not much of the time is spent on it. But in her mind gain outweighs loss, as long as some, any, attention is given to driving. Sometimes, when the little car is at rest, his hands will work their way under her kameez. Once the waist on her trousers is loose he shoves her panties to the side. Her memory burns when he is doing things like Dev Uncle used to. Sometimes she will hear him, Dev, laughing cruelly in her head. It seems another life. And yet, somehow still too close.

She lets him do what he wants. In the interest of getting what she wants. And so she allows him to flip her over, yank at her limbs, reposition her to his liking, or back her up on the steering wheel, after which there is a trail of half-moon marks from her backside up her spine. Sometimes she is able to stare out the window at whatever scenery might be in front of her and forget the moment. Dissolve it. In her mind take a trip to the imaginary hill station of long ago.

Other times he will shove her face into his lap. He will pull her head back and forth until the taste of him swims in her and makes her eyes water.

After, he adjusts his Calvin Klein briefs. He lets the elastic snap around his waist and attends to refastening his pants. She tries to convince herself that she is inching closer to her goal. But she finds herself wondering if it will take an eternity for her to achieve it.

When Dadi-ji suggests after several months that they arrange for her road test, she panics. 'I still don't feel quite ready, ji.'

'What do you mean, you don't feel ready?' An embarrassed flush creeps up her neck and spreads through her face. 'Are you so simple, girl, that it takes so long?'

'We haven't tried driving in traffic yet.'

'Not even in the traffic? Not even in traffic!' he bellows, 'Where the hell, girl, have you been having lessons if not in traffic?'

'Jovin takes me to the parking lot at the mall. I drive in the parking lot.'

'Where is the sense in that?' he slaps his hand irritatedly on his thigh and raises a flat palm in question, with his head echoing disbelief in a back and forth wag.

When Jovin returns from work Dadi blusters, 'Why is it, Jovin, that the girl is not able to drive?'

'Don't know, Dad, she's a bit of a slow learner, what can I say?' With a half chuckle and shrug he gives Aneeta a private wink. 'What can you do?'

'Take her more!'

She smoothes at invisible wrinkles in her kameez and picks absently at the soils of meal preparations. She does her best to ignore the hurt that gnaws at her.

'Busy man, Dad. Can't really spend more time. She'll get there eventually. Just not yet.'

'A simpleton. With the look of an angel. But what good?'

'Ji, it'll come.'

'Her mother said she was smart—pah! To do what? Count the grains in a pot of rice?'

In a marriage are they not supposed to stand together for one another? Unlike the defence he had mounted for Samar's return to school, this time he offers nothing to counter Dadi-ji's comments.

It is the very next day that Anju asks for Maria to fetch Raoul. Aneeta is sorting through baskets of clothing for washing. The window is open. Words are carried to her on the warming air of the mid-morning.

'Señora?' Maria asks.

'I want Raoul to give Aneeta some lessons on how to drive. Please. I wish to talk to him.' Aneeta hears the exchange as it floats downwind to her. The skin at the back of her neck pricks in a rise of leftover embarrassment.

Anju uses Maria as interpreter, speaking through her. Anju says her words slowly, loudly. In the same way as Dadi used to with her, in the early days. Maria translates the words into Spanish, but it is an unnecessary step since Raoul understands and speaks English as well as any of them. 'My boy is too busy with his work to teach the girl such a simple thing. She has led a charmed existence, left to the service of a chauffeur driven car. We need her to help with marketing and other errands, but for this she needs a driving license. Will you do it?'

Raoul does not hesitate. He gives his answer to Anju in English. 'Yes, Señora, I can do this.' There is a flood of relief through Aneeta. And gratitude. At not to having to continue the charade with Jovin.

'But please,' Anju turns to Maria, 'tell him I don't want the time he is spending with Aneeta taking away from his work. Comprendez? She is the least important of his tasks. Yes?'

'Yes, Señora.'

'We have the Corolla, but to me it is preferable...'

Raoul teaches her to drive in his small, battered, once-white Mazda pick-up truck with its cracked, brown bench seat. Tufts of blackened foam leach out in pinches from between vinyl teeth. A small crucifix dangles from the black pole of the windshield mirror. Aneeta feels comforted by its presence. She remembers the hushed chorus of voices in the school chapel: *Blessed Mary, Mother of God. In the name of the Father, the Son and the Holy Spirit.* She is looking intently at it as Raoul climbs in the other side. He rolls the window down and rests his elbow on the ledge it leaves. He looks at her, nods his head two or three times and smiles. 'You can start,' he says. She feels a flutter in her stomach. She reaches for where the key rests in the ignition. With a flush of courage she turns it heartily. The motor grabs and sparks to life. The truck lurches forward throwing her to the edge of the slippery bench and catching Raoul by surprise. He slaps his thigh and starts to laugh. While she struggles to overcome her shock, he turns to her and with mirth in his creased eyes he says, 'Manual, manu-al!' Then he points to the pedals at her feet. Of the one on the far left he says, 'Manual. Not automatic. Clutch pedal must be used too. Push. Push down. All the way. Hold. Now… ' With his hand twisting in mid-air he motions for her to turn the key once again. This time the engine sputters to life and stays running.

He takes her at his lunch break. After he has, in a few hurried moments, swallowed what Maria has brought for him, he comes to the back door. Where she is waiting. Maria smiles and shoos her from the house. In her rhythmic, accented English she says to them, 'It is a good thing. Good. Go.'

Once Aneeta gets the feel of how clutch, gas and brake work together, the way her feet must smoothly meet in opposing motion, she is on her way. It is harder than driving the Corolla because of this difference.

He first drives her to a stretch of unused road that is lined with wire fence some distance from the house. She practises the length again and again. She works the truck through its gears at varying speeds until the motion is smooth. Until the shift motions become instinctive. Until she can hear the need expressed by the revving of the engine. She learns to use her mirrors, to shoulder check, to drive in reverse. He brings a ladder and garbage can for her to learn how to park. She loses count of how many times she clips the ladder and knocks the can down. From his vantage alongside the truck he slaps his thigh and laughs. Sometimes she cannot help herself and laughs along with him. It feels good to laugh, to feel the belly open with it. She stops once or twice to touch the smile that lights her lips.

Eventually, her parking improves. Each time, Raoul places the obstacles that define the parking space closer and closer together. He makes her get out to look at the result of her efforts. Sometimes she is crooked. Sometimes too far from where he has placed the imaginary curb. Sometimes it takes her so many tries to get the truck angled right that her arms ache afterward.

One day he simply begins to clap. She can see him in her rearview mirror.

He is clapping his hands and nodding approvingly. Raoul tells her she is a good student. Her cheeks flush.

He takes her into a sleepy community of modest houses with wide tree-lined streets. He gets out and walks to the passenger side of the truck to allow her to move over and take the wheel. Her fingertips are cold and her palms sweaty that first day upon a traveled roadway; her pulse is loud inside of her head. He looks at her and smiles, 'Okay, now you.' He points at the wheel. He issues directives with his arms, turn to the right, turn to the left, straight ahead.

He saves the freeway for last. Red light, green light. Merge. Traffic seems to be whizzing by, cutting in and out on a demonic course. The first time, they stay on for only two exits, then get off and drive the surface street network to get back to the house.

When he finally tells her she is ready for her road test she is sad. Sad that the lessons are at an end. That the time they spend together has to end. He puts his arm around her and gives her a little squeeze. Maria hugs her. They both wish her *felicitaciones*. Maria claps her hands lightly as Raoul grins.

She finds white footprint outlines that toe slightly in on nubby flooring. A bland, bored voice speaks: 'Looking this way.' She raises her head and straightens herself. 'Eyes on the star.' The bored voice belongs to a round, ginger-haired woman in a tight blue t-shirt with lacquered pink nails. There is a seconds-long whirring followed by a click. 'This way, please.' She walks forward to the counter where the woman is gripping a biro pen the way one might a walking stick and busily writing upon a grid-like form. Aneeta scans the room and manages to spy Raoul, his back against the wall. He is watching her. He raises his hand and smiles at her, his jubilation clearly evident in the way it lights his facial features. Her own smile widens.

'Weight?' The query catapults out at Aneeta.

'Oh. Uh. I?' When had she last been weighed? At school. Health class. Long ago. 'I suppose…about 9 stone.'

'Huh?' The woman looks up from her paperwork, confused.

'Well, it has been some time. I am not really certain. It may be more.'

'Look, honey, I don't care about your real weight, jus' give me somethin' makes sense to have on your license. In pounds. That how we all measure weight here.'

'But I…I'm not sure, I think—'

The woman interrupts with an impatient sigh, 'Okay, let's try this another way. How tall are ya?'

'I think around about five foot six when I was last measured. At school. But I am sure to be more now.' Frustration begins to thread through her. She should know these things about herself. How can she not?

'Honey? Hon? It ain't no exact science. I'm just gonna say from looking at you right here and now that you're five seven. K? Give or take. And with your build, though it's kinda hard to figure under all that fabric, your face and arms are quite thin, so we'll say you weigh…' she pauses to look at Aneeta appraisingly. 'Ladies usually like to cut five or so pounds, make 'em feel better about themselves, you know? I'm gonna put you at one-twenty. Nice round number, that is. We good with that?'

Aneeta swallows hard and watches the woman enter the figures on the form. 'Yes, I believe that…we are good.' She says the last part slowly, feeling decidedly American as she lets the words roll off her tongue.

'It'll just be a bit to process the license. See you passed on your first try. Wouldn't believe how many don't.'

Kameko
San Francisco
2002

On her wedding day she had worn *tsunokakushi* in the tradition of centuries of brides before, to hide her jealous horns and to show her wish to become a gentle and obedient wife. Of course, no bride on her wedding day thinks of the day that might cause the horns to quiver. It is laughed away, as so many superstitions often are.

It is not accepted for a wife to make demands of a husband regarding fidelity. She looks at the American Express statement, and then squints at the figures before her. She tries to fashion them into a more convenient explanation. Tries, but fails. 02/13 in the date column of the billing, an entry for Tiffany & Co. in the amount of 1,896 United States dollars. On the same day, a charge of $2,165 at a Fairmont Hotel, San Francisco. Some days after, an entry for Victoria's Secret and a purchase for $328.97. Certainly with a name like this it is unlikely to be a purchase for Shiro. Together the items amount to just less than a half million yen. The telltale signs mock her.

She goes to the kitchen, takes a slender glass and fills it with water. She takes tentative sips but cannot seem to dispel the tightness in her throat. She fills the kettle and puts it to boil for tea. Surely tea would help to calm her.

When the water is ready, she waits for the tea to brew; she stands by the floor to ceiling window, looking out into the town. Amid all the bustle and fervor she wonders how many rush to meet a lover, even at this time of the day. How many secretly indulge in pleasure beyond the bounds of a marriage.

It would have been harder for her to discover an affair simply from credit card statements in Japan. Hostesses, bars and clubs, brothels, all facets of the water trade, are camouflaged by legitimacy. It makes it easy to look away, especially for wives. To spare the embarrassment. Even when truth is thinly veiled. Deception is good form, after all. Good to keep *tatemae*. And good to keep the twitch of horns hidden.

Here she is, no different than Mother. It is a bitter pill to taste. She finds herself trembling at the memory of old resentments as she pours the tea and raises the cup to her lips. Unlike Mother, she does not wish to look away. And there is no consolation for her in sameness. In the numbers of wives or women also like her. That she tends toward the rule and not the exception. Whether she likes it or not, she has become one of them, the stereotype, the kind of wife she had once shunned. Akira's words haunt her. Lodging themselves in her heart like sharpened quills.

Since feudal times a mistress has been a sign of status. A measure of success. And when a wife happens upon such knowledge she is expected to keep her pleasant and pleasing mask in place. These are the dictates of history.

She thinks back to years before. Her choice to spare Mother upset; loss of face. To keep harmony within the family. How her *honne*, her true sentiments, she had kept locked up inside—the anger like a poison.

And now, the knowledge she has come upon winds its way acidly through a network of old channels. Eating away at her. When she closes her eyes she can see her husband. The images she summons are cruel. Punishing. Her heart tightens. Silent tears begin to flow. She sees Shiro laughing in the company of another woman, fixing her with some jewelry, some trinket, gently brushing his skin against the faceless object of his desire, his coy smile knowing what the gift might get him in return. She imagines rumpled sheets, the remains of hotel food, a pair of figures vaguely outlined against the cover of a steaming shower, familiar hands with their long tapered fingers stroking an expanse of flesh that is not hers. She shivers despite the hot tea and bites her lip to dispel the imagery, to hold back the rising sob.

She is reminded of *The Tale of Genji*, Murasaki Shikibu's ancient musings on life and especially on love. *When there are crises, incidents, a woman should try to overlook them. It is very foolish for a woman to let a little dalliance upset her so much that she shows resentment. A commotion means the end of everything. It may be difficult when someone you are especially fond of has been guilty of an indiscretion, but magnanimity produces wonders.* She imagines this to have been the way her mother had lived, in the face of her father's indiscretions, though the age-old advice turns in her like waves on a rough sea. She hardly feels capable of being such a woman. In fact, she does not want to be.

Mother's voice suddenly ribbons through her heartache: *Lift your chin, daughter, and hope that tomorrow will be a fine day. If not tomorrow, then surely one that follows. Look toward it. And the rest will fall behind, no more than a shadow at your back. A good wife does not yield to the trifles of emotion.* A good wife. Like Mother had been. One better than she.

Aneeta
Fresno, California
March 2002

The day had begun in its everyday way. Eggs had scrambled the same. The hush of unexceptional conversation was the stuff of most mornings. Of the Monday to Friday variety. It had become so she could almost sleepwalk through it from familiarity.

Dadi-ji and Anju are expected at a ceremony for a new house. Something new should also be blessed. Sanctioned. By God. Before relations and community. They ready themselves after the boys are gone and in leaving remind her of what needs doing, of the grocery list on the kitchen table.

For Anju the new house would invariably be too big, too small, no yard, too big yard, too fancy, too plain. 'You know, I would never say to their faces, but I guess if that is your taste and the way to live for them, then okay, it is a fine place.' Dadi-ji, as was his duty, obediently trailed after her. To one event or another.

It used to be that Aneeta would have to attend with her in-laws, but after what Anju considered an appropriate length of introductory show she was not always expected to. She imagines Anju's great pleasure at explaining her newest daughter-in-law's absence. With a tilt of the head and a lift to her chin. 'Should a new house, even though it is very lovely to see, also be an opportunity for my daughter-in-law to be lazy? She has much to do, I tell you. Not every day should be an occasion for a holiday, hunh?' Anju has excused her in favour of marketing today. For Aneeta it means the peace of some time on her own.

Her step is light under the warming morning sun as she leaves the empty house, carefully locks the door behind her, and slips into the driver's seat of the car. Her skin gives an involuntary shiver of thrill. She is managing the freeways and the grids of surface streets with increasing confidence. Her destinations are not many. And they are not far. Yet they seem a whole world away. The first several times Dadi had gone with her. Set himself beside her on the other side of the car and held tightly to the handle on the roof. But she has proven she is safe, and capable.

As she pulls into the parking lot she marvels at how very similar the shopping plaza looks to its Delhi twin. With the same types of goods and merchants, the same stuccoed walls. But without boxes and carts littering and spilling things into narrow side streets and lanes, without open gutters or rotting discards. Everything here appears just so. Together the various concessions seem a proud part of the whole, not at cross-purposes, fighting or wheedling for the attention of passersby.

Dadi had been glad to be able to take leave of the marketing duties, pleased that he finally does not have to leave the comforting drone of television soap operas or miss a moment of the tangled, oily, orange-tinged wranglings of his favourite wrestlers.

No longer the useless princess, she is at last fulfilling her role. Though the others view it as mundane, having to go out to the shops is a pleasant diversion for her. For the change of scenery and more so for the sense of independence she feels. It gives her a reason to put on one of her nicer salwar kameez suits, one of the ones not suitable for household chores. Maybe with a little embroidery or some detail, perhaps fashioned from a more delicate fabric. She takes some care with her preparations on market days, for no other reason than it pleases her, because she has somewhere to go.

She has found a set of glasses with large, darkened rounds in a thick-armed, black-lacquered frame that have been left in car. She has no idea who they belong to, but has put them on anyway to block the glare of sun while she is driving. Now, as she steps from the car into the crisp morning air, she pushes them up and into her hairline, so that they rest atop her head. In loose waves her usually braided chestnut hair cascades beyond her shoulders to her mid-back. She locks the car door and deposits the key in the pocket of her handbag. Smiling, she considers the low stretch of buildings.

The list had been prepared in advance of this morning, of course. Onions and coriander. Cloves and cinnamon. Mustard greens and spinach for saag. Cauliflower. Aubergine. Lentils for later in the week. Turmeric. Tomato for the curry; lamb pieces already defrosting in the fridge. Dadi had carefully calculated expected costings and given her an amount he considered sufficient. It is taking some getting used to, these American dollars. She is most probably regarded as simple when it comes to the slowness with which she deliberately thumbs through the softened bits of paper to count out payment. She isn't about to rush and make an error. Dadi has also warned her about muggings and American goonda thieves, telling her to keep tight hold of her purse and not to openly show her money. She wants to laugh. He must know that Delhi is far worse for such things.

Dadi-ji tells her often of the importance of budgeting and planning. The importance of thrift. She is unsure as to why he delivers her so many lectures on this cause. It seems to her that the boys must bring home a respectable living, but Dadi likes to remind that living ought to be kept simple. It is the desire of God, he says. She wonders to herself, permitting a small inward smile at the thought, if he ever speaks to Anju of living simply. Life on earth could become very uncomfortable, she imagines, if Anju's desires were to be left unsatisfied.

She goes about her business slowly, lingering perhaps longer than is necessary in this California blue-sky day. All at once something within her sticks sharply in her belly. Like a length of knitting needle. She feels a slice of hot pain. She gasps and clutches tightly at a splintered wooden edge of a bin piled high with potatoes. The pain defies breath. Her fingers whiten under the pressure of her grip. And then, just as quickly as it has come, it is gone. Exiled like an unwanted ghost. But for a tiny sliver of wood that rests in her index finger to remind her.

She tells herself that it is stomach upset. But the sudden onset of the episode has left her feeling slightly uneasy. She attends more efficiently to the last items on her shopping list and settles her purchases into the little car. She gives herself a look in the rearview mirror as she starts the motor and prepares to back out of the parking space. There is something wary in her eyes. Once again she slides the sunglasses down over them. Her stomach is tight. She decides she will make tea from saunf seeds when she returns to the house. To ease it. Most likely some indigestion, from last evening's meal, or too much spice in the eggs this morning.

Late morning traffic on the roads is light. It takes hardly a quarter of an hour to retrace the route. She eases up the drive and parks the little car tightly to one side. The garage is reserved for the newer Mercedes of the two and for Samar's convertible. From the back seat she collects the bulky brown bag. She will boil water for tea and heat some of last night's vegetable sabzi for her lunch. And let the tea steep as she eats. She cannot remember the last time she had felt her stomach so hollow. Perhaps it is the nature of the errands, or even simply the outing, the fresh air, that has ignited her desire to eat. Her mouth waters at the prospect. Maybe she will have time for a short nap after, before she starts the dinner.

The overfull bag makes passage awkward as she picks her way along the narrow side of the house to the door that leads from the laundry into the kitchen. She struggles to fit the key into the lock. It is a relief when the handle pops and she pushes through, the shopping clutched tightly to her.

If the image before her eyes had not presented itself she would hardly have considered it, it would not have seemed possible. Plausible. Likely. But it is not imagined; it is reality. Reality that is hideous and ugly. Magnified in her mind. So that it seems bigger than life itself. So that it assails her in gigantic, monstrous, consuming proportions. She hears every torturous layer of sound. And is overcome by a rush of nausea. The scent of flesh, of sweat, overpowers coriander and onion; it sours the sweet tropical scent of mango.

Time stalls. To let over-hungry senses adequately digest. Thighs and buttocks thrust. A tandem rhythm pounds the metal of the washing machine. Red-nailed fingers cut sharp edges into a bare-skinned back. It is a torso that is immediately familiar. Over one shoulder, a contorted face is paralyzed; glassy red lips wide, head thrown back, dark-lined eyes closed in ecstasy. 'Yes, yes, yes!' The voice is breathless, demanding, as it always is. Flesh slaps thickly, wantonly, against flesh. Beating out a tempo of syllables over a staccato landscape, 'Don't. Stop.' Then run together, 'Dontstop! Dontstop!' The grunts, the groans, the squeals. Of sex. Between a husband and sister-in-law.

Then the crash. The grocery bag slips from her grip and lands with a thud on the floor.

'Oh, shit. Shit!' Samar's voice rings out.

She hears her own shrieks. 'Dammit! Aneeta!' Him. Limbs frantically try to untangle themselves one from the other. And scramble for discarded clothing. 'Aneeta!'

'Ohmygod. Oh. My. God! You bastard! Bastard! Ohmygod, you! You!'

Screams mix with wild sobs. There is a mighty roar in her ears, and a sudden thickness of pins and needles in her head, her hands, racing down her torso toward the floor, where her feet are cemented. Frozen in place. Unable to move, or be moved.

'Stop screaming! The neighbours'll hear!' Hands roughly grab her shoulders. Shake her. Then harder. Shaking her into silence. 'It's not what it looks like. I can explain. Aneeta!'

But it is. Exactly what it looks like. Unavoidably what it looks like. There is no explanation that could possibly change it. It loops itself around and around her, pulling, tugging, lashing away at her, taunting her.

Dumbly, she stoops to collect fallen food from the floor. Trying to put it back into the bag. Trying to ignore the rest of the scene. Their filthy, empty words blend together above her like a two-headed serpent, forked tongues flicking at her. She does not notice that the bag has ripped in the commotion; when she lifts it up, all the retrieved items simply tumble out again. It is the rusky tan onion rolling to a stop at her toe that prompts her to tears. Tears of fury and frustration. She gives it a vicious kick that sends it clanging into the washing machine. She turns her back as they hurriedly dress. Layering piece upon piece. Bra. Briefs. Blouse. She leaves the morning's purchases to the floor and walks away. Like the brown paper of the grocery sack, she feels as if there has been a great hole torn in her.

When the vision comes back, as it does over and over again, her insides revolt. And cause her to be sick. So many times after. She expels the bile violently, without a care for who hears or what they might think. She flushes the toilet, wipes her face, not even offended that the sourness lingers in her mouth, in her throat.

'What is with Aneeta? Is she sick? She is looking weak. Feeble. Wrong with her…something is wrong. Find out, Jovin. See to your wife. Talk to her.'

Haunted and listless, she moves as a sleepwalker, hypnotized but for the fire that burns deep down in her gut. She feels it, persistently in her belly. Clenching and unclenching with unspent emotion.

She considers them a group of traitors. Who have all been a part of the betrayal. Because they are all part of the household, all part of the family. This was not a new happening. Not from the look of it. The way they seemed so familiar. Husband with sister-in-law. Right under their noses. They should have known. Or thought. Or seen something. She does not wish to answer their questions or to pretend. And she does not want to slip, to lose control of her tongue and speak something of it until she has decided the best way.

On the face of things she busies herself with the everyday, but finds it impossible to concentrate. She burns samosas, roti, papadums. She leaves the dahi out too long; it sours. She burns a hole in one of Dadi's kurta pyjamas while ironing. His wounded face almost moves her to tears. She bites her lip and turns away. She ignores Anju's admonishments.

She has taken to sleeping on the floor in their bedroom. She would rather the stiff back and sore legs. She does not want to let him touch her. He does not try to reason with her or coax her from her silence. That she hears him snoring above her in the darkness makes her blood boil. How can he sleep? With such a weight on his mind? Unless, for him, it is not the weight it is for her. She lies, unable to rest, twisted up and wide-eyed upon the unforgiving hardness.

She happens upon whispering now and again. Between the two of them. Whispers of speculation. For they know they are at her mercy. It is smeared all over their faces when they look at her. Guilt. Weakness. And fear. It is a strange feeling, knowing that it is her they are afraid of.

Kameko
San Francisco
March 2002

If she were American, an American woman with an American husband, she would probably confront Shiro. Since coming to San Francisco she has spent a good deal of time with the television on. From what she has seen on the daytime talk shows she has learned that Western women are not content to pretend like nothing is out of the ordinary if they feel wronged. On such programs women often take great pleasure in formally presenting a man with their knowledge of his lack of discretion. They hire investigators, throw punches, draw out their kitchen knives.

In a silent show of defiance she had left the statement on the countertop where Shiro would be sure to discover it. To make him aware that she knew. It was a bold challenge. A finger pointed. But he said nothing to her about it, made no mention of it in his coming and going. Concocted no story, offered no apology. Life, for him, seemed to continue on around it without missing a beat. She had let it stay there, as a reminder, until, after several weeks, she filed it away with the others. Into a neatly kept accordion file separating household bills by calendar month, the tab marked February destined to forever capture her attention each time she opened it up.

And yet, in spite of everything, she needs him. Perhaps more than ever. Getting pregnant, having his baby, this is what could revive their relationship. If, she thinks, she could just become pregnant.

Somewhere along the way she had gotten so melancholy about it all, that she'd lost sight of *them*. And really, with the mounting pressure, all her desperate intentions to make a family, hadn't she been partly to blame for turning him away? If she is honest with herself—if she considers that perhaps his infidelity stems from her moods, her frustrations, her selfishness. That his indiscretions are not the root cause of the difficulties between them, but merely a symptom.

Maybe she has taken more exception than necessary. Maybe, it occurs to her, finding out was intentional on his part. He is a smart man. If he wanted to deceive her why would he have let an affair be so obvious? There are ways of hiding the kinds of things that one wants to keep hidden, especially from a spouse. Maybe, just maybe, her discovery has marked a turning point in their relationship.

She has neglected him. That is the reality, the truth. Mired in her own pity she has forgotten childlessness is a hardship that, in fact, affects them both. That they share. One that she cannot change without him. The cycle of hard and tender feelings that have flooded her spirit open her to this realization, and to an acceptance of her part in the matter. It has not been Shiro's doing alone. In some way she is the more at fault *because* of her single-mindedness. Almost as if she has pushed him to it.

Life is not meant to be simple. This is a humbling lesson. *Nanakorobi yaoki*. Stumbling seven times, but recovering eight. So they have stumbled. It isn't unusual. Not at all. Now she must persevere. Not let these early problems defeat her, or them.

But unlike Mother's comfort in her lukewarm water situation, her placid acceptance of circumstance, Kameko resolves to fight for her marriage. She will fight against being the stereotype that Akira had so scorned.

For the first time she is opening her mind in little steps to liking America, for all its foreign attitudes and differences. It can help her. To become a more assertive woman—in a way that is considered acceptable, even desirable. What she needs is to come out of her little girl tortoise shell and ease herself into the life she has been resisting. 'Like a princess locked away in her tower,' Shiro had joked. 'You need to go out, do things, meet people. I can get the phone numbers for some of the other wives. You could get to know them.'

She might have. Until the pregnancy difficulties had come to light. Then she didn't want to deal with it, the curiosities, the questions, and most of all, the babies most of these women were likely to have.

She has let desperation reduce her to a one-dimensional sort of being, one who does not exist outside of him. This is what she must change. To bring him back. She had been an independent woman once. That was the girl he had married. Once upon a time. After stumbling she must only get up and try again.

She kneels at the low table to serve the slender slices of marinated beef. With her eyes concentrated upon her task, she sets the cart wheels into motion. 'I'd like to get a job.' He just about chokes on his mouthful. She bites her lip to keep him from seeing her slight pull of a smile.

'What?'

'I said I'd like to get a job. You've been telling me to get out and do things. I'd like to see about getting a job.'

'You would?' He sounds dubious.

'I would.' She tries to maintain the serious tone of conviction in her voice, even though she wants to laugh out loud at his surprise. She has caught him entirely off-guard. A perfect point of strategy. She only wishes she'd had the sense to employ it sooner. 'I think it might help me. With fitting in here. I mean, social engagements can only go so far. And I don't feel entirely comfortable with…' shame takes over, her eyes cast downward, her voice drops to the pitch of rustling reeds, 'our…difficulties to become pregnant.' She tries for some depth to her argument, a collaborative play, 'Even the doctor has suggested a hobby. Or something.' The end of the statement rises up, sounding like a question, which is to say that it is perhaps not as strong or forthright as she has intended.

'You shouldn't be so uptight about that.' He scolds her for her weakness.

'How can I not be?' her voice jumps in octaves. She clears her throat and moves several of the platters, an attempt at distraction. It is an insult, his comment. Perhaps unintentional, but it stings, like a slap against bare skin. She changes direction. 'At least in a job, I am with people who don't know me. Don't know...' She swallows hard. 'I think this way it might be simpler. Can you understand? For me?'

'Okay, okay. I won't argue.'

'So then you are okay with it?'

'So long as it does not interfere.'

'Really?'

'Really.'

'I understand...and...I thank you, for giving me this chance.'

It is Maria who finds her, sitting in a pool of her own blood, shaken and faint. 'Madre de Dios! Señora! Mrs.! Mrs.! Come quickly! Come!' The voice rises up and out. Reaching.

'Aneeta! Aneeta!' Maria takes her gently by the shoulders. 'Aneeta! What is happening? What is wrong?' She folds Aneeta's listless hands into her own, pressing their coldness to her own chest. Aneeta can feel Maria's heart beating through her thin cotton dress.

'Oh my God, Aneeta! Ji!' the voice comes out in a siren wail that brings him to the door where the two women fuss around her. She looks over to the doorway helplessly, unable to make herself move. She hears him, sees him stop short.

'Oh my God!' his head is shaking in dismay. She wonders if his words of despair are for her or the mat she has soiled where she sits. He quietly turns himself away, his obvious discomfort with the scene before him evident in the motion. The bottom of her suit is heaped on the floor. The tunic barely covering her undergarments. She hasn't the strength or inclination for modesty. She is lifeless, frozen. Her mouth is wide in shock. She cannot speak. Every now and then there is a gush from between her thighs. Like a water pump flushing. But unlike water that cools, the feeling that comes out of her is hot and sticky. She squeezes her knees tightly together, willing it to stop. It is too late. She is too late. Droplets of blood mark a trail to where she rests, and beneath her a halo of rust spreads slowly outward along the wick-like fibers of the mat.

'Emergency call, karo! Find out what we should do. Hurry, ji!' Her mother-in-law's sound is distant and grainy.

Maria holds her and rocks her, speaking gently to her in Spanish. What she is saying Aneeta does not know, but it blooms into the emptiness.

She hears words in the distance. Explaining. 'Girl is bleeding …daughter-in-law…bleeding badly, badly…between legs…okay-okay…thank you…' The duration of the conversation is brief. He returns to the doorway. 'She needs to be taken to hospital. To see that everything is okay with her.'

Everything is not okay, she thinks dully. My baby is not okay. My baby. Is gone. What is left of him or her, this child, is only enough to stain my fingers; a sticky coating of a life lost.

'Hunh, like this?' Anju protests. 'So much blood. How will we? In the car?'

'Raoul,' Maria says. She is holding Aneeta in her arms, like a baby, a child, and rocking with her. 'He will take her. In the truck.'

'Ji, get a blanket. Call Raoul in the yard. Tell him to bring the truck to the side door. Tell him take her to Regional Medical Center. Give him some directions. Tell him we will meet him there.'

Her body is shaking and convulsing, in rhythms beyond her control. Hot blankets are being piled on top of her in layers. Her limbs continue to twitch and jerk under the increasing heaviness. It is as if she has been possessed by an angry demon. Her jaws are clenched tight, tight, so tight. She tries to still her arms by wrapping her fingers around the metal side rods of the hospital gurney.

There are voices everywhere, though she sees only the grid of eerie lights above. Some she knows. Anju, always Anju, a pitch to sit upon others. Dadi is sounding disoriented, fuzzy, asking about parking. There are calming voices between. She cannot make herself turn left or right to look. The gurney is stopped, then pushed forth and back a small amount in adjustment. After a short time it moves forward again, through a doorway and towards a brightness, like the sun shining. Suddenly she longs for the heat of sun upon her skin. Yearns for it. The Delhi sun. It could warm her in an instant. She thinks of the baby then, her baby. Playing with her child in the sun. The things they would do, the things she would teach, how they would wrap themselves in each other…All now lost in a swell of blood. She should have stopped it. Should have known. How could she have not? How simpleminded. She wants to scream. Sound scrapes like broken glass inside her throat. She hears nothing but a grunt coming out of her in response. Eyes blur.

'How far along?…Estimate the pregnancy…eight or ninth week…First pregnancy?…Spontaneous…miscarriage…Going to have to do a D and C… clean the womb…stop further bleeding…she's lost a lot….shock…going to start a drip…saline…and antibiotics…to prevent chance of infection…She'll stay the night… stabilizes…home…bed rest.'

Her fingers are peeled away from the bars they cling to beneath the blankets. A soothing voice calls her by name, 'Aneeta.' A statement. A face leans over her, gently smiling. Fair skin, green eyes. *Gori.* 'I'm just going to put this needle into the back of your hand. So that we can attach a drip. With some saline solution. To replenish some of what you've lost. You'll feel a little pinch now and a bit of a burn.' It does not matter, she doesn't care. She wants to say *Don't bother.* The sharpness happens before she can. 'Okay?' She makes no attempt to answer. She hears other voices now, in a ring around where she is lying. All are unfamiliar. The things they are saying she does not fully understand; they talk over one another with efficient quickness. Her other hand emerges then, fingers curled and stiff. 'Antibiotic.' Words drift over her, making little sense. She knows their talk concerns her. She doesn't want to think of it. She simply wants to die. Wants to be at peace. Her limbs have slowly begun to settle. Her jaw is loosening from its paralyzed clench. She is tired. So tired. She closes her eyes and drifts away.

She sees her father. She wants to cry out with joy, with sadness, with fury. He is smiling at her. He seems so far from her. She tries to reach out to him, but he is too far. Too far away. She can't move. 'Papa!' she calls to him in her dream. Then he is gone. She opens her eyes. Anju is standing over her.

'Why didn't you tell us?' her mother-in-law asks.

Her voice is barely a whisper in return, 'I didn't know.'

'How could you not know? Aneeta! How?'

'I didn't think,' no, that wasn't right, she corrects, 'didn't notice.' For how long there had been no bleeding. No monthlies.

'How can you not notice these things?' Anju demands. 'Were you sick at all?'

'Yes. Some. Sometimes. But,' she hesitates, she relives the retching she thought was coming for such a different reason. Now is not the time for telling it. 'I never…' she lets her voice trail off. There is nothing to say. Her throat is tight. She feels puffy, like a bloated sponge; she turns her head to look at the thick needles wedged under tape into her hands. Her eyes blur again, blinding her. Fierce, hot tears roll down the sides of her face.

'Okay, okay. You have given some scare. To us all. Such silliness! You should have known and you should have told, then maybe this wouldn't have happened, hunh?' A pause. Anju looks away. 'Dadi has gone back to the house. Before the traffic. He is embarrassed about women's things. Even though his grandchild was lost today. It is hard for him. Jovin is coming. He is on the way now. He will take me with him after.' She adds, 'He is very upset. Very upset at the news. Of course. But what can you do?' Anju sighs, a great heavy exhale. 'What can you do? Poor boy. Hai!' Her tone is one of exasperation. Aneeta does not wish to see her husband. He is last person whose face she wants over her. Though she knows it is an inescapable eventuality.

There is scraping and banging to mark his arrival. The rising whine of Anju's voice, then the harsh cadence of him. The exchange between mother and son is strained, rising to crescendo. His rebuke. A dismissal. Her final whimper and then silence. Anju leaves the room in dramatic atypical concession. Aneeta half expects her mother-in-law will have an ear pressed hard to the door.

Jovin moves across the room, stands with his back to her, looking out the window as day leaks out of the sky. His hands, curled into fists, bulge where they are jammed into trouser pockets. For a time there is only silence between them. Then he turns heavily and walks in sharp staccato over to her bedside. 'If I had known, if you would have told me…' his tone is low and accusing, 'things would have been different.'

Fury, like the spreading of a wildfire, consumes her. A swell of hatred engulfs her heart. For his self-righteousness. For the way he makes the fault her own. The skinny steel tower that suspends the bags of liquid that drip slowly into her cuts him in half where he stands. Into two angry slices. Half on either side of the pole. She concentrates on the silver, letting her eyes travel up to where the emptying plastic pouches hang. The images of his two sides blur. There is nothing, nothing left. Nothing salvageable. In silence she turns herself away, her face to the wall. She stuffs a handful of twisted sheet into her mouth. And bites down to control her tongue. He lingers for only a moment more.

She blames him for her loss. And Samar. She is sure they are the reason why. Why her body could not support the life of this child. To her mind, the sacrifice it has forced is unforgivable.

She does not want to go home. It is not that she likes the hospital, but more a matter that she is unsure just how she might feel. Back in that place. The way being in the house might refresh memories kept at a distance in the unfamiliar hospital setting.

Dadi-ji comes to collect her in the Corolla. Thick blankets are spread along the back seat. He has protected the upholstery. In case she should soil it. 'Mummi-ji has stayed back to make things ready for you at home.' She hears discomfort tremoring in his voice. Perhaps he says it to excuse the obvious absence. Perhaps it is an offering for the young man in the blue pajama outfit whose hands have pushed her wheelchair to the curb. She stands and, trying not to let the overtaking sense of shame prompt an unsteady flush of tears, moves wordlessly toward the open door of the back seat. 'Take care,' the young man calls after her. She hasn't the voice to answer.

When he pulls into the drive, he gives a short signal from the horn that brings Anju from the house. Anju opens the car door while he stands silently by. In the background. She leans only a little bit onto the arm her mother-in-law has offered her. Only as much as she must. Slowly but solidly she shuffles her way across the threshold. The same threshold that not so long ago admitted her as a new bride, one with hope and good thoughts for the future. What a fool she had been.

'I have moved some things for now into the guest room. So you can rest, as doctor has said, so you will not be disturbed.' Anju walks with her down the hallway and steps to one side at the doorway of the room. At the bedside a plastic pitcher filled with brightly coloured flowers beckons. 'From Maria,' Anju offers, when she notes Aneeta's gaze on them.

The baby is lost. That is what matters to them, the family. The baby only. She is cause only for the brisk chukking of tongues, the shaking of heads. A showy film of pity thinly covers irritated annoyance. *Foolish girl. How can she not have known? She must have known.* She is ushered over to the open bed. She lets herself be eased into it. The window admits a wisp of air. She is left alone. Tears soak into the pillow. She holds the sound of sobs inside. The effort wracks her weary body. Eventually, she loses herself to the thick drag of sleep.

When she wakes, light has shifted in the room. Her abdomen is tender, distended, with an overfull bladder that presses itself on that part of her that ought yet to be filled. She forces herself to the bathroom, now and then reaching her hand out for the wall to support her motion. At the door she stops to look carefully, timidly, into the room. For some sign. An image of death. Marking the space. There is nothing. Tiles have been scrubbed clean. There is a different mat. Not a sign remains. Of her baby. Her throat knots. She sucks a breath behind the hand she clamps to her mouth.

Sometimes things happen for a reason. And sometimes it is the reason that prompts things to happen.

Daylight is fading. The sounds of the household are coming to life now with preparations for the evening meal. She has heard the purr of motors climbing the drive, the sure suction of air with the opening and closing of outside doors. Low voices murmur within the house. She does not wish to see them, but she knows they will be forced to make a trip to the room where she lies. When she hears them coming she feigns sleep. She does not wish to indulge their empty pleasantries. Footsteps soon retreat.

She exists somewhere beneath a tight, dark skin of grief. Lying dormant in the narrow fix of the bed, she looks blindly out the window instead of at the mirrored sliding cupboard door. She cannot face her reflection; the sadness, the loneliness, the condemnation she is sure she would find there. She blames herself for seeing them, the lovers. For letting it affect her so deeply. And she blames herself for not paying more attention to the signals her body was sending; the sense of fullness in her belly, the nausea, the sick. Signs she ignored, that she attributed so easily to other things.

Anju comes and goes, marking her entries with a bluster of busy chatter. False cheer and enthusiasm for things Aneeta does not care about, excepting the unusual pleasantness with which she is being treated. Anju brings *panjiri* to build her strength. But *panjiri* is meant to be eaten by those who have given birth. To healthy, live and squalling newborns. After nine months. Not nine weeks. Not like her. 'It is for your blood,' Anju tells her. 'You need your strength back. You must be sensible. There will be another baby. Next time you will take care. Extra care. And we must know. You will tell us. Next time.' Anju watches closely as Aneeta feebly forces little bits past her lips, even though she has no appetite. 'I have talked to an astrologer. When you are feeling better we will see him. He will read the charts and tell us, so we can know when is the most auspicious time. For a baby.' But Aneeta cannot bear the thought of it, any of it.

Gregory
Garden State Correctional Facility
April 2002

She's hot; feverish. Sticky under the arms. She is walking. She can't believe it. Walking away. Out of here. Goodbye, Garden State. Her heart is hammering. Disbelief is dragging at her. Keeping her from bolting like some crazed lunatic streaking for the last slip of a disappearing mirage. She's trying for normal, calm. She needs to keep a lid on things. Till she's past the perimeter.

The guard leads the way. Out the front doors of the institution and toward the main gate she urges her feet, legs, her whole damn body. Aware that the eyes of the two towers at the front perimeter are on her. Watching. She sounds like a dog panting shallow in the heat. God help her, she never thought she'd be such a basketcase. She fixes her eyes straight ahead. There's prison noises coming from the yard and other buildings that flank her path. Somewhere out back there's the sound of voices, talking, mingled with shouts and high-pitched laughter. It floats to her on the thin breeze. Her mind is numb; her mouth is cotton dry. She feels like at any moment the PA will come on and they'll tell her this is all a joke. A big joke. The cruelest joke. The board has reviewed her file and there's been a mistake. That she's not actually due for release. 'Come back inside, Abbott. You've got time to serve yet.' A panicky rhythm beats through her.

In zippered canvas she carries her journals and release paperwork; GED certificate and snapshots; a scrap of paper with Claire's number; a bus ticket and an address. The ticket will take her from the middle of nowhere to the middle of everything. Back to the world, to civilization. After four years, eight months and twenty-four days. Time enough to forget what living free feels like. Before bars and fences and wire and locks.

She is even with the tower. Above her a guard walks to the side opening and salutes. His other hand is still on his rifle. She feels moisture beading along her hairline. Her heart is pounding so high in her throat she wants to gag. The guard who has led her out works the mechanism and the gate with an easy and unhurried familiarity. He pulls the heavy metal to one side. Making an opening of not more than several feet across. Enough to let her face it forward. To take freedom head on. 'Good luck,' he says to her. It seems as if she should say something, but her brain and voice refuse to cooperate.

There's no one for her at the other side. She's told Lil not to come. Not to make the long drive. She's got conditions. Has to check in. That's what she keeps telling herself. Deep down she's not sure she's ready to be with them. One thing at a time. This part she feels she has to do on her own. As if her doing it, making it, will prove to her that she can.

Once, just once, about a hundred paces out, she stops, turns her back on freedom and regards the place one final time from where she stands. She lifts her hand to her eyes to shield them from sun. The landscape blurs and blends with the rippling of the heat rising from the pavement, warping her view of what she's left. Rising above the low-slung collection of bricked-up boxes she sees the white wooden cross that marks the tiny chapel. The razor-wire has gone invisible against the blue, almost like it's not there. Something in her wants to laugh. She turns and begins walking again, letting a long slow exhale. She's done. Paid up. She owes nothing.

The group home is called Larkin House. It's three stories, the top floor under sharp peaks. The street's lined in leafy trees and other houses just like it, but in a rainbow of different colours and detail. She climbs a run of wide stairs to the porch and the broad wood-grained front door. Even though the address is a match, she's shit-scared that she's wrong. That police'll be called and in less than twenty-four hours she'll get her ass shipped back. She can't bring herself to move. She can't do anything but stand, like a wooden soldier, in front of the door. *Get it together! You have to do this!* She's tempted to run like hell when a warm light snaps on over her. But it's like she's crazy-glued to the spot. She hears a gentle slap-slap padding of footsteps on the other side of the door. What's the worst that can happen, really? *Excuse me, I'm new to the city, trying to find the halfway house for recently released ladies of Cal State?* The panic about being discovered out on the porch, just standing and doing nothing, prompts her to punch the buzzer. Better to face it, play it as it comes.

The door opens on a smiling young black woman in denim and a faded blue t-shirt that reads in red letters: *Nobody knows I'm ELVIS*. She puts out a hand. 'Gregory, I'm Linda, the coordinator,' she says. 'Glad you made it. Come on in.' She's got the right goddamn place.

Next morning, she calls. She twists the corkscrew curls of the cord around and through her fingers. 'Thank you for using AT&T. I'll connect you now.'

As the electronic ping dies away, Lil's 'Gregory?' brings her back around.

'Sorry I didn't get a chance to call before now.'

'Why're we starting with apologies? We knew you'd call soon as you could.' But she can tell by Lil's tone that they've been waiting on her.

'Day was so long. It was late by the time I got here, to the house.'

'Can imagine. And how about you? How *are* you? After all of it.'

'Just about coping. Seems harder, coming back.' She tries to laugh.

'You'll get on. I know you will.'

'Wish I could be so sure.'

'Gregory Abbott, you listen to me—you pack up all those misgivings, you pack them up and you throw them away. Where's all that piss and determination?

Settle down and get focused on starting a new life. You've got absolutely nothing stopping you. Future's yours for the making. That's all I'm gonna say on the matter. I've got your Mama standing right here. Giving me the eye. We're here for you, Gregory. Any time you need. Any time at all. You just pick up the phone.'

'I will.'

'Promise me.'

'Promise.'

'I really do mean it.'

'I know.'

Then the breathy sound of Mama's voice is on the line. 'Gregory! You're okay? Place you're in, it's okay? Safe?'

She doesn't have the heart to tell Mama it's nicer than most of the places they've lived. A good bet it's safer around here too.

'We just needed to hear your voice. Just needed to know you were okay. To hear you had made it.'

'I'm okay. I'm good. Don't worry.'

'Lil's asking if you've got a phone number there. Lil, you know, she thinks of everything. I didn't even…Of course, now we can actually call you. I mean, if it's okay—'

'You know, I'm not sure what the deal is. With the phone. If we're allowed to be accepting outside calls or anything like that.' Her finger runs itself into the grid of digits on the telephone. Avoidance? That's what the doc would've called it. Adjustment period, she thinks. 'I'll have to find out.'

'You let us know. And Gregory…?' Mama hovers on her end. Gregory shifts her position at the quiet, feeling it, and looks down at her sneakers. 'I'm so glad, Gregory. Just so glad you're okay.'

'Mama?' Much as she wants to, tries to, nothing with any meaning, any feeling, will come. 'Give Baron a good old scratch for me.'

'Oh, I will. I will. He's standing right here looking up at me with his tail wagging. Like he knows it's you. Like he knows.'

'I think…someone else wants to use the phone. I've gotta go.'

She enters a small, stuffy room. Is pointed to the back by a uniformed man. Hulking. With biceps that look ready to rip through his shirt. Her stomach twists. She keeps arms crossed, her bag tight to her. It smells like onions, urine, and body odour, so strong it makes her need to cough. She wishes she'd brought a book. To take her mind off things.

Others, she supposes parolees like her, mill about a bit like caged animals. She's early for the appointment. Intentionally. She'd been warned about being late. In one of the mostly useless *Pre-release Transition* sessions.

After she's checked-in by a burly woman behind the counter, she's given a clear plastic bottle marked with her name and file number and sent down the hall to 'collect' a urine sample. Turns out, in a filthy two-stall washroom. There are graffiti tags, telephone numbers, obscenity all over. Inside the cubicle is a landscape scrawled in pen, in thick marker, what looks like nail polish, even scratched into painted metal. But standing out from the rest is what looks to be a religious verse. It's right in the middle of the back side of the stall door. With the lines all neatly broken up and spaced apart. Who the hell does this kind of thing? And here of all places. *I AM THE DOOR*, the title says. All capitals. She's not sure it has any business on this particular door—though it's clear that somebody thought otherwise.

> *I am the Door*
> *The words are but four*
> *Millions are in*
> *But there's room for more*
> *The door's open wide*
> *Come right inside*
> *And you shall be saved*

Salvation in a bathroom stall. She drags her eyes from it and concentrates on peeing into the plastic.

As she comes out of the stall she sees herself in the foggy mirror above the bank of sinks. *I am the Door*, she thinks and sighs. She checks that the top on the specimen bottle is twisted tightly, takes a sheet of rough brown paper toweling from the wall dispenser and wipes around it. She sets it on the counter as she washes. It is still warm to the touch when she picks it up. *I am the Door, and I watched you piss in a cup. You surely do need saving.* She exits and makes her way back down the hallway.

Clutching the damn sample, she makes for the counter. She tries to be discreet as she passes it to one of the women back behind. She clears her throat. 'Do you test it right now? Here?' she asks.

'Yep, we do. We'll have results put in your file.'

'Do you tell me? My result? I mean, I'm clean, but do you tell the…uh… the…' she doesn't want to call herself a parolee, 'the candidate?'

'Only if there's a problem.'

'Oh. Okay, thank you.'

'Uh-huh.' The woman moves with her urine, her pee, into a divided area Gregory can't see behind. What if they doctor the results? She wonders if it's ever happened, ever been done, by some disgruntled worker, or even just for the hell of it.

She chooses a backward facing chair so she doesn't have to be looked at by the women working the counter. It's the most she's felt like a criminal since she got out. This way, with her back to them, it doesn't play on her so much.

'Ms. Abbott?' Then with hesitation, 'Gregory?' The question is two-fold. First meeting. And the name. Always the goddamn name. She stands quickly. 'Dan Walrup,' he says. He turns and walks. She follows, heart pounding in her throat.

The office he's in is small. Not much bigger than the toilet cubicle. Behind her is a pane of glass. To the right, the door. Open. Sitting with her back to it, instinct keeps her checking over her shoulder. He probably thinks she's paranoid. She's uneasy not being able to see what's behind her. He'll just have to put up with it.

He's reading her file. Flipping through papers. She can feel herself rocking. Nerves. She crosses her legs. Her ankle flicks. She uncrosses her legs. Puts her feet flat on the floor. Leans forward. To stop the movement. She doesn't want him to see fear in her. The uncertainty or discomfort that's got a hold.

Gregory looks around, taking in what's on the wall, the slogans of his various posters. On one a rock climber hangs dangerously at the edge of an impossible-looking cliff. Underneath: *ACHIEVEMENT Believe in yourself and anything becomes possible.* On the wall opposite is an image of the Golden Gate Bridge spires through the fog. The message: *Even if the way forward is unclear, we must still build the bridges to reach what lies ahead.* There are a few others, these obviously photocopied, stuck in place with yellowing fingers of tape at the corners. *Be the change you wish to see in the world. Gandhi.* Then: *It starts today. It starts with you.* Uncle Sam is pointing an oversized finger at whoever happens to be in the hot seat. In front of Dan Walrup. At this minute, it's her. And on the side of the filing cabinet, made to look like a cautionary road sign, a golden yellow card with black edging bellows: *Remember, I've heard it all before!* The exclamation mark is oversized. Definitely this guy has personality. On his desk in a patch covered with muddy rings is a San Francisco 49'ers mug. In the corner, at an angle, a small wood-framed print of a smiling young girl wearing a baseball uniform, flanked by a woman laughing, her arm around the girl, and on the other side, Dan. She supposes family, then feels a slight pang and a wave of guilt, as if she's seeing something private.

She has no clue what's on all the paper he's poring over. About her. Aside from the obvious; charges, court papers, prison records, psych and medical reports. The rest, and there looks to be much more, she has no idea about. He looks up at her. 'So,' he says, 'how're things?'

'Yeah, I guess…good.'

'Drugs?'

'No.'

He squints a bit. Like he's trying to read her, see if she's telling the truth. 'Education?' She takes the GED paper from her bag. Her hands tremble as she removes it from the envelope. 'Good,' he says simply. He looks over it and hands it back. 'Thanks for coming prepared.' She doesn't know what to say, but takes the paper from his hand, refolds it along the creases, slots it back in the envelope and returns it to her bag. He writes something in her file. 'Work?'

'I'm looking.'

'Where?'

'You mean?'

'I mean what kind of work?'

'Well, I was…I worked the kitchen. Inside. Before…before prison I worked in a bakery. Commercial. So something like that, I guess.'

'Good. How many applications this week?'

'Uh, I think at least…um…' Mentally she ticks them off her fingers. Remembers how she felt admitting a felony conviction. For all of them that was where things stopped, those applications. Couldn't say she was surprised. Disappointed, yes. Surprised, no. 'Half a dozen? I think. About that.' He looks up from the notes he's making in her file and just for a moment looks at her. His truth-telling register. Nodding, he looks down again. Continues writing.

'Any interviews?'

'No.' She feels ashamed admitting it. Swallows hard.

He sighs, a first sign of humanity, 'It's not going to be easy.'

'No. I know.'

'Keep trying.'

'Yeah.'

'Where are you living?'

'At Larkin House.'

He nods. 'Everything okay there?'

'Yeah.'

'Counselling.' He pushes a card across the desktop. 'Appointment.' She looks at it. Dr. Arthur Gedge. Psychologist. 'Make sure you go.'

She nods. 'I will.'

'Don't just say it. Actually go.'

She fingers the card.

'It's my job to try and keep you out of jail. It's up to you to actually do it.'

'I'll do whatever it takes to keep from going back inside.'

'Glad to hear it. Now show me.' The set on his face is grim, but not unkind. Her read of his expression: *I don't quite know what to expect from you, Gregory Abbott, but I sure as hell have been messed around by a lot of people who talk just like you.*

Kameko
San Francisco
April 2002

The sign in the bookstore window reads:

> *One dyed-in-the-wool literature/book fanatic needed*
> *For casual/part-time labour*
> *No benefits, but lots of laughs*
> *Service with a smile must be automatic*
> *Egos, ogres, and divas need not apply*
> *Make inquiries within*

She fills in an application at a table by the front window. When she has finished writing, the man who has given her the form approaches. She quickly stands and hands it to him with a slight bow.

He holds out a hand to her, 'I'm Richard. This is my partner, Matthew.'

Matthew leans in with a hand also extended and says to her, 'Matt. Only my gran really calls me Matthew.'

'Mind if we conduct a little impromptu on-the-spot interview? Have a little chat? See if there's a comfortable sort of fit?'

'Got a minute? Or two? Or twenty?' Matt jerks a thumb at Richard, 'He likes to talk.' Richard waves him away like he might a pesky fly.

She sits again and they settle into chairs around her. 'I'll keep things short and sweet, I promise,' Richard says, with a sharp look at Matt. 'For starters why don't you give us a little bit of background, tell us about yourself, what brings you our way.'

Kameko tells of the transfer from Tokyo for Shiro. She outlines her education. Her focus on literature at Waseda University. That she married before she finished her degree. That her husband has encouraged her to take up something to fill her time. The story she tells is a gentle rearrangement of fact.

'Ka-me-ko. Pretty name,' Matt says. 'It suits you.'

'Thank you,' she says with a polite bow, but thinks of her namesake, the tortoise, a creature that is hardly attractive.

'Not a chain store bookie are you? Because they're not really our type. I say this with all due respect of course, lest I get my ass in a sling.'

'Fine ass, too,' Matt says, nodding.

Richard responds by giving Matthew's shoulder a nudge. 'Focus, please.'

'Sorry.'

'Available evenings, Kameko? Weekends?'

'Yes.'

'How's your English?'

'Good.'

'Good?'

'Yes,' she does her best to sound certain and nods, 'good.'

'How's your picture taking?' Matt asks, slapping his thigh and laughing.

'That wasn't very PC. Kameko, though she seems very agreeable, may take offence. You had better watch your *correctness* young man, or that mouth of yours is going to get you in trouble.' Richard sets his features in a momentary display of seriousness.

'Who're you calling young? I think I'm offended. In fact, if by calling me young you were inferring that I was juvenile, well, I'd consider it a discriminatory slight.' She looks from one to the other and back again, a hand to her mouth to shield the widening smile. 'Besides, my comment has proven very clearly that Kameko here is blessed with a generosity of spirit in line with what the position demands. Meaning: she can take a joke.'

'You are a joke,' Richard comments as he studies the details on her form.

'Hey, listen, it's a quirky kind of test. A Human Resources placement technique. To make sure that she'll put up with us. It could save us from costly future harassment litigation.'

'You sound like a television ad. Where's the 800 number?'

'She smiles at our jokes. Sadly, more than anyone else has in a very long while. I say snap her up. '

'She'll get used to us. It's called desensitization. Yes, it's a big word. She's fresh yet. Give her time.' Richard turns to her, 'Don't suppose you've got any references local?' He raises an eyebrow, his forehead pleats above it.

'No. I am sorry.'

'Perfect.'

'I am sorry?'

'Don't be sorry.' Matt pats her hand. 'Less work for us. Besides, who's going to give a bad reference? It's more than a life's worth in this day and age. At least, in the State of California it is. As a native of these parts I can vouch for the fact that our love of litigation is inbred.'

'Less work, less baggage. We pride ourselves on being astute judges of character, don't we, Matt? And if we fail on that count, we fire your ass. Sound about right?'

'That's harsh.'

'It's honest.'

'Honestly, it's harsh. For a first interview—if that's what we're calling this.'

'Interview is done. So. Do you want the job, Kameko?'

'Yes.'

'Yes?'

'She said yes. Single syllable. In the affirmative.'

'Wiseass. Kameko, you start tomorrow, 9:00. Okay?'
'Okay! Yes, 9:00. Thank you. Thank you very much!'
'Oh, honey, I don't need you to thank me. I just need you to be here.'
She has found herself a job.

Gregory
San Francisco
May 2002

Suite 302, 1812 Legion Street. Dr. Arthur C. Gedge, Doctor of Psychology. The numbers agree with the card Walrup's given. Gregory surveys the building before her. It is a building marked for heritage. She can see the plaque left of the woodframed leaded glass door. The coloured harlequins remind her of cutting and pasting tissue on Lil's attic window. So long ago.

She doesn't relish having to start again with spilling her guts. In her head she hears Doc Ellis, the prison therapist, repeating one of his favourite lines—that therapy is a process, that healing has no set timetable. She takes a deep breath and walks toward the door.

Arthur C. Gedge. The name rings kind of phony. An image of Dan pushing the card across his table comes to her. *Make sure you actually go. Actually go.*

She steps into the little wooden shoebox of an elevator and punches 3 on the panel. There's a mighty shudder before the thing groans and starts to rise. She decides right then to take the stairs down. After she's done with Doctor Arthur C.

The waiting area of the office has the all the buzz and hum of modern convenience, but the look is a throwback to another time. Lots of wood, detailed borders, odd corner angles and rooftop gables. Long narrow windows stretch up into roofline pitches and glassy diamonds of colour spill warm rainbow light into the room. It's too nice, she thinks, to be rehabbing ex-cons.

The doctor himself is tall and broad. Blocky and square. Big hands. Built like a linebacker. Good bet he has Varsity jackets in his closet. Full head of hair. Grey at the temples. Not how she'd pictured him at all; he looks nothing like an Arthur. But then, does she look like a Gregory?

His voice is soothing, low. Carefully timed. Diplomas and certificates alternate with arty paintings in his office. Big splashy strokes of colour that don't have a whole lot in the way of shape to them. Very headshrink. He tells her that just this once he'll be doing most of the talking. He smiles like he's told a bit of a joke. He walks her through paperwork forms. Yes and no type questions. Basic stuff. About now. Being out. Living arrangements. He calls it the nuts and bolts of things. When he's through filling in file papers, he puts his clipboard on the desktop. He tells her that she has a right to complete confidentiality inside his office. That whatever they discuss stays between them. But he tells her, too, that he's required to submit quarterly reports on her rehabilitation, her reintegration efforts. 'Any questions so far?'

'Nope.'

He says they'll continue to work on overcoming the past, but that they'll also address any current issues that might arise over the course of things. It's all an effort to help her begin to build a future. Together they'll work on her developing the skills to strengthen herself. He has her records. From the police, her attorney, the courts and the prison. Now he says he wants to know her from her own perspective. 'Will that be all right, Gregory?'

Sounds fair. 'Yeah, I guess.'

'If at any time during a session you should feel uncomfortable we can stop. Just say so. What I need you to know is that you are in control here, Gregory. It's all in your hands. You need to be the driver. Never feel compelled beyond what you are at ease with. You know best.'

It occurs to her somewhere in the middle of the session that he talks in circles. Sometimes repeating what she's said, sometimes restating the idea in different words. Sometimes he turns it around, makes it into a question and sends it back at her. He tells her this is why journaling is so helpful in guiding understanding. Because it allows the writer to rethink. To revisit thought patterns. To dig deeper. He encourages her to continue the writing she's begun inside. 'Your prison therapist, Dr. Ellis, has included the journaling pieces that you submitted to him, along with references to others. His report indicates that the material might prove helpful in your continuing therapy.'

'I didn't realize that the prison would be involved in the process once an inmate's been released.'

'You might be surprised at just what they'll do when they think there is something that can be done, Gregory. It's in everybody's interests.'

He tells her that the best assistance he can offer in their sessions is to be a good listener. A sounding board. 'For anything and everything you might want help dealing with. Even the little things, the things you might think are stupid. Because sometimes they figure into something bigger.' He maintains that it is up to her to help herself, he is only a guide. 'That you made it here today is a solid first step.'

'Did I really have a choice? I figured that between you and him—Dan, my guy down at the parole office—you'd have me yanked back in for violating. Figured you'd have some kind of Hotline, Bat Phone, you know. Between you guys. In this line of work.'

'That's the impression he gave? Or the impression you formed?'

'I don't know. He told me here's the appointment, make sure you go.'

'But he didn't offer an ultimatum, did he, saying what might happen if you didn't attend today's session?'

'Not in so many words, I guess, no.'

'So what you're saying to me is that the prospect of possibly being in violation and the consequences you thought might be associated with that violation prompted you here today.'

'Pretty much.'

'May I ask then,' he holds her eyes, 'before this discussion we're in the midst of here and now, how did you feel about attending the appointment with me today?'

'Same as I feel about pretty much everything.'

'And that would be?'

'Shit scared. Like a cat that's been treed. Stuck.'

'Okay.' He says the word slowly, thoughtfully, turning it over. It reminds her of before, with Doc Ellis. She gets a little buzz at the similarity. 'Let me ask you this: When were these feelings of being treed, stuck, at a peak for you? When did you experience the most doubt, the most fear, about this session? When Dan first gave you the card last week? Maybe last night? Or this morning when you woke up? In the waiting room? Are you feeling worst at this very moment? Try and pinpoint the height of it.'

'Uh…I think it'd probably be before I left the house. Larkin. To come over here.'

'I see. And now?'

'Not as bad. Better, some. The need to puke is a bit better.' He doesn't react.

'So what I want you to think about is this: The prospect, and we're going to use our meeting as the example, was most daunting for you before you began the physical journey that would lead you to this office? You admitted that before leaving Larkin House you felt you were most afraid. You still feel that's accurate?'

'Yeah.'

'So in this instance, when you *faced* your fear, meaning you actually engaged in leaving the house with the intention of keeping this appointment, would you say that your physiological symptoms of fear decreased? Or perhaps even potentially disappeared?'

'Um, they're better, not gone. But not so bad I can't deal with them, or can't handle being here. Like I said, I don't think you have to worry about me puking in your office.' If he's taken aback by her comments about hacking up all over his fine things he doesn't show it.

'I know this may come across overly simple, but if you can think of it this way it might help you in other similar contexts where fear seems to be an issue. You were worst, meaning you feared the most, before you confronted the fear itself. Would that be accurate?'

'Yeah, I guess.'

'You see what you're saying? I'm just the interpreter here, but what I'm getting from what you've said is that by facing what you're afraid of the fear itself lessens, or rather, the symptoms become more moderate. Or, to use your words, I don't have to worry about you puking.'

'Maybe. Yeah, I guess.'

'Okay. That's a start at least. Will the insight help you, do you think?'

'Maybe.'

'You sound uncertain.'

'Not really uncertain, just really new at this game. Like I've been thrown onto the field without knowing the plays.'

'A nice analogy. What about the other players on your team? Do you trust them to help you?'

'I get what you're saying. Like you're on my team, maybe Dan at the parole office, and that you're going to help me, right? But the truth is, I'm not sure. I've been left open before. And got sacked good.'

'Okay, I hear that your fear ties into you not trusting. It makes perfect sense. Everyone has vulnerabilities, Gregory. But here's the thing—we can either choose to be hobbled by them and let them limit our existence, or we can decide to face them. Face them, and, bit by bit, deal with them. That, Gregory, will be the primary challenge for us. That means we're going to work to get you past the urge to puke, among other things. We'll take it slow, I promise. But every time you find fear taking over I want you to tell yourself: I deserve to be free, it is my right. And—I'll bet this will be the hardest part—you need to start believing it.'

Kameko
San Francisco
May 2002

She likes to come to the bookstore early, to ready things for the day. Around the broad wooden counter the floor creaks with her movement. The air carries a chill, until the heaters manage to do their work. With two hands she holds and sips from a steaming mug of tea. She gazes out at the swirl of fog. The way it shifts and changes before her eyes. She likes it like this, when the city is only beginning to come to life. Few people are on the street.

The tea soothes and warms her. Turning, she regards the shop—the high ceilings, wood paneling running the length of the walls, rows and rows of book spines stacked in neat lines. She likes that it is totally different from the shiny chrome and polished black stone of the apartment building. The clutter, the smell of the wood and paper, the sticks of incense she burns here on occasion, she finds these things refreshing to the spirit, nurturing.

Shiro dislikes incense. Complains that it reminds him of his parents. And grandparents. The shrines. Tradition. Old times and old people, he says. She has discovered a nearby temple where she can pay her respects. In some ways it is better, because she feels freer. When her whispers echo through the sacred space it is as if she is able to clear her heart out.

Purposefully, her hands begin to restore order, to undo the tangles of the day before. She works methodically: straightening, organizing, reshelving, stacking, dusting. She steps around clusters of armchairs. Closes up items left behind. Loads them into her arms. Magazines, sections of newspapers, a volume of American history, a Martha Stewart cookbook. Richard thinks that by allowing people to feel at home they will be more inclined to buy things. Let them browse, he says. Browsing brings them in. Eventually they'll find something they have to have.

The heaters hiss with life. Her flesh shivers a little, involuntarily, with the pleasure of warming. It is comforting that here things conform to a certain arrangement, a set plan. Everything has a place. Here it is possible to right the things one finds are not as they should be. Careful rows and columns are fixed in logic, they are not susceptible to the whims of emotion. She sighs. If only life were that simple. She slides the Martha Stewart volume into a yawing opening next to a red-checked cover of *The Picnic Bible*.

There is a rustling at the shopfront and the tiny brass bell above the door rings. 'Morning, Kameko.'

She steps away from the shelf and walks to the front. 'Good morning, Matt.'

'How's it going? God, yesterday was a madhouse in here. Totally wild. Don't know what brought it on, maybe a full moon or something,' he laughs. 'Wow,' he looks around, 'how long have you been here? This place sure isn't the mess I left last night.'

'I came in a little bit early,' she shrugs.

'What must your husband think of us, pulling you in at crazy early hours?'

'My husband, he is gone to work already. He likes to be early. First to the office is the most recognized worker. He is to set the example so others will follow. At earlier times.' She does not add that many nights he does not come home at all. And so he does not know the hours she keeps. A shadowy form of his mistress sketches itself across her imagination. Kameko pictures her luscious, voluptuous and tempting. Altogether different from a dull and boring wife.

'Earth to Kameko, come in,' Matt is watching her intently. 'Where'd you go to just now? And was it any good?'

'I am sorry, pardon me?'

'You looked about a million miles away just now. Are you okay?'

She pastes a smile into place, 'Yes, yes. It is nothing. Nothing.'

'Is something wrong? I mean, I know it's none of my business to ask. It's just that, well, a happy employee is a satisfied employee, and all that rah-rah. You were fine, seemed fine, until I brought him up. I have an affinity for foot-in-mouth disease, so if it's none of my beeswax, just tell me so. I might be totally off, but you just seem to look so sad all of a sudden.'

'Beeswax?'

'Um,' Matt says, 'none of my affair. If I'm being nosy, snoopy, feel free to tell me to back off, butt out.'

'Affair. Yes, that is what it is. But you know this?'

'What?'

'My husband's affair?'

'He's having an affair?'

'But, I thought…the way you have said, I thought…I am confused.'

'Okay, now I'm confused. I only meant if your sadness was none of my affair, like none of my business, or you didn't want me prying into your personal life, you just had to tell me.'

'I thought you knew!' she breathes.

'No! No, I had no idea. None.' He cringes, 'Oh God, I am so sorry. Me and my super-size piehole. I'm just a jumbo jabberwocky! I ought to know to keep my big mouth shut.'

'Is it looking,' she searches for the right word, 'obvious? In my face?'

'No, just that you seem bummed out. You look, kind of like, well, down in the mouth. Sad, a little sad. Am I making you feel worse? I am, I'm making you feel worse. I'm gonna stop. Just…stop.' He slaps himself, lightly, on the cheek. A playful rebuke.

'It is okay. I don't know why it makes me upset. I should not be so,' she thinks for a moment, 'sensitive about it, I think.'

'Well, I would think you can't help it. I mean, I don't know what kind of hell I'd go through if I thought Richard were fooling around. I'd probably want to kill the guy, or slit my wrists. God, I know it would make me nuts. You know—last thing I'm going to say—don't let him get the better of you. Maybe you should turn the tables, find a lover yourself. See if that doesn't give him a swift kick in the nuts. Reverse the psychology a little. Let him see how it feels. You know there was a woman, American woman, who cut off her man's penis with a knife. That's the way it works around here. Someone does you wrong, you get your own back. Fight fire with fire.'

'It is okay. I am okay. Okay?' She tries for a happier look. To put her private self to the back somewhere, out of sight. And changes the subject. 'I have noticed the many boxes downstairs. From the new orders? I will unpack and check the orders. Okay? First, though, I can make some tea for you?'

'Sure, I'll have some tea. And I hate that finicky paperwork, so I'd be thrilled if you wouldn't mind dealing with unpacking and cross-checking the orders. It would be a huge help. But as far as the other thing goes? I just…well, I hope you know that you can talk to me. If you want. I guess as compensation for my big mouth and lack of tact,' he smiles, 'I *am* a good listener.'

'I thank you, Matt. It is a kind offer. But you see, I am okay. It will be fine. Let me make some tea for you, and then I can begin to unpack.'

In an effort to signal an end to the conversation she nods to show him yes, she understands. A single spare gesture excuses her and Shiro both. It is a nod to keep *tatemae*. And to avoid truth. Even though, in the matter, her heart and mind do not necessarily agree.

During the day, the door to the room is always open. Probably because Anju wants to know what is happening inside. She gets the feeling her mother-in-law wonders if she might be unstable. It is something she, too, wonders given the way her thoughts sway, and the visions she sees in her dreams.

One morning, after she has heard the boys leave for the day, she sees that Samar stands at the threshold. 'Yes?' she whispers from where she sits, not wanting to stand or move or to make any sort of gesture that could be mistaken for some implicit display of welcome.

'Can I come in?' Samar asks, though she does not wait for an answer. She is dressed, presumably, in what she will wear to school. A tight-fitting pair of blue jeans and a form revealing red t-shirt with a scooped out neckline that Aneeta recalls washing. She remembered looking for the instructions. Hand wash and lie flat to dry. She had taken pleasure wringing it in the soapy water, preferring to imagine the neck of her sister-in-law instead of the knot of fabric in her wet-handed grip.

'I just thought I would stop in before I left for class to see how you're feeling. See if you're doing better, you know?' How transparent the visit is, the charade of concern for how she is doing. 'I am really sorry about the baby,' Samar begins softly, 'I mean about you losing the baby.' Her voice, while not rising in volume, becomes steely. Her eyes are hard. Aneeta turns away, pain swells and heat pricks the corners of her eyelids. She does not want this woman, this monster, to see her cry.

Samar's face with its sympathetic half-smile is a mask of falsehood. 'What happened has hurt all of us. The whole family.' Aneeta cannot believe what her ears are hearing. 'I know you think that it's only you hurting right now, but think of Anju. She's been desperate for a grandchild. You know, since Narinder and I married. You've seen how it's been for me. I think she finally had some hope again now, with you.' The witch sighs, a feigned reflection of feeling. This truly cannot be. With her hands in her lap Aneeta pinches one with the other. Hard. Needing the sharpness of pain, physical pain. To see. See if this is merely some cruel dream.

Samar continues spinning her web of artifice. It is a pattern that Aneeta knows is not as it appears. In her mind she sees the narrows of the bazaar and the snake charmers, punji flutes in hand, with covered baskets before them. There was always something about them, something sinister that she found unsettling.

She recognizes the same sensation with certainty now. 'This loss has touched us all, Aneeta. Really. Not just you. Even though I'm sure it feels that way.' A hand with familiar red-tipped fingers reaches across the bunches of over-bright flowers that dot the bedcover to touch Aneeta's own. As if scorched by flame, Aneeta draws back. The voice pries at her conscience, trying to wheedle its way into her sensibilities. A coiling she-serpent rising up. 'We're all going through this with you. You're not alone. It's affecting all of us. The whole family. We feel terrible about things. And I know you wouldn't want to make things worse.' *I know you, Rani.* An old ghost with the same reasoning. 'For yourself or anyone else either. And Dad's health—they've warned him about his blood pressure, about not having too much stress.'

Samar leans forward, her tone low. Aneeta shrinks back. She does not want to conspire with this devil. 'I'm sure I don't have to tell you what it would do to Narinder. It would kill him. Devastate him. And we both love him. Me and Jovin both. You may not believe it, but it's true. We're both sorry about what happened. '

'You call that love?' Aneeta's tone is sharp. 'Going behind his back like that and doing what you were doing? He is your husband. Jovin's brother. What you did showed him no love.'

Samar is ready. Ready for her. With words to wash it away. 'It's not like we planned it. It just happened. Sometimes things happen, you know?'

'No,' Aneeta says coldly, 'things like *that* don't just happen. Neither of you were forced to it. It was something that you chose, he chose.'

The eyes of the snake regard her, not blinking, the viper trying to hypnotise its prey. 'Jovin's really cut up about it all. He just doesn't know how to deal with it, which is why he's, you know, kind of keeping away. To let you heal.'

'He told you that?' She does not trust either of them. They will say what is needed. To suit them.

'Well…' Samar hesitates, 'yeah. In as many words.' Liar. 'We've been talking a lot about things. More than anything we're worried about the family. Both of us are. About them finding out. About you telling them. About what it would do.'

'Of course,' she acknowledges. 'I can imagine.' Aneeta straightens stiffly. A slight surge ripples through her. A small shift. Perhaps at Samar's veiled admission of fear.

The viper tongue uncurls, testing the air, testing her. 'It wouldn't be right of you to tell them. Especially now. I know you're hurting, I do. But to lash out would just add to things.' Samar pauses to let the idea settle. 'Think of what it would do to them.' Guilt. 'You don't want to be responsible for bringing their world crashing down around them.' Samar's words gather momentum, like a boulder rolled from a hilltop. 'I realize we hurt you. And I'm sorry. But don't think you can ease your hurt by making everyone else hurt too. Do you see what I'm saying?' Aneeta says nothing. 'Things could get very difficult. Very complicated.' Samar's threat trails into a venom-laced smile.

For a moment their gazes lock. This time Samar is first to look away. Aneeta knows all too well the bargains one makes to keep shame hidden, locked away. That they are not worth the cost.

In her dreams she sees her father. Like a phantom, he appears. But though she tries, exhausts herself trying, she cannot reach him. She sees only that he smiles at her. If she were able just to walk with him in the dreamscape. To share her burdens. To ask his advice. She is sure that he would give her the answers that seem to elude her conscious self. One night she wakes with a start and she is almost sure she sees the outline of him at the base of her bed. In the darkness she cries silently.

Anju pesters her about the astrologer. She wants to say that the stars cannot fix such problems, no matter the message written in them. She worries, too, what of her past might be evident. What sort of indications the heavens might provide. And if these things are alluded to, or worse yet revealed? What then?

She is wasting away. Kameez suits hang off her frame, a flood of fabric gapes awkwardly with her movement. Her body is weak. Her mind is confounded. Living feels wrong. She does not know what to do, about anything, even the simplest of things. She completes half tasks and then forgets what it is she has been doing.

It is Maria's soft-spoken 'Señorita?' that unlocks the torment she has closeted inside. Over a cup of tea and the ritual brass polishing. One room away her father-in-law alternates between sleep and the watching of his soap operas. Anju is keeping her regular hair appointment. At the end of the afternoon she will return heavily shellacked and full of salon chatter.

Through the partly open window she can smell the sweetness of grass clippings and hear the insistent rasp of Raoul's rake. When he comes to the door Maria jumps up and rattles something sharp in Spanish. She cannot see his face, but she hears his soft, questioning response. He retreats and Maria returns to sit again.

In halting whispers Aneeta starts to speak. 'I don't know…where to begin,' she says, and presses a tissue to the corners of her eyes, trying to hide the telltale signs of upset. She takes a shuddering breath.

Maria pats her hand. 'Anywhere. You must let it out. I will listen. To all you wish to say. It will stay,' she puts a hand lightly to her left breast, 'in my heart. I will share it with no one here. But only with God. I will pray for you. For your troubles. And for your sorrows to be lifted.' She nods to Aneeta, 'Yes?'

'Yes,' Aneeta whispers, barely audible.

'I pray for you. Since the day I see how quiet, how sad you are. And I pray for you after your loss. But I know there is more. Okay. So. Tell what you need to.' Maria's face is solemn.

'It was one day after the marketing….' The story reel unwinds in her head, frame by frame. She recounts the tale little by little—seeing them, Jovin and Samar; the tearing of the grocery bag and her screaming; the excuses and the veiled threats they make now. She tells of silly details that stay with her, that haunt her, like the bloodlike crimson redness of Samar's fingernails, the lopsided onion rolling to settle at her feet. Across from her Maria sits listening. Silent. More than once she makes the sign of the cross and raises her eyes heavenward.

Gregory
San Francisco
May 2002

It is a small bakery café, suspended in a sort of time warp between the fifties and sixties, at the well-traveled gingerbread fringe of Potrero Hill. Gerry's, it's called. Red vinyl booths line the walls. Filling the open checkerboard floor, table rounds are clustered with chrome-legged, red vinyl chairs. Black and white framed photographs on the walls feature what look like ordinary people in the throes of the building up a city. Lace curtain hangs from the half-pane on brass poles that stretch the length of window glass, swags of solid red are pinned off to the sides.

She's got an appointment with a guy by the name of Lenny. Sunday's a strange day for an interview, but from the looks of the hours posted in the window, it's the one day of the week the place is closed.

It hasn't taken her long to get here. By bike it's about a twenty minute ride. She'd bought the old cruiser cheap at a neighbourhood yard sale. She imagines she could easily take the bus, though she expects that it would probably be a longer trip with all the stops in between. She'd prefer the ride. Stupid, maybe, to be thinking about getting to and from already, but it gives her something to fix on.

The job suits her. They're looking for an early shift baker to prepare items they use in-house and are starting to sell on to a few small restaurants and several local retailers. This one's a job she could do, wants to do.

She's taken extra care getting ready. Wound her hair into a bun. Dressed in a cap-sleeved blouse with a small floral pattern, jeans she'd got at a thrift store, a pair of flat peep-toed sandals from the Payless Shoes in the same block. All of which she'd managed on the dwindling remains of Lil's charity. Lil, always bailing her out. She needs to work. Needs the money. Needs to start making a living so that she can really feel like she's inching toward independent.

Linda, Larkin's one woman den mother and full-time pep squad, is exaggerated in her encouragement, but cautions against expecting too much. 'It doesn't all happen at once. All in good time. Baby steps, remember? One at a time. Just getting an interview's good.' But she is getting impatient. With herself. She's put in near forty applications by her count. She's been called in on only three interviews. Honesty—that's her problem. But she can't see any way around it. Because she knows that somewhere along the line, if she's not honest, she'll get found out. Linda keeps on cheering even when hope dissolves into nothing. 'When it's right, it'll stick. Cut yourself some slack. You're doing it right. Employers don't want to find a prospective employee hiding something from them. Best just to be right up front about things. One day it'll come in your favour. Just wait. For now, it's a numbers game.' But with each new try she's getting more and more strung up about her chances.

'Hello?' she calls, stepping through the door. She hears movement in the back somewhere, and whistling. 'Uh, anybody home?' she calls more loudly, nerves shifting her from one foot to the other.

A man looks from the back of the narrow hallway. 'Somebody call?'

For a minute she fumbles, 'Uh, I'm…we…I mean, I'm here about the job. I think…we spoke on the phone. Are you Lenny?'

'Oh, right. Yeah, I'm Lenny. Refresh my memory—you are?'

'Gregory Abbott?'

'Right. Yes. Of course. Sorry…I got kind of carried away with stuff out back. I didn't think it was that time already.' As he comes forward she sizes him up. Makes her call. To her eye Lenny's caught up in the inevitable no man's land between youth and middle-age. He's got a boyish look, but signs of life and of passing time are creeping slowly in, taking hold of features. In lines around the eyes and across the forehead. His hair is thinning, and half circles at either side of the center peak are pulling back. He probably floats somewhere between thirty and forty.

He reaches out a hand and she takes it firmly. 'Let's make things official and get down to it. Don't want to be wasting your time. Give me just a minute and I'll grab a notepad and application from my desk.' He motions at the kitchen, 'Before I head back there can I get you anything? Coffee, tea, glass of water?'

'Um, no I'll be fine. I'm fine.'

'You sure? It's a warm one out there. Not even a glass of water?'

'Okay, yeah. Thanks. Water'd be fine.'

'Good. Water. Pick yourself a place to sit. I'll be right back.' He disappears into the narrow length of hallway. There's some clatter and a muffled ring of talk that comes from behind the wall.

Choosing a spot sounds more like an exercise the doc would've put on her. *And why this seat, Gregory? And how does it make you feel?* She's got shrink games working wholesale on her brain. Rather than sit she wanders the walls, leaning in to look more closely at the pictures. The subjects are unnamed, defined only by what they lens has captured them doing. They are not the typical posed, happy shots.

He clears his throat to signal his return. 'I see you've taken an interest in the photographs.'

'Yeah. They're incredible. So real.'

'They were taken by my great-uncle. He passed on long ago, as you may have guessed from the timeline of them, but he was big into photography. He was starting out when cameras were young and it took a lot more to capture the real essence of an image. To really get the full story coming out of it. A lot of his work is holed up in city archives now.'

'Looking at them you almost get a sense that you could be part of it, their scene. It's like something's pulling you in.'

He slides his papers across the tabletop of the booth she's standing by, under an image of two children behind a line of wind-curled laundry that's strung out against a towering Victorian, not unlike the style of Larkin House.

'This is for you,' he says, slipping out an application and putting a pen down beside. 'Now, foolish me, I'll have to go grab my glasses so I can read what you write, and I'll get water for the both of us. Sure I can't offer you something more?'

Just a damn job, she thinks. She says, 'No, thanks. I'm good.'

'Okay. So I need front and back completed on the form. It's just the basics. We can talk through a lot of it. Whatever you haven't managed to get through when I get back. I'll give you a few minutes. Can't recall where exactly I left my glasses anyway, so it'll depend on how quick I put my hands to them.'

She concentrates on the front of the sheet. Name, birthdate, social security. She leaves position applying for blank since she's not sure of the exact job title. She ticks off that she's okay for shift work and digs in on the work experience, starting with Lil's and working her way forward. For the last position she writes—Institutional kitchen experience. Linda has helped her with the wording. General prep and cooking duties for larger numbers. Reporting to kitchen supervisor. Sounds good. Legit. She fills in the run of time. Which makes it sound even better, having held the spot over that many years. No sign of the dreaded question yet. It's got her feeling more confident. Maybe they're too small an outfit.

'How're you making out?' He's back. With wire-rimmed glasses on. Funny, she thinks, they make him look younger in the face.

'Pretty much finished the front side.'

'Well, let's see if we can't walk ourselves through the back together.'

'Sure.'

'I'll just have a look at what you've got here so far.' He skims quickly. 'Experience looks good. You have the main qualifications we're after. This position would be going back to a baking focus, some planning and inventory, which I guess would pull on your institutional skillset. That's in a nutshell what we're after. And early morning shifts. Someone to open up, get the fires burning, get things cooking, so to speak. Or baking, more precisely. Sound like it might be up your alley?'

'Yeah, I mean, yes. Yes.' Possibility marbles through her.

'It may not give as much challenge as a big place because we don't really compete on the numbers. We're more about the old-fashioned homespun quality. That's our focus. Our niche, if you will. Though we are growing and planning to expand our supply. I guess I should also warn you that we're not mechanized or automated in a big way, we're hand doers. Pride's in turning out the real thing.'

'I'm fine with that. Actually, it's how I got my start. Honestly, it's what I'd like to get back to. It's what I like best. Get my hands into it. Not just pulling duds off a line, or flipping switches and settings on some fancy machine.'

'I think this might be a good fit. For us both. I've got to be fair and let you know, too, that we don't have a whole lot of support infrastructure. So you'd be handling a lot of the responsibility for the day's output. We need someone we can rely on and somebody who's consistent in things. In a small place like this we'd be pretty much hooped if the person in this position were to let us down.'

'That's totally okay with me. I don't rely on a whole lot of hand-holding. I like the idea of working independent. Show me how you want things and I can pretty much take it from there.'

'You sound confident in your abilities.'

'Yessir. And I much prefer the baking end of things.'

'I take it you've got a reference who can support and testify to your abilities.'

'Yes, I have.' Thank God for Lil.

He tells Gregory that his mother manages to do most of the baking herself, but it's starting to become an issue with business picking up and starting to grow. They're looking for someone to learn it fast, what needs doing, and in time, to take most of it over. 'She'll do the training of course, because no one could do it but her, but it's my intention that she be starting to step away from things.' Then he adds, in a way that makes clear his affection for his mother, 'She should have stepped away years ago. Shouldn't still be working like she is. Time she had a minute to herself. A chance to slow down and enjoy life.

'I've just got one final thing here before I get those reference details from you,' he says, 'so we can check that you're as good as you look here on paper.' From the way he's talking, she thinks excitedly, she may actually have done it. 'I've got to ask you a silly kind of question and hope you're not offended by it.' He smiles. 'Ever been convicted of a felony?'

Her stomach plunges through the floor. Like it's opened up under her. Dammit to hell and back. And she'd almost, for just a second, let herself hope she had this one. There's no way around it. Best buck up and shoot straight. Might as well get it over with. End the charade. With a hole of frustration and defeat swallowing her in, she looks Lenny right in the eye, 'Yessir, I have.' There's no mistaking the surprise that takes his features. The way the answer, the affirmative, spikes them up. Next'll come a swift run of excuses and a hasty *we'll call you*.

At her back a voice intervenes. 'Figured I'd come sit for a bit if you two're still going, have a listen. Lenny, the dear boy, thinks he's got it all covered helping me out and all, but seeing as I'm the one who handles the baking and making, there's questions I've got he likely wouldn't have thought to ask. So I'll come find out for myself what I need to know before he goes on, and try to get some help I can actually make use of. Name's Gerry,' she says, 'short for Geraldine.'

'Gregory, Gregory Abbott, ma'am. But I'm thinking that we're about set to wrap things up here.' From the look on Lenny's face she knows she's close to the mark.

'Well now,' she says appraisingly, 'isn't that something? Gregory. I like your name. Suits you well. Takes a strong kind of woman to wear a man's name with grace. Something I said, then? Or you in a hurry?' Gerry is settling into a chair and looking to Lenny, trying to read his expression.

Better to kick this one in the nuts and walk rather than wasting more time on it. 'No, ma'am. More probably something I said. I was just telling Lenny that I do, in fact, happen to have a felony conviction. I figure that probably ended our discussion right there. I don't want to be wasting anyone's time.'

'Well...' the word comes out like an exhale, 'it takes a lot to own up to a thing like that.' Gerry pauses and looks up at her, her eyes asking silent questions. 'Do you think I ought to hold it against you?' Lenny has a look of shock shadowing his features as he turns to Gerry, but he doesn't say anything. Obviously, Gerry calls the shots. 'Tell me, does it make you a lousy baker? Bread doesn't rise; crusts don't flake right? Does it take away from your know-how in the kitchen? Your willingness to work?'

'No, ma'am.'

'See, those things I'd sure have a problem with. I'm sure Lenny's asked if you've got a reference who can vouch for you.'

'Yes.'

'And do you?'

'Yes, ma'am.'

'Somebody in the business? Who'll tell me whether you've got the skills I need?'

'Yes.'

'See, it's like this with me—as far as I'm concerned, Gregory, one strike doesn't necessarily mean you're out of the game. Not a soul I know of who's not made mistakes in life. Myself included. I know only too well that second chances don't come easy. But it doesn't mean you don't deserve one. So, in calling on your reference, that's what I intend to find out. If I ought to be giving you one—a chance, that is.'

She and Lenny are both stunned speechless by the pronouncement.

'Right. Let's get those details from you before you're on your way today. Then we'll see.'

Gregory can only nod. She takes up the pen and in the space marked *Reference*, right under the now checked box saying yes to having a felony conviction, with a trembling hand she writes Lil's name and telephone number.

Kameko
San Francisco
May 2002

She does not know how to go about it. Seduction. Thinking about it is unnerving. She inspects the reflection in the bathroom mirror, checking her appearance with a critical eye. There is nothing wrong with the body. Smooth skin, narrow hips, pert breasts, flat stomach. Flat stomach. She drags her eyes upward. Away from the failure below. Fine lines, like spider silk, have begun to creep out from the edges of her eyes and at the corners of her mouth. Signs of sorrow, worry. They have aged her. She has stopped taking care; become indifferent to paying herself attention. She has been consumed with the idea of family. Making a family. She sees Mother in her eyes. Quickly, she wrenches herself from the mirror. What she needs is to be refreshed. She has become old looking. So quickly. Too quickly.

Tomorrow she will begin. To make herself over. She wonders about the lives of women who became courtesans and geisha. How they were transformed. She wonders at the divide between mistresses and wives. A woman who can keep a man's interest in bed is a different being than the woman who keeps a household and raises a man's children.

If she does not look exactly like the girl who has been a disappointment to him lately, she thinks, then maybe. Maybe. Maybe the line can blur for them. The line that separates duty from passion.

The mid-morning bustle of the sidewalk soldiers her along. When she reaches the address, the brightly coloured windows look more like a confectioner's shop, a *dagashiya* for grown women. As a child going into the small candy stalls, she never knew quite where to focus her attention; there was so much to look at, so much to see. The same is true of this place. She looks beyond, into the store, and realizes that the heaviness in her stomach is winding higher. She remembers the first time she had seen this name. On the American Express credit card statement. A pair of American girls push past her, reach for the door. Akira's voice echoes through her: 'Don't become one of them. Don't be the stereotype!' Kameko steps through the door into a whirl of black lacquer and endless shades of pink.

'Welcome to Victoria's Secret!' The word secret bounces up, then down. 'My name's Melody, can I help you?' She is a blonde-haired, black-suited woman with a high-pitched voice. Like a bowstring drawn squeakily across notes of the upper scale. Not melodic at all, as her name suggests. A black piece in her ear curls into a wire along her jawline. It stops a couple of inches from smile-starched, pink lips. Melody is sliding rainbow-coloured floss straps along a stack of pink, satin-padded hangers. A suspended television screen plays scenes of lingerie clad women, smiling and strutting jauntily with sensual self-assuredness. 'Are you looking for something in particular?'

'I am…I would like to buy something…to please my husband.' Her English sounds more heavily accented. Foreign.

'Oh, we've got lots of cute things I'm sure you'll love and he'll love.' Giant posters hang over tables and fixtures: *What is Sexy?* Melody waves with a flourish around the room, like a game show hostess might, 'What does your husband like? Teddies? Baby dolls? Bra and panties sets?'

Kameko studies the glossy floor, ashamed and uncomfortable to realize that she does not actually know what Shiro's preference would be. 'I am not sure,' she says quietly.

'That's okay! It's more fun for you! You can try some things, see what you like, what you think he might like. As I said, my name's Melody, what's yours?'

'I am Kameko.'

'Kameko, that's so pretty!' Melody is perky and frothy, just like the contents of the store. Kameko wonders what she wears under her black suit. If she wears undergarments like those swirling around her. 'Let's get you set in a fitting room and I'll take your measurements.' She is already working a yellow tape from around her neck. 'Then I'll collect a whole bunch of gorgeous pieces for you to try. Okay?' Melody shepherds her toward a pink curtained doorway near the back wall.

She is embarrassed to be taking her clothes off for a stranger. Cool hands touch her flesh, the tape slides over her breasts; she thinks she sees Melody smile a little bit at the modest cotton of her underpants and simple style of her bra. 'I'll write your size on a card. So you know for future shopping. And I'll just be a quick minute so that we can get you started trying things. Be right back.' She sounds excited. 'Some of our designs can enhance your shape, you know, give you the look of more fullness in the bust. More va-va-voom, if you get my meaning.' Melody motions across her own ample curves. '*I* will be right back.'

When she has closed the door, Kameko sinks onto the cushioned stool in the corner and regards herself in the long mirror on the wall. She is the only thing in this room not a shade of pink. Her eyes are large. There are circles underneath. She looks tired and wary. Her shoulders curl down and she crosses her arms to cover herself. Though the store is warm, she has started to shiver.

Melody's voice rings out. 'Kim-ee-ko,' she calls with an American twang, rapping several times on the door. 'I brought a ton of stuff.' She passes an armful through the door, a thick swath of gauzy underthings, 'I'm sure you'll find some things you love. That *he'll* love. If you need a different size or anything, I'll be right outside. Okay?'

Kameko hangs the grouping on the brass wall hooks and leans heavily against the dressing room door. She sighs and begins the business of trying to find, if, for her, an answer exists to *What is Sexy?* There are bras with padding and with wires that dig into her ribs, webs of lace fixed with sequins, jewels and tiny bows. A pair of floss underwear has a line of pearls that run up the back. They must be impossible to walk comfortably in, much less sit upon for any length of time. There are sheer camisoles and underpants that allow all that is beneath them to show through; covering little and hiding nothing. She tries gowns with various patterns of criss-crossed slender straps, many of which are cleaved almost to her navel and gape widely. Some are difficult to get on because of their complexity, and then even more trying to wriggle out of.

'How're we doing?' Melody chirps, 'Can I get different sizes? Or take anything away?'

All of it, she thinks despairingly. *Take it all*, she wants to say. But then, she needs at least something. 'No, no. It is okay. I am okay. Okay.' For Shiro, she alone is not enough. She has a hair appointment in less than thirty minutes that she needs to get to. She decides on a lacy one piece. It rides high in the thigh and low between her breasts, but it clings to her, and seems the best of what she has tried.

'My favourite teddy!' Melody exclaims, 'Isn't it gorgeous? I love this. And you have the perfect figure for it. I'm too busty myself. And I think black is the ultimate. Gorgeous against skin like yours. If you buy another then you get the second for half price. Do you want me to get you another? Maybe in a different colour? Pink? Or maybe red?'

'No, thank you. This will…One will be fine.'

'Oh, it's so cute!' Collapsing the lace accordion-style onto the counter, Melody wraps it first in layers of pink tissue and then slides it into a bag of horizontal stripes of pink, light and dark. 'I'm sure he'll love it!'

'Yes. Thank you. I…hope so, too.' She wishes she could share the certainty of the sentiment. Her hope is that he loves *her* in it.

When, after two and a half hours, she emerges from the hair salon she has chosen from the telephone directory, the transformation she has intended is complete. Her hair, which has always been long, straight and heavy, is now razed into gentle waves that cascade down over her shoulders and end in a gentle upward curl. A curl that she'd had no idea even existed in the hair on her own head. Golden highlights make her look as if she has been on a seaside vacation along the Izu Peninsula and the sun has worked its magic.

In fact, a sense of lightness seems to have taken hold of her entire being. She doesn't even feel so conscious to be carrying the pink stripes of Victoria's Secret. She allows a shy smile for herself, and notices with surprise, a number of lingering glances in the oncoming tide of pedestrian traffic. The girl she glimpses in interrupted stretches of window glass is a vision she finds difficult to recognize. A woman with new confidence. It serves to sharpen the earlier wavering resolve about what she is doing. She finishes the rest of her shopping for the evening and for the meal she has planned buoyed by good thoughts.

She places a call to Shiro's voicemail. With a message that she hopes will be enough to tempt him home. She also speaks to Mrs. Ueda and to Shiro's secretary. And tells them that she is preparing a special dinner. It is calculation on her part, for they will surely wish details of the meal afterward.

In a one-sided mental dialogue she reviews things she will do and say, the witticisms that she might offer to tease and spark his interest. 'What is the occasion?' he will likely ask her. She imagines the coquettish way she will look at him before answering, 'We are.' Perhaps a giggle of girlishness. But just a touch. Tonight she wants him to see her as a woman more than a girl. A girl can engage a man, but a woman, she thinks, is what will keep him. He must see her move smoothly from one dimension to another. A long ago university lecture comes to mind—and the idea that one character's turn to the dynamic renders others dynamic by return. The various facets of a personality are the tide, the push and pull effect. And the fuel for motivation.

She takes special care with preparing the meal and the table. She has purchased candles and a California wine. In her bath she gives special attention to the parts of her body that are party to pleasure, both the giving and receiving of it. Parts that begin to ache with thoughts of she and Shiro together. For a fleeting moment she allows herself the thought of a child. What good fortune it would be if a child were to come of this evening, an evening intended purely for pleasure and passion.

On bare, dewy skin she mists perfume. Pink tissue is unwrapped and the bag secreted away. She checks her appearance and butterflies take to her insides. Over black lace she dons a dress. Conservative, but fitted. Above the neckline there is a triangle glimpse of what lies beneath. For courage she has mixed herself a glass of whisky. She paints her lips. Mirrored Orchid is the shade. A rich plummy red, it is a dramatic look that appears well-suited to her fair complexion. She has purchased it at the salesgirl's suggestion. Under the tender strokes of the brush her lips seem to swell. She presses them together and pouts into the mirror. Tonight she will play hostess and geisha and courtesan. She will attend to Shiro's needs alone.

With a smile, she welcomes him into the apartment. Surprise is evident in his features. While she fixes his drink, he appraises her openly. She has caught his gaze wandering to where the lace peeks forth. A thrill dances in her.

She drinks another whisky with him and, over the course of conversation, becomes more forward in her discourse and opinions. He does not seem to mind her boldness. She has not seen him smile so much or laugh for a long time. She feels sure that this is the medicine that was needed all along. Silently, she chastises herself for not coming to such a conclusion earlier. Chastises her single-minded preoccupation with becoming pregnant.

He devours the dishes she has prepared with obvious enjoyment. As she leans in to serve him some more he gently reaches out to run his fingers along the edge of her breast. She feels her nipple rise up, straining against lace. His fingers move along the neckline and dip under it. Her breathing quickens. She smiles at him and inclines her head flirtatiously, 'How is your meal?'

'I am not so much interested in my meal as I am in you right now.' She cannot help but giggle. She can feel her eyes shining. The look upon his face is amused. He stands and moves around the table to her. When he takes her hand, she is more than ready to follow.

The first of their lovemaking is an episode of rediscovery. Sweet, sensuous and slow. Everything is, right at that moment, the way it should be. Nothing interferes. The second time is one of hunger, unbridled and raw. Unaddressed emotions are eased away in the rhythms of their loving. They share an abandon she has not experienced before, had not thought possible. As she yields finally to sleep, with his soft snoring beside her and twinkling city lights beyond, she decides that it is possible to live beyond the bounds of duty, and to love that way. To blur the line between two worlds, to inhabit them both. Tonight has shown her that she can be much more than wife alone.

When she awakens it is quiet and still around her. He is gone. She has not felt him leave her side. Wondering where he might be, she rises and pulls on her yukata. She pads down the hallway and toward the phosphorescence she recognizes as the computer screen. But for his shorts he sits naked before it. She feels a laugh rise within her. He leans into the halo of light it gives, intent upon some message in the window. He does not hear her approach. Unchecked, Kameko reads over his shoulder. The sentiment, in a single razor-sharp instant, steals her breath. She brings a hand to her mouth to cover the laugh that has reversed into a cry.

Missing you. Longing for you. Craving the feel of you, your touch, the scent of your skin, the heat of us together. Desperately needing you back in my bed.
Elaine

The noise she makes, a pitiful whimper, prompts him to close the message, tearing the words from her eyes. But it is not swift enough for her mind, which has already digested the content. He says to her gruffly, but with an undertone of a whine, 'Can't you see I am working? I have work to do. Go back to bed.' As if she were simply an errant child. He does not explain what he knows her eyes have seen.

Mishima's words flash through her, from his *Confessions of a Mask*:

> *I was so engrossed in tales of romance that I devoted all my elegant dreams*
> *to thoughts of love between man and maid, and to marriage, exactly as*

And it is clear, suddenly, that the truth of the world has crept in to upend her elegant dreams.

Aneeta
Fresno, California
May 2002

It is a tiny pink-walled room, thick with the smoky musk of incense. Charts of planets, constellations and diagrammed astral relations are hung in jagged blocks. Some are framed. Some, with loosened tapes, curl away from the walls. Cushions and boxes collect in the corners. Leaning into one another. *Diya* lamps flicker almost invisibly in the brightness of the California sun that shines through barred windows. A file cabinet bears a fax phone, answering machine, and a small radio.

The astrologer is white-bearded, turbaned in a swath of orange silk. His voice is smooth. Lilting. 'Something specific is on your mind today?'

Anju's tone is sharp and demanding. 'I have called ahead of time. We spoke on the telephone, ji. About my daughter-in-law.' She gestures over a shoulder at Aneeta. Aneeta puts her hands together and offers a slight bow. 'I am Anju Arora.'

'I see, I see. Come.' He waves them deeper. A sensation of calm fills her as his eyes settle on her. Anju moves to take a chair and motions Aneeta to another. His eyes are still on her as she slides into place at the right side of her mother-in-law.

Anju is already busy unfolding and unrolling the various forms and horoscope papers that she has brought for consultation. 'I bring you the charts of my son. And his wife. She has just recently...' there is an awkward pause as Anju considers her words, 'we want to know specifically with regard to fertility.'

'I see.'

'I am anxious to be a grandmother.' Anju's smile is tight.

'Of course, of course. Such things are perfectly understandable. Especially with first grandchild. Your eldest boy?' His assumption is a source of visible discomfort for Anju. Aneeta sees her grimace slightly.

'No. Youngest.' To conceal her embarrassment at her elder son's non-procreation she adds, 'I have two sons.' It is a fortune doubly better than daughters. By far. An enviable position. 'Here. The charts. For my son. And daughter-in-law.'

The man sits. 'Hmm.' A bony but thick-knuckled finger traces the lines of her horoscope plot. 'In Delhi born.' He looks up at her.

'Yes,' Aneeta answers.

'Myself, I have family in the city. They say it is a too-big place these days. Too much traffic, too much noise, too much pollution, too much expense. But not enough work for the everyman. Just for the rich man. Technology people. I tell them it is much the same here.' Anju clears her throat to interrupt the further exchange of insignificant pleasantries, to refocus his attentions upon the task. The guru smiles mildly, 'Okay, okay, madam. I take your meaning. You are anxious to know. I am down to work now. No more chit-chatting.'

There is tense silence from her mother-in-law while he studies. His lips move silently. Anju shifts in her seat. He looks up at Aneeta, 'I see that you have suffered a loss.' His expression is sympathetic.

'You can see?' Anju asks.

'Yes, I can tell.' He takes up a pencil and marks figures upon a paper.

'And that is mainly the reason why we are here. We want to know when is a good time for them. For a child.'

'Don't rush the girl,' he says with gruffness, 'things cannot be forced. They must be left to happen naturally. She is not strong yet. This I can also see. There must be time for healing.'

Anju stiffens, momentarily taken aback by the shift in the old man's tone. 'There is no rushing, ji. I am giving no pressure. She is on bed rest almost entirely. I am thinking only of her. Strength is, of course, top priority.'

He considers Jovin's horoscope. And his face becomes puzzled. He looks from one birth chart to the other. He pulls the divisional charts for them both alongside. He notes a trio of additional numbers next to the first set and, after licking the pencil tip, makes some computations. With two sharp strokes he crosses them out. Anju's eyebrows rise.

'We want to know ideal times for conception. Upcoming. Between these two. To try again. We think it will be good for her. To make her feel better. What better way than to become pregnant again?'

'I see. I see. Madam is very anxious. I tell you this—daughter-in-law is fertile. This is no issue for worry. But the boy seems hot-headed. May not be sensitive. Especially to her. I see Ketu figures prominently in his chart.' He taps his finger on the paper. 'Nothing is immediate in this phase. They move apart. In different space.' Aneeta thinks of the separate bedrooms. And beds. The fact that even the thought of his touch reviles her. Would that account for signs of different space?

'So when does this phase change? When do they become closer?'

'I can see that girl resolves first. Planetary influence improves. But it is the question of stars and planets being compatible. Together.'

Anju gives a brittle laugh. 'We had horoscopes matched for compatibility before marriage.'

'And what was said to you?'

'Match is very compatible.'

His finger traces the lines of Aneeta's astral coordinates again. 'Hmm. I see.'

'So I want to know only about pregnancy, ji.'

'Peace is very important in conception. Woman must be at peace. Otherwise it is no good.' The guru waves his hand to emphasize his words. 'Bad feelings and experiences can destroy this.'

'Yes, of course.'

'So you, mother-in-law, can help with that.' He nods at Anju.

'Of course,' she says with the pouty look of a scolded child.

'She will become stronger. But it will take some time, maybe. There has been conflict. Conflict that chart shows in future is resolved. After that heart is open. There is peace.'

'This is what I needed to know, ji. That the girl will be fertile. That babies can be expected. Can you give, say, some estimation as to when that might be?'

'Time of things is never absolute. Everything will happen when time is right.' He looks from Anju and to Aneeta. 'No need for worry. But for conceiving, and for full pregnancy and good children, you must nurture the womb. It will be giver of life. She is on the cusp of a much better position with the ruling planets. Karma for her is good. I cannot speak for God, but I can see situation is deserving. To restore balance. Best time lies ahead.'

'So all is well for the next time.'

'All will be well when time is right, madam.'

'And as for right time you cannot say with some idea?'

'I have told you, it is very difficult to interpret quantity of time. That is one thing that cannot be sure. If I say six days, or six weeks, or six months—if it should not come to pass in this way then you will say that I am wrong. I say only what I see for certain.'

'Then I suppose I have what I've come for.'

'Questions have been answered to your satisfaction?'

'Unless there is more to tell in the matter, then I suppose yes.'

'I tell only what can be sure to come. It would not do to have you displeased.' He gives Anju a small smile and bows. He leans forward and pushes his aged frame to standing. With the ease of familiarity he moves about the cramped setting. He takes up a receipt pad from beside the fax-phone and slides a film of carbon under the top sheet. A spidery hand makes a bill for his time and interpretations.

'For you, madam, a good price,' he says, showing her the amount.

'Fine,' she returns briskly, drawing money from her handbag.

The fertility projection would serve Aneeta well. It would allow her to escape the pressures that she had worried might lurk right around the corner. Namely, being moved back into Jovin's bed. She knew her mother-in-law's desperation for grandchildren. But Anju would not trifle with the guru's reading. And risk the outcome she so desired.

As Anju turns away to roll her various charts and collect her papers, the guru reaches out with a sure motion for Aneeta's hand. It is a gesture her mother-in-law does not see. His skin is surprisingly soft and warm, without the papery feel of age that the lines of his face reveal. She is surprised by the comfort in the current that traverses the temporary connection between them. He gives her a gentle squeeze and a benevolent smile. She senses that his eyes look into the very depths of her. That they have seen secrets that dwell within her. She knows that charts can impart such knowledge, but if he has read it, he has seen fit not to reveal what he has found. 'Girl,' he says quietly, so that only her ears hear, 'soon it will be.

Soon.' She knows, just as surely as she knows he has read her truth, that his words bear no reference to her fertility or Anju's future grandchildren. If it were not so, he would have spoken it to Anju as well. And for relaying exactly the fortune her mother-in-law had come to receive he would likely have received a substantial and generous gratuity. As a show of gratitude. To God. To the heavens. And to the messenger. That he had willingly given up the potential for a more generous return could only mean one thing. That the prophecy applies to her alone.

Soon. For her, the single syllable is more than enough.

Gregory
San Francisco
June 2002

The day is young yet. A little after 4. Darkness has yet to lift its black cloak. Gregory crosses apron ties and snakes them around her waist. Raw dough sits in mounds before her on the block, waiting to be worked into breads, pies, biscuits and cakes.

She is alone but for the squawk of the radio that sits on the shelf in the corner. *The New Day Show—bringing you classic jazz for a new day.* Ovens tick over as they warm. Billie Holiday fills up the emptiness with distinctive sound, rich and deep. Solitude. 'Only a woman with a past can sing like that; something raw lived in her,' she remembers Lil saying, 'something that had the power to just reach right through the music. That kind of hurting has to come out somehow. Ease the ache out of the heart. Some sing, others pour their pain into writing, painting, drawing. Making things. It loosens the hold of whatever demons a person's got.' Gregory presses her hands into dough, folding it in and over itself in repeated motions, shifting it on the floured board, each time a quarter turn. There is something about it that gives her a feeling of peace. There's a sense of release.

She's getting familiar with the way that Gerry and Lenny like things. Gerry starts only one shift a week now. They're talking about hiring another person under Gregory. Since she's started, pie sales have taken off. Restaurants and retailers are buying them up about as fast as they can make them. It's what Lenny's been planning all along. Expansion. He just wanted to get some help for Gerry first. 'He'd have me turning to mush. A few grey hairs and he's got to thinking I can't be lifting a finger.'

At Larkin, Linda says working early is her way of staying on the edges of things; it lets her be a bit more of an observer than an active participant in the social fabric of the community. But she says it's not bad, just cautious.

Darkness is dipping away. She can see it fading, even though she can't see the sky. Gently she places forms of equal length into floured loaf pans, the dough rounded and even. She slides them, one by one, into the hot oven. Looking forward to the scent they'll give as they bake. She wipes floured and sticky hands against the thick cotton twill.

From the making of bread she'll move on to other pastries. Gerry has everything down to a science of timing, she's been at it for so long: 'The system works, has worked for years, why change it?'

For just a moment she leans against the counter, hot mug in her hands, and watches how the coming of light changes things, transforms them. She watches the first jogger pass; birds flutter in the trees along the road's edge. A car drives slowly by, dew still coating the outer edges of windshield, wipers moving in tandem, clearing a field of vision. She takes a long swallow of coffee.

It is the first time, she realizes, that she is not looking backward in going forward. Not relying on the rearview mirror and what's behind her to measure and map things out. For a fleeting moment the future, her future, like the day, stretches out before her, untraveled and new.

She turns her attention back to the floured sideboard and the dough that waits. She is putting her hand to something. Like Lil had said. Working things out. And the shadows are starting to let her go.

Aneeta
Fresno, California
June 2002

'You should know.' Maria pushes the worn newspaper slowly across the table towards Aneeta. 'After everything, especially now, you should know. Raoul and I both think so.' Silently, her eyes scramble through the story.

Brokerage Boys Behaving Badly

Stockbroker Accused of Co-worker Sex Assault at IPO Bash

Dot-com brokerage blueblood Paradigm Group is, for a change, in the red after a female employee has filed a complaint of sexual assault and harassment against one of its brokers.

While celebrating the IPO success of client Inktomi at a well-known downtown nightclub, Paradigm broker, Jovin (Joe) S. Arora, is alleged to have pursued a female co-worker into the women's restroom where he reportedly assaulted her and kept her confined against her will. The woman was eventually freed when a female party-goer informed club management of hearing a raised male voice and a woman's cries for help from behind the locked restroom door.

Details in a complaint filed with the San Mateo sheriff's office indicate that the victim had been the subject of Arora's unwelcome advances on multiple occasions.

A spokesperson for Inktomi has declined to comment on the matter, saying the complaint, while unfortunate, has nothing to do with the popular Internet search service.

Sexual harassment claims in the testosterone-dominated securities industry have risen sharply in recent years.

Steve Santos, a media liaison for Paradigm, has indicated that the brokerage house takes such allegations extremely seriously and will co-operate fully with local authorities. Mr. Santos added that there will also be an internal inquiry into the matter.

When Aneeta looks up from the page, Maria's smile is sad. Her voice is quiet and solemn. 'What you do with the information, that is yours to choose. The way you take it. Raoul and I care about you. We think you put too much blame on yourself for the bad things that have happened. The baby…and the other things you have confessed to me. What you saw. Found out. About your husband. And Señor Narinder's…wife. So we decided you need to know what happened before. When the engagement was broken, after the news, the family was upset. They didn't like to look bad. There was so much anger and unhappiness in this house.' Maria shook her head slowly. 'That was when Señora decided that Jovin should have a girl from India. When they began to look for you. And then you came. You are like I would wish for a daughter, and for Raoul too. We don't like to see you hurting this way. I am sure one day, someday, you would come to know these things. Truth is like this. If we didn't tell, you would find out somehow. But we think you need to know this truth now, to help you see things clearly.'

Aneeta folds the worn and yellowing newsprint along the sharp pattern of creases. Lightly, she puts her fingertips to it. With a whisper, it crosses the table once more.

Gregory
San Francisco
June 2002

She holds the phone in one hand. In the other, a scrap of torn paper, its outer edges rough. On the paper: CLAIRE!!! 916 244 1892 CALL ME OR I HUNT YOU DOWN! A piece of the past. Is it something she should hope for in her present?

Might as well find out. Claire's been on her mind. And Gedge has told her she needs to be making more of a social effort. At connections. She told him she didn't need connections. He'd turned on his pity smile: 'Gregory, humans are social animals, we need to make connections. It's an important part of the reintegration process.' She wants to avoid his basketcase file. *Jesus*, she thinks, *I am a wreck*. She takes a deep breath. *Here goes nothing.*

As she begins to punch the numbers she tries to still her jangling nerves. She is biting her lip to the point of pain. The phone begins ringing at the other end. Her ears feel blocked. Like her head's up in a vise. The sound seems so distant, the way it tumbles through. Three rings. She's starting to think that maybe nobody's home. Relief, and yet not. Now four heading towards five rings. No machine. How many is enough? How long should she give it?

A weekday, 10:30. She looks at the clock on the stove. They could all be at work, Claire's son at school. Probably not the best time to be calling. Late afternoon or early evening's probably better. She can picture them. Claire at the table with her boy, rumpling his hair, making jokes. Helping him with homework. Her father reading the news or watching it on TV. Would Claire be able to talk? Would she even want to talk?

'H'lo.' A man's voice. Low and resonant, it echoes through the earpiece pressed to her head.

Under where she grips it the phone handle is becoming slimy. She studies the paper again, holding it higher. Looking intently at it. Wondering if she got the digits wrong. 'Is, uh, is Claire around?'

'Ask who's callin'?'

'Uh, yeah. It's Gregory.' Gregory from prison. Gregory her cellmate. Killer. Ex-con. That Gregory.

Sound goes muffled. She expects he's put his hand over the receiver. There's the cadence of her name with an audible question mark in it. Suddenly on the line, breathless, is Claire: 'Gregory!'

'Hey.' Her heart is thumping, her face is hot, her mouth is curling into a smile. It's good to hear her voice.

'Hey! How are you?' Claire stretches the phrase out. She sounds happy, excited.

'Doing just about okay, I think. You?'

'Good, I'm good. Wow! I can't believe it's you! I half-expected…I didn't really know if I would hear from you or not.'

'I think it says on this paper with your number that I was meant to call or you'd hunt me down, or something—your words.'

'I seem to remember I left you with an ultimatum like that, but I couldn't be sure about you following through or not. Still, here you are. Not quite as hard-assed as I figured you might be!' She laughs. 'It's crazy…it seems like yesterday, writing that paper. I was like a lunatic.'

'Yeah, I guess. Time goes a whole hell of a lot faster out than in.'

'Yeah, you've got it.' There is quiet. A pause that turns things serious. She has to know whether there's a dead end ahead.

'Claire?'

'Yeah?'

'It's nice to hear you. Your voice.'

'Yeah?'

'Sounds familiar. In a nice way.'

'Yeah?'

'I was going to send you a note. A letter. When I got out. But I never. So…' She doesn't have the *cojones* to say it. *Cojones.* The balls. That's what the Latina girls used to say in the kitchen. They used to say it to the bitchy ones who came through the kitchen looking for extras. *Bitch, watch the cojones!* What she thinks is: I didn't know if you'd even want to hear from me. She lets her back slide down the wall under the phone, settles herself on the floor with her knees drawn up. 'Claire?'

'Yeah?'

'I…really missed you, after you left. I hardly even spoke to my new mate. I mean it's not that we didn't get on, we didn't ever disagree, it was easy enough, but we just didn't…What I'm saying, or trying to, is that she wasn't you. She just wasn't ever going to be.' She takes a deep breath, 'That's kind of why I'm calling. I'd hoped that maybe…It's just…I've got this shrink they've hooked me up with, and he keeps pushing on this whole socialization thing. About fitting in. I mean, you know me and…well, maybe that's the point. You *know* me. I know I'm going a mile a minute, but just…hear me out okay? Before I lose my nerve on this. I just… wanted…to ask if…you'd want to stay in touch. If it's not a problem or anything. 'Cause I understand if it is. But, I was wondering…' Gregory's voice drops, 'It's hard.'

'I know.' Claire says it quiet. It is the voice of someone who truly does know. 'I'd like to see you. It'd be nice. To see you face-to-face. How you're doing and all. Telephone isn't the same. How about you come out here one day? Would you be up for that? For socialization's sake? Make your goddamn shrink happy.'

Silence falls again. Should she jump on the offer? If she doesn't then it might just die on the vine. She may not have the guts to follow it up. 'Yeah, I could do that.' This part is unfinished in her. Because of how fast Claire left. How fast it all ended. She doesn't have the strength yet to face all the stuff in her that remains unfinished, stuff like Mama and Lil. But she needs to start dealing with loose ends.

'What do you say? Take the bus out this way.'

'Yeah.'

'Yeah?'

'Okay, sure.'

'Okay, that was easy for a stubborn-ass mule. When?'

'When?'

Claire laughs, 'When. That's how we make plans, Gregory. For *so-shul-ization*.'

'Okay, okay! I don't know, I've got a day off next week?' Why wait? Waiting won't make things easier.

'Hey, so you found yourself a job already? That's good! Good for you!'

'In a bakery café of all the damn things.'

'So which day are we talking?'

'I'm supposed to be off Wednesday, but if it doesn't work for you I could see if I can switch.'

'I'm flexible. Wednesday I can work with. You got a bus schedule? For the Greyhound? That's probably the best way. Cheap and easy. Shouldn't be more than a couple hour ride.'

'I'll get a schedule. Can't be too hard to find. I'll check times. And call you before. Maybe Monday?' She doesn't say, *Just in case you've changed your mind.*

'Yeah. Sounds good. Plan to grab one that gets you here around 12. I'll come get you at the station.'

'I don't want to put you to any trouble.'

'No trouble, Gregory. We can maybe grab lunch. God, tell me you don't love real food. I've put on so much weight.'

'Sure it's no trouble? I'll have to leave in time to get back for check-in at the house.'

She laughs. 'Sure, I'm sure. Just call me Monday. To firm it up. And how's the house anyway?'

'It's good, nice. Like I can't believe how nice.'

'You're lucky. Some, I've heard, are real dives. You get to know anyone there? Social-like?'

'Nah, you know me. I'm happy being a loner.'

'I'm starting to think I get the shrink. He's wondering if it's an excuse. Or a legitimate defect. He's just not sure which yet. Antisocial types make the best psychopaths. Don't want him making his mind up the wrong way about you.'

'Thanks a lot. I may be a freak, but I am no, no...' she looks around for anyone in the vicinity, then lowers her voice, 'I am no psychopath, Claire Darlen!' She can hear a thread of laughter creeping into her.

'Best you start with some social exploits before the good doctor gets the wrong idea.'

'Very funny.'

'Be seeing you Wednesday, Abbott. Call me Monday with your times.'

'I will.'

'And Abbott? It's a good thing you called. To save me the trouble of having to come after you.'

'I know better than to mess with a tough nut like you, Darlen.'

'Yeah, whatever. You slay me. Take care, you.'

'Yeah, you too.'

Monday she'd been ready to cancel, call the whole thing off. But Claire would've seen through her, whatever excuse she'd have cooked up.

She takes the 9:30 Greyhound. Claire has insisted on picking her up. In Claire's words: 'Look out for a filthy blue pick-up.' It's strange to imagine her in a life outside prison walls.

It's the middle of the morning and still the bus seems at least half filled with night-walkers. People with crazy hair and wild eyes, smelling of stale cologne and sweat, arrange themselves along the narrow aisleway. She takes the first available window seat and angles toward the glass. In it she can see the ghosting of herself and what's going on behind her, as well as what's happening in the busyard.

A girl with spiked hair who's chawing away on a mouthful of chewing gum settles next to her. There's a whiff of drugstore hairspray and bubblegum. She hears distant tinny tones of music; notices a wire snaking out of the handbag. A guarantee of quiet if you didn't count the noise leaking into the air.

She holds the cloth bag on her lap, gingerly—a pie from yesterday. Apple. Because it seems to be the one everyone always takes to, without exception. She's doing a mean cherry, and peach, and a tangy rhubarb. But she'd rather hit than miss. Now, closeted in this animal farm, she wonders what the hell she was thinking. Taking pie.

Out of the corner of her eye she sees the driver step up. He's got a belly that makes him look pregnant. Thumbs are hooked into belt loops, trousers sunk low beneath his gut. Oil slicks his hair straight back. The style of yesteryear. Looks something like the way Curtis used to keep his hair. Makes her shiver, the association. He wears big mirrored sunglasses; boots with pointed toes. He looks down the aisleway to the back of the bus. Just looks. Then nods. In a way that seems more a warning of sorts. Finally, he sits. The door pulls closed with a drawn groan and the engine fires up.

Gregory leans herself into the window thankful for the cool against her skin. They ease into the street to begin the trek out of town. She watches building fronts go by. People on the sidewalks. Cars alongside. The bus is picking up speed, there's the chugging roar of the diesel shifting through its gears, the squeal of now and then braking, the hiss of air with it.

She can cope. Of course she can. If it comes to the worst. Been through a hell of a lot that the loss of one person in her life shouldn't matter all that much. If Claire's a piece of yesterday she'll be able keep, then good. If not, least she could tell the doc she'd been making an effort to socialize. That's something. Every now and then the thread of a breeze reaches her. Ruffles the edges of her hair.

Sound and tempo change regularly from the girl next to her. She turns, ever so slightly, and sees her eyes closed. Following her seatmate's lead, she shuts down for the ride.

She wakes, later, with the lean of the bus. The pull of gravity. They're coming off. Headed into Davis. Smaller scale civilization is cropping up. Traffic lights, gas stations, convenience stores, manicured lawns, coffee shops. Trees line boulevards, people dot wide sidewalks.

At the bus station she's in no rush to get out. Doesn't want to look eager. She waits until the last few are getting up and out, stretching, yawning, reaching for bags, backpacks, a guitar case. The driver is looking impatient. She lets those at the back file past, then brings up the rear. When she reaches from the last step for the curb she fixes her eyes on the low-slung stucco station building. The lot is littered with buses and people. The group opens up as she moves. At the outer edges of the human tide she spies her. Claire. Arms crossed across her chest, grinning. No glasses.

'Greg-ree!' she calls out. Throws a hand up to wave. For just a minute it's like her heart stops. Then it gives a great kick of a jumpstart like it's bucking to loose itself. It's Claire all right, there's no mistaking it, but the difference is apparent immediately. From the hug of the jeans slung low on her hips, to the fit of her shirt, the way it clings and narrows at her waist. She's neat, pretty, clean like a damn Noxzema commercial—sanitized. Not the kind of girl you'd ever imagine did a run in state prison. This Claire is All American, girl-next-door.

'Well, look at you!' Claire says appraisingly, taking a lean back. 'Mighty nice in something other'n State of California orange.'

'You too. Obviously civilization agrees with you. You wear freedom well.'

'And just who wouldn't it agree with? Hey? Who the hell, I ask you, would rather be on the inside of things?' Claire steps up and reaches for the bag in Gregory's hands. 'What's this?' Taking charge. The way she always did. The leader. Maybe that was the real seed between them.

'Pie,' Gregory offers. One word, a single syllable. Seems her tongue is all knotted up.

'A pie? And you brought it through that ruckus? Lord, girl.' Claire gives a big wide smile, 'You've got guts. With a menagerie like that. Might have turned out even worse than some of those fights in chow hall.'

'Nothing could get worse than that, Claire.' They share a smile then. 'But those are the kinds of things I'd rather not hang on.'

'Why? Some things are kind of funny when you're looking back.'

'I'd rather not be looking back, Claire.' She says it quiet and low.

Claire's eyes are intense. 'Sometimes, Gregory, it can't be helped. It's a part of you.'

Claire jerks a thumb to where the bus sits idle at the corner of the yard, 'I'm over here, behind the bus,' she says walking ahead, 'just there.' She points out a blue pick-up truck, the lower half covered by a spattering of grime. 'Tryin' to get Jace to clean my truck, but seems he's always got something better to do. Even offered to pay him for it.' She laughs. 'My, it feels strange you and me meeting like this, doesn't it? Something unreal about it all.' She shakes her head a little.

'About the pie? It's apple. Because I wasn't sure. You can take it home. For your dad and Jace. I figured best to play it safe, not knowing anyone's taste.'

'Shoot, girl! Did you think I was just going to take you to lunch up at Denny's or something? Shows what you know. We've got chicken fried and fresh biscuits and potato salad. I've been busting my ass over it, slaving over a hot stove,' she makes a face, 'and you know I'm putting you on. Kitchen never has been my domain. When I went inside, Dad got a housekeeper. For him and Jace. The reason they survived, I guess, though Jace can already do a good weekend eggs or pancakes. I just make the coffee.'

Gregory honestly doesn't know which idea she'd prefer. Both make her uncomfortable. But it seems the choice is not hers anyway. She sets the pie on the bench seat between them. The engine roars and Claire checks over her shoulder before turning a wide U. For a while they drive without talking. Windows down. Radio on. They cruise through town, past strip malls, fast food joints, chain stores, until they turn and head away from where everything has spiked up commercially. She takes in modest houses, white pickets, groups of flowers staked together, posed garden gnomes, bicycles leaned up against shadowed porchfronts. At first she finds the quiet between them awkward, but as scenery passes she feels herself unwinding. Claire sings with Chris Isaak on the radio. Sun is beating through the windshield. It is hot inland. Much more so than at the coast. Denim is sticking to her legs, pulling at the flesh under them. She shifts the way she sits and trails her forearm out the window, feeling the air lick at it. The wind on her face is drying the damp at her hairline.

The valley air is void of the salty tang of sea that she's becoming used to. Instead, memory recalls the sweet, dirty smell of grassland with a sour of fertilizer. It plays on her. Reminds her of all the driving they did together, Curtis, Mama and her. All the running. All in the name of keeping secrets.

'So tell me what you've been up to.'

'Not much,' she shrugs. She looks at the cracked earth of an unplanted field that they are passing. Dry silt blows in swirls along trenches the plough has left.

'Not much? What a crock! So tell me about the not much. Tell me something. You're too damn quiet.'

Turn the same dirt again at the next planting season and it'll give itself over to something entirely new. 'Well, I got a job.'

'Yeah, you said. In a café?'

'Yeah. Managed to keep the early morning routine. I bake mostly.'

'Explains the pie.' Claire grins.

'Yeah, I guess.' Although she thinks, no, not really, it doesn't. Yes, she's made it. But she's got nothing to prove that way. That's not why she brought it. It's more that she wanted to do something. For Claire. For hello or goodbye. For whichever it turns out to be.

'Nice place?'

'Yeah. Small. Quaint. Not modern.'

'People? What're they like?'

'Yeah, nice. The owner, Gerry, is getting on a bit, so her son wanted to ease her workload by taking on help, or a secondary, since everything they sell is baked fresh.'

'Gerry's a her?'

'Yeah. She said that's why she gave me the job, on account of my name. Said she felt we had something in common there.'

'A good thing to come out of the name, hey? So between the two of you, you and her, you do it all?'

'It's not a big place, so it's not too bad. I have help during the day. I just get things kicked off in the mornings.'

'And they know?'

'Yeah, some. Gerry was willing to take a chance on me. Helped that Lil gave a glowing reference. It's early days yet, but it's working. I like it. Like them too. See—socialization, right?'

'So that's good.'

'Yeah. It's good. You?' Gregory looks over at her, studying her relaxed smile, hair blowing about her face in the warm wind.

'Back at UC Davis.'

'They took you back?' Her voice rises with the question.

'Yeah, but it took a fair bit of wrangling. I'm only a junior research assistant, they took my seniority, they have my parole office on speed dial, and I'm on an indefinite probationary period. Which basically means the bastards have to pay me next to nothing. And if I even so much as take an extra packet of sugar from the cafeteria they've got grounds to boot my ass. I'm doing grunt work, which is bullshit. But I've got time. And I'm not afraid of work. Hell, it's work, right? It pales in comparison to some other stuff I've known, we've known. I'm not much afraid of anything anymore.' She laughs. 'Maybe it's my professional penance, like snakes and ladders. That I've got to go down to the bottom and climb back up.'

'Seen any of your old colleagues?'

'Yeah. Most have moved on, retired, transferred, moved into private industry. The way things typically work in research. There are some left, not many. And some who don't know me, but know of me. My infamous reputation precedes me in Davis U circles. Makes me a bit of a celebrity.' Claire turns and grins.

'Get out! Celebrity, my ass.'

'You know like those circus creatures with ten heads? Or maybe Medusa? People give me a wide berth. It doesn't bother me. Keeps things quiet. I can handle it.'

'Yeah. I'd just about bet you can, Claire.' She smiles at the mental picture she's imagined.

'Everybody makes mistakes. I did my time. I'm moving on. If people got a problem with that, tough shit, it's my life. Honestly, I can't waste more time feeling like I always have to apologize for it. For me that's how it's got to be. I'd rather just play it straight with people. And get on with things. Focus on what matters.'

She can feel Claire glance over at her. Can feel her eyes on her. Studying her profile. She jokes, needing something to hide behind, 'We there yet?'

'Spoken like a true child.'

'Expect anything else?'

'Patience is a virtue, pouty kid.'

'Yeah, one I don't got.'

'Bullshit. After how many years in the can?'

Gregory gives her a look. Sidelong. Sees that she is smiling ahead, up through the windshield. But she gets a sense of seriousness, despite her demeanor. 'Didn't make me patient.'

'Speaking of patience, have you seen your mother?' In an instant Claire has shifted gears.

Gregory stares into a passing field, plants flowering yellow, and squints her eyes against the sun, 'Nah… I don't think I'm ready. Something the doc and I agree on.' Not quite the truth, but an adequate sidestep. She knows her, Claire does. Enough to box her into a corner. 'You count as the first. First reconnecting connection.'

'I'm honoured, I guess, if it was intended that way. But you're just changing the subject. Trying to avoid it, Gregory. What're you waiting on?'

'Dunno. Christmas. Hell freezing over, maybe. Stigmata, or some kind of mystical sign.'

'Yeah, you go on and be a joker. You're so full of it.' Claire laughs.

Gregory sobers, 'Don't know how to handle it, I suppose, or what to expect.'

'Never know until you try.'

'Wise, kemosabe. But I'm not like you. Can't just walk back into my old life. And before you go on with the lecture, let me just point out that you didn't kill one of your parents.'

'No. Don't suppose I did.'

'So what's your dad like?'

'Got the hint. Okay, I'll let you off. Changing subject.'

'Thanks.'

'What do you mean, like?'

They're driving along a rural route now, there isn't a whole lot but large expanses of green land punctuated every once in a while by a grove of trees, barn, farmhouse, horses.

'Since you've been out. With you, I mean.'

'Well, he's been good. That's not to say we haven't had our share of adjustment, or haven't done our share of arguing. 'Specially when it comes to Jace. He sometimes forgets I'm Jace's mom. That Jace is his grandkid, not his kid. There are things we don't always see eye to eye on. He usually comes around.'

Claire slows and turns off the roadway onto a tree-lined laneway that opens into an expansive tailored clip of manicured hedgerow. The landscape speaks volumes in its carefully cultivated precision. This is not like any kind of living she has ever seen, hell, even gotten close to. So how was it that she had assumed she and Claire were so much alike? Because Claire had said *farm*. Said she'd grown up on a farm. Gregory had taken the word at face value, had wrapped her own perspective around the term and left it at that. Though together with Claire's education, which she'd known about, and her job, which to a certain extent Gregory had also known something about, the details added themselves up a lot differently than she had.

They pull to a stop. She faces a stately and pristine rise of house looking nothing like *farm* but a whole lot more like *manor*. Pillars flank a grand entryway; a long expanse of porchline runs the front from end to end. Carefully tended flowers are clustered at intervals. Willows grace a rock-lined pond. A tire on a thick length of rope hangs idly underneath a beard of branches, almost hidden from view. A tidy line-up of vehicles angles out from a trio of barn doors. In a paddocked field she can see a pair of horses. Discomfort in her rears up, rising like a rocket to the moon.

How wrong has she been? Just from what she can see it seems impossible that there be a future between them. In prison everything's stripped away. So that on the surface everyone's equal. But out here? To deny that money or things or privilege define a person would be a bald-faced lie.

'Home, sweet home.' Claire sits in the cab not moving. She must have known how it would look, feel. 'Ready?'

'As I'll ever be,' she mutters, more to herself than Claire.

'Dad's probably still in the field.' Claire hops from the cab and slams the door.

Gregory slides slowly out and picks her way after Claire. Like a kid tiptoeing her way into something she shouldn't be, pie or no pie. She feels guilty and she hasn't even made it inside. 'Does he remind you, your dad?' Gregory asks. Wouldn't this be an *I told you so* kind of world?

'No, he and I are in agreement on that. There's nothing to be gained. The future is about Jace. If Jace weren't around and part of the equation then maybe it wouldn't be so easy. But we avoid it for his sake.'

'No questions?'

'From Jace? Not really, not yet. But I have to be realistic. In the sense that I know we don't live in a vacuum.' She shrugs, 'People talk. Maybe as he gets older…I'm hoping we'll be strong enough to handle it, if and when it comes. Hoping I'll be strong enough.' They step through a screen door that claps shut behind them as they enter a room of golden yellow. There's a long wooden table surrounded by solid, sturdy and practical farmhouse chairs. The air is a heady mix of fried chicken and baking. Biscuits. Comfort food. Perfectly matched to soften the tensions of uncomfortable times. Times like these. Her stomach grumbles at her. Wary and yawing.

'Tractor's still out, but they'll be heading this way soon. Creatures of habit, these two. Dad and his hand.' Gregory slides the pie out and places it on a wide kitchen island. Claire leans in close to the golden pastry and breathes deeply. 'Smells divine!'

'Hope it tastes that way.'

Claire sets herself to pulling out plates and cutlery, readying for the meal. 'Grab yourself some lemonade. Must be thirsty.' She seems happy, satisfied, as she moves. Whole.

'Yeah, thanks.' It tastes so good going down, the tartness of lemon puckers her up and makes her mouth water.

'Lotta's already gone for the day, she's the housekeeper and cook, not to mention keeper of flowers, mender of socks, knees, just about everything. Jace adores her. I adore her. My waistline, however, does not.'

'He ever come back, Claire?' Her movements slow with the question. She knows without saying who Gregory's referring to. The reason that brought her all the trouble to begin with.

'Not around here. Not to my knowledge.'

'So you haven't heard.'

'No. Haven't heard. But I'm not really looking to hear either. In certain circles…I'm sure if I wanted to I could get a line on him. I don't, though, want to know.' She smiles, but it is shaky.

Somewhere a clock chimes noon and the men are suddenly at the door. After the basic formality of introductions, Claire's father seems to look right through her. Kind of like he's pretending she's not there. He's clipped in his way and his words. Gregory can tell he doesn't trust her. She can understand how he might be suspect. Can't blame him for it. Claire has obviously issued strict instructions about conversation lines in advance because they work carefully around the hard center, how Gregory and Claire have come to be acquainted, sticking instead to just the edges of things. Things that don't matter, really, at all.

'Ever done farm work, Gregory?'

'No, sir.'

'Lived on a farm?'

'No, sir.'

'City girl, then?'

'No, more small town.'

'Ah, well…Claire tells me you've settled in San Francisco?'

'Yes, sir.'

'How you like it there?'

'It's an adjustment.'

'I'll bet.'

She sees Claire shoot him a look. His skepticism is all in the set of his jaw and the steely grim line of his mouth.

Claire tries her damndest, but the conversation is riddled with potholes of awkward silence. Axle-breaking beasts that're almost impossible to navigate around. The closest thing to interaction between them all is when Claire mentions that her truck happens to be giving trouble on the down shift. Gregory knows her way around basic auto mechanics. How could she not? What with cars riddling the front lawns of her childhood, various varsoled parts sharing counter space with meals, Curtis making her re-fit tires on bare wheel hubs to 'toughen her up', or making her work the hand jack to 'give her some muscles'. She knows enough about working under the hood to suggest that it might be a timing issue. She also knows enough to read the raised eyebrows of the men who sit opposite her after she says it.

Claire's dad takes some time chewing it over, like the food, pushing it from side to side until the idea makes itself palatable to him. When eventually he nods, slow and deliberate-like, his man Carlos looks at him from the corner of one eye. 'Might be right,' is all he says.

Timing is at the center of everything, not just mechanics. The way things have to mesh just right for gears to match, how pieces have to lock themselves together for everything to work in tandem, without misfire or collateral damage. For everything to be smooth. She wonders about whether she and Claire still have that. Whether their gears still mesh. Or whether with time and the changed landscape they've gone out of synch.

Doing time once held them close. Prison. But it's not the bond between them any longer. There's a matter of apples to apples comparative that no longer applies. It's what one of her junior school math teachers once upon a time used to screech about fractions: *In order to compare, class, what must we have? A common denominator, missus,* the whole damn class would drone. For Claire and her, the common denominator is gone. And she's not sure what's left.

Kameko
San Francisco
June 2002

Endurance a woman should cultivate more than anything else. If you endure well in any circumstance, you will achieve happiness. It was the feminine ideal in the time of the *hakoiri musume,* the box-enclosed maidens. Inside, it still pulls at her, the idea of it, passed down through generations of women and from Mother to her. It is perhaps a lesser part of her fabric, but threads of it yet remain. And play on her, especially now.

In the quiet of the bookshop she has to try and draw the pleasant, enduring mask back into place. Before the rest of the world sees what lies underneath. She opens her mouth wide. To release the tension. No one is here to see her strange face. As if it is a shout or a scream she makes, but with no sound. It occurs to her that her eyes must also bulge with this exercise. She is reminded of a fish lying on the shore, gaping for air. She goes through the motion several times. It makes the lower half of her face a little bit looser.

Heavy steps move with her from case to case along the floorboards. Are her steps always this loud? Why has she never noticed? The bell at the door rings out suddenly. Her movement stalls, she does not feel ready to face anyone just yet.

'You're early again? This is getting to be a habit. If you're not careful I'll start exploiting it.' He shouts it out. For he cannot see her. She is removed from his eyes, in the stacks, the World Wars section at the back wall. He knows, though, that she is there, from the order of things. It gives away her presence. But he is mistaken in thinking it is purely industry that prompts her.

The patience of *gaman,* she used to think, was a sign of self-control, of strength. Now she is not sure. Some days, days like today, when the turmoil in her is so great it threatens to explode, she wishes she could release just a little. The way steam escapes a boiling pot. Without notice, simply disappearing into the air. His feet approach, seeking her out. She attempts to arrange her face in a pleasing order, to dispel the last vestiges of her fish face exercise. She prays that her tension, her pain, is not outwardly evident.

'Ah, here you are! Should have known I might find you in the wars.' Richard smiles at her. He does not realize the irony of his wit. It is a joke, of course. But she cannot find it in herself to indulge it. Instead, she gives in to exactly the opposite of emotions. In seconds, even splinters of seconds it seems, the mask and careful cloak of equanimity have vanished and she is wailing and sobbing like a person she does not recognize, in a fit of upset. She knows she ought to, wants to, but she cannot regain control. The boiling pot has bubbled over, no longer able to contain its heated contents.

'Kameko, my God, are you okay? It was a joke. Is it that I made a joke about war? I'm sorry, just, you have to stop. My God, I don't know what to do with a crying woman, jeez. Are you? Okay? Of course you're not okay. What am I saying?'

She sinks heavily onto the floorboards, her spine collapsing against the hard edges of shelving and books. She takes pleasure in the pain it causes, in the reality of a physical discomfort.

'Jesus, Matt, I don't know what's happened, okay? She's totally hysterical.' He is on his mobile phone, turning his face away from her. Like falling leaves, words flutter around her. 'No...help me out. Come down...yeah...no idea! No! I just made some stupid joke about a war, I mean, the wars....' He sounds exasperated in trying to explain.

She is suddenly embarrassed, ashamed. There is no way to escape the indignity of her melodrama. She reaches for the tissue he offers. In the other hand he holds the entire box. She smearily wipes first her leaking eyes, then her nose, and balls up the mess in a closed fist. She spasms, periodically, as pockets of trapped air ricochet inside her body. She attempts to swallow them as sobs begin to quiet and trail off.

'Wow,' Richard suddenly gasps, 'you got your hair done! How slow am I? Like, I just noticed. But, hon, it's gorgeous!' He takes a lock and winds it onto his finger. Then he slides back from her across the boarded floor and says, 'The colour, the layers— honey, it's fabulous. Really. The tears, I take it, have nothing to do with the new do.' She lifts her head to look at him, every so often she hiccups and her head, and hair, jerk with it. She can barely make him out through blurry eyes, but begins to laugh a little at him. Crazy, that he should notice her hair. Crazy. Crazy, like she has been. And yet, it is just the distraction she needs. 'I'm telling you, you look fabulous. Totally.' She is pathetic, really. Feels pathetic. Gloom is sweeping over her again. Her lips begin to tremble. She reaches for the tissue box, takes another. She twists the softness around her hands until it has taken on a crumpled, tubular shape.

She whispers, 'I did it, the hair...to please...my husband.' He is watching her, his face is sorry. She concentrates herself on the manipulation of the tissue and away from his obvious sympathy. Dully she says, 'It is...for him...not enough. *I* am not enough. But I have to...had to...try.' He slides toward her and takes her hands. Even the one with the limp, soggy twine of tissue that she clutches. Together they lean against the hard, uneven shelving.

'I'm sorry, Kameko, really I am. Honey, I can't pretend to understand— I'm the kind of guy who can't put the words serious and relationship in the same sentence. The whole idea of marriage, the long haul, it freaks me out. I have to say, I totally admire your commitment, and your determination. Matt told me about the affair. You're just too sweet a girl to have to put up with being screwed around on. The asshole's lucky to have you. I don't think it's the same, necessarily, in reverse. If it were me? I would can the man's balls. And kick him to the curb. There you have it.' Earnest blue eyes study her, the set of his mouth is straight and pinched. 'Life is too short to have to put up with that that kind of drama. To have to deal with it. Especially when you are so obviously trying to make things work. You know, hon? If you ever need some downtime, or space, or a breather, you can use the office to crash in. If you ever want some time to figure things out. Even as a place to stay. I can personally vouch for the sofa. Honestly, Kameko? You practically live here as it is now.' He smiles at her, his eyebrows rise, though in his eyes there is concern. 'And…you shouldn't have to always justify being here by working.'

'I…' she shudders, 'like to…work.' She pushes the words out, nodding. 'It helps me. To feel better. It makes me more quiet, here,' she taps at her temple. 'Takes my mind away. Otherwise, with too much thinking, it is difficult to be accepting.'

'Jesus. I don't know how you do it. You have the benevolence of a saint.'

'No,' she shakes her head, 'because I am not able to endure.' Words of Mother's come to her mind: *You must let trying matters be like water. Let them flow through, or wash over. Do not keep them for more than their time.* But her insides are like a typhoon, turbulent and volatile. It is a weakness. One that probably keeps her from the only thing that might settle the storm: a baby.

Aneeta
Fresno, California
July 2002

While she waits for fate and opportunity to agree, she holds fast to the astrologer's prediction. Soon.

It is not often she finds herself alone in her brother-in law's company. Yet this is precisely the condition she needs. Desperately, she hopes she is right in her assumptions about his sensitivities. She is counting on his outrage at the betrayal. More than anything, though, she is counting on his willingness to help.

She is home on her own for the afternoon, with a list Anju has prepared of things to attend to. The California sun is high in the midday sky. The warmth of it surrounds her. She draws a damp sheet from the basket at her side. A soft and gentle breeze blows, flipping loose ends of fabric. She pushes the drying wire along. The wind brings a scent of flowers and blossoming trees. As she is about to anchor a corner of cloth with a wooden clothespin, the wind also brings the cry of a baby. Time stops. The peg remains in her hand, suspended in mid-air. It comes again, the cry, this time with more urgency. It reaches out to her over the fence. The neighbours. The baby is a girl. Cassandra. She cannot find it in herself to feel happy for them. Anju had tsked and tutted that it is a shame. 'Nice people, they are. Too bad. It is always nice to have a boy. Then perhaps for the next one it does not matter so much.' She had resumed speculation through a forkful of biryani, 'I am sure he was hoping. Every man wants a son.' The cry rises again, and then, falls silent. Aneeta imagines the woman cradling the infant in her arms, softly singing. She plunges the peg harshly over the length of cloth and, as sobs erupt, clamps a hand to her mouth. Leaving the basket with damp contents spilling over the sides, she runs clumsily for the refuge of the laundry room to suffer her grief in private. To mourn her empty arms and her own lost child. She clambers through the door, pushing it hard behind her.

Sobbing, she sinks into an unwashed pile of garments. She muffles her sound in the first piece of clothing that yields to the clawing grip of her hands. It is a shirt of Jovin's. Still ripe with the scent of his aftershave cologne. *I hate you. Hate you. Hate you both.* The wretched scene loops again. Because there is no one else at home, she gives in to her pain, her outrage, her fury. *It was the two of you. You who made me lose everything. Everything. Something to be. A child to love. You took it. From me.* Open palms batter her message upon walls. Feet lash out to attack order in the neatly separated piles. Spindles of the drying rack collapse under a heap of damp vests and bras and blouses and shirts. Fists pound metal, plaster and wood, until despair evolves into exhaustion and finally, into silence.

The pain, however, is as sharp as ever. In her chest and deep in her abdomen. In her head it throbs behind her eyes and roars through her ears. She begins numbly to re-sort the pile of garments. To separate dirty from clean. When Narinder flings open the door, she gasps. His reaction tells her that her presence, too, is unexpected. 'Aneeta! I didn't think anyone was here.'

She tries to attempt a smile and hastily wipes a hand across wet cheeks. 'Yes, I am here.'

'I thought you would have gone with Mom and Dad.'

'No. Your mother wanted to be sure dinner was prepared.'

'Ah, you wouldn't have missed much. All those family things are the same.'

'Yes,' she whispers, suddenly conscious of being in the midst of the household's soiled garments, including all manner of underthings. She is embarrassed for him, and embarrassed for herself. But here at last is her chance. She cannot afford to lose her long-awaited opportunity to modesty. She clears her throat.

'I couldn't find my squash gear. I thought I'd put it in the laundry, so I figured I'd try here just in case. I'm going for a game at the gym. Didn't take any kit. Ah, here. Shirt. Shorts. You don't mind if I take them?'

'Narinder?'

He grabs the items from a pile heaped close to the door, raising the fabric quickly to his nose. 'Not too bad,' he comments, chuckling. 'The smell, I mean.'

Has he heard her? Has he noticed that she isn't laughing with him? Does it matter? *No.* The only thing that matters, the only thing, is that she tell him. *Tell him.* She presses on, gathering strength to face him, to look him in the eye, 'I need to talk to you.'

'Can it wait? I'm running late. When I come back. Dinner. At dinner?'

'No.' She is firm.

His haste stalls. 'All right.' He says it slowly, with a pause between the first and second parts. All. Right. But nothing is right.

She tries vainly to steady her nerves and to ease her thudding heartbeat. To focus on what lies ahead. Her voice is quiet, but sure. 'I need to speak to you about your wife.' The words echo through her. She draws a breath before she plunges determinedly past the point of no return, 'And my husband.'

His look she will never forget. Disbelief. Shock. Anguish. Emotions wring the colour from his pallor. And turn him as pale as bone grey ash. 'Tell me,' he says. In his eyes there is fire.

She has resolved to hold nothing back, not to cloud the truth for the sake of modesty, or apology. She offers what she knows humbly, without condemnation, without judgment. His features fall in a slow melt, like the wax of a candle. She is sorry for his pain. It sits heavily with her that she has been the one to cause it.

'Is there more?' His tone is grim, and yet, not surprised. This much—that he might have known or suspected already—she has not considered.

She shakes her head, suddenly cautious. 'There is no more I can tell about what is between them. But I also know, about…before. Before I came here. Before I married Jovin. And I know…that I cannot stay.' It is done. Her fingers tremble. Her skin prickles. Tension coils within her. Ice floods her veins. They are not moving. Neither he nor she. Silence cocoons them.

Without warning he shatters the quiet, his sound like jagged tin, 'Will you be going back to Delhi?'

'No.' She looks up at him with a sad smile. In Delhi they would not welcome her. They would turn her away, send her back, do what they had to. To keep old whispers stilled; to keep fresh inky secrets from staining a good Brahmin name.

'Then…I'll handle it. Just…let me think about it.' He nods sharply.

Heavy wings of imaginary auntie jackals beat down on her, scree-screeing their scorn: *Such a little thing. How weak she must be if she cannot take the smallest of transgressions. He is from a good family. With a good job. And in America. She has the sweetest of fortunes. Hai! She thinks she is the first woman to face such a scene? It is hardly different than cooking or cleaning. A small sacrifice.*

'In the meantime, I'd appreciate that you not mention we had this,' Narinder pauses, 'conversation. I'll figure things out and come back to you.'

She lowers her head. Swallows hard. Her mouth is dry and tight. 'Thank you, Bhaji,' she says solemnly. They are bound together now.

She spends three long nights staring wide-eyed at the guest bedroom ceiling. Narinder has said nothing directly to her since. And, from what she can tell, nothing to anyone else. The rest of the household follows a normal rhythm. There is nothing to alert her to any change, any trouble. She does her best to hide her anxiety. She feels like a racehorse at the Mahalaxmi track. Tiptoeing in place. Holding nervously for the bell.

On the fourth day Narinder comes from work in the early afternoon. Without warning. He comes to the kitchen door while she is chopping potatoes. She knows instinctively why he is there. He raises a finger to his lips. Has he known? Known that this is Anju's day at the beauty salon? One of Maria and Raoul's off days? Dadi, after his midday meal, is comfortably slumbering before the afternoon soap operas. His favourite is Days of Our Lives. At four o'clock. He may sleep through others, but he is sure to awaken for good at the theme song. She checks the wall clock. Shortly before two.

Vegetables are all around her. In varied states of preparedness for the evening meal. A meal that suddenly no longer matters. It is time. Her stomach flip-flops wildly. She puts down the paring knife. He raises his finger to his lips again to keep her silent, though it is hardly necessary. Neither of them wishes to alert Dadi-ji.

In his hand is a bulky envelope. On his finger is a key attached to a slender column of clear plastic through which she could see the word BUDGET in orange letters. He motions her closer. 'Where is your case?' he whispers tersely.

'In Jovin's room. Under the bed.'

'Is there anything else?'

'Just a few things. I have a bag. In the guest bedroom. I will collect them.'

'Take only what you can carry.'

She nods dumbly. With him close at her back they slide from kitchen to hallway in silence. She is intensely aware of the loudness of her own breathing, the cracks of her bones, the creaks of the floor under every step. She winces each time she makes a sound. Her heart is pounding. Breath comes icy quick. She moves with purpose. In the guest room she frantically gathers her things. There is no time for neatness, for folding and arranging. She moves across the hall to the bathroom. And recalls the blood she could not stop. The life that had drained away. Her throat buckles. She forces her eyes to the mirror and channels a message to the reflection staring back at her. *No. Now is not the time.* She takes her toothbrush and paste. Her hairbrush, comb and hairpins. Antiperspirant and perfume. Her few bottles of Cutex varnish. Finally, she bids the sad face watching the silent economy a firm but hopeful goodbye.

When Narinder meets her in the hallway with her case they say nothing. Snoring comes in even measures over the creep of television dialogue. They ease back into the kitchen. She puts the plaid plastic luggage bag on the floor at her feet. It crinkles slightly, a noise that sounds to her like thunder. Her handbag is over her shoulder. 'Ready?' He whispers. She nods gravely. He picks up her case and turns to the door. A sudden succession of coughing sputters from the living room. For an instant they freeze, stalled upon the threshold. Snoring, though, shortly resumes, and the moment of panic subsides.

He watches behind them as they step out of the house, and pulls the door gently closed. It feels like a scene from a cat burglar film. The silence, the furtiveness in their movements, the clandestine nature of what they are doing. He moves swiftly down the path at the side of the house, careful that his heels don't strike the cement. She walks on her toes to avoid the click-clack staccato of her sandals.

At the sidewalk she follows as he crosses to the other side of the street. The wind gently tugs the ends of her chunni, fluttering them at her back. She turns to look at the face of the house, only for an instant, and then quickens her steps to keep pace. There isn't any of the melancholy of leaving Delhi. There is only a sense of relief flooding slowly and hesitantly through her.

He stops at a small white car, not bigger than the Corolla, and inserts the key in his hand into the lock on the boot. He slots her case easily in. She lifts the bag in beside it. They are far enough along the block now that even if Dadi or any one of the neighbours were to have been watching, the two silhouettes would not have been easily discernible in the brilliance of the California sun.

'The car is rented and paid for three weeks. Return it to any Budget rental car outlet. Car hire outlet? You can find them in the telephone directory.' She nods, what else is there to do? 'There's a map on the seat. They're probably also listed there. At least the ones close-by are.' He hands her the thick envelope. 'A gift from Jovin,' he says darkly.

A flock of pigeons mounts inside of her. Panic again grips her. *Hunh, stupid girl!* The voice in her head is guttural and condemning. What if? What if the brothers are allied against her? Is this a trap? 'But what?' she exclaims breathlessly.

'No, don't worry, I've told him nothing. For the moment he's still blissfully ignorant. The cash in the envelope is from his trading account. At work. I took it without him knowing. He'll have some explaining to do. But I think he owes you. For what he's done. And the hurt you've been through. Besides,' he continues grimly, 'it gave me some satisfaction to be able to take it from him. He's taken enough from me. And there's this,' he reaches into his pocket and draws out a business card. It is his own, but on the back handwritten in capital letters is the name Patrick Mullen along with a series of digits. A telephone number, she guesses. 'He's a property manager. Company he's with has places pretty much throughout the state. He owes me a favour from way back. Not telling you what to do, and not saying where you should go, just that if you use my name he'll help you out. Use your family name, not ours, that way he won't know how we're connected. Jovin doesn't know him. I've told Patrick you might call. He's agreed to arrange a unit for the next few months. No charge to you. I'll cover it. If you decide that's what you want.'

'Thank you,' she says softly. 'No one…has ever helped me like this.'

'I figure it's the least I could do,' he laughs harshly and looks away.

'I'm sorry…for the trouble I've caused you.'

'Don't be. It's not your fault.' His voice is sharp, pained.

'But your parents, I never wanted…for them to suffer…' hesitating, she adds, 'or you.'

'After I say what I'm planning to tonight,' he returns his gaze to where she stands, his mouth in a small, bitter curl, 'things are going to get ugly. But I can't see them coming after you. It would only make things more public. Your being gone will be humiliation enough. All the same, you know, I wouldn't leave a trail. The only one I can't vouch for is Jovin. Obviously, I don't really know my brother at all.' He can't disguise the acid in his voice. 'You should go. We don't really want to tempt fate by standing out here any longer than we have to.'

'Yes,' she agrees, feeling somewhat dazed by her sudden shift in reality. Her insides swell and heave nervously.

He opens the driver's door for her and waits while she settles herself behind the steering wheel. 'Good luck, Aneeta.'

'And to you too, Bhaji.' Her eyes feel the heat of threatening tears. 'I… can't thank you enough. You are a good man,' she says simply, 'and a good son.'

She slots the key he has given her into the ignition and turns it to hear the engine catch. Solidly, he pushes the car door closed. She shifts from neutral into drive, once again looking to where he stands, his arms crossed tightly over his chest. How sorry she feels for him. She gives a wavering smile. Of gratitude. A single tear begins to roll. She swallows against the ache. Looking once over her shoulder, she lifts her foot from the brake and lets the car begin to slowly take her forward. As she drives down the street she glances into the rearview mirror and sees him still standing there, motionless in the road, watching her leave. Silently, she promises the timid girl in the corner of the reflection frame that it will be the last time she looks back.

The End:
The Influence of Freedom

*The gloom of the world is but a shadow. Behind it, yet within our reach,
is joy.
Take joy.*

Fra Giovanni Giocondo

Kameko
San Francisco
July 2002

English 50
Introduction to Creative Writing
This class will introduce the process and techniques of creative writing. Students
will experiment with various types of writing, including the writing of poetry. Class
readings will expose students to various writing styles and provide examples of
the successes and strategies of other writers. Class time will be spent discussing the
writer's craft, assigned readings, and the student's own creative writing pieces.
Wednesdays 6:00 to 8:00 p.m.
Arts and Humanities Building

She has seen the course description in a college catalogue left stacked by the noticeboard near the door of the shop. Something had made her flip through it as she had been straightening the things on the low run of shelving. Something.

She goes to the Tea Garden to walk quietly with her thoughts; along tidy pathways that curve between carefully tended gardens and koi ponds, beneath the rise of curving rooflines and towering pagodas. It is alive with tourists. Elderly Japanese in visors against the sharp sunlight walk with hands clasped conservatively behind their backs. Their pace is slow, indulgent, so unlike the life they have come from. Dialects of her native language swirl around her. Since she has left Tokyo she feels connection to them all. Even with their differences. The inflections that give one's origins away are all but forgotten here. It does not matter so much, the points on the compass, when one is outside of it. In a greater landscape it ceases to be a point for judgment, or for status.

Here, in the garden, she feels closer to Mother. To Akira. In her thoughts she speaks to them. They help her to think, to rationalize. It is not madness, but a trick she contrives. A scale of internal balance. Mother at one end and Akira at the other. She can hear their voices and summon their images.

'You are a wife now. Education is for girls before they are married.'
I know this Mother, her silent reply.
'You should be attending to your husband.'
In the same way he is attending to me?

229

'That is different, Kameko.'

How is it?

'It is your duty as his wife.'

Akira interjects, 'Oh come off it, Kimura-san! Your thought is so old-fashioned. Times have changed.'

And yet they have not, Kameko thinks.

'She should be concentrated on babies. Giving her husband a family. That is what settles a man to his fate.'

'Fate,' Akira spits. 'Is that what it all comes back to? The damnation to a certain fate? I don't believe that. Fate is to be decided by oneself. Not left to the manipulations of others.' Kameko can see the scowl across Akira's features.

'It is not easy, but when misfortune beckons you must turn in the other direction, Kameko, and resist the temptation to look back upon it. Otherwise its power may stay to poison you.' Mother's ear is sympathetic. But her counsel is rooted in old ways. Drawn from what she knows, what she has lived, the choices she has made.

Akira groans. 'Stop focussing always on living for him. He's surely not living his life focussed on you. Besides, neediness is entirely unbecoming.'

'So is becoming headstrong, as she is with her own job outside and with the idea of more education. That is the more undesirable.'

'So why the other woman? His little America doll?' Akira makes a sharp point, one that cuts right to the heart of the matter.

She can see Mother's face become waterlike, rippling and fading.

'What did I tell you, Kameko? Don't be the stereotype. Maybe it is good that there is not a child in this. It would cloud things even further.'

Perhaps. And perhaps just the opposite is true. Perhaps she would not *be* in such a position if she had given him a child. If she could have. She cannot know.

'Don't derive your worth from anything other than yourself,' Akira warns. 'Besides, *he* has cast his vote—for himself. But he cannot make you cast yours in the same way. It is your choice. Don't wait until there is nothing left of *you*. Then you might as well be here with us.' And with that, Akira's image also vanishes, leaving her alone with her thoughts.

One evening a week. It seems not too great a concession. Would he be irritated with her? On the days he did come home he would not likely be back from work before that hour anyway. It might also be a good thing—for him to wait on her occasionally. She puts her hands to her cheeks where she can feel heat rising at the irreverent thought.

She sits in the dimming light of day, in the car park of a shopping mall an hour up the freeway, and counts it. Whispered numbers in breathy Punjabi buffeted by the surrounding silence of the car. Her mind for counting things still seems to turn over in an Indian tongue. Stern faces, unsmiling, look severely out at her from notes of vellum and green. Some of them have stuck. Against the furtive flicking of damp and sweaty fingertips. So she is not sure that she has been correct. In fact she is more certain that she has not been. But she is close. Eighteen thousand, six hundred and fifty dollars. She breathes out heavily, overcome at the amount. There is a sudden wave of guilt that rushes through her. For having so much money. Someone else's money.

She removes three of the bills from the top of the stack. She coaches herself in English this time. Fifty. One hundred. One hundred and fifty. She tries to shorten the sound of the *-dred* sound on the hundreds. With her tongue flattening the usual rolled sound of the *r*. Nervously, she re-tucks the flap into the body of the envelope. For safety, she shoves the envelope deep into her handbag, so that her fingers scrape along the bottom before she releases it. The bills in her hand she folds in half and then half again and zips them into the small inside pocket. Then she pulls the main zipper carefully from end to end, watching metal teeth mesh together.

She pulls the lock, opens the car door, and steps out. The darkness of the asphalt is gridded by thick white lines. It reminds her of the first of her driving lessons with Jovin. The expansive space is punctuated by cars of every shape, size, colour and description. Hers is unremarkable among them. One of many.

She thinks back to how things were left: potatoes unboiled, peelings in the sink, vegetable piles. Laundry water-logged in the machine. Poor Dadi-ji. She wonders how much of the blame he would shoulder. For snoring through all of it. She can imagine Anju's scolding. The shrill of her tone. His confusion. With what Narinder is intending, she suspects that unfinished chores and an uncooked meal would be downgraded to small resentments. The missing daughter-in-law perhaps a somewhat larger one. But the truth? It will surely overtake everything.

Acutely aware of the thick envelope buried in the depths of her bag, she clutches the vinyl of the handbag strap so that her knuckles glow white. The body of it is tucked under her arm, tight to her. With a surge of determination she coaxes her footsteps out of the maze of cars and toward the halo of blue light that wraps around the wide bank of doors before her.

A blue-vested woman with thick eyeglasses chirps, 'Welcome to Wal-Mart. Buggy? Basket?' She is smiling easily, looking Aneeta up and down. 'Why, you look real pretty. Like a princess or something, I'm not sure. Can I help you find something?'

'Ladies clothing,' she says, returning the smile shyly. She thinks of the clothing of Samar's she has envied, held up against her body; freshly laundered items yet to be returned to their rightful owner.

Anju had discouraged her from wearing American styles. Whether it was because she did not want the expense of purchasing new things, or simply did not approve, was uncertain. Perhaps it was a way to assure that daughter-in-laws were kept separate, perhaps it was to keep her from becoming like Samar in other ways as well.

Once, her mother-in-law had taken her to a Wal-Mart quite near the house. To shop for a wedding gift intended for some distant relation. 'We hardly know the family, just from so far back. Why should we have to spend a fortune on gifts for someone we hardly know? This way we can get something not so costly. No one will know.' In the end, Anju had opted for decorative bowls of black glass with a thin gold band around the rim. $19.99 for a set of five. 'Who wouldn't want to get something as fancy-looking as this?' she had puffed. 'And it is such a good price.'

The blue-vested woman is pointing down the aisleway. 'So for Women's Wear you go straight up this way and take a left where you see that table filled up with shoes. My,' she coos, 'that is about the prettiest outfit I ever saw. I expect bees might confuse you for a flower!'

Something less obvious is what she needs. To fit in as opposed to standing out. She walks toward a large panel that hangs from the ceiling. On it a smiling fair-haired, blue-eyed woman stands, hands smartly on hips, her look casual in trousers and a slim-fitting sleeveless shirt. In the hazy distance one could make out bicycles and a handsome man looking on. Aneeta could just about imagine what her mother might have had to say: 'And this is why they have problems, these American women. Is it any wonder? They flaunt themselves. Always too much freedom.'

I'm about to become one of those women, Mummy, she thinks, picking a path into the spindled chrome maze of clothing.

'I'm real partial to that colour on ya,' a voice from behind interrupts as Aneeta surveys a westernized version of herself in a long mirror. 'Picks up the colour of your eyes. Kinda like the fog on the bay on a spring day.' The woman sounds wistful. 'Your eyes, I mean.' Aneeta turns. A slender young woman with a golden halo of tightly curled hair grins at her. Underneath a blue vest Aneeta can see a plunging sweater. She wears a yellow smiling face button and an *Ask me!* tag with the name Angela on it. Smiling faces everywhere. On people, pins and signs. A very happy place this must be. 'They're real unusual. Noticed 'em right off. The eyes. No pun,' she laughs, 'but I've got an *eye* for that kind of thing. And your outfit too, so different from styles you see around here. Smaller towns, we don't get anything near as unusual—I mean that in the most complimentary way—nothing nearly as pretty. Maybe up in the city though.' Angela stops just long enough for a sigh. 'I love the city. It's so exciting, San Francisco. New York's my Number 2 after San Fran. Never been to the Big Apple. Not yet. Maybe one day. Guess bein' married pretty much keeps me close to home.' A jerky tremor passes through Aneeta's body—married. 'Derek, that's my husband, says everything's too expensive up there. That it's a place for the rich, not working class folk. Why, Derek, I say, every city needs its share of both. That's what I tell him.' Angela gives a conspiratorial wink. Aneeta tries her best to smile politely in return, even though all she wants is to escape to the tiny changing room.

'Tryin' to convince him to move us on up there, or at least a little closer than we are now. What about my bowling league, he asks me, like *that's* the most important thing in his life!' She shakes her head and motions toward Aneeta's left hand, 'But I guess you understand how men can be sometimes. All stubborn and pig-headed.' Aneeta is suddenly aware that she still wears the slim gold wedding band. Her blood runs cold and thick, her heart thumps hard. 'As for me, I tell him I'm workin' for the perfect company because there's plenty of Wal-Marts across this great nation. And I can have a job in any one of 'em. That's what's so great about it.' Angela shrugs. 'One day maybe we'll up and go. You never know.

'You wear blue much? You should, on account of your eyes. And green would set 'em off. Real nice. Red, even. Or just about any colour. You're so pretty you could get away with about anything. And I am *loving* that look on you. You really got it perfect. Simple. Classic. *Classically simple.*' She giggles, then tilts her head critically, 'You got anything else to try?'

Angela has given her the idea. Though she would never actually know it. She chats and fusses over Aneeta and helps her put together what she calls 'everyday wearable outfits' when Aneeta explains her need. 'Fit for just about anything. You got some fashion pieces and some basics. So you can keep with the trends, but not lose yourself in 'em. Still think that what you wore into the store is prettier by far. But good to have options.' And now she will. With two pairs of blue jeans, one *capri*, one *bootcut*, 'to cover your bases,' several t-shirts and one knit top, with long sleeves, in black. 'Can't ever go wrong with basic black,' Angela says. She also selects a plain zip sweatshirt and a blue cardigan, a pair of black trousers and a simple, flowing skirt. At Angela's direction she adds to her basket a pair of plimsoll-type shoes. 'Keds knock-offs. Look perfectly real except for they're missing the itty-bitty blue rubber tag at the back. Nobody'll know the difference.' Finally, she helps Aneeta pick a black pair of flat-heeled shoes, 'So you can dress your stuff up some. Go from casual to ta-da!' Angela throws her arms up, sticks one hip out and gives it a wiggle. Aneeta can't help but smile. 'I can tell you, no word of a lie, this is the ultimate comfy ballerina, even better than the really expensive designer ones. Only at Wal-Mart, yes indeed!' she proclaims. 'Why would you ever pay more?'

When Aneeta finally leaves the store she wears an all new outfit: blue jeans with a grey sweatshirt zipped over a blue t-shirt and white trainers. As she catches sight of her image reflected in the glass of the door, she is surprised that she hardly recognizes the girl she sees there.

She has driven north up the freeway. With each passing mile she feels herself relax a little bit more. Ahead a motel sign blinks *Vacancy* into the coming night. Neon red-orange, like the last of the sun. Suddenly she realizes how tired she is. How long the day has been. She considers the distance she has traveled and decides to stop for the night. The parking lot is quiet. She eases the car into an open space behind a bigger vehicle, to keep it hidden from view. From street traffic. Should a familiar Mercedes or BMW convertible with its saucy nameplate happen to pass by. Along this route. In the case of a brother having had a change of heart, or a change of mind. For a time she silently sits, simply watching the busy roadway.

Her skin prickles as she pulls the key out. And reaches for her purse. She opens the car door and extends a leg, a foot. Stands. Takes a first tentative step. Heat is draining out of the air as quickly as the sun is setting. A damp cold is creeping in. She is getting closer to the water, the ocean. She huddles into the softness of the fleece jacket. Looking up into the darkening sky she can see the first of the stars.

Across the parking lot she walks toward a two-storied building where bright blue script flashes *Office*. As she steps through the door, an oily haired man looks out at her from behind a pair of fingerprint-greased eyeglasses. 'Hello,' he remarks in a lazy voice.

She tries to make her voice casual, controlled, 'I would like to see about a room? For three or four days, I think.' She holds her breath.

'Well, which'll it be?' he asks, narrowing his eyes. 'Three or four?'

'I,' she pauses, 'I'm not certain. Not exactly.'

He looks dubious. 'Start with three and you can always add to it when the time comes. If need be.'

Three would be enough. She would work up the courage to make the call to Narinder's colleague, Patrick Mullen. About a place to stay. 'Yes,' she nods, hoping her nerves aren't apparent, 'that would be fine.' Funny that what comes to mind are Dadi-ji's reminders of the importance of thrift, of budgeting.

'Three nights it is. Cash or charge?'

'Cash,' she hurries. She lifts her bag to the counter and slides the zipper along.

'Promotion running is get yer third night free after the first two nights. So it'll run sixty-five with taxes.'

'And if I decide…to stay?'

'I'll mark it down here that you may want to extend.'

Trembling fingers reach into the handbag and fumble with the wear-softened notes. Can the clerk see her hands shaking? She flicks awkwardly through, to check and double-check denominations. And then a third time. Just to be sure.

'And I'll need an imprint of a credit card. On file. For any extras.'

'Oh,' she panics, 'but I don't have a credit card.'

'In that case, I'll just need an extra fifty. For deposit. You'll get it back when you check out. Boss makes me do it. We've had a few, let's just say *accident-prone* guests in the past. Girl like you, though, surely not going to be any trouble.'

'No. No, absolutely…no trouble.' She wonders about Jovin. If he were to come after her, find her. Would there be trouble? She shakes her head to banish the thought.

'Where'd you say you're from?'

Where? Where. She hasn't thought about what she should say. Not Fresno. Not Fresno. Just say…'Delhi.'

'Hmm.' He turns away, non-committal. 'Notice you've got a rental car. It a long drive from here?'

She stifles a laugh of relief, 'You could say, yes.'

She is smiling as he hands her a key. 'Room number 206. Up the stairs. Sixth door on your left. There is no right.' He chuckles a bit, then turns quickly serious, 'Hope you can handle your things okay. I got a bad back.'

'Yes, I'll be fine.'

'Just need your signature on the paperwork. Confirming three nights.' He points. 'Discount promotion.' Points again. 'State tax. Transient Occupancy Tax. Grand total. And showing your extra cash deposit. All I need is a signature here.' He taps on a finger length line that sits between the final figure. Tap, tap.

Her mind goes blank. And then frantic. A name. What name? Narinder's warning: *don't use your married name.* Not Aneeta Arora. Or Malik. If someone was looking they would try Malik too. She looks down at the signature line. She doesn't have the slightest idea what to write. She takes up the pen in her hand and holds it, suspended, over the oblong card. Signature. The clerk regards her strangely. In a flash it comes to her. With dramatic flourish she writes…*Madhuri Dixit*. Madhuri Dixit! How ever would this man know that she has taken the name of one of the most famous Bollywood film actresses?

'Right.' He collects the card and looks it over. Tilting it to look. Then tucking it into a folder. 'Check out's 11:00. Enjoy yer stay…Miss?'

'Dixit,' she says, hoping it sounds smooth, natural. Like it belongs to her. Suits her. Her ears are ringing. Madhuri Dixit. Of all the names.

The room is small and sparsely furnished. To a lesser-trained eye it appears clean. Her eye sees differently. She notices incomplete rings that ghost the small bedside table, dark shadows that live between bathroom tile lines, dust that has collected itself in the harder to reach corners of the room, strands of cobweb that wave in slow overhead arcs.

The air behind door 206 is stale; steeped in old smoke, the oiliness of sleep and sweat, and the tang of mildew. It is ineffectively masked by an overbearing floral-type scent that she attributes to a combination of cleaning fluids and a small spray canister behind the toilet. If she takes a deep breath the air prompts her to cough a little.

She sifts through the stuffed plaid bag. Takes out the only things she needs immediately. To prepare for sleep. In the Wal-Mart parking lot, before returning to the freeway, she had eaten the tin-wrapped snack she had hastily stuffed into her bag before leaving the house. Two parathas. The potato had stuck in her throat, the dough was tough. They would have been better warm. Or with something. Perhaps even just some simple raita or a chutney. No matter. At least her stomach is not empty. She is exhausted. Truly and completely. Like she has been wrung out. It is all she can do to find the energy to clean her teeth. She swills tepid water in her mouth and spits into the basin.

Flicking the wall switches, she extinguishes the lights. Bathroom. Main room. Lamplight. In darkness she crawls into the narrow bed. A bluish finger of street light illuminates the slim opening between drawn curtains. Under the rust-red abstract swirls of the thin coverlet she shivers. With fear and cold. The bed frame creaks and groans if she moves. So she keeps herself still and rigid. Arms tucked tight to her sides. And tries to will her body warm. Her mind checks and double-checks the three locks upon the door: handle, bolt and metal latch chain. Before even putting the lights out she has tried them countless times. Her chest feels tight. Like a lime being squeezed for juice.

She finds herself listening, straining for something her senses might recognize. Voices, the sound of a car motor, boot opening or closing, the cadence of well-known footsteps along the concrete path to her door.

What would she do? If they came for her. There is some relief in the fact that she is not in India. Where the commotion of sharp footsteps and familiar voices can bring terrible scenes. To women in particular. Where bystanders know to look away. Almost as a courtesy. To avoid being tainted by the complications of an already complicated situation. In the messy business of life. *Sister, keep your nose out of where it does not belong. Keep walking, brother, it is none of your concern.* They might see, might shake their heads. But do? *What can you do? I have my own problems. What kind of fool wants to make more?*

Here in America people are not so ready to turn a blind eye. Those brave enough to intervene are held up as heroes, as saviours. It gives her a bit of peace. Knowing. Peace that at last leads toward sleep.

In her dream the day is bright. The sun high in the sky. A sky she knows instinctively is India. Delhi.

Little snippets of remembering pass by, like flotsam on water, trickling along. She watches, enchanted. As a child might watch a banana leaf raft float down a gulley stream made by the rains.

Under this sky it is not too hot, nor too cold. A warm breeze wraps around her. Taking the earlier chill. In this bright light, the way it looks, it should be much hotter. She lets the thought go. Feels the logic of it simply float away. She blinks at the sheer brilliance of the light. But she cannot look away. Does not want to look away. She tries to look into it, as though it obscures something.

The face of her father appears. Then his figure. The whole of it. He begins to move forward. Toward her. As if he is walking out of the light. At first his features are dark, shadowed, but they grow clear and strong. He is closer to her than he has ever been in her dreams, yet her heart knows that he is still far away. Too far for her to attempt an embrace, to reach out in her dream and to touch him. But that she sees him lifts her spirits. She feels joy. 'Papa!' she cries out inside herself, but there is no indication he has heard. Again, she tries calling out to him. He does not move any closer, nor does he give sign of hearing her.

The mind blinks.

This time Papa stands together with a little boy. Hand in hand. The child is young. Not more than 4 or 5 years of age. Knobby legs, knee socked. In shorts and shirt and vest. The uniform of a schoolboy. The boy's eyes are squinting into the light and the distance. There is something about him, the child, that is so familiar.

Suddenly, she is flooded with an intensity of feeling so strong it is unlike any she has ever had before. Joy mingles with the exquisite pain of sorrow. And love, so much love. Yes, that is it. Love. And in that instant she knows: the boy is the child she has lost. Her baby. A son. Impossible love for an impossible vision in an impossible dream. Her sleeping body aches with it. He smiles up at her father. His Baba. That is who Papa would have been to him. Would have been. Is. A flutter of tranquility wraps her in a soft cocoon.

The mind blinks. And they are gone.

She wakes with a start. Her heart is pounding; her throat is thick and tight. To her surprise, the pillow is damp with warm tears.

Gregory
San Francisco
July 2002

She's just home from work. In the kitchen. Buttering a thick slice of bread to go with the vegetable soup warming on the stove. There's a heavy thumping climbing the stairs at the front. Elsewhere in the house there's the grating of furtive movement.

Gregory isn't clear on what's happening. Or why. Noise stalls on the porch, then suddenly turns hard and demanding against the heavy wood of the door. Something tells her it's the butt end of a fist making the noise. It brings Linda, startled, from her office. Linda looks out the peep hole at whoever's hell-bent on getting through. From the way Gregory sees her back stiffen it isn't good. She flips the lock and opens the door. Cops. A pool of black, radios squawking, floods roughly through. The room starts spinning, flaring in and out, losing and regaining focus. Gregory's feet have rooted through the floor, she stands immobile in the kitchen, silently watching; soup and bread are forgotten.

Above her, the bathroom faucet runs. Through the pipes behind the kitchen wall she hears the sure path of water rushing by. The thing must be wide open from the sound of it. The toilet handle clinks against porcelain. Loose. There's another flush. But with the sink and toilet both drawing, the water is slow to react. Because of the quick one-two of it. Shit. Gregory's brain is starting to build a story.

There is a mix of voices. All of them, even Linda's, are raised. Heated. A lone female officer pulls away from the group and charges for the stairs. Grabs the banister. Takes them two at a time. She's grunting as she flies the length. It is not a long run. Voices roller coaster up and down in front of her.

Linda's voice is angry, 'Have your damn paperwork in order...'

'Reason to believe Lacey Holman...' she hears Cop 1 say.

'Witnesses to corroborate...' adds Cop 2.

'Stolen property...' Cop 1.

She gets pieces only. Scraps of it. They'd arrived at Larkin around the same time, she and Lacey. Lacey was first. But she guesses not by much from the way she'd seemed to be working her way through all the house rules, slow and unsure, like it was still new to her, like freedom was fresh.

'Camera caught...' Cop 1.

'Peddling for...Known pusher...' Cop 2.

'A snitch in tight on this one...' Cop 1.

The female officer is pounding on the bathroom door. 'Get out here! Now!'

'I'm having a shit!' Lacey shouts.

'Get the hell out or I'm coming in!'

A fourth cop flies through and makes for the stairs. Breathing heavy as he passes the kitchen. The door splinters open. There's a wild scramble of sounds. The thud of flesh to floor. That sound. Oh God. That sound. Gregory winces, her stomach jumps high into the narrows of her throat. Her heart jackhammers. Reinforcements step across the threshold at the front. *How many are there?*

'No. No, it's mine! My sister gave it to me! My sister! You bastards! You fucking bastards! That's…my…fucking cash! I haven't done anything wrong!'

Lacey's shouts are bucking up against the cop. 'We've got people who think differently. Willing to say different. And tape that shows it's so,' the voice sneers. A shout is hurled from the bathroom down, 'Trace residue at the sink! Get the lab in.'

One of the cops with Linda leans into the radio pick-up on his shirt, 'Yeah, dispatch? This is Alpha-40. Can you send a forensic unit? For narcotics…10-4, copy that.'

'You got nothing! Nothing on me!' There's the clatter-clang of moving porcelain, jarring and scraping as it's shunted. Gregory squeezes her eyes shut. Then, the chirring of toothed metal, a final click. Once more the same. Lacey yelling. Hoarse. Her pitch rising, coming undone. 'This is a set-up! A goddamned trap!'

Grudging motion descends the staircase. Three abreast is tight, the female officer is slightly behind on the one side. Lacey is pushed out in front. It looks like a skewed triangle. Linda stands with her back to the corner nearest the door, arms crossed tight over her chest. Her expression is pained. The cop beside her, notebook in hand, is scribbling, not looking up. Lacey is a mess. Defeated. Gregory recalls Mama then, battered and broken. She swallows back a rise of vomit. There's spit and snot running down Lacey's face. Her shirt's stretched off one shoulder, her feet are bare. Her moves are jerky coming down the stairs. Her mouth is stretched out in a clown-like, upside-down grimace. Trying to hold back. When she sees Linda, her balance gives way. Whether she's stumbled or her legs have buckled isn't plain. She's pulled roughly to standing by the grip of the hands under her arms.

Lacey's voice comes whispery and jagged, 'Tell me what I did. Just tell me what it is you think I did?' She cocks her head toward the officer standing with Linda.

His eyes glitter like he's enjoying the moment. Like a dog on a bone, he doesn't wait on laying in, 'For starters, we've got you resisting. That doesn't sit well with your claims of innocence, Ms. Holman.'

Gregory sees Lacey go into a slump, sees her shoulders give. 'Where'd you get your information from? I wanna know,' she growls. 'I got rights. Snitches is rats! You know it. I know it.' With venom she spits, 'Whatever you got, it's bullshit!'

When she turns to Linda, she's suddenly like a needy child, 'I need to get to my baby. Please.' Her eyes are wide, pleading. 'They don't have anything on me. Whatever they told you, I ain't in it. It's not my deal. I'm innocent.' Linda is struggling for balance. Her face is tight. 'I need to be with him. My little boy. He needs his mama with him. Please. He needs to know he's got a mama who cares.' Linda reaches out and with the tips of her fingers touches Lacey's arm. 'Please. Help me. Linda, you've got to help me. Tell them. I been good. Trying. And working. To get myself home. I need to be with my boy. Don't let them do this. I swear, I'm going straight, I just need a break. Just a little break. Plee-ee-ease.' Her voice shudders and heaves, gives way to sobs.

'I'll do what I can, Lacey.' It's obvious Linda's pissed. With the cops. The way things have played out.

Gregory's hands are shaking so bad she doesn't know what to do with them. Put them on something and they're going to telegraph her panic like some crazy Morse Code. Old memories—her brain called them up so fast. With a force that's kicked the wind out of her. She wishes things were different for Lacey, but she knows there's no fix for the kind of trouble she's found.

Aneeta
Modesto, California
July 2002

As she dials the number there is a jump in her throat. She clenches the receiver and whispers the words she has practised. There is a succession of connecting clicks and then the drawn out peal of the ring. She squints into the glare of sunlight. Traffic noise penetrates the box in which she stands—tires along rutted pavement, horns, the squeal of braking as signal lights flash amber, then red. She turns the card over in her fingers. Paradigm Capital. Narinder Arora, Vice President, Investment Banking. Her past on the one side. Her future scrawled upon the other in forward-leaning block capitals. Patrick Mullen. Narinder's hand is sharp and square. Partway through the third ring the hollow bell is interrupted by a staccato click. His quick 'Y-ello?' startles her.

'Mr. Mullen?' Her voice is shy, a tremor is evident. 'Mr. Mullen, my name is Aneeta.' Pause. She runs her free hand down the steel coil of cord. 'Malik.' The name that used to belong to her. 'Narinder Arora gave me your name?' It comes out with a lift at the end, as if she is asking him to know. She prays that he remembers Narinder's request. To try and jog his memory she says, 'He told me to give you a call.' She can hear a good deal of noise in the background. Wherever he is sounds busy. 'About a flat?' She wishes she could be more self-assured sounding.

'Right. Yeah. He said you might call. It's a funny thing, actually. As it happens, I've got a place. Well, a bunch, but one's just come up. One that's easy. For me, maybe for you too. Not sure. San Francisco. Downtown. In Chinatown. He wasn't sure where you wanted to be. I've got others if the Bay Area doesn't figure in your plans. But this one came up only last week, matter of fact. Kind of a strange situation. After hearing from Narinder, I thought it might work well. Since it's a pain to try and flip things mid-month. Could save me the hassle. Tenant just up and cleared out. How's that sound? You flexible? Or were you planning to be somewhere else?' There is a static and crackling looping on the line that makes him hard to hear. 'It's a one bedroom. Partly furnished. Assume that's okay.'

'Yes!' she tries to contain her excitement. 'San Francisco would be, well that would be…very good.'

'You familiar with the city?'

'Not…really. No.'

'Everybody likes it. Never met a person who didn't. There are other parts of the state, though, everybody's different in terms of where they want to be. Or what they want.'

'Yes, well, San Francisco was actually where I was planning...' *careful*, she thinks, 'to spend some time.'

'Then this unit might work out real well for you. It's fairly central. I always tell people Chinatown is a great area. Close to the core, but not too close. And not so expensive. With a real unique neighbourhood feel to it. Being on the doorstep of downtown makes it much easier to get around. Sound like a place you'd be interested in? At least in the short term? Don't know what kind of plans you've got.'

Neither do I, she thinks. 'Oh, I think so. For the moment, yes.'

'Narinder's volunteered to take care of your overhead for three months, so he's on the hook. I owe him anyway. But if you decide you wanna keep it longer you'd have to let me know.'

'Of course.'

'I'll need 30 days either way. Yes, or no. Whichever way you decide. Then it's up to you. We can talk cost if you decide to stay and we'll have to get paperwork and a tenancy agreement in place. Sound fair?' He pauses for a moment. Strains of noisy conversation bloom through. Music. There is a burst of crackling.

'Hello?' She strains for him, the return of his voice. Has she lost him? 'Mr. Mullen? Are you still there? Hello?'

'So…sorry. I just stepped outside. It was hard to hear. Hello?'

'Yes, yes. I'm still here,' she hurries.

'Sound good? This place? If you prefer, I can go back and look at my database, see what else I've got, but you'd actually be helping me out in a way if you take this. And I'll cut a better deal on the rent if you decide to keep it after the three months. I can meet up with you to give you a tour and, if you like it, the keys. How about tomorrow, 11 o'clock?'

'Fine. That would be,' she breathes, 'just fine.' She smiles widely at the blurred outline of her reflection.

'Address is 888 Pacific. Powell at Pacific. You got a car?' Talking and laughter rise and swirl away.

She fumbles to pull the motel pen from her handbag. Under his name on the business card she scribbles 888 Pacific. 'Yes.'

'Because this place doesn't have parking.' His voice hollows out, gets tinny.

'No, no. I mean, I don't *have* a car.' She is flustered trying to explain. 'I am just driving one that has been hired, I mean…rented.'

'Oh, okay. Perfect. Wondered if that might mean a bit of a hiccup. Parking's ridiculous that part of town. Spaces are pricey. But if it's a rental then that's fine. Good. Right?'

'Yes. Right.' She laughs a little.

'So, tomorrow. I'll wait for you outside the building. Probably the only suit and tie on the block. At that time of day.'

'Okay. Great, that's great.' She struggles to dampen down the rolled sound of the 'r', to make it looser, and the 'a' sound flatter. 'Thank you. Thanks.' Does she call him Patrick or Mr. Mullen? It isn't a matter she needs to puzzle over for long.

'Yeah. Sure. No problem. See you then.' Without good-bye, he is gone.

She has no idea at all where Powell and Pacific is. She has no idea where

Chinatown is. But Narinder hadn't let her down. He had kept his word. Her own flat. She cannot help the smile, even though her insides are still shaking. There is an almost giddy Madhuri Dixit lightness to her steps as she makes her way back to the motel. Sunidhi Chauhan singsongs through her mind: *Forget everybody else,* the words of the song suggest as Madhuri smiles and winks, *and come dance. Aaja nachle.* At this very moment, it feels the perfect sentiment.

She will take one of those street maps from the tourist kiosk lined with leaflets. And tell the attendant at the front desk that she won't be staying on after all. She will smile pleasantly. Practise her American accent: *I won't need any extra nights. I've managed to sort something out.*

Kameko
San Francisco
July 2002

'Hello? Moshi-moshi.' Distance swells in her ear, like the wash of the ocean. A series of hollow clicks fade with a static hiss.

'Kameko-chan?' The voice arcs, grating and stern. Unmistakable to her ear, even with the separation of time and miles. Though the caller asks for a child. A younger version of herself, a watery old memory lost to him many years before. Yet this is their connection; what links them. Since her move to America they have exchanged little communication. She can count the conversations on the fingers of a single hand. Awkward moments of cursory small talk. The things that bind them still are scant and washing away with time, like designs upon the sand of the seashore.

'Father?' If he hears the sound of surprise in her tone, he makes no mention of it. 'Are you well, Father? Okay?' How easily she embraces the return to Japanese. And the conditions it imposes upon a conversation, the polite formality.

'I am no longer a young man, Kameko. I cannot hide from it.' He gives a short, barking laugh.

'But you are not suffering from illness are you?' Mentally she adds up the hours of differing time between them, trying to gauge the urgency in his unexpected call.

'No, no. Nothing that age hasn't brought upon me. I do not move as quickly as I once did, but still I move. I am golfing sometimes. And I visit the hot springs. It does my health good, going to the springs; the fresh mountain air.' He falls silent then.

Aside from the still distinct sense she has of ocean water, Kameko wonders if perhaps they might have been cut-off. 'Father?' she prompts.

'Yes, yes, Kameko-chan. In answer to your question, I am well as much as can be expected. But I have not called to discuss matters of my recreation. I have called because you should know,' he pauses, and in the fragment of silence she hears his hesitation amplified, 'I will marry again.'

She draws breath sharply and then worries that he has heard her poor reaction. 'Why, Father, this is some news! A surprise. I must say to you,' she stutters over the choosing of what words should follow such a pronouncement, 'I, well, even more so we, would…oh, of course, want to wish you well.' Hers, though, is a conflicted feeling. A red ribbon of aching and hurt winds through the good wishes she has offered, quietly tainting them. 'When…when will the marriage take place?'

'In some weeks.'

'Quite quickly, then?'

'It has been a time. That it has been coming.'

A vision assails her. One of long ago. A man and woman, arm-in-arm, laughing in the flashing Tokyo neon. Is it possible?

She knows that calling her with such news is no more than a courtesy. It has been put before her like an already ordered boxed meal. And, now that it is present before her, it certainly cannot be waved away. Honest feelings must once again be put aside. She can only support the appearance he would like. 'I should come. Would you like me to come?'

'It is not necessary.' His protest is firm. 'You have a husband. And I know Shiro must be busy with work. It is not a choice at all.'

'I would, though. If you wanted.'

'No, no. There is no need. I would not want to interfere. There should be no such obligation for you. You do not even know the woman.'

The woman? His way of thinking, his words, remind her of the differences. The lines that separate man from woman. 'I must be pleased for you.' Pleased. Even while old and unresolved sentiment bubbles to the surface to needle her as if her discovery of his indiscretions had passed only yesterday, and not so many years before. Today, however, there is no place for such emotion. For there is no longer the potential to cause pain; no honour left to be spared. Hers is a secret whose potency died alongside Mother. And yet, she finds she cannot extinguish this flare of old upset that lies buried within her, intertwined with memories of her mother. Feeling that fires to taunt her anew each time the circumstances between them— Mother and she—see fit to align.

'I do this because age makes us frail. I prefer not to be frail on my own.' His tone is brusque, perhaps to discourage sentiment, or perhaps to cast his decision as one of practicality. Especially in light of the distance between them. A distance that is both physical and emotional. 'She has a house, away from Tokyo. We will go there. To the seaside. The weather is milder. Better for old bones. It will be better for us both. She, Mei is her name, has finished working in the city. I should like the peace of being away at last from Tokyo. It has belched me out. There is no longer a place for me here. In its overfull belly.' He laughs, a succession of gravelly barks.

'Shall I inform my father-in-law of your plans?' She already knows his likely response.

'No. When it is done, after, then fine. They should not feel obliged. It is of your choosing when to bring the matter to Shiro. In a marriage there are some things told. Some not. Perhaps when you return to Tokyo might be a more suitable time. Then it is no longer so fresh, and the news will be received more…easily. Without unnecessary bother.'

'Yes. Yes, that is true.'

'You understand, then?'

'Yes. Yes, I understand.'

'Some days,' he pauses and she hears a sigh float across the ocean waves in the telephone, 'I think of your mother. You are like her. But like yourself also.

Stronger. This is good. You will find your way, not wait for it to be shown to you. You are not the little tortoise girl who hides her head any longer.'

She is completely surprised by the nature of his comments about her character. So surprised that she has no idea what to say in return. Silence stretches between them.

He is the first to speak, to interrupt the quiet. 'I think I have been too much time on the telephone. My bill is going to be very high. The telephone company will rub their hands that this old man is going crazy talking to America.'

'Father?'

'Yes, Kameko-chan?'

'I wish you, both of you, well…in your life together.' Her voice chokes with emotion, 'Mother would have wanted it for you.' The words she has spoken on Mother's behalf are not untrue. Mother would have wanted it.

For Mother, life had been like the gradual unfolding of a painting on a scroll. She had chosen simply to accept whatever the scene happened to reveal as it was presented, and to endure it, to make peace with it. For, in her mind, the paint had already dried and her place had been set. Tears burn hot in Kameko's eyes.

'Thank you,' he says in a softer, gentler sounding tone. He coughs once and his usual manner swiftly returns, making her wonder if the moment before was either something she had imagined, or simply a trick of the telephone line, 'I must go, Kameko.'

'Be well, Father.' She bites her lip, thankful he cannot see the tears that line her cheeks.

'Be well also, Kameko-chan.' And the water between them washes him away.

Aneeta
Modesto, California
July 2002

The day begins misty and dull. It is 9:26 on the clock radio when she scans the
room one last time. From the doorway she checks the parking lot. It is a practice
she has been keeping since she has arrived. There is nothing to alarm her.

Lugging her bag and case, she makes her way down the chewing-gum
tarred walkway toward the back of the building where the car is parked. Her arm
strains to manage the awkward weight. In the side pocket of her handbag, fingers
fumble for the blue and orange tag with its single silver key. A swift turn in the
lock pops the boot. Gripping the handle of the case with both hands she lifts and
swings the oblong up and into the depths. After it goes the plaid sack. She pushes
the lid down.

Zipping her jacket against the morning cool, she moves toward the office.
She pulls the green motel key tag from her blue jeans. 206. She would remember
it, this place. Where she has lived her first nights of freedom. A different clerk eyes
her approach. She pushes the office door open and walks to the desk. 'I'm checking
out,' she says, and slides the key over the countertop.

'Uh, 206. Room 2-oh-6,' he says, inspecting the number outlined in
disappearing white on the tag. 'Let me just check there's no charges.' The clock
behind him says 9:30. One hour and a half. She shifts her weight and waits while
he moves slowly behind the counter, nodding and whispering under his breath.
From a folder he pulls a stout card and inspects it closely. 'Nothing in the way
of extras. So I guess I've got your deposit to return.' He unlocks and pulls open a
drawer from which he takes the three bills. 'And there y'are. Twenty, forty, and ten.
Makes fifty. You're good to go. Need some die-rections? I mean, to where you're
headed from here.'

'I have a map,' she offers. The clerk on duty when she returned from
speaking with Patrick Mullen had been happy to help. Had given her a city map
when she couldn't find one on the wire rack. He had told her shyly that they usually
charge a dollar, but that he'd just let her have it, since he could tell, he'd said, that
she wasn't from around here.

'Oh,' he sounds disappointed.

'But thank you,' she volunteers quickly.

He brightens, 'No problem. Have a safe trip.' He nods awkwardly and
smiles.

Before she starts the car she looks carefully at the route that the clerk had marked in fluorescent yellow. She studies the names of the streets where she is to turn. Mitchell to Gateway, then Airport Boulevard to the 101 and San Francisco. A thrill runs through her. Take the Mission Street exit. Left at Van Ness. Right at Broadway, then Stockton, and finally, Pacific. The only thing left to chance is parking. The clerk had told her that parking in town is not so easy. 'Check the side roads. You might have more luck there. But watch your signs,' he'd cautioned. 'Don't want to come back to find your car gone. Worst feeling ever.' He has told her that at this time of day the drive could take up to 45 minutes, depending on traffic, which he called 'a real nightmare'.

In all, it takes about forty minutes. She finds a parking space between an already busy Dim Sum restaurant and a yet closed Best Education Center where large posters promise assistance with math and science and offer a 30% weekend discount. There is a smiling cartoon cat pictured. Holding a stack of school books and an A+ card. As she jockeys the car into the space she imagines Raoul's smile.

From a small plastic bag she takes coins she has collected and drops them into the parking meter. The mist of the morning is rising into warming air and disappearing. Trees line Pacific, giving it an almost park-like appeal. She hears birds chirping and chittering to one another. Sidewalks are busy with people. Across the street, behind orange spires of metal, is 888. She likes the way it looks; the square cement structure, solid surrounding fence, the curve of walkways beyond a tall entry gate. Gazing up, she counts eight floors. She finds herself hoping that the apartment is on one of the higher levels. There is a certain sense of security that height gives.

An elderly woman totters up the slight slope of sidewalk before the front door. Two young men pass in front of her, laughing and speaking in a foreign tongue. A blond-haired young man in a shirt and tie rounds the corner with hands jammed deep into dark blue trousers. He moves toward the gate and she knows: Patrick Mullen.

By the time she crosses at the corner he has withdrawn a mobile telephone from his pocket. He dials and raises the phone to his ear. As he is talking he walks a short distance, then pivots to walk the distance again. When he sees her, like she has known him, he finishes his call, slides the phone into a trouser pocket, and reaches out to her. 'Aneeta?' he asks. His hand is dry and sure in comparison to her own damp and clammy version.

'Yes.' She clears her throat self-consciously, trying to dispel the nervous inflection. He is affable and polite. He talks about the city, the area, the building. He asks if she has had problems finding it, whether she has managed parking close by. She answers without elaboration. Her smile is timid.

He does not ask anything of the nature of matters that have brought her to him. He unlocks the gate using one of three keys on a small silver ring. After he allows her to pass through, he flips the keys back into his palm and walks, with her trailing behind, to a second gate. Again, a key unlocks it. He holds it wide for her and then moves past to lead her to a lift. The up arrow lights green at his touch. From where they stand she can see a leafy inner courtyard dotted with plants and carefully tended small trees.

'It's quite a nice place,' he volunteers. 'Different building, I mean, with the courtyard. Some of the residents plant their own herbs, vegetables and things. Mr. Cheung, he's a retired botanist, he's lived here something like twenty years—well before my time—he takes care of the general upkeep.'

The up arrow goes dark. The lift door grinds back. It is a small space. A metallic cube. She feels the heat of their bodies intertwine as she passes him to step in. It smells of cooking around them, and mothballs. 'You don't have any big furniture needs moving in?'

'No.'

'Almost better. Elevator's a real pain for that.' She feels embarrassed at his closeness and concentrates on the numbers lighting as they move upward. 2…3…4. The lift shudders to a stop at the fifth floor. He emerges first. '502,' he says with a lopsided smile, and walks swiftly along the corridor. Overhead lights give a dull, greenish cast. When he stops to put a key into the door lock, she looks over her shoulder, back down the corridor they have just walked, judging the distance. She hears the heavy lug of the lock turning.

'It's not much,' he apologizes, 'I don't know quite what you're used to.' She steps after him into a narrow corridor. 'Narinder said you needed someplace safe and affordable to stay.' She stiffens at the mention of her brother-in-law. 'So here we've got the bathroom,' he takes a couple of steps and turns to gesture, 'kitchen and living space.' Across the small angular floor is a length of window. 'It's nicer not facing the street. You don't get the noise.' She looks out onto the thatch of courtyard greenery below, her small smile unobserved. He moves again, and she turns back to follow the few paces to where he is already indicating the slender rectangular length of bedroom. 'So, as you can see, there's a bed and night table in here. And a chair and lamp,' he is retracing his steps, 'what must've been a dining table of sorts.' His laugh sounds sorry. 'Keep what you want. Call Goodwill or something to collect the rest.'

He holds out the key ring, 'Keys are labeled: FD front door, ID inner door, AD apartment door. ID will also get you into the laundry on 2. Machines are coin operated. And, here, I'll give you my card, just in case.' He thrusts his hand into his pocket and pulls out a business card with a design in blue like a pinwheel. 'Top number's my direct line. You've got my cell already.' She nods, not knowing exactly what to say. 'I think that's about it. Can you think of anything?'

'No,' she says with a bit of a smile, which he returns. 'But thank you. Thanks a lot.' She does not want to say much for fear it might encourage questions. He seems, like the day they had first spoken, pressed for time, rushed.

'Don't need to thank me. Thank Narinder. Anyway, if that's it, and you're good here, I'm on a meter,' he says, gesturing with his thumb, 'so I'd better get going. Oh, almost forgot, one last thing,' he points to a small grid on the wall, 'the intercom. Front and back door. But,' he shakes his head, 'it doesn't work so hot. Better to know in advance you've got company coming. Black button to talk, red to buzz someone through. You may have to go down though, to let 'em in. Thing's got a selective personality.' So much the better. It is a good thing for her that it might prove tricky to get into the building. She does not have anyone she wants visiting.

Quite the opposite.

'Give me a call thirty days out. To let me know your plans. Stay, or move on. If you want to formalize. Or if you want a line on something elsewhere.' He flashes a grin with a hurried half-shrug and then heads for the hallway. Over his shoulder he says again, 'I mean it. You need anything, just call.'

She lugs the suitcase and plaid bag from car to building. At the fifth floor the lift door grumbles open on a small and sprightly Asian lady wrapped in a too large overcoat and wearing a smallish hat with a feather on one side.

'Oh! Hello!' the lady singsongs with a bright coral smile. 'Here, I can hold the door for you.' She braces her frame against the metal track as Aneeta struggles to move her things. 'Nasty beast! I don't know how many times it's tried to knock groceries right out of my arms! Like it's hungry or something. Need to teach it some manners. You moving in? Or just visiting somebody? Don't look like you got enough stuff for moving in.' Thin eyebrows arc, 'Must have wrong floor. Nobody young like you on 5. Not your age. You sure you want this floor? Maybe 6. College boy on 6. And one girl. Or she on 7?' Her forehead creases in thought.

'Actually, yes, I am moving,' Aneeta blushes, 'into apartment 502.'

'Into 502? 502…502.' The woman taps at her chin and looks off into space contemplatively. Suddenly she exclaims, 'Oh! They gone?'

'It seems they have.'

'I'd much rather have *you* for a neighbour,' she pats Aneeta's hand. 'So pretty! And young. Make me think young thoughts.'

'Oh, I…thank you,' she manages to stammer, embarrassed, 'you're very kind.'

The elevator begins to buzz loudly. 'Better go. Nice to meet you, pretty new neighbour girl. I am Mrs. Lee. I live close to you! Number 504.' The door slides jerkily between them. 'You come visit, okay? I would like to know you.' Aneeta hears the last words stretch and fall as the lift starts to the ground.

She unlocks the heavy door and deposits the case in the narrow hallway. Beside it, she settles the bulky plaid bag. And she is officially moved in. Now she must return the car. It is the sensible thing to do. Even though Narinder has arranged for more time. Parking is difficult and expensive. Gas is costly too. She needs to be careful with her money. She pulls the door closed and looks at the trio of keys to find the one for the door lock. AD the tag says. Apartment Door. It is a silly idea that occurs to her. The initials could just as easily stand for Aneeta's Door. She clasps the ring in her hand and holds it to her chest.

The streets and sidewalks are busier now. She feels like a fish swimming against the river current after a heavy rain. She clutches her purse tightly and wonders about pickpockets and thieves. She checks faces flowing toward her. In singles. In tight clusters. In Delhi, pickpockets were everywhere—men, women, even children. In the past she has never had much to lose. She thinks of the envelope at the bottom of her bag as she makes her way back to the little car.

The rental return is marked on her map. Again with the motel clerk's help. This time the luminous line starts at Pacific and runs back in the direction of the city center. Nerves flutter. She has never driven in a big city. Raoul, when he was teaching her, probably never expected she would. *She* had never expected she would. But it is the closest Budget car hire center.

It is all new. The patterns of streets. The junctions. The way things move. One way. Do not enter. No left turn. She feels claustrophobic in the tiny car amid rows of tall buildings. She is trying to watch and keep up her speed, to obey the traffic laws and rules. When a disheveled, bearded man steps into the flow of cars, she hears herself gasp. Her face burns. There is a concert of honking and shouts as he ambles across the roadway and disappears crookedly into an alley, seemingly unaware of the chaos he has caused. Her heart beats fast and sharp. She casts her eyes into the distance and thinks she maybe sees a G on a street sign up ahead. *Please let the street be Geary.* She signals right, checks over her shoulder. Double-checks in the mirror. She hears Raoul, his gentle voice, calmly reminding her of what to do, and bites her lip. She has not had the chance to say goodbye. She changes lanes. The signal stalk clicks off. Ahead there is a sign that looks the same as her key tag. Orange and blue. Budget Car Rental.

A large orange arrow directs her into a white spiral of concrete. She carefully manoeuvres through the narrow corkscrew core, following a trail of signs and arrows. Finally a 'Return' sign flashes before her. A young man stops her and motions her window down. 'Return?' he asks. She nods. 'Take key'n paperwork. Side thu'fice.'

'I'm sorry?' She struggles to make sense of what's been said.

He must see the confusion in her expression. In an overly loud voice with excruciating slowness he says, pointing, 'Over there. Key. Paperwork. Inside. The off-ice. Office.'

Her face flushes. 'Thank you,' she manages, fumbling to get out of the car while he stands waiting, shaking his head.

A woman wearing a tag that says 'Johnny' reaches out a hand with extraordinarily long orange and blue striped fingernails for the rental papers. She clicks digits into a computer. Puzzled by something on her screen, she says, 'S'cuse me for one minute. Just a sec.' She takes the papers and disappears through a door behind the long expanse of counter where other agents process customer returns. A sense of panic thickens in her head. *Will they call? Reveal where she is?* Her mouth is suddenly dry. She waits. Revolving clock hands click through minutes as though they are hours. When Johnny finally emerges from the back she is smiling pleasantly. Confusion is gone from her expression. Aneeta gathers her splintered courage and asks, 'Is there some kind of problem?'

'No. No problem,' Johnny chirps. 'It's just that it was prepaid, your rental, and through Paradigm Investments, your company account. And you returned early is all. I just needed to get a supervisor to process the credit.'

'Oh.' The syllable sounds hollow. Johnny smiles. Aneeta attempts to return the smile, but her lips are fixed over dry teeth. 'You didn't need to call... anyone...about anything?' Her words are sticky.

'No, ma'am. The supervisor's on break. So he goes back there. Off the floor. Avoid being bothered all the time.' Johnny continues without hesitation, 'So,' she shoves a paper across the counter and stabs at it, 'you were pre-paid...to three weeks. I had to charge for today. Here's mileage...insurance...fuel...credit to account. Total.' Johnny sharply creases the paper in three and hands it to Aneeta. 'Sorry again for the wait.' A wide, efficient smile. 'You have yourself a nice day.'

No need to call. No need for worry. She urges herself toward the door. Her face is hot. There are more cars stacked behind the little white car that for the last four days has been hers. The young man is busy motioning to newcomers. She makes her way to the road and combs for street signs in the sidewalk clamor. As she grapples in her bag for the map, her hand touches the cool ring of apartment keys. Below it, her fingertips find the smooth edge of the envelope. With timid but determined steps, she begins to walk.

She has some jewelry. A few modest pieces she can sell. The wedding band. But how much could it possibly bring her? Work is necessity. The money, though quite a sum, will not last forever. Yet she has no idea where even to begin. What could she do? Serve at a tea party here and there? Tie a sari? Weave a braid with jasmine flowers? Make samosas?

By chance she bumps into her neighbour, Mrs. Lee. And it prompts an invitation from the elderly lady. 'Come to have tea with me. Tell me what you think about the city. You not from around here, I can tell.' Teetering toward her apartment door she calls, 'Come, come,' and waves her hand in the air.

Not to go when she has no other plans seems unacceptably rude. And so she follows. 'I cannot stay very long, Mrs. Lee,' she calls out at the older lady's retreating back.

'Young people so busy. So much to do. What, you got party? Date? You go to work?'

'Well, no. No. No party or date. Nothing like that, but I am...I am looking for work. So I can't stay long.'

The tiny lady pushes a key neatly into the lock on her own door and smoothly flips the bolt. She turns to give a wide, ruby lipsticked smile and pushes the door open. 'Come in, come in! I get to the water, and you,' she waves her off, 'you go sit down. Be comfortable.' To herself she mumbles, 'So busy, young people. Never a moment. Good to take time for a cup of tea. What harm to slow down? World's not gonna end over a cuppa tea.'

Mrs. Lee hums as she arranges things in the kitchen. Aneeta finds a living area like her own, this one with yellowed lace curtains. The settee is a worn deep green with plastic arranged over the arms. There is a small square table settled against the wall opposite the window. Three chairs are around it, with another backed up to the wall beside.

Photographs and collectibles line a long, shallow shelf. In black and white, a young Asian man has his arm around a white-suited and handsome woman in a jauntily angled cap, a flash of netting coyly obscuring her eyes. Aneeta imagines that the woman must be Mrs. Lee. In younger days. The man, most likely her husband. More recent images seem to be ordered chronologically. A smiling schoolboy. A young man in a cap and gown proudly holding a paper scroll. The young man, older now, links arms with a beautiful Asian woman in a western bridal gown. An infant, swaddled in blue. Another baby, this time wrapped in pink. Her belly tightens as she considers the baby pictures.

There is a disapproving cluck of the tongue behind her as Mrs. Lee enters the room, 'Everybody so busy, don't have time for anything. Young people. Move too fast. You outrun own life. Then what?' On a wooden tray she carries a painted porcelain pot with two similar cups. Aneeta smells the musk of black tea and draws it in. 'Sit, sit,' Mrs. Lee motions, pulling up a tiny side table upon which to set the tray. 'Like my son. Verrry busy.' She shakes her head gravely, as if the words are some sort of poor prediction, but there is pride in her expression. 'He is working in Bank of America,' she says, nodding. 'His wife, she is pediatrician. They meet in college. Stanford. Mm hmm. One son. Kai. 15 now. One daughter. Kenzie only 13. Kenzie dance ballet. Very good. Verrry good. Kai not sure what he is good at yet. His parents hope math. But,' she pauses in her pronouncement, 'nobody knows for sure. See what his tests like. He is more American boy, not Asian. Asian students have much discipline. Work hard to make family proud. Try to be the best. American students distracted by America too much. They want Kai to go to Stanford. Like they did. They are hoping. Hoping he can have enough good grades.'

Aneeta chooses a seat in one of two stiff-looking chairs. Mrs. Lee places cups of steaming tea on the small oblong between them and seats herself on the faded settee.

'So. Now. This is very nice. To get to know you. You go to school? You look young. Maybe you came here for school. Hmm? Stanford, maybe? Look smart to me. I know these things.' She taps at her temple.

'No, no. I've finished school already.'

'Where you from?'

She does not want to mention Fresno. Or being married. It would require explanation she is not ready for. 'From Delhi. In India,' she says.

'Ah, India.' Mrs. Lee nods sagely. 'So what you here for?' She takes a loud slurp of tea.

The question, an obvious one, is one without a simple answer. She shifts in the chair. The old woman watches her expectantly. 'Well, I suppose I'm here,' Aneeta hesitates, finishing cautiously, 'to build a new life. For myself.'

The older woman is nodding, 'Good place for that. Very good place. My husband Albert and I, we come here for doing that. Escape the war. His Korean name Hyun. Means wise. I like Albert better. But he was wise to bring us here.' Her eyes take on a faraway look, and she sighs. For a moment there is silence. Suddenly she asks, 'What you gonna do for your new life?'

'Well, I don't know yet. I…I'm not too sure.'

'What you wanna do, then?'

'Well…just…to be independent, I guess. To know that I can be.'

'How you plan to do it?'

The questions seem endless.

'Well, I guess the first thing I really must do is find a job. Of some kind.'

'What work you do?'

'I don't know, I… haven't had a job before.'

'No work? Hmm.' Mrs. Lee takes another drag of tea. 'Not many of us work anymore. Spend our time playing games,' she leans in, 'gossiping.' She says it in a conspiratorial whisper, and it makes Aneeta smile. Then she straightens up. 'Some ladies where I go to church? Just waiting to die. Terrible really, such a life.' Mrs. Lee tsks lightly and with barely a breath continues, 'God want to keep you here, you gotta live. Even if you're by yourself. On your own. He give, he take away. Like my Albert. Still, I keep going on.'

There is a moment of quiet. Until Mrs. Lee launches in again: 'I gotta friend. She works at Chinatown Library. On Powell. She's a mahjong partner. Only other friend still working owns Korean grocery. You wouldn't want to work in Korean grocery.' She waves a hand dismissively with a scowl. 'Husband drinks too much. Kids are lazy. So she have to keep the store. They don't do nothing, so she has to do it all. But maybe the library…you like books?' she asks, her penciled eyebrows peak. She peers intently over the rim of her tea cup at Aneeta.

'Why yes, of course. Yes!' Aneeta laughs.

'Let me see. I'm gonna talk to her for you. Nice lady.' She shakes her head somewhat gravely. 'Not so good at mahjong. Just let me see. See if she can help. Been working there so many years, I can't remember. From when Albert was still living. We been friends a very long time. I can ask.'

'Thank you. That's very kind of you. Very kind. I mean, I hardly know where to begin. As far as finding a job.'

'What good is a neighbour, if not to help?' Mrs. Lee pats Aneeta's knee. 'Library is not far from here. You can walk. Nice place for a job. And close. I think she can help. Her name is Beatrice Liu. That's L-I-U, but you can say *Loo*. Okay? I will tell her you need some work. That you're smart. That you're coming to see her. I call her tonight for you. Okay?'

Aneeta is surprised at such a generous turn, and grateful. 'Really, I can't thank you enough.'

'What else I have to do? Nice to have somebody for tea.' Mrs. Lee brightens, 'Hey, you could come for mahjong sometimes.' She grins at Aneeta, a ghost of red lipstick on her teeth. 'I can teach you. Sometimes we don't have enough players. Then we get stuck with gossip only. Not as much fun. You want more tea?'

She walks to the Chinatown library. It isn't far. Several blocks. Along the way she envisages herself readying for a workday, relishing the burst of fresh air, the simplicity and economy of having a job so close. It would be, she thinks, ideal. Though she does not have any idea the pay, if they are willing to hire someone inexperienced, as she is, she imagines it cannot be a lot. But then she chides herself for letting her mind wander so far ahead.

It is an older bricked building. Two identical stairways zigzag from opposite sides to the main door. Arches over long windows and details in the stone around them suggest a different time in this city. She climbs steep cement steps and takes a deep breath before she pushes through the heavy wood doors. Inside, a sound of children steals away the thick hush she has expected. There is a woman seated in a too small plastic chair, picture book held wide, with a gaggle of boys and girls before her. Most have necks tipped back, chins high, eyes and mouths wide; enchanted imaginations watch the animations of the storyteller. In a range of different voices she is telling the tale of a child who will not eat his vegetables. Aneeta smiles to herself.

Mrs. Lee has told her that Mrs. Liu will be on the second floor. Behind the desk. She makes her way past the children on tiptoe, so as not to disturb the fragile equilibrium. Up the stairs she creeps, looking back at the scene, taking it for a piece of magic.

In front of her, by contrast, the broad half-circle desk is a hive of activity. There is a sudden burst of trepidation as she waits before the hanging *Information* placard. 'Yes? Can I help you?' A woman smiles, eyes angled under gold-rimmed spectacles. Her voice is soft, gentle, in a manner befitting a library.

Nerves dance in Aneeta. 'I am here for Mrs. Liu,' she says it the way Mrs. Lee has instructed, 'Mrs. Beatrice Liu.'

'One moment. Just one moment. I will get her for you.' The desk clerk moves to a bank of glass fronted rooms and speaks to a woman with eyeglasses hung from a chain around her neck who, at the moment, is concentrated on a great stack of papers. Mrs. Liu lifts the lenses to her eyes. Her study, Aneeta thinks, is intense, almost severe. She nods briskly to the clerk and, stepping away from her task, strides toward the desk.

Aneeta draws herself up as the woman approaches.

'I am Mrs. Liu,' she says.

'I am Aneeta Malik. My neighbour, Mrs. Lee, has encouraged me to speak with you about the possibility of work?'

'Yes, yes. We spoke. I told her I have only as-needed openings now. Are you a librarian?'

'No, no.'

'But you finished school?'

'Yes.'

'In America?'

'No, India. Delhi. Complete to 12th Standard.'

'Huh.' She rolls her tongue and considers Aneeta again. 'You can carry a box with books in it? Maybe 30 pounds?'

Aneeta bobs her head, agreeing. 30 pounds. Like a box of potatoes. Maybe less, even. She had carried the last one from the Corolla before Dadi-ji could tear his eyes away from the television. 'Yes. Yes, I am quite sure.'

'Quite sure? Or sure-sure?'

'Oh, I am sure.'

'Sure.' Mrs. Lui is silent for a moment, then asks, 'Push a 250 pound cart?'

'Oh.' 250 pounds? Could she? 'Well, I think so.'

'Think so?' Mrs. Liu eyes her a bit skeptically.

'Yes.' She hoped she could.

'You can work Saturdays?'

'Yes.'

'No boyfriend-girlfriend who says no weekends for work? Everybody works some Saturdays. Library isn't just Monday to Friday. Saturday too.'

'Yes, I can work Saturdays.'

'You can. Okay. Let me get the forms. To apply. If you think you are sure.' Mrs. Liu turns and walks to a tall file cabinet. A bud of hope grows within her. Elation catches in her throat. Up the steps the storyteller's voice floats, cushioned, every so often, by a cloud of giggly laughter.

Mrs. Liu returns with a number of different coloured papers in her hand. The top sheet is one of duties and responsibilities of a position referred to in the heading as Library Page: Temporary Exempt. Aneeta isn't sure what exactly the term Temporary Exempt means, but she is certain she can manage most of the requirements outlined below it. She says a little prayer when she reaches the mention of computers that she will not be asked about her abilities in that regard.

'Duties mainly clerical, right? Some lifting, some pushing carts. You got no back problems?'

'No.'

'Health problems? So you can't lift? Hernia? Anything like that?'

'No, no. I'm…very healthy.' Aneeta dismisses thoughts of the baby, the hospital.

'So you need to complete Information, Employment Application,' she flicks through the papers, 'Conviction History Form. You got no conviction history, right?' Conviction history? 'Prison. You ever commit crime, or go to jail?'

'No. No.' She feels compelled to add, 'Never.'

'Good. Make it easier for you. Now, pay comes to about 15 dollars an hour once tax taken off. Tax taken off before you get it. Right?' Mrs. Liu asks, she thinks, to determine if she has understood.

'Yes, right.' She is breathless. 15 American dollars every hour? Why, it's more than many could even dream of. It seems almost too good to be believed.

'Pay is every two weeks. No advance money. No matter what. Your problems are your problems, okay? Library not a bank. You got education papers?'

'Yes. Yes, I do.'

'With you?'

'Yes, yes. Right here, I've got them right here.' She has thought that bringing the documentation might be a positive step to shift chance in the right direction. Out of her bag she draws the thin skin of brown paper. From it she pulls her ISC school certificate.

'Okay, okay. I'm going to make a copy so I can give it back to you.' Mrs. Lui narrows her eyes, 'Lily said nice things about you. Said she know you for a while. So I ask her, how come you never talk about her before? She make all kinds of excuses for that. Lily not good at bluffing. Why she always lose at mahjong. Everybody can see her secrets on her face.'

Aneeta uncertainly offers what she hopes to be a polite smile, 'I'm her neighbour. But I've only recently moved in.'

'She said she knows you're a hard worker. Wonder how she knows?' Mrs. Lui makes the pronouncement a bit gruffly.

'Oh yes. I am. I mean, I can be. Will be.' She worries that the words may have sounded presumptuous, too forward. That is, assuming she is given the chance.

'She recommend I hire you.' Mrs. Liu looks at her sharply. 'Says she's afraid of some of the new people we hire. Funny hairstyles and make-up. Rings all over the place. She's too old-fashioned, Lily. But she knows Mr. Ho on the Library Foundation Board. Through her son.' Mrs. Liu shrugs, 'So I listen with one ear. Because I know she would gladly fill both of Mr. Ho's ears if she gets a chance. And because she's a very old friend. I have to see her every week at mahjong. And at church. It's Albert's fault. Her husband. Too nice to her. Never could tell her no.' Mrs. Lui mimics, 'Yes, my Lily. Certainly, my Lily. Since he's gone she thinks she can do same thing with everyone. What you gonna do?' She throws up her hands. 'Read it. Fill it all in. Most I can give you, 20 hours per week to begin. You good, you can work your way up. You not, Lily gonna hear it from me. For her, I give you six weeks. I keep her, and Mr. Ho, from giving me trouble. I been here too long for that. When you finish, ring the bell on the desk.'

Gregory
San Francisco
September 2002

Guards paw through every bag and haphazardly wizard wand all *visitors*. She'd be lying if she said the security work-up didn't make her jumpy. But once she's past and in, waiting for the elevator, she's okay. She actually doesn't mind coming to these meetings. Funny, Dan Walrup she's actually gotten to like.

California Department of Corrections Parole Services. The authoritative thick black arrow directs like a pointed finger of shame. Another day, same cast of characters. The smell of urine is high and potent. The cumulative product of all the daily piss running. She tries to limit breathing in the hallway. Fans that run in the office make it weaker. She hopes for an inside seat.

She gets to the doorway and finds she has a choice of several. Lucky day. Choosing one next to an ancient looking Asian woman, she can't help wondering what the woman's here for. Maybe with a relative. A son, daughter, or something. She couldn't possibly have been in trouble herself. Or could she? The woman is bent forward in her seat, mumbling to herself and threading green beads through gnarled, chapped fingers.

There isn't room for her bag on the chair, the seats are narrow, so she puts a foot through the strap and rests the bag on the floor between her legs. She puts a hand into it. Fingers touch the new notebook she is using for her journal. She draws it out and opens to a fresh page. In the zippered side compartment she fumbles for a pen. Keeping her eyes focused on the scene around her— the flow, the shifts, the colours of character, the dialogue she catches— she tries to sketch it with words.

Plaid-shirted guy, blue jeans slung low—'Mr. Garcia your urine test is positive for cocaine.' 'No fuckin' way, I ain't done no blow. You got it wrong! You!' He jabs at the parole office worker, index finger and thumb in the shape of a gun. Woman with tightly braided hair leans in to whisper, 'It ain't right... an' I tol' him tha's robbery man, highway robbery...you takin' 'vantage of situation like that'. Tiny, nimble fingers swallow up one bead after another after another, milky green and smooth they pass through the close of the wizened woman's palm...like a magician playing sleight of hand. 'Mr. Garcia, please.' 'No way am I doing that, no way, it's bullshit. You, and the whole goddamned State of motherfuckin' California is full of bullshit.' Security cop, biceps bulging, is making for the showdown. 'I ain't tellin' you no lies'...wild eyes dart from one face to another. Man of gaunt and angular features, flesh drawn tight and thin against hard edges of bone, sits with a filthy, cracked, white-covered Bible in his lap. Yellowed fingers caress gold lettering. There is a need to believe in something...for guidance, for purpose, for survival. This is the next fork in the road. Make your choice, or let the choice make you.

'Gregory,' Dan says.

'Oh, yeah. Hi.'

'What're you doing?'

'Oh, just...' she claps the journal shut, shrugs. The elderly woman looks up, startled, from her beads. Gregory unwinds the bag strap from her ankle, jerks the weight of it and gets to her feet. Does she want to say? Can she not? Is she being paranoid? What harm could it do to tell him? 'I'm writing a journal,' she says, embarrassed, 'for a class. A writing class. Dr. Gedge hooked me up.' Pathetic and lame. Lame.

'That's great. Really. You enjoy it?'

'What, the class? Or the writing?' Duh. She's a brainless cartoon character. Hyuk, hyuk, what's up, Doc?

'Both. Either. You don't have to feel funny about it, you know.'

'About what?'

'About doing something for yourself. And about actually liking what it is you're doing.'

'I don't feel funny.' Defensive. Inside she tightens like a coil.

'Good. So?'

'Yeah. I like it.'

'I'm glad Gedge turned you on to it.' They have reached the office. He waits for her to enter. Courtesy is as foreign as compliment. Both confuse her. Her eyes drop. She grips the journal and pen tighter to her and passes him by.

'Yeah.' She settles in the hot seat.

'I'm sure he had his reasons. Gedge is not the kind of guy to knee-jerk. I've known him long enough to know that. So he must think there's something there. Good for you.' He moves behind the desk. Sits.

'Uh, I hope. I mean, maybe.' She's looking around, eyeballing for something to muddy the attention. A change in subject would be welcome.

'So what're you doing in class, besides journaling?'

'Uh. Well. We've been looking at other writers, you know, sharing stuff we think is good. He, the professor, is an okay guy. We do a lot of talking. Discussion. Back and forth.'

'What're the people like?'

'Everyone's pretty different.'

'A good thing?'

'Yeah.' She lets her eyes travel; to try and take the heat off. Every time she's here they land the same place. The photograph on his desk. It's like a magnet. The girl. It's something about her eyes. They're so bright looking. She would say, if

259

she were writing a description, that they sparkle. Even though it's not something you can get from a photo. She has wanted to ask but hasn't had the guts to. Today though, now, it might be a way of taking back the conversation. In the picture, Dan's on one side, a woman's on the other. The girl is in between. They're standing on a baseball diamond. She doesn't know what the limits are. His boundaries. About personal stuff. But it's out in the open, public. One way or another, he'll bring them back to business. 'So, this your family?' He looks just a little surprised. At the twist in conversation.

'Yeah.' He is nodding. Smiling at the image. There's gentleness in his voice.

'Nice.' She says even though her heart aches from the current of what's reaching out of the layers of the photo paper. 'How old?'

'Oh. She's nine. Just turned nine.'

'Nine. Wow.' She sifts through her memory to see if she can pinpoint something of nine. Where had she spent nine? Idaho? Colorado? Montana? 'She plays ball?' *I wanted to play ball when I was a kid*, she thinks. She doesn't have the guts to say it.

'Yeah.'

'You play together?' Little tiny fragments of a child's wishing come back to her. Too small to matter.

'Sometimes they let the parents join in, make fools of themselves. Teach us a lesson about all the heckling we do from the sidelines. Make us put our money where our mouths are, so to speak.'

'Looks happy. Your family.'

'Yeah.' He says it quiet and thoughtful.

She looks from him to the picture and then down. Away from the smiles, the happiness that is there, showing itself in everything about her, the girl. Nine. 'She's a lucky girl.'

'I think it's the other way around.' He flips open the folder and dates the entry. The tide of words in the room begins to turn once more.

Her voice is low, 'That's what makes you a good dad.'

Desks are being pulled from rows into an egg-looking shape. 'God, you guys are good!' he booms from just behind her, causing her to about jump out of her skin. 'Love it. Love you taking the initiative with the circle thing.' Turner is nodding as he makes for the front of the room. He's in blue jeans. Could be one of them, from the way he looks, the way his shirt hangs loose. Sleeves rolled casually to his elbows. Young, he looks downright young.

Tonight's episode covers *Techniques of Fiction*. They talk about various elements in a *How To* sort of way. They line up dos and don'ts in a divided list on the board. People more openly volunteer ideas now, the shyness of being strange to one another is starting to dissolve. Conversation is punctuated by laughter. Turner is reciting passages from memory. Using them as examples. To show them what's good. They consider setting. Character. Gregory is surprised to feel her hand rising, to hear herself sound like she knows something. Others agree and expand along her lines of thinking.

People are frantically note-taking. Heads bob up and down in the class. Hands shoot up. Questions are asked. Is it her imagination, or is Turner looking at and smiling a lot at Beauty? What's her name? Aneeta. She looks earnest, interested. Gregory watches her for a moment. She isn't blind to his attentions. Couldn't be, when it's such a clear read. Or is she? Beauty's eyes are bright. And they are only willing to hold his for the smallest moment before they escape to the safety of the notebook. Once, twice, three times, she counts. *Well, I'll be,* she thinks.

'Without conflict, there's no story to tell. Why? Because there would be no change or growth. Robert Olen Butler puts it in terms of yearning: Desire is the driving force behind plot. The character yearns, the character does something in pursuit of that yearning, and some force or other will block the attempt to fulfil that yearning. Do we agree, disagree? Yes.' He points in acknowledgement and voices vibrate with ideas. Flowing one way, and then another. They pare the bigger topics down to get the basics of how to go about things. The best approach.

He defines synecdoche for them. The hired hand. A set of wheels. The businessman as the suit. He cautions about language and overly flowery prose. Encourages simplicity. 'For now,' he jokes, 'until you write your Pulitzer Prize-winning effort.' More laughs.

'Dialogue plays a crucial role in the advancement of your story. Incredibly powerful, but a two-edged sword. Done well, it draws the reader into your realm. However, there is absolutely nothing worse, in my opinion, than bad dialogue. Dirty dialoguing, I call it.'

They address plot as pivotal. 'The Sun,' he quips. 'Everything else revolves around it. It's at the center of things, and it is big, and fiery, and powerful. It's what holds the reader. But there's this push and pull with character. That tug-of-war back and forth is equally driving. One affects the other and vice versa.'

China Doll, Kameko, as Turner has reminded Gregory when he first calls on her, is getting into it too. Gregory notes that she blushes when Turner compliments her. 'Whoa, that's deep,' he says when she mentions existentialism, a word Gregory has no idea the meaning of, in fact has never even heard before.

They back and forth, the two of them, Kameko in her soft, careful singsong. 'It helps to give how and why to direction. To choosing. In the process of becoming. Standing apart and beside oneself, so one can consider more objectively.' Her hands are gesturing. Her face is expressive and eager, 'It is, for a character, very different between being and knowing. In Japan, Haruki Murakami is well-known for using this technique in his stories. I look in the mirror, but who is it that looks back?'

'Yeah, I like it,' Turner says. 'Paint that into a portrait. How choices might define but also confound a being. An intelligent technique with character. But use it modestly and wisely. Right, Kameko?' He grins broadly, then asks China Doll, 'Where'd you get to studying existentialism?'

She is back to nodding, her cheeks pink, 'In Tokyo. I studied literature for a time at Waseda University.'

'Credit where credit's due. Good. Great. Thanks for sharing that.' Turner checks the clock and begins to wrap up, 'So for next week, listen up, I want you to write something about yourself. It can be in the now, in your present, or maybe the past, even in the future, but somehow *you* need to figure into the context. There has to be a personal connection. Now, here's the key to this exercise—it should raise some sort of question or conflict without actually telling us what that might be. But it doesn't necessarily require resolution in this particular piece of work. Think of it as taking a snapshot. Frame a certain point in time. Describe it. What do you want us to notice? Be broad, be wide open in your thinking and examinations. Venture outside of your comfort zone. Give yourself some artistic freedom. Put down whatever comes to mind and go with it. Nothing is ever wrong! According to Emerson: *All life is an experiment.* I couldn't agree more.'

News comes rippling through as class breaks that it's Barbie's birthday. Suburban Barbie 2, as Gregory's silently dubbed her. The blonde is Number 1. Of course. The original Barbie was blonde so makes sense in the game that she'd be the first. The brunette always seemed pretty much an afterthought, so in the classroom context Gregory's tagged her Number 2.

So Barbie 2, or Krista — with a 'K' as she keeps reminding Turner— is having a little 'fiesta', her word. She says it in a squeaky giggly kind of pitch. While sharing party plans, Barbie 2 laments that little Johnny, her 'baby-man', has a cold, a 'gross snotty nose' and a 'I could sell him to the circus' kind of 'seal-bark' cough.

'Let the hubby handle it for once,' she dismisses. 'I'm tired of being Mommy.' She half-sings a personal rendition of the *It's My Party* sock-hop standard with a bit of an evil grin: 'It's my birthday party, gonna do what *I* want to, do what *I* want to....' She invites the whole of the group for drinks at the Hemlock Tavern. 'Be easier going back to borings-ville and being up all night if I get a little buzz on first.' She works the room: 'Come with me. Say you'll come. You'll come, won't you? Just for one teeny-tiny drink. I'm buying the first round of beers if that makes the deciding any easier.' Some of the guys whoop.

Gregory gets nabbed seconds before she's ready to up-and-out. *Damn. Not fast enough.* 'You'll come, won't you? It'll be fun. A chance to hang out for a bit.'

She's not sure whether she wants to or not. Her first inclination is not. But maybe she should try. Can't hurt. *So-shul-ization.* She shrugs, noncommittal, 'Sure,' is what she says, though she isn't. Sure, that is.

Krista even talks to the professor. He smiles and she seems to swoon. But while they're still chatting he is packing. Probably not joining in by the looks of it.

She tries to gauge who's coming. Of course the guys. Free beer is too much to turn down. Beauty seems hesitant. But she can see Krista pushing until, there it is, a nervous smile and a nod. China Doll, who is beside her, seems to be hanging in a question mark limbo for Beauty's answer. Krista looks to be leaning on them a bit. Both look uneasy. 'Come on, it'll be fun, I promise.' This girl should be an evangelist. Seems to have the power of persuasion nailed.

'Okay, so we'll see you guys there!' Krista waves gaily, clearly pleased with herself. Gregory is taking her time with her things. Still sitting on the fence. Until China Doll stops in front of her.

'You will go for a drink? For Krista?' The girl is nodding at her. Maybe looking for a nod-back? Who knows? Expectantly, she waits, looking at Gregory. With a sweet smile. Wide, liquid eyes. God knows why, but she looks like some wanting little kid.

'Well...I...Yeah, I guess.' No easy out now.

'Then,' China Doll asks, nodding still, 'maybe I can walk with you?'

'Yeah, why not.'

'You know it?' It comes out like *eet-ah*. 'The bar?'

'No.'

'No?' Voice and eyebrows rise with the question.

'Krista was saying it's one block over, on the corner. I have a rough idea.' Then Beauty is there. With them. Looking like some kind of goddess you'd expect to have flowers wound into her hair.

'You will come with us too?' China asks her. The tight *oo* sounds cartoonish.

'Would that be...' she looks from one to the other. Damn, the colour of her eyes is wild. 'Would it be okay with you?' Her voice is soft and husky.

Kameko looks to Gregory. 'Yeah. Sure. No problem.' Gregory takes a deep breath. At least it makes for points in the positive column of her shrink file. In the name of socialization. Still reluctant, she heads for the door. The other two tag along behind.

'You gals know where you're going?' Beer Can Mike of the crew cut asks.

'Think so,' Gregory replies for them.

'See ya there.'

They are quiet as they make their way from the building and out into the commons. The evening is still lively on campus. But between them the staccato clip-clop of Kameko's shoes is the only thing to break the quiet. The silence, as it stretches, begins to get awkward. It's like the start of a therapy session. Waiting on some direction, a signpost. Okay, dammit, she'll be the one to break the ice, to start things off. Class seems a natural enough kick-off. 'So,' she drags the so, watching them react and turn to her, the atmosphere changed with her voice, 'what d'you think of class?'

Beauty speaks eagerly, like she's thankful for words to interrupt the chasm of empty air. 'Oh, I find it very helpful, really. Very.' She rolls her r's like the purr of a cat.

China Doll jumps into the fray and conversation is suddenly off and running. 'Yes, I think that Doctor Turner,' which comes out sounding *Doc-ah-ta Tune-ah*, 'is teaching useful techniques to help with writing. For improving style. He is a good teacher. Maybe…' she looks for the phrase and with it gives a small smile, 'because of his different approach. I have not had a teacher like him before.' She nods with it. She is soft-spoken and girlish.

As they continue to walk Beauty pipes up, 'You know how the professor has suggested that we have others review our work? To help get a more balanced view? Well, I don't really have anyone I can show my assignments to. I wonder, would you perhaps be willing to meet and read over each other's assignments? Maybe once a week? I think it could be a great help.' She ventures, 'Well, I know for my work it could. If you…would be interested, would want to…we could fix a place to meet.'

Both of them, China and Beauty, are looking at her. Waiting on *her*. To answer. Another step outside the zone. Fine suggestion, she thinks, but why do you need me? Why the hell me? Some, like Claire, are happy taking the lead. But it's not her thing. Not at all. 'Uh, well, I work odd hours,' she manages. That's her best excuse? Dimwit. Lame, lame, lame. She has to be faster off the mark with her excuses. Sharper. Then again, who else is she going to show her work to? Her shrink, yeah, that's about it so far. She doesn't know that the girls passing through Larkin House would be up for it. Of all the potential possibilities or groupings this, by far, seems the least intimidating. These two are like mice. As afraid of the shadow they throw as she is. How bad could it be? And again, a tidbit for the doc. Something like this ought to qualify her as a damn butterfly on the social scale. 'Yeah, I guess. We could try. Maybe. See how it goes.'

It was a big enough deal just taking the class. Now she's being hooked into birthday parties and a homework club. A shiver runs through her.

'Oh,' Beauty points, 'I think I see a sign. See the red lettering? Ahead there, on the left.'

'That looks to be it.' At the corner is a building with dark wood accents and white-stuccoed peaks. Windows line the front and reveal the joint to be packed with coeds.

Beauty leads the approach, at last pulling a long twist of black iron handle on a heavy wood door pocked by dark knot holes. The atmosphere inside is raucous and in-your-face. Gregory can't help but want to draw back. 'Holy shit,' she says, thinking she is quiet enough not to be heard over the ensuing craziness, but both Aneeta and Kameko look questioningly her way.

Krista is holding court at a long table on the right just inside the doorway. She spots them and shouts, 'Over here!' which Beer Can Mike accompanies with a whistle so sharp that all kinds of people stop and look. Nothing like making an entrance.

Clear plastic pitchers of beer and clusters of glasses line the tabletop, spread at intervals. 'You guys don't get out much, do you?' Krista is laughing. It must be in their faces, or in the collective hesitancy. Awkwardness.

'Yeah, well, this is wild. Kind of like the zoo,' Gregory answers, looking around.

'Caters to the young set; undergrads, frat boys, sorority sisters, party people. Loud, but lots of fun!' A roar erupts from somewhere at the back of the place. Black-aproned staffers move between tight-packed tables like zombies in a familiar maze. Working in a place like this would make her nuts.

The three of them select from the randomly spaced empty chairs around the table. She notices, however, that they choose the seats closest to one another. It occurs to her that the crazy noise level might actually be a good thing. Then she doesn't have to think about what to say. Krista shouts, 'Happy birthday to me!'

Mike is re-filling his glass. 'Drink up, drink up, before it's gone,' he urges, 'and you have to pay for your own!' There is laughter and raised glasses.

Above them on the wall is a huge screen. On it: the football game. The males seem to have gathered at the far end of the table, the perfect vantage point for the game. 49ers outstripping the Cowboys. Incomplete pass. Back to the 25 yard line. A cheer rises. 'Follow football?' Manfred, one of two males actually in the non-viewing end of the table, asks her.

'Some.' Her reply is non-committal. He doesn't pursue it.

Barbie 1, Ashley, is talking to Kameko. Kameko is nodding. It seems her chief form of expression. Barbie 1 pulls her hefty handbag from where it hangs on the chair back, points at some leather tag hanging off the handles. Kameko smiles. Barbie's doing all the talking.

She half-listens to conversations about sport and celebrities, about east-west college rivals, about the crazy price of real estate and dot-com bubbles, about nothing degrees and back-up plans, about Beer Can Mike's—bingo!— tour of military duty. She doesn't have to do much other than nod on cue. Not so hard. She catches similar motions in Beauty and China. Smile and wave, girls, smile and wave. She's only halfway through her beer, but she's had enough. Done the thing. Survived to tell the headshrink doc of it. Time to go. She stands. 'You done with that?' Manfred asks of the beer.

'Yeah. Hey! Krista! Gotta go.' She has to shout to get Krista's attention. 'Thanks for the beer. Happy birthday.'

'You going?' Krista hollers back. Her blouse has been opened a few extra buttons. The sweater has been discarded, as has the careful headband. She is swaying to a melody of music that is threading its way through the other layers of noise. Television noise, conversation noise, cheering noise, football noise. Layers and layers and layers. The music comes in choppy scraps in between.

'Yeah. Got to be on my way. Got to be at work by 5.' She says it loud enough so she knows her excuse will be heard. She turns to step away from the chair, to slide it back to the table edge, and notices that Kameko has gotten up too.

Aneeta is attempting to withdraw from a conversation. One of their classmates. Male, of course. Bent on monopolizing her attention. She slides herself away from the table and stands. Still the guy talks. She politely takes one step to the side. He doesn't stop. Even as she loops a length of scarf around her neck and lifts her coat from the chair he is still working. Aneeta somehow gracefully extricates herself, leaving him staring after her. 'He was a little intense,' Gregory says to Aneeta as they step into the brisk night air.

'There was no way for me to stop him talking!'

'You just have to be blunt with guys like him, that's all.' She shrugs.

Kameko taps at her ear, 'I heard you say you have work,' which comes out like *wahk* instead, 'very early in the morning—5 o'clock?'

'I do.'

'So early. Excuse me, but what kind of work?'

'I work in a bakery.' Then she stops. No. 'I'm a baker.' *Be precise with your words*, that's what Turner had said this evening.

'Ah,' Kameko is nodding, 'so always a very early start?'

'Always. I don't mind, though.'

'So, maybe later in the afternoons are better then for meeting to discuss writing.' Again, the *er* in afternoon and better come out sounding like *ah*. 'I have work during the day too. But not so early.' Kameko smiles.

Aneeta asks her, 'What kind of work do you do?'

'I am helping in a bookstore.'

Aneeta volunteers, 'I work at the public library, in Chinatown.'

'Chinatown?' Kameko raises her eyebrows.

'My neighbour—she's actually Korean—helped me to get the job.' Beauty presses on with the planning, 'So should we arrange then to meet one afternoon before next class? Do you know which of your days are free?'

'I think,' Kameko nods, 'that I can arrange it with my bosses.'

'Gregory?'

'In the middle of the span somewhere, so we've got time to write something frst. Let's make it...' mentally she coaches herself—*Pick a day, any day!*—rubbing against the chill moving through her sweatshirt, 'uh, Sunday? Monday? I know a little coffee shop around the corner. Biked past it a couple of times. Perk Hill? It seems quiet. Not like this.' She motions backwards. She's feeling the cold. And she's tired. Make plans and get going.

'Yes, I think Monday.' China's nodding. 'So now we must decide what time to meet.'

'Monday. Shall we say 5 o'clock?' Aneeta suggests.

Monday at 5 is agreed. Good nights are exchanged. There's a handful of cabs at the curbside. Kameko makes for the front of the short line, waving as she goes. She opens the tinny platter of a door and Gregory can see the turban of the driver in the lamplight. She hears Aneeta's drawn breath. And notices that she has suddenly huddled herself low into scarf and coat and turned to face the other way. She seems to be looking at something down the end of the street. Gregory follows her gaze. Did she turn away, or had something in the other direction entirely caught her attention? Near the end of the block a pair stand by a tree while a dog on a leash lifts its leg. *The couple walking the dog?* Kameko still waves from the back window as the cab pulls away. Once the car has turned the corner Aneeta straightens up and gives a small smile. But she's looking nervous. *You don't want to know, Gregory. Don't want to know, not your business. You've got enough shit of your own to deal with. Nothing personal.* 'So, which direction you headed?'

'Chinatown.'

'How're you getting there?' *Lives there too?*

'By bus. The stop is just here. Just past the lane. It's how I come to class.'

'I'll walk with you as far as the stop.'

'You will walk?'

'Yeah. Where I'm going, it's not too far.'

'You think it safe to walk alone? As a woman?'

'Yeah, I'm okay.' Gregory shrugs, 'I can take care of myself.' She thrusts hands into pockets.

'Even the buses are no assurance of safety in my country. Many bad things happen. To girls and women. On streets, buses, trains. Pickpockets. Assaults. Rape. It is best not to be alone at night. Anything can happen. Especially in the dark.'

The lighted bus shelter is before them. There are people waiting. What Beauty's said has tripped something in Gregory. How she seems vulnerable, fragile. Like she doesn't have a whole lot of fight in her. Why something like that would come to her she hasn't the foggiest idea. That Beauty's too nice, maybe. Too polite.

Aneeta stops at the edge of the shelter. 'Until Monday,' she says.

'Yeah, Monday,' Gregory says, wishing now that she hadn't agreed. Wishing she'd had the quick thinking and *cojones* to come up with a solid excuse to avoid the meeting. Socialization or no. In thickening fog she picks up the pace for Larkin House.

Gregory
San Francisco
October 2002

She doesn't know if classwork qualifies for therapy discussion, but it's eating at her, so rather than go through the face-scanning ritual routine of *What do we talk about today?* she leaps right into it. 'So he's given us this assignment, Professor Turner has. And, okay, I'll admit, it's been a nightmare. We're supposed to come up with some experience we've had, in our lives, and describe it without actually saying *what* it is we're describing.'

'I take it you're having some difficulty with it?'

'Damn straight.'

'Well, Gregory, we all have any number to draw upon. Surely there's something.'

'Yeah, *My Life in the Circus*, or *Extra, Extra! Let me change your take on the baseball bat.*'

'I'm sure that you could focus on something else.'

'I don't have a whole lot of Kodak moments stored away.'

'Have you ever noticed that you tend to let the negative moments define you?'

'Well, they're the things that keep rising to the surface. Doesn't that make them defining?'

'Maybe you ought to see what else you can find. Don't be deterred by what simply rises up first.'

'This is why you make the big bucks, I'm assuming.'

'Gregory, have you ever thought that if you adjust how you choose to look at things the focus might change.'

'What kind of therapy shit advice is that?'

'It means that besides the obvious, there are other things, qualities, experiences, that are more a part of you than you're even willing to consider.'

'Right.' She can't help the sarcasm, but then feels contrite, 'Sorry.'

'It's okay.'

'It's just this thing, assignment, I've been thinking about it so much, it's really getting me frustrated. And...I just seem to freeze-frame when I think about myself. On the big things. And I guess they act like blinders for anything else.'

'Maybe, if the prospect of this assignment is getting to you that much, you ought to leave it. Let it go.'

'Damned if I'm going to let one stupid assignment beat me.'

He smiles. 'You're right not to.'

'Didn't we come full circle? You say drop it and I say no, then you say right, don't. Am I wrong to be confused?'

He sighs, 'It *is* in your interest to do it, the writing. But at what cost? There's a point where you'd be better off leaving it if it's giving you so much angst, but only you can say if you've reached that threshold. I think, and this is my opinion, that you just need to relax a little and it'll come.'

'Before class on Wednesday?'

'I don't have a crystal ball.'

'No shit.'

'But still, I really think it will, if you intentionally let it loose. Free your mind—a cliché, I know—but just try to mentally cancel the hold the assignment seems to have on your psyche right now.'

'And how do you propose I do that?'

'Avoid thinking about it at all. Just for a day or two. See what happens. And don't be so hard on yourself. Remember, you're taking this class for your enjoyment and improvement. Enjoyment. Improvement. Keep that in mind.'

'Yeah, yeah. Still.'

'It's not easy. The assignment, or the healing process.'

'I get that. Boy, do I ever get that.' She grimaces and wonders about the other two in her homework trio, whether they've had trouble coming up with something. Not like she could really tell them what's got her stumped. *Hey girls, so I'm just fresh out of jail for killing my daddy who used to beat on my mama. What do you think I could write about as one of my defining moments?* Not likely.

'So taking your advice, moving on. Two of the other girls in the class, they…we've…' What does she say? Avoid the truth: that if she'd had an out she would have jumped at it. 'The three of us have agreed to meet up once a week to share our work, discuss our progress—or lack of it, as the case may be.'

'A great idea.' He emphasizes the great. And smiles.

She clears her throat, 'Well, I'm not entirely comfortable with it, but I figure it's worth a try.' She doesn't mention other details about them or the weird gravity that seems to pull at them. The way they seem to look to her for, what is it? Approval? Guidance? *Cojones*? She doesn't say, in case he thinks she really is crazy. It's not exactly need-to-know.

'It's a big step forward.'

'I think it's going to make me look a fool.'

'Why?'

'Don't know. I worry I'll get all panicky. And lose myself in *What do I say? What do I do? How do I act?* Like this brain-swarm of confusion will magnify my freak vibe.'

'I don't believe you're a freak, Gregory.'

'You're just saying that because you're my shrink.'

'No, Gregory, I'm saying it because in my experience I have found it to be true. For no other reason.'

'Then maybe you're the one that ought to be in therapy.'

'Very funny. I like this sense of humour. I only wish it wasn't so self-deprecating.'

'You want to say it in English?'

'Well, you have a tendency to be tough on yourself. Overly. To your detriment. That's self-deprecating. When you belittle or under-value yourself. '

In a deep tenor timbre she makes the statement: 'She's a decent enough girl. In fact, we find her to be really quite ordinary. If she weren't so fucked up.'

Kameko and Aneeta are already waiting in front of Perk Hill when she rounds the corner. She checks her watch, a thrift store cheapie with a stuttering second hand. It's just shy of 5 o'clock.

They file through the door: Kameko first, Aneeta following. She trails. Traffic's light. Good timing. Inside Perk Hill is a mismatched collection of corners and angles that'll come to good use given what they want it for. No Gerry's, but not bad. A goth-looking girl gives them a once-over and refocusses on a squealing stretch of shiny coffee machine. Kameko leads to a corner near the back, hangs her enormous bag on the chair and shrugs out of her coat. Out of the way is good.

Gregory clears her throat as they deposit things on the tabletop, 'I somehow don't think we'll be welcome to stay unless we buy something.' One by one, they make their way to the counter. Tea and a pecan biscuit for Aneeta; the same for Kameko. Gregory opts for coffee, adding a biscuit at the last minute, even though she feels a traitor for buying someone else's baked goods. The goth girl gives her a hard stare and she returns it, holding it until the girl looks away. So much for intimidation techniques. *Looking the part's only half the battle*, she wants to say. Probably from some middle-class, suburban neighbourhood; never seen the ass-end of any trouble. She steers herself back to where the other two are carefully chit-chatting, notebooks and pens politely poised.

After she comes up with her own pen and paper, she hesitantly takes a test nibble of the cookie sure that she'll find it stale and flavourless. She is, instead, pleasantly surprised at the way it melts on her tongue; sablé, a shortbread dough. Nicer than simple sugar cookie dough, and the chunks of pecan are actually substantial within it. Not what she'd been expecting, not at all.

From an outsider's perspective she imagines they must be a bit of an odd-looking threesome—the Japanese with her bright shiny presentation, like a glittery new toy wrapped up so perfectly; the haunted beauty with coffee cream skin and unearthly looking eyes that dart from the front door around the room and back again at nervous intervals; and, of course, the bit of rough, the ex-con freak. Beauty's taken the chair Gregory would have preferred, back to the wall. Every so often, Gregory sees her head cock a little, to one side. Like she's listening for something.

First session of Homework Helpers is underway and still she's had no luck with the assignment. Wound a bit tight, she takes a sip of hot coffee. She imagines the doc watching, telling her it'll get easier. Easier. When? She listens to their voices talk about class, Professor Turner, how they'd found out about English 50. Work at the bookstore. Work at the library. She's damn glad they don't ask her how she found her way into English 50. She looks down, fakes a preoccupation with dunking the cookie into her coffee.

China Doll's given up university and moved to San Francisco with her husband. 'I once was studying literature.' Does she imagine the note of regret? See it in the sad-sweet smile? The husband is busy, not home much. Maybe class is a time filler? Bored housewife?

Beauty's stepped up. 'I thought the class might be something to help my English.' She says it clah-ss. Laughs shyly. There is a pronounced rhythm to her speech. 'As a child, as a student, I always liked to write. The only thing about the course that worries me is the use of computers. I don't know computers at all.'

It comes before she stops to think, 'I didn't either. Well, I don't—but I'm learning. There are free courses. At the downtown library. For beginners mostly. Low-tech for the no-tech crowd.'

'Through the library? Really?' She sounds incredulous, like she's just hit the jackpot.

'Yeah. Though it may only be at the main branch, I'm not sure. I'm doing Windows for Beginners. Maybe they should have called it Windows for Dummies—capital D. Like those books, you know?' Nope, clearly they don't know about the yellow Dummies guides. She doesn't say that Linda, Larkin's den mother, has hooked her up. Told her that it would be wise to get a basic understanding of technology, computers. In the interests of expanding her skillset. 'I'm sure if you wanted,' she shrugs, 'you could turn up, see if it helps.'

'Really? You'd be willing to take me with you?'

Take her? Is that what she'd said? Offered? 'Uh, I think there's still space in the class, I mean, not all the computers are getting used—'

'Is it complicated?'

'So far, no. Far as I can tell, everybody's at the same level. We started by finding the on/off switch. Can't get more basic than that.' Here she is, putting herself on the line again. She has no clue what's prompting her. None. Beauty is beaming at her. Gregory writes the day and time on a page in her notebook and tears it out. 'I'm not sure exactly what the street address is, but since you work at the library I'm sure you can find out. If you want…well, I'll be there anyway.' Gregory slides the paper over the tabletop.

Aneeta's smile is like a megawatt blaze against her skin. Kameko smiles too. They are like two grinning Cheshire Cats at points across from her. Definitely an oddball trio.

'This is a nice place for meetings,' Kameko announces.

'Yeah, it's okay. I wasn't sure if they'd let us linger or not. The girl behind the counter, she looks a bit tough. But I don't think she'll mess with us.' She doesn't mention the stare down.

'She reminds me of a Tokyo Harajuku, the way she wears her hair and make-up. Just maybe not the clothing. Harajuku are very serious about dramatic fashion. I think maybe Harajuku point of view would be good for some assignment. Interesting.'

An *exercise* Turner's called it, this homework that's driving her nuts. Just one snapshot moment, frozen, with no past visible. Still, her brain refuses to cooperate. Not one of them has finished the work. Which makes her feel not such a complete failure for her brain block.

'I feel,' Aneeta says carefully, thoughtfully, 'that in order to describe a moment in such detail, to know it through all the senses, that I must have lived it, at least by some measure. Otherwise how can I really know its effect?'

'It is a difficult task,' Kameko agrees. 'But we can think of it or compare it perhaps to a dream, or dreaming. Dreams can be very much a sensory experience, without knowing everything, all of the other details. How or why, for instance.'

Something that sounds like TV fairy magic, like a Tinker Bell sprinkling of stardust, reaches out from behind Kameko's elbow. At the noise, discussion drops. Kameko registers a look of surprise that fast morphs into recognition, 'Oh, excuse me.' She plunges an arm into her shiny, oversized bag and grapples with the contents. Two more fairy spells ring before she manages to pull out a glittering, wafer-thin phone. There is a growl that comes out of it when she answers, a male voice. *So much for magic.* Her voice is soft between his drawn-out bursts. He fills up most of the conversation. With a fast, stamp-heeled rhythm. Her side of things is meek and thin. Facial features slip and fingers work the corner of her notebook page into a curl.

When the growl is finished with his delivery, Kameko moves the phone away from her ear. She gives them both a timid smile and a bow. 'I am very sorry. This was my husband. He has returned home…earlier than I have anticipated. And so I must go.' Her English sounds unsure suddenly. She begins collecting her things, 'I am very sorry…I was not sure he was coming this evening.' She wraps a delicately patterned scarf around her neck and scoops hair out. As she reaches for her coat, Gregory can see her face is shuttered by guilt. The expression is one she knows. From all the times she'd seen it before on Mama. Funny how it looks the same on both of them. No two more different women in the world, Mama and this girl. Obviously, making excuses for a man's bad behaviour is a universal habit.

As they sort paper and pens from napkins, cups, plates and spoons, Kameko volunteers, 'I have enjoyed our discussion. Even though today it was short. I think it could help us if we continue to meet.' She looks hopeful. Aneeta is looking at Gregory too. Two sets of damn impossible eyes.

'Yeah, I guess…it probably could help.' For some reason she thinks of the doc. Wonders how much of her agreeing to continue is about meeting the state's requirements for fitting in, and how much is because she might want to. Dirties, she stacks and walks to goth girl's counter. For her effort she gets a flinty grimace of thanks, a concession that looks almost painful.

Leaving, Kameko again leads the way, scarf ends fluttering on air. And a lightbulb trips in Gregory. She's got her subject for the assignment, the snapshot she can write about: Mama's gypsy scarves.

Gregory Abbott
English 50

A suitcase. Small and blue-black. With a shiny silver clasp. Tucked away under one side of the bed. From where she'd been playing on the floor she'd spied a metallic glint. It had winked at her and drawn her to it. In the way of a secret.

It took almost nothing by way of a tug to pull it out. Hardly any effort at all. It slid toward her so easy; like it wanted out. Like a kept animal wants out of a cage sometimes. Fingers trace spider cracks; pick at curled edges of paint and lost stiches of thread. Maybe it's been brittled by age, maybe by miles, maybe by things hard and heavy. She wonders at its journey, tries to conjure its mystery contents.

Curiosity can get a person into trouble. That much she knows. But there are times, too, when curiosity won't be denied. Times like this one, right here and now. Without any mind for what might come of it. The latches suddenly pop, sounding like rifles, splitting still air. Ice races in her veins. Slow and ginger, she lifts the top open. She draws breath so deep and quick it makes her heart ache; little black spiders prick and pop in front of her eyes.

It is a dazzling kaleidoscope collection, as bright to behold as a rainbow. The case is filled entirely with scarves. Scarves and nothing else. Squares and rectangles of different sizes; all of them beautiful and soft. Some are gauzy and sheer, some are thicker and textured. Threads are woven into delicate patterns of flowers, or paisley, or into abstract halos of rich colour. She allows herself to believe she's unearthed a treasure. A run of magic tremors through her. For the moment, worry is whisked away. Childish fingers walk through the yielding depths, disappearing beneath the cheery cover they've found. When she scoops the fabric cloud to a wanting cheek, it's like butterfly wings on her skin. But the look and feel of them is deceiving.

The truth is, she knows them all. Every last one of them. From times before, occasions when they've been needed. To pretend that things are different. They're a reminder there's a storm brewing. Somewhere not too far from now. They call to mind the unpredictable reach of lightning and the rage of thunder. After, when a temporary calm has returned, they hide the remains of a bad spell that's blown through.

Fingers tremble as she tucks them back under the hard old shell of the battered and beaten case. Until then, they stay in darkness. Out of sight. Waiting on the wind to shift, the weather to change. She puts the lid somberly over them; presses the clasps of metal hard until the teeth grab and hold, locking the secret away. And she prays that she might never have to see them again.

Aneeta
San Francisco
October 2002

'Please, I can't go in there.' In panicky desperation she pulls on Gregory's arm with perhaps more force than she needs. It stops Gregory in her tracks.

They are at the threshold, ready to step into the library's computer room. Aneeta scrambles for an excuse as Gregory waits expectantly. Stepping quickly to one side of the door, Aneeta tries to position herself out of the sightline of the dark-skinned man standing before a length of whiteboard. Presumably he is the instructor. He has stopped writing and is looking toward the door. The bangle on his wrist glints in the uplight of what seems a kind of projector. It makes him, like her, Sikh.

The threads of affiliation are extraordinary in their uncanny ability to weave themselves together. *Where are you from, girl? Which part in the country, which village? Your family name? A good family, I have heard of them. Well-known Brahmin. What brings you to America, girl?* Names, details and information so smoothly, so easily, trickle through family lines and connections. *Sistersmotherinlawsbrother. Friendofafriend.* And if she is found out, then what?

'I simply can't.' Close to tears, she fumbles for a reason to put forth. Something that sounds likely, believable. But in her panic she grasps only emptiness. Heat is rising in her, her heart flies, her abdomen twists in anxiety. She offers a basic truth. 'Because… that man is Indian.'

'Okay.' The word drags, Gregory's doubt evident in it. 'I don't get it,' she has one eyebrow raised, 'aren't you Indian too?'

Her breathing is shallow. 'Yes. Yes, I am. But…I can't explain. Not here, not now. I just can't go in there. I can't. Please, I'm sorry.' She shakes her head with vigour to affirm her decision. 'You go. I will wait.' She motions down the hallway. To a collection of chairs at careful right angles divided by low tables. It would be rude simply to leave when Gregory has tried to help. She wasn't to know. How can she be expected to understand? 'I will instead stay to read.' She attempts a smile. People file past where they are standing and move into the room. Aneeta has flattened her back to the wall, hoping to have escaped the instructor's view.

Gregory shrugs. 'Suit yourself.' Readjusting the pack on her shoulder, Gregory steps into the room.

Aneeta slides from the wall and slips swiftly along the hushed hallway in search of camouflage. The blocky backs of chairs are low; shoulders and heads stick over the tops of them. She purposely chooses one that faces out the window, so that her back is to the hallway. It occurs to her that she will have to come up with something more to tell Gregory, to explain her strange defection.

She flips blindly through a magazine left by some other patron. The title, in large bold letters: GROW. There is a profusion of plant life pictured from page to page, but she struggles to concentrate on the smaller columns of type that run alongside and underneath.

All at once, he is before her. The instructor. Sinking down into an empty chair set square to hers, smiling, teeth starkly white against the darkness of his skin. *Oh God.* Please say he is from the south. Let them have been separated by thousands of miles. Let there be no cruel coincidence, nothing that filmily ties them together. 'I am JT,' he offers by way of introduction. 'Capital J. Capital T. Period.' He uses a finger to punctuate the air and symbolize the period. 'Short for Jatinder, you know?' She does. She swallows thickly. 'I am from Punjab.' Panic seizes her. *North! Closer to Delhi!* He peers at her. 'You are?' *Ohgodohgod!* Her gaze drops. To where the magazine lies open across her lap. The cheery vibrancy of pictured flowers blurs before her. *There are millions of people in Delhi. God knows how many Sikhs. Why think the worst?*

'I am Aneeta.' She offers the fact quietly, her head bowed, not wanting to meet his eyes.

'A beautiful name. And just where would you be from, Aneeta?' His voice is soft.

She feels sick; dizzy and vague. Two tiny pieces. This much she could tell. 'From Delhi.'

'Well, Aneeta from Delhi, there is likely a good reason you've come to the class today, hmm? I'd be very pleased if you would come and join. Now that we've been formally introduced.' He smiles at her. As if that is to be all. No questions. No probing. He offers a knowing look. The kind that might be reserved for a child caught out in some small transgression.

How can she now reverse her earlier decision without appearing terribly silly? 'Oh, I...' she begins, feeling foolish. There is a flush of heat in her face. She imagines she has turned quite the colour of beetroot. His smile is unchanged. 'I...I simply can't.' *Silly girl! Look what you've done.*

'You can't? And why not? Not on account of me, I hope.'

'No, no. That's not it at all.'

'No?'

'I've just, well, suddenly found myself feeling a bit ill. A bit faint is all.' It is not entirely untrue.

'Shall I tell you what I think? I suspect that there's something, maybe something about me being Indian, or even Sikh, that troubles you.' He is nodding at her. She finds herself struck dumb. He sees her exactly. 'Just for a moment hear me out, okay? Let me tell you a little bit about myself. And perhaps it might put you more at ease. Just the basics, okay? Because we've only a minute or two before we're due to start.' He leans forward slightly. 'As I said, I'm from Punjab. Jats, my family. Farmers.' He waves his hand. 'I am the youngest. Four boys. Oh yes, lucky-lucky. Anyway, the thing of it is,' he pauses for breath and looks directly at her, his smile now one-sided, 'I am gay.' Her jaw drops at the forward nature of his announcement, but he simply continues, 'I'd known from a very young age. And then they'd caught me dressing up.' He waves his hand dismissively. 'My mother tried to push me in the other direction, but without success. My father threatened. Eventually they came to accept that it was something that was not going to be changed. So before my *character*, shall we say, came to light, they realized that with three sons already to farm the land they'd be more than happy for me to go abroad—which is what I wanted, the only thing I ever wanted. Nobody would have to know, and they'd have bragging rights. A computer programmer son working in America is a big thing. Everybody wins, you see? You…do see, don't you?' He nods at her.

'The closest relatives I have: one cousin, a cook in an Indian restaurant in New Jersey, Jackson Heights, and another distant relation who grows marijuana on the west coast of Canada. Big cash crop my parents tell me. Maybe I should turn my hand to farm export like this, hunh? Doctor-lawyer future is not so impressive anymore.' He grins at her. 'Anyway, the point is, no one from the family tree is close, so my secret is safe. Everybody is happy. No shame, no harm. I understand, Miss Aneeta from Delhi. That is what I am trying to say. I understand. Whatever it is. Perfectly. Okay?'

She could have hugged the earnest man in front of her, hugged him for the surge of relief suddenly coursing through her veins. He continues lightly, 'You see, there are those of us here —Indians, I mean—who are content in a big American city like this. Those who value the anonymity it can give. Because we are able to be okay with who we are and not worry so much about the old notions of shame. We are able to live quietly with our truths, with who we are or who we choose to be, and we don't have to give a damn. To let the family back home,' he waves mildly, 'concoct and live with whatever fairytale notion bloody well makes them happy. Here, all that nonsense cannot touch us so much. That is what I love about America. That it is 7,000 miles away makes it much harder for the gossip to pass back and forth. You see?'

She is shaking her head, unable to keep from smiling. 'Forgive me,' she manages, 'I've never met anyone so honest, so…what is the word? Forthright? Yes, forthright. Not, I think, ever before.'

He reaches his hand toward hers, his kara bangle glinting in the little remaining sunlight. 'I am pleased if it helps with your hesitation. My parents, of course, would be horrified. But they are at the other side of this world, and this is my life. Let them continue as they are, this is not bothering them. And here, love them as I do, their guilt cannot reach me. So, Aneeta from Delhi, I invite you to come with me to class and let me impart the marvels of Windows.' His hand waits, open, palm up with its contrasting pinky inner skin, 'There is nothing you need fear.'

With a sigh and a smile she puts her hand out to take his and lets him ease her from the chair. 'Thank you, JT.'

'*Koi gal nai*, Aneeta Miss. It is not such a big deal.'

Kameko
San Francisco
October 2002

The sound of the telephone in the apartment is sharp. In quick mental calculation she tallies, hoping to rule out her mother-in-law being on the other end. Pleasantries would have been trying. It is unlikely. Unless it is a matter of urgency. It would be the middle of the night in Tokyo. Perhaps the clinic. Something about the tests. Adrenalin mushrooms. 'Hai. Hello?'

'Mrs. Tanaka?'

'Yes?'

'Please don't hang up, Mrs. Tanaka. You don't know me but I need to talk to you. I know your husband, Mrs. Tanaka…I…I'm going to have his baby.'

It is as if she has suddenly been engulfed by seawater. Plunged into it without preparation. She cannot draw breath. Limbs turn to lead; tremble like jellyfish. Her hand, paralyzed, remains tightly clamped around the telephone receiver. 'But, how?' she hears her voice cry out in anguish. Instinctively her brain demands details, fact, as it always has. Even though her heart does not want to hear, does not want to listen to the thinness of the confession.

'We're colleagues at work, Mrs. Tanaka,' the voice says, as if to reinforce the likelihood of the revelation, the possibility for it to be true. The stranger's voice continues, as if unconcerned about the chaos it has created, 'We work together. And then, we… became…involved. Intimate. Lovers.'

'Oh,' is all she can manage. Shock has claimed her senses, taken her tongue, left her disoriented. *Needing you back in my bed. Elaine. On the email, the name was Elaine. Could it be?* Her mind struggles for clarity.

'You needed to know. And,' a pause, 'I couldn't be sure…that Shiro would tell you. I've been asking him to. Since I…I mean, we…found out.'

She has no reply. No words to say. *He knew. Shiro knew.*

'Mrs. Tanaka? Are you still there? Mrs. Tanaka?'

'Yes…I am here.' She says the words slowly, with a sound of calm that belies her inner tumult.

'It's hard, I think, for all of us. A complicated situation. But you needed to know,' the caller's words tumble on, 'especially since, well, Shiro told me…that you can't have children.'

It is a dagger through her heart.

'I didn't want to hurt you, Mrs. Tanaka. But, please understand, I didn't want to spend my life trying to hide it from you either. It isn't fair. For either one of us, is it?'

'No.' The syllable is monotone and bleak.

'Mrs. Tanaka? Shiro has agreed that he'll take responsibility,' the voice stills, 'for the child. But it's more than that.' Again, a pause. 'I love him.' Another icy wave washes in, dragging her deeper into darkness. 'I realize he is your husband, but you have to know that I love him. This wasn't something I planned, I…it wasn't something I'd foreseen.' A pregnancy unforeseen? In her mouth there is a metallic taste like tea steeped too long, gone bitter. 'What I'm trying to say, Mrs. Tanaka… it wasn't my intention for this to happen. Certainly not the way it has. I'm not that kind of person. Not…that kind of woman. But it means a great deal, this baby.' The caller trails into silence. A moment later she re-asserts herself with passion, 'And I'm not willing to undo it, I won't.' Kameko can hear the woman beginning to cry. 'Because it might be the only piece of him I get to keep.' Emotion strangles the voice. 'I just…I needed you to know. I don't…' sound drops to a whisper, 'expect you…I know this can't be easy. And, I'm sorry. Really, I truly am. I can't begin to imagine how you must feel. But you needed to know. I just, I couldn't have lived with myself otherwise.'

'Oh.' There it is again, a meaningless syllable. What else can she say? To such a confession, such a truth, such an irony.

'I realize,' Kameko can hear the voice drawing itself up, and she hates it suddenly, this faceless creature, hates it desperately, 'this has come as a shock to you. But, I…I want to thank you for hearing me out. And being understanding of my…of my wishes.' There is a hesitation. A waiting that she can hear in measures of her own breath. She says nothing to the empty air, though she cannot seem to find the will in herself to disconnect from it either. Nothing, and yet everything, lies in the silence between them. Eventually, there is a hard click in Kameko's ear.

Keizoku wa chikara nari. The Japanese proverb. Continuance is strength. But how can she be expected to go on? How can fate be so cruel? Her entire life, in its already unsteady state, has been dismantled by a single telephone call. In minutes it has made everything different. It has left a weary bridge between two people broken beyond repair.

And she had worried that the telephone call might have been her mother-in-law. How trivial such a conversation would have been by compare. She tries to picture the woman who has become pregnant with Shiro's child. Is her husband's lover light-skinned, fair-haired, with wide eyes in a shade of green or blue? A voice by telephone does not reveal these things, but Kameko imagines her this way. And colleagues, she has mentioned that they are colleagues. So the woman is a professional. A contemporary, perhaps even his equal.

She puts her hands to her face. Presses into the flesh of her cheeks. She begins to laugh. It is anguished, the sound. Keening and wild. Her knees give way and she collapses heavily to the floor under the weight of her burden.

He will be a father. The prospect of joy lies ahead for him. Where she has failed, he will not. It is a reality she simply cannot bear to endure.

Gregory
San Francisco
November 2002

Light's starting to break in the sky. Already they've been going for hours. They're rounding the bend on Thanksgiving and Gregory's never been busy like this in her life. All around them is a sticky, gritty storm of activity. Not more than a week to go and they've got a heap of orders. She, Gerry, Lenny, they're going full out. Even Lenny's wife, Suzanne, has taken some time off from her job so she can help out, and still it's a stretch. They've had to take on a new guy, part-time, and an extra driver just to try and manage the workload.

Gregory can hardly wait for the weekend to come, and then be gone. Gerry reminds her that Christmas follows less than a month after. 'No rest for the wicked,' she chortles at Gregory's groan. 'And dear me,' she adds, grinning, 'I've been real wicked in my time.'

Gerry is flattening and folding dough with determined vigour. Her concentrated expression makes Gregory want to laugh. An edge of silliness is settling on her. Which, she expects, is a result of the extra demands of work and not much sleep. She has an urge to throw flour. A fistful. Followed by a clutch of dough from the clippings gathered in a pile at the end of the worktop. Bits and pieces that later will be refashioned into latticework tops and used for some of the smaller savoury items. Only the thought of the added clean-up makes her resist. Every now and again she hears a laboured rush of breath out of Gerry with her pushing. She'd offered to spell her off this morning, but Gerry wouldn't hear of it. 'Are you kidding? What do you take me for? Some feeble old woman?' Her hands are practised and fast, but Gregory can sense the effort in her movements.

Even Lenny had tried to talk Gerry out of keeping such a busy routine. 'You go out and get me these orders and then expect me to just sit idly by and watch? No sir, this place has my name on it, and until I'm in the grave don't expect me to just waltz in and occasionally supervise. I'm no supervisor. I'm a baker. Have been all my life and will continue to be. I'm still your mother, mister, and what I say goes. Besides, I like doing it. You worry too much.' That was last week Sunday, when they were just starting to come up on it. Now they're in the middle of the holiday worst and it has them held fast and spinning.

Stacks of flat brown boxes reach in uneven rises from the floor. Cooling trolleys are heaped with items fresh out of the oven. Gregory rubs an escaped curl of hair on her forehead with the back of a hand. She knows she won't be able to ease it back under the kerchief without knocking the whole thing askew, so she'll just have to live with the irritation of it falling back down in front of her eyes.

Solid is how the work sounds. She lets her hands feel their way through the routine. The radio satisfies the ambling of the mind while the hands work: *Kick off a great Thanksgiving with an invigorating fun run or walk at Golden Gate Park before parades, football games, and feasting commence! Festivities get underway at 8:15 with the Kids Gobbler Run. Bring the whole family!* A sharp clatter of tin causes her to look up just in time to see Gerry crumple like a rag doll to the floor.

Everything after that seems to happen in a slow motion, shaky Panavision hand. Where it's like she is watching herself in some home movie film reel. Here, she lifts her heavy head. Her eyes widen; looking, seeing, not knowing. Then, realization. *Oh my God!* Her voice rings out, shrill and harsh, 'Gerry! Gerry! Oh shit! Gerry!' Panic hammers through her. She battles the drag of an invisible tide to get to Gerry's side. Sinks to one knee. Turns Gerry's lifeless face up. Eyes closed. Face waxy grey. *Oh God, please don't let her die. Please don't let her be dead. Oh my God! What does she do? What should she do? Think. Think, Gregory! Oh God! What if Gerry dies? What if they think she had something to do with it? Ohmygod! What will she do? What? What!*

She pushes up from the floor and makes for the phone that looms ominously at a magnified distance on the wall. *Lenny. Lenny!* Her breathing is fast. Icy. She is so slow, so clumsy. *Okay, what's the number? Think. What's the number? Think, Gregory! Remember!* Trembling fingers poke at raised digits, slipping and sliding off the push pads. The call turns over, clicks through. *Oh please! God, please! Come on, come on! Shit!* Begins to ring. *Lenny! Lenny pick up, pick up!* She is terrified, sobbing. Out-of-control. 'Hullo?' the sleepy voice mumbles.

'Lenny!' she sobs, unable to help herself. 'Lenny!…Gerry!' is all she can seem to get out.

His voice snaps to attention. 'Gregory? Gregory! Calm down. What's going on?' He takes control. 'Okay, take a breath! Gregory!'

She manages, 'We were working. She just…collapsed. Oh! God! Lenny, what do I do? What do I do?' She is panting: like a dog, like she has run for miles, like she is being pursued.

'Okay, Gregory,' he says sternly, 'you need to calm down. And do exactly as I say, you hear?'

In the background, behind Lenny's voice, she can hear Suzanne asking, 'What is it?'

'You need to find out if she's breathing. I'm going to tell you what to do, just hang on.' His voice fades, he's talking to Suzanne, 'Call 9-1-1.' And then he's back. 'Are you with her?'

'Yeah. Yeah. I'm… I'm here. Beside her.' Her tone is high and tight.

'Now,' he says it firmly, like an order, 'I need you to get her so she's on her back.'

She has the phone wedged between her ear and shoulder. It is biting into the flesh at the side of her face from the pressure. She hears that she is grunting trying to move Gerry's accordioned dead weight to lay her out on her back. 'Okay, okay,' she puffs, 'she's on her back.'

'Is her chest rising? Get low and level to see if there's any movement.'

'No, I don't think…I…I can't tell,' she can feel the hysteria swallowing her. 'Oh God!'

Sounds in the background again, behind Lenny. Suzanne. 'Gregory, the paramedics are on their way. Help is coming. It won't be long. Stay with me.'

'I don't think that…don't think she's breathing.'

'Here's what you do, okay?'

'Yeah.' Her heart is pounding. She is freezing. Only moments before, she was overheating.

'Cup your hand under her neck and tilt her head back.' The head yields to her pressure. Gerry looks like she is sleeping. Like she's been caught mid-snore. 'Right?'

'Uh-huh.'

'Make sure her mouth is open. Pinch her nose and seal your lips over her mouth. I know you won't be able to talk once you've done that. What you need to do is give two good breaths.'

'Okay. Two.'

'Put the phone down beside you and do it now.'

She feels lightheaded. Her ears are buzzing. One. Two. She pulls away and draws gaspingly on the air in the room. She gets a hint of burning pastry. She reaches again for the phone, 'Done.'

'Now. Put your hands together, one over the other. In between her breasts, I need you to give a count of 30 quick pushes. You need to press fairly hard. Don't be scared. You should go about as deep as about 2 inches into her. Okay? Do that and then give her two more breaths. Then repeat it, okay? And keep going with that. Over and over again. Unless she comes to.'

'Yeah, yeah. I think. Okay.' *She can't die! Cannot die!*

'You can do this, Gregory! You can! Put the phone down beside you while you do it and talk loud so I can hear what's happening.'

She puts the phone on the flour-gritted floor and begins to press. Firmly, like Lenny has told her. Push, push, push. It reminds her of kneading dough. She is counting with it…10, 11, 12…29, 30. Pinch nose, head back, mouth over mouth, seal. Breathe. Breathe.

She is still going, pressing on Gerry's chest, waiting for some sign, some change, some transformation, anything, when there is a banging at the front. She grabs the phone and pushes to standing. She is aware of running side-on into the countertop and it buffets her hard; her feet are slipping as she makes frantically for the door. Flashing red lights cut through the mist of early morning. 'They're here, they're here! Lenny, they're here!' she cries into the phone. She is sobbing again; fumbling to unlock the bolts. The phone slips and skitters beneath one of the window tables while she opens to the paramedics.

'Here! She's back here!' She runs back to the kitchen with them at her heels. They drop down beside Gerry, placing their cases on the floor, and begin. It is as she is standing over them, watching their precise and sure action, that she remembers the phone. She makes her way across the floor and reaches down to collect it. When she raises it to her now aching ear, she finds him gone.

She hates hospitals. The minute she carries herself through the door, things start to close in on her. There's just something about them, all of them, that's the same. The smell, for one. All those germ killing mixtures. It gets her in the back of the head. Then add to it the potato-like scent of what they pass off as food—oatmeal, chicken soup, eggs—no matter, it all smells the same. Dull and bland. Jell-O's the best they can do to liven things up. Whoever makes Jell-O, the manufacturer of it, has got to be damn glad for hospitals and prisons. Pretty much counts as one of the food groups. Claire used to complain long and loud about its prevalence in the prison food line-up—*Is it too much to ask for them to feed us something real?* Some of the girls would sing the jingle —*Watch it wiggle, see it jiggle...*

The cloying warmth gets to her too. No more than a dozen paces past the door and already she's removed her sweater. It's a wonder hospital staff can muster any energy at all. Her arm is turning clammy under where she's got the sweater draped over it.

Foil balloons float by, *It's a Boy!* She can't think what it must be like to come to hospital for happy things. She's checking the signs that hang from the ceiling. There are red arrows lined next to blue arrows in tracks along the floor. According to the colour coded chart she ought to be following the red arrowed side for the Cardiac Unit. There's a faint buzzing in her ears; pins and needles creeping in. Shoes squeak on linoleum. She squints down the corridor, trying to focus in on the up ahead signs. To make sure she's still right. At her feet, red arrows carry on.

She looks into the offshoots she passes. Each is a hive of activity; pings of call buttons, ringing telephones. Smock and drawstringed staff cluster around desk configurations. Sometimes chatter is light, sometimes serious. Some pods are populated by beds, some simply by seating. There are people everywhere. She avoids the eyes of those who visibly struggle along the corridor, those who hold tightly to poles with drip bags suspended from hooks, using the wheeled bases for support, or those who cling heavily to the wide rail that divides the wall. There is a clench of nausea in her gut.

Will Gerry be sleeping? Awake and alert? Lenny has said she's doing as well as can be expected. What the hell does that mean, exactly? The red line seems to end with a left turn. Cardiology. She coaxes herself in. The room opens out into a circular shape. At the center, by a half-moon of desk space, three women in scrubs talk quietly. Slender glass-doored slices reach out like spokes to the perimeter. To her mind, it's not unlike a pie. Sliced. The thought strikes her as queer, ironic. She pushes stale air out of her lungs and tries to muster courage. Slowly she approaches the desk, taking halting steps, like in some schoolyard game—*What-time-is-it-Mister-Wolf?* Her eyes cast for anything that might give an idea as to where Gerry is. She licks dry lips and teeth; struggles for calm. Mindlessly, fingers pick and pull at sweater nubs.

The round has no windows. She can almost hear bars sliding into place; buzzers. Perspiration is rising, creeping from her pores. It beads at her lip line, stings her underarms, stipples the back of her neck. *This is not a prison. Not a prison.* Lights over the center hub are sharp and bluish bright. She stammers, 'I'm looking for Geraldine Bukowski.' She has never said Gerry's full name aloud. It rolls off her tongue sounding choppy, as if she doesn't know her at all.

'She's in 6,' the nurse motions, pen in hand, 'at the corner.'

Gregory nods and swallows, moves like a sleepwalker. The slide of glass at 6 is open, though it has a privacy curtain pulled across. Some pinwheel segments are lit, some emit scraps of television noise and flashes of a picture changing. Blue-green. A phantasmic light. Number 6 is still and quiet. Lenny has spent the day. He called her, told her was going to go home and clean up. Have a shave. Some food. He and Suzanne are planning to return later.

Gregory lifts the fabric to one side, careful not to let curtain hooks slide their slippery rattling way along the rod, and tentatively steps through the opening. Gerry is asleep. Her face is slack. Along the pillow fine silver hair spreads outward in loose waves. It surprises Gregory, she's only ever seen it neatly kept in a bun. It is flattened against her head on one side where it has obviously been slept on. Arms lie soldier straight at her sides, tucking the blue crochet blanket tight to her. The face is childlike beneath the lines of years. Time gives back in sleep, she thinks.

In the corner, behind the bed, a green line blips peaks and valleys across a black screen. Numbers adjust themselves up and down beside the line. An IV pole stands beside the bed and feeds into the back of Gerry's hand. A metallic canister and mask stand ready on a trolley beside it.

She reaches forward with one hand, then pulls back. She feels strange watching Gerry sleep. There's a chair at the bedside. She could simply sit. But then, she should let Gerry know, at least, that she's here. She hesitates. Then reaches forward to touch Gerry's hand with her fingertips. A featherlight brush. Skin against skin. Hers hot and damp against the papery-dry cool. She whispers, 'Gerry.' Eyelids flutter briefly in waking, before opening fully.

'Gregory.' Her voice is croaky. 'Could I please,' she points, 'the water.'

'Oh. Sure.' Gregory moves nearer. On the wheeled table positioned over the mid-section of the bed is a plastic cup with water and a bending straw. Next to it, Gerry's carefully folded eyeglasses and a small box of tissues. Gregory takes the cup and hands it to her. It takes only a second to see from the way her hand is trembling that she won't manage it on her own. Gregory reaches for it. Gerry lets her. She moves the cup forward so that Gerry can reach the straw with her lips. With noisy gulps she drinks it down. When she pulls away from the straw and lets her head relax into the indent of the pillow, Gregory sets the cup down.

She can see strain painted across Gerry's face. For a moment, Gerry closes her eyes again. Then she gives a slight smile and opens them. 'I'm afraid without my glasses I can't see you all that clearly. Would you mind?' Gregory opens the arms and eases the dark framed lenses into place. 'Now that's a whole lot better.' She gives a little laugh. 'God, you look awful! Must've had yourself some kind of terrible day.'

'You could say.'

'Old lady gave you a bit of a scare?' Gerry says the words slowly.

'Just a bit.'

'I am sorry. Ticker's getting to be a mite unpredictable.'

She volleys back, 'Maybe you've got it working too hard.'

'Now don't you start on me too. Lenny's been going at me all day long. I swear, it's more tiresome than the working is, listening to all the harping.'

'Burned the first batch of pies in all the fuss you caused.'

'Oh. Oh dear,' she chuckles weakly. 'Are we still going to be able to manage the Thanksgiving orders?'

'That ought to be the least of your worries,' Gregory scolds.

'Well, I can't help it, can I? Something I'm expert at.' Her voice trails into a shallow cough.

'Easy. Better behave. Or you'll get me kicked out.'

Gerry's face turns suddenly serious. 'Listen, I'm a big joker and all, I know. But today, what you did for me? It was no small thing. All joking aside, Gregory, you saved my life.' Gregory can see tears gathering; hears the tremor in her voice. For a moment nothing is said. Gerry just holds tight to her hand. In the corner the monitor is on a steady up-count with the peaks rising higher up the scale than before. Gregory hears Gerry's heavy swallow. Tears roll down her cheeks. Gerry takes a shaky breath and lets it out in a long sigh, 'Do you think you could pass me a tissue?' Gregory offers the box. 'Thank you.' She lifts an unsteady hand, slow and careful so as not to disturb the tubing of the IV, and dabs at the glistening tracks. Her voice is thick, 'I want you to know. How much it means. To me. I wouldn't be here if it weren't for you and what you did.' With considerable effort she pushes up from the pillow. 'You,' she whispers with an intensity that takes Gregory by surprise, 'need to know that.'

Gregory
English 50
November 2002

At the classroom door she stops dead. Taped to the board at the front of the room is at least a 3 foot by 2 foot cardboard cutout turkey, complete with a kind of popped out accordion tissue paper ruffle for a middle, and a headdress that sort of looks like a crown of vegetables. Underneath it, in Turner's unmistakable hand, are the scrawled details of an invitation: Day, time and place.

Manfred of the Red Neck pulls up beside her and stops too. 'What the…?'

'Apparently, a party.'

'So he's not just saying we're all turkeys.' Part statement, part question.

'Could be.'

She knows Turner's a little goofy, but she never had him figured for something like this.

'Where do you even get something as dumb-looking as that?' Manfred's head is shaking.

'No idea.'

Turner is smiling widely at them, where they are stood frozen in the doorway, 'Okay, I'll admit it's sad as far as gimmicks go.'

The two of them make their way to open seats. Gregory chooses to be facing the door. One after the other the rest arrive, not quite knowing what to make of the festive fowl. *Smile, you're on Candid Camera!* Not really, but that's what their expressions show they're wondering.

As class starts he volunteers, 'It was a dare. My nephew picked it out. Made me promise to use it in class. Told me to take a picture. Evidence. To prove I had the guts to do it. Kids these days.' He's looking quite pleased with the effect of his bit of fun. 'Though I should really have been photographing your reactions. What's happened to the kid in all of you? It's a travesty the way we get so uptight with age.'

Boho Chick asks, 'How old's the little boss-man?'

'Six.'

Beer Can Mike exclaims, 'Holy, you've got a budding dictator on the way up!'

'What's on his head? I mean, the turkey's head.'

'Vegetables.'

'Vegetables? On his head? That's goofy.'

'Thing's a trippy turkey.'

'Alliteration—fine example.' Turner smiles.

'How about Turner's Turkeys?'

There is open laughter rippling through them. 'Even better.'

Barbie 2 chimes in, 'My husband bought a huge inflatable like that for the front lawn and I'm so embarrassed.'

'There goes the neighbourhood,' Randy's shaking his head.

Manfred asks, 'Why don't you turn the tables? On your nephew. Give the kid a dead one. Stuffed. What do they call it when they stuff the thing to keep it looking alive?'

'Taxidermy. But no, I don't think his mother would appreciate that. Not to mention the fact that I would probably be banished and made to go hungry if I showed up with something like that—I'm not going to sacrifice my Thanksgiving dinner for a bit of fun.' He laughs. 'So anyway, the turkey was meant to be the entrée—' there are more groans—'Hey! It got your attention. Okay, have it your way, you guys are no fun. How about foray, segue, introduction? I do this once a year. Host a party. Bring budding writers together.'

'To talk turkey,' a male voice ventures. She didn't catch who said it.

'Now that's the spirit,' says Turner, 'and—sort of. So you can feed off one another, figuratively speaking. Or maybe it's that I want you to feed me, literally. That's why it's a potluck affair. Do we all understand the meaning of potluck? Everybody brings a dish. Here's hoping you won't all bring Jell-O salad.'

'What, you're not into Jell-O?'

'Man, we are the Jell-O generation.'

'J-E-LL-O. Remember those commercials?' There is a chorus of yeahs and a tremble of Jell-O-ish laughter.

'You could always wrestle in the leftovers.'

'A tasty and tempting prospect, Mike, but we are straying from the original point of this discourse. So the term potluck, bringing things back around, may come from 16th century England. The writings of one Thomas Nashe indicate that what an unexpected visitor might get in the way of meal from his host or hostess is said to be the luck of the pot. Hopefully he hadn't pissed them off too much by showing up unannounced. Or there is thought that the word may have originated from the Native American term potlatch, referring to a ceremonial feast. We do know that the modern use, by that I mean circa 20th century, seems to have cropped up around us, on the west coast of the United States. Interesting, hey?'

'You must rock at, like, Trivial Pursuit,' Boho Chick offers.

Turner smiles. 'At the very least, you may have taken something new on board. One of those things you can just quietly file away for some future point when you might whip it out and call it to action.'

'Something,' says Mike, 'I'd always, in the deep dark recesses of my mind, wanted to know.' It is clear he is having Turner on. 'I only pray I don't someday succumb to early dementia with nuggets like that one carefully stowed away in my brain, it would suck to lose wisdom like that too soon.'

'Indeed, it would. Take up Ping-Pong, Mike, and stay away from women— my best advice if you want to keep from losing your mind.'

'Too late,' Mike says proudly, and channels his best Springsteen, *I'm doomed and going down, down, down.'*

One of the other guys, real quiet with crazy-wild curly hair, she thinks his name is Ruben, chimes in, 'No shit, Ping-Pong? Really?'

'Yeah, really. Something about the coordination stimulating the brain. Anyhow, back to what I was saying before the turkey ends up being responsible for *gobbling* too much time.' There is another chorus of groans. 'If you're coming, here's the potluck rote: bring a dish, or some kind of food for sharing around. It doesn't have to feed everyone, but we need to get some mileage out of it. And one caveat—this is predominantly aimed at the men—no buns, and no beer.' A spike in sound from the male portion of the class. 'Those two don't count as a potluck contribution. Nor does a lovely lady on your arm count as your *dish*. Hear me, Mike? Try for some culinary extension, men, stretch yourself a little.'

Kameko raises a hand and asks, 'I can bring some Japanese food?'

'Absolutely. Perfect. At least one less Jell-O salad on my table. Yes. Please. Great.' He is thumbing through a stack of papers. 'I printed a flyer with the details.' He sets them down at the beginning point of one side of the circle. Take one and pass it on. A girl named Grace is the first. She remembers her name because *Grace* rhymes with *brace*, and ironically, she just happens to have a mouth full of glinting metal. Grace very obviously has it for Turner. She opens up in a full-on Cheshire Cat smile every time the professor has her even remotely in his line of sight. He seems only to have eyes for Beauty, but he's pleasant in the face of Grace's attentions. Turner is still talking. 'Come by if you can. It should be fun. All my neighbours hate me for it, so I've taken to inviting them too. That way they don't call the cops if things get a little out of hand. Joking, joking. It is a civilized affair, as much as it can be. Okay, let's get down to the real business of the evening.'

The flyer reaches her. Kameko, with two hands, holds it out, nodding encouragingly. There's the beginnings of a headache flaring. She folds the paper over on itself, so that the text is covered, and slots it in the front of her notebook. Saves thinking about it until later.

They spend the class debating the paganism that tends to be associated with the harvest. The Autumn Equinox. How it's depicted in literature. How it tends to be vilified. Cultified. Spookified. Given dark, otherworldly origins. Turner covers theories on the importance of the moon. The symbolism that surrounds it. Much of which dates back to ancient civilizations. And is pinned in cultures all over the world. Beauty talks about the *Diwali* festival in India, the triumph of good over evil, the lighting of little clay lamps in ceremonial celebration. In Japan, Kameko says, *Tsukimi*, or moon-viewing, is often marked by the writing and exchange of tanka poetry. She recites a poem called *The Moon*. First in Japanese, her voice soft and smooth over the complicated sounds. Then she translates:

> *'The evening moon in autumn*
> *Still remains as it was long ago*
> *Even though so many people have passed away'*

Nice. Light and uplifting. Roger, a guy in the class she'd never really taken much notice of before, says he is part Chinese—though he doesn't look it— and talks mooncakes. Mooncakes turn the talk to beefcake, which breaks the spell. There is more laughter.

And it's where things finish for the night. 'Keep reading and journaling daily.' People are up and out the door. When she looks up from her notes the professor is in front of her desk. 'Gregory, can you do me one quick favour?'

'Such as?' she asks warily.

'Just take a picture of the damn bird, and me with it. For posterity. For the kid.'

'Oh. Yeah. Sure, okay.' What made him ask her? From his bag he grabs a serious looking piece of photographic hardware. Does she look like she has experience with this sort of thing? He passes it off to her and makes for the turkey. The camera is heavy. Solid. No doubt expensive. She puts two hands around it, nervous. 'What do I do?'

'Just press the round button, front right.'

'That's all? It seems like it should be more complicated than that.'

'Nah. It's set to automatic.'

'Oh. Okay.' She looks for the button while she holds it in front of her.

'Hey, Aneeta, come stand with me so I don't feel so silly.'

Beauty looks at him like she must have misheard. 'Me?' she questions.

'Please? Help me.' He is motioning her over. She looks unsure, kind of a mix of surprise, shock, with a confused half-smile. 'You're not vegetarian, are you?' Turner jokes.

'No, but…I don't think you want me in your photograph. It is for your nephew, is it not?'

'Of course I do. C'mon. It proves that I had it up here during class. Help me out. Or I'll have to endure some further torture. God only knows what. This way I've got all my bases covered.' She makes her way shyly forward, keeping the festive fowl between them. She gives a sort of embarrassed laugh and angles her eyes toward the turkey and Turner.

'Ready? Say…turkey!' Gregory instructs, and they do—Aneeta looking doubtful and impossibly beautiful, Turner wearing a wide, toothy grin. Freeze-frame. And click.

'There,' he says, 'dare fulfilled. Thanks for helping out.'

'Sure. No problem.' Gregory is glad to hand back the camera. Unharmed, unbroken.

He turns it over in his hands and shows the frame to them both. 'Oh, it's good. Perfect. Oughta satisfy the little monkey.' To Aneeta, Turner says, 'I'll make you a copy. I'm sure you'll want to remember the turkey.'

He is joking, but Beauty seems to take him seriously. 'Oh, thank you. That would be very kind.' Just what every woman wants. A photo of herself with a turkey.

Where her things are still spread out on the desk, Kameko is standing to one side. Her eyes and smile look sad, 'The imagination of a child can bring such a simple joy to life. It is easy to see the pleasure it gives Professor Turner to indulge his nephew. I think, perhaps, he is right, that we should perhaps not be so…' she casts for the word, 'uptight.'

Nodding, she asks, 'So I am wondering, for this turkey party? Can we go together? Because I am not so sure of myself.'

Whether something is lost in the translation, or whether she has intended to arrange the words in the way she has, it's like she's read Gregory's mind. The uncertain jumble of her thinking—turkey, party, people. A silent consideration of the kinds of things people choose to do in life. Out of a sense of some obligation, some link, some tie. To please. To spare. To appease. *Nope, honey,* she thinks, *I'm not sure either. About any of it.* But it is some comfort to know, at least, that she is not alone.

Gregory
A Potluck Party
November 2002

The plan is to meet up at the Perk Hill on the night; middle ground. Turner's place is close to Sea Cliff. She's cycled through the area before; sueded lawns, bricks and stucco, gates and walkways, arbors with flowers, carefully tended yards fronting fashionable façades. Pretty and expensive. The out-of-*her*-world part of town. Kameko convinces her they should take a taxi, then won't let her pay anything towards the fare. It doesn't sit right, but she's not about to push it. By the time they arrive, people and music are spilling into the night air. She tries, with not a whole lot of success, to shrug away discomfort, clinging to the trio of pies she's brought as her potluck offering like they're some kind of shield.

What's she been thinking, agreeing to come tonight? Kameko walks toward the front door, taking tiny tripping steps in impossible-looking heels. Gregory sighs. There's no turning back now. She does a quick swivel to scan for a nearby bus stop. No deal. She tries to remember whether she'd seen one. But nerves and memory don't mix, she draws a blank. In this tax bracket there ought to be a well-organized offering of city services. Transit ought to be one of them. Though she expects folks around here wouldn't be big users, they probably like knowing that their help are easy-in, easy-out.

She and Kameko manage their way through clusters of people on the front steps; some are chatting, some are having a smoke. They pass Manfred who salutes as he takes a steep drag on his cigarette. They press on and through the front door. *Damn!* It's like out of a magazine. Wood rails and high ceilings and rich wall colours. She half expects Turner to be clad in some sort of shiny velvet jacket with a tie, one that's knotted at his neck, like they used to wear on Dallas, Dynasty, one of those crazy-rich prime time soap operas. But when she catches sight of him he's the same old Turner, right out of the classroom, blue jeaned and dark-shirted—crisp, but with rolled up sleeves. He pulls away from a conversation with a black-haired, intense-looking woman and an equally intense spike-haired string bean of a guy.

'Hey, I'm glad you could make it. Let me show you where the kitchen is so you can unload. What can I getcha to drink?' He leads down a ruby red hallway that opens onto a monster kitchen. A wooden table with a pricey-looking patina and black iron brackets for legs is loaded to overflowing. Obviously the whole potluck thing has been taken seriously.

Gregory whistles. 'This is some food!'

'Yeah,' he says with a laugh, 'you never quite know what to expect. Sometimes it pays to preach at people.'

In the corner sits a life-sized, housedress-wearing blow-up doll. Across her front is a sign that says Bunny. Gregory gestures, 'Guess someone took literally the comment about the buns.' Kameko's hand flies to her mouth to cover her reaction.

'Yeah, Manfred,' Turner says, nodding in the direction of the doll. Explanation enough. 'But to give him credit, he brought perogies too.'

'Manfred? Wow, who knew?'

Kameko has busied herself removing protective coverings from her oblong platter. From a glitzy-looking carrier bag she pulls a long tin cylinder, which when she whips the top part off holds sets of paper-wrapped chopsticks. She digs in again and pulls out a bottle of soy sauce. Talk about thinking of everything. 'Incredible,' Turner laughs.

Gregory pulls the three pies from her canvas bag and sets them in a stack on the table. 'Oh my God!' Turner breathes.

Boho Chick has come to look over her shoulder and groans, 'Pie! I can feel my waistline expanding already.'

The Barbies are gathering too. Barbie 1 raves, 'Oh, I love Asian food! Sushi is my absolute favourite. And it's supposed to be so good for you.'

Barbie 2 steps up, 'You didn't make the pies. Tell me you didn't make them. I can never get my crust to look like that.'

Gregory assumes she is talking about the twirled latticework on the apple. 'Yeah, I made them.'

'But,' Barbie 2 blusters, 'these are bakery boxes, and they say,' she flips the lid and smiles triumphantly, 'Gerry's Bakery Café.'

'It's where I work,' Gregory says.

'You're kidding.'

'No joke.'

'You've got to be kidding.'

'Why's that?'

'You just...' she giggles, 'you don't strike me as...I mean, you just don't look like...a baker.'

'And what does a baker look like, exactly?' The hair on the back of her neck is starting to stand.

'Well...jolly. And maybe round, a bit round.' Barbie carves an air figure with her hands.

Turner interrupts to ask, 'Drink, ladies?'

'Yes please,' Gregory says emphatically, turning to follow him to a countertop lined with glassware, grateful she's got an out. Jolly. *Why I oughta,* she thinks, silently mimicking Jackie Gleason, *Pow, right in the kisser!*

'Wine? Beer? Vodka, scotch, bourbon?'

'Beer'd be good.'

'Light? Or regular?'

'Make it a regular, I'm working on rounding out my baker's figure.' She pats her stomach meaningfully. Laughing, he grabs a bottle from the fridge and reaches for a glass. 'Don't worry about the glass,' she says, taking the bottle from his hand.

'Kameko?' Turner asks.

'I will have one too,' she says pointing at the beer in Gregory's hand.

'In the bottle or a glass?'

'Glass,' she says so that it sounds like *grass*. It makes Gregory smile. Turner twists and pours, the perfect host.

'*Kanpai!*' Kameko says, raising her glass.

'No Aneeta?' Gregory asks. 'I thought for sure she'd be here.'

'I thought she might've come with you guys. I was hoping.' He says it kind of sheepishly. 'Did she say anything?'

'I just assumed,' she says.

'Yeah, well,' he shrugs trying to feign indifference at Beauty's absence, but his hangdog eyes tell another story.

A male voice hails from the hall, 'Neil!'

Better to move out and mingle rather than get into something un-jolly with the Barbies. She looks to where Barbie 1 has draped herself over some unsuspecting frat boy type. Barbie 2 is holding forth among a group of unfamiliar but perfectly turned out college females, 'And so I said to her, you can't possibly expect me to pay that much when it's clearly last year's line.' The sorority clatch seem to hang on her words. Manfred has taken a chair in the corner, next to Bunny, balancing an overflowing plate of food on his knees. Glass doors are opened out onto the back of the property; a deck and a yard with little ornamental lamplights all around. She sees the glow of cigarette tips, hears the rasp of conversation.

Kameko is decidedly un-clingy, considering her initial uncertainty about coming. She sees her talking with a very red-faced Andy, the science guy. He keeps pushing his glasses higher on the bridge of his nose. Kameko looks as if she is enjoying their chat. She wonders mildly about Kameko's husband. Whether he's at home waiting on her or not. She bets on the 'or not' side of the coin.

She walks through the house and pretends to study the art on the professor's walls. If she is ogling Turner's wall-ware she can sidestep eye contact and conversation. Just for now, she tells herself. Until she warms up a little. He has a big collection, which makes the depth of her dragged out interest more convincing. It's while she is studying a large abstract of orange and gold off the entryway that Aneeta arrives.

There is a collective in-breath that ripples through the space. She wears an exotic outfit in a bright green. A beaded tunic and narrow-legged pants that fall in soft folds. Her neck is draped in a long scarf, ends trail down her back with loose waves of hair. She looks out of some fairytale storybook. *Way to dull down the rest of the room, sister.* Aneeta smiles tentatively into the room, looking quickly left and right, holding out and forward a black lacquer tray piled high with golden bites. Gregory hears tunneled whispers. From the women about the striking outfit; from the men about the woman who wears it.

From where she stands, Gregory can see them both. Turner's got his back to the door, he's talking to a bearded guy in tweed. But he must have figured out Aneeta'd arrived because he lit up a bit like an over-amped Christmas display. The story it tells is plain. All at once he's off at speed to meet her. Aneeta notices Gregory and lifts a hand from her tray with a shy smile. Gregory raises her bottle. Grace, Dr. Turner's most obvious admirer, is partway up the stairs with a young man easily her equal in the awkward looks department. With Aneeta's arrival and Turner's reaction Grace has completely dropped the conversation ball to watch in mute, horrified fascination. In the quiet of her preoccupation, the guy fidgets uncomfortably with his eyeglasses and sweater cuffs. Grace's mouth is open and she's got a kind of hypnotized stare fixed on Turner; a *Fatal Attraction* kind of look. Gregory doesn't think Grace has it in her to be a psycho bunny-boiler, but then again, appearances have a strange and unexpected way of being deceiving.

Eyes lock, and as much as she wants to look elsewhere, to look down or away, she finds she cannot. Heat fires in her cheeks. She recalls a physics lesson, and the intense, angular face of Sister Agnes, sternly clinical in her explanation of magnetism and poles. This, though, is not a classroom experiment. That such principals have demonstrable capacity in human attraction is almost unthinkable, laughable. Especially for someone like her.

He is smiling widely as he makes his way to her side. 'I am so glad to see you.' A thrill ripples inside of her, against the tide of wary. A path opens for them as they move; he guides her, his hand gently at her elbow. 'I thought that maybe you weren't planning on coming. Gregory and Kameko said they weren't sure.'

Not come? 'Oh no,' she breathes in a way that comes out sounding girlish and silly. 'I wouldn't have wanted to miss it.' The latter part is better. More formal. Though her insides tremble.

'I kind of figured you might have come along with them, so when you didn't, I wondered. I'm pleased you're here.'

Her laugh is nervous, but woven with threads of pleasure. 'Thank you,' she offers simply. They pass into a sprawling space at the back of the house. To one side copper pots hang in abundance, like a tree endowed with heavy clusters of fruit. A great rectangular slab of blackened stone beneath it is laid with glassware and bottles of all kinds. A long wood table is laden with food. 'My goodness, I see that people have taken you quite seriously.'

'You included.'

'Yes, well...' she slides the tray, borrowed in last minute haste from Mrs. Lee, into an open rectangle of table space, 'it would have been unwise not to, wouldn't it?' He looks at her and down at the platter with the undisguised eagerness of a schoolboy. Others have drawn close to the table. She takes the top from the also borrowed lacquer bowl with Chinese characters circling it, releasing the fresh tang of chutney. The same smell that yet clings to her hands. She has rushed. Rushed to finish preparing. Rushed to come here. Rushed to see him.

She hears over her shoulder, 'Oh my God, Indian food is, like, to die for! Spicy food helps you lose weight, did you know that? I read it in *Cosmo*. Honestly, no joke. Because it heats things up inside of you. Makes the metabolism move faster to burn up fat cells. Between Indian and Thai take-out, I figure I'm sweating it off my thighs.' There is accommodating laughter.

'I just love your outfit, Aneeta. Let me see.' Krista lightly fingers the beading at Aneeta's shoulder, 'How cute is that! You look just like Princess Jasmine.' She speaks rapidly, sharply, like a clucking chicken. 'So what'd you bring? Oh, those look and smell so delicious! You absolutely have to tell me where the best Indian food in this city is. One of my husband's friends is from London,' her voice rises up with the mention of London, 'and he swears by Mehfil. He says it's totally authentic. Not Americanized.' Krista rolls her eyes. 'Do you know it?'

'I made pakora,' she smiles faintly, 'several kinds of fried vegetables.' She points to the clusters that she has taken care to pile separately, 'Aloo,' she says, but realizing her mistake she corrects, 'potato.' She points again, 'In the center is cauliflower. At the far end is aubergine—what you know as eggplant, perhaps? In the bowl is a mint chutney for dipping.'

'Are they really spicy?'

'Not so spicy.'

'Mmm. They're warm.'

'Are they vegetarian?' The question comes from a gangly, ginger-haired man with waxen looking skin and a pullover the shade of ripe mango flesh.

'Yes, they are vegetarian.'

'Cool. Outta sight. And vegan? 'Cause I don't do eggs or dairy either.'

She laughs. 'Yes, they would be vegan too.'

'Wow, awesome! I have a hard time finding something I can eat at these kind of things.'

'Don't eat all of them, Blinker,' the professor says. 'I know you're a growing boy, but leave some for the rest of us.'

Blinker holds his hands up in mock surrender, a slab of potato pinched like Buddha between thumb and forefinger. Krista nibbles at a bit of cauliflower. Eating. Inspecting. Inspecting. And eating. She looks uncertain. Her prior enthusiasm for Indian food has all but vanished. Continuing talk and other questions have thankfully freed Aneeta from needing to answer Krista's question. The best Indian food in San Francisco? She couldn't say. Because she has purposely kept herself away.

'The sauce is so refreshing, I love the flavour. What's in it?' Crystal, the Canadian woman, has her eyes closed. She is chewing slowly.

'A mix of coriander and mint. Some chillies.'

Sweeping crumbs from his hands after sampling each kind, the professor— Neil, as he had asked her to call him the day he took her to tea— says, 'Every kid in the world would eat vegetables if they were served up like this. Write a book, Aneeta. Make a video. You'd be an overnight sensation. Make millions. Angst-ridden Moms of children who don't-like won't-eat vegetables would adore you.' He grabs another chunk just as a broadly smiling man claps a hand on his shoulder and leans in to admire the table.

'Now here's a gourmet offering! Quite the spread from a confessed culinary deadbeat.'

'Ed!' The professor laughs and gives the grinning man a great hug, slapping him heartily on the back. 'I resent that comment, true as it might be. But coming from the likes of you?'

'I may have similar leanings, but I can hardly compete with the Takeout King!'

'Okay, okay. Got me. I beg your humble mercy. Please don't be spilling my secrets. Especially in the presence of those who don't know better. I have a reputation to uphold. Glad you could make it, you globetrotting son-of-a-gun. How the hell are you?'

'God, it's good to see you haven't changed. We're good, things're good.'

'Forgive my manners. Aneeta, Ed. Ed, allow me to introduce Aneeta.' He does not mention the fact that she is one of his students only. Whether the omission is intended or not, she is secretly pleased. She finds she does not wish to be thought of as merely a student. The by-product of his work.

'It is my pleasure, Aneeta,' the man makes a gallant bow, garnering further laughter from Neil.

'Look what the Brits have made of you. Breeding manners in an old dog.' He explains, 'Ed's the envy of the entire English department because he's on a year long sabbatical while his wife lectures at Oxford. She works and he gets to pretty much bum around and play the impoverished writer.'

'A role I play exceedingly well.'

'I see,' she nods, not quite sure what to make of the back and forth parry. 'I'm very pleased to meet you.'

'Is that an English-English accent I'm hearing, or Indian-English accent?'

'Aneeta's here from India,' Neil volunteers for her.

'We love India, my wife Jill and I. Spent six weeks there year before last. Something we'd always wanted to do.'

'You two compare notes and I'll fix you something to drink. It's the least I can do if I'm going to let him monopolize your time. Aneeta? A glass of wine? White? Red? The white's Italian. Nice for sipping.'

'Okay, thank you, if it's not too much trouble.'

'Not at all. And you, you hound? How about a scotch?'

'Yeah, twist my rubber arm. I brought you a bottle, by the way. Though it's buried in a suitcase. When I manage to unearth it, I'll invite myself over.'

'I'll look forward to it,' the professor says, grinning.

Ed turns his attention back to her, 'I think Jill and I both felt that even after six weeks in India we'd only just barely scratched the surface. We did Agra first, to see the Taj Mahal, went on to Varanasi, the ghats and the Ganges. Jill loved her time at the university. Spent a week in Darjeeling. Took the train to Kolkata. And finished in Mumbai. I think my wife is already planning for us to go again, some sort of yoga retreat this time, bit of work sandwiched between to legitimize things. And we want to see Goa.' Aneeta feels a rolling sense that alternates between pride and homesickness. A smile tempts at tears, and then births a prickle of fear with a wave of clammy nausea. She swallows hard at the knot in her throat.

Neil hands her a wine glass that is clouded on the outside by the chill of the pale liquid. She raises it to her lips and hopes it can help to loosen the tension inside her. He passes a heavy tumbler of amber to Ed.

'We were there for a wedding, actually. That was the main reason for the trip. Neil, you know Rav, don't you?'

'Yeah, sure. Nice guy.'

By way of explanation Ed volunteers, 'Rav's a fellow professor. Lectures with my wife. Anyhow, we thought this guy was the consummate American bachelor. Always a rotation of women, big into American football, fast cars, weekends in Vegas, the lot of it. Then he says to Jill, I'm going home to get married. Jill thinks fine, nice, whatever, he's locked onto *the one* as it were, taking her home to meet Mom and Dad. Bollywood wedding. Very chic, worldly, that kind of thing. So Jill being Jill, she asks after the lucky woman. And he tells her his parents have found him a wife. No, correction, I think *girl* was the word he used because Jill came home so pissed off at his terminology.' He laughs then, 'My wife the demi-fem. I mean, you could have knocked us over with a feather. It was just so out of left field. Especially for him. Educated here. Masters. Doctorate. Working here. Living here. Total playboy. The full-meal American Dream deal. Then all of a sudden, whammo! Major reversal. '

'I can just about imagine Jill's reaction.' Neil is chuckling.

'Yeah, so that's the thing. It's totally out of character, totally out of the blue. Rav wants some representation of his American life there on the big day—well, not a day, is it? More like a whole week, right?—so he invites Jill and a number of his other colleagues in the department to come to Mumbai for the wedding. And Jill, even though she's still well ticked at him and his whole *regression*,' Ed curls fingers into half-moons around the label, 'we figure what the heck, why not? It gave us a reason to go, and we'd always wanted to. But the strangest thing, I think, for both of us, knowing him the way we thought we did. He didn't even know this girl.'

'At all?' Neil's face and voice betray surprise.

'Man, I kid you not,' Ed is shaking his head, 'the parents set the whole thing up. Apparently, they sent suggestions to him. Little *Hi, my name is…* ads, complete with a picture, and Rav either says yep, interested, or no, not. It was like running a round of job interviews. Only this was for choosing a wife. After they agreed the selection there was some communication on the phone, by e-mail, but that's pretty much the extent of it, until he goes home to marry her.'

'So how does a guy like that set up house with a woman he hardly knows, let alone take her as his wife?'

'Man, beats me. From what I hear getting a guy in the States, or in Europe, especially London, is quite the achievement. Am I right, Aneeta?'

She has been hoping that the subject of things would naturally shift somehow. Simple sightseeing talk would have been preferable. This is too close. And still too tender. She struggles for detachment, 'Marriage prospects in western countries are desirable to parents, and often to girls as well.' *It was a chance at a new beginning.*

'So would a woman, say, prefer to marry an Indian in America as opposed to a prospect in her own country?'

'It is hard to say. There are so many things that are considered. For the family. And the girl.'

'So you're saying the girl *does* have a say.'

'Some say. At times a yes-or-no say.' She can hardly weave the words into sense.

'But not always? Even today?'

She is trembling. Can they see? She wants to drink, but to lift the glass would surely reveal the shaking. *Then there are times when the girl has no say, where the power of circumstance overrides everything. Where the good of the family must be the central concern. Where duty and honour are more important.* Those words do not pass her lips. 'Not always,' she volunteers weakly.

'So, Aneeta, not wanting to seem too forthright or anything, considering we've only just met—'

'Uh oh. Here he goes.' Neil laughs, 'Watch out, he's coming for you, Aneeta.'

Ed holds up his hand in mock effrontery, 'Hey, enough out of the peanut gallery, I'm just trying to understand. Let the lady speak. You're obviously a modern woman, you're living in liberal, cosmopolitan San Francisco, what do you think of the whole arranged thing?'

Her ears are ringing. The inquiry is innocent. There is no presumption. Even so, she feels herself falling. Through a tunneled hole of time. She can see herself back in the Delhi front room. She remembers the rolling gait of the bichola, the squint of appraising eyes, the way roughened thumb and forefinger pinched at flesh. It was the only solution. Her knees are weak, her head light. Past and present mingle. She draws a shaky breath. They are waiting on her. *Stop!* she scolds silently. *It is not you they are talking of. They have no idea of the truth.* She has only to present a point of view. It need not reflect her own experience. 'Well, in the history of our culture arranged marriage is a tradition, one that persists. It is a funny thing about India. We move forward, but we still hold closely to the pieces that define our past. Marriage, I think, is one of those.'

'So how do you reconcile that? How do the young people of today—who, from what Jill and I experienced, are far more western and liberal than their parent's generation—justify the whole notion of having a partner picked out for them?'

'If you consider the term *arranged* you see that it refers to something more pragmatic than love, perhaps,' she offers a half smile, an apology for a defence she hardly believes. 'It applies to a broader circle than only the two at its center. It is more about the families involved.'

'So—and I hope you don't think I'm getting too personal—your parents? Were…arranged?'

'Actually, my parents' was a love match, but they had the approval of both families because it was a suitable pairing.'

'What makes it suitable?'

'That would depend upon the families. Mainly things like standing, circumstance, education, religion. Really, so many things affect a decision.'

'Standing? Like caste? I thought the whole notion of caste had been outlawed. You're saying it still exists? That people still marry according to caste?'

'I can say only that the past yet guides the present.'

'Are you an only child?' The abruptness of the question Ed asks catches her off-guard.

'No…I have a sister.' The sound of her own voice turns thick, strained. Curd pressed through cloth. Neil's expression registers surprise.

'Older, younger?'

'Older.'

'So your parents were in love, and married because of it. Surely they wouldn't force an arranged marriage on the two of you. If theirs was based on love. Hypothetically speaking, of course. I'm not trying to criticize, just to understand.'

'Love cannot cancel ties to tradition.' An ache spreads in her.

'So they would?' The would rises up like a tightrope walker, inflected with disbelief.

'My sister Asha, like my parents, has a love marriage. But again, both families approved the match, so, technically speaking, it could be considered arranged.'

'And Asha, like you, is here? In the States?'

'No.'

'Where does she live?'

'Delhi.' *Don't look back.*

'Ah. And your parents?'

'My mother only. She is in Delhi also.' Balance. One foot toes tentatively in front of the next.

'So you've chosen to come here, to live a modern life in the west?' Aneeta lets it be, the assumption. She is keening. Afraid to stumble.

Neil turns to her. His face is serious. 'Would you ever let your marriage be arranged?'

Shadows enter the circle of conversation. They listen, cocking their heads, taunting her with their truth. Her voice is low, but determined, 'No.' It is an uneven truth. The shadows flicker. *Not again. Never again.*

'Well, there. That's settled. Aneeta, you're proof positive that things are changing. I rest my case, Ed.'

'And you have to know my wife, Aneeta. Jill said Rav should have had the balls to stand up to his parents. Tell them if it wasn't what he wanted. But seeing them together, Rav and his now wife, I mean they were shy in a getting-to-know-you kind of way, but you could definitely see that they had a thing.'

'A *thing*?' Neil laughs. 'Mister A type, the most unromantic and totally pedantic guy I have ever met, would you care to elaborate on what kind of *thing* you might be referring to? Please.' Neil sweeps his arm in a wide arc of invitation.

'A chemistry. Even Jill couldn't deny it after seeing them together. So all was well in the end. My borderline feminist wife was at least semi-appeased. After all her rumination and criticism. American women can be so difficult,' he sighs in mock exasperation.

'How are they now, the happy couple?' Neil asked.

'Wouldn't know, you're the only sod I've been to see since we jetted in.

Cheers, buddy.' Ed holds his glass to meet Neil's in a thick crystalline chink, 'Good to be back.'

In America, she has come to understand, tradition is rewritten with every passing day. Out with the old and in with the new. Her ties reside in a different world.

Later:

Gregory

Barbie 1 is dirty dancing in the center of the room with a happily obliging Beer Can Mike. They are gyrating out of sync with Turner's tunes and letting hands hotly traverse each other's bodies. Mike is wide-eyed, but Barbie has her eyes closed in a look of far-out ecstasy. Quite the floor show.

Manfred and Blinker, sat on either side of Bunny the blow-up doll, watch like spectators at a ball game. No, make that a circus. *Ladies and gentlemen, boys and girls… Prepare to be entertained. Prepare to be amazed.* Blinker's popping what looks to be the last of Aneeta's veggie treats into his mouth and licking his fingers after. Bunny is losing air. Her head is starting to nod and there are creases in her previously plump form. Even Bunny knows it's time to bow out gracefully.

Barbie is obviously over her limit. And Mike is Mike, a ready opportunist. Gregory doesn't want to have to witness the inevitable implosion. Better let Kameko know she's going to go. She finds her in the front room, in a smaller, more well-behaved group intent on talk as opposed to teenage variety exhibitionism. Interesting how the two segments had separated themselves naturally, without coaxing. The way the back room antics seem not to have reached into the front. Kameko's talking with a bearded guy in dark-rimmed glasses. One of Turner's colleagues, she imagines, from the look of him. A bit of a stuffed shirt. Upright and slightly puffed at the chest, in a tweed and elbow-sueded blazer, one that he hasn't removed in spite of the crushing warmth. Kameko, with lollipop-red cheeks, looks even more doll-like. She is talking and motioning in a mix of words and hand action. Her English is loosening ever so slightly around its normally carefully contained edges. *How many beers does it take to topple the little Japanese girl?*

His eyes, magnified behind thick lenses, are intense. He leans toward her, which, given the noise of the room, is understandable. But the way his mouth is forming the words and the volume of them makes it sound like he thinks she's damn near deaf. 'As I say, I was only there for a semester, but…very learned institution…' shreds of his side of the conversation rise out of the fieldspace they share, Kameko's voice is lost under blanket layers of music, conversation, laughter. 'Our department would be very pleased to have someone of your background… Asian literature courses…Talk to Neil.'

Gregory moves in. 'I don't want to interrupt….' They both look up. Talk stops. The man takes a step back. 'I wanted to tell you I'm heading out now. Leaving. Just wanted to let you know.' The man looks at her with a hard set to his jaw. She has clearly been an interruption here. His annoyance with being derailed is plain. How, she wonders briefly, does he get the lines of his beard so straight? Must take a whole lot of face-in-the-mirror time to get the outlines of it so zip-perfect. What does that say? Pretty particular about things. Picky. About being interrupted, she'll bet, too.

'Oh,' Kameko is still smiling and nodding in half bows at the man, the way she does, with that upward hook at the end of it, 'please excuse me, but I must go. I have very much enjoyed talking with you.'

'It's been my pleasure, Miss Kimura. You have my card if ever you need. I do hope you'll consider what I've put forward.' He bows. She does the same.

As they step away Gregory motions, 'I didn't mean to shut your conversation down. It's just that things are getting strange in the back. I'd rather hear about it on Wednesday than see it with my own eyes.'

'I will come then,' Kameko has screwed up her mouth in a funny way that looks a bit like concern.

'You don't have to,' she says. 'It's…making me feel a little itchy is all.'

'Itchy?'

'Um, yeah. Uncomfortable.' *God, the limitations of language.*

Kameko considers for a moment, and reaches out for Gregory's hand. 'I am happy to go. With you.' Again her head is bobbing. Gregory feels a sliver of something like satisfaction. Kameko whips the jeweled cell phone from her white and cherried handbag. 'I will call a taxi for us.'

'I can just grab the MUNI.' I. Wasn't the 'we' of their leaving already established and settled? She wished her brain had better control of her mouth. Gedge said she *used deferential language in an attempt to limit her significance,* called it *marginalizing. What gets spread on toast!* she'd shot back. At that, his sigh.

'No, no.' Kameko flutters her protest. 'It is not a worry.' Her head is shaking, her brows knit slightly, this time to reassure. 'No trouble. Okay? But I must tell Aneeta too. She wishes to come with us.' There is something about how she tries to form the certain English sounds, how she works at them. Even when she doesn't quite get there, it comes off sounding soft, cute, pixie, exactly the way she looks.

'Just got to look for Professor Turner.' Kameko takes Gregory's comment literally, missing the joke altogether.

'Yes, I think so.'

A quick scan of the area says nope. Aneeta wouldn't have been missed by the eye. The exotic flash of green. Though she gets a fix on Turner. Positioned in the round entryway, he is anchored in the tide of comings and goings.

So much for getting out with some speed. But then there's the cab. That would force a wait. In the last moments the initial desire to leave had morphed into something like panic.

Kameko mounts an impromptu search, heading in the direction Gregory does not want to revisit. Knowing that if she stands still she might attract party guests seeking interaction, she casts her eyes again over the art upon Turner's elegantly decorated walls. And in her scan arc, she finds Aneeta. At almost the same time Kameko emerges from the other side of the floor. Beauty is maybe a dozen paces from Turner. Gregory knows he can see Aneeta from where he stands. Has clearly made it a point to. The man is so obviously sweet on her.

Aneeta is chatting with Grace's Number 2, the band-aid and glasses guy. Poor Grace. Tonight, hers is destined to be a losing battle. The guy is clearly putty in Aneeta's radiant company.

Gregory leaves Kameko to do the honours of letting Aneeta know they're going. Graciously, with a smile that would surely set ice alight, Aneeta shakes the boy's hand goodbye. He turns to watch her walk away.

Kameko comes for Gregory. Aneeta goes the other way. Kameko is nodding. 'She will come with us. She has to collect her things. From the kitchen.'

A mismatched older couple are carrying on a very one-sided chat with a now totally sidetracked Neil Turner. Gregory stifles a laugh. His head is spinning like a barn owl. The couple talks, totally oblivious to the fact that they've lost him. He smiles half-heartedly, says something, and steps away. Looking momentarily put out, they head off into the better-behaved front room as the good professor makes for the back. He is a man definitely on a mission.

Aneeta

'Here you are!' He seems pleased to have come across her.

'Oh. Yes. I just had to come and collect my tray,' she corrects, 'my *neighbour's* tray and dish.' There are only a few crumbs remaining; faint smears of chutney line the rim of an otherwise clean bowl.

It has become quite loud in this part of the house. A number of people are gathered in a knotted nucleus and are attempting to dance in a small square of floor space. Some keep time with the rhythm of the music while others simply cling to one another and sway. It is hard to see just where one dancer ends and another begins.

She tries to ignore the display of intimacy before her. It unsettles her, especially with him so near. She raises her eyes to his, willing herself calm, 'I... We...I mean, Gregory and Kameko and I...we have to be going. A taxi should be arriving any moment now. So I have to...collect these things. Thank you for a lovely time, a lovely evening. I apologize that there is nothing left for you. I should have, perhaps, made more.' Her fingers find and fumble with the lid for the chutney bowl. It drops into place with a porcelain clink.

'Please, don't apologize.' The flecks of gold in his eyes reach magically out to her, warming her, gooseflesh rising in their wake. 'It shows you how good they were.'

'I am pleased if you enjoyed them.'

'I did, very much. I also very much enjoyed the chance to talk with you. I only wish there were fewer people, less noise, more time.' The smile opens up. 'I wish you could stay.'

'I have to go.'

'Just a little longer? Please? Would you? Stay?'

'I wish that I could…but…I can't.' Why can't? Why only wish? She feels herself holding back. As though she does not trust the feelings heating her blood, does not know what to make of them. Or what they might make of her. She shakes her head. At him. At the confusion inside. She is afraid of old ghosts. Afraid of what might happen if the dark parts of her were to come to light. 'I simply can't,' she says quietly, 'I'm sorry.'

'Don't be. I'm just being selfish. But I…'

'Yes?' There is laughter around them. 'They will be waiting for me.' She tries for a smile. Her face feels tight. She looks down as the forced bloom of it fades.

He touches her hand with his fingertips, just for a second, where she holds the tray. Then lets them drop. His voice steps in. It lifts her, holds her, embraces her, 'I'd really like to get to know you better.'

She looks up at him. Amazed. This kind of feeling is not meant for her. Not for someone like her. She nods at him slowly, she hopes he cannot see the warring of her emotions, 'I…would like that too.'

'Cab's here,' Gregory calls to her.

'Another time?' he asks with a quiet smile.

She nods, her heart pounding, 'Another time.' He leans in to let his lips brush her cheek. She can feel the outline of fire that lingers. With the dishes hugged tightly to her she moves quickly for where Gregory and Kameko wait. She can sense his eyes on her. She turns once to look and sees him mouth the words: another time. He raises his hand in goodbye. Inside, her heart agrees: *Yes, there will be another time.*

Aneeta
November 2002

She waits for Mrs. Lee to return from church. The dishes are cleaned and waiting. Yet she is reluctant to let them go. Only dishes. Lacquered plastic and porcelain. But to her they are a bridge, a connection. She sips tea and lets her mind wander. Behind closed eyes she can live it again. In pieces. The touch of his hand. The way he had looked at her. His compliments. His smile. His lips. The pleasure within her. The fluttering of her heart. Memories she turns over and over again, like a new trinket in a child's hands.

There is a rise, suddenly, of contrary feelings, old feelings, that interrupt the vision. They taunt her, as they always do, remind her of what is real. Why would such a man have an interest in her? Someone like her. Indeed. Such fancies are the indulgent frivolities of schoolgirls. Like a movie star crush. Acceptable in the private darkness of the theatre, but in the plain light of day another matter entirely. The practical thing to do, she knows, is simply to discount it all. To see it for what it is, this daydreaming, simply a mirage.

Locks chuck over in the hallway. There is the creak of widening hinges. The solid thud of a closing door. She stands. With a sigh, she takes up the dishes and coaxes herself out of her own door. At apartment 504 she raises a hand and knocks. Inside she hears sound responding. There is the shuffling to the opposite side of the door and a pause. Then the scrabble of yielding bolts. The door opens. Daylight spills weakly into the hallway. 'Mrs. Lee,' Aneeta reaches the tray and covered bowl forward, 'I wanted to return your things. And to thank you for the use of them. I had many compliments.'

'Oh, no need to rush! I hardly ever use these things. Too fancy just for me. You shouldn't have troubled yourself. Hurry is not necessary. Come in for some tea? I was just going to make some myself. Much nicer for two. Like the song?' She sings in a lilting voice, *'Two for tea, and tea for two...*You know it?'

Aneeta smiles, 'But I don't want to trouble you.'

'Noooo trouble,' the tiny woman waves dismissively. 'Got nothing to do anyway. Nobody got time for me. Too busy with other things. Too, too busy. Nobody wants to come sit with an old lady. '

'I can't imagine that.'

'Come, come inside. So how was your party, then? You enjoyed it?'

'Tea would be kind. Thank you. Yes, I very much enjoyed myself. It was my first potluck event.'

'Ladies at church like potluck. Get good leftovers. Little bit from everything. We share it. Keeps everyone from getting bored with own cooking.

You know, I was going to come by and see you myself.'

'Oh?'

'Yes, because of the young man. Looking for you. Yesterday. I'm coming home from mahjong, and he's out front.'

'A man?' Her mind reels and her stomach flip-flops. A freeze starts inching it's way up from the soles of her feet. In icy metallic tines. Her brain flashes through possibility like a neon sign in the night. Chaos scrambles reason.

'Anyway, he asks if I know you. If you live here. Says he has this address. But not the apartment number. Kind of looks like you. But taller. Maybe you could be related?' Mrs. Lee looks quizzically at her, 'But you must not be close or else he would know apartment number. And you would know he's coming.'

Has she been found? After all this time? She'd let herself relax. Let her guard down. *Has she been foolish, thinking they would allow her to simply disappear? Could this all have been part of a plan?*

'I say I know you. But I can't let him in. Security reasons.' Mrs. Lee says it proudly. 'He says okay. He says he doesn't want to bother you. I think it must be okay.' Numbness is spreading through her. *But it's not okay. You shouldn't have told him. You should have saved me.* She wrestles with an oblique sense of futility. Defeat. There are things, though, that don't make sense. Why the concern about bothering her? Mrs. Lee is still talking, '…didn't need to see you. Just that he got something for you. Important papers he says. Personal, he tells me. Would I be sure it gets to you?

'He showed me a picture. He asks if it looks like you. This girl all dressed in red. Fancy. Lots of jewels. Up arms, around neck. Long earrings.' She gestures with her hands. 'Face was looking down, so it was hard to see. Could be, I say only. He thinks it's enough, I guess.'

The foolish fantasy fairytale notions of earlier now seem absurd. This is what comes of such hopes. She is caught in a web that will not let her go. If she is honest with herself, she has known it all along. The border, the limit, the miles of divide that she had trusted, relied upon to keep her safe, have all but vanished. Just like that. And she has known it could be so. That if they wanted to they could find her. But this is America. America.

'He asks if I can give it to you. That he doesn't trust leaving it at the front. He gives me a big envelope. He has nice smile. Good teeth. Very even-white. Seems nice enough. So I say okay. He says thank you. Polite. Clothes are expensive looking. Then he goes. Just like that.' She reasons, 'He must think I have honest face, maybe. To give important papers to me. That's why I don't win much mahjong. I can be tricky, though. Annie Yu, she says that I can be very tricky player. You should come play sometimes.' She smiles. A helpful neighbour smile. Behind it, inquisitive. 'I will get it. I put it somewhere safe. Because, I thought,' she taps lightly at one temple with a curved finger, 'they are important.' Her voice dims as she moves down the narrow hall, 'Just one minute.'

A thought comes. A wisp. A curl. Aneeta calls after her, 'Did this man say his name, maybe? Or occupation?' She is grasping at chance, flimsy and thin. At anything that may dull the sharp edges of fear.

Mrs. Lee turns at the hall's end, and in what seems barely a heartbeat emerges with a large white envelope. 'No. Not my business to ask questions. Too many nosy old ladies around. Don't need another. Here you go.'

On the envelope her name is handwritten. And the street address. There is no apartment number. She runs her hand slowly across the surface. The surname is that of her husband. There is no Kaur between first and last names. Aneeta is written in full as opposed to only the initial A. The letters of her name are not joined in cursive, but printed; sharp, angular and oversized. *We know where you are*, they mock. The whistle of the boiling kettle cuts in. There is a flash. A recognition. Her mind recalls a similar look.

Mrs. Lee follows the insistent shrill to the kitchen. 'I hope it's some good news for you,' she muses brightly. 'Maybe lucky, like Publisher Clearinghouse winner.' Luck owes her no favour. It would be a false hope to think it might smile on her now. There is no return address. No postmark. She scissors hotly through the top crease. A pit twists in her abdomen. Her pulse drums, heavy and fast.

That she is living in hiding Mrs. Lee wasn't to know. She pulls paper forth with a trembling hand. The sound is like the rasping draw of blade against sheath. Her eyes ravage the page. Her name. First name only. Dear. Dear? Syllables, sounds, half words. Her mind is unable to make sense of what she reads. Mrs. Lee is still chirping, but it comes to her ear through a thick fog. She scans blankly to the final words: Sincerely, Narinder. Narinder.

The second time through Aneeta reads without the same haste. And this time her brain agrees to give meaning to the words.

Dear Aneeta,

I hardly know where to begin. I hope that this has reached you and finds you well. I also hope that you have not been caused undue anxiety by having me seek you out this way. I have asked the family to allow only me to have contact. They have agreed. They will not be informed of your whereabouts.

They've found another girl for Jovin. But the immigration process cannot begin until your marriage is dissolved. The legal papers that follow are divorce papers, and, assuming you agree, will require your signature. Legal costs will be taken care of. Please don't worry yourself with any of it. I managed a deal on the fees since I am also in the process of divorcing. 2-for-1 affords some bargaining power. After the initial upset had worn off, Samar and I both decided it best to formally end our relationship. Of course, Mom is less than pleased with the fact that she is no nearer to having grandchildren. That's partly why the urgency on the girl for Jovin. She volunteered to find a new wife for me as well. I told her that I needed some time. She told me I didn't need time, just babies. Some things will never change, I suspect.

I should also let you know that your sister called here asking after you. A little over a month ago. I thought if you had wanted her to be able to reach you, you would likely have contacted her. For that reason I told her I was unable to help.

Maria and Raoul, too, were distressed by the suddenness of your leaving. Maria spoke privately with me and confessed that she felt somehow responsible. I told her that wasn't the case. That much more was involved in your decision. She told me they are praying for your wellbeing and for your happiness.

There is a key in a small envelope included in this packet that belongs to a safe deposit box in your maiden name at the Bank of America main branch in downtown San Francisco. In it I've put your mother's jewelry and gifts from the marriage. They belong to your family and should be returned to you. It is only right. You can close the box once you retrieve them.

The petition for divorce seemed the natural and final conclusion to things; to free you to build a future, Aneeta. I wish you all the best.

Sincerely,
Narinder

'You win anything?'
The remnants of panic are beginning to subside. She smiles weakly at the expectant, elderly woman. 'Not exactly.'
'Oh. Too bad.'
There is no way to explain that freedom is perhaps the richest prize of all.

Gregory
Thanksgiving
November 2002

There is a cream-coloured length of cloth, uneven, on the rollered table that cuts across Gerry's hospital bed. On it are the remnants of turkey dinner. With all the fixings. Cranberries, gravy, mashed potato, a platter holding scraps of a damn large bird. Suzanne and Lenny have missed nothing. Gregory was charged with bringing the pie. Of course.

'Since I landed here I've been dreaming about pumpkin pie.' Gerry has instructed that it be divvied up and passed around at the nurse's station too. Manuel, the dishwasher and delivery driver at the café, and his wife, Lupita, have stopped by. They can't say no to Gerry's offer of pie. They stand and eat awkwardly off blueflower-edged paper plates with plastic forks. Once they have finished they hug Gerry and offer get well wishes. They tell her they don't want to tire her out. 'Tire me out,' she moans, 'all I do is sleep all day. Nothing else to do around this joint.' Everyone laughs. Gerry has spirit, though Gregory is not entirely sure how much may be an act for their benefit.

Gregory has never had Thanksgiving this way. Holidays, her and Mama counted themselves thankful if they managed to avoid pissing Curtis off. That's what they celebrated. That's what Thanksgiving was all about growing up in her world.

In prison, it was one of the few days in the year that supplies in the kitchen were a little better. There were a few extras—like having turkey, or getting stuffing and buns both, makings for some pie. Quantities were a bit better. Inmates seemed better behaved too. Maybe because they were all forced to attend chapel. Every year the message was the same. Because every year there were new ears to hear it for the first time. The Book of Philippians. Christ's disciple, Paul, being held in a Roman prison, writes a letter to his people outside—*'Not that I speak from want; for I have learned to be content in whatever circumstances I am.'* The focus always on that particular verse. The chaplain's yearly appeal: 'Even in Paul's dark prison days he was content. We need to respond with gratitude for the ups and downs, the changes life may bring our way. And the truest form of contentment is in thanksgiving.' Right. In other words, it's all good. Don't worry, be happy. For the razor wire and steel barred pit-stop along the way. The various versions of hell they'd come from didn't seem to figure in things at all.

And this? Now? She feels guilty for living it. Some circumstances are so much the better than others they're almost more difficult to make peace with. And yet here Gerry is trying to apologize. 'Well, it's not the kind of sit-down I'm used to, but after the hospital food of the past week I'll say it's more than a welcome change. I intend to be up and ready for Christmas. So we can do things right.' She pats Gregory's hand in a gesture that includes her in the plans she's already making.

'Now, Ma, don't put that kind of pressure on yourself.'

'Lenny, how can I not? Then I've got nothing to shoot for.'

Suzanne inclines her head slightly and raises her eyebrows in a look at Lenny that very clearly says *leave it alone*. Lenny reads her expression and falls silent.

Gerry pushes straighter in the bed. 'Remember the times we used to go up to Uncle Henry's farm and he'd chase the turkey around the yard? I do recall the first time you saw what he'd done to that bird there was no consoling you. Remember?'

Lenny smiles, 'Yeah, well it's a lot of trauma to inflict upon a five-year-old psyche.'

'Oh, you were older than five.'

'Still, for any kid I think it would be a big deal.'

Gregory shares a look with Suzanne at the way the two of them carry on.

Gerry chuckles, 'Your dad, bless him, said to me: Well Geraldine, there goes my hope of that boy ever being a doctor.'

'I wasn't that bad.'

'You were doing some mighty fine squealing about the whole thing, let me tell you. And you were having none of that bird for your Thanksgiving dinner. '

'In spite of my adverse beginnings I've grown into a guilt-free, turkey-eating adult.'

'Oh you!' she scoffs, waving her arm at him.

Suzanne reprimands, 'That's about enough. We don't want the patient getting too worked up.' She slaps Lenny's upper arm lightly in mock rebuke. As she starts to pull away he grabs her hand and folds her into a hug. At first she acts exasperated with the way he has subdued her, but then she relaxes into it. Gregory feels a twinge of longing, watching them, one that catches her by surprise.

Some of the earlier animation has left Gerry's face. Her smile is tired. 'I think I've had about enough fun for one night,' Gregory says. 'Better get going before I turn into a pumpkin.'

'I wouldn't want to be responsible for that,' Gerry says with a short laugh. Suzanne has begun returning lids to food containers, but Gregory notices that she has piled one high with a variety of leftovers. 'Suzanne's fixing you a care package.'

'Oh no, really...' she starts to protest, but they won't have any of it.

'You have to,' Lenny asserts. 'How are we,' he waves at the enormous supply of food, 'going to ever finish all this? Save us. From some of the overindulgence.'

'You'll make me feel better if you take some,' Gerry adds.

'When you put it that way, it'd make me a heel to argue.'

Gerry reaches her hand across the bed to grasp Gregory's, 'Happy Thanksgiving.'

'Yes,' Gregory murmurs, surprised to find it true. 'Happy Thanksgiving.'

She unbolts the door and opens it outward. For a moment she stands and closes her eyes; lets the fine mist in the air refresh her, the cool slip itself over her. She hears the approach of footsteps and opens her eyes. 'Morning, Bill.'

'Gregory. How're we doing this fine morning?'

'Don't know if it's fine or not. Don't know much of anything. Coming, going. Just the kitchen, oven, dishwasher and back again. I'm a walking zombie.'

He takes his cap from his head as he passes though the door and rests it reverently on the window ledge beside his favourite table. Placing the newspaper on the table, he removes his leather bomber jacket and drapes it on the chair.

Way back at the beginning Lenny had told her he was a regular. 'Can pretty much set your watch by Bill Sterling's timing.' Retired structural engineer. Originally from back east somewhere. Widower. He'd sit in his corner nursing his coffee through the morning rush. Reading, watching, thumbing slowly through his paper.

She gets things ready. On platters, in pans. Sets some items on the countertop, some under the glass display. Slices the first pies of the day. She takes him a steaming mug of coffee from the pot just finished brewing. And a scone still warm from the oven.

'So how's Gerry?' he asks.

'Doing okay, I think, from what I can tell. Looking more herself. Joking with the nurses and doctors. Gerry thinks it's all too much fuss, and Lenny, he tends to go the other way completely. So I guess somewhere in the middle is about right. She thinks she'll be home early week. Lenny thinks late. We'll see.'

'This her first heart attack? You know?'

'Think she's been having some problems for a while now, but from what I gather, never a heart attack. Never anything like this.'

'Lucky thing you were here.'

'I suppose.'

'No suppose about it.'

He means it as a compliment. But she finds it hard to take. She steps away and busies herself at the counter. It's pretense, since things are pretty much set. But it short-circuits the conversation. She takes to chalking the board with the day's offering. Manuel ought to be in soon. Lenny has been working until close. With Gerry out they're in need of more help. Even with Suzanne pitching in it's not enough. They are all more than exhausted on account of the demands of the holiday run-up. Lenny has eased off commercial orders until something can be ironed out. Under the circumstances, they're doing the best they can. She wipes at her forehead with the back of a hand.

When she hears the door chime in the back she figures Manuel must be early. She is surprised to see Lenny down the corridor. 'What're you doing in?' He has not shaved. His eyes are red-rimmed and tired. He rubs his hand against the stubble along his jawline.

'Wanted to have a chat.'

'With me?' The *me* see-saws.

'Morning, Bill.' He lifts a hand in greeting.

'Lenny.' Bill seems to know this is no ordinary visit; without a word further, he drops his attention to the leaves of newsprint spread before him.

'Over here.' Lenny pulls two stools out at the counter. 'Wanted to catch you before the morning got going. Have a seat.'

She leans herself onto the vinyl covered round with one leg supporting her half-on, half-off positioning. Lenny goes and pours a cup of coffee. 'Something wrong?' she asks, suddenly jumpy.

'Been doing some thinking.' He comes back to where she is and settles onto the second stool with both hands wrapped around the mug of hot liquid. He looks down into it. 'A lot of thinking, in fact.' He sighs. 'They're letting her home Thursday.'

'Well that's good news.' But then she hesitates. What if there's something else? 'It *is* good news?'

'Yeah, it's good. But they've told her she really has to slow things down. Like I've been telling her all along. She's been doing too much. Not that she'd take notice of me. She's had heart troubles for a couple of years. But after this she can't pretend like they don't exist. Which she's done real well. Until now. Thing is,' he looks intently at her, 'I need someone to take over for her. Someone who won't mind her butting in here and there, can handle her. You know what she's like. She won't be able to give it up completely. We think you're that person. Or you could be. We wanted to put it to you. See if you'd consider it. We can't pay a whole lot more, but what we can offer is lodging. The upstairs. I mean, she's been using it mainly for storage, sometimes an office. Nothing a hammer and nails couldn't easily fix. It's more hours. More responsibility. I wasn't sure it'd be something you'd want. But think on it, okay?'

She is stunned at the offer. At the trust, the belief. In her? Her. They want her to run things. In Gerry's kitchen. Before she can recover, before she can say anything at all, he is up and off the stool, taking himself to where Bill is. Her mind is like a frantic expressway. The what-ifs flow on and off, weaving themselves in and out of her buzzing thought.

Bill looks up from his paper, asks Lenny, 'How's your mother doing?' She watches as Lenny settles in for a chat.

The day she moves her meager belongings from Larkin and into the apartment is a dirty one. The light is wan and watery. The trees along the boulevard verge upon the skeletal. Odd leaves in hues of crimson, gold and brittle tawny brown dangle listlessly from outstretched bones.

It is a small space, but it is her own. She feels a tightness in her chest.

Lenny has been true to his word. Hammer and nails and a coat of paint have made all the difference. He'd asked her to select the colours. Afraid of a mistake, she'd stayed neutral. 'You can always change them,' he says. For the bedroom she has chosen Butterfly Bush, a creamy vanilla. Guacamole lights the walls in the main space. And if it doesn't look exactly the hue of mashed up avocado. The walls of the tiny bathroom are clad in a shade called Nickel; it calls to mind an ocean water and fog mix. It'll be such a luxury not to have to share. Furnishings are limited to an old desk and worn two-seater; a double bed takes the bulk of space in the narrow bedroom. Suzanne and Gerry's obvious considerations include a couple of black-framed pencil sketches of San Francisco landmarks, the Coit Tower and Golden Gate bridge; linens on the bed, in the bath, even in the kitchen; hangers and spare blankets in the closet. Without so much as a word they'd done it. They know her well enough to know she'd have said no if they'd asked. Behind a short length of counter stands a small stove; under it, a miniature refrigerator. They look positively puny compared to the monsters downstairs. Lenny has even installed a run of cupboards. Inside there are stacks of some of the older crockery and dishes, marred ever so slightly with chips or darkened webs of spider veins. It's the stuff they take pains not to use for paying customers. She doesn't mind the look of them, there's a comfort in the imperfections.

Access to the apartment is by way of a steep planked ladder of inside stairs. Through the back entrance off the alley. Lenny is apologetic, but it's fine by her. Isn't like she'll be expecting visitors, or even wanting them. She prefers the layer of insulation, separation. Just being on her own is a big enough shift for the time being.

She'd used the fixer-upper lead time to talk it out with Dr. Gedge. 'Some fear is natural, Gregory.' Yeah, some. 'It's a healthy and normal dynamic. As I've said before, what sets us apart is the different ways in which we choose to deal with it.'

'How about Valium or Prozac?' He had smiled, said he thought the move was a good thing. And the added responsibility. A positive growth opportunity. That he is pleased with the way she's making a place for herself as a contributing member of society.

Lenny asks her if she needs help with her things, she lifts the plastic bag and says she can manage. He doesn't know where to look, how to look; she sees something in his eyes. All her earthly possessions fit the one garbage bag. Hefty Sack, Linda called it. Hefty. Funny word. Makes for an easy move, that's for sure. She remembers back when she and Mama would scramble to pack for a move. How it seemed so overwhelming. How Curtis used to insist on traveling light. Ironic, her single sack relocation now.

She'd felt herself go misty saying goodbye to Linda at Larkin House. Linda had given her a squeeze on the shoulder and wished her luck.

Things were in full-swing downstairs when she'd arrived. The lunch rush. 'So if there's anything else you need,' Lenny says, 'give me a holler. We've got Chipotle Bean Soup today in case you want.'

'Yeah, sounds good. I'll be down. A bit later. I'll just get sorted in here.' It is not the things that need sorting. There are so few. It is the invisible that needs to be sifted, ordered, addressed, taken stock of.

'You know where to find us.' He smiles and crabs side-on down the stairs.

'Yeah,' she says, smiling back, 'can't really miss you, can I?' She waits until he reaches the bottom and turns out into the hallway before she pushes the door closed and turns the lock.

The scent of fresh paint is strong; she walks across the space to open the front windows. Winter air pushes eagerly past her, smelling of mulching earth and the tang of sea. She thinks, in passing, about dressing the glass in tissue the way she used to at Lil's. How coloured shades of light might look cast on these walls; the patterns it might make. The kinds of imagining it might inspire. Because where she's at now? It's already more than she'd ever let herself hope for.

Aneeta
November 2002

She signs the documents, HERE, HERE, and HERE as luminous yellow tabs instruct. The signature on the various lines is, to begin with, like the jerky strokes a child might produce. Aneeta Kaur Arora. Once, she had thought it was a name to signify a new beginning. It had given her a means of escape. Now she is closing the chapter. In many ways she still feels a stranger to it, to that life and to the person she was meant to have grown into as Jovin's wife. Maybe her awkwardness is a sign that the marriage was ill-conceived all along.

At the very least, it has brought her here. She creases the papers into three equal segments and inserts them into the enclosed and already addressed return envelope. *Attention: D. Gideon, Esq. Universal Law Group.* It seems almost too easy, to end it in this way. At a distance. In pen and ink only.

She moistens the adhesive and seals it, running the heel of her palm along the length. How clever that postage has been affixed to the front of it as well. All the little things have been attended to. To make it easier for her to complete the one big thing that is necessary. She has flipped through the pages in review, to be sure they are initialed and signed at all the designated places. Once, and again once more. So that she is certain it is done as required, so that she has fulfilled the last of her duties to this man, her husband.

Narinder. Sincerely, Narinder. Thus far her brother-in-law has been true to his word. Where he is concerned, she keeps a fragile kernel of trust. She does not wish to tempt fate. But if the family is moving ahead with plans for another marriage, perhaps then there is more reason to hope.

She walks from the building, not more than twenty paces, to place the envelope, minus her brother-in-law's letter and the tiny toothed key, into the metal jaws of the post box outside the corner convenience market. When she pushes the yawing mouth closed, the slippery sound of paper is followed by a resounding metal clang of finality.

She will claim the jewelry from the safe deposit box tomorrow. And turn the key over. Narinder's letter she has tucked beneath the layers of coloured silk in her suitcase, along with the other things she keeps, reminders of a life lived in days gone by. Small things. And yet substantial effects. In how each has undertaken to shape her. They are, these assorted joys and sorrows, what prompts her forward.

Gregory
December 2002

'Gregory, there's somebody to see you,' Lenny calls out the back. She's sat on an overturned plastic milk crate taking a break. Getting some fresh air. Middle of the morning and she'd needed to get off her feet. The place is humming, but everybody's in now, so she can afford a few minutes.

Adrenalin fires at the announcement. An involuntary shudder sloshes coffee into one side of the mug, like a wave on a rolling sea. Quick and unsteady, she stands. She sets the drink on a wooden window ledge. 'Who?' Her question curls up. She can hear fear in her voice.

'Don't know. Woman. Nicely dressed. Want me to ask?'

'Huh? Nah.' She gulps. Her heart kicks heavy. Damn Doc Gedge and his empty promises, fear still plays her, it doesn't feel like it's getting better at all. *Face it, have to face it.*

From the shift in his look he's twigged to the way she's taking it. 'I can,' he says with a hitchhiker's thumb, 'you know, if you'd rather...' He lets the thought drift.

'Nah, I'm coming.' She exhales, a white puff in the cold air. The tremor she feels isn't owing to caffeine. But she's clean, staying inside the lines, playing by the rules. So why does it feel like she's been caught out?

Lenny turns to head back inside. She coughs anxiously, shallow and thready, into a curl of fist and wonders if she ought to remove her headscarf. She decides against it, concluding that the hair under it probably looks a wild mess. She watches Lenny's back disappearing. Whoever it is obviously hasn't seen fit to have words with him. So that's good. Must be good. Anyone from the state would likely be nosy—want to be finding things out about her, sneaking around—before they get face-to-face. The hum of the café reaches along the corridor; voices, the chirr of porcelain, the sound of coffee grinding, the high scree of steam frothing milk. She moves toward it.

She can feel herself starting to perspire. She squints as she comes into the room, on account of the bright morning light spilling in the front windows. Her eyes need a moment. To adjust. And then it's all up in front of her, grey-green outlines closing in with the changing of her pupils. Ghosting. She's drawn stiffly into a hug. There's a voice she knows. Tension begins to unwind. A spike of annoyance shoots through, and she pulls back to let her visitor have it. 'Jeez, Claire! You had me totally freaked out. I ought to break your scrawny neck! Why'nt you tell Lenny it was you? I'm back there having a full-blown panic attack, imagining all sorts!'

'Are you serious?' the look on Claire's face falls. 'I didn't mean to spook you. I guess I didn't think I needed to announce myself. You don't seem the kind of girl who'd require it.' She cocks her head with a goofy look, 'Why? Who're you expecting?'

'I don't know—does it matter? I'm jumpy. You'd think you, of all people, would know that!'

'Don't be sore with me. Least it's only me you've got to contend with. That's a good thing. At least, I hope it is. I'm just happy I managed to find you in the first place! Traffic was a total nightmare. God, I can't imagine *that* as a regular commute! So I crawled in. Went to Larkin. And they tell me you're gone. Can't tell me where. Just that you're gone. Moved out. Course, didn't help that I hadn't heard any of this from *you*. All I could do is stand there looking stupid. Woman I spoke to was pleasant and polite, but was not buying the close personal friend thing. Wouldn't give any details at all. Zip. Some strange-ass *I'm Elvis* t-shirt.'

'Linda.'

'We didn't exchange introductions. Anyway, I'm stood inside her doorway wracking my brain trying to figure out the name of this place!' She looks mighty pleased with herself. 'And it came to me: Gregory, Gerry, things that start with G? Lucky thing, otherwise you could've slipped off into the sunset on me.' She laughs. 'Sure smells good. You got yourself a nice slice of outside life, Abbott.'

'You hungry? I can get you something.'

'I'd like that.'

'Coffee? And? Cinnamon twist? Scone? Muffin? Pie?'

'Coffee for sure. Maybe a cinnamon thingy. Something for my troubles, hey?'

'Grab a seat. I'll bring it.'

'Wow, and service too.' Claire shakes out of her coat, 'I'm just glad.'

'Why?'

'That I managed to find you. Hunt you down. You make a girl feel awful insecure, ditching like that. I mean,' she laughs, 'you don't call, you don't write. Was it something I said? Did I smell bad?' She pouts like a disappointed child.

'God, Claire,' Gregory scoffs. 'Truth is, I wasn't so sure you'd be interested in finding me.'

Two little old ladies gawk at Claire's play. Two pairs of circle-rouged cheeks and penciled eyebrows, with almost-matching smudged pink bows for mouths. They look to be trying to figure details of the scene. Real life soap opera? Long lost reunion? Friends or lovers? Lovers or friends? Some gossipy chatter to liven the morning. Twittered imaginings between them. So be it.

'What makes you say a thing like that?'

'Well, I just wasn't sure, after your place, that we had anything in common anymore.' There, it was out. 'I wasn't sure you'd be wanting to keep up with someone from the past. You know, somebody like me.' She's made her confession in full.

'Now wait just a minute, Gregory Abbott! All the things we've been through together? You and me are bigger than that. Our bond goes beyond the wire and walls.'

'Let me just…get that coffee. Before we get into it.'

'And the cinnamon thingy. I'm starving.'

'Still black?'

'Still black.'

'Be right back.'

'I'll be right here waiting on you. Don't you be doing a back door slide on me.'

'Apparently, I can run, but I can't hide.'

'Best you remember that.'

'Sometimes, Claire, you scare me.'

Claire gives her fiercest look in return. 'Better believe it, baby. Tough love.'

The ladies are leaned in, teepee-like, heads together, silent, ears intently tuned into the conversation beside them. Two little birds; eyes wide, mouths in open O's.

Gregory shakes her head, 'I'm going for that coffee now.'

Claire smiles wickedly in their general direction. 'If you know what's good for you, hon.'

'Right. Going.'

'And some sugar. I need sticky, sweet sustenance,' Claire calls after her.

When she returns, Claire is staring blankly out the window. She sets coffee gingerly on the tabletop, unwinding her fingers from the V she has made of the two mug handles. She slides a warm cinnamon twist in front of Claire. 'Earth to Claire. Penny for your thoughts,' she says, as Claire pulls herself back to present.

'Is it still only a penny? Hasn't there been some sort of COLA clause? Some re-evaluation for undermining brain output? The Brain Trust lobby. Storming the capitol, or God only knows.'

'It's only a saying. Not a money-making enterprise.'

'Still.'

'Wow, you're in a strange way.'

Claire sighs, 'I'm doing my best to try to avoid what I came to talk about.'

'You think pinching thought pennies is going to help you with that?'

'For a little while.' She sips coffee and tears a jag of caramel pastry. Then she shoves the plate toward Gregory. 'I can't eat it all. Have some with me. I won't feel so guilty if I'm at least sharing the calories around.'

'Oh, stop!'

'No, seriously. I can't stop eating. Making up for lost time, I guess. I'm carrying like twenty extra pounds. Every other week I'm having to up a clothes size.'

'That's because in jail you never ate.'

'Prison food, no offence, was not my idea of good eats. I know you guys in the kitchen did your best. This, however, is delicious. And,' she moans, 'headed straight for my thighs!'

'God, stop your whining. You're eating, you're coffee-ed. What's up that brings you all this way?'

Claire sighs. 'I know exactly what you're going to say.'

'Fine. So enjoy the snack, the joe, a this-and-that chat, and then, whatever, off you go to battle the freeway again. If you already know.'

'Maybe I know it, but I think I still need to hear it. If I want to make it stick. Me imagining what you're going to say isn't exactly the same as hearing it straight from you. The horse's mouth. So to speak.'

'I'm not sure I like that comparison.'

'You know I don't mean it unkindly, so don't take it that way. I guess the point is…I trust you. To be straight with me. Because you're balanced. And, Lord knows, I need some balance and perspective right about now.'

'That good, huh?'

'Yeah, well,' she shrugs, 'Grant's back.'

'Back how?'

'Back in town. Looked me up. Called me. Took me out. He came back, he says, to apologize. To explain. Says after I got caught he delivered and told the boss he was out, done, finished. How they wanted his head on a platter. How it was the hardest decision he's ever had to make, to let me take the fall. Says he missed me. Missed us. Misses us. That he wants us back together. So we can be a family, make a life together. He said…if he could go back and change things he would. Said he was proud of me for being so strong. So committed. Gregory, he was in tears. He got down on his knees. God, I felt so…seeing him…like that.'

'Just one little question I've got, Claire. One minor detail I'd like to understand.' Her sarcasm is sharp. 'Where was he when you were doing your time? If he really cared about you, Claire? And about his kid? Where the hell was he?'

'He said he was getting himself clean. Cleaning his life up. Cauterizing loose ends. Turning himself around. Starting again. Building a respectable life. Trying to go straight. He's in real estate now. He's…doing well for himself.'

'Sounds mighty convenient, if you ask me. You are asking me, aren't you? Not just telling me. You see the difference, Claire?'

'I see the difference. I see it. So, yes, I am asking, Gregory. Because I know I'm too close to it. Even though I want, more than anything, to believe him. To believe it's real, that he's sorry for what he did, that he's changed.'

'You're willing to let him off the hook for letting you rot, alone, in prison. For not taking any responsibility for putting you there? You're fine with that? For him doing the easy thing and walking away. That with sorry and a few tears he's going to make everything okay?'

'He said he had to walk. To avoid having Jace dragged into it. The people in that business, they look for that kind of weakness to exploit. I know it would have been complicated. I'm glad he had the good sense to leave Jace out of it, to protect him. I'm thankful to him for that.'

'You're *thankful*? Oh, thank God for the small things, the littler gifts. Where the hell do *you* figure into this fucking lopsided equation? The *small* matter of jail time, life put on hold, your kid's childhood sacrificed. Of course there's the even more *insignificant* matter of a criminal record, in your name, not his, that's not going anywhere. Ever. And now? You're willing to just take him at his word that things have changed? You know, for a really smart woman, Claire, you sound like you've got a brain the size of a pea!'

Gregory pushes back to consider Claire, 'Tell me you haven't slept with him. Tell me, Claire. That you haven't gone there.'

'You make it sound so ugly. I'm not an animal, Gregory. I'm a human being. It's not just about the physical. We share a child together.'

'So let's explore this happy families thing. What does your daddy say about the return of the guy who sent you up to the big house? Was it a happy reunion? Was there feasting and celebration in the manor?'

'That's not fair.'

'Oh, please!'

Her eyes and voice lower, 'My dad doesn't know.'

'Why? Because the dog is afraid to come sniffing around? Why don't you just come clean to your dad? And tell Grant to fuck off. Right? Not the easiest of things to do, but not the hardest either.'

'It's not that simple.' Claire clears her throat. 'My dad doesn't know it was Grant who got me in trouble,' she pauses, 'on both counts.'

'What the hell?'

'Okay, so I'll admit, I've not been real honest about things with my dad. When I got pregnant, I…wasn't thinking straight. The reasoning behind my motivation doesn't really matter now.'

'Does Grant know this? That you've kept it all quiet?'

'Yeah.'

'Of *course* he does. Boy, the way things are playing out here, I shouldn't have even had to ask! Let's take it one step further then, since we're on a bit of a run, was it your choice not to mention his…*involvement*, shall we call it?'

'We agreed. Both of us. Together.'

'My God, Claire! You should hear yourself. So really, all he's got to do is work his way around you. Ought to be a piece of cake. Got you like a puppet on a string. Give your head a shake! What the hell are you thinking?'

'You don't know him like I do. You think he's all manipulation, but it's not like that, we agreed. It was mutual. We had reasons for doing things the way we did.'

'I can't believe how gullible you are!' Gregory's laugh is hard. '*You don't know him like I do.* I lived it. Lived it. Please, let me recite for you: *I'm sorry. Truly sorry. More sorry than you can imagine. I messed up. It won't ever happen again. I swear. I swear on my life, your life.* All the bullshit promises, excuses, apologies laced with crocodile tears. You have no idea how many times my mama made excuses for Curtis over the years. Just like you're doing now. But the one thing you could bet on, even if you weren't a betting sort, was that it would come around again. It was a sure thing, history repeating itself.

'You, Claire, here and now, are *not* the same woman who swore, on her life, on the life of her child, that she would never go back. That she would never let it happen again. You cannot be the same woman. You paid the price for him. Do you want to keep paying for his choices? Is that what you want for your life? The rest of it? The part he hasn't already taken from you? And do you want that for Jace?'

Claire's tone rises defensively, 'I want nothing but the best for Jace. And I think the best for him is having a family. He needs it. He deserves it. Jace didn't ask for any of this. I owe it to him.'

'You think it was best for me having a family? See where it got me? How good it was? There's no doubt in my mind I would have been better off not having Curtis around. I'm not saying I don't agree Jace deserves a family. Just spare him the pain of the wrong kind of one. Please. Be clear-sighted enough for that. I wouldn't wish that on any kid.' She pauses. 'You know I'm right, Claire. Tell me you know it.'

'I know you're right, Gregory.' Her voice is soft. 'In my heart of hearts, I know you're right. I just don't know if I'm strong enough.'

'Give yourself some credit, Claire. You've been through a lot, you're tough, you've got this. But know I'm going to come for that bastard if he messes with you.' She smiles grimly. 'I'm here for you, if you need me. But I can only help if you let me. Please, be strong enough for Jace. Especially for Jace. Promise me. Promise me—for *him*, for your son's sake.'

Claire's eyes are ringed red, she can see the threat of tears. The whisper is barely audible, but it's there, 'Promise.'

'Don't look back, Claire. Don't let him fool you. Somebody like that doesn't change. They'll take your legs out every time. If you let them.'

Aneeta
December 2002

His back is to her. She stands and watches. He is lost in what he is reading. A brown volume that requires both hands. Hair curls over the edge of his collar. Just for an instant, like a curious child, she longs to move forward and touch it. Embarrassed at her bold wishing, she clears her throat, alerting him to her presence. He swirls in his chair at the noise. To face her. The late afternoon sun at his back makes his hair light like spun gold. His eyes smile before the sentiment boldly spreads across his features. Her heart jumps and seems to expand in her chest, suddenly leaving her short of breath.

'This is such a pleasant surprise!' he says, jumping up.

'I hope I'm not intruding,' she offers with a sudden wave of hesitancy.

'Not at all, not at all.' All at once he is in motion, commandeering a chair from the opposite wall. 'Here. Come on in,' he enthuses, gesturing widely.

'I didn't call ahead or make an appointment.'

'No, not necessary. Not necessary. At all.'

'Well, quite presumptuous of me, really.'

He has fixed the chair next to his own. 'Just so happens I had nothing to do until class.' Her eyes look to the book splayed face down upon his desk. 'I was catching up on some reading. But I'd much rather be catching up with you. That leaves,' he consults the watch on his wrist, 'a fair chunk before time has a claim on either one of us. Have a seat. Please. What brings you by?'

He is careful, but there is a sliver of hopefulness around the edges of what he says. Although he does not outwardly allude to the way things were left. The words he had spoken as she was leaving the party. The kiss. It is enough that she is here. Regardless of the premise. This implicit agreement, it seems, suits them both. Butterfly nerves have fashioned themselves into a sensation of giddiness. This is how he makes her feel. She gulps it back, tries to steady her insides.

'There is a piece of writing that I wanted to have checked for grammar.' It is not entirely true, but not false either. 'I am not so sure of my written English. I had hoped, if it isn't too much trouble, you might look it over.' It seems plausible on the surface of things.

A glimmer of something in his face extinguishes like a falling star. 'Absolutely. Though I doubt very much you need my two cents worth. Your composition so far has been exacting, to say the least.'

'That is kind of you to say, but this, well, I think it could very much use your attention.'

'On one condition. I'm starving. On an empty stomach, me and grammar—or better, grammar and *I*—don't mix. Let me take you downstairs and get us something to eat before class. Guaranteed I'll be far more productive that way. Ever tried Alfredo's in the Student Union? Pasta is the perfect solution to everything.'

She laughs, 'I suppose it wouldn't hurt?'

'Quite the opposite. Good food makes everything infinitely more pleasant.' He stands and moves swiftly. As if he is afraid that she might change her mind. It is the slight invisible push of encouragement she needs. For it is too soon yet to expect the past to have simply melted away. *The evil that men do.* She thinks of Shakespeare's Caesar; the passage they used to recite in elocution drills. Old wounds take time to fade.

They step out of the tiny room, she before him, but with him so near that she can feel the heat that reaches out to her. He pulls the office door firmly closed. 'You're in for a treat. My stomach is grumbling just thinking about it. Let's be off!' He jabs the down arrow at the lift and smiles at her. He has the look of a little boy with a surprise to share.

There is a chill in the air as they cross the courtyard in fading daylight. She wraps herself into the felt of the coat she has recently purchased. He, though, is in only shirtsleeves. He plunges fists into trouser pockets and shrugs his shoulders higher.

When they reach the other side of the square, he flings the door wide on the bustling Student Union. Standing to one side, he holds it to admit her first. A flush of warm air pushes past. She slips by, close to him, and shyly lowers her gaze. He steps after, letting his fingertips gently touch the small of her back. Leaning in, he says, 'This way.' Side by side is difficult. So he stands slightly to one side at her back. His fingertips move round to the side of her, at her waist, gently guiding her way through the oncoming flow. A rush of heat surges through her at the intimacy of his touch. Deftly, he steers through the boisterous crowds. It is a cacophony of laughing, talking, yelling, sing-songing; a spiraling fever of sound. It reminds her of a thronging crush thousands of miles away, worlds away. And she feels a small pang. Yet in this wild maze of strangers she is happy; trading fear for shyness, for excitement, for possibility. He opens another door and steps to the side again, admitting her first. The air behind it is fragrant with food; a sharpness of garlic and onions, tomatoes and cheese, the yeast of freshly baked bread.

She smiles up into his eager eyes. 'I told you, didn't I?'

A young woman approaches. 'Hey, Dr. Turner.'

'Liz,' he acknowledges, still with the same smile, the same warm tone.

'For two?' she inquires.

'You guessed.'

'Follow me.' They move through a labyrinth of dark wood and fabric with red checks. Once more, fingertips ease her ahead. The same flutter twinges and turns over deep in her belly.

Left to their table, he helps her shrug out of her coat, pulls out a chair and waits, lingering there, for her to sit. Once seated himself he reaches for the paper she has extended. Fingers brush hers as he takes the assignment she has brought to disguise her desire, her longing to see him. She watches his hands and the taper of his fingers against her work and finds herself hoping for more than just an inadvertent touch.

'Let's order,' he says. 'To get it out of the way, before we get too deep into things,' he smiles. 'Everything's good.' Another young woman, this one with a pencil through the loose bun of hair at the nape of her neck, recites the day's specials: Spicy penne arrabiata with Italian sausage, and fusili with pecorino cream sauce, pancetta and fresh peas. Aneeta chooses a half order of the spicy penne. He nods his approval and asks for the classic lasagne.

'Full or half order?'

'Full,' he says. 'With any luck, I'll have some left for lunch. Or a midnight snack.'

The girl laughs, 'Sounds good.'

'Would you like wine?' he asks.

'I'm afraid I might be tempted to sleep in class,' she admits.

'I'm that exciting a lecturer?'

She can tell he is teasing, but she protests, blushing, 'It's not that at all.'

He laughs at her and orders a large bottle of mineral water. The golden flecks in his eyes warm her; tell her she doesn't need to make excuses. Her heart blooms.

'I'm glad you came by today.'

'I'm sorry I didn't make an appointment. I hope at least that I haven't interfered with your schedule.'

'Not at all. I can tell you this is infinitely more pleasant than a lonely sandwich at my desk. You're actually doing me a favour. Speaking of which, you didn't drop by purely to rescue me from the doldrums of daily routine and a solitary supper. Shall I read this now?' he asks, holding up the paper.

'Yes, please do,' she urges. It is not a long piece, but she feels it very intensely. The thoughts and ideas she has cobbled together have bubbled up and onto paper from some inside well-spring. In the guise of allegory, it is much like her own story.

While he reads the words she tries very hard to read his eyes. To get a sense of his thought, his feeling, his impression of the woman she has portrayed. He does not take up his pen, which she takes to be a good sign as far as grammar is concerned. Instead, he devotes himself intently to the paper. When he looks up, they both exhale. Hers is an internal release, his is a low whistle. She has not realized she has been holding her breath.

'It's beautiful,' he murmurs, 'extraordinary. In its simplicity, and for its underlying complexity. It is luminous and…horrifying and bittersweet, all at the same time.'

'You like it?'

'Very much. I could feel it. Envisage it. I have to ask, how did it feel to you when you were writing it?'

'Well, honestly, it just kind of came. Without having to think all that much about it.' She doesn't tell of the sense of relief after the finishing of it.

'There is a realness to it, a rawness. That kind of emotion doesn't translate easily to words on paper.'

Food arrives to momentarily interrupt the conversation. He passes the paper back to her. She tucks it into her bag. 'So the grammar appears okay?'

'Grammatically, it's in order. But, for me, the embodiment of the story—the style, the voice, the character—totally outweighs the mechanics. Anyone can learn mechanics. Not everyone can put their heart onto paper. Have you considered taking the story further? Exploring her in greater depth?'

'No.' The food allows her to sidestep whatever questions may have remained on the subject. It is utterly and incredibly delicious, mouthwateringly so. The amount of chilli in the tomato sauce is perfectly sharp to the tongue.

'Good?' he asks.

'Mmm.' She answers, nodding, her mouth full. For a moment she feels embarrassed at her pleasure, but he laughs it away.

'Told you so.'

As food disappears talk begins to resume, but the subject is changed. And she is grateful. Instead, they talk of class, the people in it. And about the Thanksgiving party. The strange dynamics between some people. After she, Kameko and Gregory had already left. He confesses he'd had to call Ashley a taxi. And help her into it. That she had been very drunk. He lightly laughs it off. 'No big deal for me. But I hope her husband wasn't too offended by the way she turned up.'

She thanks him again for his hospitality. 'I'm just glad you came. I really did mean what I said to you that night at the end of the party. If you even remember it. I feel like I've been spoiled today. With you coming by. Now this,' he waves at the table, 'getting you all to myself, and pasta too.' He laughs.

Conversation turns to the impish antics of a six-year-old boy. 'Max loved the picture of us with the turkey. Calls you the Turkey Lady. I hope you're not offended. Says he wants to meet you. Make sure you're real. He's got his mother's bossy temperament. My big sister Charlotte always got her way. She was a great wheedler. I can see the same thing in Max. My brother-in-law, poor guy, doesn't stand a chance. I think payback will eventually come when Max and Charlotte start to lock horns. I give it until the teen years. Right now, though, the bossiness is still endearing.' There is no mistaking the depth of his affection for this little boy.

'You know,' he muses, 'I've got Max for the day next Sunday to free Charlotte up for Christmas shopping. We were going to head out to Fisherman's Wharf and then the beach. Why don't you join us? Seriously. You'd be helping me out, and he'd get his wish to meet you. We'd both be ecstatic. And Charlotte thinks I'm a bit cavalier as far as the childcare routine—not making him wear his scarf and earmuffs, not making him eat his vegetables, letting him have ice-cream after he's brushed his teeth, that kind of thing. I'm sure she'd see you as a moderating influence on my bad habits.'

That night she dreams her dream of a little boy until her heart is aching with it. And she knows that she will go. The balance of the scale is tipped. She will go to satisfy the part of her that longs for the things that live in an awake world. Things that could be reached out for and actually touched.

Aneeta Malik
English 50
The Washerwoman

A washerwoman makes her way through a waking Indian village. Although it is yet early, the light from the rising sun is punishing. When she squeezes her eyes shut, jags of red pass across a shadowy canvas. If not for such a bright light, she thinks, the stains she carries would not be so obvious in appearance.

On her back is a heavy passel of things for cleaning. Her heart worries about the task she must attend to. She hopes for pity; that somehow, against all likelihood, fate might favour her good intentions and her industry.

At the river's edge she carefully unties her load. The brackish swill is already host to numbers of washers, water gatherers, and farmers tending thirsty animals. She eases into the slurry and raises a last pleading look to the heavens for mercy. With legs braced against the flow, she labours. Forcefully trying, with all the might she possesses, to turn the clock back on itself. To undo what is already done.

Hers is such a determined and rigorous effort that there are those who begin to talk of it among themselves. They wonder what it is that drives her, some demon perhaps, or an old karmic debt. Speculation fuels their words. They make up ugly stories with her fixed at the center. In the tales they imagine they do not see her as she truly is. As a sister, a daughter; once accepted, once loved, once no different than a child of their own.

Again and again she plunges into the murky water, but the morning light heartlessly highlights her shortcomings. She knows the level of expectation; eyes will be critical and conditional. They will hold only her to account, even though the stains she works to banish have been created by their own deeds. Once she had been foolish, thinking that such marks might be overlooked or forgiven. But that naive simplicity is hers no longer. Her eyes have no choice but to see through the clouded judgments of others. If she cannot meet their standards, their whispers—of fault, of blame—will see her good name turned to ruin. Without her reputation, her honour, she will be worth less than nothing, no better than gutter trash, a disgrace.

As she regards a particularly fine length of peacock-coloured silk, she is taken by a sense of overwhelming futility. It is a cruel design of destiny that holds her to this ransom. One she fears she will never be able to settle. Despair tempts her easily into the deeper water, where she no longer has strength enough to withstand the current. The weight of failure circles around and around her, until at last it swallows her whole, condemning her to darkness. She does not resist. For in death, the stains that plague her will no longer matter.

But even as she yields to the claim of shadows, the rhythm of the river comes to her and rescues her. Folding her in arms like a newborn child, it whispers to her soul and fortifies her weary spirit, casting her burdens into the flow. With strength restored, the waters return her to the shore. The scene before her is the same. As if she had never left it. Washers yet wash, water gatherers continue to fill empty earthen vessels, animals yet drink. Outwardly, nothing is different. But inside she is changed. The divine wisdom of the river echoes through her:

Light is not your nemesis, nor something you need fear. Free yourself to it; accept the truth it reveals. Only then will you come to know its grace.

Kameko
December 2002

They are collecting books and papers at the Perk Hill coffee house, their discussion session over. Outside, darkness has settled. Through window glass she has felt the air change. The sulphured light of the street lamps is brightening. Kameko would prefer to stay in their company. To avoid the pain of truth. At least for a little while longer. And so she offers an enticement that comes to mind, as if it had been waiting only to step forward and save her from herself, from the loneliness she dreads.

'I would like to invite you to join me for Japanese food. To share something of my country with you. It is my…treat,' she offers, pleased to have remembered the expression. 'Maybe…now could be a good time?' She looks inquiringly from one to the other. 'If I am not interrupting anything. Other plans?'

Aneeta shakes her head, 'Oh, I've no other plans. I'd like to.'

'Gregory, you will come?' Kameko asks.

'I…' she stops, sighs, 'sure, yeah, why not?'

They layer themselves in clothing, coats. 'There is a place not far,' Kameko volunteers, 'we can walk. And Mizumi is true to Japanese tastes.' As they exit, the sharpness of the cold travels through her bones like a spirit. The air stings bare skin, she can feel her blood rising to meet it. Like Aneeta, she wears a scarf and gloves. Gregory wears only a short coat against the weather. It is interesting how blood can be so different; to experience the very same conditions so uniquely.

Mizumi had been recommended by another transferee in Shiro's office. They had tried it the first time, Shiro and she, soon after they had arrived in the city. Then, they were missing Japan. It had been a comfort, a good way to feel closer to home.

It is only three blocks, the walk. As they approach from the opposite side of the street, she points it out to her companions. Light floods warmly from the windows. It occurs to her suddenly how awkward it might prove if they should happen upon Shiro. An encounter that would be all the more unpleasant if he were to be in the company of his pregnant mistress. Humility burns at her cheeks. Thankfully the sentiment is invisible in the darkness. She strains to see if in the few early guests there is one whose look is familiar, but she does not detect her husband's presence among them.

She hopes there might be a tatami room available. For a time to keep the world out. To separate themselves from other things that might interfere with the simple enjoyment of the experience.

Stepping through the door she calls, '*Shitsurei shimasu!*'

'*Irasshaimase!*' the chorus in return.

For her companions she translates, 'They welcome you.' Turning to the blue robed hostess she asks, 'Have you a tatami room available?'

'Hai. For three? Please, this way.' She bows and leads them in.

Like the core of a fruit, the center spine of the restaurant is a segmented row. The hostess motions to an opening near the middle of the run.

'We remove shoes,' Kameko instructs, 'before entering.' She places her boots neatly side by side on the floor and slides in first. 'You can sit on the knees, or with legs under the table. Whichever is most comfortable.' Both women wear uncertain smiles as they adjust themselves. With a bow the hostess slides the screen closed, separating them from the main room.

Aneeta's hand lightly travels the wall beside her. 'This room is beautiful. It makes me feel like I should whisper, everything is so quiet in here.'

'The screens contain sound very well. People choose these rooms because it gives the freedom to behave as one wishes. And preserves an appearance of modesty to those beyond. The tatami floor mats for which such rooms are named in ancient times were a sign of importance, of position. Japanese use such rooms to entertain, conduct ceremonies, sometimes to keep religious altars. The famous geisha of Japan entertain in tatami rooms of prominent Teahouses.'

She smiles, 'But tonight we should not drink tea, I do not think. Tonight, if you are willing, we can have sake. Yes? You know sake? Rice wine? It is very popular, perhaps even most popular in Japan, along with beer and also whisky. I think you will like it. If you don't, we can choose something else for you to try.'

A discreet tap and the screen slides open to reveal a smiling waitress. Kameko requests sake and a selection of food.

'I have asked for the most well-liked of Japanese foods for you to try,' she explains.

Moments later the screen opens again, and the waitress kneels to pour sake.

'For Japanese, drinking is a big part of socialization. I think mostly because it makes people relax. Ordinarily in daily life, one is very careful about how to behave. But drink gives certain permission to say things, do things, that one cannot without it. To be more open.' She smiles and takes her cup. Again, the waitress takes her leave. 'Before we drink we say *Kanpai!*'

'I heard you say that at Turner's party.'

'It is like a command to drink. To empty your cup.'

'The first lesson is complete, then.'

'Yes,' Kameko laughs, 'I suppose it is.'

Aneeta sips. 'The flavour is lovely and mild, but when it goes down it has the sensation of the brandy I used to be given when I was unwell as a child. It's like fire!' She gives a small, choked gasp and laughs.

'I think it is stronger than wine from grapes. That is my only caution. Sitting down, the body does not notice. But when the body must again stand, it can be another matter. Here is the next lesson: in Japan it is considered poor manners to pour one's own drink. Hopefully, whomever you sit with is attentive to the changing level of your cup. It is a very important task for any club hostess or mama-san, for a friend or colleague, even for a wife to do for her husband.'

'Speaking of which, how long have you been married, Kameko?' Gregory asks.

'Oh, it is already more than two years.'

'So before you came to the States?'

'Yes,' Kameko nods, feeling suddenly uneasy. Questions, though, are inevitable, understandable.

'How did you two meet?'

'Our fathers were acquainted through work. They…arranged our introduction.'

'Really?' Aneeta sounds surprised.

'It was at the encouragement of my mother. She was ill. Her desire was to see me marry. Before she died.'

'Oh, I'm sorry. I shouldn't have—'

'No, it is…to talk of it is something of a relief.' Her smile is sad, both at the memory and for the way things are now. 'It was her one wish. And so, when I knew it could bring her a measure of happiness…' She shrugs, an indifferent finish to the idea.

'How is it that you came here, to San Francisco?' Aneeta inquires, her voice soft.

'My husband came for work. With his company. It is a temporary posting. Eventually, he will be called back to the main office in Tokyo.'

'So you're just here passing time?' Gregory asks.

The tap on the shoji relieves her of the need to respond. 'Thank you for waiting!' the waitress chirps, leaning in to arrange food on the tabletop. At the moment Kameko cannot be sure of the future. Any of it. About whether she is simply passing time in this country or not.

'Ah, rice, something I recognize,' Gregory jokes. There is a stifled giggle from the waitress.

'With food we say *itadakimasu*, I receive gratefully.' Bows are exchanged as the service is completed. The screen slides closed.

'Perhaps you already know, but if you don't, the main lesson for tonight— chopsticks.' Deliberately making a silly face, Kameko demonstrates positioning and shows how to achieve the scissor effect. 'If it proves tricky, please do not worry. Simply use fingers. The experience should be about enjoyment of the food, not about how it travels into your mouth.'

She identifies the various dishes: 'Sashimi and sushi is fresh fish and also fish with rice. The green paste? Is wasabi. Spicy. Also, some smoked eel and egg nigiri. And okonomiyaki, like Japanese pizza. The fish flakes on the top wave because of the heat, not because they are alive.' She giggles at their quizzical smiles. 'Gyoza are dumplings; here with pork and chives inside. The tempura is of assorted vegetables. On the bamboo sticks is yakitori chicken. Please, take as you wish. I hope very much that you like it. You already seem fast learners with chopsticks.'

'I don't know about fast learner,' Gregory argues, 'I feel like my hands are going to freeze in this position.' She awkwardly mimics the pincer motion and they all laugh.

The screen slides, and the sake bottle is exchanged. The colour of the wine is in their cheeks; conversation between them is beginning to flow more freely.

'So, along the lines of recent class discussions on the subject of character, and, as you've suggested Kameko, in the spirit of being more open—which is something I seem to be unable to make my chopsticks do—' Gregory struggles to urge the two pieces of wood apart, 'I have a confession.' Her face tenses as she concentrates; eyebrows draw down and in, the line of her mouth tightens. 'I have this character game I play. A habit. Something I've been doing since I was a kid. Because I moved around a lot. Back then,' she strains at pinching the levered wood around a gyoza, 'it kind of helped take my mind off the awkwardness of being *the new kid*. So what I'd do is make up nicknames for people: stack up the things that stood out about a person and try to come up with something fitting. For my own entertainment.' She has managed to get a dumpling to her plate, and for the moment lets it rest. 'Now, without really even thinking about it, my mind just invents these…names. Anyhow, the confession is that I've done it for a bunch of people in our class. I figured I'd better say something in case I call somebody by their made-up name and you wonder who the hell I'm talking about.'

'What do you call Professor Turner, I wonder?' Aneeta muses.

'Mmm. Do I detect an interest?' Gregory's look is sly.

Aneeta looks shyly down, smiling, 'He seems an obvious place to start.'

'No name for Turner, sorry to say. Nothing has really come to me that sort of, you know, sums him up. Got any ideas? Romeo, maybe?' Gregory teases. 'Here's one for you. Mike? Crew cut, army dude? I call him Beer Can Mike after the poem he read. By Updike. And Manfred? I call him Manfred of the Red Neck because if you've ever noticed his skin, especially at the back of his neck, is always really red. That, and he tends to be a little rough around the edges. In true redneck fashion. Ashley and Krista? I call them Barbie 1 and Barbie 2. You know, as in the plasticky perfect Miss All-American.'

'But do you have names for Aneeta and I?' Kameko asks.

'Embarrassingly, yeah, I do. You were actually two of the first to come by your names. Right at the beginning of things. I actually can't believe I'm sitting here about to tell you, but,' she shrugs, 'I guess there's no point in it being secret. Aneeta I called Beauty, because I've never seen anyone who looks like her before, exotic, especially her eyes.'

'A good name, I think, and very true!' Kameko agrees.

'Oh no. I'm not, really,' Aneeta protests.

'And you, Kameko—this was before I knew you were Japanese—I nicknamed you China Doll, because of how perfect and doll-like you look. And your skin is smooth like porcelain. The first day of class you reminded me of one of those collectible dolls. That's what came to mind, my first impression of you.'

'Oh, I do not know that I agree with this so much!' It is flattering, to be compared to a doll, but sobering too. Inasmuch as a doll has no will, no capacity to think or act for itself. It is ironic that Gregory should choose to think of her in this way.

'So that's my little character game. And it's just kind of stuck with me. All these years. A harmless enough pastime, I guess.' She shrugs, and concentrates on moving a piece of fish to her tray. 'There you have it. Enough about me. What about you, Aneeta? What brought you to California?'

Aneeta looks down, her face serious. 'Well…' she straightens, and with a tight smile says quietly, 'I suppose I'm kind of like Kameko. Marriage brought me to America.'

'What?'

'Oh!' Kameko breathes, 'But…I did not know. You wear no ring. I never—'

'No. It is all right, really. Like you, I feel…it's a relief, to talk about it. It wasn't good, my marriage. And so I decided I had to leave it. That was when I came to San Francisco.'

'So you weren't living here, in the city, with your husband?'

'No. I lived further south.'

'Do you have family here, in California?'

'No. My family…is in India. And…I don't really have contact with them. Anymore.'

'At all?' Gregory asks.

'No.' There is sadness in Aneeta's voice.

'And your husband's family?'

Aneeta shakes her head slowly, 'I…I don't want them to know where I am. The city seemed…well, it seemed like a good place to get lost in.'

'Marriage can be very complicated. It takes great courage to do something when it is not good. Like you have done. I admire you for this. For having such strength.'

For a time there is silence between them. The focus shifts to food, and to eating. Aneeta and Gregory prove determined with the chopsticks.

Kameko finally interrupts the quiet, 'When I was in school, I said to my friends that it would never be my life. The kind of marriage I have, it was not something I wanted. Being young you can say such things. Have such ideas. I suppose, because of my mother, her illness, I gave up my ideas.'

'You don't sound as if you're happy about it,' Gregory says.

'In America things are different, maybe I am too,' she reasons. 'Here, I think I have changed my view of certain things. Maybe it is more of a return to the thinking I once had. And it has caused me to question things that a woman more like my mother would not have. Things that are connected with tradition, like duty and expectation. I remember watching the television when I first arrived. During the days, while my husband was at work. I did not like to go out very much. I thought the programs could help me to understand the language and the way to act. But on some of the shows I was shocked to see people reveal their feelings so freely, or choose to pursue their own desires so easily. To choose to live life as they alone would wish to live it. To care for their own happiness above all.' She sighs, 'I find it is hard to know what is best, what is the right thing to do.'

'Do you think it's the effect of America, of coming here, that is responsible for the change in your thinking?' Aneeta asks.

'Maybe. Maybe because here it is the way women are…I do not want to use the word permitted, because it is not a matter of permission, but this is the way that is… accepted, maybe.'

'In India there are expectations about the behaviour of young women, especially for those not yet married. My mother had strict rules. She was stricter, maybe, because my father died when my sister and I were young.' Aneeta grips her sake cup with a faraway look, 'But maybe living in such a controlled way, by all the dos and don'ts, it keeps many girls, girls like me, from even knowing themselves. I still struggle with the idea of what people might think of me or say about me if I don't behave as is expected.'

Kameko nods, 'In Japan, girls, women, are supposed to be meek. In marriage we say a woman should be a good wife and wise mother, this is considered the right kind of character for a woman. The husband at the center of the universe. After him must come the children. Anything else…well, it is not easy being measured this way.'

'In India there's a great deal made of a woman's honour. Before and after marriage. It is so easy for women to be judged, or shamed. Punished. You hear of women burned by fire, by acid. Killed. Many times by their own families. And for things that are often beyond their control. In many ways I was lucky, coming here to marry. Even though the marriage turned out poorly.'

'Your troubles make my confusion seem simple by compare. My difficulty is more a matter of endurance. In the face of unpleasant circumstances. It was the way my mother lived her life, and although I am grateful, for it was I who benefitted, I also came to resent her for it. For her willingness to simply accept things, even the things that must have caused her pain. I am finding that I am not content to simply play this part. When I agreed to marry I had thought perhaps I could be. A good friend told me I was not being true to myself.' Her smile is rueful. 'I refused to see it. Now I think she was probably right.' She shakes her head. 'And though I know I am not happy to live the same as my mother, I am terribly confused about what I should do. *Should*, you see? Still I am looking outside of myself for my direction. For some guidance.

'For many Japanese wives, children can make it easier to overlook other things. A child…helps. When things are not pleasant in a marriage.' She does not have the courage to speak further of her difficulties in this way; the ironic news, the confession that haunts her.

Gregory interjects, 'My shrink calls that avoidance. According to him: not good.'

'Shrink?'

'Doctor. Therapist. Somebody I talk at once a week. What I've come to think of as the *How Does That Make You Feel?* hour.'

Gregory, with her sharp manner, so reminds Kameko of Akira. In the way she tries to make fun of serious things. In some joking way. With faces or silliness or mimicry. Akira, who kept her true feelings hidden by comedy. By acting out for the rest of them. 'You are very much like a friend I once had. She was always trying to bring a smile to a sad face.' Without thinking, she takes Gregory's hand. It is solid and warm. For a moment when she looks into Gregory's eyes, it is as if she is seeing Akira all over again. As if she has found some version of her in a world thousands of miles away. If only in a different incarnation. 'Oh, I am sorry,' she breathes, then laughs, 'I have forgotten.' She releases Gregory's hand and draws back, suddenly embarrassed. 'I was lost in old memories. Forgive me.'

'Nothing to forgive,' Gregory says, with what looks a puzzled sort of smile, one that reflects Kameko's own feeling. It is a question left unspoken between them.

Only scraps of food remain. Tail shells of prawns. Shavings of pickled ginger. Pasty bits of wasabi. The sake bottle is empty. And yet, she does not want this time to be at an end. Masks have been let down. And truths revealed. Truths that have shifted her perspective, and helped her to see things differently. Helped her to see herself differently.

Aneeta
December 2002

She stands before the computer. The screen, unlike those around her, unlike Gregory's next to her, is still black. Little white letters unspool in rapid strings. Left to right. Left to right. She's afraid to touch anything.

When there are questions from students in the class regarding oddities within the fleet of machinery, JT, with palms up and shoulders shrugged, smiles an easy smile. He seems amused that there should be any confusion regarding the workings of computers. 'Inside. Outside. No big mystery. Outside, you tell computer what to do. Inside, the machine only follows what you tell it. Like master and servant. You are the master. It can only perform as you instruct.'

But this computer is flashing and whirring without her instruction. A spinner of secrets. Beside her, Gregory is already at the familiar *Start* rainbow and squinting at JT's written first steps on the white board. JT is capping a black marker pen. INTRODUCTION TO CHARTS AND TABLES is written very cleanly in tall, square capitals. Instructions below are numbered in three-part sequence:

1. 1. 0

1. 1. 1

1. 1. 2

Concise. Orderly. He takes teaching quite seriously. Even though, as he says, he is only 'moonlighting' at it. He had to explain to her the meaning of moonlighting. He is moving now along the classroom rows, checking progress. She is in the third row. Beside Gregory. As she is every week. Gregory always chooses the same seat in this row. On the aisle. Right beside the door. But today Aneeta is afraid to claim this computer as her own, wondering if she should choose a different seat, where the display is already at the familiar *Start* screen. Her teeth bite at the corner of her lower lip. The ongoing activity is like a little firefly bug dancing in the darkness. Now and then there are little blips of sound. Aneeta raises her hand partway into the air, fluttering it, to try to catch JT's attention. He acknowledges her with a wag of the head and a smile. Sidestepping bags and coats and books, he inches along the narrow laneway of chair backs.

'JT, I don't understand what's happening with this computer. The screen is black. I can't even get to the starting page.'

His eyes flick to the screen. 'Not to worry. It's in the midst of a boot sequence.'

'A boot what?'

'This is like its warm-up. A check that everything is as it should be. All parts working. Responding.'

'So then nothing is wrong?' Aneeta asks.

'Nothing is wrong. Patience please, only. Just wait.'

'Achcha, okay. I feel better.'

'It is almost completed, Master Aneeta-didi.'

Gregory offers a chiding grin. 'What did I tell you? Worrywart.'

'What? Wart?'

'A joke. Instead of standing there looking at the thing like it's going to explode, why don't you sit?'

'Okay, okay.' She settles into the chair and slides her bag under the table. Every now and again there is a flip-flash of transformation. She keeps watch, channeling her energies into urging things along. Gregory, she can see, is watching her.

Around the room there is a swell of tick-ticking. Scrambling fingers on plastic keys. Masters giving beginning orders. Commands. JT is waiting with her, but at the same time surveying the group. For signs of their collective progress.

Gregory says, 'Today's tour of charts and tables promises to take us into previously *un-charted* territory. Sorry, couldn't help it. Corny joke.'

Aneeta makes a face. And JT begins to laugh. Clucking her tongue with mock severity, she says to Gregory, 'That was poor. A real poor one, I tell you.' Behind her JT has dissolved into a burst of belly laughter. She turns to look at him, hands clutching his stomach, loudly haw-hawing so that others, too, have turned. Masters and servants are, for the moment, paused. Puzzled expressions watch JT in a hilarious, clownish fit. Aneeta covers her mouth, to hide her surprise and to hold back the laughter now bubbling in her.

Gregory, eyebrow cocked, catches her eye. 'It wasn't *that* funny. This guy must not get out much. Maybe it's because he spends all his time around *machines*. Whatever it is, his humour outlet is severely repressed.'

JT is shaking, completely lost in spasms of mirth. Tears stream from his eyes. His sound reminds Aneeta of a braying mule. Eyes at every workstation are on him. People are stopping to peek in the door of the classroom.

'Oh my God!' Aneeta suddenly raises a pointed finger and gives in to a burst of giggles, 'Just now…you looked like Johnny Lever!'

'Johnny who?' Gregory asks.

'A famous Indian comedian. Terribly funny. Makes such silly faces,' she explains in bits and pieces.

The comment, though, has broken the spell. With a few stray haws the hysteria of the moment is smothered. And JT is restored to the proper demeanor of sensible systems analyst. 'A-heh. A-heh. My Bibi-ji loves Johnny Lever. I love him. Everybody in India loves him. But look like him? What would ever make you say such a thing?'

'But you did,' Aneeta says earnestly, 'you really did. Just when your eyes went wide. It's the crazy eyes, I think. And maybe your eyebrows. You know how he manages to make his jump to impossible heights? For a second it was there. I saw it. Really.' She teases, putting two fingers up to show by width the measure of time she is referring to. Very small. 'Otherwise, with a serious face, you look nothing like him.'

'Okay, sister, thank you very much for making that clear. I am happy to bend to your fancy. But now that you've had your fun at my expense, *I* have one small thing to ask of you.' He measures with his fingers the same as she had. Not more than an inch of air between. 'A small request. To make things even.' The air is light from the joke, but she senses a change of atmosphere. A seriousness. He focuses himself intently upon her screen. But she can see that it is merely his way of avoiding her eyes. It is flashing through whole screens now. Black and white. An audible thrum spurs it through the automatic motions.

She attempts to coax him back to light-heartedness. 'Okay, okay. You might as well ask me now since I'm still at the mercy of what did you call it?' she waves at the screen, 'This boot thing. What is it, this request of yours?' All of a sudden his is the face of a boy, shy and uncertain. 'JT, what? What is it?'

He sighs and, at last, commits himself. 'A photo.'

'A photo?' Gregory queries.

'I need a photo. A picture. Would you allow me one?' There is vulnerability in his tone. It makes her heart go out to him.

Gregory chimes, 'You wouldn't be the first guy asking. Though the other one made her pose with a turkey.'

JT looks confused. 'You're joking?' His eyes are wide again, his mouth rounded by surprise.

'No, serious.' Gregory nods sagely and winks. 'Gobble, gobble.'

'Let me explain!' Aneeta protests, embarrassed. 'It isn't at all how it sounds. It was a *paper* turkey! My writing professor had mounted it on the wall in our classroom. He needed proof for his nephew. That he had hung the creature in the room. The child dared him, a six-year-old. Can you believe it? He asked for me…to join him. In the photo. So I stood there with him. Beside it. While Miss Whatsit, here, worked the camera.'

'He's in love with her,' Gregory adds. 'The professor, that is. Not the turkey.'

'What?' JT gives a low whistle.

'Oh my God! Gregory, you are mad.' She gives a dismissive laugh to cover the swoon of her heart and the pleasure she takes at the notion.

'Okay, whatever you say. But he is. So, JT, what kind of proof do you need *your* picture for?' Gregory asks.

He wears a sheepish grimace. 'I feel very badly. For having to ask. No, having to ask is not right. For choosing to ask. But I suppose I feel, Aneeta, that you understand. These sorts of things.' With downcast eyes he takes his voice lower, 'Only these small concessions I make. I feel I must make. I need something for my mother. She simply wants just a picture…to show.'

'You're serious?' Gregory asks.

'Quite.' His tone is a mix of grim and pleading. It is the ransom of ancient ways. 'I'll understand, Aneeta, if you don't wish it, but it would help—a great deal.' His uncertain lopsided grin is not one of humour now, only chagrin. He blows out of puffed cheeks, 'Something to pacify the gossips. I cannot blame my mother for asking. It's not enough that her son is a computer programmer in America. People are nosy still, for the next bit, the next morsel. Like hungry dogs they wait. If they can just be shown something. Then, for a while, their sly questions will stop. Of course, given an image of a beauty like you, the tongues will wag in completely the opposite direction.' She cannot help but feel affiliation, and sympathy, for his plight. 'I didn't want to ask, but I honestly couldn't think what else to do. Every time we speak she hounds me.' In a put-on woman's voice he mimics, 'Can you not help an old woman? Please, son. So I can end all this nonsense. Surely you must be able to do something. A nice girl at work? Ask some desi friends?' He laughs drily.

'Of course I will do this for you. I can help with this,' she shows a thin slip between her fingers and teases, 'small request.'

'This is the way it is,' he shrugs. 'Always there is the pressure to give the right impression. Or people talk, whisper. After all my parents have done for me, all the sacrifices, I can't bear the thought that they be fixed in gossip on my account.'

'So you're gonna fake it,' Gregory says.

'You might say. A bit of fakery. A tiny bit. Just to keep tongues still. Eyes and minds convinced. And with thousands of miles between, who's to know different? Great job, beautiful girlfriend. For a time at least. Until I confess that she's left me. For another programmer. Torn my heart in two.'

'Man, you've got it all figured out.'

'Until the part where she crushes me underfoot like a stray ant. And to see her, with her Bollywood looks, who wouldn't believe it?'

'Crush you like an ant? That's a horrible thing to say!'

'This is fiction, remember? But somebody like you, anyone can see, is too good for a boy like me. Even a computer programmer in America.' His smile is restored.

'JT, that is absolutely not true.'

'Oh come on, Aneeta, you know it is. Both in fiction and in fact. Back home would two like us ever have ended up together? On the basis of surface considerations only? Realistically speaking?'

'I suppose not.' Differing shades of skin, hers like honey and his like darkened chocolate, would typically have been enough to interfere. And caste difference? On Indian soil a relationship between two like them would rarely have a chance even to begin. 'The thing is, I don't have a picture of myself, well, aside from a few childhood snapshots,' without thinking, she muses, 'a wedding photo.' But her brain is too late to catch the tongue. His eyes widen at her revelation. She rushes on, words tumbling out, trying to minimize the significance of the admission, 'I don't suppose you'd like the one of me with the turkey?'

She has not even noticed that the computer's boot sequence has finished. None of them has. That on the screen in front of her waits the start-up rainbow. At last.

Kameko
December 2002

'*This is Memorial Hospital calling for…Shiro…Tanaka? I couldn't reach him on his cell phone; someone at his office gave me this number instead. Is he available?*'

'*He…is not, no.*'

'*He's a hard man to reach. I'll just leave a message, if you don't mind. If you could let him know that his wife is resting comfortably, everything went just fine. We've moved her to a recovery room in the Delivery Unit. Visiting and viewing for anyone other than the new father is from 2 until 6. Obviously, he's welcome anytime.*'

Pieces of the puzzle come together in her mind, and she knows what she must do.

In that first tangled glimpse of horrified fascination Kameko tries to summon hatred, tries to summon anger, but she cannot. As much as she has wanted to. Shiro's baby is at perfect peace; tiny cherubic rosebud lips putt-putt with every miraculous exhale.

As she watches in awe, in a shocked haze, an ache of agony swells. She stuffs the knuckles of a fist into her mouth and bites down hard on the flesh, hoping to distract herself. Hoping the pain will be enough so that the turbulence of anguish might be dispelled somehow, but a low gulping sob escapes the opening that flesh and bone have not succeeded in blocking. Torment screams through her like a wild ghost, threatening to consume her. *Gaman.* The surface tries to stifle the turmoil that rages inside. It is conditioning. To keep the outside peaceful and pleasant. To keep true emotions from showing. To keep them contained. *Tatemae* before *honne.* Harmony before the self.

She raises her free hand and opens it to its fullest, stretching and reaching through her fingertips so that they strain away from the palm. For a time she simply regards it extended in front of her. Then she gently places the hand, in sorrowful longing, against the clear window barrier that separates her from the child. A miracle, new life. But one that is not to be hers. She watches, bewitched. Her chest heaves with a fiery rawness unlike any she has ever experienced. Time passes imperceptibly. Five minutes, ten, thirty, one hour or more; she is unaware of how much escapes.

Whether it is truth or simply what she imagines, the child is already the very mirror of Shiro's image. Through all of the difficulties, the tears, the heartache, it was all she ever hoped for. For herself. For him. For them both. To keep their marriage alive, to keep their futures bound together. To give her own life meaning, purpose. She cannot help her feeling. She will resent Shiro forever for having succeeded where she has failed. For having what she will not.

But this innocent does not deserve the ugliness of envy. In flashes before her she sees a chubby, gurgling toddler taking first wobbling steps, a shy child posing for a baseball photograph, a teenager with the same grin and sweep of thick hair as her husband.

She pulls her outstretched hand sharply away from the glass, willing a stop to the transferring flood of imagery. Tearing her eyes away from the sleeping infant, Kameko looks down the corridor into the ward. Several women take proud, careful steps toward the nursery viewing area. She is so unlike them. So alone. Joy surrounds them. In a radiant halo. She has no place here, she does not belong. She spins blankly into the open corridor, threads of conversation circle around her:

'Gallbladder. Terrible, the pain…'

'Dr. Kinman said…'

'Four kids, now twins…'

'Biopsy came back positive…heartbroken…'

The cadence of English phrases rise and fall as she blindly pushes her way to the exit. Doors slide open to bathe her in a rush of cool evening air. She takes one slow backward look and begins to run. Away. From the child, from the hospital, from the life that is no longer hers. She runs like she is sure she never has before. In her mind she hears children chant the schoolyard rhyme from so long ago: *Why do you go so slow-slow-slow?* And she promises herself: *I am not the tortoise. I will not be. I will not hide myself in this shell any longer.*

She drags the night into her lungs. Her body is pushing and pumping. She can feel the searing heat of exertion beneath her ribs. Like a jackrabbit fleeing the chase of a fox, her heart pounds. Blinded by misery, gasping and choking, she stumbles with the unevenness of the pavement. To keep *tatemae* is too great a concession. One that she is no longer willing to make. Sharp quills poke into her consciousness. Out of the chaos and confusion, an old saying rises. The words cleave through her, their truth searing and razor sharp: *Fukeba tobu yo na sonzai.* A puff and it is gone.

She is stranded in a sea of holiday festivity. The streets have become very busy. The bookstore too. The guard behind the front desk in the apartment building lobby smiles and greets her by name as she enters. 'Good morning, Mrs. Tanaka.' A Christmas tree, heavy with lights and ornaments, rises up behind him. Today she finds the recognition, and especially the use of her married name, overbearing. He is friendly, as he always is, also making comment about the chill of the winter weather. Maybe he has commented because he sees she is hunched into her scarf and coat. Perhaps he thinks she is cold. She manages no more than a nod.

The face of the double walking quickly with her in mirrored walls to the bank of elevators is tight and pained; a pale image with a pinch of cold spread high in her cheeks. It is the middle of the morning. A 'coffee-break break' Richard has called the timing. Both Richard and Matt have volunteered to help. 'Honey, no offence, but you're not built to sherpa.' With what she hoped had looked a strong smile she had assured them that she would take only a few things, that it would be simpler than they imagined because her case had wheels. Gregory and Aneeta had also offered. Said that they would go with her. Gregory had wondered about Shiro. About his reaction. But she has explained that Shiro will be at work. And since he is not aware of her intentions there is little need for concern. She has tried very hard not to offend by refusing assistance. Today, though, is something that she must do alone.

As the building is home to many city professionals, professionals who by now are peppered at desks in offices throughout the city, she is alone to go up in the elevator. She tries to avoid the disturbed eyes of her twin looking nervously at her from shiny steel as the cubicle climbs swiftly into the sky. Instead, she tells herself that what she is doing is not wrong. It is not the natural thing, that a woman should choose to leave her husband, but in this case she has no doubt it is the right thing. Right for them all.

A growing sense of dread accompanies her to the apartment door. The tortoise in her creeps timidly around the seed of resolve; slowly it nibbles at tender, young edges. Trembling fingers fumble with keys. The sharp sound of the lock turning echoes in the empty hallway. She pushes inward. Bright morning light spills from the wall of windows. The look is the same. The smells are the same. And yet, everything is different.

Like a vine creeper, disharmony had crawled slowly and insistently between she and Shiro, clinging to weakness, rooting in spider-cracks, growing and spreading with each successive disappointment along the way. Until it had become a thriving, choking divide.

She tiptoes across the black marble hallway to the doors that hide the laundry machines and storage cupboard. How convenient she had thought it when they first moved in. For so many things to hide right here. Inside the home. It holds their suitcases. Hers. His. A set of luggage given as a wedding gift. She takes one of the larger cases and returns to the bedroom.

In the closet she gropes blindly through hanging garments. She feels the back wall and lets it guide her until she is able to put her hand to what she seeks. From the narrow top she walks her way down to the hard leather handle and lifts it clear. Sinking into a corner chair she lays the case gently across her lap. She flicks the clasps and opens the lid; the violin lies in a crush of velvet lining. Gingerly, she trails her fingers along the polished wood. She gives a gentle pluck to assess the loss of tune. Then she draws her hand back.

When had she given up? She could not pinpoint it exactly. Details become muddled with years wedged among them. With the lightest touch she lifts the instrument out, as if she does not wish to disturb a slumber. It is smaller than she remembers. But of course, the feel of it depends upon a frame of reference. She was but a child. Nervous anticipation floods her. She worries she might be frustrated if her long dormant technique is lacking. She moves the case to the floor; takes and rosins the bow. For a moment she considers it in her hand. Finally, she lifts the violin and tucks it under her chin. How welcome, the familiar sensation. Beginning with the A string, she adjusts and refines tension. There is no question in her mind about what she wishes to play. Already she can hear it, feel it communicating itself to her fingers. She is longing for the melancholy of Chopin's Nocturne in C-sharp minor. Standing, she moves to the window. Surroundings fall away, as if stroked by a watery brush.

She begins with soft and careful steps, slowly. At first her fingers stumble in their dance with an old friend. But something in her fights. Fights against reserve, against inhibition. Rigidness loosens as instinct threads through. She coaxes the hair of the bow across the strings. How bitterly sweet this reunion. A catch, and for an instant sound is suspended. She hears Sensei in her mind, barking instruction; immerses herself in long ago. Keep moving. Find the place again. Don't give in. Persist. Again, the slow cadence of beginning rises up. She makes it sing to her. And takes from it. She reaches deep into it. Reaches and pulls. The hairs at the base of her neck stand to attention. Gooseflesh stipples her arms and spine. Music spills out of her like blood, in a pained and pulsing tide. Music is an acceptable outlet for *honne*, for the feelings she keeps buried and silent. Fingers are merely a vessel for the deeper message of the notes, a channel for what lies behind the melody. She knows that now. She lets the music take her heart and lay it bare. *You see, Mother, I have it now. I have what was lacking from before. Too late to be the gift you were hoping for, but it has come for me at last. And it plays through me.*

When she finishes the piece her intention is stronger. Lovingly, she returns the instrument to its case. She empties the closet of the rest of her things, stacking them in arbitrary piles in the suitcase. From the other rooms she gathers the last of her belongings. Fragile items she cocoons in clothing. There is a single wedding photograph. The bride looks brightly into Shiro's eyes. His smile is broad. As if she has told a joke. But she is not a joke-teller any more than she is a fortune-teller. Which is why she could not see then that bittersweet happiness would become such heartache. This is the way of fate. One knows with certainty only those things at one's back. The things that have already been. She leaves the picture in its place. Those who stand in it, they are strangers now.

She summons the remains of her courage for what she has decided must be done. In the interests of a child, an innocent. And for herself as well. She leaves the letter on the table in the main room. Where it will surely be seen. When he returns. When that will be she does not know. It is not a matter for her to mind anymore. When he will come, when he will go. What he will say, think, or do.

Toshiro-san,

I write this because I cannot stay silent any longer. I put words on paper to save dignity for us both.

I have tried to be a good wife. Perhaps it was not enough, or perhaps I did not go about it in the right ways. I accept this as my own fault.

My inability to become pregnant has changed me, and, too, has changed our path in this marriage. In my heart I must acknowledge my shortcoming. It is my greatest failing.

I am aware that there is one who has given you the child that I cannot. The child is deserving of a father. And is deserving of none of the complications that will come if I remain in this marriage. And so, I must find some other way of living. For I am not content to exist only as a shadow.

I hope you can forgive such selfishness in me.

Kameko

Turning away, she rolls the wheeled case along the marble hallway, collects the violin, and takes one last look at what remains. She pulls open the heavy black door, holding its weight with her foot, and puts the two pieces into the hallway. Stepping through, she lets the door go. She waits for it to travel the slow weighted arc to closed; to separate yesterday from today. And she wonders at what might lie ahead.

Aneeta
December 2002

It is 11:30, as they have agreed. She stands on the sidewalk by the wharf, before the roadway starts to curve up and away. Shifting from one foot to another in anticipation, she cranes to scan the oncoming tide of people. Chilled fingers hold tightly to a tissue-wrapped copy of Rudyard Kipling's *The Jungle Book*. A favourite of hers. She is terribly nervous. She so wants the child to like her. This child. Living. Breathing. Heart beating. Real. A parallel. With what she has lost.

She keeps her watch intent upon approaching faces. In a blink, an instant, like a trick of magic, he is among them. Familiar features peek between the bobbing sea of strangers. Excitement fills her. The child at his side is too small for her to glimpse yet. He turns his head to look down. Lips moving, he leans. And disappears from her view. When he straightens, he raises a hand into the air to show that he has seen her. She does the same in return. She tries to imagine what might have been said to the boy. Instruction. A review of manners. Reminders of things allowed and things not. Things to say and things not.

As they draw nearer on the sidewalk, bodies part and her desperate eyes finally find him. Slight and fair with golden hair, he is smiling up at his uncle. In the same way the boy in her dreams looks to her father. With a trust, an innocence, a purity of heart and spirit. Her throat catches. She blinks hard. It is not being dreamed, this. The heat of forming tears blurs her vision. She wills them away, furtively wiping at escaped moisture with one hand. She is trembling under the various layers of clothing she wears, and not from cold.

When they are at last face-to-face, Neil reaches out and touches her arm lightly in greeting. Then he looks to the boy at his side. 'Max, I'd like you to meet Aneeta.'

'How d'you do?' says a little-boy voice full of adult seriousness. With solemnity, he offers a mittened hand.

She can't help but laugh, though she might just as easily have cried. Crouching, she gently takes the mitten into her own lonely, wanting hand. 'I'm very well, thank you. I'm terribly pleased to meet you, Max.' She gives it what she thinks might be considered an appropriate number of shakes before reluctantly letting it go. 'I've heard so much about you from your uncle.' With both hands, she extends the blue tissue package and smiles into hazel green eyes with the same golden flecks as his uncle. 'I've brought something for you.'

'For me? You did?'

'Yes, I did.' She looks up at a grinning Neil.

'Oh boy, Uncle Neil!' His eyes widen at her and, gift in hand, he turns to his uncle.

'What do you say, Max?'

'I *like* her, Uncle Neil! I like her already, I do.'

Aneeta looks to one side and bites her lip to keep from laughing.

'Max,' he chuckles, 'what do you say when someone gives you a gift?'

'Oh, I forgot.' The boy looks suddenly sheepish. 'Thank you.'

'You are most welcome. I hope you like it.'

'Can I open it now?' he asks.

'Of course.'

'Whoa, whoa, whoa! Hold on a minute, buddy. Why don't we wait till we're in the car? Then you can open it.'

'Oh Max,' Aneeta nods, 'that sounds like a wise idea. Let's do that, shall we?'

'K. K, Aneeta. Let's go! C'mon, c'mon,' he urges, 'me'n Uncle Neil wanna take you to lunch. Let's go!' He reaches a woollen hand to claim her own.

Over a little boy's carefully slicked hair, their eyes meet. And her heart jumps with a rhythm that is entirely new.

'We're gonna look at the crabs and lobsters. Uncle Neil said we can look at them in their tanks. Have you ever seen them? Do you like crabs and lobsters? C'mon, c'mon! Follow me! Let me show you.' A golden-haired imp tugs at her attentions and her heartstrings. It is impossible to resist the contagious lightness of his enthusiasm. 'So see, the fishermen? The fishermen on the fish boats? They take out their traps in the morning. The traps are like wire baskets. And they put them in the ocean and let them sink way down. And look what they catch. Just look, Aneeta!' Max gestures wildly and proudly in front of the great tank in the entrance of the restaurant, taking obvious pleasure in the moment. Mirth is unmistakable in Neil's eyes.

'Wow! That is...well, it's amazing, Max.' She looks for words. Little boy words. She is totally inexpert in such ability. 'D'you think that these crawly creatures just creep right into the baskets when they see the traps lowered?' Aneeta watches the hard shells try to clamber one over another, as if they suddenly know their fate. Out of the darkness and into the world above. For such a short time.

'I think they get like the big *splaaaassshh!* and they see, like, this shine coming down at them? And maybe, maybe they wonder where it's from, and they say, hey, I wanna go there, I wanna try it! Like an elevator, except with no buttons. And then it's like uh-oh, too late!' He is jubilant and bouncing. The creatures behind the glass are heaped up at his back. 'Youuu'rrrre lllluuunchhhhh!' She cannot help laughing.

'Okay, okay. I think Aneeta gets the idea, Max. So how about that lunch? Max, are you ready for lunch?'

'Lunch, lunch. Yup. Let's have lunch. So after we can go fly kites at the *beeeeeach!*'

For Max, lunch is fingers of fish and french fried potatoes with a wash of tomato ketchup. Neil encourages her to join him in the crab, which arrives at their table on a large oval platter, legs arranged on either side of a now detached red-orange back. 'Can I keep the shell, Uncle Neil? Can I?'

'I don't think Mom would be too impressed if I brought you home with a fishy-smelling treasure, would she? How about you have a play with it now, instead?'

When he sees the way her hands clumsily attempt to manipulate the entirely foreign utensils he asks, 'You've never done this before?'

'What this?' She lifts a leg jokingly, and Max giggles. 'No, never.' So much of this she's not done before. Her admission is an umbrella truth.

'Why don't you let me? We don't want you going hungry. You're going to need your energy for running the beach. Max here's an ace kite-flyer. Aren't you, Max?' With his mouth stuffed under chill-rouged rounds, Max nods vigorously, his eyes bulging. Neil cracks and shells the crab for her unpractised hands. Pulling free thick and tender morsels, he generously douses them in lemon. There is an air of intimacy about the way he shares it out that makes her self-conscious. He serves her far more than he eats himself and so she starts to protest the continuing offering. 'Good?' he inquires.

'Mmm,' she manages by way of an answer, 'delicious. But you need to eat as well. You wouldn't want Max and I to outrun you.'

'Yeah, Uncle Neil. You don't want to get beat by a *girl!*' His tone is so full of horror at the possibility that both she and Neil laugh heartily at it.

'Well, I wouldn't want to completely sacrifice my dignity.' Outside, the gulls shriek and rollick at the prospect. 'But, Max, I've got to tell you, buddy, sometimes the girls are going to win. And that's good too.' Max nods sagely at his uncle's grown-up advice.

Aneeta tries to contemplate the scene in which she is fixed. She can feel the warmth, the fullness, the rightness of the portrait. The incredible sense of agreement between the three bodies. The feeling that she belongs. Here. Now. She would never have believed it, had it once been suggested to her. And yet. Somehow it feels as if she's spent her entire life inching toward this very moment.

The sky is a bland wash of winter blue. The water is dotted with sharp white triangles leaning into the bite of the wind. The air is perfectly accommodating for kite-flying. A little boy's legs zig and zag the uneven pathway. Amid logs and stones in water-washed disarray. Laughter carries on the curling gusts. Six cheeks are stained tingling red. A green-skinned, pipehorn-eared ogre and toothy donkey grimace down on them with red-blue-black streamers waving.

'Don't you know *Shrek*, Aneeta?'

'I'm afraid I don't, Max.'

He sings in looping circles, 'He's *soooooo* funny!' Thighs and knees and feet pump. In furious motion. To help guide the path, the Shrek path, along the stairway to the heavens. String is unraveled and unknotted and rewound and tugged. Hands touch. Eyes meet. Grey and green. Green to grey. 'Are you having fun, Aneeta? Uncle Neil says if you have fun you might want to come out with us again.'

'Am I? Why, Max, this is the most fun I can remember having in such a very long time. I would love to come out with you again. In fact, I can't imagine anything nicer.'

The little boy beams at her.

Who runs the fastest in the back and forth along the sandy slope turns out not to matter at all. But when a little boy happens to stumble, losing his footing over a length of driftwood, a childless and lonely once almost-mother rushes to his side. To brush a pair of knees, to tenderly wipe away his tears and to receive, in wonder, the tight embrace of two small arms. Arms whose size belies their altogether surprising strength. In that single moment, in that perfect embrace between woman and child, it is as though wholeness and order are righted within her. And her soul trembles with joy.

When it is time for bed, with shreds of tissue discarded all around, she reads from the book she has gifted—at Max and his uncle's insistence—the story of Mowgli the man-cub. As she does, one pair of hazel green eyes yield finally to sleep. And so she whispers the end of the tale: *'Hsh! He is asleep. We will not wake him, for his strength is very great. The kites have come down to see it. The black ants have come up to know it. And there is a great assembly in his honour.'*

Gregory
December 2002

The card is simple. A ribbon of red around the edges, beside it a thinner ribbon of silver. At the center is an abstract form of an evergreen tree. Inside it there's no over-the-top sentiment. It's just not in her to put herself out there like summer laundry on the line. She cares, sure. She knows it. They know it.

The whole thing makes for strange and hot debate in her. They've been patient with her excuses, but since her release there's a silent expectation hanging on. She can sense it. And there isn't much of anything she can lean on to excuse herself anymore.

She feels a certain obligation. Perfectly natural, Doc Gedge says, at this time of year. Though the good doc won't steer one way or the other. Sometimes it makes her want to scream. His unwillingness to say right or wrong, to tell her do or don't. The decisions have to be your own, he says. Made in your own time. And on this one, she's copping out.

Truth is, there's a niggling inside telling her she isn't ready to face them, Mama and Lil. Nobody's fault and nobody's doing. It's a silent tide, curling and pulling just under the surface, the ghost of him, Curtis, that she's not feeling strong enough to deal with.

She's picked up a packet of notepaper for writing a message to explain. Or at least to try and put her feelings into words. She'll include it with the card. Hopefully, they'll understand. When she slides a sheet of paper from the tight plastic skin, it makes a clean, clear sound. The smooth blankness of it jars her. She looks up and into the pitch of roofline above her. There is a hollow tick of plastic from the tapping of the pen against her cheek. She worries it's going to be a hard pull. Getting to the words she needs.

She imagines Mama reading. Lil reading. They're both going to see and hear her different. Then they're going to combine it all, like mixing up a cake. She lets a big exhale into the quiet and offers up a silent plea—please, Turner, let the classes have been good for something. The best she can do is be honest. She brushes the back of a hand across the empty white and squints at it. Then she puts the pen tip to paper and begins.

Dear Mama and Lil,

I guess seeing how Christmas is sneaking up you both are getting ready. We're taking orders for mince pies here, but Gerry says that San Francisco is not a mince-loving city, so we expect numbers to be small. Apparently, though, her shortbread has quite a reputation, so I imagine it'll more than compensate for a lack of interest in mince.

You may be a little surprised at getting a holiday card from me. Mainly it's because I have to confess that I am truly afraid of stepping wrong between us. I feel a little like I'm walking a path of eggshells. I just really don't want to hurt you, either of you, with what I say or do. And I'm worried sick that I will screw things up. Writing to you lets me think about what needs saying and what's the best way of putting it. Plus, it lets me get it all down at once. It's one-sided, I know. But maybe it's better since you both get the whole of it, all the same bits. You've got it all there in black and white, for considering.

Here goes, the best that I can get it out, the things I feel I have to say—

Sometimes I can't even believe you would want to set eyes on me again after everything. And I have to also be honest and tell you—you, Mama, especially— that I can't be sorry for what I did. I've got to make absolutely sure you know that. Because it's probably the biggest part that will figure into how we try and make peace with the past.

I know you never said one way or the other, but I got the feeling that you might've been thinking I would come for Christmas. Maybe I'm mistaken. If I am, I hope you'll forgive me. But if my feeling is right, then I wanted to tell you that I don't feel ready. I've come to the realization that I've got to get things right with me first. That's what I'm working on every single day, but I didn't bargain on how hard it would be, or all the hang-ups that would come with being free.

All I'm asking is that you please be patient with me. That you not be thinking I don't want to see you both, because I do. A little like the sketch on the front of the card, there are bits I'm still missing, bits I need to get in place to make me complete. Whole. So that I can be sure I'll be strong enough. Then I will come. If you decide you want me to.

Gregory

Kameko
December 2002

Night swirls like ink. Thick and viscous. As if painted out of a calligraphy pot. Tonight she is part hostess, part planner, part geisha. Waiting to entertain.

She wears a kimono for the occasion. They have asked. *Did she have one? Would she consider wearing it?* To add to the *cachet* Richard had said. The robe is emerald green with a patterning of white and silver blossoms. The accents are red and gold. It is a lighter weight silk. More a springtime garment. But here it will not be noticed. Her thicker kimono is of a vivid blue with fuchsia and orange-gold accents in the form of a trail of whimsical carp. But it seemed altogether too bright for such an event, and too girlish. The only other of her collection is her wedding kimono. It had hurt to see it in the case, but she had tried, as much as was possible, to ignore the pull of the past, to instead focus on the party ahead.

She has often been told that her form is a good one for traditional garments; that she is shaped much like a stick of bamboo. Tonight, though, she takes liberty in the way she dresses, to allow for greater freedom. She does not wrap the gown as tight, nor tie the obi as high as is customary. The adjustments she makes are in the interests of comfort. And she realizes that for the first time she is molding tradition to *her* desires and not the other way around.

Forgoing traditional tabi socks and wooden geta footwear, she has instead chosen a pair of high, dark sandals with straps that cross and hug at her heels. Her hair is pulled into a bun at the nape of her neck. The shorter layers closest to her face are unwilling to be held, and they escape in loose wisps to frame her face. At the top of the bun she slides a comb decorated with tiny white blossoms. She has lined her eyes in black and drawn the outline of her lips in red. As a final preparation she paints in a similar but lighter shade of red lipstick. She has not applied traditional white makeup, choosing to maintain her natural skin tone, lightening it only with a little bit of face powder.

As for the demands of the evening ahead, she cannot say whether her greater involvement has been incidental or by design, but she is glad of the distraction it has offered. She knows enough of the efficient way that Richard and Matt manage their business to have been slightly suspect at their reliance upon her as the night had edged closer. Whatever the matter, she was grateful to have been absorbed in attending to many of the final details for them. It is a small offering on her part. Given all they have done for her.

It is already busy in the store when she finally steps out of the room she occupies. That, for the moment, she lives in. Black-shirted and bow-tied waiters move elegantly with trays through the wooden maze she looks down upon. It takes only a moment for Richard to notice her standing there. He gives a low whistle. 'Matt c'mere,' he beckons. 'Come check this out.'

'Oh my God! Can it not wait? I'm trying to get these napkins to fan. There has got to be an easier way!'

She begins down the steps, holding the rail with one hand and a fist of silk with the other in order to keep from stumbling.

'No, Matt, look at Kameko. How incredible!'

He spins to see her. 'Wow, honey! You are breathtaking! Oh my God, where's the camera? Richard, did you remember the camera?'

She has forgotten the way a compliment can make her feel. Like a flower in the sun, she basks in the glow of their attention. 'Thank you. You are very kind.'

'Uh, camera?' Richard is holding the camera high with one hand on his hip.

'Oh, thank God!' Matt sighs with relief, his hand to his chest. 'Where was it?'

'In your satchel. Behind the desk. With all the other goodies you'll no doubt be looking frantically for at some point this evening.'

'But that's why I have you, babe. You keep me organized. On the narrow, if not the straight,' he laughs. 'Excuse me, handsome?' Matt motions to one of the black shirted waiters, 'Would you mind getting a picture of us?' To Kameko he says, 'Wow, he's cute. Don't you think he's cute?'

'Stop flirting with the help,' Richard advises gruffly.

'I'm just having a little fun with him is all. He knows it's just a bit of fun.'

The young waiter smiles engagingly and indulgently raises the camera. He looks at them from the screen at the back. '1...2...3...happy holidays!' he coaxes.

'Happy holidays!' both men chorus back. There is a burst of flash, and the young man moves forward, handing the camera back.

'I can help to arrange your napkin fans,' Kameko volunteers.

'Oh, you're such a sweetheart. I just don't have that kind of patience. Mine look like leftovers from some ticker tape parade.'

She laughs. 'I am happy to do it.' She looks appraisingly about the room with a quiet sense of pride. It does indeed look festive. Decorations of silver, gold and green give the ordinarily rough-hewn feel of the shop a look of elegant sophistication. She takes small steps as she moves, conscious of how the kimono limits her stride.

Another black-shirted young man is stacking glassware on the opposite end of the table. As Kameko begins to re-group and adjust the arcs of coloured paper she can feel his eyes on her, but she does not look up. She can hear Matt behind her somewhere. 'It had to be black, so it didn't interrupt the colour theme. White isn't uniform enough, it has a tendency to look yellow. And at this time of year, my God, we all look so pale! Besides,' he laughs, 'I'm not sure how many of these boys even know what bleach is.'

'So what do you call that ...uh, outfit you're wearing?' the voice at the other end of the table asks.

'It is a kimono.'

'Are you one of those…what do they call it? Geisha?' He says it gee-shaw.

'No, I am not geisha,' she says with a smile, pronouncing the word in the correct way.

'Did they get you from an agency?'

'Excuse me? An agency?'

'Will you stop distracting the help, Kameko?' Matt has moved in to where she is standing. 'Don't be looking to get busy on my time, little boy beefcake.'

'I'm sorry.'

'Um-hmm, you should be. Don't you have a tray you should be filling?'

'Yes, of course.' With that, the young man steps away.

'I love it!' Matt enthuses. 'Kameko, that looks so much better.'

She shakes her head mildly, 'Only small adjustments I have made. Almost nothing.'

'I definitely prefer the way you kept the colours blocky. It's a huge improvement on my psychedelic kaleidoscope. In other words, my mess.'

'I think to keep similar colours together makes them look stronger.'

'Absolutely,' he nods, 'and, I have to say, it's amazing because even *you* fit in with the colour theme tonight.'

'There is a theme to the colours you have chosen?'

'Silver, gold, green—It's for the money, honey. It's *our* personal Christmas wish. And for the store. Obviously, for the store. Without the store doing well *we* won't be in the moola. Can't have one without the other.' Again he laughs, his mood is high. 'Plus, I really do have to say, you've been so good for us.'

She gives a small bow. 'It makes me happy that you think so.'

He scans the room, the high wood-beamed ceiling, the green wreaths along the windowline, the gold and silver painted antique glass accents, the large globes that hang on fishing wire over their heads. His delight is akin to a child's. 'I can't wait to see people's reactions. I don't think we've ever had such a incredible looking Christmas soirée. It's you, honey, you're the difference this year. You've made everything so beautiful. Obviously, we needed your touch.'

'Oh, but you are too kind, really. I thank you, but I am simply an extra pair of hands.'

Richard raises a champagne glass as he joins them. 'Are we ready? It's showtime! Marco,' he motions to yet another young man dressed in black, but who also wears a tuxedo tailcoat and white cotton gloves, 'is ready at the door.'

'Marco.' Matt puts his hand to heart and sighs, 'Of course. How could I have not known he'd be Italian?'

'I feel like I should be clapping and saying, *Places everyone! Places!*'

'You are such an eighties TV junkie. But FYI? I'm no small man in white, and I don't do sidekick. Something written into my contract. Hey, I've got it! Our super-hunk Marco's given me a great idea.'

'Of course he has.'

'Oh, don't be so catty. It's on account of his Italian roots. Next year let's add in some purple and take it to a Venetian theme. Masquerade. We'll get all the boys dressed as Renaissance clowns. In tights, with a harlequin look. Now that would be a thing of beauty.' He sighs wistfully.

'Yeah,' Richard rolls his eyes at his partner, 'save your money.'

'Oh don't be such a killjoy! Besides,' he pauses, grinning, 'I could be your masked mystery lover.'

'All right, okay!' Richard throws his hands up in mock surrender, 'But please, let's get through tonight first.'

'Can you just imagine the suspense, the tension, the drama, when masked eyes meet across a crowded room? I know. I'm a diva. But you love me.'

She admires their wit and comfortable joviality. Their affection. A small sentiment of sadness creeps in, but she pushes it away.

She has invited Gregory this evening to come as her guest. Such a solitary personality, Gregory. And a character that recalls so much of Akira. She finds a comfort in the similarity. It is strange, the way of fate, drawing her to this woman.

She recalls on the day of her wedding, she and Shiro standing side by side on the bridge in the park. In posing for a photograph they had been directed to gaze at the tableau of their faces joined in the water's reflection. But the flow of a small incoming stream had rippled and distorted the image, because the water would never quite still. Now, she cannot help but feel that this is the very nature of life itself. Like water, it shifts and changes constantly.

People spill into the store and thread through the aisles. Laughter and conversation swirl and spin, wrapped in silken jazz music; sultry instruments and velvet voices. The waiters, like black-suited soldiers, turn briskly through the room, with all the precision of a carefully choreographed dance.

She tries to busy herself, but cannot resist the temptation to keep watch as Marco admits arriving guests. Many comment on her dress, exclaiming how lovely she looks. Some ask after the traditions of Japan, or inquire as to the significance of the ornament in her hair, the detailing on her robes, the difficulty of wearing such a gown. She is very flattered at the interest.

As time passes, she wonders about Gregory. She finds herself becoming preoccupied with silent speculation. Perhaps something has happened to prevent her attending. Or perhaps she has been too forward in extending the invitation. Or perhaps, Kameko thinks, her sense about Gregory has been wrong entirely. Is she imagining something that does not exist in a desire to make it so?

Richard sidles over to her then and winks, 'Hon, there's a pretty little carp out of water at the door for you. I don't think she'll come any further unless you bait a hook and reel her in. Our stallion of a doorman is getting a bit touchy. The way she's standing there, her body language is threatening to haul off and hit him if he so much as tries to suggest that she shift herself by moving any further into the room. I don't want to see blood. Especially not from a wound on *his* gorgeous face. Can you please rescue her? Please? To rescue him.'

She almost stumbles in her haste. She cannot keep the smile from her lips. It is true that Marco and Gregory look very much like two fighters squared off and waiting for the bell to sound. 'Gregory! Gregory!' she calls out with a wave. The recognition of Kameko's voice prompts her to turn to it. She is beautiful, Kameko thinks. Her hair is slicked back and fastened in place with a large black clip. She wears wide-legged black trousers and an elegant satin vest.

Reaching her side, Kameko links her arm in Gregory's and leans in to whisper, 'I think the doorman, Marco, is afraid of you.' She giggles. 'But I am glad to see you. That you could come. I very much like your outfit,' she says. 'It suits you, this style. And your hair is very pretty. We must have a picture together, I think. Just a moment, I will find my boss, he has a camera to take a picture for us. Come this way.'

'Whoa! No, no, no.' Gregory shakes her head emphatically. 'Pictures, they're not my thing,' she protests. 'I mean, you? You look amazing. But I'd rather not be in any photo.'

'But this is a special occasion. It is not often that we dress in such fancy things. Please.' She steers in small steps toward where Richard and Matt are. A smiling waiter offers champagne. 'This will help you to at least make a smile for a picture. *Kanpai!*'

'*Kanpai*,' Gregory says, reluctantly sipping and making a face.

When Kameko touches Richard on the shoulder, he and Matt excuse themselves from the group of guests they have been chatting among. 'I would like to introduce my friend, Gregory Abbott. And these are the hosts, my bosses, Matthew-san and Richard-san. They say I cannot use their last names because it makes them feel old.' She bows deeply.

'Great party,' Gregory says.

'Glad you could make it,' Matt says.

'Well, I'm glad you spared Marco,' Richard jokes.

With a backward glance toward the door Gregory says, 'He seemed a little uptight.'

'It's probably because you have a cooler outfit than he does.'

'And the hair—very Josephine Baker. I love it.' Matt turns to Richard, 'Is her hair not just like Josephine Baker's? On the cover of the Entertainers book we've got?'

'Excuse me, Richard-san, but I wanted to ask if you would take a photo for us?'

'Hon, I'd love to. The two of you look gorgeous together. Real yin and yang.' He shoos them with his hand, 'Stand over there, under the mistletoe.'

'Mistletoe?' Kameko asks.

'See it over there, the ball of waxy green leaves? Matt, let's show the girls what to do under the mistletoe. It's my favourite holiday tradition.'

'My pleasure to demonstrate. So, stand here like this, right underneath, and the person closest—who, by sheer genius design, is Richard—gets a great big kiss.' With that he takes Richard's face in his two hands a gives him a loud and flirtatious kiss on the lips. 'Your turn, Kameko!'

With some protest from Gregory, Kameko pulls her under the plant and leans in to kiss her. They both are still laughing at the spectacle of Richard and Matt before them. Intending a quick, lighthearted indulgence, Kameko is shocked at the seriousness that takes over as their lips meet. Frivolity disappears and her heart flutters wildly. Electricity burns through her. As she pulls away, Richard and

Matt are whooping and clapping. What must surely be a vivid blush flames at her cheeks. The kiss remains, in a lingering sweetness, on her lips.

'Stay cozy. Just like that. Beautiful!'

'Kameko, what do Japanese say when they pose for pictures?' Matt asks.

'We say *cheezu*!'

'Both of you say *cheezu*!'

Kameko laughs at his silliness. She gives Gregory's hand a squeeze. The camera freezes the moment. One that is hopeful and happy. And she knows that the expression she wears is not a mask.

Richard looks down at the small frame. 'Perfect!'

'You see?' Kameko laughs, 'It was not so difficult was it?'

'Cheezu? How corny is that?'

'That is what we say.' Kameko shrugs, trying to look serious.

'Who wouldn't crack a grin?'

'I am glad to be the one to make you smile.'

It is as midnight approaches that Kameko asks Richard if he can excuse her. 'Of course, hon, of course. Go! My God, you've been worth your weight in gold tonight. Skedaddle! We'll see you when we see you.'

Arm in arm they walk, as a pair of schoolgirls might. Against the chill of winter air, Kameko leans into Gregory. Suddenly, a cry cuts through the darkness; hard-edged guttural bites snap syllables like a brittle stick in autumn, 'Ka-me-ko!' She knows the voice instantly. The thick-throated uprising cadence in tone suggests drink. Panic spikes and she freezes. Gregory turns. Toward them, with an unsteady gait, moves the tuxedoed form of Shiro. He crosses into and out of lamplight circles and shadow. 'My, you look so…traditional, Kameko. And here I thought that the ways of home no longer flowed in your blood.'

Kameko can see that the path his feet choose for him is not straight. 'Shiro, you are drunk!'

In defiance he spits on the sidewalk, and then, silent for a moment, he regards them both. His eyes narrow and glint in the sphere of the street lamp. When he speaks next, it is in Japanese. With his tongue he excises Gregory from his confrontation. 'And you, Kameko, are only able to see the obvious when it stands immediately before your eyes. But I have to wonder, what is it that *I* am seeing here?' He motions his hand at them, 'What exactly is *this*?'

'What do you want, Shiro?' She hears herself waver.

'I want what any man in my position would want. A little help, dear wife, to figure out what is between you two.'

'I don't understand.'

He snaps acidly into the darkness, 'Of course you understand. You understand perfectly well.' His voice thins to a hiss, 'I saw you.'

'What?'

'At the party. With my own eyes, I saw. How…friendly you were, how cozy. Oh yes, but I had almost forgotten about your friend, what was her name? Akira, I think it was. Didn't she hang herself…for you? I hadn't known that *your*…interests…tended that way as well. I wonder, is this the cause for your recent convictions? Is your latest *girlfriend* responsible for your decision to leave?' His words are edged with malice. His lips are stretched thin, revealing the points of teeth. She is reminded of a snarling dog, the way he looks.

Though Gregory cannot understand his words, she has stepped her body between them, her shoulder is in front of Kameko as a divide, a physical interruption of the open space. A gesture at once both protective and possessive. While Gregory is smaller than he, her position is one of challenge. For a woman, it is a surprising posture. A stand of strength. Against his intimidation. But Kameko can also feel the way Gregory's body has stiffened.

'You think I do not know of you? How you spend your time? Where you study? What you do?' He snorts his contempt. 'You are my wife. It is my right. No,' he stamps his foot, producing an emphatic crack, 'it is my responsibility. Because of how it can make me look. I have told you of the importance. I have told you of my desires. As far as my career. My intentions for this post. You agreed with them. Once.' His voice is bitter. 'I will not suffer for your foolishness. I will not allow it.

'I can see,' he jerks a thumb in the direction of Gregory and she catches, with his movement, the sweet scent of alcohol, 'the kinds of things you have been doing. You have lost yourself. And your place. America has re-made you. It does not suit you, I do not think. You even choose your words in English.' His bark is one of scorn. 'One would have hoped you had more modesty than that.'

'I have nothing to hide,' Kameko cries angrily, 'that my friend should not know.'

'My mother always said you thought too much of yourself. I told her I needed a woman with something of a brain. Some thoughts of her own. She warned of the delicacy of such a balance. The educational leanings you favoured she felt were too great. That they were a mark contrary to a more favourable personality in a wife. And I ignored her caution. It pains me that she has been right.' His dark eyes flash, telegraphing anger. He pokes his finger like a sword through the air to emphasize his point, 'It is you, your blame to bear. But this?' His hand slices the air angrily in warning, 'I will not let you disgrace me.'

'I disgrace *you*?'

'I have my reputation to think of!'

'Were you thinking of your reputation when you made your co-worker pregnant?' His features rearrange themselves at the boldness of her accusation. 'What would you have me do? Curl up and die? To save your face? Your honour? What about my own? I am finished with posing for your honour! What is more, if you persist, I will come to your office and say as much. To the faces of your superiors. I will say it loudly enough so that all hear more than just the whispers that creep around on timid insect legs.'

'You would not dare.'

'And why not? Can we not then both be measured by the same stick?'

'You will not speak a word to tarnish my reputation. You are far too meek for such threats.' His eyes narrow cruelly.

Kameko is trembling. With anger and fear and cold. But she does not want to appear weak. To withdraw like the tortoise. She is determined not to give in. Whether she feels something in the current of words, a shift, Gregory chooses the moment to interrupt, 'Listen, it's been great catching up like this, but we're going to be on our way.'

In a return to English, Shiro sneers, 'What makes you think that I was quite finished talking with my wife?'

'Well, unlike you, I'm getting the message that Kameko is more than done here. So,' Gregory asserts meaningfully, 'we are going to turn around and walk away, whether or not you've finished. Got me?'

'You think you are funny?'

'I'm not trying to be funny. I'm being polite. Now, as I was saying, we are done. Through. Going.' Headlights wash over them. A car slows, passes by.

'This is not finished, Kameko, between you and I.'

Tears threaten as she raises her voice up in anguish against him, 'It has to be finished! There is no way to change things. Don't you see? For the choices you've made. That I cannot bear to live with. And for the child. You have chosen first, and that has left me no choice. It is better for us all. So let me be! Please! It is all I ask.'

Gregory encircles Kameko's shoulders, drawing her in. 'Come on,' she urges, and, turning away from Shiro, they begin to walk. Kameko has to take two steps to match every one of Gregory's. She strains her ear but cannot hear footsteps following. Their pace quickens as they move toward the flashing lights at the corner crossing. She is on tiptoe to keep up the tempo. She does not let herself look back. Just before the corner they slip into a narrow walkway between buildings.

Gregory peers out and back down the avenue, the way they have come. Traffic is thin given the late hour. Kameko squeezes her eyes tightly shut. 'He's not out there, not coming. Coast is clear.' Gregory tries for lightness, but panic still buzzes through her. 'Hey. Hey? Look at me, Kameko. It's okay. He's gone.' She lets herself collapse weakly against Gregory. 'Sorry, these last few blocks have never seemed like such a long way.'

'I am afraid it is the fault of my robe and foolish shoes.'

'Now I'm thinking it would have been smarter just to have let you call a taxi.'

'You were not to know. You could not have known.' Both of them edge around the unpleasantness of what has taken place. 'Even I would never have expected this.' She shakes her head. 'Thank you.'

'For what?'

'For helping me.' Kameko attempts a smile.

'But I didn't do anything.'

'Just by being here, my arm in yours, it helped me to be strong enough not to hide from the truth. But to face it. That has always been the hardest thing in my life.' Kameko touches her fingertips lightly to Gregory's cheek. Gregory does not pull away. They study each other quietly, intently, as if this is the very first time that they are seeing one another. Truly seeing. With hearts as opposed to minds. It is barely more than a whisper when she speaks next, 'I am very grateful. To you.' Desire has fired in her, from some unknown place, and it is blazing a trail of longing, of need. Hungrily, but so very tenderly, her lips seek out those of her protector. She can feel the rush of her blood, the pulse of it heavy and thick. The sensation of the kiss is at first questioning, soft and careful. Then, as a bud gives itself to the spring, it opens into something full and unguarded and ripe. When at last she pulls away, tears slide slowly down her cheeks.

'What? What's wrong? I don't understand.' Gregory's voice is husky and low.

'It is not wrong,' Kameko manages, in a half-sobbed laugh. 'It is, at last, right.' Together under the dark blanket of night they cling to one another. Where her ear rests she can hear the echo of another heart. One that shares the rhythm of her own.

Aneeta
December 2002

Panic runs fleet-footed through her as he leans in. Like a monsoon flood, in seconds it has risen up to overrun the banks of self-control. He must sense the change, her sudden hesitation. He draws back. Shadows close in. 'I...I just...' she shakes her head. Old nightmares tighten around her like a coiled serpent. Reasserting a claim. Reminding her of the power of the dark.

What must he think? I am weak. And needy. That he has made a mistake, misplaced his affection. I am soiled and dirty. He is wrong to care. It is a mistake. Despair has made her its puppet, pulling at every part of her. Fingernails dig deeply, bitterly, into palm flesh. There is no escaping the need for explanation now. But what can be told? What? Without risking everything. Her face burns. Skin pulls tight against her cheeks. There is an insistent throbbing ache at the back of her skull. She wishes she could simply close her eyes and escape. All along she has known that at some point truth would have to interfere.

'Aneeta,' he whispers in the semi-dark. Candle flame flickers. Beyond the windows streetlamp halos glow. She fixes her concentration on the warm light they cast. 'Was it something I...have I done something? Something wrong? To offend you?' For a time they sit in silence. She does not trust herself to speak. Instead, she bites at trembling lips and tries to swallow pain away. To hold the tightness back. To keep it squeezed within her chest. She shakes her head mutely, numbly, in response.

'Can I?' He motions at the physical distance between them. She can only nod. He eases himself slowly closer to her, stopping at intervals to test her permissions, her reaction to his nearness. It is, the thought occurs, a bit like a man might approach a wild animal, inching cautiously toward it, trying to gauge its trust. She longs to tell him that it is not his fault, that it is her defect, that she can never be worthy of somebody like him. That much he should know.

Though they are not touching, he is seated close enough that she can feel the heat of him escaping, melting into her. It is madness for her to have thought, dreamed, that things could have been different. At last, he speaks into the trembling electric air in front of him, 'I want to help.' His throat catches and breaks slightly on the word help, bringing it out with more depth. 'I want to know. From the very first time I laid eyes on you, I could see it. Something in the way you carried yourself. It pulled at me. So proud, so beautiful, but in your eyes, the message is so...full of pain. You're like this wounded, fragile bird. Let me help. Please.' A warm hand settles on her frigid and tightly interlocked pair. A gentle reassurance, it takes her by surprise. A candlelight mirage trembles and dances in her blurring vision. His arm circles her shoulders, tenderly pulling her to him, 'Let me help. Please.' She collapses willingly, wantingly, into the warmth of his embrace. 'It's okay, Aneeta. I'm here. I'm here and I'm not going anywhere.'

Lines, boundaries, separation dissolve. She tries to convince herself that tomorrow does not matter. That the cold, steely edges of reality are irrelevant. That for right now, just for this single hourglass grain, she chooses to believe the arms that hold her are those of love.

He does not move, does not shift away. He lets her cling to him and cry herself dry. When she has finally calmed, he whispers through her hair, so she can feel the heat of his breath, 'Can I make you a cup of tea? I think I have something herbal.' She pulls away from where she has left a wide halo of damp on his shirt. In the dimness of the dying candlelight she looks up to study the outline of his face. She cannot discern the set of his features. She wants to laugh. To laugh, and at the same time to cry. Tears, this time, of an entirely different nature. For this turn of fate. Who is this man? A man who has let a woman wring her heart out, a woman he hardly knows, a woman who has yet to offer a single word of explanation. A man now offering to fix her tea? What kind of man?

'You have herbal tea?' Her sound is nasal and raw.

'As a matter of fact, I do. I confess I don't often drink it, though I do happen to know all about its many virtues thanks in large part to Charlotte, who stocks it in my cupboards.' Taking her hands in his, he draws her up and leads her into the light of the kitchen. He settles her on a stool and walks to flick a switch on the kettle.

'I must look a mess.' Embarrassed, she wipes where tears have soaked her skin, at what she imagines is a face of smeared kohl tracks. She tries to coax a smile. Lips quiver at the strain of the effort.

'You most certainly do not. You look beautiful, as always.' His smile at her is easy, though she can read sympathy in his expression.

'I'm sorry for spoiling the evening.'

'I don't consider it spoiled. Regardless of what you may think. I got to know you a little bit better, which, if you remember, is exactly what I told you I wanted.'

She forces a half laugh, 'I'm sure it wasn't at all what you expected.'

'I'm not sure it's wise to have expectations. As far as I'm concerned there is nothing to be sorry for, so stop feeling bad.' His look is earnest.

'But I've behaved altogether terribly,' her voice catches, 'especially after you'd gone to so much trouble.'

'So what? You think that you owed me something? Is that what you think? This evening was all about the enjoyment of each other's company. Pure and simple. Just you being here was enough for me.' The kettle begins to whine and he turns his attention to the making of tea; he rummages through cupboard contents. 'As it happens, I've got chamomile, peppermint and jasmine. What be your preference, m'lady?'

'Oh dear. That sounds far too proper.'

'Okay, so pick one. What flavour wins your favour?'

'Jasmine, please.'

He pours the tea too early. She wouldn't dream of saying so, but it makes her smile ever so slightly. She folds her hands around the cup. They sit opposite one another. She is surprised how much larger the kitchen seems than on the evening of the Thanksgiving party. The countertop is a disarray of foil tins and cardboard covers. All the spoils of Italian takeaway. A wine cork lies idly alongside the remains of the breadbasket. There is a companionable silence between them, even though she feels shy in it.

The eventual sound of his voice breaking through the quiet startles her. 'The woman you wrote about? The washerwoman? She's you, isn't she?' His tone is gentle, soft. 'That kind of passion doesn't come through in writing unless there's authenticity to it, unless it's been lived.'

He knows. Not the details. But the outline. Isn't it what she had intended? To reveal herself, in a sort of abstract parallel? To test his reaction? And yet she can't help but worry that his knowing is already more than enough. To drive him away. She concentrates her gaze on the pale liquid in her cup. What comes next?

Again, he speaks. And saves her. 'I'm not trying to push. When you share, whatever it is you decide you want to share, I hope you'll do it because you trust me. Nothing you tell me will change the way I feel. But I want to know. To help. Okay? And, just so you know we're on equal footing with the whole thing, anything you might want to know about me, anything you want to ask, I'll tell. Any details, anything.' He is smiling encouragingly at her. At *her*. Is it possible? 'I'm happy to start things off. Get the ball rolling. I realize I'm about to thoroughly embarrass myself. Uh, okay, where to begin? At the beginning, I suppose. Born March 28, 1970. Neil Calvin Turner. Calvin for my great grandfather on my dad's side that everybody hated but wanted to please. Yeah, I know, I don't look like a Calvin. I thank God every day they didn't make it my first name. As you know, one sister. Charlotte. Tortured me mercilessly. Called me Nu-nu as a baby. Still calls me Nu-nu. I flunked Grade 4. Because I stunk at math. Especially long-division. I can't function without a calculator. Words were always less threatening. When I was young I thought I would grow up to be The Fonz. Not that you would necessarily know who that is. But it meant I used an awful lot of Bryl Creem as a young-un,' he leans back and sticks both of his thumbs straight up, 'and said *Aaaaaaayyyyy!* a lot. Too much. I had a dog I named Ranger. Even though she was a girl dog. I thought if I gave her a boy dog name, none of my friends would figure it out. They did. For years they teased me.' He falls silent. Smiles at her.

Her heart pounds at the contemplation of what she might volunteer. Safely. Her smile wobbles. Self-conscious and uncertain. She raises a finger up to still it. Her stomach drops. 'As you know I have an older sister as well,' she whispers. 'But,' she pauses and forcibly holds the smile, 'we've lost touch. Since I left India.'

His eyes are sympathetic. He takes her hand, cupping it in his own. 'Tell me if I'm poking my nose where it doesn't belong. Just say the word. Yes?' He nods. Aneeta cannot tell if her own nod is merely mimicry or actual agreement. 'Were you two close?'

'When we were still young. Oh, you know, I suppose children, siblings…
they can disagree.' She is letting herself think back, and is surprised that the smile
feels more real. 'There was quite an age difference. I was the baby. Too much
responsibility for Asha, perhaps. Especially after my father passed away. The
distance between us because of the age gap became more pronounced as we grew
up. Then she got married.'

'And?'

'And became part of her husband's family.'

'Is that why you lost touch?'

'Maybe part of the reason.' The smile tightens. She shrugs. Something in
her shifts and gives way to a small sigh. A resignation. Other bits and pieces jockey
themselves about.

'Was it a physical distance? Did she move away?'

'She went to live in her husband's family home.'

'Not a very nice husband?'

'On the contrary. He was very nice. His family too.' She does not add: I
wished for someone like him. Or that what she got for her wishing was altogether
different. Altogether. Different. It stopped her wishing. And destroyed her girlish
notions about love.

'Okay.' She can hear the question in his tone, though he does not probe,
and it has the strange effect of making her want to offer some response.

'There was…a disagreement…of sorts. And then I…left India. Now, well,
we are too far apart….'

'But I can see it upsets you.'

'Yes. But I can't change it. Even though neither one of us was at fault.'
Sides have to be taken. Sides that divide. Separate. Alienate. 'Attitudes toward some
things are…It's just the way things are.' Rules unwritten. Set down by time, by
history, by whispers.

'You would want things to be different. I can hear it, see it.'

'Of course.'

'Could they be?'

'I don't know.'

'What about your mother? Would she step in? Mend fences between you
two?'

'No.' Her voice is small but certain with knowing, just as she had known
before. It is a push and pull tug-of-war tangling the hold of silence within her. She
is so used to keeping the darkness of the past locked inside that it is hard even to
try to let it out. Words struggle against the tide of shame, against old wounds, the
long ago touch of hands. Once upon a time. In a land far away. Far in time, far in
place, far in culture, in tradition. But fate has brought her, too, to this place, to now,
and to the man whose compassion she can see and feel. A man instinct is telling
her she can trust. Somehow.

Her heart hammers wildly. Her voice sounds wrapped in cotton, thick
and distant. 'It all began…on the night of my sister's wedding. Many years ago.'

Her mind ricochets through time. 'I was only thirteen…I remember thinking everything was so romantic, so beautiful.' She feels the bitter curl into the confession, 'After the wedding party…my uncle…he…forced himself on me.' Her voice pleads for understanding, 'I was only a girl. I didn't know what to do. How to stop it.' It feels like there is something in her throat. Almost as if she cannot breathe because of it. And then it is reaching, not able to be stopped. Words fly out of her. No longer willing to be contained. 'I was his favourite. Always his favourite. They…they blamed me. Thought it was my fault. My fault. What he did.' Clammy old hands grip her, squeeze her heart hard. But, this time, the truth of her story slips around and through them. 'For years I prayed for it to stop. I begged him, I threatened. And I lived silently with the secret. The shame. I wanted to die. I did die, little by little. But as I grew older fear turned into something like anger. Eventually, I couldn't bear it…any more. It was something no one wanted to hear, to know. No one could understand…my mother and sister were deeply hurt…he was my uncle. They worried that the family…our reputation…could have been ruined…if others came to know. It was decided that it was best if I was sent away. Married…away.'

She has watched his features transform. From shock to fury. From grim to aching. In her memory vault a peacock-coloured sari blazes, burns, and at long last, with a final sigh, turns to ash.

Kameko
January 2003

The sky is a vivid blue. The wind is up. Sea birds wheel and cry in loud, looping orbits. It is a brisk winter day. They meet at Perk Hill. And sit outside. At a small, wobbling table for two that angles into the corner of the building, beyond the bite of the wind. There is no one else around them, others preferring the comfort of the indoors.

'On such a beautiful day, there is something serious troubling you?' Kameko puts her hand to Gregory's face. The sharpness in the air has drawn colour to her cheeks. There is copper glinting where sunlight touches her hair.

'I have to tell you something,' Gregory says. She says it quietly, pointedly. Before shifting her eyes to the cloudless sky above. 'Something that I'm afraid might change things. I've been putting it off, but I can't keep doing that. Much as I might like to.'

Kameko moves her hand from Gregory's cheek and pulls back to search her features. There is a flutter of uncertainty low in her belly, but she tries to smile. Imagination casts about. Gently she asks, 'Is it something about what has happened? With Shiro? With me?'

'No, nothing like that.' Gregory's words are like water overflowing the edge of a tub, at first an eager rush, and then slowing, with hesitation, to a trickle. 'It's something I don't like to talk about.' She squints her eyes and looks away. Kameko is reminded of a warrior. Bloodied and wounded, but resigned to battle. 'Avoiding it...is something I've become very good at. But because of...what's happened between us, happening...I hope...I don't know, I don't even know if I've got a right to hope.' The words are clipped and punishing. Her gaze shifts and settles into a steadied concentration where restless fingers trace the ring of cup upon saucer and fiddle with the spoon that balances beside. 'And even though it was a long time ago, it's a big part of me, of who I am.' Like a swimmer preparing to launch into a frigid ocean surf, Kameko can feel that every part of her is tensed. And yet, one is never adequately prepared for the first shock. 'I killed a man. He was my... my father.' Gregory's face is a storm of turmoil, of anguish. Time seems to stop, suspended in the space between them.

It is a truth shared with a sense of great fragility. Passed from one being to another like the most delicate of artifacts. Kameko struggles to keep her composure as she tries to make sense of what Gregory has said. Her pulse is thready and quick. The revelation is shocking, yes. But threatening? No. A killer? Heart and head agree a definite no. No. The scene starts a slow thaw, released from the grip of a temporary freeze.

'And you need to know…I'm not sorry for it.' There is a pause as Gregory struggles to go on, her voice choked and breaking, 'He used to hurt my mother. Beat her. I came home one night and he had her head in a sink full of water. He was drowning her. I had to do something. When I did, he turned and came at me. He would've killed us both. I know it. If he'd had the chance. If I hadn't done what I did. Stopped him. For good.' Gregory looks away. After a moment, she faces Kameko again. 'I got out of jail in May. I've done my time, but I have parole requirements, I report to a parole officer. And that's why I need to see a shrink, a therapist. My shrink got me into the writing class. Because he and Turner are apparently connected. Friends, I don't know, or professional colleagues. I'm trying, really trying, to put it behind me…looking to get to the right side of normal.' The expression Gregory wears is bleak, 'Never would've imagined, right? Pretty crazy. Pretty damn crazy.' Grimly she is shaking her head, as if she herself is struggling to believe it.

Kameko's heart has begun to steady. The draw of breath is deepening. The nature of her initial stunned reaction is transforming. And in its place a wave of sympathy rises. She cannot imagine what it must have been like to endure such violence. To see it, live it, over and over again. Kameko puts her hand over Gregory's, hoping that her touch might be a comfort. Before she speaks, she considers her words carefully. 'It is true that I would not have anticipated such a confession. But I would rather honesty, however difficult or unpleasant it seems.'

Gregory's voice drops to a jagged whisper, 'You must think I'm some kind of…freak.' Her words are condemning. Her shoulders tremble. She shields her face, putting her hand to her eyes.

It is all clear now. The hesitations, the rigidness, the cover of humour. Even the instinctive protectiveness. The way Gregory had acted with Shiro, in the face of his threats and intimidation. Even though she couldn't understand his words. The edges of her are honed so sharp.

But what is the right thing? To say? To do? Is there anything? She needs to loosen, if she is able, the grip of hurt that is so plain. To take the sting of the wounds Gregory continues to inflict upon herself, the self-condemnation. 'What you chose to do for your mother took great courage. She was very lucky, I think, that you could be strong enough for her. To save her. To protect her. I don't think you can blame yourself for the challenge fate put in your path. It compelled you to act.'

Kameko leans forward, looks into Gregory's eyes. 'You are a defender, a protector. I know this from what you have done for me. With Shiro. To defend another being is an honourable thing. My feeling is based on what is here,' she places a hand over her heart. 'One Japanese hero, a samurai, wrote that the real power to see comes from what the heart knows.' Gregory's look is one of doubt.

'How can I explain? To make you understand?' She combs her mind for an appropriate answer. The explanation comes to her in what seems a strange analogy. 'You know a persimmon? It is a favourite fruit of autumn in Japan. The only way to get to the best of a persimmon is to cut it open. Then it can be enjoyed. It may not be pleasant to look on, as the softness of the ripe fruit makes it messy.

But only when it has been opened in this way can one enjoy all of it. In the same way, when you are completely open to me, that is when I can get the best of you.'

'Oh, I'm wide open. And sure as hell about as messy as it gets.' Gregory looks away. There is a couple coming along the sidewalk, walking a small dog. Laughing. Lighthearted. As the couple walks by, she turns to Kameko again. 'I needed you to know. For the first time…it mattered to me. I didn't want to have to hide. It's a lot to deal with, and I'm sorry for that….' Gregory falls silent.

When Kameko speaks her voice is soft, 'It is not possible to go back. To change the life that has been lived. But it does not have to be all that is responsible for defining the future. What is past should not be allowed to have such a tight hold over you.' An idea lights in her mind. 'Will you allow me to share a traditional Japanese pastime? In this city there is a bathing house, a *sento*. In Japan bathing is considered a very important ritual, for cleaning not only the outside, but inside as well. For healing. Maybe this way we can help painful memories to flow out of your spirit. Wash them away. And then perhaps we can begin cleanly. From today.'

'A bath? You're serious? It sounds a bit New Age for my psyche. But…if you think…' Gregory shrugs, 'I guess it can't hurt.' She makes a face. 'Though I'm not sure how I feel about the whole public aspect of a bath. Like out in the open?' In any other situation Gregory's look of concern would be almost comical.

'It is not a show. Do not worry.' Kameko puts a hand on Gregory's shoulder in a way she hopes is comforting. 'There is great respect for privacy. Please. Come with me. I think it can help.'

'I guess…I'll have to take your word for it,' Gregory offers uncertainly, with a weary attempt at a smile. Kameko stands, and after her Gregory rises, though she seems unsteady on her feet. She stacks together the dishes and pushes them to one side of the table. 'Habit,' she says, and sighs heavily. They sidestep table legs and the black iron of chair frames.

As they begin to walk, Kameko links her arm through Gregory's. The wind has calmed. The sun has begun its certain descent toward the busy skyline. 'Gregory?'

'Hmm, yeah?' She seems absorbed in thought, her expression unsure.

'How you see yourself? It is not who you are. It is not what my heart knows.'

Gregory

It's a low boxy building on the edge of Japantown. From the outside she'd never have guessed it to be a public bath. Inside is a mix of stone and wood. Shades of brown, grey and green mimic a natural outdoor setting. The air is heavy and damp. There is a trickling sound of water. A girl with heavy blonde dreadlocks works the desk. So not Japanese. Kameko insists on paying, waves her off.

They must have lucked out or timed it right because there are not a whole lot of people in the shower area. There are varying levels of inhibition, or exhibition, on display around her, which makes her feel a little better. Some women are wrapped in terry towels as they move around. Some wear them as white capes. Some are completely without. Maybe it's the concentrating on Kameko's what-to and how-to explanations, but her tension has let up some. Her guts aren't churning as bad, she isn't as frayed. The shower room smells of sweet, wet wood. Incense sticks in a sanded base release drifting curls of thin smoke.

They've stuffed clothes and everything else into two narrow lockers and are slap-slapping in rubber soles over tile to where, as Kameko has just explained it, they will have an allover wash.

They settle on low wooden stools. Nervous hands are clumsy with the showerhead. In the facing mirror she sees that her movements are disjointed and jerky, like a Pinocchio puppet. *What the hell has she gotten herself into?*

A run of adrenaline suddenly kicks her backwards. Old memory muscles in: *What the hell you got going on in there girl? Get your skinny ass out and give someone else a minute before it's cold. Who she think she is, hoggin' all that water? I got half a mind to drag her out! Hey, hot stuff! The rest of us waiting out here are freezing our asses off. Hurry up, bitch!* Ears echo with the remembered rhythm of boots, the heavy ominous chink of metal on metal.

Only a cruel trick of the mind, but she's shaken by the vividness. The way it's all still so fresh. Even though here, now, is peaceful and quiet. There is no one trying to hurry her ass along. Nobody hooting about titties or cootchie. Here, not a soul gives a damn that she is sat in the altogether taking her time. Letting the sharp spray ripple over tight muscles. She looks down the line of bucket stools. Shoulder checks in the mirror. What's there to be afraid of? Getting Ninja chopped by some ornery old Japanese lady? Four stools down there is a woman half-asleep, like a lizard in the sun, skin sagging, eyes heavy-lidded and lazy. Sedated by heat and water. Not a likely scenario for upset.

A hand comes to rest on her shoulder. The current it sends through her is electric. She doesn't catch the words Kameko speaks in the rush of water: wash or watch? The assumption is wash. Vigorously Kameko soaps her back, kneading ridgy knotlines along the spine and shoulder blades. 'It is very tight.' Touch is heavenly. She could stay here, this way, forever. With Kameko's hands on her under the hot wall of water. It is so seductive, the feeling. Her body has come alive. And the mind skips again to an entirely different scene—hands running over one another, they caress, touch, explore.

In the mirror Kameko's smile is coy, knowing. 'We are ready to steam now.' As she turns and slips the shower nozzle to the wall-mounted chrome holder she leans in and lets her lips graze the back of Gregory's neck. They leave an outline of fire. Her heart trips and her guts somersault. Kameko passes a towel and she winds herself into it. They do a slow shuffle to a door with a sign that in English says *Steam*. Underneath the word are lines of different characters. 'Japanese and Korean,' Kameko points, 'the last line may be Turkish.'

'So this is an international thing. This whole idea of public cleansing.' It's a weak try at funny. A poor cover. When she feels like she is melting inside.

'Very much.' Kameko, back to matter-of-fact and smiling, pushes open the door. They are assaulted by a rush of vapours in an escaping cloud. Light is dim.

Form is obscured by what looks like a pillow of cotton. They are swallowed into it. Fingers find the bench edge, and they sit, sliding themselves along moisture-slicked tiling. 'Here, we allow the things we wish to clean to rise to the surface.' Kameko lets toweling drop and smoothes it down around her. Gregory stays wrapped. Fingers find fingers, trace the outline of bare thigh and rest there, upon heated skin. Beads of moisture prick Gregory at her hairline, along the ridge of her upper lip. Sweat and water mingle. She can taste it. The weight of her is lost to the caress of warm mist. Eyes close; tension is letting her go. So far, the fallout she imagined would come from her bombshell has not materialized. *You're too hard on yourself.* Gedge's words. Maybe, and maybe not. She still has the sense of walking a tightrope. Of needing to hold her breath, of not looking too far ahead.

When she feels the outline of lips at her ear, her insides tremble. Kameko's words breathe into her, 'I think we are ready to go to the bath.' Gently pulled to her feet, she feels like she is floating. Her head is light and her legs are weak. With Kameko's arm at her waist, she lets herself be guided into the cool beyond the steam room door.

They slip-skate gingerly into another room entirely and submit to a shocking cool rinse. Further on, a round circular space is filled with what reminds Gregory of a giant Old West washtub. There are few other occupants. Two older Asian ladies chatter swiftly back and forth like nattering squirrels. A heavy-featured woman with eyes closed is buried neck-deep. After hanging towels and slipping out of sandals, they settle themselves slowly in the tub, letting dark water creep along skin, inch by inch. There is a languid sensuality in being swallowed by the silky heat. She watches Kameko's breasts disappear and sees eyes wander over her. From her slowly vanishing body up to her face.

'Not too hot?' Kameko asks, her voice low. Hers is a lazy, liquid smile.

'No. It's…wow,' Gregory inhales deeply. 'You're right, the heat, the water…it's breathtaking. It's like…I don't know…like I'm coming undone. Like everything's letting go…of me…*in* me,' she murmurs. 'Like I'm adrift in some kind of dreamworld. My body is like lead.' Words are thick and slow, like molasses, 'Mmm. I'm seeing the bath in a new light. Maybe replacing therapy entirely. Would mean a whole lot of out of work head doctors. I guess they could become towel jockeys.' She grins at the idea, at the way she imagines Doc Gedge.

'Your body has the right idea. In relaxing. Now, perhaps, the mind can follow.'

Gregory begins to sift through memories like one might a deck of cards. One by one, with Kameko's encouragement, she deliberately deals them out. Pouring her past into the water. There is Curtis and Mama. Playing gypsy. All the moving around of those years, the secrecy. The hiding, how she would run when things got bad. The way she'd take care of Mama after. There's Lil. And prison. Getting through, day by day; looking forward. Keeping herself fixed on that invisible someday. And then, finally, getting out. The crazy fear of freedom. How she can't seem to bring herself to go home. All the while Kameko's eyes are fixed on her. What Gregory sees there doesn't flinch or change.

Not once does Kameko look away. Nothing is held back. Confession simply floats away; slipping on the liquid surface, sinking slowly into the depths. Until she is empty, and there is nothing more that needs saying.

Gregory
English 50
January 2003

Hope sees the invisible, feels the intangible and achieves the impossible. Anonymous.
The quotation stretches the length of the front board in Turner's blocky hand. He's reading from something as they arrive. He looks up. A smile lights his face, 'Welcome back.' He has similar greetings for everyone. It hits her out of the blue that this was never what she had expected. This class. That she feels good for seeing Turner again. And the others. That she's gotten used to the mix of personalities and camaraderie inspired by the once-a-week session. There is joking and laughter. A comparing of holiday happenings and, of course, gifts. Barbie 1 is showing off a bulky silver bracelet in the presence of Boho Chick and Barbie 2. They *ooh* and *aah* appreciatively.

Aneeta is already sitting in the room, also lost in some book that sits open on the desk before her. A graceful hand thoughtfully flips pages. She lifts her head and smiles as Kameko heads toward her.

'You have had a nice Christmas?' Kameko asks.

'Yes,' she says quickly, her look suddenly shy. The good professor is written all over her reaction.

They take side-by-side seats next to Aneeta. Gregory wonders if the new closeness between them will be noticed. She's told Kameko she wants to keep things quiet. For no other reason than to protect their privacy. She tries outwardly to appear the same as before. To maintain her space. But solitary now is hard. Foreign. Can things have changed so quickly?

'You both have had good holidays also?' Aneeta asks, closing the book.

Kameko looks at Gregory wondering who should answer, and for a heartbeat says nothing. At exactly the same time, they both say, 'Yes.' Kameko lifts a hand to hide her smile. Aneeta looks amused, and for a here and gone flash, just the slightest bit puzzled. She inquires about Kameko being apart from her husband, asks if things were okay. 'Yes,' Kameko answers with her trademark head bob, 'I am good now.'

Beer Can Mike shows up without his signature crew cut, his head instead shaved bald. 'A bad buzz?' someone inquires.

'New year. New me. It's a statement,' he responds with a grin, sliding into a desk. He has cultivated an exactingly manicured goatee instead. 'The chicks dig it.' His fellow classmen nod appreciatively. She wants to laugh out loud at them.

Barbie 2 makes her way over and, with hand extended, asks for a touch.

'Ooh!' she enthuses with a breathy sexpot kind of wonder, 'Smooth.'

'See what I mean?' Mike drawls. Again the guys wag heads, slap palms, knock knuckles. The primitive rituals of inter-male acknowledgement.

'Okay,' Turner admonishes the small flock of bald-curious females, 'enough touching The Mike. Ladies, back away from the genie and take your seats.' There are giggles at his intimation and a smile from Mike, who happily offers to indulge them after class.

Turner shakes his head with a smile and gestures at the quote on the board. 'I offer the entreaty because it seems particularly appropriate given the fact that we have rounded the corner on a new year. It's a big idea. Though it seems a shame that we can't give some recognition to the sage who offered it in the first place. Actually,' he continues, 'the quote came to me by way of a Christmas card from a law firm. Surprising. Goes to show that if something like this can come from a lawyer, then truly anything *is* possible.' He gets a ripple of laughs. 'Such is the profession that they would choose something from a source that is anonymous. No copyright obligations. No lawsuit potential. No harm, no foul. But enough of my lawyer jokes. That's not what we're here for. We don't have any lawyers in our midst? Any wannabes?' There is no response. 'I thought not. No, it would be contradiction entirely to have a lawyer with a penchant for creativity, especially in writing. Perhaps excepting John Grisham. My brother-in-law is a lawyer, so I like to think the criticism is my entitlement by marriage.' Again, laughter. 'No, really, my brother-in-law is a good guy. For any who do have ties to the legal world or who happen to be affronted by my comments, I do deeply and humbly apologize.

'Anyway, to carry on to conclusion the last of the holiday theme—I propose that the festive season is an intensely high-stakes emotional roller coaster. The ride is a wild one, boasting both highs and lows. We have all lived this, have we not? Perhaps it is fresh in your minds yet.' Somewhere in the group there rises a groan. 'You, my friend, have been away from this clever class for too long. Hear me out. The roller-coaster is a comparative, dramatic perhaps, but relatively apt— depending on the personalities, vices, or even sanity levels,' he looks at Manfred, 'of those who may have been part of your festive celebrations. Bear with me, I'm getting there. My point: in the same way, so is writing like that coaster. One day so good, so smooth, so swift and unencumbered; the next day, it's all uphill, a battle. On those dry days you may wonder if creativity will ever come again. Okay, now I see you nodding.' He shifts forward, 'Thing is—creativity is not learned. That much we know. Abilities can be honed, refined, but creativity? It just *is*. Entirely inexplicable, unpredictable, finicky and fickle.'

He throws his hands up, 'Because I know it's hard getting back into things after a break we shall *ease* ourselves back slowly into the world of words. And hopefully, what we're going to do tonight will kickstart your creative juices, get them revitalized and flowing again.

'Remember, no one ever ran a marathon without regular training. In the same way, you have to train the mind. Exercise it. Regularly. In all sorts of different ways. To keep things keen. And if it can be fun, so much the better.'

They'll play what Turner calls Quotable Quotes, a game in which they attempt to name the person responsible for certain well-known quotes. 'We are working to get through the rough, to blow out the cobwebs, to rev the motors. Some of the quotes,' he says, 'are gimmes. Others have been used in class.' Mike rolls his shirt sleeves, rubs his hands like he's getting psyched and leans into his neighbour, Andy, bookish and unkempt, the Science guy. Manfred's dubbed him Kid Nobel. The name's a good fit, Gregory will give him that. Andy's eyebrows shoot up and he laughs a little at whatever Mike has said.

'Never hurts to expand the brain capacity—hey, Mike?' Turner teases.

The professor announces that the class will be divided into teams along gender lines. A hearty whoop-whoop rises from members on both sides as desks are re-shuffled into groups. 'Get thinking caps and game faces on!' he booms. He warns the guys, who are rumbling with manliness at the prospect of pairing off against the Chromosome X team, that they are likely to succumb to the superiority of the female brain. Known, he says to them, for having better memory and superior language-associated thinking. Of course, his comment inspires good-natured laughter, and sparks determination in all.

He lays out the rules. He will read a quote. The object is to correctly name the individual responsible for the quote. A team is able to confer, or not, before arriving at an answer. In order to be granted permission to speak first, the chosen communicator for the round must be the first to rise. Turner tells them that as a kid he loved Name That Tune. This, he says, is not a whole lot different, except that they're dealing with words as opposed to music. Into the frenzy he interjects that they must be silent and hear the entire quote before being permitted to give a response. Everyone nods their okay to the rules. Classic game show format except for the lack of an oversized red dome buzzer to hit.

'Contestants, are you ready?' There is a chorus of yeahs, some clapping, whistles from several on the male side. He says in his best game-show drawl, 'Then let's get *staarrrtteddddd!*' He rolls his r's and holds the d long. 'A reminder that cheaters and troublemakers will be ejected from the classroom. May the best and brainiest team win! Are you ready—Ladies? Gents?— for the first Quotable Quote?' She can see Mike rubbing his hands together, the cocky grins on most of the Team Guy faces.

'*Oh, East is East and West is West, and never the twain shall meet,*
Till Earth and Sky stand presently at God's great Judgment Seat.'

Aneeta leans quickly forward into the female circle and whispers, 'I think I know this one. In fact, I am quite certain of it.'

Confusion, not surprisingly, is manifest in the male camp.

Aneeta stands.

'Okay, this isn't gonna be fair!' some jockey whines. The women laugh.

'Ladies, you have an answer?' Turner is taking Aneeta in with the biggest, broadest, most beaming smile on his face. There is no denying the love connection between them.

'Was it Rudyard Kipling?' she asks tentatively.

'That is correct! Point 1 for the ladies.'

They wade through: '*The difficulty of literature is not to write, but to write what you mean.'* Robert Louis Stevenson. Point to the men.

'*Know thyself.'* Words of Socrates. Boho Chick, it turns out, takes philosophy too. Point 2.

There is a surge for Team X. The female contingent wins points for: '*Begin at the beginning and go on till you come to the end; then stop.'* By Lewis Carroll. '*It was the best of times, it was the worst of times; it was the age of wisdom, it was the age of foolishness.'* The first lines of *A Tale of Two Cities* by Charles Dickens. Quiet, soft-spoken Maddy, a literature junior, wins the point. Team Guy collectively moans because they knew it, but were not first to stand and so sacrifice the round.

'The ladies are on a roll!' Turner exclaims. 'Here's your next quote: *Be still when you have nothing to say; when genuine passion moves you, say what you've got to say, and say it hot.'* Again, thanks to Maddy, the women win the point, naming D.H. Lawrence. High-fives are exchanged all around.

There are grunts and the beginnings of frustration. And then a guy-side rally thanks to Manfred who leaps to his feet like a shot out of a cannon at, '*Brevity is the soul of wit.'* The wit has just barely died on Turner's lips and Manfred is on it.

'Shakespeare!' he cries out in a rush. 'From *Hamlet!*' He dances a red-faced, cackling jig before collapsing into his customary slouch in the desk chair. There is enthusiastic backslapping for him; the return of boisterous bravado.

Randy, baby-faced and mocha-skinned, beautiful model-actor-poet jumps in, 'Yeah. It's like that! My boys are on the rebound!' He does a funky dance step, 'Watch your backs, ladies!' He is laughing the whole while.

Innocent looking and usually reserved Maddy wolf-whistles at him. The girls look at her in surprise. 'What?' she says, 'I'm a hip-hop fan.' This strikes most, including Turner, as comic. There is a loud outbreak of laughter.

'And here I thought I had you pegged,' Turner jokes.

Randy checks her up and down, nodding, 'Mm-hmm. You're probably like…some b-girl dancer or something in your spare time, right?' Maddy's cheeks burn red.

'Wouldn't you like to know!' Krista shoots back without missing a beat.

'*Ooh!*' is the collective male camp response.

'Gimme a high-five, girlfriend!' Krista demands, and Maddy shyly does. Grace's jaw is on the floor. For once she's not ogling the dear professor.

They work through quotes by Emerson, Oscar Wilde, Gandhi, Maya Angelou, Wordsworth. Ironically, Grace jumps up first for: '*How do I love thee?*' Calling Elizabeth Barrett Browning. Somehow the guys get one from Chaucer that the girls have no clue about. Mike stands for it, though she has doubts that knowing it was down to him. Then Turner reads:

'I will die Before my time

Because I feel the Shadow's depth'

'Oh yeah!' Randy just about hits the roof. 'That's kickin' it! That's my man Tupac! Tupac Shakur, modern-day Machiavelli. Man, may he rest in peace.' He puts his hand to his heart, and bows his shaking head, 'One of the greats.'

The teams back and forth over the last few, but in the end, the women dominate and easily clinch the victory with a final of 19 to 12.

Amid groans of defeat Manfred crows, 'We need a re-match. I vote for sports trivia next time.' In seriousness he asks, 'Can we add cheerleading as a category?'

Turner's grin is wide and he is laughing. 'Manfred, I don't know that sport, or cheerleading for that matter, fits with our mandated curriculum. So, people, I truly hope that great words will inspire you. And spark the creative fire within. Now, as we wade into the second half of the course, I want to give you a heads up on what you've got to look forward to.' He takes a deep breath and tries for calm in the room, 'We are going to tackle point of view and setting. We're going to look at nonfiction in the form of memoir. We're also going to spend some time on revision techniques and how to use them. But,' and he speaks more loudly to top the conversational din, 'I wanted to tell you that we're going to have a reading night, where, as part of your final evaluation, you will present a piece of your own work in front of an audience.' There is a dive in the tempo and noise-meter of the room, a swell of nerves stalls the buzz as they process what's been said. 'I thought that might get your attention. I'll give more information as we approach the final stretch. You can choose anything you've written, any one of your pieces, even entries in your journal if you decide that's your best writing. It's entirely up to you. It may be a piece not yet written. That's a possibility too. Don't panic, you will all be great. It should help that you're facing an audience of friendlies. No one is going to be critical. We are there purely to appreciate one another and what we've achieved.'

Despite what Turner has said there are still looks of fear and heads shaking at the thought.

Manfred raises a hand and asks, 'Will there be food at this thing?' In that instant, the spell of anxiety breaks. Trust Manfred. Laughter returns to the group.

'You could bring Bunny,' Mike pipes up, 'your blow-up dollie chica!'

'Maybe I will,' he teases back.

Turner puts his hands up, 'Okay, okay, I just wanted to put it out there. On the radar. So there's no whining later. Yes, Manfred, there will be food and drink, and yes, significant others are invited to attend. Though I thought, Manfred, that things with Bunny were a little, pardon the pun, *deflated* since her Thanksgiving outing.' Books snap shut. Groans float away as ones and twos make for the door.

Manfred, in typical wiseass form, shoots back, 'Nothing a little patchwork can't fix. I'll have her pumped again, my Bunny. Ready for all the action. She's my favourite airhead, she is.'

More laughs as they file out. Kameko is smiling at her. And it feels good on her, in her. The business of being back to class.

Gregory
January 2003

It is Sunday and still quiet. She wonders if calling now might be too early. She checks over her shoulder at the wall clock. 9:20. 'Just do it,' she says into the silence of the empty café. 'Do it.' She picks up the telephone receiver in one hand, the dialing hand holds the paper with the number. This time she smiles at the all caps threat to hunt her down.

Claire's voice interrupts the third ring. 'Hullo?' She sounds awake, alert.

'Hey, Claire? It's Gregory.'

'Hey! What's new? Hadn't heard from you over the holidays.'

'Hadn't heard from you either.'

'Busy time.'

'Here too. Glad to be done with the insanity of things.'

'Bit different from inside?'

'I'll say.'

'Things good?'

'Good. Better, I'd say. Takes getting used to.'

'Gregory, everything takes getting used to. Everything.'

'Yeah, I know.'

'For me, man, I get weirded out by the whole Santa routine. And Jace still gets so excited. He made me sit on Santa's knee with him this year. Told me I needed to do some wishing too. How crazy is that?'

'Somehow I have a hard time with that visual. And did you?'

'I said something or other when the guy asked what I wanted. I mean, I was truly pathetic. You should see the picture. Jace is from ear to ear grinning. And me? You can see nothing but terror in my face.'

'Really?' She is smiling at the idea of it. Picturing Claire.

'Sure was glad to get the hell up and out. I'm sure I sprinted out the Winter Workshop gates. The whole episode felt like a cheap slice of *Alice in Wonderland.*'

'And Jace?'

'God, he was so proud. It made me want to cry. He must've seen or smelled the fear because after he kept patting my shoulder, saying *Good job, Mommy. It wasn't so bad, see?* Give me a mean sonofagun anytime, but Santa? Scares the goddamn life out of me.'

She is laughing. 'I wonder what my head doctor would make of that one, Claire. Something to discuss at my next session. Santa-phobia.'

'How about you focus on the sack full of your problems, wiseass, and leave me the hell out of it?'

'Okay, ouch. I get it. But it could be so interesting, or twisted, this difficulty of yours. Don't you want to know?'

'Yeah? No. It's a mere hiccup to me. A once a year blip. Just like that. Here and gone. Remember Christmas inside? Those sad little paper chains we used to make and hang? The Charlie Brown tinsel tree in the television room? Oh, and remember how Donna used to weave all those bookmarks?'

'Yeah, I remember. Still got one. Somewhere.' She can't remember when she'd last seen it. Since she moved to the apartment? At the thought of having lost it she feels strange. Badly. Like it might've meant something to her.

'She put out those bookmarks like the Gideons put out Bibles. Everyone had one. As I recall, she made the designs more elaborate for the people she liked. I think I had maybe two shades of blue. If I remember right, yours were always elaborate.'

'How do you know two shades of blue yarn wasn't the only thing commissary had at the time?'

'May well have been. But there wasn't anything but two stripes to it.'

'Well, she might've used me as her design tester. Or something. I don't know.'

'She liked you.'

'Yeah, yeah.'

'Imagine how long the collection'd stretch if they were laid out end to end somewhere. Like a Hands Across America.'

'Well, you know, it was her thing. Kept her occupied. Distracted. A time-passer.'

'Remember Reba complained, after her, God knows, tenth or something? Told her she was using the extras for maxi pads and cleaning rags.'

'And Donna's reaction? She had such a mouth on her. It's funny. Sometimes you almost forget. Life inside. Reminiscing makes me feel almost like I miss it. Almost, but not. I do wonder about some of the girls. Every now and then.'

'Pinin' for prison? Got the Cal Correction blues?' Claire sniffs melodramatically.

'Oh get off it. You're so full of it.'

'Yeah, I know. So. How'd your first Christmas out of the joint go?'

'It went.'

'Uh huh. That's pretty non-committal. Do I have to out and say it? Honest to God, it's like I have to pry every little thing out of you.'

'What?'

'You know.'

'Know what?'

'Did you do it? Go home. See your mama. Lil. Finally?'

'Nah.'

'Are you serious? *Still*?'

'What? What are you up in my face about? Even the doc agreed.'

'Bullshit! What's he gonna do? Tell you otherwise? Upset the balance? The choice was yours. All along it's been yours.'

'Based on what I'd said he agreed I wasn't ready.'

'Is that how therapy is supposed to work? He's just your parrot? You know,' Claire says in her finger-shaking voice, 'the longer you leave it the harder it's going to be for you. You see that?'

'I know, I know. It'll happen. At some point.' She shrugs. 'Why do today what you can leave till tomorrow, or next month, or next year, or till hell freezes over? Let me put it this way, Claire, my mama is like your Santa. You get me?'

'Lame example, Abbott. Difference is, I did it. I sat on his lap. I asked him for something. Okay, this is bad. It sounds so wrong!' Claire laughs.

'Now I know you've got bigger Santa issues than I thought.'

'Stop. Stop putting this back on me. You are so slick with that. This is about you. You! Not being able to get your sorry ass back home. You can't leave the past in the dust until you square up and face it. You need to put it properly behind you.'

'Yeah well, I just thank God you're not my therapist, Claire.'

'Fuck you, anyway!' she whispers it, quiet but terse, so other ears that might be around don't catch it, then returns to a normal pitch, 'That's the thanks I get for trying to help?'

'You know me well enough to know I'm joking. I sent a card. With a letter. I tried to explain. The way I felt about things. Gedge said it was a step in the right direction.'

'I swear, Gregory Abbott, you're going to be putting flowers on your mama's grave if someone doesn't push you to this. Then see how you feel. When it's too damn late.'

'I won't.'

'Dead woman can't release you. From the guilt you're still so tied into.'

'I won't wait that long.'

'Just a little word of caution, me to you. So if you didn't go on home like you should have, what did you get up to over the holidays?'

'Went to a party Christmas Eve. Went to dinner at Gerry's Christmas Day. Worked. You? Besides coming to terms with Santa?'

'I am really regretting ever telling you about that. Me and my big mouth. Honestly.' She drops her voice down again, 'We had a bit of special holiday drama.'

'Claire? Did something happen? With Grant? I thought I told you to call me if he turned into trouble.'

'Yeah, well it wasn't exactly the first thing to occur to me at the time. And before you go getting all high and mighty, you can't even face your own demons.'

'But I would have been glad to come and bust his ass for you.'

'And I told you that you had parole to think about. And keeping yourself clean. Out of trouble. Unless you've got a longing to be going back and getting yourself another one of them bookmarks of Donna's. Anyhow, turns out my dad did it in your stead.'

'Your dad? I thought he didn't know. About… all the details.'

'Well, unlike *you*,' she pauses to let her meaning settle in on Gregory, 'I decided I'd better deal with old ghosts. Set things straight. So I told him. It was about time I came completely clean.'

'Wow. So? How did he react? Your dad, that is, at the news?'

'Less than pleased. But he was glad to know. You should've seen how he stepped in and handled things. It was downright impressive. And the little weasel literally turned tail and ran.'

'So Grant got pushy?'

'Yeah. Maybe had designs on Jace. Showed up at his school. Not really sure. What started out all sweet and nice got creepy pretty quick. Guess I was stupid for not knowing. For wanting to believe his bullshit. Again. You, Gregory, had best keep your I-told-you-so's to yourself.'

'I didn't say anything. Wasn't even thinking about saying.' She could imagine Claire's doe eyes concentrated on her feet. Her toe playing with something invisible.

'Didn't need to. Such a shithead.'

'You referring to him? Or you?'

'Oh, me. Of course, me. For a smart woman I can be pretty stupid. Not too long ago I heard those words. That's what you said, right?'

'I didn't mean it. You know that.'

'Anyway, the long and short of it is he's gone. If I were a betting woman, my money would figure he won't be back this way anytime soon. He had special help getting out of town. Thanks to Dad and the Sheriff being old hunting buddies.'

'Now *that* is handling things. So I guess you really didn't need me.'

'I always need you, Abbott. I just want you staying out of the can.'

'How're you holding up?'

'Me, I'm fine. Getting over it. Getting on with things. Jace keeps me up. Sometimes I feel like he's the grown-up and I'm the kid, the way he tries to look after me. Makes me feel bad for him.'

'Why feel bad? He's got people that love him, Claire. He's got you back. That's all he needs.'

'You've got folks who love you, Gregory. Why do you keep putting them off?'

'Well, in a roundabout sort of way, that's kind of why I called.'

'Why? What? I thought we had been through that.'

'This is…different.'

'You're not making any sense. Spill the beans. Pronto. Before this becomes a no holds barred cross-examination. What exactly are you referring to—that's why I called?'

She turns the words out slowly, 'I guess I wanted to tell you…I met someone.'

'No! You're not shitting me? You're not. You're kidding? You're also not saying anything. Gregory? Speak to me. Tell me.' The outright surprise in Claire's voice makes her smile. It's getting easier to do that. Smile.

'Well, and I'd like you to meet her.'

'I'll be damned, Gregory Abbott. I am happy for you. So happy. I really am. So when? When do you want to get together? Now you've said something, better make it soon. Or I'll show up uninvited. And I know how you hate me dropping in.'

'I was kind of thinking…you know, that new year is coming up.'

'Honey, I hate to burst your bubble, new year's already been.'

'No, I'm talking Chinese. Chinese New Year. In Chinatown. They put on this big parade. And have fireworks. I heard from Louie, one of our dishwashers, it's supposed to be incredible.'

'I know it.'

She tucks the plastic between chin and neck and attempts to scrape at a squared fingernail still slivered in white, dough that has resisted scrubbing. 'So anyway, I was wondering…if you and Jace, uh, want to come into town and take it in, the parade, with us?'

'We will be there. Absolutely. Would not miss it. For anything.'

They fill in the blanks with all the relevant details in an excited blur. She hears Jace in the background asking questions and Claire is distracted, though still bubbling like a shaken soda. There's the haste of a final exchange and goodbyes and it is done, set. Suddenly, she's aware of what it is to be looking forward.

Gregory
Chinese New Year
2003

They're picking their way down Market Street. Through a sea of waiting people. There are thousands out for the parade. Sidewalk is all but invisible thanks to the bodies draped in various ways attempting to claim pieces of it.

'Maybe we should've come earlier. This is mad!' She has to pretty much shout to be heard by Claire.

'Huh?'

'It's mad. Madness.' She bulges her eyes to make the point. 'It scares me, all these people.'

'Honey, it isn't a prison break,' Claire laughs. 'Don't worry. You can put those eyes back in your head.'

They walk by twos. And even that proves a challenge. Snaking their way through moving holes and openings. Kameko and Jace walk ahead. They look for a good vantage point, their own scrap of pavement. Cymbals clang and incense infuses the air with an eastern presence.

'What was I thinking—this would be a good chance for you to meet Kameko?'

'Oh, *stop*. Relax a little.'

'I have a thing about people, crowds.'

'What?'

'Crowds,' she raises her voice to be heard over the clamor, 'freak me out.' A ten-legged goat zig-zags along the street with shoes of Nike, Adidas, Reebok. The golden head bobs left and right, to the delight of the children who squeal at it, many from perches upon adult shoulders. Gregory cranes to keep Kameko and Jace in her sights as they slip in and out of sliding human waves. When the goat reaches where they are, it makes a jaunty, rolling sidestep. Kameko and Jace have turned, hand in hand, standing momentarily still to watch it. It snorts smoke in their direction and bobs its head. Both are laughing at the antics.

'See? They're loving it. It's great. Don't be so hard on yourself.'

'I guess it wasn't really what I had in mind.'

'It's a parade, Gregory, what exactly *did* you have in mind?'

'For starters, not quite so many people.'

'I think it's one of the biggest events in the city.'

There are uniformed police officers standing by at intervals, surveying slices of the group. It makes her more than a little nervous. 'Jee-sus! And all the cops. I should've thought this through.'

'Well you can't blame the city—especially after 9-11. These days, they see the potential for a bulls-eye target just about anywhere.'

'Yeah, well, my stomach feels like it's in my throat.'

'That explains the green colour in your face.'

'Seriously?'

'Or maybe it's because you're jealous of Jace. Up there holding hands with Kameko.'

They dodge a double stroller being shunted madly down the packed walk by an elderly Chinese lady. 'Watch your toes!' Claire laughs. 'Now she's someone you'd be right to be scared of. I always find the stroller pushers are the worst at these kinds of things. They use the contraption more like a battering ram.'

'Kameko and Jace are cutting left. Maybe they've spotted a place to sit.'

'So tell me, before we get settled, since I've kind of got you to myself here for the moment, is this serious? Between you two?'

'Serious how?'

'Oh, come on!' Claire cocks her head, 'Is it a fling, or something more?'

'I don't know. I don't know this kind of thing well enough to know.'

'You've got to at least have some idea.'

'Well I don't think it's just a bit of fun, if that's what you're wondering. I would say…I care for her. Is it serious? If I said it was?'

'I would say dammit, you deserve it. Yes, you,' she jabs her finger in Gregory's direction and exaggeratedly mouths the words she shouts over the din, 'deserve it.'

Gregory grins and scans for the pair up ahead. Every now and again she sees them turn and check back over their shoulders to be sure that Claire and she are following. It would be too easy to get separated in a throng like this. People are bunching up in layers with parade time now upon them. 'I hope those two know what they're doing.'

Claire waves it off. 'We'll find something. I just want to be able to plant my butt rather than standing.'

'It looks like butt-land is getting scarce.'

'I'm gonna trust that they know what they're looking for. You know, Gregory, she's adorable. You just want to eat her up. She reminds me of one of those Kewpie dolls. Remember them? Like a little cupcake. Tiny package, all frothy and sweet.'

'You did not just call her a cupcake!'

'Yes. Yes, I did.' She throws an arm around Gregory's neck to pull her in. 'And…I like her. She's good for you.'

'Like a breakfast cereal.'

'Get out!' Claire gives her a shove and a look.

'I'm kidding!'

'Well, I'm not. Look how she is with Jace. She's just met him. He's just met her. He's usually reserved around new people, but they're getting on like a house on fire. Kids know. They have the best kind of people radar. You should have seen him when his father came round. If that kid were a cat his hair'd have been standing on end.'

Kameko and Jace are sharing a conversation that cannot be heard, though what they can see, even at a distance, speaks volumes. They lean in. They swing their hands in happy arcs. They are smiling. There is something genuinely touching about the way they are with one another.

'She can't have kids,' Gregory says.

'Shit, really? She'd make a great mom.'

'Hmm. Yeah. It's part of the reason her marriage fell apart. The guy screwed her over good.'

'She divorced?'

'No. Came here from Tokyo with her husband. A transfer. Separated though.'

'Fresh?'

'Yeah, pretty.'

'Because of you?'

'Nah. I think I'm a rebound.'

'Doesn't matter how you got together. Just that it's good together.'

'She's had an offer. From a guy our writing professor knows. To help teach or something. Asian literature. And finish her degree. Here.'

'Wow. There's an opportunity.'

'Yeah.' A longing stirs in her. She watches Claire's son and Kameko laughing. Their almost skipping steps. 'Or she might go back.'

Claire grabs her arm, stops short and looks at her hard. 'She makes you happy. I can see it in your face; in fact, in everything about you. Give her a reason to stay. Don't let her go. You need her. You need this. Give her a reason. To stay.'

Aneeta
Perk Hill
March 2003

The last of the day's sun reaches into Perk Hill in long window-length fingers. Gregory slides her coffee onto the table and pulls out a chair.

Aneeta looks up and offers, 'We were talking about influences, writing influences. The part family plays. I was just saying to Kameko that my life changed with my father's death. I was young, a child. I felt I still needed a way to communicate with him, and for some reason I thought the way was to write my thoughts and feelings and questions on paper. I think much of what I tend to write, even now, I write with him in mind, maybe because he's not here. I wonder if it's how I include him. In my life.' She does not mention how she sees him in dreams. How, in sleep, he comes to share her child with her. But that she cannot cross the divide to communicate. That some part of her hopes that the words she writes can.

Gregory exhales and concentrates on her cup, sliding the tiny spoon back and forth in slow arcs. 'Mine, my old man, was a big part of what made me write things down, but that's where you and me, I guess, we part ways. Where we differ. My writing has always been about forgetting. Getting him out of my system. All the dead wood that's left behind because of him. Harsh, but apparently, as I've been told, necessary.'

'For me,' Kameko muses, tapping a finger to her lips, 'it is thanks to my father that my perspective in life changed. My innocence disappeared. I grew up. Matured, emotionally. And I think because of this change, I detached from my parents. To be more objective. To see their humanity. And to see that each had flaws.'

'And your mother?' Aneeta asks Gregory.

'Not really that close,' she shakes her head, looks down, continues stirring black coffee.

'No, neither am I.' Aneeta tries to smile.

'But your family, I mean, your mother, is in India. That, I guess, makes things harder.'

'It wouldn't change things, I don't think. If she were here, or I were still there.' History cannot be adjusted, words cannot be taken back, reclaimed, to remain unsaid. 'I did something…' The words surprise her. That some part of her fabric should still feel this way. Responsible.

'You? I can't believe that. You were probably the perfect child. Every parent's dream. Everybody's favourite.'

Everybody's favourite. The idea yet strikes a chord of unease. 'For a time, maybe.' She envisages Mummy's face. The shock. The way her skin seemed to sag suddenly. The way the revelation had changed her whole physical being. The way it felt to have hands, hands that had reached out in apology, in deference, kicked away. 'But things changed.'

'When my mother became sick, I felt guilty.' Aneeta is relieved that Kameko has stepped in. 'Because she did not have such a happy life. I felt a sense of responsibility for her disappointments,' Kameko continues, 'for disappointing her. And so, to try to make up for the unfairness in her fate—maybe even to make *myself* feel better for failing her—when she encouraged me to marry, I agreed. I tried to convince myself it would work. I tried to make it work. Now, I may be sorry about Shiro, but I am not sorry for where it has led me.'

'And that is how, I must say, I have come to think of it too. In what we do, what we face, for every bad turn there is some good.' Aneeta nods.

'All these things, they change us us, who we are and who we are becoming,' Kameko says. 'But, speaking for myself, I think it is bad experience especially that seems to have a stronger influence on the words that come. In writing. Why, I wonder?'

'Maybe because we want to get rid of them. Get them out of us. Like taking out the trash.' Gregory laughs, 'Life's trash disposal. And, no joke, mine really would be dispose-*all*.'

Kamkeo is contemplative, 'It is much like one might pull weeds out of a garden. To let the beauty, the goodness, stay.'

'That's a poetic idea, Kameko.'

'Certainly much prettier than my taking out the trash picture. Then I have to ask, have either of you composed a piece that's purely happy or positive? Something that you think is a strong sample of your work? I know I haven't, I'm not sure even that I could.'

Kameko offers, 'Maybe it is because the process of writing acts as a way of letting go. Perhaps it is a catharsis. One of the ways we can try to feel better. To heal.'

'I'm thinking of sharing a poem on the reading evening,' Aneeta offers. 'It is certainly not a positive or happy reflection. Have either of you made a selection?'

'I'm a natural procrastinator. It's still out there as far as I'm concerned. Give me a month or so before panic takes over.'

'I am leaning toward poetry too,' Kameko says. 'Traditional Japanese. A very old style. But it is merely a budding idea. In my mind. It has not yet begun to take shape.'

'The problem I'm having, that I'm struggling with…this poem tends to bring painful memories. I'm not certain I would read it well, even though I feel it is one of my better pieces. I'm not certain that I could make it through without ending up in tears. Do you recall my first reading in the class? I made such a fool of myself crying over the poetry of Tagore. And that wasn't even my own thoughts and feelings.'

'Have you tried,' Kameko inquires gently, 'to see if this is the case?'

'No. Just talking about the very idea of reading it is making me uncomfortable.' She takes a swallow of tea.

'We can hear it. This poem. I know we would be happy,' Kameko includes Gregory in her offer, 'to help you see. If, for the reading, it is possible. Would that be better? If you try only for us?'

'It would, I suppose. I just feel, I must admit, a little embarrassed, because of the harsh nature of the words. They don't come easily to me. I mean…for me to *voice* them. Such images and ideas, I find them strange to say. Even though to write them was entirely natural.' A chill of hesitation threads possessively through her. She has re-mapped the boundaries of her life, but she has yet to exorcise the demons of memory completely. They skitter through her on spider legs. The chowkidar's distant watch whistle. Hot hands creeping along skin. Thieving. The smug smile of a once-loved face. A knowing look, a glint in brown eyes. 'It's a good idea, reading it for you. At least to see if I'm capable. Initially, I felt as though putting it down on paper could help me resolve, you know, the things I was upset about. To some degree, at the time I wrote it, it did. But when I speak the words, it's like it makes that time, that moment, real again. It makes it seem almost as if it were the present. Now. And it conjures all those old feelings, sentiments, as if they were simply asleep in me. Only dormant. I need to try, though, to see.'

Summoning courage, she turns the pages of her notebook. Back and back and back again. To find what she is looking for. To a very different chapter. A chapter she knows is long behind her. But knowing and feeling are two very different things. She settles the page. Presses and smoothes it open along the spine of her book. 'Ready?' It occurs to her that the question is perhaps more to assess her own readiness. Lowering eyes to paper, she steels herself against the image of the familiar face that seems to hover; watching and listening. Her throat catches. The cloying smell of hair oil seeps in. There is tightness in her chest. A sudden lack of breath. Memory so easily recalls the details. Her voice comes quietly at first, speaking the words she has written in hardly more than a whisper, but with every line it grows in strength, drawing from some unknown force:

'Hell is a place where I have no voice;
Where, though I cry, my sobs are mute,
And in silence they have no meaning.

Hell is a place where the way of what is past
Carves out the future;
Where I am clothed by only my shame,
Where the nightmares I dream
Are my reality,
Where I fear I have not the courage to escape them.

Hell is a place where those I have trusted and those I have loved
Choose to turn away,
So they do not have to see truth in my eyes.

Hell is when I realize
That what I believed to be salvation
Is but a reflection of another time, another place,
And all around the ghosts of yesterday press in on me.

But hidden in a space hell cannot claim,
I have buried seeds
Of hope;
That one day
From where they are scattered
Light may coax them
Beyond the shadows,
At last to bloom.'

She has stumbled several times to struggle for composure; to fight her straining vocal chords and to blink away the liquid heat that blurs her vision. She comes to the finish slowly, and back to present. A silent surprise is burned into their features and fired through their posture. She senses the need for explanation. Some explanation. There is no point in fabrication. 'Yes, I once was a favourite. But things changed. I was sent away…because my uncle, he…abused me. It was some time this went on for. When I eventually spoke up it was decided that I should marry. Ideally, in some other country. To keep my secret quiet. It could have disgraced my family. If it were found out.' She draws her shoulders up. 'I thought, hoped, that America would be a chance at a new life. But my marriage…didn't work out that way.' Her heart thunders, the hooves of a thousand horses beating through her, 'And then…I lost a child, miscarried, and…I don't know what came over me. I can't explain it. I changed. I didn't want to live my life being ashamed or avoiding the truth. You know what we were saying about the bad things? Yes, they changed me. A bit at a time. Eventually they brought me to the realization that I didn't want to live my life for anyone else. I decided that I had to save myself…' she trails off, smiles faintly. 'And here I am.'

Kameko
March 2003

She does not recognize the digits, but answers anyway, raising the phone to her ear as she walks, tucking the hair behind it, 'Hello?' She is working hard to master the difficult sounds in English. It pleases her that she does not hear as much foreign inflection in the tones, that the pronunciation is becoming more natural, not as laboured.

'Kameko?' The voice is hesitant on the other end. Shiro. 'I need to speak with you,' he rushes, lapsing into Japanese, 'Hear me out. Please. Please!' His voice is urgent. 'I needed to talk to you. I needed…to say…I am sorry. Sorry for what happened.'

She is startled by his call. After such a time. 'I…must accept your apology. But this call…is quite a surprise.'

'I…I have been reposted. Back to Tokyo. Things are not going as well anymore in America. The office is closing.'

She knows the tide of fortune is turning. Boom times are slowing. 'So when will you be leaving?'

'At the end of the coming month. Obviously, there is paperwork. That must be undertaken. And I wanted…needed to ask you—'

'Is it a matter of the paperwork?' She does not tell him of her inquiries into a visa. 'I am not sure I understand.'

'I wanted to ask you to return to Tokyo with me.' He blurts it in one breath. Her mouth drops wide. Words vanish. Silence stretches like an invisible chasm between them. With irritation he calls to her, 'Kameko? Kameko. Are you still there? Kameko?'

She is tempted to simply disconnect the call. Turn the telephone off. But it is a childish thought, and at best, only a temporary solution. 'You are asking me seriously?'

'Such a question? Of course it is serious. I must go back. I do not wish to return without you. To have to explain your absence.' His assertion is gaining strength.

'I…' she tries to think what she might say. 'Shiro, you must imagine my considerable surprise at such an unusual request. Especially with the way things are between us.'

'Why unusual? You are still my wife.'

'I don't understand. What purpose would it serve?'

'Purpose? You are my wife. It is your life.'

'My life?' She is incredulous. 'Have you not told them? Your parents? That we are no longer together?'

'We have not divorced, so technically we are still together.'

'You must stop being a little boy and confess it.'

'Confess to what? There is nothing formal in place.'

'After everything? How could you expect me to agree?'

'I can finance your schooling. If you return. With me.'

'You?'

'You know what I mean, my family. You can finish your degree. There is not a finer institution than Waseda. And surely not here,' he scoffs.

'This is a course of bribery you are pursuing.'

'Not bribery—'

'My feelings, they are not so easily mended. I cannot be bought, Shiro.'

'You will face difficulties with the authorities if you stay without the adequate permissions. They will be difficult for you to come by. And expensive. Really, Kameko, be sensible. You are in no position. The Americans are very particular about such things.'

'How very quickly the tone of this conversation has changed.'

'I am simply making you aware. You are being stubborn and irresponsible. I am only trying to help you see what is best. For you.'

'It has been some time since what was best for me mattered to you.'

'My motivation is not completely selfish. Contrary to how you see it.'

'You have a child now. Why drag the past into it? They are your future.' But as she makes the remark she knows, with a dawning certainty that settles itself on her in a sense of dread, that she must be wrong.

'No.' There is audible pain in the word. It shocks her. She has, albeit unwittingly, grazed a raw wound. She is perched precariously, her footing less sure. An animal wounded is an unpredictable beast. 'They will not be...returning with me to Tokyo. She has refused. She wants the child raised here. In America.'

Carefully, carefully, she must tread. 'But you asked? And she said no?'

'She said no.'

'But this is your child! Your flesh and blood. The child should not be denied a father.'

'It is not *I* who has chosen to deny the child. It is she. This is the fault of American women. They think they should be able to do as they wish. The obligation is now only one of finances.' He sounds suddenly defeated. 'It would have been too great an expectation for her to adapt to Japan. A completely foreign situation. And for her to leave her position here. Too much to ask, really. Maybe it is better.'

'You cannot mean that,' she says softly, imagining the newborn child in the hospital nursery.

'Of course I can.' She can hear frustration in his tone.

'I am sorry, Shiro.'

'If you stay, Kameko, you will regret the choice you are making.' There is a low growl of aggression that echoes in the words. But she also knows there is weakness. She has to carefully navigate it.

'At last, Shiro, you realize that it is my choice to make.'

He sidesteps the comment, refusing to acknowledge the position it confers. The shift in the balance of things. For them. 'Here you will be alone. It will be difficult to manage on your meager bookshop finances.' His disdain strikes her.

'What do you know of my finances? Of my need? I can manage. I will.' She tries her best to make her words and her voice sound assured. 'It would not be much different than Tokyo. I think I would rather take my chances here.'

'Divorce will not be kind.'

'Divorce will not be kind anywhere, Shiro. But it is better than to go on living a lie. It is not fair to either one of us to deny the possibilities of the future. It may seem the harder path now, but one day—'

'One day?' he interrupts harshly. 'My concern is for today, tomorrow, not some distant shore I cannot yet see. What I need is my wife beside me. For my parents to see. My superiors and co-workers to see. Not to be the subject of their gossip and speculation if I return alone. I can make up some story after that. After an acceptable length of time. It is simply a courtesy. Surely you won't deny me that.'

She has to take care to keep herself not too adversarial. Or risk provoking him. 'I wish you well, Shiro, I do. But we cannot pretend. It is not right to continue living a divided life for the sake of appearances only. It may not seem so to you now—'

'No, in fact, you are right. Your way of thinking does not show any practicality. A typical female shortcoming.'

'But what you are suggesting, asking, it can never work. It would tie us to a sinking weight. Hold us tightly and miserably in place. I need a life of my own. I was wrong to think I would find it in a marriage. *I* was wrong. That is why I cannot go back with you.'

'So you would rather I am forced to suffer for what you admit is your mistake. All I am suggesting is that you rectify things by thinking less of yourself. Come back to Tokyo. We can seek some help if you like. Then if you decide that it still isn't what you want, I won't stand in your way.'

'I will forever be grateful, because I realize that it is because of you and our marriage that I am here, but Shiro, I cannot do as you ask. I have to move forward, not back. To find my own way. This marriage, our road together, is at an end.'

He grunts his response and falls silent. Clearly, this was not how he intended the conversation to flow. Now she simply has to try to leave him with honour. 'You are a busy man, no doubt with many details that require your attention. I think, Shiro, that I no longer belong among them. It would be selfish of me to consume any more of your time or energies.'

Her message to him is clear. He could protest, but he will not. As with the finality of a game of chess, additional play would simply be superfluous. The outcome will not be changed.

Kameko Kimura
English 50

The zuihitsu style of writing is symbolized by the joining of two kanji characters. Taken together, the literal translation means: to follow the brush.

Zuihitsu emerged in the Heian Period with Sei Shōnagon's The Pillow Book. Shōnagon, a member of the Heian Imperial Court, kept a private diary to note her observations and musings about courtly life. The words I have written take a similar format, but are observations drawn from my own life.

Things that are bothersome;
Secrets
Questions without answers

Things that are worrisome;
When the telephone rings unexpectedly
The denial of honest feelings
The invisible outline of tomorrow

Things that are near yet far;
The heart and the mind
The distance between a husband and wife

Things that defy logic;
Love
Creativity
Trust
Dreams

Things most difficult to accept;
Lies passed from a parent to a child
The shortcomings of the physical body
Bad news
Death
A compliment

Things that move my heart;
The return of blossoms in springtime
Warm air against skin
The sound of water meandering among a bed of stones
Desire

Aneeta
March 2003

She has volunteered to cook an Indian meal for Neil. Heaving a bag laden with food and cookware, she climbs the steps to his front door. She has butterflies, a nervous excitement that intensifies as she reaches to ring the bell. Chimes echo solidly through the house. A voice calls out and makes its way closer. She tries for a relaxed smile. The door swings wide. He stands in the opening, grinning at her. 'Do you know how long this day has been? I've been counting hours since something like seven this morning. Come in, come in.' He reaches forward to claim the bag, and she follows him to the kitchen.

'*Mi casa es su casa!*' he says broadly, placing the bulging carrier gently on the wide countertop. 'My home is your home.'

'I ought to say thank you. *Gracias.*'

'No, it's *my* pleasure. Considering you've agreed to feed me this evening. To entice me with the exotic flavours of India. I'm in your debt.'

'Goodness, that sounds as though making dinner is a most impressive feat.'

'That it is, that it is. Especially for those, like me, who are card-carrying members of the fraternal order of non-cooking bachelors. I think I may be developing carpal tunnel syndrome from too much take-out ordering.' He flexes a hand, 'My dialing fingers are suffering considerable strain.'

She laughs and sets about emptying the sack of various containers and ingredients. He follows, lifting lids to inspect contents, to inhale the scents. 'Mmm. I can tell I am in for a delicious treat.' He reaches into a steel cup of cashews and with a cheeky grin tosses several easily into his mouth.

'If you continue like that there will be nothing left to cook with,' she scolds. She moves with some familiarity, but not so much as to suggest a presumption toward his things, or a sense of entitlement. She is an invited guest, after all. She asks after knives, chopping boards, bowls, and after the operation of the cooker, oven, and dishwasher. Then she turns her attention to meal preparations. She adds herbs and spices in combination to other ingredients. Sets pots and pans to heat. The oven to warm. Before long, cooking dinner smells begin to flavour the air. They cling and hover, their silent presence permeating the space. She wants desperately for this meal to be perfect. This is a part of her that she is proud to share.

'This looks quite a feast for two. Or did you put invites out to the whole neighbourhood?'

'Well, I wasn't sure exactly what would be to your liking, so I planned a variety of things: rice biryani; yellow lentil dal; spinach with mustard greens, we call it saag; sabzi of mixed vegetables; a chicken curry. Besides,' she teases, 'I thought you said you liked leftovers.'

'Oh, I do. I definitely do. You'll have no complaint from me, if there should happen to be anything left.' He looks at her, his eyes glinting with humour. 'If I can coax you into making this a regular sort of gig, maybe you could teach me to cook. Think of the fusion potential! The East-West hybrids we could concoct. We could make beautiful food together, you and I. What do you say?'

She laughs, 'Don't get too far ahead of yourself. Indian is about the only cuisine I have any ability with. And there are those who would argue that. After this evening you may be happy to go back to your takeaways. Better wait and see.'

'How could you say such a thing? Impossible. It will be delicious and I will love it because,' he pauses, 'you made it for me. And because I,' Aneeta looks up at him from the aubergine she is slicing, 'have become rather fond of you.' His eyes are no longer swimming with comedy. They are, instead, serious. She fumbles with the knife, and the blade clatters defiantly to the floor. 'Whoa, careful!'

'If you are at all fond of eating this evening I would suggest that you allow me to concentrate on what I'm doing!' There is a tingling rush through her veins.

'I mean no harm. What would the lady have me do?"

'Perhaps see to the table? Maybe some music?'

'A glass of wine?' he offers.

'Would be lovely.'

'It's settled then. Uncork a California Cabernet. Push play on the jazz. Lay the finest of flatware and china. Knives, forks, spoons.' He ticks the items off on his fingers.

'If you like, but traditionally we use our hands to eat.'

'Messy. I like it. That sounds especially appealing.' The grin returns.

'You are terribly silly.'

'You saw the signs in the joke repertoire months ago. You know, elephant with the bun and all?'

'I don't think I've ever known a man to take himself less seriously than you.'

He staggers toward the dining room, clutching at his chest dramatically. 'She has wounded me,' he jests.

'I don't mean it badly. I actually find it…' her voice sobers, 'I appreciate it. I know, also, that some of it is for me.'

'Really, I take pride in being a serial goof.' His tone becomes serious, 'But I like to make you happy. Like to make you laugh. Now, without further ado, I'm off to see to my duties.'

She smiles to herself. Strains of music begin to float smoothly into the kitchen. The low pitch of the voice is husky and distinctive and sings of a wonderful world. She turns her attention to the hissing and bubbling of the food before her.

By the time he returns to the kitchen she is adding the last of the seasonings and preparing the rotis.

'Your wine,' he says, offering the glass with a flourish.

'Oh, thank you.'

'Everything looks and smells amazing!'

'Well, let's see how you like it.'

'Have no fear.'

Diligently, he parades dishes to the table as they are readied. At last, she follows with the stack of fresh rotis. The place is awash in candlelight and flower petals. How he has managed, she has no idea. He watches for her reaction. 'It's beautiful,' she remarks in a whisper.

'And so are you,' he says, taking the plate from her and putting it in an open spot between the two place settings. He pulls out her chair and motions to her, 'Please. Sit.' When she is settled, he seats himself and lifts his glass, 'A toast to firsts, and to the sharing of many more. To cross-cultural osmosis. To fusion. And to you. Especially, to you.'

'Thank you.'

'Please, show me the ropes. I'm famished!'

She explains the dishes once again, serving him in small portions for trial. She adds yoghurt raita and chutney. Lastly, she offers a warm roti. 'May I show you?' she asks with sudden shyness. She pinches the food into a small pocket of bread, and with her fingers takes it to his mouth.

'I could really get used to this. Especially the feeding part.' His lips graze her fingertips and unleash a flood of excitement.

'Now you see how to do it?' Aneeta asks, her voice catching.

'I do so like you doing it for me,' he says with a cheeky grin.

'Well, you will have to do your own if you wish to allow me to eat.'

'Oh, by all means, how selfish of me. But...I could wait,' he teases.

'Then everything will have gone cold.'

'Right. You have a point.'

'So please, eat. Enjoy.'

He dives in with relish, pinching and mixing and eating as if he somehow has *desi* blood running through his veins. It pleases her, the sight of it. 'I hope you don't mind,' he says, adding seconds to his nearly empty plate.

'Not at all.'

'My friend Ed? You met him on the evening of the potluck party. The one whose wife teaches at Oxford? He was telling me about this time he was out with some business chaps he wanted to impress. They go to this Indian restaurant, and he orders this dish. So the waiter asks him how he'd like it, and playing the big man he tells the guy he wants it hot. Well, whatever he had ordered,' he nods vigorously between mouthfuls, 'was so intense, he says that it made him feel like his mouth was going to explode. Literally had to marinate himself in beer. He said his eyes were tearing, his nose was running, his forehead just kept beading in perspiration. Totally embarrassed himself.'

'When I was only little I used to take a very small taste of a dish to begin. If I found it hot I would whimper and completely refuse to touch any more. They used to say I had gori-tongue, a light-skinned girl's taste. My Papa, he used to eat bowls of chillies with his meals. Some really enjoy it. But it can get very, very hot. Tonight I made it mild,' she teases, 'for your light-skinned tastes.'

'Well, I thank you for taking it easy on me, the novice, but I love it. All of it is delicious.'

He asks if she's decided on her reading. She says she isn't sure. He tells her that her piece about the washerwoman would lend itself well. She asks after Max. He laughs as he tells her that Max insists on Kipling for his nightly bedtime story, but that he complains no one reads it with the right voices or accent.

She tells him that the library has given her one storytime session each week. How she loves reading to the children. They talk about Winnie the Pooh and Beatrix Potter and modern kiddie lit, as he calls it. They touch on her weekly sessions with Gregory and Kameko. She tells him how much she likes them both, that they share many similarities. They discuss some of the other personalities in the class. Ashley is going to share a work she has titled *Lust at the Fashion Parade* about her longing for handbags and shoes. They laugh. He says he finds it especially interesting to see what inspires and guides a person's creativity. He tells her that Manfred has written about his high school football glory days—from the point of view of the football. Entitled it *Pigskin*. He explains the term to her. Talk flows smoothly back and forth without hurry and without searching for things to say. He regales her with stories of his schooling, his travels, his work, his love of the city. To her he is a fascinating man. Worldly. Charming. Charismatic.

A twist of fate has brought her to him. Across thousands of miles. Across multiple lifetimes. Into his world. There is no why. No how. In her wildest dreams she never could have imagined this. In the candlelight she studies him. She cannot deny the force of attraction. Nor can she explain it. There is just something about him—so many things, really. His lively green-gold eyes. His hands, the way they move so naturally in expression. His confident posture. The sureness of him. The slim hips and broad shoulders. The golden hue of his hair, the darker gold of his skin, the way each sets the other off. And his lips. The myriad of ways in which they smile. The way they light his features. Now, as he speaks, she imagines them softly against her own. Her pulse skips. A blush rushes to her cheeks and burns there. As if he might somehow know her mind. Her heart. Her insides somersault.

In a sudden move, he pushes back from the table and stands. 'Creator of this truly divine meal, would you care to join me in a dance?' He offers a hand.

'Oh, I…' she stammers, 'I'm not terribly good. I've not danced with someone, a partner, a man, before. We…that is to say, girls…tend to dance among girls.'

He pulls her to her feet. Violins weave and rise into an impassioned crescendo. 'I've no fear of you treading upon my feet,' he says. 'Dance with me.' With an encouraging smile he draws her to him, and she feels herself melting into his embrace. As they begin to move, a woman croons, *'At last…'* The words are drawn long with emotion. Music enfolds them. His arm presses possessively against the small of her back. They sway gently, turning with the melody. The touch of him, where their bodies meet, ignites a current that flows hotly through every part of her. Is it a dream that she has found, as the song suggests? Will she wake from it someday? He pulls away slightly to look down at her. She meets his gaze. Wondering. What he might find. What she might find. She loses herself in him, in the music, in the dance. As the last notes of the song finally fade, they pause, yet holding each other. She is reluctant to let the moment go.

'I've always loved that song,' he breathes the words into the dimly lit room, 'but it's never felt the way it did just now. With you. It's like some kind of spell, voodoo, magic, whatever. I can't even put one foot in front of the other.' She can sense his smile. 'I don't know if you noticed, but *I* stepped on *your* toes. Me, the one who's supposed to be teaching you.'

'It's all right,' she whispers. 'I don't mind.'

'No. Of course. You wouldn't. That's who you are. A very rare and incredible woman. The likes of which I never thought I'd ever encounter. My heart is so full. And in it there's this peace. But at the same time there's this desperate, hungry insanity.' He shakes his head. 'Somehow you come into my life and turn everything I thought I knew upside down. For reasons I can't explain, and believe me, I've tried…for me, with me, you fit.' Gently, tenderly, his lips find hers. The longing with which she responds surprises her. 'Please,' he pleads, his voice thick, his hands cupping her face, 'I can't begin to make sense of it with words. Let me show you. Can I?' His last words are whispered, 'Can I share that with you?'

'I…can't believe this is happening. To me. For me.' In a rush she confesses her fear, 'I worry that I don't deserve it, that like a dream it will vanish.' Because? Because.

'Touch me,' he takes her hand and presses it to his face, 'I'm for real. I've told you before, I'm not going anywhere. That's a promise I will swear to. I love you, Aneeta, so deeply, so instinctively, that it's almost as if I've known you before. I know you feel it too. Let me show you how sweet love can be. Let me help you heal. Nothing else matters to me.'

In flickering candlelight her hand strokes his face, along the angular shadows she traces the bone of his cheek, her fingers soft against the slight rasp of skin. She stops at his lips. Those lips. Her thumb lifts to brush the outline of them. He kisses it, holding it there. Her heart jumps. Her hand traces a path from cheek to jaw, along the edge of his collar and down to the front of his shirt. She sees him swallow heavily. She is amazed. At herself. At this boldness that seems to have taken her over. Desire urges her forward. With both hands she pulls herself to him. Her message is clear.

He picks her up. Curling her arms around his neck, she puts her face to his chest and lets herself be carried. At the table he leans in and, with a single breath, extinguishes the remains of now drooping candles. 'Hot enough in here,' he says in a voice that sounds more serious than joking.

He moves into the entry hall and toward the stairs, his eyes fixed on hers. As he walks with her they watch. To be sure that there is no question. For either one of them. When he reaches the bedroom he very gently sets her down on the bed. He takes her face in his hands and kisses her forehead, her eyelids, the tip of her nose, her lips. Eagerly, her lips meet the tenderness of his own. He pulls away then. To look at her. Gauging her permission, her certainty. She reaches with trembling fingers for the buttons that fasten her jumper. His hands cover hers. 'Let me,' he says.

Air caresses bared skin. He pulls her to her feet. His touch raises gooseflesh. His eyes are still locked on hers. 'You are…so beautiful,' he murmurs low in his throat. Reaching into the waistband of her blue jeans, now soft with wear, he releases the button, then more slowly, the zipper. Denim slides to the floor. 'So incredibly beautiful,' he lifts her chin. She can see the question in his eyes. She responds by working the buttons on his shirt. One by one, with nervous and fumbling fingers. Fingers fired by desire, by need, by want. To touch, to discover, to claim. When she reaches the end of the run he stops her, 'Are you…do you want… to do this?'

'Yes…I do. I do. Want this.' There is a raw yearning in every division of movement. Gently, he lays her on the bed. Languidly, lazily, his lips taste her. At her hairline, the lobes of her ears, her neck. A small moan escapes her. It seems to take him by surprise and he stops. Again his eyes meet hers. 'Please,' she pleads. From her neck his lips travel to her breasts. Deftly reaching beneath her, he releases her bra. He takes her erect nipples into his mouth and teases them with his tongue. 'Oh…my…God,' she breathes. He ignites a line of fire as his lips travel down. At her navel, he stops again. His fingers trace the beginnings of lace. Her belly twists and expands at his featherlight touch. She draws a shuddering breath.

'Aneeta?' His own breath, fast and shallow, is audible in the stillness.

'Yes…oh, please…yes!' He slides the silken slip of fabric from her arching hips. His lips meet the rise of her body and kiss her softly, slowly, tenderly. She hears her voice cry out for him.

Remaining buttons and zippers and fabric give way. She opens herself to him hungrily, achingly. She is starving for him. Wanting nothing more than this, than him. *I am yours.* Passion is a dance without inhibition. Without rules. Fear is swept away. And pleasure surges. *You are mine.* Fevered skin upon skin. Shimmers. Like a mirage, a dream. Two kaleidoscope into one, losing boundaries and barriers. There is no separation. A crest of lightness weaves among the heavens. At last, her spirit realizes a wonder she has never known.

Gregory
April 2003

Uncovering our truth is the first step in recovering our truth. She hasn't seen this poster before.

'Sit.' Dan motions at the chair.

'Thanks. New?' she asks, nodding toward the saying.

'Yeah.'

'Come up with that gem yourself?'

'Nah. Far too big in meaning for me to have thought of it. Doesn't mean I can't admire it. My thinking, though, tends to lend itself to a much smaller field of vision. Like arm's width circumference. It's enough.'

'I like it.'

'Me too.'

'Bold.'

'Always. Actually, we could back and forth like this for the duration, but I have news,' he says with a smile she cannot read.

'What news? What kind of news? News makes me nervous.' Her stomach flips.

'Good news, big news.'

'Good news. Good. God, that's a relief.' She exhales slowly.

'That I hope will make you happy.' He reaches behind his desk, to where his in-tray sits below the new poster, and proceeds to paw through the stack of paper there.

'Don't keep me in suspense. My nerves can't handle it.'

'Okay. Here it is.' He slides it across the desk. 'Know what it is?'

She looks at the black and white of newsprint, confused. 'Yeah. *Chronicles of Courage.* Prison journal.'

'That's right.'

'We used to get it inside. Use it for toilet paper.' She laughs.

'Really?' He laughs too. 'I guess it's appreciated for being multi-purpose, then.'

'No, I'm kidding, we didn't really.'

'I'm going to miss your wit now that we're pretty much done with our sessions. Or not.'

'What's that supposed to mean? Or not?'

'Well, have a look at the toilet paper. See anything that catches your eye?'

'Not particularly.'

'Come on, look at it.'

'Fine, I'm looking.' She is scanning headlines, masthead, bylines, content and then…her name. 'Holy shit!'

'Congratulations.'

'How the…? What the…?' She looks up at him, dumbfounded. 'I don't get it. How?'

'Oh, it's a murky old chain into this dungeon, I tell ya. Actually, I'm kind of hoping that you're not going to take to the warpath or anything. I wasn't exactly sure how you would react. But I hope you can see the bigger picture here. From a broader perspective. So, let me at least explain. After that, I'll take whatever it is you're in the mood for dishing. Gedge sent it to me, the piece you had written.'

'Gedge, the good doctor, my mind shrink-ologist? Doesn't that mess with the whole doctor-client privilege thing? How the hell'd he get this piece? I wrote this for my class!'

'Now don't be too quick to jump to conclusions. This is my understanding of how it went—Apparently, your professor thought it was good shit. Pardon my blunt French. Since Gedge was the connection and they're pals, the prof and he, I'm guessing that was Step 1 in the chain. You already know that the good old doc is connected by the state to this office. When I sent him a requisition to get his commentary on how your therapy rehab was progressing—since we're closing in on the end of things—he sent me his report along with this. So, Step 2. He obviously thought it a good mark of your healing evolution. At least that's what he wrote as his motivation for including it. See the chain? And I, as the final link, thought it deserved a wider audience.'

'You pulled strings.'

'I did not. I simply sent it to the editor. No more. The merit of the message and the accessibility is what won you the space.'

'No way. Not buying it.' Her head is shaking in denial.

'Buy it, or choose not to. It's the truth. Scout's honour.'

'You were a Boy Scout? I'd never've guessed.'

'You should see me tie a slip knot.'

'*Riiiight*. You're trying to get away from this, this thing. We're not done with it. Keep talking while I make up my mind about what I think.'

'So. Back to the state of the nation. You, at the moment, are a Department of Corrections poster child. Why? Because you've turned things around. To the good. And you can bring that to others, who really need something to hang on to. Inside-outside. Do you know that *toilet paper*, as you so eloquently put it, has as big a readership outside as inside?'

'Fucking unbelievable.' She is shaking her head.

'You see that it's good, right? That we were never conspiring to be exploitative. I gave it a great deal of thought before I sent it off. I lost sleep. Lost hair. Hair that, clearly, I cannot afford to lose. Only because I was thinking about you. How you might take it. It was not a decision made lightly. In the end, I figured because you had submitted it in your class it was okay for public consumption.'

'Would you have told me if it hadn't been…put in here?'

'Published? No, I probably would not have. What would be the point? It would only have been a downer.'

'I just…I've never seen my name in print before.' She looks from the paper to him. 'Except in court transcripts and police documents. I…it just seems unreal. I feel kind of numb, to tell you the truth. Holy shit. It's a bit much for me to get my head around.'

'There's more. I know I should give you time to digest, but why don't I just lay it on you, so you can sift through it all. So, there's a national syndicated journal for prisoners and past prisoners as well. It's been put forward to them too. Or so I'm told. I didn't have anything to do with that. The info came back to me simply because you're my file. So it could go even farther. You know, hope is a message that's real high on the Corrections priority list.'

'I still…shit, I just can't believe it.'

'And—hold on to your seat cushion—the department has also asked *me* to ask *you*…if you would consider going back in as a speaker for the pre-release program. You know, deliver the same kind of message about getting by on the outside. Sort of a motivational-inspirational pitch. About your experiences. They think it would really resonate.'

'Oh, fuck. *Now* my world is completely upside down.'

'You helped yourself. You could help others too. Consider it. I know it's a lot to process.'

'You're joking? Kidding, right?'

'Did I mention also that it's a paid gig?'

'You hadn't. Though it seems a bit of a cheap play at bribery. Especially for someone who is just about eking out a living. God.' She forces another slow exhale. 'Where do I go with this? I had just gotten myself into a comfortable rhythm. Why is life all about messing with that?'

'I was hoping you'd be proud.'

'Proud? How does one *do* proud? I wouldn't know where to look for proud inside myself. Well, except maybe getting my GED. That felt good.'

'Use that. Draw on that. It's a good place. For a start. Do you remember your pre-release?'

'Yeah, total bullshit. How to rent an apartment. Techniques for managing stress. How to find a dentist in your area. How to dress for success. I kid you not. Like a recently freed ex-con is going to be able to afford a solo pad, yoga class, having her teeth re-done, or anything other than thrift store duds.'

'You could make a change. Offer some authenticity. Usable advice. Real life experience. At least think on it.'

'I just can't believe it. This is crazy. I can't write worth shit.'

'Obviously, Gregory, others would disagree.'

'God.' She is holding the journal up, looking at her words, her name, in disbelief. 'Do the others know? In your little daisy chain? That it came out like this?'

'Nah. I figured that should be left to you. The trickle down was natural, Gregory. But the success—and what you choose to do with it—is yours alone.'

'Oh, so that's great, just great. You put me here and now you're going to leave me in the wide open by myself. Great.'

'It is great, Gregory. It's opportunity. Do with it what you will. But bear in mind, it knocked on your door. You can hide from it, and lament your exposure, or you can open the goddamned door and see what it's bringing. Be glad at least it isn't Tupperware or Avon.'

'Damn, you're funny.'

'I try.'

'Wiseguy. Man, I don't know whether I should be celebrating or screaming at all of you for violating my rights.'

'Celebrate, Gregory. It'll do more for you, I swear.'

A sign on the front door says *Closed: Private Party*. They are it. The gang is all here. Present and accounted for. There is a tremendous buzz in the room, either from the nervous excitement of the night's performers, or because her head is threatening to self-destruct. The chance for fight or flight is past. Though flight, by her sweating armpits and hammering heart and cotton-dry mouth, seems now to have been by far the better option.

Tonight, there is an audience just for her. A group that a year ago she would not, could not, have imagined. There is Dan. There is Gerry and Lenny and a newly pregnant, glowing Suzanne. Lenny confesses he has never been to a reading. Gerry laughs and says that considering her younger life, the amount of protesting she'd done and festivals she'd attended, she's shocked she'd never dragged him to at least one. 'Not that I remember,' is his reply. With the baby coming they're trying to talk Gerry into retirement. Gerry being Gerry has told them that once the baby is here she might think about it. But Lenny and she both know it's not terribly likely. There is Claire, who has driven in. There is even Gedge, the good doc. She'd made a comment in a session—fear-related, of course. He had said he'd like to come. If she would be all right with it. Like she'd have been able to turn him down. But, to be fair, she probably wouldn't have turned him down anyway. And he couldn't analyze what she was reading because he already had. That's some comfort. However small.

JT has brought his partner, Alex. They're standing with Aneeta and Turner who can't hide the fact that they are very obviously together. No big surprise. Everyone is talking and milling about. Manfred, in a suit, keeps pulling at his shirt collar, which, for some reason, makes her smile. He has brought a repaired, shoulder cross-patched and re-inflated Bunny to sit as class mascot. Or, as he has said, for something inanimate to focus on. He has referred to the X of band-aids that cover the hole in her as her tattoo. Krista has said that a good trick for keeping the jitters at bay is simply to imagine everyone in their underwear. 'I'll just bet,' Mike's teasing reply. Gregory spies Kameko across the room; they lock eyes for a moment, Kameko gives a little wave. She is talking to Turner's professor friend, Giles. Who has officially offered Kameko a teaching assistant position in the fall. She can't begrudge the guy Kameko's time, since he has, after all, cemented her ability to be staying in the country.

There is a table with wine and beer. Another with iced tea, water and coffee. Another laid with food. Of course, there's pie. Gerry'd given her what-for when she'd been shy about asking. She's got to give it to him, Turner has splashed out on this.

A shallow-ish stage at the front of the room is backed by a maroon curtain that gives an old theatre effect. Off to one side there's a podium and microphone. At center stage is a single wooden stool and another mic that bends at the middle like an arm at the elbow. Cane chairs curl around small table rounds. People are dotted among them, chatting, laughing, looking at the single page program with the order of delivery. She is number seven. About in the middle of things. Before her: Mike. She tells herself to remember that. The idea occurs that it might just be nice to be passed over. But she knows Turner would never let it happen. Aneeta is third in the run of names. Kameko twelfth. Her buffers.

It is 7:30. Showtime. Now she's shaky. Kameko is making for her, a smile on her face. She sees Turner excusing himself to make his way to the front. Her heart leaps into her throat. 'If I can have everyone please take a seat,' he pauses, 'we'll get things underway.' People are settling themselves. It is fascinating to see who is with whom. Ashley, Barbie 1, is with a guy who must be her husband, but who is the absolute antithesis of a Barbie's Ken. He is oversized and beefy with a jowlishness that makes him seem like he's got no neck. Barbie 2, Krista's guy, is smaller than her, carefully mustachioed and decidedly mousy. Manfred sits with his arm draped around the back of Bunny's chair. To his left, Mike. Boho beside him, then Maddy. Lights lower, blending individual outlines, joining shadows.

'Good evening.' Turner leans into the mic that is too low for his height and jams his hands into his pants pockets, an act that flips the sides of his jacket back into paper airplane pleated wings. He does not adjust it upward, she assumes, knowing that Maddy is first to speak and shorter by a head at least. His introduction brings a burst of applause, whistles and cat calls. He beams. 'Thanks, I needed that. No seriously, this evening is about you. You. Save the applause, the cheers, I'm not the one who deserves them. I'll keep this short and sweet. So we can get to the good stuff. I want to thank all of the significant others who've accepted the invitation or been forced into accepting the invitation to be here this evening. Though I have to say,' he points out to Manfred, arm draped casually around Bunny Blow-up, 'some of us have a slightly skewed vision of the term.' There is, again, a roll of laughter, a smattering of noise. 'Thank you, on behalf of all the students—for sacrificing the cereal box to early morning read-alouds; for learning to interpret and respond to language based largely upon animal grunts; for understanding vain attempts to extract exactly the right word or phrase from unyielding grey matter; for suffering all the strange and obsessive tendencies that writers seem to indulge in. We salute you.' Applause. In the audience there are leaned-in silhouette kisses. Kameko squeezes her hand.

'I can say it's been a remarkable journey to witness, this forging of literary personality. You've refined your craft with dedication. And you've come together as a group to connect with and learn from one another. Be proud of your accomplishment, be proud of the writer in you. In the words of Sylvia Plath: *Everything in life is writable about if you have the outgoing guts to do it, and the imagination to improvise.* I would encourage you to go forth and wield your pen, or your computer keyboard, mightily, boldly, and with confidence; the world is waiting on your minds and your words.' He steps away as applause and cheers resume. The show is on the road.

The program really is a mix of people and personalities and styles. It's kind of nice not to have known any of it before. To be surprised. Entertained. The material and deliveries are creative and inventive. Maddy speaks about her love for her native Puerto Rico. The mic and stool are for Boho Chick. She plays Joni Mitchell's *Both Sides Now* on her guitar and sings in a similar sweet soprano. Aside from the chorus, the lyrics are her own. Aneeta has decided against the poem she read at their Perk Hill session and instead brings to life a fable-like depiction of a village washerwoman in India. Manfred becomes teary and choked reading a piece he has called *Pigskin*, a reflection on the glories of high school football. Ashley, in true Barbie fashion, gets laughs with *An Ode to Shoes and Handbags*. Krista gives a heartfelt memoir-type account of the birth of her son. *Deployment* is Mike's piece, a sentimental reflection on the brotherhood of soldiers.

Then, she's up. She gets through her reading without coming undone. The first sentence is tough. She finds the doll. Bunny. Fixes on it. And then somehow, she's not sure at the change, it becomes a bit like having a conversation. One-sided, but still. Jitters settle. She finds Kameko, looks at her, gets a boost at being wrapped in her smile. After that she is brave enough to look to others. Gedge, she sees, is nodding. She can feel the audience listening to her. Wanting to hear, wanting to know. That she has something to say, to share. Inside dialogue has gone quiet. Her heart slows to a more normal rhythm. Her voice steadies. Gedge has told her she has demonstrated maturity and healing. The realization: she isn't just Gregory, the girl who killed her father. The misfit. The outcast. The past alone doesn't define her anymore. There's more to her now. She's someone different. And she isn't alone. She's got people in her corner. Suddenly there's cheers and applause. She's done it. Mentally she casts back to the question she'd asked Dan: How does one *do* proud? She's learning, bit by bit.

Randy does a rap, *Against Type*. He has a friend on stage beatboxing with it. It gets the crowd into clapping and cheering and whooping. Andy, the awkward looking science major, delivers *Progeny: The Evolutionary Art of Science*, totally justifying his Manfred-given nickname, Kid Nobel. Ruben, the wild-haired guy who has maintained a decidedly low profile in the class, gives a comedy monologue *The Life of Ruben: A Jewish Boy from the Bronx*, which, he says by way of introduction, is his personalized take on Monty Python's Life of Brian. He literally has people coming apart in tears and hysterics, he is so funny. And there is sweet, adorable Kameko, who teaches them. Gently, delicately. About the writings of a courtesan in the Imperial Palace in ancient Japan. She offers her own personal rendition following a similar style and explains how the ancient form is still a very valid structure. That it is, in a sense, thought and feeling laid bare; a portrait of individual humanity. 'Imagine,' she says in her soft voice, 'if Sei Shōnagon were alive today, what she might say about her life, what kinds of things she might consider affecting.' Kameko will be a great teacher. Instruction seems so natural to her. The professor's friend, if his expression is anything to go by, seems to think so too.

After, when the program is done and Turner has heaped even more praise upon them, there is relieved chatter and congratulations and high-fives and planning for future writing: groups, classes, more readings. Kameko's bosses, Richard and Matt, enthusiastically offer up the bookstore, even volunteering to look into self-publishing a volume of written work. Excitement rises three levels at the idea, the place is absolutely humming at the possibility. Manfred gets talking about book signings and rooming with Mike on a future book tour, 'I have to warn you, I snore. Oh, and in case you didn't know, I do my best writing at night. I get these creativity blasts. And then I'm up and down. A real night owl. Man, I'm a martyr for my craft.' Mike groans and they all laugh.

Gregory gets hugs from Claire and Suzanne and Gerry, even Dan. She has thanked them all for coming and received their compliments and tried, really tried, not to be *self-deprecating*, as the good doctor would say. Claire apologizes for having to up and run, but with the drive and traffic, and work and school in the morning, she has to hit the road. They promise to get together soon. Kameko says she would like to do something with Jace. Claire gives her an amazing hug and kiss on the cheek, and whispers, 'I'm proud of you, kid. You done good.' She darts through clusters of people, and with one last turn to wave, disappears out the front door.

Out of the corner of her eye Gregory has spied the doc watching her as people come and go. Finally, he makes his way over to her. She is just shaking Gedge's congratulatory hand as the professor approaches.

'She has talent, you know,' Turner says. 'Thanks for steering her my way.'

'I know she does. Now if she would just accept that strength in herself.'

'In all honesty, Gregory, you have a voice that's easy to read. And a refreshingly raw take on realism.'

'I would have to agree,' Gedge concurs.

'I hope she'll stick with it,' he nods to the doc.

'I do too. I do too,' Gedge says slowly, meaningfully, with his assessing look.

'Is this some kind of writer press gang?' she jokes. She can hear the version of Gedge inside her brain asking her why she felt the need to resort to joking. She could make another smart remark but it would probably compound things. Instead, she chooses to offer the truth, 'I actually enjoyed it, so yeah, I can see me continuing, you know, much as I have the time, or the creativity. One of the hard lessons I learned over the year; sometimes it comes, it flows, you're feeling good, sometimes it doesn't at all. I hate that. Doc knows, I can get ugly about it.'

Kameko has left Richard and Matt laughing with JT and Alex and joins them. She takes Gregory's hand, squeezes it. 'What is ugly?' Kameko asks.

'Frustration with the creative ebb and flow,' Turner offers.

'Creativity, like a lot of things in life, will not be forced,' Gedge says.

'Defies logic,' Kameko puts in, from the list she has composed for her own reading.

'Exactly right,' Gedge agrees.

'Oh. Kameko…Kimura,' she chooses not to use Kameko's married name, 'this is Dr. Arthur Gedge.'

'It's a pleasure to meet you, Kameko,' Gedge smiles warmly at her, and, Gregory notices, doesn't give her the know-all-your-secrets look.

'And very nice to meet you,' Kameko says softly, bowing.

Gedge expresses an interest in Shōnagon, asking Kameko how to spell the name so that he 'might seek out', as he puts it, *The Pillow Book*. He tells her he finds the title fascinating in and of itself, and they are off into discussions of the ancient world. Secret thoughts, desires, wishes, and the origins of diarizing.

Manfred approaches with Bunny under his arm. 'Hate to interrupt this powwow, but we've got to be heading out.' He raises the doll head up so her blank expression and O-shaped mouth are visible. 'Got a babysitter to pay, and Bunny and I have to take the dog for a walk and a poop.' Gedge raises an eyebrow and looks bemusedly at Manfred. They all laugh, Manfred included.

'They look like they're having fun,' Gregory gestures at the guffawing foursome Kameko has left, and Aneeta has since joined.

'Yes. JT is telling stories. He is very funny to listen to.'

'Apparently, a lot like Johnny Lever. Some famous Indian comedian. Ask Aneeta.'

'I think I will,' Turner says. 'Good to see ya, Art.'

'And you, Neil.'

'Thanks for coming.'

'A pleasure. I enjoyed it. Gregory, thank you for allowing me to be part of your evening. I learned a great deal.' He smiles, but not the secrets smile.

'Yeah,' she says, 'I think I did too.'

'And it was nice to meet you, Kameko.'

Kameko returns the same and bows. Gregory has noticed that the bowing has eased a little since she's known her. She wonders if it will ever totally disappear, or whether it will be one of the little pieces of Japan that will stay with her.

Randy has music set up and playing from some makeshift apparatus that reminds her of one they used to sell in the prison commissary. His beatboxing buddy plays DJ. Boho Chick, Mike, Ruben and Maddy are dancing on a smallish open space that has been made over into an impromptu dance floor—probably also of Randy's creation—and are trying to emulate some of his dance moves as he stands to one side clutching his belly laughing hysterically and pointing at them. Even Kid Nobel Andy looks like he might give it a go and put his foot in the ring. When he eventually does, he looks quite comfortable wearing Randy's technique, and very determined. There is cheering for him, and a circle develops to watch. Kameko is smiling at the scene, her eyes wide.

She thinks about her name game then, and the realization hits her: how there is so much more to a person than what the eye can see. What is the truth, the reality of a person's story, is often in the invisible. Detail that cannot be touched, measured, labeled. Life that attaches itself in layers; thick, thin, weak, strong. Each one building up to the outer skin, the veneer of just that moment alone.

Aneeta
May 2003

Until now, she has made wide arcs around the South Asian parts of the city. But it is Max's birthday. And she finally feels ready for past and present to meet.

JT has recommended All India Emporium for the items she wishes to find. She feels foolish in recalling her initial fear of him. Now he is like a brother to her. And a connection to home.

As she steps across the threshold while Neil holds the door, her senses are instantly seduced. Bits and pieces, threads of days gone by, wrap themselves comfortingly around her. *Lost child, where have you been?* they inquire. So long ago, India seems. So far away. And she realizes how much she has missed it. Her eyes well and her smile wavers in a proud-sad way. Proud of her heritage, proud to share it. Sad that necessity has forced such a distance.

The front portion of the store is devoted chiefly to movies. Postered walls feature adored Bollywood actors and actresses posing against overbright studio-lot sceneries. Paper incarnations look out over a domain of tightly packed wire shelving sandwiched with foodstuffs. Pickle, masala, namkeen. Packets of haldi, seeds of fennel and cardamom. On the far side of the shop, a glass case shows off stacked geometric arrangements of ice-cream coloured confections. Beside are gold-orange pyramids of laddus and jalebi. Boxes of cardboard, marked in red with the name of the shop, stand on top of the glass, together with a weigh scale.

Beyond where hungry stomachs are tended and entertainment needs seen to, dazzling islands of rainbow-coloured packages escape at odd angles from an overstuffed cubicle wall. Men's, women's and children's plastic forms hang from the ceiling and dance lazily in the breeze of a standing fan. Wide display cases feature an assortment of gold. Bangles, chains, rings, and elaborate engagement-wedding finery wink under tracks of hot lights. A low run of half-sized cubicles is packed with a tight and tangled press of practical chappals, strappy sandals, and variations of slipper. Bolts of bright fabric run the length of back wall.

Sardar-ji uncle behind the cash register, his head tightly wound in a length of beautiful saffron that reminds her of Papa, has been watching them carefully. He keeps his expression bland. But the eyes, she can see, are curious. He tries to conceal his interest in a quartered form of newsprint. Eyes flick up and over. And retreat. Then again. Sly sparks wonder at the image of coffee with cream and cream with coffee. *Desi* with *gora* and *gora* with *desi*. With-with. If it were *gora* alone. Or *desi* alone. Or *gora-gori*, two light skins, it would not be cause for such attention. But mix the two? Her kind, his kind?

As she draws closer there is further ignition of surprise. Light eyes. And so he peers a little more carelessly. A little more openly. At her. In a palette confined mostly to brown, grey doesn't come along every day.

A handful of braided and hair-bunned women—a range of generations: daughter, niece, mother, auntie—bustle back and forth, with a crackling plasticky assertion of industry. Like scattered pigeons they cluster, break apart, and re-cluster. Curiosity is plain in their faces. English lapses into Punjabi. Since they can't be sure how much she knows, their Indian words tiptoe around her.

The women make no overtures without direction. They wait on uncle. After a respectable interval he clears his throat and lowers the paper. 'Halloe,' he calls.

'Hello, ji. Sat Sri Akal.' He appears pleased by her show of respect.

'You are looking for something?' he inquires.

'Sherwani suit, or kurta pyjama. For a boy. Little boy.' She holds her hand, in a height estimate, at her own waistline.

The suggestion had come to her in a dream. From a slight, mocha-skinned, knee-soxed little boy with a quick smile. In the unreal way of dreams, lips had moved with silent words, channeling thoughts and ideas into her. Of course, she had felt it instantly perfect. Especially given Max's fondness for *The Jungle Book*.

'Boy is how old?'

Though she knows, she turns to Neil, to include him in their conversation. 'Seven.'

The women are listening.

'And Maharajah slippers?'

'For child?'

'Hanji. Yes.'

'I think we do not have,' he says, his head shaking.

One of the women breaks in, 'We have some with open back, so it could be okay.'

'She will help you.' He points with his chin. To the woman who has volunteered the information.

'Thank you, uncle.'

'Okay, okay.'

Aneeta turns and asks the woman, 'And turban? Very small, perhaps with a quill?'

'You are going to a parade or something?'

'No, it is for his birthday.'

The shop woman's eyes ask without words, *He is yours, this boy? Yours with the gora? Or yours with another? Or gora's with another?* Her lips purse tightly. Disapproval is clear. 'Boy is seven? I think size 26 or 28 maybe. Big seven? Or not so big?'

Aneeta turns to Neil. 'What would you say? Is he big for his age?'

He shrugs, 'I don't really know. Maybe about average. Is that the safest answer?'

The woman gives Aneeta a knowing smile that asserts with a silent flash of pleasure that men never really know these things.

'If you could show us, I'm sure we could get a better idea,' Aneeta urges.

'The boy likes some colour? You prefer some colour for him?'

'Neil?' Aneeta prompts.

'Uh, green, I think. Maybe red.'

'Achcha.' The woman reaches into several cubicles and, squinting, peers at size labels. She tosses half a dozen packages on the glass top. Colour, size, detail and workmanship are shaken out and inspected while the woman looks on in bland silence. They debate over a dhoti or pyjama style bottom. Aneeta wonders aloud if the traditional dhoti might seem too much like a girl's skirt. In the end, they decide the pyjama pant to be more practical. Because of the drawstring they can buy a larger size, which seems wise given their uncertainty about his height. Together, they settle on red brocade with a gold embroidered Nehru collar and pants of plain gold. The chosen items are folded back into plastic.

'Turban, we have. But I think it will be too big, even smallest size.'

'We could try?' Aneeta suggests. 'It doesn't have to be an exact fit, does it?' Neil tries at least a dozen. She even tries several. They are laughing at the silliness of their turbaned reflections in an oval countertop mirror. Even auntie cannot help a fleeting smile. By chance they find one, bright gold with a large center jewel and decorative quill, that is too small for either of them.

'It might roll around on his head, but I think it will be fun. A chinstrap could always be attached. Since it is only for play.'

'For play?' the sharp rise of auntie's question tuts her scorn at the idea.

'He is interested in things of India,' Aneeta volunteers. 'Stories and such. I thought it might be nice.'

'Here. Some slippers.' Auntie points to the lowest rung of cubicles, 'Mostly ladies in small-small sizes, we have some, not many. You have to see if you can find something.' She flicks a slipped chunni end over her shoulder. With something that glows like resentment in her eyes and a small semi-satisfied smile she watches Aneeta squat to sift through footwear.

The woman asks Neil, 'Your child?' She needs something to satisfy the others who watch and wonder.

'No, my nephew.' Neil is happy to explain. 'He fell in love with Aneeta. A little like me, I suppose. Now he's infatuated with all things Indian. I think he fancies himself kind of an American Mowgli. This one,' he motions toward Aneeta, 'she reads a mean Bagheera and incredibly believable Kaa.' The woman nods blankly.

The smallest slippers Aneeta can find are a peacock blue, the shade so close, so spectrally similar in likeness, that for an instant it whisks her back. To a young girl's enchantment. The swish of silk. In the mirror turning this way and that. A shy smile. Her heart trips. She sees the little girl dancing. Waggling her finger coyly at herself. Like so many film actresses. A first sari. And then. A stone thrown against glass. The image shattered. But no. That was long ago. She clutches the slippers tightly to her chest and stands. Turning, she looks into Neil's golden, chiseled features and a sense of gratitude takes her. 'I think these would do. What do you think?' She can feel the embrace of his smile.

'Wow, I love 'em. Very Ali Baba and Arabian Nights with the curled toes and all. I bet we'll be hard-pressed to get them off him.'

She laughs. 'You really think so?'

'I really do. I know he's going to love it all. I have to say, I think you're spoiling him. I'm sure my sister is going to give me a hard time for letting you do it.'

'Oh, but I want to. I do. I think it is as much for me as it is for him. Does that seem selfish?'

'I don't think there's any way you could call it selfish. Not at all. I think it profoundly generous.'

In some small measure it helps to soothe the rawness of grief. Her own child would still have been younger than Max, but she likes to think that they might have been contemporaries. That is the way the mind has orchestrated things. She does know, however, if the child had lived his very presence would have altered her journey dramatically. For him she would have sacrificed her own life. Everything. Without hesitation. Without regret. With a child, especially a boy child, she could not have left. Ever. There would have been no choice in the matter.

She recalls the visit to the astrologer. The comparison of charts and stars. To predict her future fertility. The way the wizened old man had held her hand at the end of the meeting. The simple word he had spoken: soon.

The walls behind the jewelry counters feature magazine images of bridal prospects. Girls who look shyly into the camera lens. She remembers her own wedding. Her hope that marriage might give her the chance to begin again. Her mind recalls breaking the laddu for placing in Jovin's mouth. To symbolically mark her commitment. To bind one soul to another. And she remembers how Jovin had grabbed hold of her wrist and grudgingly taken what she had offered, telling her later that he didn't like laddu. How, together with his reaction to her misstep around the altar, something had stirred in her. Even then. A quiver.

'Whom shall I ask about sweets?' she says. It is uncle who moves behind the display case. Perhaps a sign that his own curiosity is winning out. Perhaps he wishes to find out for himself.

To Neil she says, 'I'd like to take some for the party.'

Uncle asks, 'Girl party, boy party?'

'Boy party.'

'This is a good thing,' uncle offers. 'A boy party. Better to be watering own garden for future, hunh? You are married?' the chin inquires of them both.

'No.'

'I think that you are looking familiar to me. Eyes I have seen somewhere, I think. What is the family name?'

It is a question that at one time she would have been afraid to answer. 'Malik,' she says firmly, without hesitation. His eyes are impressed at her origins. The Brahmin caste ties that become apparent.

'Achcha? Family here? In America?'

'No, in India.'

'Big place. In India.' He chuckles and looks to Neil to share his joke. 'Where they are there?' Not to answer would be difficult given the fact that she has not yet told him what sweets she wishes to buy. He holds the empty box, and her with it, hostage to his interrogation.

'Delhi.'

'You are here, only?' His voice acts in surprised concert with his eyebrows. 'For little while? Visiting?' He is perhaps wondering whether or not he might be able to finagle a good Brahmin stopover in Delhi the next time he is back that way.

'No, uncle, I live here.'

'For school? Computers? Medical doctor? Maybe lawyer?' He eyes Neil now with some suspicion.

'No, uncle-ji, because I have chosen it. No American doctor-lawyer. No computer programmer-PhD. Sorry to disappoint.' She shakes her head and smiles widely at him to cover the pointed impertinence of her words. *Hai! Who does she think she is, this girl?* She hears a soft chorus from the women behind, a twitter of laughter.

She has caught him off guard. He covers it swiftly with a jump of joking bravado. 'Oh-ho, she is spicy girl. I cannot take such spice myself. My constitution does not favour it. For me, milder taste is more appealing. I think it is the same for many Americans too.' He looks pointedly at Neil in an attempt to recover both his footing in the conversation and his ego. His criticism does not bother her. There is a surprised realization, in fact, that quite the opposite is true.

With conviction she gives her order: 'I should like 3 each of the burfi, 9 jalebi and 9 laddu. But please keep one laddu out for me.' The time has come to mark a new beginning. She takes the golden round that uncle hands her on a thin paper napkin. Soft and sweet. Chickpea flour, ghee butter and sugar.

She remembers the scratchy feel of Papa's beard when she used to feed him. How they would eat one after the other. It was their favourite treat. And she would giggle with delight at the shared secret mischief.

She is reminded, too, of the flitting tree-bird of her seven-year-old poem:

In a leafy tree-top
I flit from branch to branch
I sing a happy little song
And dance a happy dance

I live a life of fancy
A life without a care

And nothing in the world below
Could ever tempt me down
For I'm up above the worries
Of a life upon the ground

All those years ago, without knowing it, she had given the little girl she once was a gift in seeing herself as such a creature. A creature happy, hopeful, and free.

Now, with all in the shop standing as silent witness, she pinches a piece of laddu and offers it up to Neil's smiling lips. He takes it from her, kissing her fingertips tenderly in return. Then she takes some herself. She does it because she wants to. Because she is ready. He may not know the greater significance of the gesture, but the others surely do. Their momentary hush speaks volumes. Chatter may rise at her back, but what they say, whatever they may think, cannot touch her.

As the sweetness melts slowly into her, she silently gives thanks to God: for the father who smiles in her dreams, for the child at his side, for the man who has shown her the beauty of love, and for the finally apparent grace of destiny.

Gregory
May 2003

Light creeps across the sky, bleeding into the retreating night. A growing gold-hued force to overtake the last of darkness. Dawn.

Below, there's the sure sounds of the café coming to life. The voices of Louie and Manuel. The clang of pans. Laughter. The hiss of steam from the espresso machine. The grinding of coffee beans. The groan of floorboards under shifting racks. She'll meet them in a moment, just to go over things once more. Before she and Kameko have to go.

A new day. And with it a reassurance. A sense she hasn't known before moves through her. Behind her, Kameko sleeps with abandon. Hair fanned across the pillow, her face childlike and serene.

She has finally felt that pull. Like it would be okay. Though she still worries about how the ghost of the past might catch her. Whether it could pull her back. Send her down. Like a game of snakes and ladders. After she's fought hard for every inch of ground she's gained. But no amount of imagining beforehand can change the eventuality of things. However things might go. However they turn out.

Gedge has told her the downs are dependent on how one takes them, tries them on for size, and treats them. That they shouldn't be responsible for defining a life, just for shaping the individual.

She remembers as a kid once marveling at a fallen tree. She can't think where it was they were living at the time; it didn't much matter. The thing that had struck her about the tree were the rings that forged its insides. From the center of the wood out to the bark. One after the other after the other. Different in thickness, different in shade, some infused by the patterns of holes, some grown right around thick, interfering knots. The layers of a life. Each one adding its own unique characteristic to being, to living, to becoming. Each making the tree more sturdy, more established.

There's a solid strength in the latest of her life's layers. And a new acceptance for the layers of before. For every texture, every detail, every imperfection. For their collective role in her growth.

She sets her coffee mug gently on the ledge, careful with her sounds. Time and circumstance have made her an early morning person. The glow of light intensifies in the room. Birds are beginning to add their chorus. She picks up a copy of the prison journal Dan has given her. Eyes are drawn to it again, her name. In bold letters under the masthead. *Chronicles of Courage*. The sight of it causes a tremor somewhere in her that surfaces in a shiver. Is she? Courageous? In all this? Has she been? *You should be proud*, she hears Dan, his voice an echo in her head.

Proud. She folds and slides the journal into an envelope, along with a short note. To explain. She seals the top and flips it over, running her finger over the postage.

Professor Neil Turner
c/o College of Liberal and Creative Arts
HUM Room 465
San Francisco State University
1600 Holloway Avenue
San Francisco, CA 94132

She'll have Kameko remind her to mail it on their way to the Greyhound station; her mind will be all over the place today. At least now he'll know. She wants that. For him to understand the why of her words. For him to know the context of the story she's telling.

Doc Gedge comes to mind—*We can think of life as a mountain. There are countless ways we can get from bottom to top. But we each have to forge our own individual path. You, Gregory, are the only one who can decide the way of your journey.*

It is a clear and welcoming morning. And it is time. In her journey. She is finally ready. For whatever lies ahead.

Gregory Abbott
English 50

The Process of Becoming

I used to put coloured tissue on my windows. With tape and sometimes a thin frame of cardboard to protect against the damp. I started doing it when I was a kid. I'd stick it up wherever light would reach out to touch glass. It was my way of making things around me more beautiful. A sort of patchwork paper rainbow to cover up the things I thought were ugly about myself.

I don't have a history of Kodak moments. I always thought that made me not worthwhile; a freak. Too crazy-different to fit into this jigsaw puzzle world. I worked so hard at hiding all the bad things in my life, keeping them in the dark, making them like shadows. There, but not. Things about me I didn't want finding their way to light, into a space where others could see them, know them, judge them and me. I was so afraid of what might happen if my secrets got found out. But all that hiding ever did was keep me a prisoner in my own skin. Fear was my own personal jailer. Finding the courage to face it, my fear, is quite possibly the hardest thing I've ever had to do.

413

Writing helps to make sense of the parts of me that still live in shadows. Words on paper. It was an idea that once I didn't have a lot of time for. But now I know that words are the voice I never knew I had. E.M. Forster said, 'How do I know what I think until I see what I say?' Writing is kind of like having an emotional rummage sale. It's a way to get things out in the open and then decide what's worth keeping, and maybe more importantly, what's worth letting go of.

Little by little, what I put on paper is allowing me to make peace with where I've come from. It's helping me to look beyond the ugly things I used to be so afraid of; all the things about myself I used to try so hard to cover, to hide.

The coloured tissue I used to tape up? I realize now that it was about giving me hope. Keeping it where I could see it. Even on the darkest days, hope kept me focussed on something brighter. It's hope that has helped me get through all the rest. And hope is one thing I choose to keep.

A Note

***Backshadow* is a work of fiction, but the issues faced by the three main characters are not. In fact, they are decidedly prevalent in modern society.**

Globally, World Health Organization statistics indicate that at least 30% of women have suffered some form of domestic violence.

In the United States, physical violence is estimated to occur in 4 to 6 million intimate relationships each year.

Between 133 and 275 million children in the world are estimated to witness domestic violence annually.

Many children who are present during acts of domestic violence try to help. A study conducted in the United States and supported by UNICEF found that in 15% of incidents of domestic violence where children were present they tried to prevent the violence, another 10% actively tried to intervene to protect the victim.

A 2003 study indicated that the more severe the abuse against the mother, the more likely a child is to attempt to intervene in an incident.

While parricide remains rare, accounting for about 2% of homicides, most cases involve teenagers who kill abusive parents. Many parricides occur when a child is on the cusp of independence, about to break away from an abusive parent's domination. Most have above average intelligence and are generally well-adjusted in school and the community, though they tend to be isolated, without many friends. They commonly have no prior run-ins with the law. Sometimes the killing is triggered by a desire to protect the other parent or siblings.

The most common form of child sexual abuse is incest.

Data gathered by the World Health Organization estimates that up to 36% of girls and 29% of boys have suffered child sexual abuse.

In India, figures indicate that at least 25% of the adult population has been molested by the age of 16. More than 27 million females are survivors of child sexual abuse.

416

Findings of Delhi-based NGO RAHI suggest that 76% of upper and middle class Indian women respondents suffered sexual abuse as children. Of those, 40% were abused by at least one family member.

A 1996 survey conducted in Bangalore by NGO Samvada found that in cases of child sexual abuse 75% of abusers were family members. 50% of the incidents were reported to have taken place in the child's own home.

Childlessness is stigmatized.

Estimates indicate that infertility affects between 80 million and 168 million people worldwide; that number equates to approximately 1 in every 10 couples of reproductive age.

A survey by Schering-Plough revealed that 61% percent of infertility patients hide the struggle to get pregnant from those around them.

In a 2009 study conducted by GfK Roper, 71% of women respondents who were having difficulties with conception said that infertility made them feel flawed.

Additional Information

Domestic Abuse

Violence against women: a 'global health problem of epidemic proportions'
World Health Organization
http://www.who.int/mediacentre/news/releases/2013/violence_against_women_20130620/en/

UNiTE to End Violence Against Women
http://endviolence.un.org

STOP VIOLENCE IN THE HOME
A joint campaign by The Body Shop and UNICEF to inspire and support those affected by domestic violence
http://www.thebodyshop-usa.com/values-campaigns/stop-violence.aspx

Incest

RAHI Rape and Healing from Incest
Delhi, India
http://www.rahifoundation.org/home.html

Tulir: Centre for the Prevention and Healing of Child Sexual Abuse
http://www.tulir.org

Bitter Chocolate: Child Sexual Abuse in India
by Pinki Virani

RAINN: Rape, Abuse & Incest National Network
http://www.rainn.org

Parricide

Understanding Parricide: When Sons and Daughters Kill Parents
by Kathleen M. Heide, Ph.D.

When Battered Women Kill
by Angela Browne, Ph.D.

Infertility

World Health Organization: Sexual and Reproductive Health
http://www.who.int/reproductivehealth/topics/infertility/en/

Resolve
The National Fertility Association
www.resolve.org

Breaking the Silence on Infertility by Jennifer Wolff Perrine
Self Magazine
http://www.self.com/health/2010/08/breaking-the-silence-on-infertility

Recovery From Traumatic Loss: A Study Of Women Living Without Children After
Infertility by Marni Rosner
University of Pennsylvania
http://repository.upenn.edu/cgi/viewcontent.cgi?article=1020&context=edissertations_sp2

Acknowledgements

I am truly indebted to Paul, Charlie, Doug, Kitty, Emily, Hannah, Rosie, Mary Lou, Ruth, Ann and Iris for suggestions, advice, support and encouragement. I couldn't have done it without you.